Penguin Books

The Julian Symons Omnibus

Julian Symons made a reputation before ~~the Second World War~~ as the editor of *Twentieth-Century Verse*, a magazine which published most of the young poets outside the immediate Auden circle. He has since become a celebrated writer of crime fiction and is also recognized as the greatest British expert on the genre. His history of the form, *Bloody Murder*, was called by Len Deighton 'the classic study of crime fiction', and was awarded the Mystery Writers of America Edgar Allan Poe Award in 1977. He has also written extensively about real-life crime in *A Reasonable Doubt* and *Crime and Detection from 1840*, and has written many articles on the historical background of both real and fictional crime. In 1976 he succeeded Agatha Christie as the President of the Detection Club, and was made a Grand Master of the Swedish Academy of Detection in 1977. He was created a Grand Master of Mystery by the Mystery Writers of America in 1982. Mr Symons also has quite a separate reputation as a biographer and as a social and military historian. In 1975 he was made a Fellow of the Royal Society of Literature. His recent crime works include *The Blackheath Poisonings*, *Sweet Adelaide*, *The Detling Murders*, *The Tigers of Subtopia* and *The Name of Annabel Lee*. Several of his books are published in Penguins.

The Julian Symons Omnibus

THE MAN WHO KILLED HIMSELF

THE MAN WHOSE DREAMS CAME TRUE

THE MAN WHO LOST HIS WIFE

Penguin Books

Penguin Books Ltd, Harmondsworth, Middlesex, England
Penguin Books, 40 West 23rd Street, New York, New York 10010, U.S.A.
Penguin Books Australia Ltd, Ringwood, Victoria, Australia
Penguin Books Canada Ltd, 2801 John Street, Markham, Ontario, Canada L3R 1B4
Penguin Books (N.Z.) Ltd, 182–190 Wairau Road, Auckland 10, New Zealand

The Man Who Killed Himself first published in the United States of America by
Harper & Row, Publishers, Inc. 1967
First published in Great Britain by William Collins Sons & Co. 1967
Published in Penguin Books in the United States of America by arrangement with
Harper & Row, Publishers, Inc.
Published in Penguin Books 1977
Copyright © Julian Symons, 1967

The Man Whose Dreams Came True first published in Great Britain by William
Collins Sons & Co. 1968
First published in the United States of America by Harper & Row, Publishers, Inc.
1969
Published in Penguin Books in the United States of America by arrangement with
Harper & Row, Publishers, Inc.
Published in Penguin Books 1977
Copyright © Julian Symons, 1968

The Man Who Lost His Wife first published in Great Britain by William Collins
Sons & Co. 1970
First published in the United States of America by Harper & Row, Publishers, Inc.
1971
Published in Penguin Books in the United States of America by arrangement with
Harper & Row, Publishers, Inc.
Published in Penguin Books 1977
Copyright © Julian Symons, 1970

The lines on page 508 from 'No Orpheus No Eurydice' by Stephen Spender
appeared in Great Britain in *Ruins and Visions* and are used by permission of the
poet's publishers, Messrs Faber & Faber. In the United States of America they
appeared in *Collected Poems, 1928–1953*, copyright 1942 by Stephen Spender, and
are used by permission of Random House, Inc.

This collection published as *The Julian Symons Omnibus* 1984
Copyright © Julian Symons, 1984
All rights reserved

Made and printed in Great Britain by
Richard Clay (The Chaucer Press) Ltd, Bungay, Suffolk
Set in Plantin

Contents

THE MAN WHO KILLED HIMSELF   7

THE MAN WHOSE DREAMS CAME TRUE   171

THE MAN WHO LOST HIS WIFE   407

The Man Who Killed Himself

Note

My thanks are due to Mr A. J. Nathan of L. and H. Nathan, the famous court, theatrical and film costumiers, for information about wigs in general, and for taking a benevolent interest in the affairs of Major Easonby Mellon. Readers will be reassured to know that Major Mellon's deception is practicable, and in fact is not unknown in real life.

For George Hardinge

Contents

PART ONE
Before the Act   11

PART TWO
After the Act   95

Chapter 1

Mr Brownjohn at Home

In the end Arthur Brownjohn killed himself, but in the beginning
he made up his mind to murder his wife. He did so on the day
that Major Easonby Mellon met Patricia Parker. Others might
have come to such a decision earlier, but Arthur Brownjohn was
a patient and, as all those who knew him agreed, a timid and
long-suffering man. When people say that a man is long-suffering
they mean that they see no reason why he should not suffer for
ever.

Major Mellon met Patricia Parker on a Wednesday in April.
On the day before that Arthur Brownjohn returned to his home
in Fraycut at about five in the afternoon. The house was called
The Laurels, although there was no remaining trace of a laurel
tree. It was a small square detached house made of red brick,
with a neat garden in front and a larger one, just as neat, behind.
There are hundreds of such houses in Fraycut, and they are
loved by those who live in them because they establish so satisfactorily their owners' position in society. Arthur's wife Clare
greeted him with a fierce peck on the cheek and the news that
the hedge needed clipping. She was a powerful woman with one
of those red healthy faces that carry with them a suggestion of
hunting and horse shows. Clare was two inches taller than
Arthur, and it might have seemed that she was physically better
equipped for hedge clipping than he. It was her expressed belief,
however, that it did Arthur good to get out into the air, and now
she stood with hands on hips watching him from outside the
french window in the drawing-room while he unsteadily climbed
a pair of steps and snipped at the hedge.

'Not quite even, a little more off there on the right,' she said
and then, like a sergeant-major calling a recruit to attention,
'Arthur. What are those trousers?'

He looked down from the steps. 'Trousers?'

'They are your best gaberdine.'

'Not my *best*.'

She did not relent. 'You know you don't wear them for gardening. Go up and change.'

Arthur had already changed once, from business suit to gaberdine trousers, but he changed again. Clare went into the house.

Clip the hedges, trim the edges, mow the lawn. These were among his duties. It was half past six when he put away the gardening tools in the garage that contained no motor car, and then it was to find that Clare was dressing. Time for him to change again. The Paynes were coming for bridge.

'I should really like to have a bath.'

'Can't,' she said. 'I've just had one, water won't be hot. Besides, there's no time.'

The Paynes arrived just before seven-thirty. They were one of half a dozen bridge-playing couples with whom the Brownjohns exchanged visits. The procedure on these occasions varied very little. The visitors had one or perhaps two drinks, a rubber of bridge was played, sandwiches and coffee were served by the hostess, more bridge was played and at some time between eleven and twelve o'clock a good-night whisky was offered. The whole thing made, as Clare said when she won, a thoroughly nice evening.

Mr Payne was the manager of the Fraycut branch of the bank at which Arthur and Clare had a joint account. He was not, as Clare had often said to her husband, quite out of the top drawer.

'Funny old weather we're having,' he said as he sipped his sherry. 'Rain and shine, rain and shine. April though, I suppose you must expect it. How was it in London?' He spoke as if Fraycut were at the other end of Britain, instead of half an hour's journey from London.

'About the same as here.' Mr Brownjohn twiddled his glass.

'You can't trust the English weather.' Clare mentioned the weather as if it were an unreliable servant.

'That's just what I always say.' Mrs Payne said it, as she said everything, with a nervous rush. 'What's the summer going to be like? You can't tell. So George and I are going to Spain.'

'The Costa Brava?' Clare asked with a note of ennui. The Brownjohns never went abroad for holidays, and indeed had not been away together for years.

'The Costa *Blanca*. They say it's nicer, so much less crowded.'

'How odd,' Clare bayed in her deepest tones. 'I was in Penquick's yesterday. The Penquicks are going to the Costa Blanca. Perhaps you may see them there.'

There was silence after this remark. The Penquicks owned a grocery shop in the High Street. Mr Brownjohn offered more sherry, poured it into three glasses. His wife said sharply: 'Arthur.'

'My dear.'

'No more for you. You know you haven't a head for liquor.'

Arthur left his glass unfilled. Mr Payne and his wife exchanged a meaningful glance. They had heard similar conversations in the past.

'Well,' Mr Payne said, 'bring out the devil's playthings. After all, that's what we're here for.'

'I think it's absurd to call them that,' his wife riposted. 'As long as you don't play for high stakes and don't take it too seriously, there's no harm in it.'

Clare made no comment. She played with a concentration that was terrifying to behold.

Eight, nine, ten, eleven o'clock. Husbands and wives played together, and the Brownjohns held bad cards or had bad luck or played badly. They lost every rubber. The financial deficit was small, the mental irritation extreme. 'What made you double that heart call?' Clare asked her husband. 'Surely anybody with eyes in his head could see that wasn't what I wanted. Just because you're sitting with the king and two others.'

Mr Payne wagged a finger. 'Now, now. No inquests.'

'The trouble is Arthur's not here half the time.' She spoke as if her husband were physically absent. 'I don't know where he is. In cloud-cuckoo-land.'

'Or in the attic,' Mr Payne said with a loud laugh. 'Racing those cars round the track.' It was a source of amusement to all visitors that Arthur kept a complete layout for model electric car racing up in the attic with a quadruple track, a special Le Mans start, bridges and cross-overs, and twenty different cars.

'We had bad cards, my dear.' Arthur was pouring whisky into cut-glass tumblers.

'Give you your revenge next week,' Mr Payne said. 'Tuesday, Wednesday? The Grevilles are coming over for a game on Monday.'

Arthur coughed. 'I'm afraid I may be away in the middle of next week. Shall we let you know a little later on?'

'You do that,' Mr Payne said heartily. He finished his whisky. 'Come on, my dear, we've made our fortune, let's go and think how to spend it.'

'I feel so *sorry* for him, George,' Mrs Payne said as he drove sedately home. 'I mean, it's downright humiliating, telling him not to have another drink.'

'I believe he has got a weak head.'

'I dare say. But she doesn't have to say it like that. He's such a nice little man.'

'Not much meat in those sandwiches.' He negotiated a traffic light. 'You know, she was a Slattery before she married. It makes a difference.'

'I don't see that.'

'She married beneath her,' George Payne said in a tone that denied the possibility of further conversation on the subject.

Back at The Laurels they were stacking plates in the kitchen. There was no need to wash up because Susan, the daily, would do that on the following morning. Arthur interrupted Clare's analysis of his failings during the second rubber.

'My dear.'

'What?'

'I wish you wouldn't say that about my not taking another drink.'

'You know the effect alcohol has on you. Remember the Watsons.'

'That was seven years ago.' But he knew that the occasion, on which he had danced and sung and tried to take off all his clothes, would never be forgotten. He said feebly, 'I'm sure the Paynes thought it odd.'

'The Paynes.' Clare snorted quite loudly, like a horse. 'A jumped-up fellow. In trade.'

'A bank manager is not exactly in trade.'

'As good as. Going to Spain with the grocer.' Abruptly she said, 'What are you doing next week?'

'I shall be away tomorrow. I have to visit Birmingham and Manchester.'

'You're away as much as if you were a commercial traveller.'

'I *am* a sort of commercial traveller. If you want to sell car parts –'

'Spare me the details.' Clare turned away her head. 'I shall go to bed.'

'I'll bring up your drink. Then I shall tidy up.'

The Laurels was a tidy house. In the small square hall there was a square Baluchistan rug, a good rug as Clare often said, which belonged to her family. Above the rug hung a portrait of her father, Mr Slattery, a square-jawed man with large square nostrils. He stared across at the opposite wall with fierce contemptuous eyes. The sitting-room led to the left off the hall. It contained a sofa and two matching armchairs with loose covers, set at precisely the proper angles to each other. A glass-fronted cabinet was filled with books, most of them inherited from the Slattery connection. Little Victorian tables were dotted about and room had been found for a television set, which Clare moved about frequently because she felt that really it did not belong. Victorian ornaments stood on the mantelpiece, together with an old photograph of the Slattery family in Calcutta, Mr Slattery with arms folded, his wife wispy in something loose, Clare holding a tennis racket. The dining-room was on the right of the hall. Six chairs sat in it round a gate-leg table and beside one wall stood a twin cabinet to the one in the sitting-room containing the best china used only for visitors. More utilitarian crockery hung from the kitchen dresser. In the kitchen larder various spots were labelled 'Jams', 'Cereals', 'Tea', because Susan constantly put things away in the wrong places. A plastic chart with differently-coloured pegs reminded Clare what to buy and when to buy it.

Arthur made Clare the drink of hot whisky and lime which she invariably had as a nightcap, and took it up to where she sat waiting in her single bed, face creamed and hair in a net. They had played bridge in the sitting-room, which did not look as it should have done. Arthur put away the card table, returned chairs to their places, plumped up cushions. Then he went up past the bedroom to the attic. This large windowless coved room (a window would have disturbed the outside symmetry of the house) ran almost the whole length of the house. Half of it was occupied by the slot racing layout, the tracks bending in a double eight with two exciting chicane sections where cars could really go all out. Spectator stands with people in them, car pits with engineers waiting for cars to come in, television camera crews, hay bales, banking at bends, were all in place. Four cars stood ready to start. He thought of racing them, but knew that the sound would keep Clare awake. The other half of the attic contained much china discarded from down below, framed water colours painted by his mother when he had been a child, and his old roll-topped desk. He unlocked this with a key from the ring at his waist. A loose-leaf book in a black cover lay on the desk. It was his diary.

The first page said: 'A. Brownjohn, The Laurels, Fraycut, Surrey, England, Europe, The World.' Below there was a little rhyme which he had once read and repeated, perhaps inaccurately:

> He who unbidden looks within
> Commits a fearful wicked sin.
> Peeping Tom, filthy fool,
> I bet you were a sneak at school.

He opened the diary, read one or two of the entries, ran his fingers over an untouched white page, decided that he was too tired to write and locked the desk again.

In the bathroom he paused while brushing his teeth to consider the face that confronted him. It was pale, thin-lipped, distinctly rabbitish round the nose and doggy about the eyes. Worst of all was the billiard-ball smoothness of the head. Arthur had started losing his hair at an early age, and by the time he was in his early thirties the whole lot had gone. He had once seen Yul Brynner on the screen and had tried to convince himself that baldness was attractive, but examination of his head in the glass had made it clear that the total effect produced by his features did not at all resemble that of Yul Brynner's.

He went into the bedroom. Clare was lying as he had known she would be, on her right side with her eyes half closed. Her face was covered with shiny cream. He kissed the top of her head, undressed and got into bed, turned out the light. In the darkness he repeated what he said earlier. 'I wish you wouldn't say that about my drinking. I don't like it.'

She made no reply. Five minutes later she began to snore.

Chapter 2

The Affairs of Major Easonby Mellon

On the following day Major Easonby Mellon turned into one of
the side streets on the good – that is to say the Hanover Square –
side of Regent Street, walked into an office block named Romany
House and took the lift to the second floor. He used a key to
open a door that said in black lettering 'Matrimonial Assistance
Limited, Major Easonby Mellon', and stepped inside. He was at
once ankle deep in letters, a delicious sensation. He picked up
the armful of letters and went into his office, which had a window
looking out on to the street. There was a large chair behind his
handsome desk, and a couple of other chairs for clients. Opposite to his desk stood a filing cabinet and also another smaller
desk with a covered typewriter on it. Visitors assumed what
seemed obvious, that this desk was used by Major Mellon's
secretary, but the assumption was wrong, for the Major had no
secretary.

Major Mellon took off his pork pie hat, sat at his desk humming like a bumble bee and opened the post with a neat letter
opener. There were nearly seventy letters, and some half of them
contained cheques or postal orders. He was a dapper little figure
as he sat behind the desk, occasionally whistling a little at what he
read, for people write odd things to matrimonial agencies. He
wore a suit in a dog tooth check that was perhaps a little loud,
gay socks, and well-polished brown shoes. His tie and shirt were
reasonably sober, he had a good thatch of brownish hair with a
tinge of red in it, and a neat beard. When he had read the post he
carefully put all the cheques and postal orders into a drawer,
separated the first applications from the follow-ups and went
across to his filing cabinet.

Matrimonial Assistance Limited operated in a manner similar
to that of some other, although not the largest and most reputable,
matrimonial agencies. The Major advertised in local newspapers
and on dozens of newsagents' boards. His correspondents re-

ceived an encouraging letter saying that there were hundreds of bachelors, spinsters, widowers and widows on his books. A small remittance would bring the correspondent a list of a dozen names of ladies (or gentlemen, as the case might be) who wished, in the words of the duplicated letter, to assume 'the sweet bonds of matrimony'. The brief descriptions did not include addresses because, as the letter explained, it was a fixed rule that all introductions must be handled through Matrimonial Assistance. 'This is our pleasure and your safeguard,' the letter said. Letters came in and were forwarded, correspondents eventually met in the office (by appointment only, for the Major was not there every day), and marriages no doubt took place. It was not Major Mellon's part, as he had sometimes to say firmly, to examine the antecedents of people who wrote to him. He credited them all with honesty and common sense, and if some were lacking in one or other of these qualities that was hardly Major Mellon's business.

He looked at his diary and saw that he had only two appointments, one at eleven-thirty, the other half an hour later. There was time to do some typing. The first applications received his duplicated letter, signed 'Easonby Mellon' with 'Major, R.A.C. (retd.)' beneath. Major Mellon signed these letters, dashingly, with his left hand. Then came the follow-ups, from people who had responded to the duplicate letter and sent remittances. They got their list of names taken from the files with a request that they should not write to more than one name on the list at a time – although, of course, this request was not always obeyed. That left four letters needing more personal attention. He skimmed through one of them, in a woman's hand:

'. . . seemed a perfect gentleman, or otherwise as you can imagine I should never have invited him into my home, but as soon as he was inside he began to behave like a wild beast, I feel sure that you . . .'

How foolish people were! He chuckled a little at the thought of it. The man described himself on his record card as 'Poultry breeder (55) of loving disposition', and he lived in Norfolk. The Major reflected that he would have to write to the fellow seriously, and of course he must send a sympathetic note to the lady

19

('Widow, petite, early 40s but attractive'), something about her fatal charm perhaps? It was now, however, time for his eleven-thirty visitors.

These proved to be a Mr Lake, a gangling Australian with a terrible squint, and a nervous ageing spinster named Amelia Bonnamie. Could that really be her name? But there again, what she chose to call herself was not his concern. He said that his secretary had just gone out, expanded on it a little ('To tell the truth I asked her to step out for a few minutes, thought it might be easier for everybody') and talked briefly about the sacred bond of matrimony. They seemed pleased, with him and with each other. As they were going he tapped Lake on the shoulder.

'Just a moment.' He closed the door on Miss Bonnamie, leaving her in the tiny outer hall. 'When an introduction is effected a small fee is payable by the gentleman. Three guineas.'

'Of course. Sorry I forgot.' The Australian almost fell over himself in his eagerness to get out the money.

The Major took it, gave him a receipt and said with what might have been a twinkle in his eye, 'I hope your intentions are serious.'

'You bet,' said Lake, and was gone. It was a nicely ambiguous reply.

The other appointment – well the Major drew down the corners of his mouth as he thought of that, and re-read the letter on his desk signed in a neat hand 'Patricia Parker (Miss)'. The letter said that the writer was in her middle twenties – add ten years on to *that*, the Major thought – and unattached, and that she wished to meet a gentleman rather older than herself with marriage in mind. Miss Parker said that she had been a secretary, but was not working at the moment. She wrote from an address in one of London's northern suburbs. In the last paragraph she wrote in her neat, rather characterless hand: 'I understand the usual thing is to put applicants in touch by letter, but before deciding whether I wish to avail myself of this service I should be glad if I might see you personally, as there are certain points I would like to discuss with you.'

Something about the stilted phrases had caught the Major's attention. He knew from past experience that the point for discussion would probably be the revelation that Miss Parker had an old mother who would be expected to share the home of the married pair, or was handicapped in her search for a husband by a wooden leg, or wanted to put before him some other mental or physical problem that, so far as he was concerned, was insoluble. It was unwise to see her, no doubt about it. Yet there had been occasions in the past when such letters from women clients had led to delicious little romances of a personal kind. There was something about this letter, although he could not have said what, that made him answer it. Now, as he re-read the letter and waited for Miss Parker, he told himself that he had been foolish. It was obvious that she was one of the wooden leg brigade.

'Half an hour,' the Major said aloud – he often talked to himself when he was alone. 'Half an hour with Miss Pegleg and then a spot of lunch.' And after lunch he would pay in the cash to the bank, an occupation which always gave him pleasure. The outer bell rang. He went outside, ushered in Miss Parker, asked her to sit down. As she sat opposite him, demure and not quite smiling, Major Mellon took a good look at her and was frankly bowled over.

Patricia Parker did not look a day over twenty-five. Her face was pretty rather than characterful, but pretty it undoubtedly was. She had a beautiful skin, her brown hair shone silkily, her figure – well, it was not easy to judge when she sat in a chair but she was obviously shapely, and it was just as obvious that neither of the legs she displayed to him was a wooden one. Miss Parker was no dazzling beauty but she was a pretty young woman, and pretty young women did not often come Major Mellon's way in the course of business. For a moment or two he goggled at her. Then he recovered.

'My dear Miss Parker,' he leaned forward conspiratorially. 'I have sent my secretary out for half an hour. Unfortunately these offices are not as spacious as I could wish, and I thought that perhaps you had something confidential to discuss . . .'

He left the sentence unfinished. Miss Parker said that was thoughtful of him. Her voice was low, pleasant, unemphatic.

'You wanted to have a chat with me in person. Here I am.'

'Yes.' She seemed to find it hard to know how to begin, and

Major Mellon continued. Suspicion had quickly replaced pleasure in his mind. Was this girl trying to play a trick on him? His next words were spoken bluntly, almost harshly.

'Forgive me for saying so, but it surprises me that you should have any difficulty in finding a husband. I am here to help, but I doubt if there is anything Matrimonial Assistance can do for you that you couldn't do quite easily yourself.'

'Don't say that.' It was the first sign of emotion she had shown. 'Please don't say that.'

The Major softened but only slightly, and suggested that she should tell him about it.

'It's difficult. I don't know if I can.'

'Try.'

'I can't if you're looking at me. Will you close your eyes – or look out of the window. Then I might be able to.'

So Major Mellon swung round his chair, turned his back on her and looked at the people passing below in the street while he heard the story Patricia Parker told in her even voice. It was not, after all, such a very unusual story. Her name at birth was not Patricia Parker but Hildegarde Sommer. She was a German, and had been living in Germany with her mother – her father had been killed on the Eastern front – when the Russians swept in. As a child of five she had seen her mother raped by half a dozen Russian soldiers. Afterwards her mother had committed suicide. Hildegarde had been placed in a camp, and had come to England when she was in her teens to do housework. When she was twenty-one she had married a man named Parker, with whom she had been going out for some time. A week after their marriage he had asked her to do certain awful things – she did not specify their nature – and she had left him and later got a divorce. She had qualified as a secretary and could earn her living, but she did not feel it was enough to earn a living. She wanted to be married, and had gone out with several men. 'But it was no good, you understand? Yet I feel that I wish to be married, I could make a good wife for a man who was kind, a man perhaps older than myself, do you understand?'

'Can I turn round now?'

'Yes. Thank you for listening to me.'

He turned. She was staring at him as though he were an oracle. Was the story true or not? Upon the whole he thought that some of it was true and some invented, but it did not seem to him that this mattered very much.

'Do you think you will be able to help me?' she asked solemnly.

The Major got up, came round the desk, and lifted one of the pretty hands that were crossed in her lap. She allowed it to stay in his hand and sat looking up at him.

'I know what an effort it must have been to tell me that, Patricia – I may call you that, I hope, my dear? And if we can help you we shall. But I tell you what we're going to do first of all. We're going out together to have a spot of lunch at a little place round the corner, just the two of us. If I'm to help I shall have to know a little more about the sort of person you are. That is, if you're free for lunch.'

'I have no other engagement.' Major Mellon was delighted with the simplicity and candour of her reply.

As he was closing the door she remarked, 'Your secretary has not come back.'

The Major rode that one easily. 'She has her own key.'

The little place round the corner was also an expensive place, the spot of lunch included lobster thermidor and a bottle of excellent white burgundy. Pat – by the time that lunch was over he was calling her Pat – viewed it all with open-eyed wonder. She loved the alcove in which they sat, where the Major's hand occasionally and as if by chance touched hers, she exclaimed upon the excellence of the service, she wondered at her host's expertise in ordering the wine. Did a warning sense tell Major Mellon that there was something not quite right, not quite real, about Patricia Parker's childlike delight at being taken out to lunch? Perhaps, but it seemed that any game she might be up to could not possibly affect him. And in any case he was charmed, scenting as he did a delicious little romance. When they parted it was with the assurance that she would come to the office again tomorrow, by which time he would have thought over the problem further, and might be able to suggest some correspondents who could be recommended as potential husbands.

Major Easonby Mellon returned to the office in a daze of

pleasure. He had three more interviews with couples during the afternoon which he handled rather absent-mindedly. At half past five he closed the office and went home.

Home was Number 48 Elm Drive, Clapham, a street of solid grey Victorian houses leading off Clapham Common's south side, which had so far escaped the maw of the developer. The Major and his wife had the upper part of the house, which was divided into two. When he opened the door he smelled cooking, a smell strong, spicy and not at all disagreeable. Joan was in the kitchen and Major Mellon crept up behind her and put his arms round her plump waist. She gave a delighted scream.

'E. Supper's not ready. I didn't expect you yet.'

'But here I am,' the Major said gaily. 'And very very hungry.'

'You'll have to wait.'

'That's not what I'm hungry for.' He stroked his little beard. 'I am a traveller in a desert who has just reached the longed-for oasis.'

'Don't be silly. I've got supper to look after, it will spoil. E, whatever are you doing? Put me down.'

The Major, who had begun to carry her from the kitchen to the sitting-room, complied, for he was a small man and Joan was a fair weight. In the sitting-room he took her on his knee. 'And what has my little lady been doing while I've been away?'

'Oh, nothing. It's what *you've* been doing that's interesting. I think women have an awful time.'

'Men must work and women must weep.' He made an adroit move, and Joan found herself beneath him on the sofa. She protested.

'Stop it, E, I said supper will spoil, there really isn't time. Oh, not here please, let's go into the bedroom at least.'

'Here,' said Major Easonby Mellon firmly. And there it was. It was enjoyable, and would have been more enjoyable still if the image of Patricia Parker (Miss) had not remained so persistently in his mind. Afterwards Joan sighed.

'Trouble is I don't feel like getting supper now. Shall we just go to bed?'

'Certainly not. The labourer is worthy of his hire.'

While they had supper she said, 'Come on, what have you

been doing? Tell me some of the things that have been happening, the way you always do.'

In a way Joan was not unlike Pat, he reflected, the same sort of round face and almost the same shade of brown hair. And Joan, of course, had very good legs. But the likeness only showed how unwise it was to let yourself go to seed as Joan had done, because there could be no comparison in their attractiveness. Mark you, Joan was thirty-five, or was it thirty-six? But she could never have been in quite the same class as Pat . . .

'What's been *happening*, I asked you.' Joan's voice had a note of querulousness, and the Major brought himself back to matters in hand.

'Let me see, now. Friday – on Friday the chief sent for me and said the job in Norway had fizzled out. Our chap over there, Bjornson, had been selling stuff to the Russians all the time, and this story about a new rocket device was just a plant he was trying on us.'

'He was trying to trick you? To get you sent out there so that they could kill you?'

'Oh, I don't suppose so. Just trying to mislead us, you know, both sides are doing it all the time.'

'And what have you done about him, this man, Johnson?'

'Bjornson. Nothing much. I believe the chief's making a higher bid for his services. We want him to go on working for the Russians, naturally, that's the chief's whole idea.' The Major was familiar with the work of Mr John le Carré and Mr Deighton, and moved easily in this world of the triple- and quadruple-cross. In the manner of the masters he added, 'Spying's a dirty business.'

He embroidered the theme. It had long ceased to be a matter of surprise to him that Joan accepted his inventions so readily. The first step, by which he convinced her that he was an agent, had been the big one. With that surmounted, why should she not believe the tales he told her about the dingy office in Soho and the erratic-tempered chief, the internecine warfare between the rival Department AX 15 and his own UGLI 3 which as he often complained occupied the greater part of their time, the troubles with men in the field and his own occasional trips abroad to rebuke one agent or bribe another, the very infrequent spurts of violence? He congratulated himself sometimes on the fact that he never pitched the stories too steep, so that there were no incidents which moved beyond his powers of invention or which seemed too outrageously unlikely. The struggles between the Chief and Birkett, who was the head of AX 15, were rather like those of a television serial in which different characters come out on top in successive weeks, and at one time Joan had got bored with them as a viewer gets bored with the repetitious activities of a favourite television character. Tonight she gave up after five minutes, and they went to bed.

'Shall I tell you something, E?' she asked, and went on to do so. 'I don't know you, do I? Not the real you. Perhaps the real you is a different person altogether from the one I know.'

He protested vigorously, but as she drifted into sleep it struck him that the phrase about being a different person embodied a truth, although she did not know it. Remove Major Easonby Mellon's good thatch of hair to reveal an egg-bald scalp, take away his beard to show a weak chin, slip out the contact lenses which changed the colour of his eyes from brown to blue, replace the dog tooth check with a suit of indeterminate grey, put him down in Livingston Road, Fraycut, and he would have been recognized by everybody as Arthur Brownjohn.

Lying beside Joan, who within a few minutes had flung out an arm and like Clare in distant Fraycut begun to snore, Major Easonby Mellon thought of Pat, then Joan, then Clare. There could be no doubt that two women and two lives presented a problem, especially when a man was really interested in a third. And then, as naturally as a coin drops into its appointed slot, it occurred to him that this problem would be solved if Clare did not exist, and that it must surely be possible for a man of his ingenuity to bring about that desirable state of affairs. A life without Clare! The prospect was almost too heady to contemplate. Contemplating it, he fell asleep.

Chapter 3

Background of a Deception

Arthur Brownjohn had always been of an inventive turn of mind, and when the war ended he joined with a man in his regiment named Maser in the purchase of a firm called Lektrek Electricals. Arthur's share of the necessary capital had been provided by his army gratuity, together with a small inheritance he had received from an uncle. Lektreks was a flourishing little firm of electrical contractors, and the partners expected it to provide a living for them while they developed the Brownjohn Patent Clutch. This was a type of automatic clutch that had been invented by Arthur during his long periods of idleness as a sergeant in the Catering Corps. He had demonstrated it to Maser on a number of toy battery-operated motor cars, and he was certain that with a reasonably well-equipped workshop he would be able to make a prototype. The construction of this prototype, however, proved more complicated than he had expected. Months passed before it was perfected, or almost perfect, and then the blow fell. A very similar device was put on the market by one of the big car manufacturers, a device so similar that there was no question of going ahead with the Brownjohn Patent Clutch. A few weeks later Maser disappeared, and Arthur discovered that his partner had been fiddling the books by the simple process of having cheques for some accounts made payable to himself instead of to the firm.

Arthur was reluctant to close down Lektreks, for he had half a dozen other ideas in his mind for which an electrical firm would provide ideal backing – an everlasting torch with a battery which recharged itself automatically, an electrical shock cure for hay fever, an electrified rocking chair, and a vibro pad that would open the pores far better than any cream. At the same time it was obvious that the firm would not provide him with a living unless he gave to it the time that he devoted to his blue prints and experiments. Arthur saw that what he needed was, quite

simply, money, but where was it to come from? He had a painful interview with his widower father, a retired customs and excise
official who refused to lend him a penny and advised him to do a
steady job of work. That avenue was closed, and he had no other
approachable relatives. It was at this point that, like many men
before him, he realized the immense usefulness of a rich wife.

Arthur's contacts with women had been slight and few, and
although he had a strong fantasy life it was not associated with
girls. In adolescence he became a surprisingly good tennis player
and won the championship of the local club two years in succession. The champion of a tennis club, particularly if he is young
and unmarried, is a desirable object to many of the women
members, and Arthur had plenty of opportunities for what in
such clubs is still euphemistically called flirtation. At this time,
however, he rather resembled the man who maintained that if the
concept of love had not been invented people would never have
experienced the state itself. He was timid, even fearful, in the
presence of women, and had had sexual intercourse only once
before entering the army. On this occasion he was playing for
the tennis team in an away match, and one of the ladies' doubles
pair took him home and seduced him in the back of her car. In
the army his sexual experiences were more frequent, but equally
brief and unsatisfactory. It is not surprising that when Arthur
contemplated marriage he went to a matrimonial agency. He
soon saw that he had been mistaken in thinking that he was likely
to acquire a rich wife by this means, but the set-up of such
agencies engaged his mind. Obviously an agency needed very
little capital. Might it not be possible to make money out of it?
A few weeks later his agency, Marriage For All, was born.

It is hard to say what might have become of Arthur if he had
not one day met a friend from his old tennis club, been persuaded
to rejoin, and been partnered in a mixed doubles by a meatily
handsome woman named Clare Slattery. They found that they
made a good doubles pair, and although Arthur was too much out
of practice to do well in the singles, they reached the final of the
mixed doubles. When Clare had hit a forehand into the net to
lose the final she shook Arthur's hand vigorously and said:
'Damned bad shot, partner, I'm sorry. Come and have a drink.'

They had two or three drinks, and under questioning from Clare, Arthur found himself telling her what he did. Marriage For All was already showing signs of being profitable, but Arthur kept this activity a close secret because of its faint absurdity. Instead he talked about his inventions, in particular about an idea he had for driving cars by a series of belts and pulleys which would dispense with the need for gears. Clare listened patiently, although with obvious scepticism.

'Very clever. Be a long time before you make any money out of it, though.'

'Oh, I don't know. It's just a matter of getting going.'

'Not relying on it, I hope?'

Arthur laughed. He had a pleasant laugh, and although his hair was rapidly thinning he was still an engaging young man rather than a rabbity middle-aged one. 'Of course not. It's just a side-line for my firm. I put a couple of men on it from time to time, under my supervision naturally.'

'Not your main source of income?'

'Oh no. We're importers of car spares. We can undercut most British manufacturers by thirty per cent.' In saying this he was telling part of the truth. When he and Maser had bought Lek-treks there had indeed been a flourishing business in the importation of cheap spares. Neglect of it, coupled with the defalcations of Maser, had led to the loss of most of their agencies. The small workshop in Bermondsey had been sold and the staff dismissed, and Lektreks now operated from one room in an office block called Paget House, filling orders sent in by long-established clients. With what was for him considerable boldness Arthur asked, 'What kind of job do you do?'

Clare gave one of her gusty laughs. 'Just a bit of part-time work for the W.V.S. I'm independent.'

There was a pause. Then Arthur suggested that they should have another drink.

During the next few weeks they played a great deal of tennis together, and Arthur made some tactful inquiries about Clare. The results were encouraging. Her father had been a fairly important administrator in the Indian Civil Service. Clare had gone to school in England but spent the holidays out in Calcutta, and after leaving school had gone there to live. When her father retired, just before the war, he had bought a house called The Laurels in Fraycut, a prosperous little town in Surrey. Arthur's lodgings were at Stonehead, the next station up the line and a mile or two away, and he fully realized that Fraycut was one social step up from Stonehead. Rich commuters had built houses that were almost small estates on the edge of the town, and he spent an interesting afternoon looking round the place. Livingstone Road was not on this high income commuter level – in another place it might have been called suburban – but still, when he made an exterior inspection of The Laurels, he was impressed by the good bourgeois solidity of the house. Mr Slattery had been dead for a couple of years, his wife had predeceased him, and there were no other children. Altogether, Clare must be quite comfortably off. She was an attractive proposition, and the attraction was if anything increased by the fact that there was, as he put it to himself, no nonsense about her. Something about the sturdiness of her legs and the rough, slightly chapped nature of her skin seemed to put nonsense quite (to use a tennis term) out of court. After one rather gay evening at the club he proposed, standing with her just outside the club-house. He was faintly disturbed by the alacrity with which he was accepted. It was rather as if he had put his head inside the jaws of an apparently stuffed alligator and had found them decisively snapped together.

They were married at a registry office, and given a good send off by the tennis club members. His father met the bride for the first time on the wedding day, and expressed his opinion of her briefly. 'You won't get much change out of *her*, in bed or out of it,' he said. Clare had mentioned more than once that the rest of the family would be coming to the wedding and that she didn't know what they would think about it, and at the reception Arthur first really became aware of the Slattery connection, in the form of two immensely old men called by Clare Uncle Pugs and Uncle Ratty. Uncle Pugs, whose name was Sir Pelham Slattery, made a short but still rather incoherent speech about Clare being a sweet little girl who had grown up to be a lovely young woman. There was a drop on the end of his nose and

Arthur waited for it to fall off. Instead tears from his eyes coursed down his cheeks as he was heard to say, 'Wish every happiness . . . and all the best of . . . ship never . . . rocks . . . Mr and Mrs Browning.' He sat down with the drop on his nose still there. It did not seem worth correcting his error.

A little later Uncle Ratty cornered Arthur. Redfaced and apparently in a state of permanent anger, he was a more formidable proposition than Uncle Pugs. His first words were, 'Now you've got her I hope you can keep her.'

'Keep her?' Arthur had a vision of Clare as some great furry animal escaping from him across fields.

'Look after her, man. Pay the bills.'

Arthur goggled. The idea was quite the reverse of that with which he had married, but he realized that this must not be admitted. 'I have my own business.'

'So Clare said. Selling bits of cars or something. Doesn't sound like much to me.'

'We have agencies.'

Uncle Ratty stared hard at him, and it occurred to Arthur that this terrifying specimen of prehistoric man from the Lincolnshire fens probably did not know what an agency was. All he said, however, was, 'Stand on your own feet. Like cattle.'

That was what it sounded like, but Arthur thought that he must have been mistaken. 'I beg your pardon?'

'Thought it would have been plain enough,' Uncle Ratty said, and moved away.

Arthur never discovered what he had said, nor did Uncle Pugs and Uncle Ratty appear again during his married life. They sank back into the fens from which they had emerged, communicating only by means of cards at Christmas. It was not, however, the last he heard of the Slattery connection, for it was made plain to him that the reception had been a crucial test which he had failed. He later discovered that Uncle Pugs and Uncle Ratty were distant cousins and not real uncles at all, and that in fact Clare had no close relations, but that did not affect their plain perception that he was not up to the mark. It often occurred to Arthur in later years to wonder why Clare had married him. He came to the conclusion that the idea of marrying

31

somebody socially beneath her was really positively congenial, although she pretended otherwise. To social inferiority was added Arthur's natural timidity, which made it easy for her to overbear him on any point, and when these qualities were topped by his disinclination for nonsense he became (as he saw afterwards) an almost ideal husband. Even the failure of the Slattery connection had its compensations so far as Clare was concerned, for it provided permanent proof both of her superiority to her husband and of the sacrifice she had made for him.

The many respects in which he found her less than an ideal wife are too obvious to need cataloguing, but one must be mentioned specifically. So far from marrying a wife happy to provide financial backing that would make it possible for him to give all his time to research, Arthur found that Clare kept her private income intact, and expected him to give her a fixed sum each week for housekeeping. Certainly he lived rent free at The Laurels, certainly also Clare was an economical housekeeper, with a liking for salads and rather sparse vegetarian dishes, but he speedily found the untruth of the old saying that two can live as cheaply as one. The truth was, as he acknowledged in his diary, that he had not grasped the realities of marriage. He had been looking for a bank account, Clare had been looking for a necessary social appendage, and she had got much the better of the bargain. Indeed, her life changed very little from what it had been when she was single. She had a number of regular commitments, which included an afternoon a week at the local Liberal Party offices, one morning a fortnight on a Children's Care Committee, and a visit to Weybridge every Wednesday to shop and attend an art class. She took up other occupations from time to time, including prison visiting, Oxfam and the W.V.S. work which she had mentioned to him, but these were abandoned for one reason or another. Her only problem was that of fitting a husband into the busy round. There was also the tennis club, but the charms of that faded for both of them soon after marriage. And there were social occasions on which a husband was undoubtedly useful, little evenings at home sometimes associated with the Liberal Party but more often with bridge, which both of them played. Arthur's life was a blend of such evenings with gardening and the variety of duties that Clare found for him about the house. It was from the emotional pressures of such a life, and the financial pressure of having to pay for it, that Major Easonby Mellon was born.

Perhaps Arthur did not know himself what he meant to do with the Marriage For All Bureau after his marriage, but it was soon clear to him that it or some similar business would have to be continued, since it was his only considerable source of income. Marriage For All had the disadvantage that he was connected with it in his own person and under his own name. Supposing that he started another agency of a similar kind but run by a different person? Acting was one of the few spheres in which he had shone at school, and he had always taken an obscure pleasure in dressing up.

The idea presented several problems, but they were of a kind that Arthur took pleasure in solving. The name of Easonby Mellon, derived partly from the financier Andrew Mellon and partly from the hero of a book he had enjoyed as a schoolboy, was the least of them. The military rank seemed appropriate and the clothes, wig and beard were designed as suitable to it. The wig maker he went to appreciated the interest shown by his client. He was surprised when Arthur said that he did not want to match his original faded light brown colouring, but he asked no questions. Arthur had been keen on a red wig, which he felt would express Easonby Mellon's personality, but he had been persuaded that a brown one with reddish tints would be far less conspicuous.

'The usual problem of course, sir, is matching the natural hair colour at back and sides, but in your case –' The wig maker coughed, and it was true that Arthur was quite remarkably lacking in hair.

The wig was thick and curly and he was delighted by the fact that he could comb it so that (as he was shown with mirrors) perfectly genuine scalp would show through the invisible net foundation. 'Nobody would know,' he said exultantly.

The wig maker, who had himself a splendid head of hair, was solemn. 'Nobody at all, sir. I know husbands whose wives have no idea that they wear a wig.'

'Is that really so? Even when –'

'Even then, sir, certainly. And if I may suggest a small but possibly useful refinement –'

'Indeed you may.'

'It may be an advantage to have a trio, showing various stages of development.' Arthur was baffled. The wig maker explained that he could have three wigs, Number One showing the hair cut rather short, Number Two of normal cut, and Number Three with hair growing rather long at the back of the neck. 'I have a client whose wife tells him that he really must go to the barber when he is wearing Number Three. It positively makes his day, sir.'

'I'm sure it does.' He ordered Numbers One, Two and Three accordingly. The wig maker was less enthusiastic about the idea of a beard, saying that this would need great care when eating and shaving, in case it got wet and lost its shape. It seemed to Arthur, however, that a beard was an essential part of Easonby Mellon's personality, and by having it cut well away from the mouth he managed to deal with it successfully.

He was delighted with the result. 'You are an artist,' he said to the wig maker, a wizened, aged figure who perhaps proved his artistic nature by going out of business shortly after executing Arthur's commission, and dying in poverty a few months later. A six-line obituary appeared in *The Times*, referring to him as 'a character of the theatrical world'.

There was also the matter of renting an office and of opening a bank account. His first office was down a dingy side street but when a room in the Romany House block fell vacant he took it, signing the lease with his left hand and giving as reference Mr Brownjohn of Lektreks, who duly sent a letter certifying Major Mellon's reliability as a tenant. He used his left hand also when providing a signature for the bank. It was Arthur Brownjohn, bald, rabbity and darkly suited, who left The Laurels each morning. In the Lektreks office he kept Easonby Mellon's clothes, and he installed a mirror by the help of which, at first with infinite care and some difficulty, he fitted wig and beard. A perfect fitting took nearly half an hour, although under stress he could manage in fifteen minutes. After changing he went down in the self-operating lift and walked to Romany House, which was only a couple of streets and five minutes' walk away.

At first this double identity was a game, a way of safeguarding the shameful secret represented by the fact that his income came from a matrimonial agency, but such games have a way of developing their own meanings and subtleties, so that although we begin by playing them self-indulgently they end by taking charge of us and revealing unexpected facets of our personalities. As months changed into years, and Matrimonial Assistance flourished, and the deception remained immune from detection, its author found a positive pleasure in accentuating his own meekness and timidity at The Laurels in a way which gave additional zest to the exhibition of the very different characteristics of Major Easonby Mellon. There is no difference, Congreve observed, between continued affectation and reality, and Major Mellon proved to Arthur Brownjohn the truth of this aphorism. He was self-assured where Arthur was hesitant, brusque where he was compliant, an eager eater and drinker where Arthur was a frugal one. That is, Major Mellon became all of these things by pleasant experimentation. He developed also a quite un-Arthurian liking for a bit of nonsense, first made manifest when a woman aspirant to marriage began to take off her clothes in the office one day, and the Major found himself eagerly helping her.

Joan was the most notable of several bits of nonsense. She had turned up one day after writing a letter, a good-natured plump woman in her late twenties, whose husband had been killed in Korea. On that first afternoon she had succumbed to the Major's advances, and thereafter he took her to a hotel every weekday for a fortnight. It was the sort of situation that had to be resolved in one way or another partly because Joan, although rather vague, had realized that the matrimonial agency did not occupy the whole of his time, partly because he felt an urgent need for some relief from Clare. Marriage was the answer, marriage and the setting up of a second, quite distinct home for his second personality. Arthur Brownjohn was terrified by the idea, but Major Easonby Mellon carried it through joyfully.

He explained to Joan that his status as a member of UGLI 3 was supposed to preclude marriage, but that for her sake he was prepared to risk it so long as the ceremony was kept absolutely quiet. They signed the register at Caxton Hall in the presence of witnesses brought in from the street, Joan found and rented the apartment in Clapham, and Major Mellon transferred his effects to it. These chiefly consisted of clothes, and Joan exclaimed in wonder at the quality of his suits. Arthur Brownjohn bought his clothes ready made, but Easonby Mellon's tweeds came from Corefinch and Burleigh just off Savile Row, one of the most expensive tailors in London. Clare had always been incurious about Arthur's business, and when he said that he would have to be away very often in the middle of the week because he was taking over the work of their Midlands and Northern representatives her reaction was simply one of alarm that business might be falling off. Reassured on this point she adapted herself with only occasional grumbles to the absences from home necessitated by his additional work.

So a new pattern of life was fixed for him. From Friday to Monday Arthur Brownjohn was to be found at The Laurels, from Tuesday to Thursday Major Easonby Mellon put up his slippered feet on the sofa at Elm Drive. The wig and beard proved to be the triumphant success that had been predicted. He shaved each morning with an electric razor, and washed only cursorily, taking care to keep water away from the beard. Even in the greatest ardours of their married life Joan did not suspect his secret. Occasionally he varied the pattern of his weekly activities a little but not very much, for he felt in it a symmetry like that in a work of art. At times he really did make a tour of Birmingham, Manchester, Leeds and other cities in which Lektreks still had customers. And if Joan, that perpetually amiable and resilient cushion, was an almost perfect partner for the part of his nature represented by Major Easonby Mellon, there could be no doubt that Arthur Brownjohn had a basic desire to be dominated by some Clare-like figure. To possess and be possessed by both was almost perfect, or seemed so until the advent of Patricia Parker, which had been preceded early in March by the disastrous affair of Mr Clennery Tubbs.

Chapter 4

Wypitklere

Clennery Tubbs had appeared on the day that Arthur went to demonstrate a simplified automatic dishwasher of his own invention to a firm named Inter Commerce. This was something on which he had worked intermittently for some years, and it had at one time been in the kitchen at The Laurels. Often it worked perfectly, but upon occasions a destructive gremlin seemed to occupy the washer. The gremlin wrecked this demonstration, at which the activating rods got quite out of hand and broke half the plates. Arthur had been sadly packing it up afterwards, and was on his way out when he was stopped by a small man with wild sandy hair and markedly protruding eyes.

'Rotten luck. Bet it works nine times out of ten.'

'You weren't at the demo, were you?'

'Couldn't help hearing what Jenner was saying.'

'You're quite right. If only they'd give me another trial after I've ironed out that little trouble.'

The man shook his head. 'No good. Won't do it.'

'Certainly Mr Jenner seemed rather abrupt.' Jenner was the chief engineer of the company, and he had been caustic.

'Jenner's a pig. Won't even touch my invention.'

'Good heavens. And you're part of the firm.'

The man held out a hand. 'Way it goes. Name's Tubbs, Clennery Tubbs. Come and have a pint.'

Over the pint Tubbs talked about his invention. It was a cream that prevented the windows of cars from misting or frosting up, not just for a few hours or even for a day, but for several months. After that you put on some more cream. 'Firm tested it out. Worked perfectly. Even Jenner said so.'

'What was wrong then?'

'Inter Commerce make a windscreen wiping cloth, new pattern, big sales. Offered me five hundred to buy up my cream, then scrap it.'

'That's really dishonest.'

'Should have known better. Jenner's jealous.'

'You can offer it to another firm.'

'He'd see I got the sack. Couldn't afford to take the chance. Like to see Wypitklere?'

'What's that?'

'Wipe it clear, see? Name it's patented under, mustn't use the actual spelling of words. I said, like to see it?'

The demonstration took place on a moist, misty day. They set out for a drive in Tubbs's small car, and before they left he wiped over the screen with Wypitklere. The screen remained clear throughout the drive when, as Tubbs triumphantly pointed out, the windscreens of almost all the cars they passed were misted over. Arthur was impressed but not yet convinced.

'Try it on your own car,' Tubbs said almost angrily.

Arthur was compelled to admit that he had no car. At one time Clare had driven a car but after being involved in an accident in which the other driver had been seriously injured she gave up motor cars for ever. She had made it clear to Arthur before their marriage that she would not expect her husband to drive or possess one, and at the time this had seemed unimportant. In the end Tubbs gave him two small pots of the cream and Arthur used one on the windscreen of Payne's car and gave the other to their doctor, a man named Hubble. On Payne's car it worked like a charm.

'I really think you're on to something this time, old man,' Payne had said, and he had implied that the bank might even consider giving it financial support.

Financial support was what Tubbs required. He was insistent that he must on no account be telephoned at Inter Commerce, and they always met in pubs. It was a different pub every time and Tubbs, who was a rather seedy little man, always looked nervously around. He said that somebody else was interested in the idea.

'They're talking about putting up five thousand quid for a twenty per cent interest. Could you meet that?'

'I'm afraid not.'

'Money's not important,' Tubbs said, rather to Arthur's

surprise, for he had gathered the distinct impression that the other was in need of it. Tubbs ran a hand through his hair so that it stood up like a golliwog's, and stroked his rather indeterminate little beard. 'What I mean, Brownjohn, I'd consider less cash and a bigger percentage for myself.'

'If this stuff does all you say why don't you develop it on your own, borrow from your bank?' Arthur asked, with what he felt to be considerable shrewdness.

Tubbs moved his glass of beer about uneasily. Then, as if coming to a decision, he looked up and met Arthur's gaze. He had an intermittent pant like that of an exhausted dog, which he attributed to a weak heart, or in his own words a funny ticker. His eyeballs were enormous. 'Must be straight. I've got a record.'

'You've been in prison!'

'Right. Bank won't touch me, can't get backing, wouldn't be trying to sell Wypitklere if I could develop it myself. Strictly confidential, keep it to yourself, Jenner would have me out in a minute if he knew.'

'What was the offence?'

'I was *accused* of embezzlement. It was all a mistake.'

Somehow this admission convinced Arthur of Tubbs's good faith, perhaps because he felt that nobody would admit that he had been in prison if he were intending to commit a fraud afterwards. Money, however, was the problem. Payne had again spoken glowingly of the cream, but if money was to be borrowed from the bank Clare would have to know about it, and he knew that she would never agree. After much discussion Tubbs had said that he would take a thousand pounds for a twenty per cent share of all profits, but where was the money to come from? Easonby Mellon had to provide for two homes. There was very little money in his bank account, only just over five hundred pounds in the joint account Arthur shared with Clare. It was when he thought of the harmless deception that he practised in the role of Easonby Mellon that Arthur contemplated extending that deception. He flattered himself (or rather, he did not flatter himself) that he had some skill as a copyist, and Clare's signature was almost as familiar to him as his own. She had recently received the quarterly bank statement for the money in her private account, which he knew to be a considerable sum. He signed Clare's name to a cheque for five hundred pounds, which he transferred from her private to their joint account.

Looking back afterwards he thought that he must have been temporarily mad, but at the time he could think of nothing but getting a share of Wypitklere, and he persuaded himself that the deception would never be discovered. By the time she got her next quarterly statement at the end of June he would be able to repay the money through a loan. He would even repay it with a hundred pounds' interest, so that if she noticed the unauthorized withdrawal her anger would be changed to pleasure.

The agreement was signed in the office of a solicitor named Eversholt, who had drawn it up. He appeared to regard Arthur, and indeed the whole affair, with an air of faint astonishment, and pronounced the name of Wypitklere as though it were a a bad joke. In the end Tubbs agreed to increase Arthur's share of profits to twenty-five per cent. It seemed to him that he had driven a hard bargain, and he was pleased that Tubbs appeared satisfied.

'Here's my hand, partner.' Tubbs's hand was rather damp. 'What are the development plans?'

Arthur had not really considered this problem, beyond feeling that it must be possible to get backing for such an obvious winner in half a dozen places. Tubbs, however, did not seem disturbed by his vagueness. 'We'll be in touch then. 'Cheeribye,' he said. It did not occur to Arthur until afterwards that there was anything valedictory about his tone.

The blow fell within a week. Arthur had had several pots of Wypitklere made up from the formula given him by Tubbs, and had spent some time in making sketches for a wrapper to go round the container. He had also worked out on paper the costing of several thousand pots of the cream, the profitable retail price allowing for a handsome discount to distributors, and the likely profits. This delightful planning was disturbed by a telephone call from Payne. He asked Arthur, in a tone lacking his usual false joviality, to come and see him at home on the following morning.

When Arthur arrived Payne led him to the garage. He said

nothing, but pointed to the windscreen and other glass sections of his car.

Arthur stared, aghast. In some places the glass was streaked as if somebody had drawn a cutting knife across it, and in others it was deeply pitted as though some glass-eating animal had been burrowing within it.

'Well?' the bank manager said.

Arthur wanted to say that it was not his fault, but what he actually said was, 'I can't explain it.'

Payne nodded grimly, as though this was what he had expected to hear. 'You don't deny that your *invention* is responsible for this.'

'I suppose it must be.'

'I shall have new glass put in throughout the car, and I shall charge it to you.'

'Of course. Of course, yes, please do.'

'Very well. I should have known better. In the meantime, I can't use my car.'

'I can't think what's gone wrong.' He had hardly known what he was saying, but the full horror of his situation was borne in upon him. 'I hope there isn't any reason – I hope you won't mention this to Clare.'

As Payne said to his wife afterwards, in that moment he felt really sorry for the poor little beggar, angry as he had been when he discovered the state of the glass. That his first thought should have been not of the failure of his invention, but the need to keep that failure from his wife. It was pathetic. 'Served me right, really,' he said to her philosophically. 'I should have known that anything he invented was bound to be a dud. You can't help liking Arthur, but he hasn't got much in the top storey.' They both made a point of being particularly nice to Arthur afterwards, and never mentioned a word about the matter to Clare.

Arthur went home a stricken man. He talked to the firm of wholesale chemists who had been making up Wypitklere and told them what he was using it for. They told him that the agent which cleared the windscreen had a corrosive effect upon glass. He paid a visit to Inter Commerce and saw the objectionable Jenner, but he was not really surprised to learn that no Clennery

Tubbs had ever worked for them. He timidly recalled the occasion on which his dishwasher had been tested and Jenner remembered the man, who had come to show him some kind of demisting cream. Jenner had seen something similar before, and had not been taken in. Arthur saw the solicitor, who shrugged his shoulders and said that he had been approached simply to draw up an agreement and knew nothing about Tubbs. He went to the address given on the agreement and found that it was a tobacconist's, a mere accommodation address. The man remembered Tubbs but said that he had not been in for some time. He realized that Tubbs had spotted him for a possible gull when he came out from the demonstration and had taken advantage of Arthur's mistaken belief that he worked for Inter Commerce. He had been the victim of an obvious confidence trick.

The effect upon him was, superficially at least, an odd one. He felt angry about Tubbs, but his bitterest feeling was reserved for Clare. At the back of his mind, as he now dimly realized, there had been a belief that one day he would be free of his thraldom to her, one day an invention would make a lot of money and the money would give him freedom. Now this would never happen. He had no faith any longer that he would ever make money out of an invention, and just a few weeks ahead of him there loomed the terrible day of reckoning when Clare received her quarterly statement.

Chapter 5

Right Approach?

Arthur had often thought of abandoning the Lektreks office, but he had always decided against it. There was still a certain amount of business which came in automatically, and it helped to maintain his commercial identity. Supposing that one of his Fraycut acquaintances decided to pay him a visit, there was the office and there, during part of every day, was Arthur with the appurtenances of office life around him. He spent much of his time there in reading about old murder cases. He had always been fascinated by the idea of a murder so dazzlingly ingenious that its perpetrator could never be convicted even though his identity was known. He had a cupboard filled with volumes from the Notable British Trials series, and he read them again and again, observing where these aspirants to perfection had gone wrong. After the idea of Clare's death had come to him he jotted down some notes in the black-covered diary, which he brought up to London in his brief-case:

DIARY

Problem. A wishes to dispose of C. He inherits money, will be obvious suspect. *But:* A's reputation is such that suspicion will not be automatic. *Conclusion:* A must proceed by a course avoiding usual means, i.e. death must appear either natural or somehow completely detached from him.

Why do I write like that, all rubbish? A and C. If a man can't be honest with himself in his diary there's nothing left for him. I want to see Clare dead. (Waited five minutes before I could write that down. Having written it I feel better, relieved. Know I shan't do it, only write. I've never done anything I wanted.)

Consider it, though. How would A. Brownjohn do this? Nothing easier. Obtain gelignite, fit it to vacuum cleaner, cleaner switched on, up goes she. But suppose Susan used the cleaner first?

Second idea. Clare often uses motor mower. Make ditto arrangement with it, simple enough. Mower and Clare vanish together. Yes?

Or electric shock, but not in bathroom, played out. Do it through

43

electric iron in kitchen, fix wire so that she touches it while she's doing some washing? Think again, A. Brownjohn. *Not advisable*.

Why not? Too ingenious. A. Brownjohn is known to be a bit of an inventor, always fiddling with gadgets. If Clare's thoroughly shocked or blows up (joke) friends will say: 'Ah ha, Arthur B plays with racing cars, invented a dishwasher, etc. He's the man, needn't look further.' Somebody tells the police.

Stick to old favourites then and make a note, you must use nothing original, nothing mechanical.

Be honest with yourself, AB. You can write and you can think, but you're not going to do it.

Safety valve.

He finished the diary entry, which was less coherent than usual, and closed the book. But he went on thinking. He was precluded by natural dislike of shedding blood from anything that involved the use of an axe, hatchet or bludgeon. A gun might be clean and humane, but he neither possessed nor was skilled in using one. Drowning was ruled out by the fact that Clare had a firm objection to going in or upon the water.

The longer Arthur thought, the more he became convinced that he would be wise to stick to those old favourites, fire or poison. He considered, as he had often done before, the Rouse and Armstrong cases, and the Croydon murders.

He may have been drawn to Rouse and Armstrong by the similarity between their situations and his own. Rouse had tried to escape the burden of a bigamous marriage and not merely two but several establishments, as well as a number of maintenance orders, by setting fire to his car with a body in it that he hoped would be identified as his own. The body was thought to be that of a tramp whom he had met. Like Arthur, Rouse had wanted to start a new life, but what absurd mistakes he had made! Letting himself be seen climbing out of a ditch after setting fire to the car, and then going straight off to one of his girl friends. Arthur would never have been so foolish. The case fascinated him, but he had to acknowledge that even if he could have brought himself to kill a completely harmless stranger, the result would not really be what he wanted. It was true that he could simply disappear, but the truth was that he did not fancy being Easonby Mellon for ever. When you came right down to it, he had to admit that he wanted the money of which Clare had so unfairly deprived him by keeping it in her personal account, and if he wanted the money Arthur Brownjohn could not disappear.

He considered Armstrong, the timid little solicitor who had borne so meekly his wife's rebukes about his smoking and drinking, and had killed her by the use of arsenic. Here again he was struck at every re-reading by the stupid mistakes that had led to Armstrong's downfall. With his objective successfully achieved, what must he do but try to poison a rival solicitor! And the carelessness of leaving a packet of arsenic in one of his pockets was really inexcusable. If only he had been content with a death that had been certified as heart disease, if only he had not been subject to the hubris that seems so often to affect the successful poisoner. The Croydon poisonings showed what could be done by somebody whose feelings remained firmly under control. Here, in 1929, three members of a united family had died, one probably by arsenic put into his beer, another by arsenic in her soup, the third by arsenic in her tonic. Nobody had been tried, let alone convicted, for these crimes, and – this was the really vital point that must be latched on to – the first two deaths had been certified as due to natural causes and there would have been no trouble at all had not the mark been overstepped by a third death. Again, there was no question of Arthur's going on from one person to another in such an unreasonable and, as it might almost be called, orgiastic manner. And there was one decisive point in favour of poison. In both the Armstrong and Croydon cases the doctors concerned had been friendly with the families, and had therefore been readier than they might otherwise have been to give a death certificate. At this point Arthur thought of old Doctor Hubble, and a warm delicious sense came to him that his problem was solved. He made a further diary note:

'The *modus operandi* is ordered by the means that are to hand.' He admired the phrase, which seemed to him like a maxim of Napoleon's. Doctor Hubble was the means and the *modus operandi* would therefore be poison, although it would probably

45

be desirable to avoid arsenic. When Arthur had settled this he felt much easier in his mind. He donned the clothing of Major Easonby Mellon, and went to meet Miss Patricia Parker.

'Your secretary's out again,' she said when she arrived.

'Yes. The fact is you're rather a special case, Pat. I've got half a dozen names here, and I can give you them if you like, but frankly they're not good enough for you.' She did not comment on this, but smoothed her skirt over her knees. 'You said you weren't working?'

'Not at the moment.'

'I'm wondering if we can't find some crackerjack job.'

'I can find a job easily enough. I thought this was a matrimonial agency, not an employment bureau.'

'So it is.' The Major laughed heartily. 'But you present a problem we don't often meet, Pat. I'll be frank and say I find you damned attractive personally. I was hoping you'd come to lunch with me again today.'

She looked at him and said, with complete self-possession, 'Are you married?'

It was an automatic reflex that made him say he was not. She nodded, and they went to lunch at the little place round the corner. This time she did not comment on the service, drank her share of the wine, and accepted the brandy that he offered to follow it. When he murmured over the brandy about somewhere he knew, she interrupted him. 'Your flat?'

Such brusqueness slightly disconcerted him. 'As a matter of fact it's a hotel. Very discreet, I can assure you.' She simply nodded again.

Over lunch he had been making a reassessment of her, and had come to the conclusion that she did not want to get married but simply wanted a man. Such a phenomenon was not unknown to him, and her conduct in the hotel room (it was the same hotel to which he had taken Joan and other ladies) confirmed this hypothesis. They stayed there until six o'clock, and he reflected at one point that the things she had refused to do for Parker must have been very unusual. Perhaps there was no Parker, he thought sleepily, perhaps she had been telling lies, but what did it matter? He closed his eyes, and opened them again to find her unmistakably ready for another bit of nonsense.

'You're finished.'

'No no,' he said gallantly. Major Easonby Mellon was never finished. It could not be denied however that he was distinctly exhausted when they parted, and not wholly sorry when she said that she would be out of London for three or four days and would get in touch with him when she returned. When he got back to Joan he ate the enormous meal she had cooked and then fell asleep in the armchair watching television. That night in bed she dug him in the ribs.

'I'll tell you one thing, E.'

'What's that?'

'All these books now, they keep saying there's no romance in being an agent, but I'll tell you what, there's no romance in being an agent's wife. It's just plain dull.'

He did not reply. He was thinking about being married to Pat, which might be exhausting but would also be exciting. Then he began to think about Doctor Hubble.

Doctor Hubble was a hairy man. Hair sprouted from his ears, nostrils and wrists and, although he must have been sixty years old, a thick thatch of glossy black hair lay on his head. He was big, red-faced, and had the reputation of being still a very useful golfer and a hard drinker. Tales of his going round to see patients when he was so drunk that he was hardly able to walk straight or write a prescription were legion, and Arthur had had confirmation of this on one occasion when Clare had influenza and Hubble came round to see her reeking of whisky. It was generally believed that he had once diagnosed acute appendicitis as a bit of a stitch from too much exercise, and that the patient had died. Clare liked him because she had known him for years and he was, as she said, a proper doctor who came when you asked him and had a real bedside manner, not like these young whippersnappers who just looked at you and then prescribed some drug or other. Doctor Hubble was a great man for a good old-fashioned bottle of tonic. His capacity for the part Arthur meant him to play was confirmed as soon as they began to talk in Hubble's sitting-room.

'You'll have a drop of the hard stuff.' He barely waited for assent before pouring two liberal tots of whisky. 'And if you take my advice you won't spoil it with soda.' Arthur, who did not much like whisky and preferred soda to plain water, meekly took what he was given. 'You said this wasn't a professional visit.'

'I owe you an apology.' Hubble stared at him. 'About Wypit-klere.'

'Wipe it clear? Oh, you mean that stuff for the car. Your invention.' He laughed as if this were a joke. 'Tell you the truth I haven't used it yet. Slipped my mind.'

'That's good. I've discovered a small flaw in the formula, it doesn't work quite as it should on certain types of glass. I don't think you should use it. Perhaps you'd let me have it back.'

The doctor rooted about uncertainly in a desk that was filled to overflowing with papers. Then he shouted for his wife, a thin wispy woman whose pallor provided a strong contrast to his abundant vitality. 'Know where that whatyemaycallit is, tin of stuff Brownjohn here gave me a few days ago? Hope I haven't given it to someone for rheumatism.' He roared with laughter.

The tin proved to be in the garage. When it was back in Arthur's possession Hubble suggested another drink.

'Thank you. Not quite so strong this time.' He saw with pleasure that the doctor gave himself another generous measure. 'There's something else I wanted to mention. I'm a little worried about Clare.' He launched into an exaggerated description of the gastric symptoms from which Clare said she suffered. 'I wondered if you could come round and give her a check-up without, you know, mentioning that I'd been in to see you.'

'Of course, of course. Let's see, today's Friday. I'm playing a round on Sunday morning. What say I look in afterwards, we met in the street and you asked me in for a drink before lunch? Don't suppose there's anything in it, but no harm in taking a looksee.' Arthur assented. A visit after Hubble had played a round of golf and had several drinks in the club-house should be ideal.

A hasty study of medical manuals had left him undecided about what poison it would be advisable to use, but he carried out these preliminary moves with what seemed to him considerable ingenuity. Clare used a tooth powder, not paste. Arthur had bought a jar of this and spent some of the time in replacing about half of the contents with powdered *nux vomica*. The change in appearance was almost undetectable, and on Friday night he substituted his jar for the one in the bathroom cabinet. The results were gratifying. Clare was slightly sick in the middle of the night and sick again in mid-morning. The beauty of this device was that he could end the sickness whenever he wished by replacing the harmless tooth powder. He did this on Saturday night, and then put back the powder containing *nux vomica* again on Sunday morning. Clare was sick during the morning, and when Hubble arrived she was ready to be examined and to tell him her symptoms in detail.

The doctor was upstairs with her for thirty minutes. When he came down he said, 'I'll take that drop of the hard stuff you were offering.' His eyes were slightly bloodshot. He drank half the whisky at a gulp. 'That's better.'

'What do you think?'

'Wrong eating.'

'What's that?'

Hubble glared at him. 'I said, wrong eating. All these filthy health foods. I've told her so.'

'But I thought they were good for you.'

'They may be good for *some people*.' Hubble sounded as though he were referring to Trobriand islanders. 'Not for her. She needs red meat. What did she have last night? Grated stuff.'

'I had it too.'

The doctor ignored that. 'I've put her on a high protein diet.'

'But there's nothing serious?'

'Nothing at all.'

Clare was more indignant than upset, but small steaks and chops made their appearance on the table and her attacks of sickness ceased. A brilliant idea had come to Arthur about the *modus operandi* – he did not care, even in his mind, to use the word poison. It had been given him by Hubble and it was especially gratifying because it fulfilled the maxim that out of defeat shall come forth victory. The ingredient in Wypitklere that had produced such drastic effects on glass was zincalium, a derivative of a metallic acid based on zinc. Would it not be possible to use zincalium as the *modus operandi*? On Tuesday morning Arthur left to take up his mid-week residence at Clapham. He left Clare the tooth powder containing *nux vomica* so that she might be satisfyingly sick in his absence. Perhaps she would call in Hubble, perhaps not. It really didn't matter. When he returned next weekend he hoped to resolve the Clare situation for good.

Chapter 6

Wrong Effect

Nobody loves a poisoner. In the long lists of means of murder it would probably be true to say that poison is the method most generally abhorred and despised. People will express sympathy with axe-killers, stranglers, gunmen, even with those who chop their victims' bodies into bits, but not with poisoners. Yet Armstrong was thought of by acquaintances as an agreeable little man, and Crippen was in many respects amiable. Some poisoners like Neill Cream are far from agreeable characters, but many more are commonplace, emotionally undeveloped people who find themselves in a position from which murder by poison seems the only, or at least the simplest, way out. Once this has been decided the controls operating in their everyday life cease to be effective. So Arthur stopped thinking about Clare as a person at all, and managed to regard her as solely an object to be removed.

He spent a large part of his three days at Clapham reading about the effects of zincalium and deciding on the best way of using it. 'If zincalium is used with sufficient care and cunning for homicidal purposes we may get a succession of mild attacks of the acute symptoms with remissions,' he read in one text-book. There was no time for that, but happily the tooth powder should serve the same purpose of providing a case history which stretched back a little way in time. If there was one aspect of the affair that gave him satisfaction it was the ingenuity of using a preliminary emitic that was perfectly harmless. Had that been done before? He thought not. He was pleased to learn that zincalium was not an exceptionally painful poison. It was accompanied by 'nausea, vomiting, general uneasiness and depression', but did not cause a burning sensation or have the drastic effects of some other metallic poisons. It would have been pleasant to use a drug that caused Clare to cease upon the midnight with no pain, thereby avoiding all unpleasantness, but

51

one must use the means that are to hand. What really disturbed him was the possibility that he might not be able to distil enough zincalium out of the Wypitklere to achieve the desired result. He distilled the zincalium in the kitchen at Elm Drive while Joan looked on, fascinated.

'E, whatever are you doing?'

'Distilling this, my dear.'

'I see that, but what's it for?'

He looked up. 'You've heard me talk about Flexner in the department?'

'The expert in all those terrible germs and poisons. But I thought he was down at that place, what is it, Porton?'

'Most of the time he is, but he's been in the office recently, advising the Chief about disposing of a rather awkward customer, a Rumanian. He's given some advice which the Chief is slightly doubtful about, and I'm just checking one of his conclusions. You know what the Chief's like. He thinks someone from the other side may have got at Flexner.'

He poured the mixture into a beaker. 'If everything's in order there should be a sediment at the bottom and a colourless liquid at the top.' He watched the sediment settle with satisfaction, strained off the liquid above it, and poured it away.

'Is that the way it should be? That powder?'

'Precisely.'

'So Flexner hasn't been got at?'

'Evidently not.'

'The Chief knows he can rely on you, doesn't he?'

He shook his head. 'Not a bit of it. He's probably got somebody else checking my conclusions. It may even be that this bit of research is a blind, and that we're going to use quite a different method to deal with our Rumanian friend. But if the Chief hasn't been fooling me there is enough of this powder here to kill a hundred people.'

Here he was being optimistic, for the truth was that the textbooks he had consulted were extremely vague about the amount of zincalium needed. He would have to experiment, that was all. After the powder had dried he divided it carefully, putting the larger quantity into one envelope and the smaller into another.

He sealed both packets and put the two of them into one big Manila envelope. Shades of Armstrong! But there was this difference, that he would burn the envelope immediately after use. No tell-tale traces would be found in *his* pockets.

'A hundred people. Oh, E, I wish you could get out of it.' Joan was almost in tears. He stroked her hair.

'Sometimes I wish I could too. But once you're in the service, you're in it for life.'

DIARY

Sunday, 18 May

2 a.m. Sitting at my desk. Peaceful. Just been down to see Clare. She is sleeping quietly, one hand clutching the coverlet. Stood looking at her, all colour gone from her face leaving it like milk. She seemed very young, I felt sorry for her. But the person I have to feel sorry for is myself. I have ruined everything.

After Hubble had gone this evening I thought about my life and saw it as a record of failure. I have never done anything that succeeded, never carried through any idea, although I do believe I have had some good ones. Sometimes I have been really stupid, as I was about the cleaning cream. I trust people too much. I remember Mother putting her hand on my head and saying she hoped I should find somebody to look after me, because that was what I should need in life. I didn't understand her then, but do now. Remember also Roberts, headmaster at the grammar school, telling Mother that I lacked resolution. He was right. Sometimes it seems to me that what we do is a matter of the way we look. If I looked different I should *be* different. I think I have proved that through EM.

Putting it down here may make me feel better. Tonight shan't be able to sleep. Desperate.

Came back on Friday, asked Clare how she had been. Tuesday night she had been sick, she said, Wednesday morning sick again. Said perhaps she'd had too much protein after all, had she rung Hubble?

'I nearly rang him. And then I thought I should be able to find out what it was myself. Couldn't be the food. I'd been ill before that. And I did find out what it was.'

'What?'

'My tooth powder.' I was aghast, terrified. I stammered something, said it couldn't be. She gave me a glare of hideous triumph.

'Don't you see? Every time I brushed my teeth I was sick. There was something wrong with that tin, it must have been bad. I've changed to a tube, had no trouble since.' I asked what she had done with the tin and she said she'd thrown it away. Also said she would tell Hubble when she saw him tomorrow.

'Tomorrow?' I must have looked foolish, but then she always thinks I look foolish. She said she had asked some people in for drinks, Hubble one of them.

After thinking about this I realized that perhaps it was all to the good. When Hubble came I should be able to drop in a worried reference to her gastric trouble, even mention in a joking way her attribution of it to tooth powder. Then tomorrow night a small dose of Z in her nightcap. The large dose the following weekend.

We played bezique (let her win) and I made the nightcap and took it up. She said I made a good whisky toddy. Expect I looked strange at that, because she went on: 'Not been drinking, have you?' I said of course not. 'It's for your own good I'm saying it, you know you can't drink.'

She put her hand on mine, then belched. I was disgusted, it was all I could do not to turn away my head. Her hand is very coarse with the veins standing out, actually it is bigger than my own hand which is small and rather delicate. There is something coarse altogether about her which I find repulsive.

That was Friday. Saturday was routine. Up at seven-thirty, break-fast, potter round the garden in old clothes, out with the shopping basket. Clare doesn't like me to go shopping. However. *I* like it so why shouldn't I do it? Why should I feel guilty as though I were letting her down, shopping isn't a thing a Slattery man would do?

Damn all Slatteries.

Remember thinking, soon I shall be able to go shopping without worrying, all on my owneo, buy what I like. That would be a real pleasure. I wonder if it's true that all the most intense pleasures are solitary? After all, I haven't joined a slot racing club. I say it's because Clare wouldn't like the members to come here, but perhaps it's because I like slot racing on my own.

Perhaps. Doesn't matter. The question's not going to arise.

3 o'clock. Wide awake.

Went to the supermarket in the High Street, marvellous place, met Mrs Payne and of course she asked about Clare. Said she was better, saw my opportunity.

'I'm not quite satisfied, though. Do you know what she says caused the trouble? Her tooth powder.' Mrs P stared, as well she might. 'She's thrown it out. I don't think tooth powder could cause sickness, do you?'

'I never heard of such a thing. Is she getting fancies?' To Mrs P 'fancies' are like scarlet fever. Had a little talk with her about prices, very interesting. Corned beef in the supermarket is ninepence a tin cheaper than at Penquick's. I believe the day of the private grocer has gone. Went home feeling pleased with self at mentioning powder. A good general is a bold general I thought.

Drinks in the evening, representative Fraycut selection. Payne and wife, retired naval commander named Burke, Charles Ransom secretary of local Liberal Party, one or two others. And of course Hubble plus wife, H smelling of drink. Susan handed round hot sausages and bits of things on toast, I looked after drinks. Had one or two. Told tooth powder story to people, including Hubble, asked him what he thought, had the powder caused the trouble?

He glared at me, made me feel uncomfortable. 'Told you what I thought.' He said something about high protein diet.

I was going to ask him how he explained the tooth powder and have another drink when Clare put her hand over mine (again!) said I'd had enough. Caught sight of self in a glass tie askew and head shining, was inclined to agree. I knew I had to keep absolutely clear-headed, in command of events. Clare introduced me to a ghastly man named Elsom, engineering executive, face full of teeth, recently came to Fraycut, Clare met him at some Liberal do. Conversation:

E   How's it going, old man?

Self   Very well, thanks.

E   Must have a bit of lunch one day. I mean, we're more or less in the same line, I believe. What's your office number?

Self   I'm in quite a small way, you know.

E   Still, I'd like to have a natter. Might be useful. Nothing too small to interest GBD.

Self   GBD?

E   Gracey, Basinghall and Derwent. My outfit. They tell me you're by way of being an inventor.

Self   Just an amateur.

E   Don't be modest. You must make your money out of something.

Obviously a pest. But I've dealt with people like this before, have a good technique of brushing them off, even though I say so. Introduced him now to Mrs Payne who started on at once about disgraceful English weather and their holiday in Spain. Had to give Elsom office number but got away after that. Subsequent technique will be to say I have another engagement if he rings, and if I'm not there then naturally there's no reply.

Half an hour later they'd all gone. Clare in a filthy temper when we cleared things away, seemed to think I'd had too much.

'Arthur, how many times have I told you not to take more than two glasses?' Couldn't say, my dear. Unanswerable question. Didn't try to answer it. 'A glass filled with tonic water looks just the same as one filled with gin. No Slattery has been unable to hold his liquor, but you are not a Slattery.' Unanswerable again. 'I remember when Uncle Ratty was out in Africa . . .'

Soon I shall be free of this, I told myself, I shall never hear the name Slattery again. Parties like these tire Clare out, and at ten-thirty she said she was going to bed. Self: 'I'll bring up your nightcap.' Somehow I felt it was certain she would say she was too tired this evening, but she simply nodded.

Got the *small* Manila envelope out of brief-case. Made the drink. Hand trembling? Not at all. Put powder carefully into it, dissolved almost at once. Didn't cloud the glass which stood, browny-gold, steaming a little. Took it up. I *still* believed something would happen to stop her drinking it, but nothing did. Afterwards all she said was: 'Rather strong.'

'I mixed it as usual.'

Brought down glass, washed it, put envelope back in brief-case (too soon to burn, think of smell), and relocked. Came up here, sat down to write diary, couldn't because of excitement. Analysed my own feelings. To do something that causes pain to another person, I've always believed that to be wrong. *I am not a cruel man. That is the truth.* But think of the way Clare has behaved to me, *that's* what is responsible for my actions. The truth is I really cannot think of her as a person at all. She is an object, an obstacle. I have done my best to treat her well, but it is impossible. Summing up my analysis I have to say that what I felt was a sense of achievement.

I was wrong.

(Just been down to look at her again. The thought crossed my mind that she might be dead. Thought, believed, hoped, what is the word? Nonsense, I knew it wouldn't be so. She was sleeping quietly.)

Settled down to wait. Went to see her, she was asleep. Came down, took all the sitting-room ornaments into the kitchen and washed them, something to do. Had just decided nothing would happen when there was a noise upstairs. Then moaning. Went up. She was on the landing outside the bathroom bent almost double, retching. Got her out into the lavatory – but I can't write about all that, it disgusts me! She was in pain, and that is something I can't bear. Rang Hubble. It seemed a terribly long time before he arrived, just before midnight. She went on being sick. He was drunk, I'm sure of it. Had to hold on to the rail as he came upstairs. Left him with Clare. Twenty minutes before he came down. Knew what he'd say, severe gastric upset. Offered a drink, but he refused!! Had one myself. Then the conversation. Said, how is she?

H   Washed out her stomach, given her an injection, she's asleep. (*Then terrible glare*) What did she have tonight?

Self   You were at the party, you saw for yourself. (*Nice touch.*) I'm afraid she sometimes drinks more than is good for her, with her stomach.

H   Afterwards?

Self   Nothing afterwards. Except her usual nightcap, hot whisky and lime juice. (*Boldly*) I made it for her.

H   Glass.

Self   What's that?

H   Glass, man, where's the glass?

Self   I washed it up and put it away.

H   Ha (*Two letters only, but an awful sound.*) Bottles.

I got him the bottles of whisky and lime juice. He sniffed, tasted, recorked them. I thought of saying, 'You should know the smell of whisky if anyone does,' but didn't of course. Had to say something though, asked if it was gastric attack. I shall never forget his reply.

'If you call poisoning gastric.'

Poisoning! What a dreadful word! Don't know how I managed to look at him, but I did. I even managed to say something about it being possibly one of the canapés. He answered as if he were talking to a child, didn't sound at all drunk.

'When I saw your wife recently there was nothing at all seriously wrong with her.' I said quietly that she had been sick. 'I said nothing serious. Now she's had a violent stomach upset, caused by something she's eaten or drunk. The two things aren't connected. I've an impression it was something corrosive, a mild solution of some metallic poison possibly. Something she drank would be more likely than food.'

'I don't see what it could be.'

'Mystery then. But she'll do, no need to worry. I'll look in tomorrow. Be careful what she eats and drinks for the next day or two. I'll tell her when I see her. But you might bear it in mind too.'

Harmless words? But they weren't, I know they weren't. I know they were a warning. He is not the fool he looks, he *knew*. But why should this happen to me? In the Croydon case the doctors never had any doubt it was gastric trouble, any more than Armstrong's doctor had any doubt. Why should I be so unlucky? I'm sure that *anyone* would have thought as I did about Hubble.

When he had left I knew I dare not go on. Unlocked brief-case, took out rest of Z, flushed it down the lavatory, burned both envelopes. All right then. But what happens now? I must write out the words of my humiliation plainly.

I have failed.

Chapter 7

The Man from UGLI

Clare made a quick recovery. He seemed to spend Sunday in making little milky dishes and taking them up to her. Hubble paid a visit on Sunday afternoon and expressed himself satisfied with her progress but still mystified by the origin of her illness. His manner was neither friendly nor hostile. The only solace was the slot racing layout. Arthur spent most of the afternoon in the attic, rearranging the track to make a Silverstone circuit and putting the pits and spectator stands into new positions. He did not race the cars because Clare was having a nap, and he was afraid of waking her.

By Monday morning she was up and about the house. She attributed her illness to Hubble's unwisdom in urging her to eat bloody bits of meat and other heavy foods, and her return to semi-vegetarianism began on Monday evening with a dish of grated cheese and carrots. On Tuesday morning Arthur gratefully escaped, telling her that he had an important engagement in Bristol, followed by a tour of the West country. He had more or less recovered what he thought of as his poise. Something, he said to himself in the train on the way up from Fraycut to Waterloo, something will have to be done. But what? In a sense there was no need to do anything at all, for it was hardly likely that, when Clare received her bank statement, she would take legal action against him. He rehearsed in the train a dialogue in which he rebutted her complaints of fraud and forgery. 'You have only yourself to blame . . . a wife's money should belong to her husband . . . if you had not deliberately denied me the capital I needed to develop my inventions . . .' He shook his head sadly. All that might be true, but it really did not matter if it was, because he would never be able to bring himself to say such things. He saw instead a future in which Clare's domination over him would be unbearably complete.

On this Tuesday he found it difficult to slip into the personality of Easonby Mellon. He did not open the post with his usual zest nor interview clients with his customary conviction. The shadow of Arthur Brownjohn hung over him like a heavy cold, and it was only partly dispelled after a telephone call made to Clare to say that he had found it impossible to postpone his West country tour – he had promised that he would try to do so – and would not be home until Friday. He had four days of freedom, but what were they worth? It was a gloomy Easonby Mellon who went home that evening to Clapham and to Joan. A bit of nonsense revived him slightly, and the meal of liver and bacon followed by steamed sultana pudding which they ate afterwards confirmed him in a feeling that life might have its silver lining. They sat out in the little back garden listening to the purring lawn mower next door. The sound induced a sense of peace. He closed his eyes and did not hear her properly when Joan said something. He asked her to repeat it.

'I said, having ructions at the office?'

There was something odd about her tone. He opened his eyes. Her face wore what she no doubt thought of as a cryptic smile. He said with an effort, 'If I've been out of sorts it's not because –'

'I wondered. Because he's been here.'

'Who?'

She looked round, leaned over and whispered. 'The man from UGLI.'

Was she out of her mind? Was there to be no peace even in Clapham? He sat up in the deck-chair. 'Joan, what are you talking about?'

'It was exciting. Tell me, what does he look like?

'What does *who* look like?'

'Flexner. I'm sure that's who it was.'

He restrained an impulse to say that she was talking nonsense. How had he described Flexner? 'He's tall, over six foot, always dressed like a city man, dark grey or blue suit, umbrella and bowler hat –'

She was nodding. 'He hadn't got the bowler hat, but that's right. And you said he was swarthy.'

'Dark. Not swarthy.'

'And a pigeon-toed walk, you mentioned that. Very sinister, I thought he was.'

He was suddenly angry at this tomfoolery. 'It can't have been Flexner.'

'Oh, I'm sure it was. Why not?'

'He's out of the country. What did this man say?'

'But E, I feel sure –'

'What did he *say*?' He was almost shouting. She looked alarmed. 'Let's go inside.'

In the flat she described him. 'He was a tall man, swarthy, and he asked for you so I said you weren't here, and then he said he wanted to contact you urgently and I thought I recognized him from your description so I said, "You're attached to the Department, aren't you?" I thought, you see, it wouldn't mean anything to him if he weren't. And he smiled, and it was one of those smiles you said he could give, that cut like a razor, and he said, "You might say I'm attached, yes." So then I told him I expected he'd know where to find you and *he* said, "Ah yes, but there's been a spot of trouble, I didn't want to contact him there." So I said I couldn't help him and then I knew who he was and I said, "You're Mr Flexner, aren't you?" and he said with another smile, "That's right." So then I said would he leave a message, but he just said tell you that he would be in touch when the time came. I'm sorry if I did wrong, E.'

'You didn't do wrong.' He let the waves of her talk move over him. In bed he felt such a chill of apprehension that he had to go out to the lavatory. On his return he did not go to sleep for a long time, and when he slept at last it was with one hand coiled tightly round the thumb of the other, a habit which belonged to his childhood.

At breakfast Joan talked about Flexner and the Department until he could bear it no longer, and shouted at her. She began to cry.

'You don't want me to have anything to do with your life. I'm just something to cook meals and go to bed with.' This was so nearly true that he found it difficult to answer. 'It's not like being your wife at all. I thought I was really going to be part of your life, but you won't let me. I hate the Department.'

'You're sure he didn't say anything else? About getting in touch, I mean.'

'No. Just when the time came. And he smiled. He's got a nasty smile, hasn't he?'

He agreed absently. 'Chin up, old girl. Sorry I can't tell you anything. It's the old struggle for power.'

'With AX, you mean?'

'AX is playing a part, but it's our own lot I'm worried about. There are moves to take us over, merge us with another department. That may be why Flexner was here.'

'You said he was out of the country.'

He said snappishly, 'Obviously I was wrong. Since he's come back it must be about something important.'

He left her eager for a further instalment of Department news. His room in Romany House held the usual bunch of letters and postal orders. He dealt with them efficiently, but that sense of impending doom lay heavy as a ball in his stomach. The morning was alleviated only by a telephone call from Pat. She asked if they could meet and when he invited her to lunch she said that she would be too late for that, but could meet him at three o'clock in the hotel. This bold declaration of the fact that her interest was purely sexual flattered him, and gave savour to the quick lunch he ate in a pub. It was an expectant Major Easonby Mellon who entered the hotel, to be told with a smirk that his wife was already there.

He found her on the edge of the bed in bra and knickers, a cigarette in her mouth. She put out the cigarette at once but somehow her appearance on the bed, smoking and nearly naked, upset him. She looked, if he had to put the thing crudely, like a tart, and he wondered again why she had come to him. Sex, however, is a solvent for doubt, and by the time she had pulled him on to the bed and helped him to take off his clothes he was in no state to be concerned about her motives. He was astonished when she rolled off the bed and put on her knickers, which he had removed in the course of the scuffle. He was about to remonstrate when she jerked a thumb behind him. He turned.

A man was in the room with them. He was tall, thin and dark, he wore a dark grey suit, and he was smiling disagreeably. There could be little doubt that he was the man Joan had described as Flexner. In his hand there was a tiny camera, which he put away in his pocket. He nodded to Pat, who put on her frock. Then he said amiably enough, 'Hi. Time for you and me to have a talk. I'm Jack Parker, Pat's husband.'

Major Mellon felt at an enormous disadvantage without his clothes. He dressed quickly but in a fumbling manner, having difficulty with his trousers. His mind was empty of thought, he did not know what to say. Parker was quite at his ease.

'Little club round the corner. I'm a member. No hurry. Talk round there when you're ready.'

Suppose I'm not prepared to come, suppose I say no to your little club, he thought. But he knew that he was not capable of this, that coming on top of everything else this misfortune had stunned him. He followed them obediently into a sordid basement club down a side street. The room was small and dirty, the barman was a Greek or Cypriot in need of a shave. Parker ordered three whiskies and they sat at a small table. He was completely self-possessed. He might have been talking about the weather.

'I'll put the position to you, Major, so that you know just where you are. First of all, the Major. You're not entitled to call yourself that, there's no Major Easonby Mellon in the Army List. Next your firm. You've got no licence to operate as you should have – I've checked – and you haven't got a secretary. You're only in the office part time. It's just a trick for making money. You've kidded your wife that you work for some mysterious Department or other, so I played along when I came last night.'

'Outrageous.' Major Mellon had found his voice, although it came through as a croak.

'I thought you'd be pleased.'

'How did you know where I lived?'

'Followed you. Been keeping an eye on you ever since the day Pat came along. Careless of you not to notice. Another point, I just mention it in passing. You don't go home to Clapham every night. I'm only making a guess, but do you know what it smells like to me? It smells as though you've got a little love nest tucked away somewhere else.'

'He couldn't have,' the girl said. 'He hasn't got the guts.'

'Shut up. Am I right?'

Alarm struggled with relief, alarm that the man had got so near to the truth, relief that he had not discovered it. 'Of course not.'

Parker shrugged. 'I could easily find out, but to me it doesn't matter. This is a business deal.'

'The badger game.' He knew the phrase from books.

'Not really.' Parker smiled again. He looked like a large well-dressed rat. 'I sent Pat along thinking you might put her in touch with a rich mark. She's a clever girl. She spotted right away that you were a mark yourself.'

He sipped the whisky. It tasted disagreeably of oil. 'How do you mean?'

'Suppose it got through to the Greater London Council – they issue your licence, I've done my homework – that you're operating under a false title and without a licence. Suppose Pat makes a complaint about you and I back it up with these pictures, you'd be for the high jump, agreed?'

'You'd never dare to do it.'

'We're clean. We've never been inside. The point is, you wouldn't want us to do it. I'd lay odds Mellon's not your real name. I dare say the bogeys would be pleased to know where you are.'

With a sense of shock he realized that they thought he was a crook like themselves, operating a racket. The fact that this was in a sense true did not make him less indignant.

Parker went to the bar and brought back three more whiskies. The girl was becoming impatient. 'Get to it, Jack. You're too fond of the sound of your own voice.'

'We'll do it my way if you don't mind.' She flinched slightly. 'I want the Major here to know just where he stands. Then we can fix the deal.'

'The deal?'

'It's a business deal. I said so from the start, no hard feelings.'

He sipped the second whisky. The inside of his mouth seemed to be numb. 'What sort of deal?'

'Twenty a week.'

'Pounds?' He could not take it in. 'You want me to pay you twenty pounds each week?'

'Every Friday. One of us will drop in to collect. Probably me. You might forget yourself with Pat.' He smiled again.

'Impossible.'

'Don't say that. Let's keep it friendly.' Parker's mouth when he did not smile was like two lines of steel. 'I tell you what. There are two ways of doing this. Twenty a week straight, and that's what I'd like. Or a fiver a week and you give Pat some introductions to marks.'

'No, I can't do that. I don't work in that way, I couldn't possibly –' He left the sentence unfinished.

'It would have advantages.' Parker was watching him. 'You'd get a cut. Twenty per cent. And you don't have to know anything about it, there'd be no trouble. Pat's clever. She can tell which ones to take. And you can trust me, I know how hard to squeeze.'

The walls of the room were lime green, and one was discoloured where damp had seeped through. They made him feel sick. 'That sort of thing, I can't involve myself in it.'

Parker took out a long thin cheroot from a case and lighted it. The cheroot stuck out sharply from a face composed of a series of angles. 'I'm being patient, Dad, but you haven't grasped it. You're over a barrel. You don't have a choice. It's twenty a week, or five and a little cooperation, a partnership. I'll be frank, we don't want trouble but that's nothing to the way you don't want it.'

'I must have time to think.'

'No. Here and now.'

He seemed to be incapable of thought. Major Mellon had shrivelled to Arthur Brownjohn, and it was Arthur who said miserably, 'Five. And the – the cooperation.'

'Sensible.' Parker gripped his hand. 'Let's get along.'

'Where to?'

'Where do you think? The office.'

The next hour was one of the most miserable in his life. They took a taxi to Romany House and went to the office of Matrimonial Assistance. He gave Parker five pound notes and then the

65

Parkers went through his files, looking for possible marks and making rude comments. They picked out a dozen possibles, mostly elderly men who said that they had a private income, or middle-aged business men. He agreed to send them Pat's name, with a special recommendation.

'After that you have nothing to do with it. Leave it to Pat. She can size 'em up in ten minutes. The ones we want are married, out for a bit of fun on the side. They have their fun, but they pay for it. What's fairer than that?' Parker was in high good humour.

When they had gone he sat in the little office with his head on the table. The humiliation of watching them go through his files and read the letters on his desk was somehow the worst thing of all. The business he had built was dishonest, yet he took a pride in it and felt it to be something he had created. That he should have been forced to allow these crooks to use what he had done as a basis for their filthy game was hard to bear. He realized that this was what Parker had intended from the start, and that if he had agreed to pay twenty pounds a week something more would have been demanded of him. It was his list of gulls they were after, to make some quick killings. The future was foreseeable. The Parkers might bring off half a dozen coups, but at some time they would choose the wrong person and one of their marks would go to the police. They might be arrested or they might get away, but either way he would be dragged into it, and his complicity would be obvious. And of course his double life would be revealed by any serious police investigation. What sentence was likely for bigamy? In the general wreck of his fortunes that did not seem particularly important. Whichever way he looked, disaster lay ahead.

Chapter 8

The Solution

The solution was simple enough in its essential elements, and it occurred to him almost immediately. It was that he must say good-bye to Major Easonby Mellon. What was he, after all, but a wig, a beard, some loud suits and an accompanying loud manner? If he were to disappear tomorrow who would be the wiser? The clients of Matrimonial Assistance would write letters, come to the office, and eventually no doubt report his absence to the company that ran Romany House. The company would write to him and get in touch with his bank, but he would have drawn out all except a nominal fragment of the money he had in credit. Joan might be approached, but what could she say except some tales about UGLI 3 and – a nice confirmatory touch – about the man who had come to see him? And who would suffer? Honesty compelled him to admit that Joan would be left high and dry. He felt sorry for her, but was able to console himself with the thought that she was the kind of woman who would always, somehow and somewhere, find a man. To live with men and be deceived by them was her destiny. No, the real sufferer would be – himself. If he was to go on living with Clare the emotional release afforded by Easonby Mellon was a necessity. And the suffering would not only be emotional. If Matrimonial Assistance closed down, what would Clare say when he told her that he could no longer pay the expenses of the household? He shivered at the thought of her endless wrath. The solution so simple in its essential elements was thus no solution at all.

On Thursday morning he sat brooding in the Lektreks office over a volume dealing with the James Camb case. Camb, a steward with the Union Castle had been accused of strangling a girl in her cabin and then pushing her body out of the porthole. He had no doubt relied upon the absence of a body, but he was found guilty just the same. If only, Arthur reflected, he could make Clare magically disappear so that her money came to

67

him! But of course it was not possible. He closed the book with a sigh at the very moment that a knock sounded on the door. He opened it expecting to see the caretaker and was disconcerted to be confronted by the fine white teeth of – it took him a moment even to remember the man's name – Elsom, the engineering executive.

'Hallo there.' Almost imperceptibly Elsom was in the room, which he stared at quite frankly, his gaze passing like a rake over the dusty box files, the single desk with its typewriter, the gas ring for making tea, the blueprints of the Everlasting Torch and its successor the Hammerless Screw Inserter, the notices on the walls certifying that Lektreks was incorporated as a company and that Arthur was a member of the Society of Inventors. Elsom, carefully regarded, was an objectionable-looking man. He had close-cut sandy hair and a sandy moustache, vertical nostrils which seemed distended by curiosity, almost lashless eyes and extremely large square competent-looking hands. He was the sort of man who in that quick glance round would have photographed and permanently recorded anything possibly useful to him. 'So this is where you tuck yourself away,' Elsom said. 'I was passing by and thought I'd look in to see if you were free for a spot of lunch.'

Arthur intended to say that he was not, but reconsidered. He felt certain that something lay behind Elsom's casual dropping-in. If he was put off he might drop in again or become a pest on the telephone. There had been occasions, although they could be counted on the fingers of both hands, when people from Fraycut had visited the office, and Arthur had always firmly stressed that it was no more than a receiving place for correspondence, and had got them out of it as quickly as possible. Clare herself had been to the office only twice, conveying both her contempt for it and her astonishment that he was able to make a living from such a place. She had conceded that it was a good address, but the whole ambience was obviously a wretched one when put beside the Slattery connection. Arthur felt that it would be a good idea to get this grinning bristly Elsom out of the office and also to damp any curiosity he might be feeling. He said that a spot of lunch would be very nice.

They ate in a pub not far away. Elsom was known in the Grill Room. He took charge of the meal, giving particular instructions about the way in which their steaks should be done, and going into details about the wine. It struck Arthur that he was being treated with some attention. When the steaks came Elsom attacked his savagely, and kept up a flow of conversation about people in Fraycut until he had eaten the last scrap. Then he asked how things were going.

'Going? Oh, business you mean. I mustn't grumble.' He added untruthfully, 'Very glad you found me.'

'You don't put up much of a front.'

'What would be the point?' Arthur had countered this remark before. 'My business isn't done in London, it's personal.'

Most people left it at that but Elsom, at the same time that he gestured to a waiter to bring a tray with the puddings on it, said out of the side of his mouth, 'No girl to take messages.'

'It's difficult to get efficient staff. I use an answering service.'

Elsom nodded and transferred his interest to the trolley, ordering what proved to be a huge portion of trifle. He disposed of it in a few gulps and Arthur, toying uneasily with crème caramel, had the feeling that his companion needed something crunchy on which to sharpen his teeth. No wonder that a trifle was quickly disposed of. Elsom's next remark took him by surprise.

'Can't help feeling a bit sorry for old Clare.'

'You mean her illness? She was much better when I left yesterday.'

'Don't mean that. Being the grass widow was what I had in mind. I mean, you're away three, four nights a week.'

'Oh, not always. It varies.'

'If I were you I'd be feeling worried.' The words were alarming. What did the man mean? 'She's damned attractive, your good lady.'

'Clare?'

'I wouldn't go off and leave her half the week, I know that.' Elsom took a mouthful of scalding coffee and roared with laughter. 'Just pulling your leg, old man. Perhaps it's the other

69

way round, eh? A few home comforts up in the Midlands?' He laughed again.

Those were the vital words, although their possible implications were not borne in upon him at the time. It had never crossed his mind that anybody could think Clare particularly attractive. 'You don't really mean that you think Clare is –'

'Not a bit of it. Shouldn't have said anything of the sort, schoolboy sense of humour, it's got me into trouble before. Still, I expect you'd like to get home a bit more often.' He leaned over the table. 'GBD might make it possible.'

'What?'

'I'll lay it on the line. We're interested in acquiring firms that are going concerns but aren't, how shall I put it, flourishing quite as they were. That doesn't matter, positive advantage in fact. Don't ask me why, it's one of these financial fiddles about stock distribution, I don't understand it except that after every little take-over the directors get richer on paper. Well, Lektreks sounds like a candidate to me.'

'For take-over?'

'Hardly that, old boy. Not much to take over, is there? It would be acquisition, absorption, call it what you like. Where do you come in, you ask? No taste in nothing, we all know that.' He showed his teeth. 'This is all unofficial, you understand, but I think you'd get a parcel of stock in GBD.'

'I should?'

'And then, this is my own idea entirely, but I think we'd like to put you on the payroll. That glass cleaning device was damned clever. I know it didn't work out, but perhaps the next one will.' It was strange to have repeated to him the things he had told himself for years as consolation. Surely this was all too good to be true? Elsom's next words made this plain. 'The boys with slide rules.'

'I'm sorry, I didn't quite hear that.'

'I said, talking about terms, the boys with slide rules will settle all that.'

Arthur was unused to such terminology. 'I don't understand.'

'Accountants. We all have to do what they tell us, more's the pity. They come in, look at the books, fix a price. You can use your own chaps of course, but GBD will give you a square deal.'

'I see.' And he should have seen at once, should have known that it was impossible. The accountants would report that Lektreks did only a few thousand pounds' worth of business a year, and was worth almost nothing. When their report came through Elsom would see it and wonder where Arthur Brownjohn got his money. A whole trail of inquiry would be set up. GBD was not a promise but a menace. 'I shall have to think about it.'

'Do that. I think you'll find it will be to everybody's advantage.'

Elsom insisted on walking back to the office with him, telling him what a splendid outfit GBD was, and saying that independence was a wonderful thing and it was a shame the little man was going to the wall, but you couldn't hold out against the winds of change for ever. He left with protestations of goodwill and an assurance of not losing touch. Back in the office Arthur slumped in his chair and gave himself up to total gloom. Elsom was a fool, no doubt, look at the way he'd talked about Clare having a lover, but he was the kind of fool who didn't easily let go of an idea once he had hold of it. He had managed to conceal the Camb volume when Elsom came in and now he put it back on the shelf and took down a book in which he never failed to take delight, the account of the Wallace case. The beautifully logical complication of its structure somehow resembled music or chess. Wallace, a Liverpool insurance agent, had been accused of murdering his wife. His defence was an alibi based upon a telephone call from a man named Qualtrough which had taken him wandering round Liverpool in search of a non-existent address. Had Wallace made the call himself and murdered his wife after stripping naked, as the prosecution suggested, or did Qualtrough really exist, was he the pseudonym of a shadowy figure thus dimly and momentarily seen, who then disappeared for ever?

He felt his eyes closing, and remembered that he had drunk half a bottle of wine. And then something jerked open his lids as though he had been given a small electric shock. The nerve ends of his body seemed to be tingling. Two completely separate ideas had come together in his mind. Major Easonby Mellon had to disappear. Clare also had to disappear. Why should they not run away together? Clare was thought by Elsom to be the kind of woman who might conceivably take a lover. In fact Clare would be dead, and her body would be buried in some conveniently undiscoverable spot, but it would seem that she was having an affair with Mellon and had gone off with him. There would be letters left to prove it. And the beauty of the idea was that Easonby was no Qualtrough, no mere name without a body. When the police investigated him they would find that he had an office, a business, a wife and a home. His existence was as real as that of Arthur Brownjohn.

That was the beginning of the idea. He thought about it with rising excitement that afternoon and all the next day. Its prime requisite, of course, was the creation of a relationship, in fact a love affair, between Easonby Mellon and Clare. He bought a copy of *The Man Who Never Was*, which told the story of the deliberate creation during the war of a non-existent character, supported by all sorts of documents. Its use had been to deceive the Germans, Easonby Mellon's function here would be to deceive the police, and he had one immense advantage over the organizers of that realistic spoof, in the sense that Mellon was an established figure. On the other hand, there were difficulties which the secret service had not encountered.

The first of them was the question of Clare running away with the man. When a wife disappears, even though she may only have gone off for a week's holiday, her husband is likely to be suspected of killing her. How, to put it crudely, was her body to be disposed of? He did not drive a car, and he really could not imagine himself digging a hole in the garden and staggering out at night with a great wrapped bundle, even had such a procedure seemed judicious. To hide it inside the house or to dig up the garage floor would be dangerous as well as uncongenial. After a day's thought he gave up the elopement and decided on a bolder course. Clare's body should be discovered. She must be seen quite plainly to be a murder victim, and her murderer must be seen just as clearly to be Easonby Mellon.

Other problems to be solved, or relationships to be established, occurred to him. The project filled his mind completely. He jotted them down under three headings:

(1) Eliminate any link between E.M. and A.B.
(2) Establish relationship of E.M. and C.B. over period of time. First met in childhood?
(3) Decide precisely how project to be accomplished. E.M. is to be wiped out. How?

Under these main headings he made a number of notes. When he was sure that he had absorbed what was in the notes he burned them. The burning was a kind of smoke signal. It was time for action.

Chapter 9

Preparations

May became June, and this was a fine June. The days were sunny, the nights mild. In the second week of the month he walked often in the Green Park, entering it from Piccadilly and then going through to Buckingham Palace, where he stared at the soldiers on duty as though they might have answers for some of the questions that still bothered him. On the way back he looked at the young couples who walked along oblivious of other people, like solicitor and client in consultation. He often had a feeling of isolation, sometimes doubted his own identity. He did not put it to himself in quite that way but the thought disturbed him, and once, when he was looking at the letters and postal orders for Matrimonial Assistance he asked aloud: 'What am I like then? What am I really like?' He was inorgiastic with Joan. He attributed this to the shock of discovering Pat Parker's treachery and this was in a way consoling, but at times it seemed to him that his hold on existence itself was failing. Who was he trying to protect? Did he want to live out the rest of his days as Arthur Brownjohn?

From such vague depressing thoughts he was roused by the need for ingenuity and for action. When Easonby Mellon disappeared there must be nothing left that could possibly connect him with Arthur Brownjohn, and this meant that his fingerprints must be eliminated both from Mellon's office and from the Clapham flat, in case some inquiring police officer noticed that the two were identical. This created a further problem because some prints must be left, at least in the office. How were they to be obtained?

He investigated the forgery of fingerprints. He found with pleasure that several methods were open to him. He could photograph a print in a book, have a rubber stamp made from the photograph, hold the stamp in his hand to impregnate it with body sweat, and thus leave impressions of the stamp in suitable places. Or he could have a print copied on to latex and glued to rubber gloves, using the gloves to leave prints. These methods had their dangers, however, since he would have to employ somebody to make the stamp or to have the prints copied, and he settled finally on a third method, involving the use of cellulose tape. He went out and bought a soapstone statuette of Buddha ('soapstone', said one of the books he consulted, 'is an excellent print-taking surface'). He admired but did not touch it himself, and the dealer held the statuette firmly while extolling its beauty. Afterwards he was in agony while the man was wrapping it in tissue. Supposing the prints were destroyed! They survived, however, and on the following day he bought a pair of rubber gloves and completely cleaned the office. He paid particular attention to everything on the desk, the chair and the files, but he did not forget the door handle, the window sill, and other places likely to bear traces of prints.

Then came the ticklish part of the operation, the 'lifting' of the prints on the statuette. He used for this purpose a roll of cellulose tape. By rolling this tape gently over the Buddha he obtained a number of reasonably good prints. The last part of the process involved pressing the tape on to the best print-taking surfaces he could find on his desk and the filing cabinet. These 'roll-ons' a technical term which he had used in his own mind) became fainter with use, but he managed to take a few more which he dotted about the room. These were the presumptive fingerprints of Easonby Mellon. They were not likely to deceive any serious police examination with a hand-lens, but the beauty of the device was that in his particular case this was all to the good. 'Ah ha,' the fingerprint expert would say. 'These prints are fakes. The man Mellon is obviously a criminal, trying to leave false prints.' And the joy of the whole thing was that he wanted them to think just this. When he had done with the statuette he sold it in the Portobello Road for less than a quarter of what it had cost him.

The problem of his prints at the Clapham flat was less easily solved. He considered and rejected one shocking idea, and decided that something was bound to occur to him in a day or two. In the meantime he had to provide Easonby Mellon with a background that was so far lamentably lacking. He took Joan to see a film called *The Eye of the Past*, of which he had read reviews. It was about a business executive who had risen to be the president of a corporation. Unknown to his friends he was the son of a convicted murderer, and had been prone to fits of uncontrollable rage in his youth. He was afraid that at some moment of crisis he would be moved to injure somebody because of the bad streak in his heredity, and his concern about this was shown in several dream sequences in which he was shown committing violent actions through a kind of fog which swirled about the screen. Sure enough his secret became known to a subordinate, a man who nursed a grudge about having been passed over for promotion. He now tried to obtain his ends by blackmail, and up to a point succeeded. The president paid him money, but when the man demanded promotion as well the president hit the man with a tyre lever, drove his car on to a rubbish dump, and set light to it. The body was identified, however, and the president was implicated because he had been seen leaving the dump. He fled to his home town, where he went to see an old nanny, who was the only person who had been kind to him when he was at home. In the end he was captured in her sitting-room, where she had given him the cookies he had loved in childhood. Under the influence of a long speech from her he gave himself up peacefully instead of fighting it out with the police.

'It was good,' Joan said afterwards. 'But very psychological. I mean, it couldn't really happen.'

He was sober, even grave. 'Something like it happened to me. My brother Chris went to prison. Robbery with violence. It killed our mother.'

'Go on.' Her mouth was agape. 'You never told me. Where was that?'

'In Canada. I left home when I was sixteen. Cut myself off.'

'You don't have any accent.'

'It was a long time ago. I've often thought that was the thing that made me go into the Service. I've been alone ever since.'

'E, you've got me.' Joan threw herself into his arms. She had been making coffee, and the milk boiled over.

In bed later on he said, 'Sometimes I read about Chris. Not

Chris Mellon, that was just a name I took. He's always in and out of prison. And I know I've got the same thing in me. Violence. I could be violent.'

She shivered delicately. 'Well, you have been. That man you shot with the harpoon in Iceland.'

'That was in the way of work. I meant personally. If it came to the point I'd use violence.'

She shivered again and held him close. He thought it was a conversation she would remember.

On the following day Major Easonby Mellon visited Weybridge. He wore a green tweed suit which contrasted markedly with his hair. He ate lunch at a good hotel, where he made himself unpopular by loud unfavourable comments on the food and service and then by questioning his bill. He asked the hotel porter, as he had already asked two publicans, if he could recommend a really discreet place. Such a hotel is not easily found in the respectable commuter land of Weybridge but eventually he was told that the Embassy, by the river, might be the sort of place he was looking for. The reception clerk proved to be a bored young man who booked without question a double room for the following Wednesday.

'Just the one night, sir?'

'Not sure we shall stay the night. I'll pay for it, of course. May have to get back to London in the evening.' The clerk nodded. He hammered the point home. 'Been meeting elsewhere, you understand. Had to change because of damned snoopers. Must have discretion.'

'I understand.'

He paid for the room in advance and returned to London well satisfied.

The most difficult part of this phase in the operation remained, and he proposed to take the daring step of using Pat Parker to help in it. When Parker came in to the office he broached the matter. Parker was not in a good temper. The names they had taken from the files had almost all proved to be duds. One of the elderly gentlemen with an independent income had proved to be a retired dustman, and another was a widower at Bournemouth who was anxious to see something of London's famous night life. Others had written mere filth. There was only one possible mark, Parker said indignantly.

The Major shrugged. 'You chose the names.'

'You mean you'd have picked different ones.'

'Perhaps. After a time you get to know who's serious.'

'You'd better find a few serious ones. Otherwise we'll go back to the twenty a week, you wouldn't like that, would you?'

'How would Pat like to earn twenty-five pounds next Wednesday?'

Parker was smoking one of his cheroots. He took it from his mouth. 'For what?' When he was told he said suspiciously, 'What's the game?'

The Major hesitated, as though reluctant to confide. He saw Parker now with new eyes, a man of narrow vision who aspired to be nothing more than a petty crook living grubbily off a woman. In his new-found confidence he admitted that Pat would indirectly be helping him to nail a mark of his own. He did not go into details.

Parker was at sea. 'It's worth fifty.'

In the end they settled for forty, to be paid when the job had been done on the following Wednesday. Arthur Brownjohn travelled home in the train to Fraycut that Friday well pleased. In his brief-case were letters in Easonby Mellon's erratic, dashing hand.

23 March

My dearest,

Next Wednesday then. Will it be like last Wed? You know it was marvellous, ecstasy, don't know how to say it. I love you, love seeing you in our little room. Sorry you thought it was dingy, but we have to be careful. Don't ask me about myself, can't tell you, too complicated, I've made silly mistakes, can't go back on them now. And you too? Is that what you meant when you talked about him?

E

2 April

Clare my darling,

Your body is white as the moon, your eyes are stars. If I were a poet I'd be able to write properly about it. After each meeting I feel more jealous of *him* and angry that he doesn't appreciate the treasures he's got. But I'm glad too, glad you don't belong to him because then you wouldn't belong utterly to me. I know you do.

Ever your devoted E

Dearest dearest C,

Dearest I was so upset, hurt and angry too – not angry for long, I never could be with you, but my anger when it comes is so *intense* it frightens me. What was there in my letters that made you tear them up? Why is it wrong to wish we could be together always? Don't you know, dearest C, that I love you with every nerve and sinew in every possible way, mental and physical. I cannot bear to see you only once a week when you come to art class, it isn't enough. Why should you worry about him, whether you are deceiving him or not, it does not matter since you say he doesn't care. I don't understand your feelings. I have ties too, I told you that, but you know I will break them as soon as you say, so that we can be together. And we *shall* be together, we *must*, I cannot bear it otherwise and I cannot bear to think of him with you. I'm sorry my darling for writing like this. It is not physical, it is everything. You are so cool and calm it exasperates me but you know I love you always.

E

There were a dozen letters altogether. He had composed them after careful study of the letters written by Edith Thompson to her lover Frederick Bywaters. Did they show obvious signs of their origin? Reading them through again with the attempted objectivity of an artist looking at his own work, he did not think so. Would it be possible for a handwriting expert to recognize Arthur Brownjohn's hand? A comparison with Mellon's correspondence would show they had been written by him. Why should anyone seek to identify them with Arthur in view of that? Some of the sheets would have Clare's prints on them, even though they might be blurred, because they came from a packet of blue Basildon Bond paper that she had bought and handled before she took a dislike to the colour. They would not show Easonby Mellon's prints, but that could not be helped. He was pleased with the occasional irrelevancies he had put into the letters. 'Do you remember that day in the little tea shop at Sevenoaks … you looked like raggy Maggie today but I loved you just the same … rather worried in case Jamie recognized you … you ask what we'll live on, darling, we'll manage, lovers always do.' He was pleased also with the increasing hysteria of the letters' tone and the preoccupation which they showed with Arthur, referred to always as *him*. The last two or three letters were undated and the writing was much more erratic, to indicate excitement. It was obvious from them that Mellon had told her of his marriage and that Clare had refused to go away with him. His language became almost abusive:

I can't stand it and *won't*. If I give up Joan why should you feel bound to *him*, what has he ever done to make you happy? You say I must not come down but I shall if I wish, why not, I am so wretched, what harm can it do, I would sooner come down and have it out once and for all. *I shall not give up because I love you* and if you do not love me any more I would sooner end everything.

It was repetitive stuff to read, like all love letters, but it seemed convincing. At least, it convinced him.

Chapter 10

Finishing Touches

DIARY

Friday, 13 June

Friday the 13th, unlucky, rather worried. But it wasn't. Not that I am superstitious anyway, but you never know. Clare now quite usual self. Said she heard I'd seen Elsom. Yes, I said, had to be in London and he'd dropped in. His proposition sounded interesting but I'd have to investigate it, didn't want to lose my independence. She agreed, but *wasn't interested*. Why should I worry about that? But I do. Went on to talk about discussion in local Liberal Party. Man named Ffoliot-Jenkins says they are too much like Labour. Why should I have to listen to that, what does she take me for?

Saturday, 14 June

Shopped in morning. Hubble called while out, gave Clare clean bill of health. Later she went to Liberal committee. I talked to Susan, asked her if she had seen strange man around.

Susan What kind of man?
Self Reddish-brown beard, loud clothes.
S Don't know who you mean.
Self Yesterday I saw him leaving this house just before I came in.
S Better ask Mrs Brownjohn about him.
Self I did. She didn't know what I was talking about.
S No more do I. Probably some sort of hawker and Mrs Brownjohn didn't open the door.
Self He didn't look like a hawker.

I *hugged* myself during this conversation. Susan doesn't like me, all to the good perhaps. I think it sunk in, left her curious.

Sunday, 15 June

Houses are built of single bricks joined with mortar. Today went for drinks to the Paynes'. Had a chance to talk to Mrs P, their daughter goes sometimes to Clare's art class at Weybridge. I asked what time she got back, Mrs P said about 7 o'clock. I said that was funny, I'd rung Clare last two Wednesdays about 9.30, no reply. Mrs P pricked up ears, didn't think Wendy came back with Clare (I knew she didn't,

Clare can't stand her!) but would find out. No no, I said hurriedly, don't do that, probably the line was out of order. We agreed telephone service was terrible. She *will* ask her though. I let Mrs P see I was worried, said it was a pity I couldn't be home more. Every little thing tells.

Monday, 16 June

Why do I have to do it? Today C came to me, said suddenly it was a pity I had to go away so much in mid-week, she missed me. I said she had the Liberal Party, art class, etc. 'Yes, but we could go out together. To the theatre perhaps. I haven't been to the theatre in years. Perhaps if Elsom –'

Perhaps, I said. Then she looked as if she was sorry for having spoken. 'You know I never interfere.'

Why do I have to do it, I wondered then? I felt sorry, but it's no use. Events have a logic. They must work themselves out. And what has C ever given me in the way of companionship or sex or money? Silly to be sentimental, but I am sometimes. Life is a terrible tangle. Why can't it be straightforward? Today we gardened together. In the afternoon a new American car came. I had to adjust it before it fitted the slot, but then it worked marvellously. Raced it against several British cars, American won easily. Clare made milk jelly, horrible.

On Tuesday he was again in London. At Romany House the cares of Arthur Brownjohn were sloughed off from Major Easonby Mellon. There were letters to be sent out, some introducing Patricia Parker, there were people to see. Then a quick, early lunch. Then Major Easonby Mellon went to Waterloo Station and took the train to Fraycut. Was it Easonby Mellon who took the train? In the carriage which he occupied alone, he considered the question. Could Arthur Brownjohn have done what he was going to do this afternoon? It was one thing to drop hints and make discreet suggestions, quite another to mount the frontal assault that was to be essayed now. No, Arthur could not have done it. But the hand of Easonby Mellon was firm, the smile with which he viewed himself in the carriage glass had about it a touch of bravado.

Arthur Brownjohn had never done more than say a timid good morning to the ticket collector, who looked remarkably like the comedian Phil Silvers. Major Mellon first handed him the wrong half of his ticket and then asked the way to a house called The Laurels.

Phil Silvers lacked patience. 'Never 'eard of it.' He turned away.

The Major bristled. 'Just keep a civil tongue in your head when you're asked a civil question.'

'I said *never 'eard of it.*'

'The Laurels, Livingstone Road.'

'Down the High Street, first left, second right.'

The Major fumbled in his pocket, produced a shilling, handed it over, nodded, walked away. A sideways look revealed Phil Silvers looking after him with a stare that blended surprise and disdain.

Major Mellon sauntered up the High Street and went into the Catherine of Aragon, a pub which Arthur Brownjohn had never entered. He ordered a double whisky and asked the barmaid whether she knew The Laurels in Livingstone Road. He had received directions at the station, but couldn't find it.

The barmaid, by contrast with Phil Silvers, was made up of good humour. She laughed heartily. 'You're walking away from it.'

'Right about turn, is it?' The Major suited the action to the words, to the amusement of half a dozen regulars in the bar. 'Never had any sense of direction. Will you take a drop of something, my dear?'

The barmaid took a drop of gin and remarked, after the Major had had two more drinks, that he seemed to be in no hurry.

'In a manner of speaking I'm not. I'm not damn' well supposed to be here at all.'

'You're not?' Laughter rumbled in the barmaid, then became quiescent.

'I've come down to see a filthy rotten little skunk and tell him what I think of him, that's all.'

'And I bet you will, too. But don't go doing anything you shouldn't. What's it about, a woman?' When he nodded she laughed, in relief at something so familiar. 'You know what they say, a woman's not worth it.'

'This particular lady is.' He took out silver, placed it on the counter. It was nearly three o'clock. The bar was almost empty. The barmaid poured another whisky and, in response to his imperious gesture, another gin for herself.

'You think a deal of her, don't you?' she said perspicaciously. 'What's this man done, then?'

'Nothing. I am in the wrong. I should not be here at all.' He added reflectively, 'I meant to purchase a weapon, but I refrained. I feared I should do someone an injury.'

'A weapon!' The laughter coiled back into her stomach, leaving a fat tense face. 'I'll have no weapons in my bar.'

'I said I haven't bought it. I shall try reason first.'

She opened the flap of the bar counter. 'Closing time.' As he walked out her speculative gaze followed him.

Ten minutes later he turned into Livingstone Road. This was the ticklish part of the operation. Clare was, or should be, at a Children's Care Committee. Susan was, or should be, working in the house. He walked past the front gate two or three times, apparently unobserved. Then the milkman came along the road. The Major had his hand on the gate. He turned away, came face to face with the milkman, who gave him an incurious glance as he passed carrying milk and eggs. When the man had gone the Major returned, pushed open the gate, walked round the garden to the side of the house, picked up a handful of gravel and small stones from the garden path and threw them at the first floor bedroom window. There was a ping as the window cracked. From the bathroom window adjoining Susan's head peered. She shouted something that he could not hear. He shouted unintelligibly back and then left at a smart trot which slowed to a walk as he turned the corner of Livingstone Road. He caught a bus in the High Street which took him to Esher, and from Esher a train back to Waterloo.

DIARY
Thursday, 19 June

> Stone walls do not a prison make
> Nor iron bars a cage.

Very true, that poem. Prisons are mental. It's as if you were enclosed in a room for ever *with other people*. I often feel I'd have more chance inside the stone walls of a prison. There you can cut through the bars and get out. In the room with other people you can't get out except by getting rid of them. Isn't there a play about all that?

Writing this in train on the way up to Birmingham. All part of the plan.

Notes on progress. Contradiction here, have to admit it. I really *like* all the complications, pitting my wits against 'authority', solving problems as they come up. I've done so much since Monday and it's all so clever, so well arranged, that I can't help being pleased with it. I said I'd never do anything, but I've proved myself wrong! Have to be careful, though. This liking for complication is my weakness.

Notes, then. Tuesday night bought the gun at a shop in Brixton which has lots of flick-knives in the window. Told the man I wanted it to protect house against burglars, had no licence. Paid through the nose for it, naturally. Smith and Wesson ·38, same thing that American police use, the man said. Surprised it was so big. Unpleasant, don't like the look of the thing. Left it with Joan, said if Flexner reappeared show it to him. Seemed to regard it all as a game, extraordinary woman.

Then Wednesday. What a day! First arranged to go up to Birmingham today, a.m. to see Gibson of Steel Alloys. Said I wanted to talk to him about whether he'd be interested in new lines I'd been offered by U.S. firm (True!). Then rang Elsom, arranged to look in and see him tonight about 6 o'clock. Then sent telegram to Clare saying meet me Waterloo Station 4 o'clock Wednesday. Point was to keep her away from Weybridge art class that afternoon. Thought of her waiting at Waterloo getting angry, hugged myself. Appealed to sense of humour, I must say. Then the tricky part of the operation which was not pleasant, taking Pat (Bitch) Parker to Weybridge. Was this a mistake, over-complication, should I have made some other arrangement? Still worried about it.

First she came to the office with the man. He asked again what it was all about. Said divorce case, that seemed to satisfy him. Then he demanded fifty pounds instead of the forty we'd fixed. Blackmail, but what could I do? Very angry, but no good showing it. Had to agree. At least she'd bought a good thick veil as I'd asked. Couldn't see features clearly behind it.

Got to Weybridge just after 3.30, signed register 'Mr and Mrs John Smith', classical. Same desk clerk, gave him a fiver, ordered bottle of champagne in room. She perked up at that. Sent her into bathroom so that he shouldn't see her when he brought it up.

Then gave Miss Pat a real shock. As I opened the bottle, poured it, she said archly, 'What happens now?'

The bitch was ready for anything. She disgusted me. Took out a pack of cards, asked if she played bezique. 'You've brought me up here to play cards!' Didn't want to cause a scene, said this was strictly business. Glared at me. 'I always knew you were a creep.'

EM could have made a blistering reply, really given her the rough side of his tongue. Didn't do so, just said she was getting well paid for it. Didn't play, however, so played patience alone. She sat smoking, said I hadn't even brought bloody papers to read, called me a creep again. Sticks and stones, etc., but words will never hurt me.

At a quarter to six mussed up bed thoroughly, creasing sheets and denting pillows, while she stared at me. At six o'clock we left, she wearing veil. Looked at her figure as I walked out, stockier than I thought, really quite like Clare, especially legs. Travelled up together to Waterloo, not speaking. Gave her the other twenty-five pounds, took it without a thank-you. Good-bye Miss P (B) Parker.

Then to Clapham. Ought to write about that, but can't. Makes me shiver to think of what I had to do. It makes me angry to think I should have to work by such deceits. Why does society punish a man for going through a social form with two different women? And if all the things said about the sacrament of marriage, one flesh, etc. are true, why should a wife be allowed a separate bank account? Absurd. The habits by which we live and think are not what we believe.

Only writing this to avoid saying anything about last night and Joan. Ashamed, I don't know why.

It was those hours of Wednesday evening that he fought to eliminate from his mind afterwards. Recollection of them brought terror to him for he knew that what he did, even though it had been forced on him, was wrong.

Seven-thirty. He opened the door, Joan greeted him. He met her with a deliberate brightness that oppressed him by its falsity. 'We're going out.'

'Out?'

'The flicks. *La Ronde* is on at the Globe, you've always wanted to see it.'

'But E, I've got some nice chops I was just going to grill.'

'No time for that, my girl. *La Ronde*, it's –' He kissed the tips of her fingers. 'Anton Walbrook.'

'I know but.' She did not complete the sentence, peered at him. 'Something's wrong.'

'Nothing. Don't be absurd.'

'It's to do with the Department, that man coming. You're going to leave me, E, I know you are.'

The image crossed his mind of a bitch knowing that it is going to be put down. Why should he feel like this, when he was doing nothing to hurt her? She clung to him. 'You don't love me any more.'

'Yes, yes.'

'I love you, E. If I didn't have you, there'd be nothing left, I should kill myself.' To this he made no reply. 'Come to bed. Now.'

He removed her arms from his neck. 'You said the Tallises are away?' They were the occupants of the other maisonette in the house.

She stared. 'You want to get me out of the house?'

In your own interest, he said to himself, while aloud he told her not to talk nonsense, he was coming with her. The stresses of the day had overcome him. He felt as if he were running a high temperature, and when he put his hand to his forehead it was covered with sweat. In the end she agreed to go, but insisted that he come with her while she put on her coat. When they were outside the house she said abruptly, 'The garden shed.'

'Yes?'

'Why is it locked? What have you done with the key?'

He did not answer, but wrenched her arm so that she cried out. The night was hot. He could feel the sweat rolling down his body, dropping from the torso and pouring down his legs. His collar was wringing wet. Involuntarily he looked down to see whether water was staining his shoes. He swayed, and she caught his arm. 'What is it?'

'Nothing.'

They crossed the road and walked along beside the common. The scent of grass was strong in his nostrils, the roar of traffic exceptionally loud. Suddenly the grass scent was replaced by that of petrol, moving over him in sickly waves. The gears of a lorry grated, and the sound broke on his ears like a shriek of pain. In a field boys played cricket, the ball thudding on bat like a drum. Was it the traffic noise or something wrong with his hearing that made the words she was saying merge into indistinguishable blobs of sound? He turned his head to speak, but she shrieked something and made a gesture. He turned back. Slowly, as it seemed slowly, a cricket ball, reddish brown, moved through the blue air. A long way back on the field the players all stood turned towards him, a theatre audience waiting for something to happen. Joan was calling out, he moved his head, the ball went past (with a super-sensitivity of hearing that replaced his deafness he heard it pass, making a distinct train-like whistle). Then it was in the road and had banged against the tinny side of a car.

'That almost hit you.' Her voice sounded faint now, as though wax were in his ears. He shook his head and smiled slightly. A man picked up the ball and threw it back to the cricketers.

The cinema was half empty. They sat in a row with only two other people in it. They arrived near the end of the first scene, the soldier's encounter with the prostitute. The darkness surrounding them seemed to have something physical about it, like a blanket. He was jerked sharply into attention by a new theme in the music, and turned to look at Joan. She was staring straight ahead at the screen, and in profile her face had a crumpled, folded expression. Tears crawled like snail-marks down her cheek and she made no attempt to wipe them away.

This dumb-animal misery was too much for him. The day had been so full of anxiety and there was still so much to do, including what lay ahead of him that evening, that he was incapable of making the consoling gesture she needed. He closed his eyes against the images on the screen which mocked his own situation, and let the music flow over him. Within his head there moved incoherent abstract forms. Bright lights converged, met and noiselessly exploded, to be replaced by waves of sound and colour moving restlessly like the sea. They gave way to pictures of people – Pat Parker was there with a veil thickly covering her face. He removed it to find another veil which he pulled aside, and another and another. The important thing was seeing and touching, to assure himself that it was Pat and not somebody else who had come with him to Weybridge. When he touched her hand he knew that something was wrong.

He opened his eyes. The screen was in front of him, figures

moved across it as they should do. What was wrong? He looked down to see Joan's hand inside his trousers, felt the desperate groping of her fingers which moved as if she were trying to bring back the dead to life. She was still staring at the screen, and her hand might have been an agent remote from the rest of her body. He removed the hand, buttoned his trousers, stood up. She clutched his arm. He whispered: 'Got to make a phone call, back in five minutes,' walked up the aisle and out of the cinema. Less than half an hour had passed since they entered.

And less than half an hour after that he had done the thing that terrified him. He spent the night in a London hotel. In the morning, before taking the train to Birmingham, he read the papers carefully. Two of them reported the incident. 'Mystery Fire at Clapham. Arson Suspected.' Number 48 Elm Drive had been gutted, and people had been evacuated from Number 50. Nobody had been hurt. An empty petrol tin had been found and also some cotton waste in the garden shed belonging to the house. Arson was suspected.

He shivered as he read. It had gone as he intended, with no damage to anybody except an insurance company, yet he still felt uneasy. The crime against property seemed in a way to be a crime against himself. But it had been effective. There would be no personal trace left at Clapham of Major Easonby Mellon.

Chapter 11

The Act

He had not decided upon the method and manner of committing
the act without thought. It was tempting to play with the idea
of planning some deliberate deception about the time of death.
'It is not possible to be certain about the rate of cooling of a
body': those encouraging words had been written by no less a
medico-legal expert than Sir Sydney Smith, and books of medical jurisprudence all spoke with delightful uncertainty about
establishing the precise time of death. Suppose that one placed
an electric fire near to a body, the time of death would appear
to be an hour or two later than was actually the case. Or suppose
– more ingenious and interesting – that one took ice cubes from
the refrigerator and placed them in plastic non-leaking containers
at various points about the body, the normal cooling process
should be speeded up. He reluctantly rejected such ideas, partly
because of the distaste that he felt for having anything to do with
a dead body, but chiefly (or so he felt) because such ingenuity
was in itself to be deprecated. If the police happened to notice
that the electric fire, although turned off, was still curiously
warm, if ice water somehow leaked out of the plastic packs, if in
fact the police thought that deliberate deception was being
attempted, might they not immediately suspect him? The
strength of his position was that Arthur Brownjohn and Easonby
Mellon were two wholly separate characters, and that there was
no reason in the world why they should be associated. This was
what he must remember. The act should be simple, quick and
obvious. His plan was simple, and entailed practically no
risk.

At Euston Station, on his return from Birmingham he telephoned Clare, and cut short a burst of recriminatory phrases by
saying that he was coming home and wanted to see her.

There must have been something strange in his tone, for she
checked abruptly as a horse coming to a jump. 'What about?'

'I can't explain now, but –'

'You can't explain,' she said incredulously.

'You're alone, aren't you?'

'Of course I am alone. I am just finishing my lunch.'

'I shall be back soon. Don't tell anybody I'm coming, will you?'

'Arthur, have you been drinking?'

'I'll be there soon after three.' He put down the telephone. His hand was shaking.

In the station lavatory he changed into Easonby Mellon's clothes, and carefully adjusted the wig and beard. He went out carrying Arthur Brownjohn's clothes and diary in his suitcase. He caught the two-thirty train from Waterloo for the half-hour journey to Fraycut.

This time Major Mellon made his way straight out of the station in the direction of Livingstone Road. Phil Silvers was not on duty, and the man at the barrier took his ticket without a glance. The Laurels stood foursquare in exurban dignity. The rest of Livingstone Road appeared to sleep. He opened the gate, which gave its accustomed small squeak, walked up the path, inserted the key in the lock, turned it, was inside. Mr Slattery stared at him accusingly, as though aware of the revolver in his jacket pocket. The door of the living-room opened, and Clare came out. 'What –' she said, and stopped. He found himself holding his breath, as if something important depended on her words. Then she completed the sentence.

'What are you doing in those ridiculous clothes, and that –' She seemed to find it impossible to specify the wig and beard. 'Take it all off immediately.'

She had known him at once. It was awful. His fists were clenched into tight balls. 'I can explain.'

'Your telegram, what was the meaning of that? I waited for more than an hour at Waterloo. And now this fancy dress.'

'I said I could explain.'

'I doubt it very much. I cannot think what possible explanation there can be.'

He heard himself saying that it was quite simple, and knew with dismay that the tones were those of Arthur Brownjohn, not of Easonby Mellon. How could boldness have so speedily and humiliatingly abandoned him? One hand went into a pocket and drew out the revolver.

'What is the *meaning* of this masquerade?' Clare was becoming angry, it could be seen in the thickening of her neck muscles and the spot of colour in her cheeks. He was near the door of the living-room and she stood in the middle of it just beside the mottled grey sofa. She saw what was in his hand, and her reaction was one of pure exasperation. She spoke like a mother to a misbehaving child. 'Arthur, what are you doing? Put it *down*.'

'No.' He found it impossible to speak, then swallowed and managed it. 'I really must explain.'

She took a step towards him. He retreated. 'If you could see how silly you look.'

'Silly!' he cried out. The word moved him to anger. He raised the revolver, squeezed the trigger. Nothing happened.

'Of course you do. Just get that stuff off and wash your face and you'll feel better.'

'I am not silly,' he shouted. Why didn't she realize that he was a dangerous man? He realized that he had not moved the safety catch and did so. Suddenly the revolver went off, making a tremendous noise. The kickback jolted his arm severely. What happened to the bullet? He became aware that Clare was strangely pale.

She took another step towards him and said in a low voice, 'What is the matter with you, Arthur?'

He retreated. He had his back to the door. The revolver went off again, almost deafening him. This time she put her hands to her stomach, so evidently the bullet had hit her, but she did not fall down. Instead she put out a hand, and he felt that if she succeeded in touching him something terrible would happen. He cried out something, he could not have said what, and fired again and again, he did not know how many times or where the bullets went. There was a ping of glass and he thought: 'Heavens, I've broken the french window.' He looked and saw the window starred at one point, and with a deep crack down the centre. He was so much distressed by this time that his attention was temporarily distracted from Clare. He saw, however, that she was badly hurt. She appeared to be trying to speak to him, but failed to do so. Blood shot in a stream from her mouth – he jumped back hurriedly so that it should not touch him – and she fell over the back of the sofa and then down the side of it to the floor, clawing at the sofa for support and making unintelligible noises in her throat. She seemed still to be trying to say something to him, but he could not imagine what it was. She lay on the carpet groaning. Blood continued to trickle from her mouth. He found it unendurable that she was not dead, perhaps would not die. The revolver was empty, but in any case he could not have fired it again. He stood and watched helplessly as she tried to inch her way across the carpet to – what would it be? – of course, the telephone. There was blood on her face now, and she moved more slowly. He could not have said whether it was seconds or minutes before he realized that she was not moving at all.

It would have been impossible for him to touch her with his gloved hands, but he moved across with the caution he would have used in approaching a squashed but possibly still dangerous insect, and rolled her over with his foot. She lay still, staring at the ceiling with her eyes open. She was, she must be, dead.

He felt that he could no longer bear to be in the house. He dropped the revolver to the floor, looked round him without seeing anything, and ran out of the room. His case stood in the hall. He picked it up, opened the front door, and began to run down the path. Then he checked himself. In the garden of Endholme old Mr Lillicrapp was at work with his fork and trowel. He straightened up and said, 'Afternoon. Some boys been breaking windows round here. Heard the glass go. Thought it might be mine, but it wasn't. Not next door, I hope.' He laughed heartily, but the man leaving The Laurels in a hurry made no reply. Mr Lillicrapp leaned on his fork and stood looking after the man as he walked down the road. Discourtesy was rampant nowadays. He ascribed it less to rudeness than to the hustle and bustle of modern life.

PART TWO

After the Act

Chapter 1

Discovery

Major Easonby Mellon died in a train lavatory somewhere between Fraycut and Waterloo. The clothes, wig and beard that had been the corporeal marks of his existence went into the suitcase. The police, when they checked, might find that Mellon had got on to the train at Fraycut. From that point onwards he would have vanished. They would check at Waterloo and at the intermediate stations, and would find no trace of him. Arthur Brownjohn, a man totally inconspicuous except for the bald head concealed by a trilby hat, got off the train at Waterloo, deposited a suitcase in the Left Luggage office and put the ticket carefully into his wallet. He spent a few minutes in the buffet and then bought a ticket and caught the next train to Fraycut. He walked from the station to Elsom's house, which was ten minutes' distance from his own.

The Elsoms lived in a new development of what were called superior town houses, and he was happy to feel that the man who walked up their short drive and rang their three-tone chiming bell, was in complete command of himself. The revulsion he had felt during and after the act remained, but the terror accompanying it had vanished when he shed the appurtenances of Easonby Mellon in the lavatory. Waiting at Fraycut Station, as he had had to do because the train was late, he had been dreadfully agitated. The fear had possessed him that a policeman would come up and say, 'You were seen leaving The Laurels a few minutes ago under suspicious circumstances, and I must ask you to accompany me to the police station.' When he became Arthur Brownjohn again he shrugged off these fears, and indeed was able to see that everything had happened for the best. That Mr Lillicrapp had seen the murderer leaving, and that he should have displayed such obvious agitation on the station platform, must surely remove any doubt that might linger in the official mind. If he had planned all that – and it was with a shade of reluctance that he acknowledged what had happened as unplanned and at the time distressing – it could not have worked out better. The call on Elsom was a precautionary measure designed to show that at (he looked at his watch) six o'clock he had been perfectly calm. And he congratulated himself that he had passed the test, that he *was* calm. Many men, after all, would not have been. It was with insouciance that, as the door opened, he faced Elsom's fine teeth.

'What a very nice place you have here.' In fact he detested the appearance of the living-room, the picture window, the differently-coloured walls, the rugs placed with careful carelessness on the wood block floor, the absence of a fire-place. How could you possibly call such a place a home?

'We like it. Melissa's done the furnishing. She's got taste.' All Elsom's statements were positive. They both invited contradiction and implied that it would not be tolerated. Melissa, a wispy blonde with a tiny triangular face, came in and said that she was sorry.

'I beg your pardon?'

'Melissa couldn't get along to your party. She had one of her heads.'

'One of my heads.' A red-tipped claw was placed upon the longest side of the triangle, the forehead. 'I believe your wife has heads.'

'What? Oh yes, she does have heads.' The conversation was proving less easy to maintain than he had expected. An image flashed across his mind of Clare with two heads. He rejected this, and it was succeeded by one of her face as he had last seen it, with blood trickling down the chin.

'I find the only thing is a darkened room. Does your wife find that too?'

He began to wish that he were alone with Elsom. However, it proved that Melissa had come in only to make polite conversation. She extolled the virtues of the new development, said how pleasant it was to be among people who were really your sort, expressed a hope that she would meet Clare very soon, and drifted delicately from the room.

'She's very sensitive.' Elsom closed the door decisively.

'What'll it be, gin, whisky, vodka, sherry? You name it, we have it.'

'A little vodka.' He coughed. 'I believe that has no smell. I mustn't go home smelling of drink.'

'Clare wouldn't like it, eh?'

'The truth is, I must confess, I have rather a weak head.'

'You haven't been home yet?'

'I came straight from London. I wanted to see you.'

'Here I am. Anything I can straighten out, be happy to do it.' Elsom settled himself in an oddly-shaped chair. 'Fire away.'

'The truth is Lektreks hasn't been doing very well lately. In the last couple of years, I mean.' Elsom's brisk nod showed him to be unsurprised. 'And Clare is not very keen on my giving up.'

'Doesn't want you round the house all day.' Elsom guffawed, gulped at his drink. 'So?'

He said carefully, 'It might be a question of what terms you have in mind.'

'I told you, that's in the hands of the slide rule boys. But I've never known anyone who dealt with GBD who had any complaints afterwards.'

'You did say you might employ me. My inventions.'

'Your inventions, yes.' Elsom was obviously about to launch on a long speech, and Arthur took the chance to look surreptitiously at his watch. Just after half past six. How long should he go on with this, when could he decently leave, having established the fact of his calmness and coherence? He listened for what seemed like minutes to Elsom circuitously conveying that what really interested GBD was Lektreks and that the offer of a job was conditional on the purchase of the firm. He nodded occasionally, and was astonished to find that his eyelids had actually closed for a moment. He jerked into attention at mention of Clare's name.

'Why not give her a ring?' Elsom leaned forward doggily in his chair, ready to spring.

'Give Clare a ring?'

'Unless you've any more problems, conference is finished, agreed? Why not ask her round for a drink, Melissa would love to meet her, won't take a couple of minutes in the car.'

'We haven't got a car.'

'Shanks's pony then, it's a fine evening. Or I'll nip round and fetch her.'

Why not, he suddenly agreed with doggish Elsom, why not give Clare a ring? There was something gruesome about the thought of the telephone ringing in the empty house, the body on the floor with blood coming out of the mouth, but it was necessary not to think of that. You must be brave, he told himself, you must not draw back now. He saw the sequence of events, the telephone call, no reply, where can Clare have got to, must get back at once, no doubt she's just slipped out for a few minutes but still. Perhaps Elsom would drive him back. If he did, so much the better.

'Very good idea. I'll ring her now if I may use your phone.'

The telephone was in a corner of the room, beneath a grinning mask. As he picked it up and dialled he saw with extreme vividness the telephone at the house. It stood in the hall, an old-fashioned black instrument, different in colour and even in shape from the red telephone in his hand. Burr-burr, the telephone said in his ear, burr-burr. It would take Clare four burr-burrs to get there from the living-room, a dozen from upstairs. He would give it something over a dozen before turning to Elsom, brows knit together, to say that there seemed to be no reply.

The burr-burr stopped. A man's voice said, 'Yes?'

He thought for a moment that he would drop the telephone. Then he managed to say, 'What number is that? Who is it?'

The number was his own. The speaker did not give his identity.

'I want to speak to my wife. Mrs Brownjohn. Call her to the telephone, please. And who is that?'

'Just a moment.'

In the next seconds he expected to hear Clare's voice and to be assured that nothing had happened, the whole thing had been something merely imagined in his diary. A different man's voice said, 'Mr Brownjohn?'

'Yes. Who are you? Where is my wife?'

'Coverdale, sir. Detective-Inspector, C.I.D. I've got some bad news for you.'

He did not have to make his voice quaver as he asked the nature of the news, and was told it. How had the police got there so quickly? Was there something threatening in the Inspector's voice? He was asked where he was.

'A friend's house. Very near.'

'Give me the address, sir. I'll send round a car.'

He put down the telephone for a moment. 'Not bad news, I hope,' Elsom asked eagerly.

'The address, what's the address?'

'I don't get you. What address?'

'The address *here*, you fool.' The actions and emotions of the day were too much for him, and he began to weep. Elsom looked at him appalled, called his wife, and then picked up the telephone. Even in the grip of the hysteria which was not checked by the huge drink Melissa poured for him, he could not help noticing the businesslike way in which Elsom received the news, opening his jacket to reveal a battery of pens and pencils and selecting one with which to make notes. He chose a ballpoint which wrote in red, and as Arthur remembered the trickle of blood, this seemed to him absurd. The tears streaming down his cheeks became tears of laughter. He made a gesture at the ball point, and the laughter grew higher. Elsom put down the telephone, turned, said, 'Sorry about this.' He saw nothing, but felt a tremendously hard blow on the jaw, one that rattled his teeth and knocked him off the chair arm on which he had been sitting, on to the carpet.

Melissa's triangular face bent anxiously over him. He looked up, unable to focus properly. 'Oh, Derek,' she said, 'I hope you haven't hit him too hard.'

Chapter 2

Conversation with Coverdale

Everything seemed to be happening at once, and everybody treated him with a totally agreeable care and delicacy. When the police car arrived he was still on the sofa, with Melissa holding a damp towel to his jaw and Elsom full of apologies for not knowing his own strength. Then into the car – it was the first time he had ever been in a police car, and he said so to the detectives – and in a flash they were back at The Laurels. He was still feeling shaky, and entered the house holding the arm of one of the detectives.

In the hall Mr Slattery gave him his customary look, but otherwise everything was changed. As always happens when the police enter a house where a violent event has occurred, the whole place seemed to have been taken over by them. There were cars outside the house, men dashed in and out carrying bits of equipment, and they talked to each other briskly. 'Got all you want? . . . Is Jerry at the station . . . Finished the downstairs and the hall, trying upstairs.' Feet clattered in and out, up and down. He tried to look in the living-room, but was not allowed to do so. A man appeared, nodded, said 'Mr Brownjohn, come along.' Where were they going? It proved to be the kitchen. Clare wouldn't like this, he thought as they sat in chairs on opposite sides of the kitchen table, she wouldn't like it at all.

'My name's Coverdale.' He was a big man with a lumpy, knobbly face and a bulky body that seemed to be straining out of his shiny blue suit. 'Sergeant Amies.' Startled, Arthur looked round and saw another man beside the door. 'Cigarette?'

'Thank you, I don't smoke.'

Coverdale lighted one himself, staring across the table all the while. Was it the prelude to a fierce interrogation? Instead he said, 'Put the kettle on, Bill. Mr Brownjohn could do with a cuppa. You've had a shock.'

'Yes.'

'Stands to reason it was a shock.'

'I was a little hysterical. A friend had to hit me.'

'He made a job of it. You're going to have a nice little lump.'

'I don't really know what's happened.'

'Stupid. Course you don't.' Was he guileful, or as straight-forward as he appeared? 'Somebody broke in, that's the way it looks at the moment, burglar perhaps. Your wife surprised him.'

'She – she is dead?'

'I'm afraid so. I told you on the telephone.'

'Yes. Somehow it's hard to believe.' This was true. Clare's presence seemed to him to hang like a gas cloud over the whole house.

'You need that cup of tea.'

'Tea coming up.' The Sergeant poured it into mugs instead of the cups Clare would have used. The tea itself was strong and sweet, and he did feel better after drinking it.

'Amateur,' the Inspector said.

'What?'

'If it was done that way, somebody breaking and entering and then your wife surprising him, it was an amateur. Pros don't carry guns.'

'She was shot?'

'Didn't I say?' It was the first hint that guile might lurk behind the blue marble eyes. 'Emptied the revolver in a panic, fired all over the place. Amateur sure enough.'

What was the the best question to ask? 'When did it happen?'

'Round about three-thirty.'

'I don't think that's right.' Surprise showed on Coverdale's lumpy face. 'I mean Clare has – had – rather fixed habits, for being in and for being out. She was almost always in on Friday afternoons. So it's not likely she would have come back and surprised a burglar. I mean, she would have been here.'

'Interesting.' Coverdale drained his cup. 'Eh, Amies?'

'Interesting.' The Sergeant whisked away the cups, began to wash them up.

'You think it was personal, some enemy?'

'Oh, I didn't say that.'

'You got any enemies, your wife got any?'

'No. Nobody who would do this.'

'Happily married? No quarrels?'

'Certainly not.' He was genuinely shocked by the suggestion. 'We were quite happy. My work takes me away from home rather a lot. Clare had developed interests of her own. I was pleased about that, but I suppose in a way they tended to separate us.'

'Tried to ring you this afternoon.' Coverdale's voice was casual. 'Your office. No reply.'

'It's a small office, just an address. I don't have a secretary.'

Silence. Amies turned from the sink. 'Going to ask him, sir?'

'May as well.' He could feel his legs trembling. 'Any idea where you were this afternoon around three-thirty?'

'I went up to Birmingham this morning to see a client. I caught the two-fifteen back. I was in the train from Birmingham to London.'

'Mind telling us the client's name?' That was Amies again.

'Steel Alloys Limited. I saw Mr Gibson, left him soon after twelve, had lunch –'

'Mind telling us where?'

'A pub called the Dog and Duck, just off the Bull Ring. I got in to Euston – oh, I can't remember, but not before half past three.'

'They're not that quick yet, are they?' Coverdale laughed heartily.

'I don't understand why you're asking me these questions.'

'Shouldn't have done perhaps. Don't want to upset you. Leave it until tomorrow if you like.' Coverdale got up. 'Like us to fix a hotel for you? Don't suppose you'll want to stay here, wouldn't advise it anyway.' Amies had washed up the cups. The two men moved to the door. He felt a passionate reluctance to let them go.

'There was a question I wanted to ask you.'

'Yes?'

A man put his head round the kitchen door, muttered something to Amies, who went out. Coverdale looked inquiring.

'How do you know it was half past three when it happened?'

'Your next door neighbour, name's Lillicrapp. Heard some glass breaking, saw a man run out of your house and down the road. Went round the back to have a look. The glass was your french window, broken by one of the shots. He looked through the window, saw your wife on the floor, rang us straight away. That's the sort of cooperation we like to get from the public.'

'This man he saw. You've got a description?'

Coverdale nodded. The door opened again, Amies said, 'Spare a minute, sir?'

He was left alone in the kitchen. His existence with Clare surrounded him. The plates had their own place on the dresser shelves and she had been especially pleased by the mats beside them, a series called 'Cries of Old London' which she had bought only a few months ago. Attached to the gas cooker was an automatic lighter which he had bought for her. He sat at the kitchen table and put his head in his hands. His jaw ached.

'Mr Brownjohn.' Coverdale was looking at him with what might have been pity. Beside him, Sergeant Amies was holding the Easonby Mellon letters. 'No more questions for tonight.'

Chapter 3

Life Goes On

He stayed that night, and for two nights after it, with the Elsoms. Derek – he had insisted that Arthur should call him by his Christian name – had come to The Laurels and taken him back. No sooner was he in the Elsoms' home than a doctor arrived. He turned out to have been sent by Coverdale. He took Arthur's pulse, listened to his heart, looked into his eyes, ordered him to bed immediately and gave him two pills which, with the accompanying glass of hot milk, sent him to sleep in five minutes. He woke next morning to find that Elsom was working in the garden – it was Saturday. Melissa brought him coffee and toast on a tray.

So began two of the most enjoyable days in his life. Melissa was prepared to treat him like an invalid, and he stayed in bed that Saturday until lunchtime. It occurred to him that he had not spent a whole morning in bed since he was a child. All sorts of people left messages of sympathy. 'I told them you were not well enough to see anybody yet,' Melissa chirped. The doctor returned and pronounced him much improved. When he got up he wore Elsom's dressing-gown, which was far too big for him. In the afternoon Elsom brought a caseful of clothes from The Laurels.

'You're very kind,' Arthur kept repeating.

'Not a bit of it. You stay as long as you like, that's the way we want it. What are friends for if they don't rally round at a time like this?'

You're not a friend of mine, he felt inclined to say, I hardly know you and don't even like you. But the doggy managing quality of Elsom proved very helpful. 'Hate to bring it up, Arthur, old chap,' he said, 'but there'll be the question of the funeral. Would you like me to see Jukes, they say he's the best local man?' Then there was the coffin. Was it to be the finest quality oak with specially designed handles, or standard pattern? His choice of finest quality oak met with approval. The inquest was fixed for Tuesday, and Elsom had gathered that it would be more or less a formality.

'I think Coverdale's got a line he's working on, though he won't say much about it.' He held out a small paper bag. 'I got this for you.'

Arthur opened the bag. It contained a black tie. He saw that Elsom was wearing one.

'Just a formality, but you have to show respect.'

'Very thoughtful of you.' He took off the tie he was wearing and put on the black one. 'Thank you very much.'

That evening Melissa suggested that, if he felt up to it, they should ask one or two people in tomorrow who wanted to express their sorrow in person. He dimly perceived that the Elsoms were using the occasion to establish themselves in the community, but what did it matter? A dozen people came in before lunch on Sunday, and the occasion turned out to be something between a cocktail party and a wake. The Paynes were there, and so was the retired naval commander. A dwarfish man from the Liberal Club told Arthur what a great loss Clare would be to the whole community, and Miss Leppard, secretary of the Art Society at Weybridge, said that Clare had a real talent for painting. Miss Leppard was a tall peering woman, and she brought her face very close to Arthur's as she said, 'I have had a visit from the police.' He moved back a little. 'They were interested in your wife's attendance at our classes. I told them that she had one of the most original approaches of anyone in the group. I'm not sure if that was really what they wanted to know.'

So they were on to the Weybridge art classes! He knew that they must be, but it was good to have this confirmation of it. Had they got on to the hotel yet? The trouble was that he felt a need to give them some direction. He wanted to go to Coverdale and tell him the name of the man he was looking for. That was obviously not possible, and he felt the pangs of the artist unable for private reasons to make public acknowledgement of his work.

'Wonderful weather.' That was Mrs Payne. Had she not been saying a few days ago that the weather was incalculable? 'I shall never forget the chats poor dear Clare and I had about her garden. She loved growing things.' She put a hand on his arm. 'You mustn't take it too hard. George and I were *very* fond of you both. We always thought you were perfectly suited.'

The strange thing was, he reflected, that in many ways this was perfectly true.

The inquest was a formality as Elsom had suggested, and indeed it was rather too much of a formality to suit him. The doctor gave evidence that death had been caused by a bullet which entered the stomach and was responsible for an internal hae-morrhage. The deceased had also been hit by two other bullets, one penetrating the ribs and the other grazing the left arm. Mr Lillicrapp made a brief appearance to say that he had heard glass breaking, gone round to the garden, seen the body, and telephoned the police. Nothing at all was said about the man he had seen. Coverdale popped up to say that police inquiries were continuing. The coroner adjourned the inquest *sine die*, which Arthur gathered meant until they had some more evidence. The funeral was interesting in its way, although it was something of a trial because certain members of the Slattery connection re-appeared, among them Uncle Ratty. He was visibly older and now walked with a stick, but age had not made him less choleric. 'Should never have left her.'

'What's that?'

'Used to write, say she was lonely.' This was a new light on Clare. Had she really been lonely? Such a possibility had never occurred to him. 'Left her at the mercy of these damned young thugs. That's who it was, take it from me. Army discipline, that's what they want.' It did not seem worth arguing the point.

After the funeral he returned to The Laurels. The Elsoms protested at his going, but not very fervently. He guessed that they had had enough of him, or to put it unkindly that there was no more publicity to be got out of him. Before he went Elsom said, 'About that little deal, it's still on.'

'What deal?' He really had forgotten.

'Lektreks.' Elsom showed his teeth. 'You said Clare had ob-jections.'

'I can't possibly consider it just now.'

'I realize that, Arthur. When you're ready GBD will still be there.'

Back at The Laurels again his first sensation was a feeling of freedom. There were certain things about the house that he had always wanted to change and now – how extraordinary it was – he could do whatever he wished. He put Mr Slattery up in the attic and brought down one of his mother's old pictures of the Sussex downs. To his surprise Susan was enthusiastic about the change, and revealed that she had always thought the portrait very gloomy. Her attitude towards him was one of protective flirtatiousness. 'I expect you'll like me to come in a bit more. I could cook lunch and then leave something for the evening.'

'That's very kind.' He hesitated before asking her to help him change round the furniture in the living-room, but about this too she was approving. The bloodstained sofa cover had been sent to the cleaners.

'You'll be staying here, then?' she asked after he had been back three or four days.

'I don't know. I haven't made up my mind.'

'After all, it's your home.'

'It's a big decision, Susan.' He found it easy to call her Susan now, where before it had been difficult. 'I have to try and adjust to a new life.' He longed to ask whether she had talked to the Inspector about the man she had seen in the garden, but appreciated the need for restraint.

'I can see that. Must be lonely.'

He agreed, but in fact found that he did not miss Clare at all. He seemed to be busy from morning to night, shopping, doing little things about the house and in the garden (he chopped down a vine that darkened the living-room which Clare had always refused to remove), answering the telephone, accepting and refusing invitations from people he knew only slightly. He realized that some of these people asked him as a social obligation owed to the bereaved and that others were eager to hear the unpleasant details of the act, but still the invitations pleased him and he accepted a few of them, although he was careful of what he said and careful also not to drink more than one glass of spirits or three of wine. He was even asked to a Liberal Club social, but this was one of the invitations he declined.

At two or three of these functions he saw George Payne, and the bank manager invited him in for a chat. Payne began by asking him about the crime. Were the police any nearer to finding the murderer? Arthur said he didn't know. He hadn't spoken to Coverdale since the inquest.

Payne lighted his pipe and sat back behind his fumed oak desk. 'I tell you what, the police aren't all they used to be. I don't believe all the tales I hear, but I can tell you this, if they spent their time looking for criminals instead of giving motorists tickets for doing five miles over the speed limit, we'd all be better off.' It seemed safe to agree. 'And how are things going, Arthur? How are you keeping in yourself?'

He was used to being questioned as if he had just recovered from a serious operation, and had even come to like it. The question, in any case, was a formal approach to the production of an array of papers which Clare had lodged with the bank. A solicitor could handle some of these things if Arthur wished it, but otherwise Mr Payne would take the whole burden of them upon his shoulders. He murmured that that would be very kind, and Mr Payne said with a brisk smile, 'That's what we're here for, to help. I wish more people understood that. Now, you might like to have a look at *these*. If you come round this side of the desk I can explain.'

He explained and Arthur listened, although without full comprehension. There were stocks and Defence Bonds and things which should have been sold but hadn't been, and other things which if he took George's advice he would hang on to. There was the pass-book in which he noted, but did not mention, that large withdrawal from Clare's private account. The private account in any case contained only a small fraction of the sum that would be coming to him. With a flash of indignation he realized that Clare had had a good deal more money than he had known. He would not be a rich man, but there was enough to provide a tidy income, which indeed she had been enjoying throughout their marriage. No wonder she had been comparatively unconcerned about his earnings.

The little chat lasted more than an hour, and ended by Arthur expressing his complete faith in his friend George. 'He's really still in a state of shock, poor little chap,' the bank manager said to his wife afterwards. 'It's a good job he's got us to look after his money. I'll tell you what he is, he's unworldly.' And as a mild parting jest he said to Arthur, 'No more investments like that car cream you know.' Little Brownjohn looked quite startled for a moment.

During these days Arthur did not once go up to London. He knew in a way that he ought to put in an appearance at the Lektreks office, but there seemed to be no hurry. If orders had come in they could wait. That was what he told himself, but the truth was that London represented to him things that he wanted to forget. There was the suitcase in the Left Luggage office, there was the Matrimonial Assistance office which was now forbidden territory, there was Joan. He had a vision of the Matrimonial Assistance office with the letters inside the door piling up and up, until at last the postman was unable to get them through the box. Or had Coverdale got there first, were his men even now going through the files? He felt that he had to know, yet there was no possible safe way of finding out. In case he should be tempted to do so, he stayed in Fraycut.

One day he saw an interesting item in the paper:

BLACKMAIL CHARGE. COUPLE ARRESTED

Patricia Parker, 26, a secretary, and John Termaxian, said to have posed as her husband, appeared at Bow St yesterday on a charge of attempting to obtain money by blackmail from Mr X, a businessman. Mr X said that he was in a hotel room with Parker when Termaxian, whom he believed to be her husband, burst in and demanded money. Mr X has an invalid wife, and according to him threats were made to send her photographs of him with Miss Parker.

A meeting was arranged after Mr X informed the police, at which £200 in notes was handed over to Termaxian, who was then arrested. Det. Sgt. Rose said Termaxian stated on arrest: 'I only did it to put the wind up him.' Termaxian and Parker were committed for trial. Bail was refused.

So they had come unstuck, probably with one of the people on his list. He couldn't help feeling pleased. He worried for half an hour over their connection with Easonby Mellon, but there seemed no danger to him in their arrest. It was unlikely that they would admit to any connection with Matrimonial Assistance – why should they? No, it was a matter of blackmailers getting their just deserts.

A couple of days after reading this newspaper item he had his second conversation with Inspector Coverdale.

Chapter 4

Second Conversation with Coverdale

He was sitting in the garden after lunch drinking hot tea with lemon when Susan announced the Inspector. Arthur said truthfully that he had been wondering what progress was being made.

'That's why I'm here. But there's something I must say first. I'm sorry if we gave you a hard time the other night.'

'A hard time?'

'That's right. I'll admit I was a bit worried about you though my sergeant, Amies, said I had no need to be. He's got a head on his shoulders, Amies. But there's no rough stuff in this force. Police are the servants of the public, is what I say.' Coverdale's face was as shiny as his suit. 'I don't mind saying we checked on your story about going up to Birmingham. I mention it in case you're talking to Mr Gibson. Hope it doesn't cause you inconvenience. And we checked on the train times too. There was a train at twelve-thirty you could have caught.'

'Is that so? But I didn't.'

'I'm sure you didn't, you *could* have caught it is all I'm saying. I'll be frank with you, when a married woman is killed my first thought is about her husband, especially if he gets the money. And when his business is a bit shaky –' He paused.

'Yes, it's true mine is. I'm thinking of selling it.'

Coverdale nodded. He had obviously talked to Elsom. 'I'm being quite frank. You didn't have an alibi, you could have been on a train which got you down to London in time to get to Fraycut. You were an obvious suspect but for one thing.'

Arthur sipped his tea and put down the glass on the bamboo table by his side. Coverdale did not seem to know quite how he should go on. As he said afterwards to Amies, he felt sorry for the little devil, he looked so trusting even if he was a bit silly. When he broke the news as tactfully as he could, by saying that

Mrs Brownjohn had been left at home a good deal and that it was not unusual for women in such a situation to look for other masculine company, the little man was incredulous.

'I can't believe it. Not Clare. Why didn't she say something to me, I'd have done something, tried to come home more.'

She wanted a bit more than you could give her, Coverdale thought, and then reproached himself for coarseness. He produced photostats of the letters they had found, and watched the bewilderment with which Brownjohn read them.

'You found these *here*?' Coverdale told him where they had found them. Brownjohn sat shuffling the photostats, reading bits of them. 'She didn't leave me. You see what it says in this one, she wouldn't leave me.' He continued reading, rubbing his bald head. 'I suppose it's true. I never did make her happy.'

Coverdale, who had been married since he was a copper on the beat, had two teenage daughters, and liked to think that he had always been master in his own home, felt sorry for him. 'You're right about that, she wouldn't leave you. That seems to have been at the back of it. Ever heard of a man named Easonby Mellon?'

Brownjohn shook his head. 'Was that the man? I don't know the name.'

'He wasn't a friend of the family? Your wife's family?' Brownjohn said he thought not. Coverdale told him about the hotel at Weybridge. It was the only meeting they had been able to trace, but it was obvious from the letters that the lovers had met elsewhere. 'This meeting must have been some sort of crisis. She was due at her art class, but she didn't go to it, left a message saying she had another engagement.'

At Waterloo Station, Arthur thought. Aloud he said:

'What was he like? Is he like?'

'Pretty shifty customer. He ran some sort of shady matrimonial agency. But he's disappeared. And there's no doubt this was a premeditated thing. He took care to cover his tracks.' He described the gutting of the house at Clapham.

'What did he look like? Did he look like me?'

It was a bit pathetic. From what Coverdale had gathered, Mellon couldn't have been more unlike Brownjohn. 'Brown hair and little beard, loud clothes. Aggressive type, from what I can gather.'

'He was married.' At Coverdale's look of surprise Brownjohn explained. 'He mentions someone called Joan.'

'Yes, he was married.' The Inspector remembered the ludicrous story told him by Mellon's slatternly wife in the furnished bed-sitter where she was living, the tale about her husband working for some cloak and dagger organization. She had seemed very upset by the news that he had been carrying on with another woman. It had occurred to Coverdale that the tale about being in some sort of Government service might be true, all sorts of unreliable people were employed nowadays, though he had been unable to get any confirmation of it. But the odds were heavily on Mellon being some sort of crook, and the 'Flexner' who had called on him being a fellow crook who had been looking for him. The likelihood of this was emphasized by the fact that a number of fingerprints had been found in Mellon's office which, when checked with the photomicrograph, revealed themselves as obvious forgeries, lacking the sweat pores of genuine prints. The obvious conclusion was that Mellon's prints were on file, and he had taken the wife along for a session with the Rogues' Gallery pictures, although he had known in advance that the session would be abortive. Indeed, she had told him as much, and the truth was she seemed quite besotted with the man. 'If he is there I shan't tell you,' she said, but he had been watching her, and he did not think she saw a face she recognized. The problem was to find Mellon.

'Was she upset?'

'Who? Oh, the wife. Yes, she was.' She did seem to have had a presentiment about his not coming back to her on that night when, for some unexplained reason Mellon had walked out on her and set fire to their flat. *I knew he was going for good,* she had said. *I knew my life was finished, finished.* The things people said! 'She seemed very upset.'

Brownjohn had put down his unfinished glass of lemon tea and was standing up, looking over his neat garden. 'You think he did it?'

'He was seen leaving the house at the time, sir. By your

neighbour, Mr Lillicrapp. That and the fact that he's disappeared –'

'Is there any news of him?'

'We shall find him,' Coverdale said, with a confidence he felt. 'When we really spread the net, sir, the fish don't wriggle out of it.'

Brownjohn turned to him. His voice was high. 'Thank you for telling me.'

Coverdale felt more uncomfortable than ever. 'I left it a day or two until you were feeling better. You had to know some time.'

'Quite right. You've broken it to me as gently as possible.' Hesitantly, like a schoolboy asking whether he might be allowed to leave the room, he said, 'Do you want me any more?'

'Want you?'

'This has been a shock. If I had that man here I might – I don't know. Why did he do it?'

'Looks like jealousy, sir. It's in the letters. If you'd like me to leave them –' But Brownjohn was thrusting back the photostats at him with a shaky hand.

'I don't want to read them, how could you think I should want to read them again.' He checked himself. 'I'm sorry. What I wanted to say was that I think I shall have to leave here.'

Stolidly but with sympathy the Inspector said, 'I understand.'

'It all belonged to Clare and not to me. Everything reminds me of her.' He waved a hand that embraced the garden with its rockery and the foursquare bulk of the red brick house.

Coverdale said again that he understood. He went away and left Brownjohn in the garden staring at the house in the sunlight, with the half-finished glass of lemon tea beside him on the bamboo table. He may be a silly little man, the Inspector thought, but I shouldn't like to be in Mellon's shoes if this chap ever caught up with him.

Chapter 5

A Car and a House

He had told Coverdale nothing but the truth. As he sat in the
house every evening, eating a meal which he bought from the
deep freeze at the grocer, and switching the television set on and
off in the hope of finding a programme to interest him, he felt
Clare's presence pervading the rooms as tangibly as a scent. He
was not burdened by guilt about the act, which seemed something remote and belonging to another person, nor did he feel
any sense of triumph that things had gone as he intended. It was
rather as if Clare was not dead at all but might walk through the
front door at any moment, criticize the changes he had made in
the house and demand that everything be put back in its proper
place. He had moved the television set to a part of the room where
it was possible to sit and watch in comfort, but he knew that she
would be annoyed because it made all the furniture look un-
balanced. He hung up some curtains that Clare had discarded
because she thought them too bright, but they gave him little
pleasure. There were some things that he enjoyed doing himself,
like paying the milkman, and there was the daily pleasure of
shopping, but even about such things there was something dis-
concerting, because he was constantly reminded that he was
shopping not for two but for one. After buying a chop one day
he remembered that Clare did not like chops, and felt irritation
because she would not be there to see his gesture of independence. He was irritated also by Susan's complaisance, which had
pleased him so much at first. Why was she so unctuously friendly,
why could she not behave more as she had done when Clare was
alive? He contemplated getting rid of her, but found himself
unable to make the effort.

He spent the whole of one evening up in the attic, dismantling
the slot racing track with the intention of bringing it down and
setting it up in the dining-room, which he hardly ever used.
After all, he could do what he liked, he could even knock two

rooms into one to accommodate the track if he wished. But he found that he no longer had any interest in slot racing, and never put up the track again. He advertised and sold the whole thing through a local paper.

He found himself unwilling to leave the house for any length of time. He was not afraid that something might be discovered in his absence, for there was nothing to discover, but each time he opened the front door he had a feeling that something terrible might have happened. This sensation became so strong that he was increasingly reluctant to go out in the evening. There was no lack of invitations, from the Paynes, the Elsoms and others, but he refused them with transparently untruthful excuses. Nor did he go up to London. Easonby Mellon's clothes were in the Left Luggage office still, together with the diary, and he knew that he must do something about them, but he stayed at The Laurels.

One evening Payne came round, bringing with him some papers for signature. He accepted a glass of sherry.

'Nice bright curtains. You've made some improvements.' He peered at Arthur as if he were an object at the end of a microscope. 'How are you keeping, old chap? Sorry you haven't been able to manage an evening for bridge.'

'I've been busy. And you need a couple.'

'Nonsense,' Payne said heartily, although it was obviously true. 'You're looking a bit peaky.'

'I'm all right.'

'Partly the weather, I dare say. It's a funny old summer all right,' the bank manager said judicially, although it had been very much like all the summers Arthur could remember. 'You want to get away. And you're a lucky fellow, you can do it.'

This was a day or two after Coverdale's visit, and the words seemed to harden the resolution in Arthur's mind. 'I thought of selling the house.'

'I quite understand. Though of course we shall be sorry to lose you. Where did you think of going?'

Nothing so tangible as a particular place had been in his mind, and it was with surprise that he heard his reply. 'A little place by the coast. Somewhere near Brighton.'

From the moment of speech he knew that this was what he wanted. It was as though a gate had been opened by the words, and after Payne had gone he brought down from the attic the other water colours and sat in a chair looking at them. The memories they evoked filled the room. His mother's sprawling hand had given them titles: 'Devil's Dyke in Summer', 'West Blatchington, the Mill', 'Penn's House and Cottage, Steyning', and so on. The longer he looked at them the more attractive they seemed. They were very different from Clare's pictures, in which great blocks of vivid colour filled the canvas, barely recognizable as tables and chairs. What nonsense Miss Leppard had talked about Clare showing talent – his mother's water colours seemed to him ten times more interesting. When his mother painted she had worn always a large floppy hat which kept away the intense sunlight. He had asked her once whether she could see clearly enough, and she had laughed and said coquettishly, 'Even a lady painter has to look after her complexion, darling.' It was true that she had a complexion of beautiful pallor with just the faintest hint of colour in it – or had the colour, now that he came to think of it, been added by art?

They had lived at Brighton for only twelve months, after she separated from his father, but in retrospect the time seemed to have been much longer. In his recollection that had not been a funny old summer, but one in which day after day had been hot with a sky of endless blue. He did not know until years later that his father had gone off to live with the other woman whom he eventually married, only that there were no more quarrels every evening, and that he must not mention his father's name. 'You're all I have now,' his mother said to him. 'We shall never be parted, shall we, darling?' Every day they had taken a picnic somewhere on the downs and there, on a green breast of hill, she sat and dabbed paint on to cartridge paper while he read historical tales and funny stories, or rolled on the grass.

He remembered vividly being at the top of a hill, calling to her to watch and then rolling down, over and over until he came to rest at the bottom. He saw that blood was running down one of his knees and began to cry. He looked up then to the top of the hill, an immense distance, and saw her against the skyline, arms spread out like a bird's wings, and then descending to him with little musical cries of alarm. They went almost always to the downs, because his mother said that Brighton itself was vulgar. Sometimes they caught a bus and had tea at Steyning in a little low-ceilinged cottage where he always drank milk with soda water, which she said was good for him. Was it possible that this period in his life had lasted for only a few months? He had never returned to that part of Sussex, but looking at the water colours with their patches of green, gold and blue, he knew that this was where he wished to live.

Later that evening he contemplated his own naked figure in the full-length bedroom mirror, the spindly legs and sloping shoulders, the beginnings of a paunch, and below the paunch the thin fuzz and the small useless-looking penis. He examined closely the egg head with its small sorrowful eyes like raisins, and the poached egg pouches beneath them. 'Not much of a body,' he said aloud, and it occurred to him that it was the same body with which Easonby Mellon had been so successful. That too seemed a long time ago, everything before the act was a long time ago.

For a few days after the act he had felt an intense urge to recommence writing his diary, and suffered the sense of deprivation that a smoker feels on giving up cigarettes. He actually bought a note-book and sat down to write in it, but the words refused to flow as they had done in the past. After a couple of days in which he found almost nothing to say, he tore out the sheets on which he had written and burned them. This gesture seemed to have a symbolic value. After it he was better able to accept that he had entered a world in which the pressures and pleasures of the past no longer existed. He did not want the things that Easonby Mellon had taken so greedily, nor was he the Arthur Brownjohn who had been married to Clare. The act had in some mysterious way set him free to begin a new life. He felt himself able to go to London.

He went to the Lektreks' office in Romany House and found there a few orders and several sharp letters from his American suppliers asking why they had not heard from him. In a burst of energy he typed twenty letters in a day, informing suppliers and customers that because of family troubles Lektreks was closing down. Then he invited Elsom to lunch and told him the news.

'But you can't do that.' Elsom was amazed and indignant. 'Why not?'

'I told you, GBD are interested. You're throwing away money.'

Although the problems of the past were remote he recognized that they existed, and that it would be foolish to let GBD see the Lektreks books. He said curtly that the closing down of Lektreks was his affair.

'Of course it is.' Elsom spat out bits of food in his earnestness. 'But I'm speaking as a friend, Arthur, you understand. You can't do anything but lose by this.'

'It's what Clare would have wished,' he said piously, and added with more truth, 'It's for my own peace of mind.' The meal was concluded in gloomy silence.

There remained the question of Easonby Mellon's relics and the diary. They could not be left indefinitely at Waterloo Station, but he had not faced up to the problem of their disposal. When he had collected them, where were they to be buried or burned? It struck him suddenly that he must buy not only a house but a car. If he possessed a car, the disposition of Mellon's belongings would be simplicity itself.

No sooner had the idea occurred to him than the purchase of a car seemed a matter of urgency. He had learned to drive in the army during the war, but he took a few lessons and surprised his instructor by his aptitude and the quickness of his reactions. There was little point in having a car until he had passed the driving test, but he was unable to deny himself the pleasure of spending money. He did not buy a new car because part of the pleasure lay in bargaining about the price, and after visiting half a dozen dealers and trying out twice that number of cars he bought a two-year-old Triumph, guaranteed by the dealer to have had only one owner and to be in splendid condition. The car was driven back to The Laurels and put into the garage, which had been cleared to receive it. He waited eagerly for the day when he would take the test.

In the meantime he was engaged in selling The Laurels and buying a house on the Sussex downs. He slightly scandalized Jaggard, the estate agent, who hinted delicately that the recent tragedy might affect the price, by asking what would be a reasonable figure and then naming a sum two hundred and fifty pounds below it. The Laurels was bought by a civil servant who had a wife and family, and the sale was completed in August. Arthur had, however, already moved out. There was a sale of effects, a symbolic severance of the bonds that linked him to Clare. He included all of their household belongings in this sale, even things that would obviously be needed in his new home like kitchen utensils and the lawn mower. He did not attend the sale, but was pleased to see that the picture of Mr Slattery had fetched only three pounds, the cost of the frame.

He said as few good-byes as possible. What, after all, linked him to Fraycut now that life with Clare was over? The Paynes, the Elsoms, one or two others, said how sorry they were to see him go, but he did not feel that they were in any way his friends. Perhaps it was a good thing that Arthur Brownjohn, starting a new life, should have no friends. He gave Susan a cheque for a hundred pounds, saying that Clare would have wished her to have it, and was embarrassed by a flood of tears. He had a slightly disturbing encounter when he was almost knocked down while crossing a street one day by a car which swung without warning out of a side road.

The driver poked his head out of the window and shouted at him. 'You want to bloody well look where you're going.' It was Doctor Hubble. He got out of the car and stood swaying slightly. 'Oh, it's you. How are you? Hear you're clearing out.'

Arthur agreed, although they were not the words he would have chosen.

'Don't blame you. Shouldn't want to stay myself in the circumstances.' What did he mean by that? 'Still haven't got the chap who did it?'

'No.'

Hubble stood glaring at him, and Arthur felt a twinge of uneasiness. How could he ever have tried deliberately to deceive a man who resembled more than anything else a dangerous wild animal? Then the doctor stuck out his hand, said, 'She was a damned fine woman,' got back into the car and drove away.

Before he left he went to see Coverdale. The Inspector's reception of him was friendly but gloomy. There was no news of Mellon.

'We've found somebody who saw him on the platform. Carrying a blue suitcase.' A shiver went through Arthur's frame. This was the suitcase in the Left Luggage office. If the police ever thought of searching there . . . but why should they do any such thing? Coverdale was still talking. '. . . up in London I guess, hiding out. A crook like Mellon knows plenty of places. But we'll find him.'

'You don't think he's gone abroad.'

'I don't. One thing, far as we can tell he's got no passport. No, he's hiding out. Trouble is, we don't know who his friends are. Can't find out how he got to know your wife either.'

Arthur shook his head to show that he also could not imagine how this had come about. Then he said with careful slowness, 'You've questioned his own wife again, I suppose?'

Coverdale stared at him. The shiny lumps on his face were more than usually apparent. 'You hadn't heard?'

'Heard what?'

'She's dead. Put her head in the gas oven.'

On the wall behind the Inspector there was a photograph of police sports, with a man doing the pole vault, twisting over the bar. Arthur stared at this photograph.

'Can't think what made her do it. Wish I had talked to her again, got to the bottom of all that rubbish about Mellon being an agent.'

'When did it happen?'

'Fortnight ago. It was in the papers. She left the usual note, can't go on, that kind of thing.'

A secretary came in with letters to be signed. Coverdale said, 'We'll keep in touch. Don't worry. The usual channels work slowly sometimes, but everything comes through them in the end.'

After leaving the station he walked to a small public garden and sat down on one of the green wooden benches surrounding a dry fountain topped by a mournful bronze bust. Below the bust it said: 'These gardens are the gift of Ezekiel Jones, citizen of this borough, educator and philanthropist.'

He knew that he should feel sorrow and remorse, but in fact he felt nothing. What had she said to him on that last evening?

Can't live without you, I shall kill myself, something like that. People really do kill themselves, this is something that happens, he thought. He tried to remember what Joan looked like, but was unable to bring her face before his eyes. He seemed insulated from emotion, as though some fibrous barrier had been interposed between his feelings and what went on in the world.

An old man sat down on the bench, produced a bag of bread from his pocket and began to break the bread and throw bits to the pigeons clustering round him. One of the pieces fell beside Arthur's foot. He picked it up and threw it to a bird that seemed weaker than the rest. The pigeon looked at the bread, pecked at it ineffectually, then moved away. None of the other pigeons came near it.

He found a house soon after he moved into a Brighton hotel and began to look for one. He found the house quickly because he knew what he wanted. The area between Devil's Dyke and Brighton, which he remembered with pleasure, proved distressingly urbanized and unattractive. Perhaps the beauty of it had been invented by him and it had always been like this, for he learned with surprise that a railway had run to the Dyke before the war. The triangle to the east of this area, however, topped by Ditchling Beacon, with its small villages and relics of ancient earthworks, fascinated him. He knew from the map that this was not where he had come in childhood, yet it seemed to him that he recognized landmarks, the Iron Age fort of Hollingbury, Plumpton Plain, and the black and white windmills known as Jack and Jill. It was here, near to the road running from Ditchling to Brighton, that he bought a small bungalow, surprising another estate agent by his acceptance of the price asked for it. The bungalow had been built in the nineteen thirties, of ochre brick now weathered to neutral brown. It had a square living-room with french windows, two bedrooms of which one was minute, a surprisingly large kitchen with a good deal of electrical equipment in it, and a bathroom with green tiles on the wall and mustard coloured plastic tiles on the floor. Geese flew on the living-room walls. It was not pretty, but nothing could have been less like The Laurels, and the setting was delightful, sheltered in a small cleft between hills. Outside there was a garage and a quarter of an acre of wilderness which had once been a garden. He was able to move in before the end of August, and he drove the Triumph into the garage himself, for a week before the move he passed his driving test.

Almost the first thing he did was to put up his mother's water colours in the sitting-room. For some reason he did not take down the flying geese. Did he leave them because, like the water colours, they would have offended Clare? Had he bought the bungalow because it was what she would have described as a potty little place? He could not be sure, but in any case this was a line of thought that he did not care to pursue. The furniture came from a Brighton store. It was all new and mostly finished in light woods, polished pine and afromosia. On the afternoon that he moved in, there was a knock on the door. He opened it to find a diminutive couple standing there smiling at him.

'Mr Brownjohn?' The little man took off a check cap and presented a card. 'George Brodzky.'

'And I'm Mary,' the little woman chirped. 'We're your neighbours.'

'Neighbours?'

'Over the hill. From Dunroamin. You must have passed it. So amusing, English names, are they not?'

That was George. Mary chimed in. 'And we thought as you were moving in – I mean, we know what it's like – you would come to tea.'

'Come to tea!' The note of horror in his voice escaped them.

'Tea is on the hob.' Little George rubbed his hands.

'You're very kind but –'

'I won't take no for an answer,' said little Mary. 'I've made some buns, and although I say it myself my buns are good. And you'll find the men get on *much* better without you, isn't that right?' She called this out to the foreman, who agreed enthusiastically. Arthur had been altogether too fussy about occasional bumps and splinterings.

'Her buns are the tops,' said George.

He went to tea with the dismal knowledge that he would regret it. The Brodzkys lived over the brow of the hill, five minutes' walk away, in a bigger version of his bungalow. Brodzky was a

Jewish tailor who had come over as a refugee from the Nazis, and had evidently done rather well. Sufficiently well, at least, to retire and buy the bungalow which had been named Dunroamin in what Mary told George was the English tradition. It was not about themselves that they wanted to talk, however, but about their new neighbour. They knew he was alone, but what had happened to his wife? Arthur said she had died recently, and did not expand on it. He did not need to, however, for Mary Brodzky read about every case of criminal violence in the newspaper.

'Not *the* Mr Brownjohn?' She saw from Arthur's hesitancy that he was. 'George, Mr Brownjohn's wife was – this was the case that – you know, you read about it –'

'The lady who was murdered?' Little George rubbed his hands together.

She lowered her voice respectfully at mention of the tabooed word. 'Such a terrible thing, and they still haven't got the man, have they?'

No doubt the manner of Clare's death would have become known quickly in any case, but he felt that acceptance of the invitation had been disastrous. When he went into the local general shop or into the nearby pub conversation ceased for a moment before being abruptly resumed, and he saw people looking at him with sidelong expectancy. Mary Brodzky twice telephoned him with invitations to meet people, both of which he refused, and one day she called to ask if she could do any shopping for him in Brighton. He replied politely that he was driving in himself. On the following day George called. It was raining.

'We have here in the village our society for amateur dramatics. I am to ask if you would like to join.' His smile was wide.

'No, thank you.'

'It is very amusing. Perhaps if I should explain it –'

Brodzky was not wearing a coat. Rain spotted his shoulders. It was outrageously rude not to ask him in. 'Go away,' Arthur said.

Brodzky was dumbfounded. 'I beg your pardon?'

He was dismayed to hear his voice rising to an undignified squeak. 'I don't let nosy parkers into my house.' He stepped back and slammed the door. After that there were no further invitations from the Brodzkys, and they did not acknowledge each other in the street.

That was really the end of his relations with the village. In the shop he was greeted politely but without warmth, and he stopped going to the pub. The milkman said good day to him and the butcher delivered three times a week. The vicar called once, but lost interest when he learned that his new parishioner did not go to church. The Brodzkys had offered to try to find a woman who would come in and do for him, but their relations had been severed soon afterwards and he felt reluctant to allow anybody to intrude on his affairs, asking personal questions and poking about among his things. The bungalow was small, and it was quite easy to clean it himself without the nosy assistance of some Sussex Susan. He had escaped from them all, Susans, Elsoms, Paynes and the rest. He was, as he had often wished to be, alone.

He found sufficient occupation inside and outside the house. He bought a multi-purpose electric tool with which he sanded and polished the floors of both living-room and bedrooms, repainted them, built some bookshelves and also a cupboard for the living-room. The making and fitting of this cupboard, which was made of a polished wood named sangrosa, gave him great emotional satisfaction, and he put a small compartment inside it, with its own separate doors. The latch on these inner doors did not fit perfectly and had a tendency to come open, but still he was delighted by his own skill. The garden also took up a good deal of time. What could be done with a quarter of an acre? He bought half a dozen books on gardening and cut out articles that appeared in the papers. He would have liked to see things flowering immediately, but it proved that September was not a good time for planting. However, there were things that could be done. He reduced the wilderness of the lawn with a scythe, mowed it, and then spiked the mossy weedy surface with an aerator. Every day for a week he carried out destructive operations, pulling up weeds and nettles and burning them in a new kind of incinerator which he bought. Sodium chlorate extinguished weeds on the paths. There was broken fencing at the back of the house which he mended with new palings and wire.

127

He worked every morning and afternoon, eating a quick lunch of bread and cheese with an urgency he could not have explained even to himself. In the evening he cooked something, often out of a tin, and settled down to read the papers and watch television. The news seemed unreal to him, the capers on the screen even more insignificant, and watching them he often fell asleep.

One day he took the train to London, went across to Waterloo Station, collected the blue suitcase and came straight back again. In spite of his advance trepidation he felt no flicker of fear when he handed over the ticket and was given the suitcase. He would have been quite prepared to meet Coverdale at the station. Easonby Mellon had had a blue suitcase, he was carrying one too. What was strange about that? He was strong in the assurance of success. He would not have been so boastful as to call what he had done perfect, for he recognized that he had been helped by one or two fortuitous circumstances like Mr Lillicrapp's sight of Easonby Mellon leaving The Laurels, but still he was satisfied.

He deliberately delayed opening the suitcase until the evening, leaving it to be savoured like a favourite sweet. As a further congratulatory gesture, a measure of Brownjohn's confidence in Brownjohn, he opened the sangrosan cupboard, considered the bottles which had been lined up there – gin, whisky, vodka – and opened the whisky. Gobble gobble, went the liquid in the glass, giving him a delicious feeling, not unlike that felt by Easonby Mellon when having a bit of nonsense. A zizz of soda and there it was, ready for drinking. He drank. Then he took the little key from his ring and turned it in the lock of the suitcase. Was everything there? He checked, hugging himself.

Item. One suit in loud gingery tweed, jacket and trousers only, in good condition.

Item. Tie decorated with small coloured horseshoes, sporty shirt and ditto socks.

Item. One fine head of glossy red-brown hair, one small beard of slightly different colour. One small bottle of spirit gum.

Item. One pair of contact lenses in small box.

Item. One diary in black cover.

The rest of Easonby Mellon's clothes, together with two of his wigs, had been incinerated at Clapham. He stroked the crisp hair.

'Safely home,' he said aloud. 'Safely home, my beauties.' He drained the whisky and poured another, then opened the diary and sat down to read, absorbed by the account of problems that had loomed so large in the past and now looked trivial. All the fear he had expressed about Hubble, for instance, and his feeling that the doctor had been suspicious. Obviously what he had taken for suspicion was natural drunken rudeness, the 'terrible glare' he had noted was annoyance at being called so late at night. At the same time he was pleased that he had given up the zinca-lium scheme, which as he saw now had been clumsily conceived. When he came to the passages about Clapham the past flooded back unpleasantly. To stop himself from reading further he took out the sheets, tore them up into small pieces, and put them into a cardboard box. Tomorrow would be D-Day, D for Destruc-tion. His glass was empty, and he poured another drink. He took off his jacket and trousers, put on the tweed suit, clapped the wig to his head without bothering to use the fixative. Easonby Mellon walked agin!

Not quite, however, not really as he should be. He used the spirit gum to fix the beard and put in the contact lenses, which were more trouble than they should have been because his hand was shaking slightly. 'Not a bad little bachelor establishment you've got here, Brownjohn,' he said. 'You don't mind if I look around?' He strutted into kitchen and bedroom commenting loudly on them, bouncing up and down on the bed. He went to the front door, opened it with a little difficulty and staggered slightly as he walked out to the garden, looked up at the green swell of hill. 'Nestling under the down,' he said. 'Very nice, though it's nicer to nestle between the sheets.' It was twilight, and the air was filled with the sweet scent of early evening. He sniffed this air, opened his mouth and drank up the air in great gulps, staring at the green hill. A tickling sensation at the back of his neck made him turn.

The Brodzkys stood beside the gate, arm in arm, staring at him. The little man with his check cap, the little woman gazing eager-eyed – for a few seconds they stared at him and he stared back at them. Then the Brodzkys, still with arms linked like some four-legged creature, scuttled away up the road to their bungalow, and he returned to the house. He stared at himself in the bedroom glass. He seemed to have shrunk within the clothes, which hung on him with curious looseness – could he have lost weight? With furtive speed he took them off, together with the wig and moustache, and slipped out the contact lenses. Safely back in Arthur Brownjohn's nondescript old flannel trousers he recorked the whisky bottle and returned it to the cupboard. The latch came open and he closed it with a thump. The genie who had come out of the bottle lacked his old magical power.

On the following morning he put a barrowful of weeds into the incinerator, stuffed the suit on top of them together with the box containing the torn-up diary, and added the beard. He broke up the contact lenses with a hammer and added them to the pile, and did the same thing with the bottle of spirit gum. Then he put on more weeds and set fire to the lot. Blue smoke swirled upwards. He placed the top on the incinerator and left the past to burn. At the last moment he found himself unable to dispose of the wig. As he stroked the crisp reality of the hair tears came to his eyes. He put it carefully into the inner compartment of the cupboard, promising himself that he would destroy it very soon. At midday he lifted the incinerator lid and stared at the contents that were reduced to satisfying but saddening ash.

Although so much of the past had gone his mother's water colour scenes remained. He took down the little pictures from the walls, put them into the car, and drove out over the downs. During the afternoon he revisited the scene of each picture, and found them all changed. 'West Blatchington, the Mill' had been shown as an idyllic rural scene, but it stood now among a spate of suburban building. 'The Downs at Peacehaven' bore no resemblance to the hills dotted with a pretty house or two shown in her mild greens and blues. Instead, a great mess of brick sprawled over the whole area like some terrible red growth. Not one of the scenes was as she had shown it. He knew that this was to be expected, yet it troubled him. The country today belonged to the new housing complexes and the petrol pump. The world of his childhood, the world his mother painted, had been destroyed. Back in the bungalow he pored over the water colours as though they could provide an answer to the problems of his life, and realized what was wrong. According to a book he had read about Sussex the picture of the Devil's Dyke should have shown a railway where she depicted a green wash of down. She had left out the railway because it would have spoiled the picture. Were the other paintings equally remote from reality? When he looked up other books he found that Peacehaven in the early nineteen twenties could not possibly have looked as she had shown it, and it seemed to him that this doubt about the veracity of the pictures must extend to the whole of his childhood life. Had it ever really existed as he remembered it? His mother had died of what was then called heart disease when he was twenty-one. How much did he really know about her? Did this image of a woman in a floppy hat, this indulgent mother trying to preserve him from the harshness of the world, correspond with the truth? How deep had been her disappointment when it became clear that he was not bright enough to get a University scholarship and would have to take a job when he left grammar school? What had she felt during the last years in the little flat at Swiss Cottage where she died? It was not until the funeral that he had seen his father again, and then he wondered how he had ever felt the fear he was now able to acknowledge of this outspoken but meticulously neat and dapper man. They found little to say to each other, but they met two or three times a year, conversing with the politeness of strangers. His father had written a letter of sympathy after Clare's death which remained unanswered.

These events were clouded in his mind, he had always refused to discuss them with himself, and it seemed to him that the rest of his life must consist of such an unending discussion. He could remember nothing at all of the years before his mother's death when he had left school and gone to work at the insurance office in which he had stayed until his call-up. Had he come home each evening to a cooked meal, did they ever go out together? He could remember nothing except the three heart attacks she had suffered in the months before she died, the rest was the woman in the floppy hat on the downs painting her untrue pictures. He had shown the pictures to Clare just after their marriage, and a little later she had begun to attend art classes. Was it possible that his feelings about his mother had affected his relationship with Clare?

He hung up the pictures again, ate a tin of food and went to bed. He lay sleepless until four in the morning. Around him in the darkness stretched the barren land of freedom.

Chapter 6

The True Identity of Arthur Brownjohn

He saw the Identikit picture in the paper the next morning.
Under the heading HAVE YOU SEEN THIS MAN? was a composite
picture of a man with thick hair, a squashy nose, large staring
eyes, a little beard and the caption: 'This is an Identikit picture
made with the help of eye witnesses of a man the police would
like to interview in connection with the Fraycut murder case.
Further details: brown hair and beard, about 5 ft 9 inches tall,
stockily built, possibly wearing tweed suit or sports jacket.' He
looked at the picture and hugged himself because of its unlikeness
to the facts. Two inches had been added to his height, and
'stockily built' was a tribute to the effect of the suit. At the same
time he felt a little indignant about that squashy nose. His nose
certainly could not be called squashy.

The Identikit picture had appeared before, although he had
missed it, in the paper. It was the joint product of the recollections of the Romany House porter, the barmaid at Fraycut (who
had insisted on the staring eyes), the clerk at the Weybridge
hotel and Mr Lillicrapp, as interpreted by the artist who had
drawn it for the police. Inspector Coverdale had no great faith
in the accuracy of the Identikit, and as usual the people who had
seen Mellon were by no means agreed about such vital matters
as his height, which had been placed between five feet six and
five feet eleven inches. Indeed, Coverdale had no longer much
expectation that they would find Mellon at all. He believed the
man to be an experienced crook known to Scotland Yard under
another name, that the murder had been prompted by Mrs
Brownjohn's discovery of his real identity, and that Mellon had
almost certainly left the country. The best chance of laying hands
on him would come when he started up another Lonely Hearts
agency elsewhere, as he almost certainly would do, and Interpol
had been duly alerted. In the meantime it was necessary to go
through the motions.

The issue of the paper containing the Identikit picture recorded also the verdicts in the case of John Termaxian and Patricia Parker, who had received sentences of four years and nine months respectively. Termaxian had been in prison twice before for similar offences, and the Judge had referred to him as 'a blight on society, feeding on the weakness of foolish and lecherous men'. He had regarded Parker as Termaxian's agent, and very much under his influence. There was no mention of the source from which they had obtained the name of Mr X.

Strangely enough this paragraph depressed rather than pleased him. After reading it he went out into the garden, but worked there for only half an hour. He was in the act of turning over earth in a patch destined to be a flower border next year when an almost physical revulsion from what he was doing made him stop. He cleaned the fork and trowel he had been using, put them back in the garage, and returned to the bungalow. In the kitchen he drew himself a glass of water, sat down at a table and stared at the refrigerator. It had occurred to him that, in any meaningful sense, he did not exist. He remembered a strange novel he had read, about a man whose whole inner life had been destroyed by the things that happened to him, but who functioned perfectly to all outward appearance and even flourished, so that when he was offered an academic post 'the Faculty had no idea that it was a glacial shell of a man who had come among them' instead of a real human being. Was this his own situation? Arthur Brownjohn had wished to be free of Clare's domination, Easonby Mellon had been trapped in a net from which it had seemed essential to break out. He had escaped from Clare, he had broken out of the net, he was free – but he was forced to the conclusion that freedom only existed in relation to restriction. 'The habits by which we *live* and *think* are not what we *believe*' – that, or something like it, was what he had written in his diary. But what did he believe, what did he wish to do with his freedom? The things in which he had taken pleasure, the slot racing layout in the attic, the piles of letters round his ankles, even the bits of nonsense with Joan, seemed to have had no existence independent of the people with whom they were associated. 'I could have had the biggest slot racing layout in the country,' he thought, and had a vision of the kind of house he might have bought, a Victorian barracks with a great glass-roofed room like a monster conservatory in which the whole floor was covered with a network of tracks, bridges, fly-overs, along which there raced twenty different types of car. He could have bought such a house, he could still buy it, but he knew that he would never do so, for although he was able to conjure up the vision it no longer excited him. Slot racing had not been a passion but a reaction, a means of asserting his identity against Clare. Now that she was gone he no longer needed it. What was the true identity of Arthur Brownjohn? Surely he must take pleasure in sights and sounds, must enjoy food and want sex as Easonby Mellon had wanted it? He remembered Joan's desperate clutching at his parts in the cinema, and shuddered away from the thought that he was no more than 'a glacial shell' able to dig gardens and make cupboards but totally without emotion because heart and guts had been removed. There must be people and situations who would revive the sleeping soldier, and reveal his real nature. It was to discover them that he went to Brighton.

He watched himself with detachment, in the spirit of a doctor trying out various forms of treatment. The drive through the downs and along the main road, now, did that excite him? The sense of achievement he felt in first handling a car had long since vanished, but now he deliberately accelerated to pass other cars on bends and at the brows of hills, answering blares of protest with furious hooting of his own. At one point he passed another car near the top of a hill to find a great Bentley coming at him. He cut in sharply on the car he had just passed, which was forced to brake suddenly. Both the Bentley and the car behind him hooted, and this time he did not trouble to hoot back. 'Any emotion involved there, Mr Brownjohn, exhilaration, fear, anything at all?' the doctor asked, and he had to shake his head in reply. He had felt nothing. Yet that was not quite true, for he had taken avoiding action, so that the instinct of self-preservation must still exist. In the pleasure of realizing this he passed and cut in on another car. In the town he parked the car just behind the Palace Pier.

Come to Doctor Brighton who cures all ills. Is the prognosis favourable, Doctor? Too soon to tell, my son. For an hour he bathed in the fantasy of the Royal Pavilion. Below the onion domes he wandered in a Chinese and Indian dream, columns sprawling out as palm trees, tented ceilings down which crawled gilded dragons, great wall paintings of Chinese landscapes like those that made the Music Room resemble a lacquer cabinet. Would it be possible to live in such a cabinet, in such a world? Pagodas and temples, formal rippling rivers with sampans frozen on them as though in the performance of a ritual, palm trees and bamboos, furnishings that dazzled the senses by their colour and disturbed them by their ornamentation – he found himself thinking first that these existed in a different world from that of his mother's water colours and then that the furniture would never have done for Clare and The Laurels. He laughed aloud at the thought, and an attendant gave him a reproving glance.

After the Pavilion the Lanes, those narrow alleys right in the heart of the town, bounded by North, West and East Streets, and stuffed with antique shops where in the summer American voices could be heard translating everything into the music of dollars. He drifted from shop to shop, staring at collections of Victorian fire irons, at panelled pine mantelpieces, at windows full of old medals. One shop window had a crowd around it, and mixing with them he saw that it held a collection of chamber pots of different sizes. He was about to turn away when he noticed a number of soapstone figures on a shelf above. One of them was his Buddha! He pushed his way through the crowd and entered the shop. A woman in a green dress greeted him. He pointed to the figure.

'The Buddha?' She took it off the shelf, her red-tipped fingers caressed it. 'You like him? I think he's fun.' She told him the price on the base. It was half what he had paid in London.

'I wanted to know – I wonder if you could tell me where you bought it?'

'I'm not sure that I know, and even if I did know it isn't policy to say.'

'I have a special reason. I believe it is – that is, it once belonged to me.'

She nodded in a humouring way and went to the back of the shop. When she came back she said, 'I bought it at a country sale. Nearly a year ago. Shouldn't admit I've had it for a year, should I, but you see I'm frank.'

A year ago! He said something confused about that being impossible. She raised her thin, plucked eyebrows. 'They're not very uncommon, you know.'

'Not very uncommon?' The man had told him it was a piece of individual Indian craftsmanship.

'I'm a terrible saleswoman, but yes, that's right. Quite a lot of them were made in several sizes. I'd consider an offer. Since we've had it so long.' Her lips curled. They were thin, but a Cupid's bow had been painted over them.

'No, thank you. I'm afraid it's a mistake, I thought it was the one I had.'

'Perfectly all right. Don't you think it's a fun window?'

'Window?' He stared in alarm at the clear glass.

'*You* know. The indispensable article of bedroom furniture. Draws the crowds, but nobody comes in to buy.' She smiled now with an open mouth. He saw her teeth, white and regular, and the dark cavern behind them.

'No, thank you,' he said meaninglessly, and edged his way out. It did not matter, nothing at all was affected by it, but he was upset by a feeling that he had been tricked again.

What did he expect Brighton to do for him? He hardly knew. He walked uncertainly along to the Marine Parade, along the promenade towards the West Pier, and then on to the beach. He began to throw stones into the sea. The stones were smooth and cool in his palm, and as he flung them, with a jerky round arm motion, some memory stirred in his mind which he was unable to trace. There were few people on the beach, but a boy came and stood beside him and then began to pick up and throw stones himself. The boy made them skim over the water, bouncing several times before they disappeared.

'That was a sevener,' he said after one particularly good throw. Arthur flung a stone which sank ignominiously without bouncing at all. 'You don't do it right.'

'I expect not.'

'You want to get flat stones. Then like this.' He sent one skimming like a speedboat. 'See?'

The memory came back to him. On one of the rare days when they stayed in Brighton his mother had left him playing on the beach. He had joined half a dozen other boys around a boat, and they had laughed at him first because he would not go into the sea (his mother had told him it was too rough) and then because he could not throw stones properly. 'You throw like a girl,' they said. He had been weeping when his mother returned.

'You got the time, mister?'

'Ten minutes past six.'

'I got to get back to tea.'

'Wait a minute, I'll walk with you.'

The boy looked at him with the fearfulness shown by the young at any kind of involvement with their elders, then backed away. 'Wait,' Arthur appealed. He put his hand in his pocket, took out a coin, threw it. Silver glinted in the air. The boy snapped up the coin like a lizard stretching its tongue for a fly, then ran. Arthur climbed wearily up the beach, the stones hard under his feet.

Later he went on to the Palace Pier and rode on the little electric cars. All the other cars seemed to be occupied by couples, the boys driving, the girls beside them shrieking with laughter. He steered his own car deliberately at others. After the crashes the girls laughed louder than ever. One pretty doll-like girl wore a paper hat in red, white and blue, and a badge pinned over one breast which read I AM A VIRGIN. Beneath these capitals was a small longer word – what was it? He peered to see, without success. When the ride ended and he walked off the shiny floor the couple came up to him.

'What's up, Jack?' the boy said. He was a head taller than Arthur, and he wore long sideboards.

'I beg your pardon.' He could see the word now. It was *Islander*.

'You do, eh? I said, what's up?'

'I don't know what you mean.'

'You don't? You wouldn't. He's a creep, Marilyn, I told you.'

'He's creepy,' the girl agreed, and burst into fresh peals of laughter.

He walked away down the boards of the pier. Unintelligible threats and obscenities followed him.

Seven-fifteen. He was sitting in a bar in a road parallel with the sea front sipping gin and tonic. Brighton had solved nothing, the doctor had failed. It was time to drive away again. The barman said, 'You want to see some action?' He slipped a card across the bar's shiny leatherette surface.

He nodded without knowing what was meant.

'Members only, but this'll get you in. Say Carlo sent you.'

He nodded again. The card said simply *Robin Hood*, with an address in Kemp Town. The place, when he found it, looked like a restaurant, but the door was closed. On the right-hand side of it a painted and tipped arrow pointed to a bell, and he pushed this. A slit in the door opened, an eye looked at him.

'Carlo sent me.' The door opened. He confronted a girl dressed in a short jerkin and tights of Lincoln green. A green forage cap with a feather in it was set on her head, and a quiver containing arrows was slung over her shoulder.

The door closed again. The light was dim. What looked like real trees were growing on either side of him. Straight ahead he saw an oak door with the legend above it: 'Robin Hood's Cave.' To the left stood a realistic gibbet with a noose hanging from it. A voice shrieked in his ear: 'Eat ye and drink ye, my merry men.'

'What was that?'

'Jock.' The girl indicated a parrot which glared from foliage. He touched one of the trees. It was made of plastic.

'I didn't know they had parrots in Sherwood Forest.'

'Don't touch him, he'll have your finger.' Without taking breath she went on: 'A guinea, please.'

'Carlo said this would get me in.'

'So you're in. You still pay a guinea if you want the action.'

'What action?'

She stared. The oak door opened and he saw beyond it bright light, glimpsed a roulette wheel, heard the murmur of voices. A fat man with a cigar in his mouth passed, took the coat the girl offered, and went out without speaking. 'Make up your mind,' the girl said. He paid his guinea and went towards the oak door. A figure stepped from beside the gibbet and said, 'Not carrying anything?'

'What do you mean?'

He was a large man with a broken nose, wearing jerkin and tights that seemed too small for him. His face, pitted with scars and with the eyes tiny in their folds of flesh, peered.

'That's all right, sir, you're okay.' His voice came out like water through a choked pipe.

'Why do you stand by that thing?'

'I'm supposed to be the hangman, see? They had me dressed up right, in a black mask and all, but it was too hot.' He gestured towards doors which said: 'Ye Olde Taverne of Sherwood' and 'Ye Banqueting Hall,' but Arthur went into Robin Hood's Cave.

It was a large room with panels let into the wall, depicting scenes among which he noticed Robin Hood embracing Maid Marian, giving money to the poor, defying the Sheriff, and with hands tied behind his back staring up at a gallows. Trophies of the hunt were hung about, including rather surprisingly a bear and a tiger. The brightness he had seen from outside was deceptive. Most of the room was dim. Concealed lights illuminated the wall panels and pools of light flooded down upon the tables where people were playing roulette and several card games, among which he recognized baccarat and vingt-et-un. The faces round the roulette table were reverent. They were not particularly rich faces, nor of any special class. Few were very young or very old. They were middle-aged middle-class humanity.

A hand touched his arm, a voice murmured, 'This way, sir.' A young man in Lincoln green led him to a corner of the room. 'Just to get it straight, minimum stake half a crown, maximum fifty quid, fair enough?'

'I suppose so.'

'What d'you want chips for?'

A Lincoln green girl behind a counter smiled at him invitingly. Different coloured counters were arranged in front of her. He had just over twenty pounds on him. 'Five pounds' worth, please.'

The young man raised his eyebrows, said something inaudible to the girl and drifted away. He took his counters to the roulette table and put a pound on black, ten shillings on the first twelve numbers. The number that came up was red, nineteen. This was another aspect of Doctor Brighton's treatment. Did he feel any emotion when the black and green counters were swept away, would he feel anything if he won? He could only find out by playing. In less than ten minutes he had lost his five pounds and had cashed five more. He decided to stop playing when he had lost fifteen.

His luck turned when he had three pounds left of the allotted fifteen. Numbers in the first twelve, which pays two to one, came up six times running, and when he changed to groups of four numbers, paying nine to one, he had three successive wins. He was now fifteen pounds up, and put a couple of black counters, worth a pound each, on numbers eleven and thirty-three. Number eleven turned up, a win of thirty-four pounds. He had set himself no winning limit, but it seemed a good time to stop. As his counters were translated into five-pound notes he examined his feelings, and discovered in himself no more than a mild pleasure at having beaten the table.

In Ye Olde Taverne of Sherwood, where crisps, olives and lumps of cheddar cheese came free, he ordered a large whisky. A voice behind him said, 'I saw you, you lucky man.'

The lady of the antique shop was smiling at him. She was dressed now in a black and white op art dress, the effect of which was spoiled by a conventional thick cluster of what must surely be artificial pearls. She readily accepted his offer of a drink.

'A little drinky would be very nice. It's not *my* lucky night. '

What could one say to that? He considered several conversational returns and rejected them all. They sat down at a table which had on it an ashtray shaped as a boar's head, with a hole in the mouth for the ash. She smoked a cigarette through a long holder. 'Are you a real true gambler? I *am* you know, or I would be if I had what my sainted aunt used to call the wherewithal. This is a fun place, don't you think?'

'I suppose so. It's just a gambling club, really, isn't it?'

'But don't you think the décor's brilliant? A friend of mine did it as a matter of fact, Seamus Macpherson. Of course he's really an artist, he did it to oblige Robin.'

'Robin?'

She pointed to a swarthy man wearing a dinner jacket and called, 'Yoo hoo.' The swarthy man came over. 'Robin Hood,' she said. 'Meet a new member, I don't know his name.'

'Arthur Brownjohn.'

'Welcome to Sherwood Forest. Enjoying yourself, Mr Brownjohn?' Robin Hood had a pencil line moustache, and looked like a Hollywood romantic actor of the nineteen thirties. His foreign accent was strong.

'He's been winning, Robin darling, of course he's enjoying himself.'

'Splendid. I hope you haven't taken us to the cleaner's.'

'What? Oh no, I only won a few pounds. I'm not a gambler.'

A bottle of champagne appeared in an ice bucket. 'To the victors the spoils,' Robin Hood said. 'That is a quotation. Don't be worried, Mr Brownjohn, this is on the house.' Glasses were filled. 'Have you finished for the evening, or are you playing again?'

'I'm retiring while I'm a winner.' He laughed inanely, and they laughed with him.

'A wise man. But come back and see us again. Just one question.' His mouth approached Arthur's ear. 'You like the way we've fitted it out?'

'Most original.'

'A friend of Hester's. A genius. You'll forgive me.' He seized Hester's red-tipped hand, kissed it, uncoiled from his chair, and moved across the room.

'Isn't he darling? And I'll tell you something, everything he does turns to money.' She contemplated the kissed fingers as if in the hope that a Midas touch might convert them to gold. 'Of course he's not really Robin Hood. His name's Constantin Dimitrop-something-or-other. You know those Dimitrop names. But would you believe it, I knew him when he was a waiter in a little Greek café. I don't know, do you?' He shook his head. More champagne was poured. 'D'you live around here, Arthur?'

'Just a few miles.'

'You often get in, then?'

'Sometimes.' The bottle was empty. He waved a hand, another bottle appeared, the cork popped.

'You're a bit of a dark horse,' Hester said as she drank her first glass from the new bottle. Her lips left a red smear on it. 'When you came in the shop I said to myself, "Well, you may sell him something, but be careful not to scare him off, he's the sort who scares easily." Now here you are, cool as a duke, going home with a nice little profit. How wrong can you be?'

He felt an impulse to confide. 'I do get scared, as much as anybody. But I do things, even though they scare me.'

'That's psychology. I'll tell you something. I've had that bloody shop for a year, and I've found something out. It just isn't me.'

'I thought not,' he said vaguely, although he had not thought about it.

'Oh, you're clever. You're a real dark horse.' She stubbed out her second cigarette, put away the holder, leaned over the table towards him. 'What would you say I *was*, really?'

The black and white of the dress dazzled him. Above it, above the diagonals that fled to infinity, was the choker. Stretch a hand, pull and the little white blobs would fly all over the room. A prize for the first man to pop an artificial pearl into the boar's head. And above the pearl choker the neck, full and unwrinkled, above the neck smooth cheeks, an inquiring nose, the red mouth a cavern. None of it excited him, he felt no stir of lust. 'An actress.'

She leaned back. 'Oh, you're so *right*. You really are a dark horse. Lavinia Skelton.'

'What?'

'My stage name. Do you like it?'

'Not very much.'

'Exactly what I said. I told that bloody agent, I told him, "Lavinia, that's Victorian, and Skelton, do you know what people will think, they'll think of a skeleton." But he was supposed to know, he said it was contemporary. Then he thought he'd done marvels when he fixed me up in a crumby little rep.'

Her face approached his. 'Darling, you're cute. Why don't we have another little drinky round in my flat?'

The temptation was too great. He bent forward so that their faces were near to each other. His hand moved, pulled, the choker came away. The string broke and the pearls rolled about, just as he had foreseen, most of them on the floor but a dozen meandering across the table. He picked one of them up and put it into the boar's mouth. 'Pearls in the mouth of swine,' he cried. 'First prize to me.' Laughing helplessly, he raised his champagne glass.

She clutched her neck. 'My God,' she cried. 'You bloody little barbarian.'

Things happened quickly. It seemed that everybody in the preposterous room converged on him, and that they were all angry. Without fully understanding what was happening, or why, he felt himself jerked to his feet. The glass dropped from his grasp to the floor and crunched under a foot. A hand was clasped inside his shirt collar so that he almost choked, another hand dived into his breast pocket and found his wallet. He tried to protest that they were stealing his money. Robin Hood's face appeared before him in close up, the lips bent back to reveal pale gums. 'The champagne,' he heard. 'You pay for the champagne.' Helpless, he saw a five pound note extracted from the wallet, which was then pushed back into his jacket. The grip on his shirt did not relax. Twisting to see his captor, he found that it was the man with the broken nose who had been standing beside the gibbet. In turning he tightened the grip on his neck and gasped for air.

Hester was weeping. 'My pearls. Make him pay for my pearls.'

Robin Hood's hand patted her shoulder. 'I'll buy you some more, honey. Don't worry about him, he's not worth worrying about.'

He felt himself being marched, almost carried, out of the bar. The girl who had let him in surveyed him critically. 'He got an 'at?' Broken nose asked, and when she said no, his grip relaxed. 'Don't let 'im in again. Trouble maker.'

'You wouldn't think it to look at him. What did he do?'

' 'Aving a go at Hester. Trying to tear her dress off. Listen.'

He pushed a big fist under Arthur's nose. 'Get out and don't come back.' The door was open. A push sent him reeling into the street. It was empty except for a man walking along the other side, whistling.

For a few moments he could do nothing except gasp. When he had got his breath he felt his neck in a gingerly way and straightened his collar. The whistling man crossed the street and walked towards him. He took out his wallet and examined the contents. They were intact except for the five pound note, which he supposed was fair enough. He became aware that something had happened, and then realized what it was. The whistling had stopped.

The man had reached the entrance of the club but had apparently changed his mind about going in. His face was half-turned away. There was something familiar about him. 'Just a minute,' Arthur said. The man quickened his step. Arthur caught up with him, put a hand on his arm, swung him round. He was looking at the sandy hair and greasy beard, the exophthalmic eyes, the twitching features, of Clennery Tubbs.

Chapter 7

End of a Journey

He was so surprised that he let go of Tubbs's arm, but as the other accelerated, moving away from him in a walk that never quite became a trot, Arthur felt indignation move in him. But for the crookedness of this man none of his troubles would have occurred, or at least this was what he felt. 'Here,' he cried. 'Come here.'

He put a hand on Tubbs's jacket, getting a grip which was a parody of Broken Nose's hold on his shirt. The jacket began to slip away from Tubbs's shoulders, and it seemed that he might leave it. Then he stopped, turned, and said, 'What the hell d'you think you're doing?' The look of outrage was succeeded by one of astonishment which merged unconvincingly into pleasure. 'Mr Brownjohn,' he said, as though the name were the answer to a prayer. His gaze looked beyond Arthur who half-turned with him to see that the door of the club was open and that Hester stood there. She stared at them both for a moment and then retreated. The door closed again.

'I've been looking for you,' Arthur said, which was hardly the truth.

'Thought you were one of the Granger Boys. Nasty lot, have to be damn' careful down here. That place.' Tubbs jerked a thumb towards the Robin Hood. 'Some hard types in there, I can tell you.'

'You were going in.'

'Not me. I wouldn't trust myself there, not in a million years.'

'I've just come out. I won fifty pounds.'

'You did? There you are.' He spoke triumphantly, as if Arthur had proved the truth of his words. 'You can buy me a drink.'

The suggestion incensed him so much that if he had been a violent man he would have struck the other. 'You cheated me.' Unable to compass the enormity of Tubbs's offences he took

146

refuge in a single phrase. 'You used an accommodation address.'

'I've been on the move.' Tubbs leaned against the wall under a street lamp. 'Haven't been well.'

'Rubbish.' Beneath the cloth he felt the thin bone of the arm. 'You're a scoundrel.'

'Mean it. My heart. Give me a minute.' His colour looked bad, but perhaps this was the street lighting. 'Buy you a drink.'

He continued to pull Tubbs along. He had little confidence in his power to pin the man down. Tubbs would go to the pub lavatory and never come back, or he would see some barfly acquaintance and slip away with him. 'Come home,' he said suddenly. 'I'll give you a drink there.'

'Home? Live in Brighton now, do you?'

'Just outside it. I've got my car here.'

Tubbs gave him a quick glance. 'All right then. Call at the bus station. I've left my case.'

They walked to the bus station in silence. Arthur went in and stood near while Tubbs handed over a ticket and came back with a battered fibre suitcase. 'Not sure where I'd stay,' he muttered. 'Been on the road.' When they reached the car he got in without a word.

For five minutes Arthur drove in silence. Then Tubbs spoke. 'Sorry I dropped out of circulation but I can explain, you know. Explain the whole thing.' He paused. His voice was thick, throaty. 'Something else I must say. Sympathies.'

'What's that?'

'Read about it. Very sorry.' He had linked Clare's death up with the man he swindled. 'Got the bastard who did it, have they?'

'Not yet.'

'Very very sorry, old man.' His hand snaked out and gave Arthur's a pat. 'They've got no line on this chap yet then?'

'I don't want to talk about it.' He was already regretting the impulse that had induced him to take Tubbs home. What was the point of it? The man was on his uppers and there was not a chance in a thousand that he would recover any of the money. Why had he exposed himself to this wretched little crook? What did it matter? His spirits sank steadily on the way back while those of Tubbs appeared to rise. When they got out of the car he looked round inquisitively. 'Marvellous. You know you're in the country all right. Lead the way, squire.'

Would it be a good thing to drive him to the nearest station and give him his fare to London? Instead he opened the front door. Tubbs dropped his old suitcase in the hall, went into the sitting-room, sat down and looked round again.

'Very nice, very cosy. Been here long, have you?'

'Not long.'

'Moved after the tragedy from – where was it? – Fraycut, yes. You could have knocked me down with a feather when I read about it, saw your picture in the paper. I know that face, I told myself, then it clicked. It's Brownjohn, my partner. Thought of writing, never got round to it somehow.' He glanced continually at his host and away, his eyes clicking like a camera shutter. There could be no doubt that he was in a bad way. There were grease spots on his trousers, his jacket cuffs were slightly frayed, his shoes dirty. 'So you came down here. On your tod, are you?'

'I live alone, yes.'

'Live alone and like it, eh? I'm on my own too, told you that, but don't know that I should want to stay here, I have to keep moving.'

'You owe me an explanation.' He felt the absurdity of the words as he said them.

'Too right. And you owe me a drink.' He amended this hastily. 'Promised me one.'

While he opened the sangrosan cupboard and poured two whiskies the nervous yet predatory gaze of the pop eyes followed him. Tubbs talked in jerks with pauses between them. 'Had a run of bad luck since I saw you last. Left London in a hurry, put some money in a business, went phut. Went up to Manchester, lost three hundred quid in a poker game. Played against Steady Jack Malory, know him? Course, you wouldn't. Cheers.' He drank greedily.

'You swindled me.' It was difficult to feel anger. 'Wypitklere was no good.'

'No good? Oh, come on now, old ma   He hardly even pretended surprise. 'If there are any kinks in it we can straighten them out. What about putting me up for the night.'

'Certainly not.' He could not feel anger even at this suggestion.

'Really get down to details then. Still, if you won't, you won't.'

'What would be the point? I shan't see my money again, shall I? I'll write it off to experience.'

'I'll be off then.' He got up, walked over to the window, turned. 'Fact is, I'm in a temporary difficulty. Couldn't arrange a small loan, I suppose, a fiver say? Had a win this evening, you said so yourself.' *A temporary difficulty*. It was really too much. He began to laugh, then took a five pound note from his wallet, put it on the table.

'Thanks. You'll get it back, don't worry.' Tubbs picked up the note, slipped it into his pocket, looked at his empty glass. 'Don't mind if I have a nightcap.' He calmly opened the cupboard, took the whisky bottle, poured from it. There was a faint click. 'Hallo hallo, what have we here?' The compartment door had opened. Tubbs held the wig in his hand.

'*What* have we here?' Tubbs repeated. He looked at the wig, smelt it, then pointed like a terrier, staring at the bald head opposite him. He came towards Arthur, shuffling his feet a little, the wig hanging from his hand. Arthur stayed still as Tubbs deftly placed the wig on his head, then chuckled and stepped back. His eyes stood out, the balls of them a dirty white. The tip of his tongue came out, washed round his mouth, went back.

Arthur snatched off the wig, threw it on to the table. Tubbs stared at him, raised the glass to his lips, sipped, put it down. 'I think I'll stay the night.'

'You will not.' He was surprised to hear his own voice so mild.

'We've got things to talk about. Explanations. You said so yourself.'

'I'll drive you to the station. Now.'

'I like it here. Country air. Good for the old ticker.' He placed his hand on his heart.

Arthur ran into the hall, picked up a loaded walking stick he kept there, came back. 'Get out. At once.'

Tubbs did not look alarmed. 'You don't mean that, you don't want me to go.'

'I do, I do.' He was not sure of the truth of his words. He advanced, holding the stick threateningly, loaded end pointed at Tubbs.

'You're being silly, old man. And you look silly too.'

Arthur struck at him across the table, a wild blow that missed completely, hit the table and chipped off a large splinter of wood.

'Steady on.' Tubbs snatched up the wig and moved round the table with it. Another blow struck his arm and caused a yelp of pain, but he did not drop the wig. Arthur suddenly reversed – it was like a sinister game of musical chairs – and stretched out a hand. Tubbs wriggled away from him, laughed, skidded round the end of the table, slipped and fell to the floor. Arthur pounced, grabbed the wig, stood over the prostrate man holding the stick menacingly, told him to get up. Tubbs did not move. Arthur prodded him with the stick, half-rolled him over. There was blood on his forehead. Where had it come from? Arthur knelt down and with a feeling of repugnance lifted the inert head. The blood came from the back of it. 'Tubbs,' he cried out. 'Stop play acting, Tubbs.' He let go of the head and it dropped to the floor. Obviously Tubbs had been taught a lesson. There was blood on the wood block floor which annoyed him. He brought in a damp cloth from the kitchen, wiped it up, gave the inert figure another prod. Two or three minutes passed before it occurred to him that Tubbs might be dead, and another two or three before he confirmed this with a small mirror put to the lips. Even then he did not truly believe it, searching desperately for a heart-beat and putting the glass again to the mauvish lips before acknowledging the truth. Among all the lies that Tubbs had told him there must have been one decisive fragment of truth. He really did have a weak heart. He had slipped, caught his head against the corner of the table, and been killed by the shock. Or perhaps he had a very thin skull, the exact cause of death did not seem important. What was he going to do about it?

In extreme situations action is for many people a kind of solace, and the logical reasoning that prompts it may be deliberately avoided. He could not have given reasons for his actions in the next hour, but if he could have formulated them they would have been that somebody in his position did not call the police. For such a tragedy to occur in the house of a man whose wife had so recently been murdered must arouse comment and investigation. And then think of the questions, who was Tubbs, why was he in the house, what was the connection between them? Once admit to knowledge of Tubbs and the police might go on to discover the swindle practised on him, find the solicitor who drew up the agreement, ask where the money had come from – there would be no end to it. The police had believed in Easonby Mellon because Arthur Brownjohn remained untouched by suspicion. Once cast a doubt upon him, and investigations would be made. But nobody knew that Tubbs had been in his house, and by his own account he had no dependants and no permanent lodging. If Clennery Tubbs disappeared there was nothing to connect him with Arthur Brownjohn.

He did not think like this, he did not think consecutively at all, while he acted. He opened the fibre suitcase and found in it a change of clothing, shaving things, a set of rigged cards for playing 'Find the Lady,' and some pornographic postcards. He put a couple of brown sacks that had been in the garage when he bought the house into the boot of the car, picked up the thing that had been Clennery Tubbs, half-dragged and half-carried it to the car and put it on top of the sacks. There passed through his mind the recollection of an American case in which a woman, after killing her husband, had disposed of him over a bridge by tying heavy weights to his feet and hands and then tipping him over. It had been important to her that the body should not be discovered, but for him this did not matter because nothing connected him with it. He put the fibre suitcase into the boot and drove out into the night. The time was half past ten.

His road lay through small villages lying under the downs, Westmeston and Plumpton. He turned on to the main Lewes road at Offham, skirted the town, and drove down through Ilford and the tiny hamlet of Rodmell which is strung out along the main road. The night was fine and there was little traffic. He had just passed Rodmell when a vehicle behind him flashed its light on and off and then sounded a single sharp toot on the horn. In a momentary panic he accelerated and took a bend on the wrong side of the road. The toot was repeated. A motor-cycle passed, and cut in front of him. A hand waved. He stopped the car, wound down his window. The night was black and still.

The head that appeared was large. A policeman's helmet

topped it. 'Take a bit o' stopping, don't you? Good job there wasn't a car coming round that corner. Bad bit of driving.'

'I'm sorry. I thought –' What could he say?

'Thought I was one o' those young tearaways, did you?' A flashlight appeared. 'Could I see your driving licence?' The light played on the licence, then on his face. 'Thank you, sir. Did you know you were driving with only one rear light?'

So that was all! Gratefully, almost eagerly, he got out of the car, walked round to the back and tut-tutted. 'I'll have it seen to. Thank you very much.'

'Can be deceptive. Might think you're a motor-bike.'

'Of course, yes. I assure you it was perfectly all right yesterday.'

'Faulty connection may be. Or the lamp gone.' The policeman put his hand down to the boot and before Arthur could complete his agonized restraining gesture gave it a sharp blow with his clenched fist. The rear light came on. 'There you are, faulty connection. Bit of brute force, that's all you needed. Want to get it looked at, though.'

'Thank you very much. I will.' He began to move towards the driver's seat. The policeman, large and black in the black night, blocked his way.

'Tell you something else. I believe you've got a puncture. Back tyre, nearside.'

'Oh, I don't think –' But the policeman was already there, flashlight in one hand, tyre gauge in the other. Arthur took the flashlight and aimed it down at the stooped figure while the gauge was inserted. The policeman straightened up. His face was round and young.

'Down to twelve pounds. Slow puncture. Better change that tyre.'

'Yes.' The spare tyre in the Triumph is kept in the boot, beneath the luggage, together with the jack.

'I'll give you a hand.' The policeman repossessed himself of the flashlight.

He took a deep breath. 'Look, officer, I'm in a desperate hurry, my wife's ill, and I've only got a mile or two to go. This should last out till I get home and I'll change it then.'

The light moved from the boot to his face, back again, was switched off. 'Reckon so. Sure I can't help?'

'It's very kind of you, but I can get home.'

'Right then. Get that rear light seen to, sir, won't you?' He moved away, kicked the motor-cycle into action and was gone along the Newhaven road, leaving the night still again. Arthur leaned against the car. A spasm of nausea bent him double, then passed. When he began to drive again he felt as if he had suffered some physical attack. At the sign that said *Southease* he turned left past the church, down a narrow road. In less than five minutes he was at Southease Bridge.

There were other bridges in the district, but most of those that crossed fast-flowing rivers, like the bridge at Exceat, were on main roads. Southease Bridge, however, was on a tiny side road joining the main Lewes–Newhaven road from which he had come and a minor road winding from the coast up to the downs through the villages of South Heighton and Tarring Neville, to pass a cement works and rejoin another main road out of Lewes at the hamlet of Beddingham. The side road is little used even in the daytime and the wooden bridge is not constructed for heavy traffic. Beneath it the Ouse flows swiftly down to Newhaven and the sea. He tucked the car in off the road beside the bridge and turned off the lights. A sign beside the point at which he had stopped said: 'Southease Bridge. Maximum Safe 2 tons, including weight of vehicle.' There were chalk deposits opposite. He had no flashlight, but he did not need one. He took the suitcase from the boot, walked to the middle of the bridge, dropped it over and heard a splash. Then he put his arm round the body, lifted. It did not move. He pulled at it in panic, felt resistance, pulled again. The strength to lift seemed to have gone out of his arms. He dragged the thing along the road up to the bridge and along its planks. A last effort was needed, and he made it. He lifted, levered. Another splash and it was gone.

With a sensation of total disbelief he heard a vehicle coming towards him from the Tarring Neville road.

He had no time to think, no time even to get back into the car. He ran off the bridge and stood with his back to the road in the attitude of a man relieving himself, as a lorry moved on to the bridge and clattered slowly across. Headlights blazed, he seemed to feel the heat of them on his back. The bridge was so narrow that the lorry almost touched him, and for a moment he feared that it would stop. Then it moved on up to Rodmell, leaving only a tail light which vanished as it turned a curve. He was safe. He got back into the car and drove home by way of Beddingham. He did not change the tyre, and by the time he limped back into the garage it was almost flat.

On the following morning he put the sacks, which were spotted with blood, together with the wig, into the garden incinerator. In the afternoon he had the puncture mended at his local garage. There was no trace left that Clennery Tubbs had paid him a visit.

The disastrous excursion to Brighton had cured him of the desire to discover his true nature by contact with other people. One fine October morning he looked up at the green slope behind the house, seemed to see himself rolling down it as a child and his mother in her floppy hat above, and realized that he wished to paint. Why had he not thought of it before? At school he had painted with enjoyment. Perhaps he had always wished to paint, perhaps Clare's visits to her art class had involved an unconscious rivalry with him instead of with his mother. He bought an easel and paints and in the mild October days went out and painted the countryside round Plumpton and Ditchling. At first he put awkward blurs on to the paper, but within a week he was producing recognizable shapes, and as he compared his work with his mother's it seemed to him that he had a delicacy and exactness of touch which she had lacked. He felt also that he was truly emancipating himself for the first time from the feminine influences that had pressed on him throughout his life – his mother, Clare, Joan. He lived frugally, taking date and banana sandwiches on these expeditions and cooking omelettes at night. The sensation of peace was strong. When he met the Brodzkys one day he greeted them smilingly, but they ignored him. This might have upset him in the past, but it did so no longer. He had been living in this way contentedly for two weeks when he returned from a day's painting to find Inspector Coverdale's black Humber in front of his gate.

Chapter 8

Last Conversation with Coverdale

It was Sergeant Amies, as Coverdale generously admitted, who made the vital discovery in the case, although neither man fully realized its significance at the time. Amies had become really rather obsessed by the affair, and had taken to brooding over the files of statements and documents when he had a spare half-hour. One day he came in with one of the documents and said: 'Just take a look at that, sir. What do you make of it?'

Coverdale looked and made nothing of what Amies showed him, except that it was certainly odd. 'There must be some simple explanation.'

'Nice to know what it was though, eh, sir?'

Coverdale sighed. The case had hardly been a triumph, although he was not inclined to attribute the negative result to his own handling of the investigation. With retirement looming ahead his chief desire was to forget about it. 'A minor point. It's difficult to see what bearing it can have.'

'It may be a minor point, but it's a discrepancy.'

'Yes. Well. I don't feel we should use a day of our time to clear up a discrepancy of that sort.'

Amies's silence showed disagreement, and indeed Coverdale had the prickly feeling in his fingers that he associated with something left undone. He was not sorry when Amies reopened the matter by coming to him one day and saying: 'What do you think of *that*, sir?'

That was a report from the Sussex police that a body, so far unidentified, had been found by some boys in the River Ouse near to its mouth at Newhaven. The body was that of a man about five feet seven inches in height, and he was already dead when he entered the water. Death appeared to have been caused by a blow on the head delivered with some severity, which had caused a skull fracture. He had been in the water for about a week and would not be easily recognizable. He was fully dressed in cheap clothing, with the exception of the fact that he was wearing only one shoe. There was no clue to his identity in his pockets. A cheap suitcase which had been found a couple of miles farther up the river might possibly be connected with him, but in any case its contents were of no help in tracing him. He was fairly well nourished, about forty years of age, with brownish sandy hair and beard, no distinguishing marks. A shoe which appeared to be the fellow to the one he was wearing had been found on the ground just beside a place called Southease Bridge, so there was a strong presumption that he had been thrown into the river at that point.

Coverdale read it and said: 'Well?'

'I've been in touch with Sussex and made a few inquiries. There's another little report here.'

The little report was from P.C. Robertson of the Sussex constabulary, to the effect that on the 30 September he had stopped a Triumph car number 663 ABC near Rodmell on the Lewes–Newhaven road, because it lacked a rear light. The car also had a slow puncture. The driver had seemed agitated and had refused P.C. Robertson's offer to help him change the tyre, saying that he only had a mile or so to go to see his wife, who was ill. His driving licence bore the name of Arthur Brownjohn. P.C. Robertson had returned to Newhaven and had seen no more of the car.

Coverdale tapped the paper. 'Why did Robertson report an incident like this?'

'I gather Sussex asked for reports of anything out of the way near the Ouse in the week before they found chummy. It meant nothing much to them but it does to us, wouldn't you agree, sir? I mean we know he hasn't got a wife for a start.'

'We certainly know that,' Coverdale said cautiously.

'And the bridge at this place Southease is only about a mile from Rodmell.'

'It's all a bit conjectural.'

'Yes, sir. I wonder, how would it be if I went down and had a look round for a day or two, see what I can dig up. In cooperation with Sussex, of course.'

So that was the way it was done. Amies in fact took a little more than a week, but the result fully justified it, and Coverdale went so far as to congratulate the Sergeant on the skill with which he had followed up the leads he had discovered. It was time for action. Strictly speaking it was a Sussex affair since the body had been found in that county, but the circumstances were exceptional, and cooperation presented no problem. So it was Coverdale and Amies who walked to the garage as Arthur was putting in the Triumph.

He was carrying his easel and paints. He stopped when he saw them. 'You've got some news?'

'We may have, sir, and we may not,' Coverdale said heavily. 'We thought we'd stop by to have a chat.'

'I'm sorry if you've had to wait. If you'd let me know –' He opened the front door.

'Perfectly all right. We've been admiring the scenery. As a matter of fact the Sergeant here has spent the last few days in this part of the world.'

Brownjohn led the way into the living-room, where he put down his painting things. 'Very tidy,' Coverdale said approvingly. He looked at the pictures. 'Local scenes. Are they yours?'

'No. My mother painted them. Years ago. Will you have a drink?'

'Nothing to drink, thank you.' Both men sat down, Amies in a circular chair, the Inspector in one of modern design which suddenly tilted back, taking his legs off the ground. Brownjohn gave a giggle bitten off like a hiccup. Neither policeman laughed. Amies looked for somewhere to put his hat and placed it carefully on the floor, then took out note-book and pencil.

'So sorry, I should have warned you. About the chair I mean.' He went to a cupboard made in some light wood, opened it. They watched in silence while he poured whisky. 'Made this myself. Turning into a handyman. Inside compartment too.' He opened it to show them. 'Had a faulty catch, but I've put it right now.'

He sat down and sipped his whisky. His face and his bald head were shiny, his nostrils twitched. He looked like a rabbit, and about him there was as always the air of being slightly lost, unable to cope with the pace and roughness of life. It was not easy to imagine him hurting anybody.

A great deal might depend on the way in which the interrogation was conducted, the order in which things were said. Coverdale had discussed this at length with Amies, and they had settled both their tactics and their technique. With the most casual possible air, like a centre forward beginning a game of football by a pass tapped only inches to his inside left, Coverdale said: 'I wonder, do you know a man who goes by the name of Clennery Tubbs?'

It was a fine evening. Behind the two policemen little chips of white cloud scudded across a blue sky. Outside there was the garden, beyond the garden a road, a hill, freedom. Inside these walls was the force that threatened freedom. Arthur could feel it emanating from the lumpy Inspector and his sharp-nosed Sergeant. He knew that battle was being joined, and that his fate might depend upon the quickness of his reaction.

First move, time-wasting evasion. 'Has he something to do with my wife's death?'

'I didn't say that.'

A pause. Amies spoke. 'Clennery Tubbs, unusual name, you wouldn't forget it.'

'I was just trying to – your saying *goes by the name of*, you see, rather – let me think. Yes. I remember. I met him at a demonstration some months ago, when I was showing one of my inventions, a dish washer.' He was conscious of waffling. 'He tried to interest me in an invention of his own, a car cream. I looked into it, but it was no good. Why do you ask?'

'You haven't seen him recently?' A shake of the head. 'He was fished out of the river a few days ago.'

'I'm sorry. Though I can't say I cared for him.' Self-possession recovered.

'He was a bad boy,' Coverdale said. 'Went inside seven years ago for frauds on women. Prints on file, that's how we traced him.'

'Our information is that you saw him recently. Just before his death. Which took place on or about September 30th.' That was the Sergeant, sharpish.

'Met him?'

'Perhaps you'd like to tell us what you did on that day. Not so long ago. Just over two weeks.'

'I'll need to look at – I've got a calendar in my kitchen.' Amies went to the kitchen door and stood there while he stared at a calendar on the wall. Then he came back and they all sat down again. 'Of course. I should have remembered, I went to Brighton. Somebody told me about a club called the Robin Hood and I went in there and played roulette. I won some money. Then I left and came home.'

'You left?' Amies said. 'You were thrown out, weren't you?'

A flicker of alarm stirred in Arthur's stomach. They had traced his movements in Brighton.

'My information is that you attacked a Mrs Hester Green, tore off and broke her necklace and had to be escorted out.'

'I had a little too much to drink.' He pushed away the whisky glass. 'I can't be quite sure about my movements afterwards.'

'I suggest that you met the man Tubbs.'

'No,' he said firmly. 'I'm quite sure I didn't.'

'Mrs Green saw you talking to a man resembling him outside the club.'

Just as firmly he said, 'She's mistaken. Or telling lies.'

He felt the tension in the other men, and relaxed a little. They were guessing, they only had Hester's word for it that he had met Tubbs, there could be no proof that he had visited the bungalow.

At the same time Coverdale, in his ridiculous tilting chair, knew that a trick had been lost. Amies should have phrased his questions differently, he had failed to maintain the pressure, they were not exactly back to square one but they would have to approach from a different angle. As Amies began to ask another question the Inspector cut him short.

'You agree that you attacked Mrs Green?'

'Oh no, Inspector, of course not.' Brownjohn laughed, moved his chair nearer to the table in the middle of the room, rested his arm on it. 'I'd met her – I didn't even know that was her name – earlier in the day in the antique shop she runs, and when I saw her again in the club it was natural to buy her a drink.' Amies tried to interrupt and Coverdale checked him, saying that they must let Mr Brownjohn speak. 'I didn't attack her – what happened was that I lurched across the table because I'd had one too many, slipped and caught my hand in her necklace. It's true that she was angry, but I assure you it was an accident.'

'It's not important,' Coverdale said soothingly. 'And after that you can't remember driving home?'

'That's right. But I did.'

'You left the club at about nine o'clock, right, Amies?' The Sergeant nodded sulkily. 'Did you drive straight back?'

Arthur thought: you've telegraphed your punch, my dear Inspector. That damned policeman on the motor-bike has reported seeing me. 'I just don't know. I know I got home, but I don't know the time.'

'Your car was seen near Rodmell, a few miles south of Lewes, by a policeman. He stopped you and talked to you, and you showed him your driving licence. You had a dud rear light. This was just before eleven o'clock. Two hours to get from Brighton to Rodmell, which isn't more than twelve miles. How do you explain that?'

'I can't. I told you I had too much to drink. I just drove around, or at least I suppose so. I do have a vague recollection of talking to a policeman.' He actually smiled and asked if they would like a drink now. He was pouring another for himself after they had shaken their heads when the Inspector said that if there was such a thing as a bottle of beer in the house, he did feel thirsty. As Arthur got up to fetch it he saw the surprised, almost hostile glance that Amies gave his superior, and thought: *I've convinced the Inspector, he's on my side now, I just have this surly brute to deal with.* Amies said: 'He was thrown into the river at Southease Bridge, not far from where the policeman stopped you.'

He did not falter in pouring the beer, but he thought: how can they know that? The Sergeant provided the answer, in his voice that sounded like chalk on a blackboard. 'You wonder how we know? Because one of his shoes was left beside the bridge, that's why.'

The tug I felt when I got him out of the car, he thought. Amies went on.

'You were seen on the bridge. By a lorry driver. You'd just thrown the body over.'

He felt mildly contemptuous. Really, the man's *modus operandi* was crude. 'That isn't true.'

'If you were so drunk, how do you know? If you were drunk, why didn't P.C. Robertson notice it?'

He shrugged and decided that it was time to move on to the attack. 'I think you'll agree that I've answered your questions patiently, but now I'm going to refuse to say anything more until you tell me why you're asking them.'

A short silence. Then Coverdale. 'All right, sir. Tubbs was thrown into the river. He was dead when he went in.' Another silence. Should he comment? Better not. 'He had a slight heart condition, but the cause of his death was a blow on the head which fractured his skull.'

'A blow on the head.' He wanted to say that Tubbs had hit his head against the table, but of course that wouldn't do.

'Might have been from your stick.' That was Amies, who now fetched the stick from the hall, thwacked his palm with the loaded end, nodded.

Indignation came up like bile. 'How did you know my stick was there? You've been inside this house. Illegal entry.'

'I happened to notice it as we came in.' Amies laughed in his face as he spoke, unpleasant. 'Handy weapon.'

'Outrageous,' he said. 'Outrageous.'

Coverdale finished his beer and said pacifically: 'Let's not get heated. Cards on the table is my motto. Your car was stopped a mile away from where Tubbs went into the river, it was identified by a lorry driver beside the actual bridge.'

'He was mistaken.'

'I'll be frank. What he saw was a figure near the bridge and a Triumph Herald car. He didn't get the number. Cards on the table. We were justified in asking questions, don't you agree?'

'And I've answered them.' Clouds were rolling up the sky, darkness softened the outlines of the room. The two figures sat like squat bugs in their chairs. He rose, turned on a standard lamp, drew the curtains across the windows, looked at his watch. 'If there's nothing more –'

'Just another couple of questions,' Coverdale said apologetically. 'About Mellon.'

'You've caught him?'

'I doubt we shall ever catch him now,' Coverdale said with a glance of meaningful directness. 'But the first question is this. Did you ever meet Easonby Mellon?'

'Certainly not.'

'Absolutely no question of it? You got that, Sergeant?' Amies had been making notes, and now made another. 'I want a positive answer, Brownjohn.'

'I've given it, haven't I? Damn you, how many more times?'

'Then how do you explain this?' A letter was thumped down on the table. He bent over it, unable at first to see anything more than the signature, 'Arthur Brownjohn' on the Lektreks paper. He began to read: 'I have known Major Mellon for several years, and it is my opinion that he will prove a reliable and respectable tenant . . .' It was the letter he had written long ago to the owners of the Romany House block as a reference. Who would have imagined that it still existed or that it would have come into the hands of the police? When he looked up his face was stricken.

'Credit where credit's due,' Coverdale said. 'Sergeant Amies spotted this.'

Amies had got up. 'Come on. Explain it.' They were both standing, one on either side of him. If ever a man looked guilty, the Sergeant said later to the Inspector, this wretched little figure looked guilty then. They asked questions in turn, so that his head moved first this way and then that, Coverdale's voice confiding, Amies's creaking with an occasional shrillness as if the teeth of a saw were being run over metal.

'On your firm's paper.'

'And your signature. We've had handwriting experts on the job.'

'So when did you first meet him? In the army?'

'No point in holding back any longer.'

'If you feel like making a statement now.'

'Make us do it the hard way and we'll be hard too. You wouldn't like it. How much did you pay him?'

The little man surprised them then. He got up, pushed past them, took one of the paintings off the wall (a hill, clouds, a house or two, they all looked much the same) and began to stamp on it. He burst into tears, his face contorted like a child's and suddenly grotesquely red. 'Lies, lies,' he cried out. 'The world's not like that, it's filthy.' He got his heel on to the pretty little picture and screwed it round. Coverdale, no art lover, felt quite upset. They stopped him as he was reaching for another picture. 'Steady on, now.'

Amies was not to be moved. He poked a bony finger into Brownjohn's chest. 'How much did you pay him?'

'Lies, all lies.' The voice was a scream. 'I don't know what you're talking about.'

'Sit down.' They had to push him into the chair. Coverdale said: 'Begin at the beginning. This letter. It was typed on your office machine. Your letterhead. Your signature.' Coverdale felt – well, hardly nonplussed but a little taken aback – when Brownjohn denied all knowledge of the letter. A simple denial is often the most effective defence an accused man can make in the face of what may seem overwhelming facts. Here the facts were powerful enough, but the man's admission of them would be extremely helpful. Instead he sat there blubbering and refusing to admit the obvious. Now he had put his head on his arms and was saying something unintelligible.

'What was that?'

'Go away. I'm not going to talk any more.' Just like a small child.

'Just as I said, sir, we'll have to take him along. No use doing it here.'

He looked up, showing a little tear-stained red face. 'Along?'

'To the station. To help us with our inquiries.'

'No.'

'It's no use getting into a tantrum.' With one hand Amies began to pull him up from the table.

'Stop it. You've got nothing against me. What do you want me *for*?'

Coverdale put his lumpy face close to Brownjohn's tear-stained one. 'I'm going to tell you what happened. I'll tell you our conclusions, and the evidence they're based on. Cards on the table. When you've heard us you can decide whether you want to make a statement or not. Fair enough?' Brownjohn sniffed, found a handkerchief and blew his nose.

'First of all, you wanted to get rid of your wife. You were too cowardly and too careful to do it yourself. So you hired a man to do it, a man you knew named Easonby Mellon. He ran a shady matrimonial agency, and the proof you knew about it is the reference you gave him. The idea, a clever one I admit, was that Mellon should write some letters pretending to have a love affair with your wife. You paid him to kill her.'

Brownjohn's fingers moved to his bald scalp, caressed it. 'That hotel in Weybridge – you told me Clare was there with him.'

'Mellon was there, but not with your wife. The woman with him wore a veil, but we've shown the hotel clerk pictures of your wife and he's sure that the woman at the hotel was a good deal younger. And we've never been able to find any other occasion when they met. Funny that, don't you think? Looks like a put-up job.' He waited for a comment but none came. 'Now, Sergeant Amies has been doing quite a bit of work on your affairs. You drew out five hundred pounds from your joint account in March – you drew it, not your wife. Why?'

'I –' Brownjohn fluttered his hands ineffectually. 'It was for Tubbs. For his invention. The car cream.'

'But you said you had nothing to do with that, you said it was no good.'

'It *was* no good, but I put some money in it. I was stupid. I bought – bought a share of the cream, I paid him the money, a solicitor named Eversholt drew up the agreement.'

Coverdale nodded, and Amies nodded in time with him. 'Now we're getting somewhere. You may be surprised to know that Sergeant Amies has talked to Eversholt.'

Amies took it up. 'He said the whole idea was so obviously potty he couldn't understand anyone with any sense putting money in it. He told you something to that effect, I believe.' Brownjohn fluttered his hands again. 'It was a cover, wasn't it?'

'I don't know what you mean.'

'When anyone asked why you'd paid out the money you'd tell them this story. It was a cover for the murder money, right?'

'I don't understand.'

'Then I'll tell you.' Amies thrust his razor nose within six inches of Brownjohn's rabbity one. 'Tubbs *was* Easonby Mellon.'

Brownjohn began to laugh. He stopped and then started again upon a higher note. Amies brought his hand round in a semi-circle. There was a sharp crack as it struck Brownjohn's cheek. The laughter stopped. Brownjohn put a hand to his cheek, nursed it. His reproachful eyes went from one of them to the other.

'The Sergeant had to do that, he didn't want to,' Coverdale said gently. The wounded eyes looked at Amies, who appeared ready to repeat the slap. 'And let's be frank about this, there's no proof of what we're saying. We know it's true, mind you, because of what happened afterwards, but there are no pictures of Mellon, and the only ones we've got of Tubbs are the prison pictures. So Eversholt can't help, and though we've shown the shots to people where Mellon had his office the results – I'm being frank – are inconclusive. Of course they're old pictures. We've got no positive identification. This is conjecture.'

'But it's impossible.'

Brownjohn looked as if he were about to giggle again, stopped when Amies asked sharply: 'Why?'

'We don't have any doubt that Mellon killed your wife, but we can't prove that you were an accessory. Can we, Sergeant?' Amies muttered something, got up from his chair and rubbed his bottom. 'But what we can prove is that you knew Mellon years before your wife's death, knew him well enough to give him a reference. And that he visited you here.'

'That he *what*?' Brownjohn took his hand away from his cheek. 'You must be mad.'

'The evidence, Sergeant.'

'Couple named Brodzky, live just up the road. They were walking past one evening – not September 30th, a few days earlier – and saw this man in the garden. Very good description they give, brownish or reddish hair, beard, ginger tweed suit. They realized who it might be at the time, being interested in the case, and they made a report to the local police.'

Coverdale coughed. 'Unfortunately it was ignored.'

'They were mistaken.'

'Oh no, they weren't. Mellon, or Tubbs whichever you like to call him, was here. You disposed of his clothes, didn't you, got rid of that ginger suit. Or you thought you'd got rid of it. You've got the doings in your brief-case outside, Sergeant, haven't you?'

While Amies was out of the room Arthur stared at the face of the Inspector as if he were examining the physical features of some unknown country which held the secret of his fate. Below thick dark-silvery hair a low forehead and then that worn knobbly face with its shallow bloodshot eyes, cheeks and chin full of unexpected promontories, the whole a mottled red in colour and bordered by a pair of ears so incongruously small, neat and pale that they might have been made of wax. Was it possible that they might have been made of wax. Was it possible that this coarse and clumsy figure – the body below such a face would be clumsy, the feet certainly clodhoppers – could be in charge of his future? When he tried to move his left leg he was alarmed to feel that it was paralysed. He had the sensation, common to those who have lost a limb, of making an attempt at movement and at the same time being aware of its impossibility. He bent down so that he could look under the table. His leg was moving when he gave it instructions! It moved quite definitely, made a little twirl in the air, twitched as though a jumping bean were inside it. Why did he feel that it was not moving at all, why was it dissociated from him?

'The Sergeant took a bit of a liberty. While you were out on your painting expeditions I mean.' That was Coverdale, his mouth opening and closing like a dummy's. He did not hear the next words properly because he was conscious of the fact that his leg was still moving although he had given it instructions to be still. He caught the last phrase: '. . . in your incinerator.'

It startled him. 'What is that? What did you say?'

To his bewilderment they did not answer. Instead the Sergeant, with a smile like a shark's, drew something slowly out of a black brief-case. He watched fearfully until the thing was right out and then relaxed. It was only a sheet of paper! Then with a pounce Amies had put the thing in front of him and asked if he recognized it.

He stared at it, seeing a large photograph of what appeared to be some kind of medal, with a fragment of a flag (was it a flag?) adhering to it. He looked up questioningly.

'Come *on* now.' That was Amies, a nasty customer. 'Look at it, man, look.'

The thing he had taken for a medal was a button. There were letters on it and he spelt them out soundlessly. I-N-C-H-&-B-U. What did the ampersand mean? Then he looked up.

'I see you've got it. Corèfinch and Burleigh. High class firm, they put their name on the fly buttons. And the material, recognize that? High class again, they knew the customer it was made for. Guess who? Easonby Mellon.'

'Fly buttons,' Coverdale said meditatively. 'Old-fashioned now, everyone wears zips, but they're old-fashioned tailors.'

'You know where it came from.' That was Amies, and it was not a question. '*Look at me.*'

He looked, at Amies's dead sallow face and Coverdale's bumpy one, and saw no help in them. Then he glanced down. Below the table his leg kept up its jigging without prompting from him. He put a hand to his face and felt nothing, although he knew that finger must have touched cheek.

Amies had his hand in the brief-case again. Another photograph was put in front of him. He turned his face away and refused to look, until Amies raised a menacing fist like a parent threatening a child. Then he did not understand what he saw.

'Bit of sacking,' the Sergeant said. 'From the incinerator. Careless you were, just a few inches not burned, but enough. Stain on it – *there* – look.' He did not look. 'Marvellous what the boys can do now. They say it's blood, group AB, very unusual. Know what Tubbs's blood group was? AB.'

Sacking, sacking? He remembered the sacking in the car, but it belonged to another time. He glanced down again. His leg had stopped twitching, his limbs were dead.

'Let's recapitulate,' Coverdale said. 'We believe you hired Mellon to kill your wife and that afterwards he tried to blackmail you. We believe that, but we can't prove it. This is what we can prove. You knew Mellon years before your wife's death, and you lied about it. You paid Mellon or Tubbs, whichever you like to call him, money for a completely useless invention. Mellon came here to see you – we've got witnesses to that. You were seen to meet him in Brighton on the night of September 30th. You burned the clothes Mellon was known to wear in your incinerator, and you burned the sacking with bloodstains that are the same blood group as Tubbs's on it. Your car was positively identified a mile from where Tubbs went into the river, and almost as positively identified at the very bridge. Mellon and Tubbs have both been here, we can prove it. There's a strong presumption they were the same person. If you say they're not, you've got to answer one question. *Where is Easonby Mellon?*'

The Sergeant echoed the question, and he knew he could not answer it. Beyond Amies, directly behind his head, was one of the little thin paintings on the wall, but it gave him no help. There was no way out.

He opened his mouth. 'I –' He was unable to go on. He felt the paralysis creeping up his body.

'I think he's ready to make a statement now, sir.'

His hand clasped his throat, plucked at it to release the words that at last came up. 'I killed Easonby Mellon.'

Coverdale let out breath in a sigh and said gently, 'Come along with us.' They lifted him, but when they tried to stand him up he slipped sideways like a rag doll. In the end they had almost to carry him out to the car. He appeared to have lost the use of his legs.

Arthur Brownjohn did not stand trial. He was found unfit to plead under the McNaughten Rules on insanity and this, as Coverdale said to Amies, was just as well, because the medical evidence about the blow and some of the other evidence too was distinctly shaky. The temporary hysterical paralysis he had suffered from soon passed away, and in Broadmoor he was a quiet tractable inmate who spent a great deal of time in painting. Most of his paintings were water colours of imaginary Sussex landscapes, and some of them were displayed in prisoners' art shows. His work in oils, however, was quite different. It depicted scenes in which a lusty naked man with thick hair and curling beard, rather like a Rubens satyr, stabbed or strangled a naked woman who limply submitted to her fate. These pictures obviously excited him considerably, and they interested the doctors, but they were not thought suitable for exhibition. As time passed he painted fewer of them, and at length he stopped asking for oil paints. He ate voraciously, grew fat and seemed quite happy.

The Man Whose Dreams
Came True

Contents

PART ONE
Misfortunes of a Young Man   175

PART TWO
A Dream of Loving Women   211

PART THREE
Dreams and Realities   301

PART FOUR
How the Dreams Came True   391

PART ONE

Misfortunes of a Young Man

Chapter 1

When the alarm bell rang Anthony Scott-Williams lay quite still and let the warm sun of Siena seep through his eyelids.

The day stretched out in front of him, an endless tape on which he would print the pleasures of eye and ear. He would rise and dress leisurely, leave the small hotel and go out into the whisky-coloured town not yet noisy with cars and scooters. Coffee and croissants on the pavement outside a small café and then the morning walk which would include perhaps the Duomo with its historical figures set in the marble that covered the whole floor of the church like an immense carpet. After the Duomo perhaps the Pinacoteca Nazionale, home of the Sienese painters, perhaps simply a random walk through the narrow streets, soaking up sun without bothering about churches or art galleries. In any case by midday he would be sitting in the Piazza del Campo, that wonderful shell-shaped open space, looking at the hard elegance of the Palazzo Pubblico, drinking the first apéritif of the day and letting the liquid Italian speech flow over him.

He yawned and opened his eyes. Siena disappeared, but he retained it for a few moments more by looking at the guidebook beside the bed. Had he placed the Palazzo Pubblico properly? Yes, here it was: 'The Public Building, now used as Town Hall, is erected in the Piazza del Campo, a proud specimen of Middle Age architecture . . .' And so on. Would he really have visited the Duomo, might he have been bored? In any case he was not in Siena but in Kent, and it was time to get up.

A look round the bedroom usually gave him pleasure. The Morris wallpaper – oh yes, he knew that it was Morris – with its great splashy purple flowers and delicate biscuit-coloured background, the dressing-table with silver hair brushes set out on it, the plain pile carpet, the comfortable bed in which he lay with its polished brass rails, and best of all the door leading to the green and black tiled elegance of the bathroom, really, what more could one want? And then to pad across the spongy carpet in bare feet as he did now, turn on the shower and adjust it so that the water was at just the right temperature, expose oneself to the hot water and end with the sharp ecstasy of the cold, all these were undeniably pleasures. He told himself so as he looked in the glass after shaving. 'You're a clever boy,' he said. 'But you're lucky too.' He stuck out a tongue which was revealed as perfectly pink. The glass showed him a leanly handsome face, yet one by no means cadaverous. Good teeth, a wide sensitive mouth, none of your nasty little rosebuds, a straight small nose, yes, he really congratulated himself on his face.

It was certainly a cushy billet. The drawn curtains revealed the long lawn, the pond beyond it and past the pond a glimpse of cattle grazing, the grass shining wetly under weak April sunlight, it was all quite perfect in its way even though it was just a tiny bit boring. He dressed with care – not that he ever dressed carelessly – in a light weight grey suit with just a hint of tweediness about it, and went down to breakfast. A dish over a hotplate revealed poached haddock when he lifted the lid, coffee bubbled faintly over another hotplate, the toast was crisp outside and soft within. Something was added to his pleasure by the knowledge that the fish knife and fork were Georgian silver.

Beside the plate lay the post, three envelopes addressed to the General. He slit the envelopes with a paper knife. An account from a builder for dealing with the dry rot in the attic, a request from the local branch of the British Legion for the General to give away the prizes at their yearly fête, and a letter from Colonel Hasty with whom he had been conducting a long correspondence on the General's behalf about the movement of tanks in the Western Desert in June 1941. He skimmed through the letter, which contained mostly military information. It ended: 'Re my suggested visit, my dear old Bongo, nothing would give me greater pleasure than to see you again and have a natter. It so happens I shall be down your way Wednesday the 21st, will you let me know if this suits you and at what time.' A twinge of uneasiness touched him like a momentary toothache, but he ignored it. Why shouldn't the old man have a natter with a friend? After breakfast he rang the little silver handbell on the table, and Doris came in.

She was one of two daily girls from the village who did the chores and lent a hand to Mrs Causley, the cook-housekeeper. Both girls were on the plump side for his taste, but he felt sure that Doris was ready for anything he cared to suggest. This sensibility to a woman's feelings was one of the things upon which Tony prided himself. He couldn't have said exactly how he knew, by a glance, a laugh, even a smell, but he always did know when a woman was ripe for love. It would be a mistake to do anything about Doris, who had a clodhopping boyfriend in the village, but he couldn't resist a smile that brought a smile back, like a return of service at tennis.

'Well, Doris, what news?'

'Mrs Causley's just taken up his tray.'

Everything was as it should be, but that early morning glimpse of Siena had unsettled him. He was really not prepared to cope with one of the old man's moods, and he saw as soon as he entered the bedroom that the General was in a mood this morning. The breakfast tray had been pushed aside almost untouched and he was slumped in bed, his fine white hair unbrushed, the corners of his mouth turned down.

'How are we this morning?'

'Don't know what you mean, *we*. *I* am not very well, I had a bad night. My back.' The glare from under his brows might have terrified once. Now it asked for sympathy.

The *we* had been a mistake, too much like a male nurse, but what an irritable old thing he was. For that matter, he thought as he patted the pillows and eased the thin body up on to them and held the glass while the General used the brush painfully with rheumaticky hands, and gently massaged the area between the shoulder blades where the old man said he felt pain, for that matter he was a bit of a male nurse at times.

'That woman will have to go. D'ye call that a three and a half minute egg?' Tony looked at the top of the offending egg and made a clucking sound. 'Can't think why you don't see it. She drinks.' The remark seemed to call for no reply. 'Don't know why I have these pains. I know, I know, Moore says it's muscular rheumatism. Moore's a fool.'

'What about getting up? Shall I help you?'

The old man looked up at him. 'You've no idea what it's like to be awake all night. I think about Miriam. Things were different then, I sometimes think my own life ended when she died.'

Miriam, the General's wife, had died five years ago, long before Tony had come on to the scene. A photograph of her, aristocratic and disdainful, stood beside the bed and the General kissed it each night before he went to sleep. He sometimes wondered whether he would have got on with Miriam. Certainly he admired her flair for interior decoration as shown in his bedroom, in the striped wallpaper and chairs of the drawing-room and even the peacock blue walls and very pale blue carpet of this bedroom. But would they have found each other sympathetic? Looking at the jutting jaw he thought not.

'Shall I give you a hand with dressing?'

'Not a bloody invalid yet. Sorry, didn't mean to snap.' The knobbly hand touched his own for a moment. Filthy old devil, Tony thought, I know what you're like, Miriam or no Miriam, soldiers are all the same. 'You're good to me.' The chalky fingers touched his again.

'You might like to see this.'

The General read Hasty's letter and began to snort like a horse. 'The man's a lunatic, a bloody imbecile. Look at this. He's got the audacity to say here, "I had the impression at the time that we were unprepared for the speed with which Jerry moved his armour. Anyway, it caught us on the hop." I told you Hasty was an idiot, didn't I?'

'Do you want to see him? You see he's coming down this way tomorrow.'

'See him? I should think I do. I'll rub his nose in it, I'll rub Ted Hasty's nose in it. Call him up and ask him to lunch.'

'There are a couple of other letters, one asking you to open a British Legion fête.'

The General had been bouncing up and down in the bed. He stopped suddenly. 'Can't do it. Not well enough, no time anyway.'

'And here's Clinker's account.'

The General examined it through a pair of rimless pince-nez. 'Hell of a lot of money, should have got an estimate.'

'If you remember he said he couldn't give one, couldn't tell how much work there was until he opened up the timbers.'

'It's robbery, but make out a cheque and I'll sign it. Later. And get out all the Western Desert papers, I want to go through them. I shall have something to say to Ted Hasty about the use of armour. Don't forget to call him up.'

Tony did so half an hour later. A surprisingly quiet and cool voice (surprisingly because 'Ted Hasty' conjured up a choleric personality) said that he would be down at about twelve-thirty and sent kindest regards to Bongo.

Chapter 2

Tony had been at Leathersley House for just over twelve months. He had answered an advertisement in *The Times*, come down by train and been engaged on the spot. The General had barely glanced at the letter from Sir Archibald Graveney, written from Throgmorton Hall, Glos. 'Don't worry about that stuff. I judge by what I see, Scott-Williams. No relation of Scotty Scott-Williams, I suppose, in my class at Sandhurst?'

'I'm afraid not.' He had been appealingly frank. 'My father's name was Williams. He died when I was three, gold mining out in Australia, and my mother married a man named Scott. Then she left her husband and called herself Scott-Williams.'

'Brought up among the Anzacs, were you? Can't say I hear the accent.'

'We left when I was ten, came back to England. My mother inherited a little bit of money, just enough to keep us going but not to give me an education, if you know what I mean, sir.' He had practised his smile in the mirror, and it did not fail him now.

'Play billiards?'

'A little.'

There was a pause. 'Job's yours if you want it,' the General said, and told him about it. He lived alone, looked after by a housekeeper. He was writing his memoirs and his secretary's prime task would be to work on them, but he would also deal with correspondence and help to look after affairs generally. Tony gathered that there had been a succession of secretaries who had been sacked because they were lazy or had left because they were bored. The pay was not high but the job seemed to have possibilities, and he took it.

Leathersley House was small as the Victorians counted size, but absurdly large for a single man. It had eight bedrooms, half of which were shut up, a billiards room and a library. The house had been constructed in the middle of the nineteenth century to solid Victorian ideas of space and seclusion. There were more than three hundred acres of land, most of them taken up by two farms which were let, and looking after affairs meant visiting the farmers once a week, talking to their wives and patting their children on the head. Most of the correspondence was from ex-servicemen's clubs and societies in which the General took only an intermittent interest, and Tony soon learned that he was expected to deal with most of it himself. He was expected also to check over the accounts that Mrs Adams the housekeeper brought him every month. But the essence of the job – and this no doubt had been the downfall of other secretaries – lay in the General's billiards and his memoirs.

Like some motor cars the General was a slow starter in the morning, when his rheumatism was at its worst. He would soak some of the pain from his joints with a hot bath, be moving with comparative ease by midday, and in the afternoon was ready for work on his memoirs. These existed in various forms, housed in two large grey filing cabinets which stood in the gloomy library, a room untouched by Miriam's restorative hand. There was a typescript of the book's first half which was several years old, there were revisions of it made over the year, there were bits of many chapters in the second half of the book, there were several thousand notes which had been filed in boxes by other secretaries. Most of the book was concerned with the General's (he had been a Brigadier then) command of an armoured column in the Western Desert, and his replacement and relegation to a home command after the disastrous failure of Operation Battle-axe in June 1941. What precisely had happened, why were both official and independent histories so inaccurate, where did responsibility really lie for errors wrongly attributed to the General? It was such questions that the memoirs set out to answer, and the secretary's task was that of blending all the notes into a harmonious whole. Or at least that was his nominal task for in fact, as Tony soon realized, the memoirs would never be completed. The General revised notes, elaborated incidents, re-read histories of the desert war and dictated furious refutations of passages that concerned him. These sessions gave him great emotional satisfaction. His blue eyes would blaze, his white hair become pleasingly disordered, he strode up and down the library thundering denunciations of G.H.Q. and individual commanders. The resultant typescript took its place among all the other notes and fragments of chapters.

In the evenings after dinner they played billiards. The flexibility of the General's fingers had by now greatly increased, so that he could make a bridge with comfort, and his movements which in the morning were jerky as a puppet's had become smooth and easy. He was a poor player, and Tony had to play with some care to make sure that he sometimes lost a game without seeming to throw it away. The General liked a close finish and when he won by only a few points would say: 'Nerve, that's what you need. You're a good player, Tony, but in the last stretch you lose your nerve.' They generally played three games, then spread the cloth carefully over the green baize, had a nightcap and went to bed. There was a companionship about it that delighted the old man. 'I enjoyed that,' he would say after a close finish. 'A damned near run thing, as the Duke of Wellington would have said.' It was during a game of billiards that he became Tony instead of Scott-Williams.

The life was boring, but the situation might have been designed for him. Mrs Adams made it clear at once that she would tolerate no interference with her handling of the household accounts, and within a month he had persuaded the General to get rid of her. She had been followed by other cook-housekeepers, of whom Mrs Causley was the most amenable. She took no interest in the household accounts, and indeed could hardly add up. After Mrs Adams's departure Tony kept the ledger in which bills were entered with scrupulous accuracy and insisted on showing them to the General until one day the old man waved them irritably away and said he never wanted to see them again. After this Tony arranged what he thought of as his commission. He changed the butcher and came to an understanding with another local man, who put in bills for steaks and chickens that never appeared at Leathersley House, in exchange for a percentage of the proceeds. He was able to make a similar arrangement with the local garage who serviced the General's Jaguar, which turned out to need a good deal more attention than it had received in the past. The invoices were rendered, Tony drew the cheques and the General signed them. It proved impossible to do the same thing with the grocer, and Tony shopped personally for groceries, adding his commission to the cost. He was at times inclined to resent the pettiness of all this, but the builders' work had provided an opportunity of which he had taken full advantage. The cheque signed by the General for Clinker included a hundred pounds for Tony. He would take the cheque to Clinker tonight and collect the money.

Yet there were periods of discontent, and this fine April morning was one of them. Retyping 'Off to the Western Desert,' which contained an account of the General's feelings on learning that his only son, a fighter pilot, had been shot down and killed, the vision of Siena – at other times it was Florence, Monte Carlo, the French Riviera – became increasingly strong. When would he get away? A few pounds here, a few pounds there, even the money from Clinker, what did it amount to? He had occasional fantasies of forging the General's name to a really sizeable cheque. He had practised copying the signature, simply for the fun of it as he told himself, but of course had never done anything about it. On this morning he contemplated, as he had done before, the rich opportunity that lay under his hand if he dared to use it. One of the first jobs he had done after coming to Leathersley was clearing out the contents of a lumber room. The tin trunks and suitcases were mostly filled with ancient movement orders, menus of regimental dinners and copies of unintelligible or uninteresting army memoranda. He turned it all over quickly, and then his attention was caught by some letters from Miriam which he put aside for possible use in the memoirs. Beneath them was a thick sealed envelope which he opened. It contained more letters addressed to 'My dearest G' or 'My own darling G' (the General's name was Geoffrey). They were love letters, signed 'Bobo', and he had read two of them through before he realized that they were addressed by one man to another. Some of them made the nature of G's relationship with Bobo absolutely plain.

He had shown the General the letters from Miriam, thrown out the rest of the stuff, and kept the Bobo letters in their envelope, locked up in the chest of drawers in his room. He had a vision of himself confronting the General with them and asking for some really substantial sum, say a thousand pounds, which would be more money than he had possessed at any one time. With all that money in his wallet he would go to the south of France, stay in a good hotel, meet a rich woman older than himself who fell in love with his looks, marry her and live in luxury ever after.

But he knew all this to be a dream. It would be blackmail, and he had never blackmailed anybody. And the dream conflicted with another, entirely different, in which the General's obvious liking for him was translated into practical benefits. In this vision he took the place of the long dead son and a will was made in his favour. But this meant staying for some years, since the General was only in his early seventies and seemed healthy, apart from the arthritis. 'You've got to do something about it,' he would tell himself, and the fact that he did nothing increased his irritation. He found it hard to work on the dreary old memoirs that day, and when the General mentioned billiards gave a reminder that this was one of his free evenings.

'Shan't be having our game tonight, then.' He would have been annoyed had the old man asked him to stay, but somehow it was almost equally annoying that he simply said, 'Have a good time.'

'Is it all right if I take the Jag?' There was another car, a rather ancient Morris, which he used for shopping. The General looked at him from under thick white brows, then nodded.

Chapter 3

Gravel crunching under tyres on the drive, speed on the road moving up effortlessly to seventy at the touch of his foot – he felt exhilarated always behind the wheel of a car. 'There goes a lucky one,' people would say to each other as he passed. 'Young, handsome, well-dressed, big car, yes, he's got it made.' The sense of exhilaration grew, he wondered why he had been low-spirited. After all, he was about to profit from the Clinker coup, and surely it was not beyond his ingenuity to find some new ways of obtaining commissions? He felt extremely cheerful when he drew up at Clinker's yard which was on the edge of Landford, ten miles away.

The builder was in his office. He was a dark squat morose man with a powerful sweaty smell about him. He took the cheque, looked at it, then put it in a drawer.

'You'll send a receipt. Got to keep the books in order.' He was aware that his jocosity sounded uneasy. He was slightly afraid of Clinker.

'I'll send it.'

'Then there's just the question of settling up.'

A pause. Was there going to be trouble? Clinker slowly lifted his black head, looked ruminatively at Tony, then went to a safe and unlocked it. A cash box inside was filled with notes. He counted, keeping his back to Tony, put the cash box back in the safe, relocked it, thrust the bundle of notes forward.

Tony counted. They were one pound notes and there were fifty of them. 'This isn't right.'

Clinker was at his desk, short powerful legs thrust out in front of him. 'How's that?'

'It's not what we agreed. A hundred.'

'That's right. Fifty each.'

'No no.' The injustice of it overcame him, his voice rose. 'A hundred for *me*. You – I arranged it so that you didn't even have to give an estimate. You could put in any price you liked.'

'It was steep enough. Couldn't make it any more.'

'I want a hundred.'

'That's all you get.' The builder rose and came near him, measuring his own squatness against Tony's height. 'Not bad for doing nothing.'

'I'll see you're not employed again.'

Clinker laughed in his face. He stuffed the notes awkwardly into his pocket and retreated. As he drove away he saw the man standing in his office doorway, grinning.

Landford was a town without many attractions. There were two cinemas, eight churches and twenty-seven pubs. It had once been a market town and there was still a Thursday market, but the town lived now on industries brought down from London, canning factories, bicycle manufacturers, a steel pressing firm. Londoners had come to live there and complained that there was nothing to do, the place was dead. It was designated as an over-spill town, and the council after long discussion had permitted the opening of a ten pin bowling alley with a casino attached to it. He paused before the entrance to the Golden Sovereign, then walked quickly past. Farther down the High Street a fascia said *Allways Travel*. When he pushed open the door, still smarting from the Clinker humiliation, it was like putting salve on a burn.

A poster inside showed a gondola, a bridge, water, beneath them the word Venezia. The maps, France, Spain, Greece, Italy, made him glow inside as if he had been drinking. Two girls sat behind a horseshoe desk, deep in train times and air connections. He waited his turn impatiently. One of the girls looked at him with a mechanical smile. He had been in here before.

'I'm interested in Italy.'

'Any particular area? What time of year?'

'I'd thought of Venice.' She reached for a folder. 'But Venice in September, that's when I'd be going, I mean, will the season be over?'

'Our last Venice holiday, 837 B, starts on the sixteenth.'

'A package tour.' He laughed easily. 'I don't want that. An

individual holiday is so much more – well, agreeable, isn't it? The thing is, is late September quite the time for Venice?'

'If you're going on an individual flight you can go any time.'

'Yes, I know, but that's not quite what I meant. The canals are liquid history, but they do smell, don't they?' He gave her a confidential smile showing – he glimpsed the glass on the wall behind her – his beautiful teeth. The smile was boyish, it would always be boyish. 'So I did wonder about Athens.'

'Individual flight again?'

She was the dullest of girls. 'I'd never think of anything else.' 'Here's the folder.'

'Thank you. What hotel would you recommend? I stayed at the George the Fifth last time, but perhaps I might make a change.'

She goggled at him. 'Hotel list inside. Did you want to make a booking?'

It was almost as if she did not take him seriously. He spun the conversation out for another couple of minutes and left when the man behind him began to mutter about people who couldn't make up their minds. It had not, after all, been very satisfactory.

Later, sitting in the American Bar of Landford's best hotel, he became convinced that Fiona Mallory would not turn up. She was something different from the usual run of his girls, the daughter of a business tycoon with a house outside the town and a flat in London (Tony had looked him up in *Who's Who*), and at their only other meeting she had seemed obviously keen on him. He had met her in the Golden Sovereign, where she had watched him playing on his final disastrous visit, and as she told him afterwards had admired the calmness with which he faced a losing streak. Later they had had a drink together and he had taken her back to Frankfort Manor in the Jag, dropping her in the drive. She represented an agreeable variation on the vision in which he married a rich woman, in the sense that she was younger than he and had the wealth of Mallory Textiles behind her. But obviously she was not going to turn up.

He was sipping his second Manhattan when she said, 'Sorry I'm late. Daddy dropped me off on his way to London and he kept dithering about. I thought we'd never get away.'

She was a tall slender girl with a good figure and a long, slightly horsy face. Dark glasses with jewelled frames concealed her eyes. Her blue dress had obviously cost a lot of money.

'I've kept you waiting *hours*. I hope you're not getting sloshed.'

'Only been here a few minutes. Hell of a lot of traffic coming down.'

'You've not driven down specially?'

'When I make a date with a beautiful girl I keep it.' He smiled. 'What are you hiding?'

'How do you mean?'

'The glasses.'

'They're a thing I've got at the moment. You don't mind?'

'They add a touch of mystery,' he said, although in fact it made him feel uncomfortable to talk to somebody whose eyes were invisible. 'Anyway I had to come down to see my aged uncle.'

'Oh yes, the General. You told me about him. How is he?'

'Just about the same, one foot in the grave and the other in the Western Desert. I shall stay there tonight, combining pleasure with duty. Shall we eat? The roast duck with orange is rather good, or they grill a steak quite decently.' He had looked up the place in the *Good Food Guide*. 'Of course it's not London.'

'If you ask me this place is just about the end, I can't think why daddy likes being here. He's divorced, you know that?'

'Yes.'

'The bore is he wants me down here too. I'm useful as a sort of hostess cum housekeeper.'

'And you always do what he tells you?'

The dark glasses were enigmatic. 'Almost always. I'm a dutiful daughter. But I hope he'll get married again soon, then I'll be free.'

Throughout dinner he was bothered by the glasses, which made him feel as if he was naked while she remained fully clothed. But still he seemed to be keeping his end up. It was lucky that she went to London very little, and to theatres and cinemas hardly at all, so that he did not have to admit his own ignorance of current plays. He talked vaguely about the firm of stockbrokers in which he worked and in more detail about his clubs and the famous people to be met in them. These were stories he had told before, with a few variations, and they came easily enough. Her own life was humdrum, friends of her father's to dinner always at weekends and sometimes in the week, a few stuffy dances with dreary local escorts. She wanted to get a job in London but her father wouldn't hear of it, or not at the moment anyway. It would be different if he got married again.

She pushed aside the food, at which she had only picked although she said it was delicious, and said suddenly, 'Would you like to come back for coffee?'

'Back?' For a moment he did not understand.

'Home. Where I live.'

'It's those glasses. They confuse me, I wish you'd take them off.'

'All right.' Her eyes were a shallow blue. She put the glasses carefully into a case.

'That's better. I felt as though everything I said was bouncing back at me. Yes, I'd love that.'

Driving back through the lonely country lanes, the situation became real to him. They were married and Mallory had given them the house as a wedding present. They had been driving round Europe on their honeymoon and now they were returning. Fiona was fully provided for, and there was no question of working or of having to worry about money ever again. He placed a hand on her knee.

She took it off. 'I don't like one handed drivers.'

Why did she have to spoil it? But five minutes later this annoyance was forgotten as they went past the entrance gates, up the long drive, skirted the servants' quarters and entered the house. How could he ever have thought Leathersley House impressive? This was the real thing, an entrance hall with big brown pictures on the walls and lots of furniture that was obviously old and valuable. A great staircase led out of the hall, of the kind he had only seen in films when the ambassador received at the top of it, and she led him into a drawing-room so big that if you put it jokingly you might say it was hard to see from one end to the other. This too was full of pictures and, yes, he could hardly believe it, but there was actually a marble statue at the other end of the room.

He nodded approvingly. 'Is that your father?' He pointed to a big head and shoulders. The man who looked out of the frame was tight lipped, unsmiling.

'Yes. You are clever.'

'I thought I recognized him.'

'Everyone's gone to bed.' For a moment she looked directly at him with her blue shallow eyes. 'I'll make coffee.'

'I don't want coffee.' He took one step forward, held her in a powerful grip. She nibbled his ear and murmured something. 'What's that?'

'My room's upstairs.'

He would have liked to see the upper part of the house, but the thought of the magnificent staircase intimidated him. He led her towards a sofa that was bigger than most beds. 'We'll stay here.'

Mr Mallory watched their later proceedings. At the climactic moment Tony felt a pleasure that was by no means wholly sexual. I am making love, he told himself as he ardently kissed the body writhing below his, to the daughter of a millionaire.

Chapter 4

On the following morning he woke feeling shagged, and more than shagged, depressed. He had got only fifty pounds instead of a hundred, had spent several on Fiona when no doubt he could have had her for nothing, and in addition – this crowned his depression when the post came – there was a letter from the Golden Sovereign phrased in what could only be called threatening terms. It mentioned taking further steps regarding settlement of his debt to them of nearly a hundred pounds, including 'getting in touch with your employer, if this regrettable necessity should be forced on us.' If they got in touch with the General they might not get their money, but he would almost certainly lose his job.

Gambling was his one weakness, or that was the way he sometimes thought of it. More often it seemed to him to be the way in which he would eventually make his fortune. The club, where he had played roulette with reasonable fortune until two unlucky sessions saw him nearly a hundred pounds down, had allowed him to give cheques for his chips because he had played there so often. After he had been cleaned out he had explained to the manager, a man named Armitage, that it was no use presenting his last two cheques because he was temporarily out of funds. Similar things had happened before in other gambling houses but then he had always moved on quickly, changing his job and his address. He took his usual line, that the amount was trivial and that he had no doubt they could accommodate him. Armitage had shaken his head and said that he would have to speak to Mr Cotton.

'Who's Mr Cotton?'

'He's Number One. Up in London.' He asked a switchboard girl to see if Mr Cotton was free and then shook his head again. 'Mr Cotton won't like it.'

'You'll get your money,' Tony said easily.

He was startled when a voice in the room said, 'What is it, Armitage?'

The voice came from a box on the desk. When Armitage leaned forward to speak into it his voice was that of a supplicant.

'You should have known better.' The voice was mild, but Armitage flinched. 'But forget it. I told you, no trouble. What's the name again?'

'Scott-Williams.'

'I don't want him in my clubs. Tell him that.'

Tony had been greatly impressed by this casual demonstration of power. Impressed and relieved, so that the letter upset him more than it would otherwise have done. He telephoned the Golden Sovereign, but found only the cleaner there.

The morning did not recover from this unhappy beginning. At breakfast his bacon was underdone and the toast burnt, and when he spoke to Mrs Causley she said insolently that perhaps he would like to cook it himself. The General was up early, in splendid spirits and eager to get back to the Western Desert. He began to comb through the mass of notes about his tank operations there, so that he could refute Ted Hasty. It was on the third mention of Hasty's name that the faint twinges Tony had felt on the previous day turned into the pain of realizing the truth. He had met Colonel Hasty, and their meeting had had unhappy consequences. It was at a time when he had been working as a salesman for AtoZed Motors, a firm which specialized in buying cars written off after involvement in crashes and putting them back on the market when they had been resprayed and reconditioned. He had sold Hasty a ruined Peugeot which contained several parts grafted on from some quite different car. Within a month the semi-Peugeot's steering had got out of control and the Colonel had driven it into a brick wall. AtoZed had professed their good faith, the Colonel had got most of his money back, and the affair had ended short of the Law Courts, but he had been indignant about Tony's selling methods and was not likely to have forgotten him. It was in total despair that he helped the General to sort out papers.

'Tank training, where the devil are those statistics about tank training?' The General looked at him. 'What's the matter, my boy, you're looking pale.'

'I'm all right.'

'You don't look it. Leave it to me, I'll sort through this stuff and we'll see what Ted Hasty's got to say.'

He lay down in the bedroom, stared at the Morris wallpaper and felt no better. He could stay in his room, refuse lunch and avoid meeting Hasty but if, as had happened before when the General met old army friends, the discussion went on for hours and he stayed the night, a meeting was inevitable. And what was he to do about that letter? He walked gloomily round the room and then went into the little study where he kept the estate papers and accounts. On the desk lay the cheque book in which yesterday he had written out with pleasure the cheque for Clinker.

In ten ecstatic minutes he burnt his boats. After half a dozen trials on a sheet of paper that he tore up at once he produced the signature itself on the cheque, done with the bold characteristic flourish the General gave to the tail of the 'y' in 'Geoffrey'. He made out the cheque for two hundred and fifty pounds. If the thing was to be done it might as well be done properly. The General saw his pass sheet only quarterly. By the time it arrived, no doubt he would have paid back the money. And if he had not – well, he kept at the back of his mind like an insurance policy the thought of the Bobo letters. Later, when he drove in to town and presented the cheque across the counter a part of him admired his outward coolness. He felt a surge of self-congratulatory pleasure when the clerk cancelled the signature without question and asked how he would like the money. This was the first really criminal act he had ever committed. How simple it was, how calm he felt. The thick wad of money in his pocket gave him such a warm feeling that he decided to wait a day or two before paying the club.

He had forgotten all about Colonel Hasty, but as he drove the old Morris back into the garage he saw a car in the drive. He avoided the front door, but just as he was about to go up into his room the General's head popped out of the drawing-room.

'Feeling better?'

There was nothing for it but to say that he did.

'Come in, join the party. Ted, this is Tony Scott-Williams.'

A sharp bird-like look at his face, a quick bird-like peck at his hand. He felt recklessly confident, even when the man said he thought they had met.

'I've got that feeling too, but I can't remember where.'

'Too young for the war. Were you out in Kenya in the fifties?'

'I'm afraid not,' he said truthfully. 'I was secretary to Sir Archibald Graveney for some time. If you ever came to Throgmorton Hall –'

'Never did. Dead now.'

The remark threw him for a moment. The *Who's Who* he had looked up was three years old. It was bad luck to have picked a man who had died since then. 'Yes, of course. I left a few months before his death.'

'Used to see him in London sometimes, at the club. Never knew he had a secretary.'

'I hardly ever came down to London with him.'

'Yes yes.' The General had been waiting with obvious impatience for this exchange to end. 'As I was saying, Ted, the whole question of preparation goes back to G.H.Q. More than that, it goes back to the Government. We were landed with these Crusaders straight out of the factory. If we'd had time to train –'

'It's a matter of logistics.'

'If you mean they had more tanks than we had and better ones, you're damn well right.'

The Colonel said something, but his mind did not seem to be on the argument. Throughout lunch, which was served by plumply attractive Doris, Tony was uneasily aware of the bird eye swivelling round to examine him. Occasionally Hasty seemed about to say something decisive. Suppose it was, 'I remember you, you're the man who sold me that dud car,' what would he say? Perhaps an outright denial would be the best thing. But lunch passed without the decisive word being spoken, and over coffee he saw a chance and took it. Hasty had been talking about spending some time in Edinburgh, and Tony repeated the name of the city.

'What's that?' The bird eye swivelled.

'It's where we met. You say you were up there on the Common-wealth Research Board. I was working with a group collecting funds and goods for the underdeveloped countries.' It was true that he had worked in Scotland for eighteen months as local representative of an insurance company that had gone suddenly into liquidation.

'Maybe.' Hasty did not sound enthusiastic. 'Some of those crackpot committees did more harm than good. No use coddling these chaps. Got to tell 'em, not ask 'em.'

'Just what I thought. That's why I gave it up.'

'Finished your coffee?' The General was fretting. 'Come on then, Ted. I've got something here that's going to shake your ideas up. Not logistics, just plain common sense. I've got some letters that will surprise you.'

They went to the library. The General was exhilarated by such discussions, and today his back was straight and his manner commanding, as they must have been twenty-five years ago. Tony excused himself, saying that he wanted to go round the farms. Before doing so he rang the Golden Sovereign again, spoke to Armitage, and learned that the letter had been sent by mistake.

'You can tear it up, though I wouldn't say that if it had been left to me.' Armitage sounded venomous. 'Cotton makes us pay five per cent of bad debts.'

'I didn't like the tone of it,' Tony said boldly. 'If I had a word with Mr Cotton he might not like it either.'

The telephone was slammed down without reply. He need not have drawn out the money, but there was no need to worry about that for some weeks. He drove round the farm and had a long talk with one of the farmers about repairs needed to one of his barns. Tony promised to look into it. Whatever builder was employed, it would not be Clinker.

When he got back Hasty's car had gone. He met Doris in the hall and asked her if anything had happened.

'Only one telephone call. For the master. He's in the study, asking for you. Soon as you came in, he said.'

So Hasty had remembered. Well, he would simply deny it, that was all. It was one man's word against another's. He gave Doris a little pat on the bottom as she turned away.

In the library the General sat at the desk with some of the precious papers in front of him. His knotted hands rested on them. Against the light from the window his fine profile looked weary.

'Sit down.' Tony sat. The General did not look at him, did not speak.

He felt it necessary to break the silence. 'I don't know what Colonel Hasty has said –'

'Hasty?' Eyebrows were raised in surprise. 'He thought you seemed a nice young chap.'

Everything was all right. As a gambler he knew that if you played your luck you couldn't lose. But why was the old man so silent? 'How did the discussion go?'

'I'm an old fool.' Was that a reply to what he had said? 'Should have known better.'

What was he going on about? From the papers on the desk the knotted hand picked a piece of pink paper, held it out. He stared at it unbelievingly. It was the cheque he had cashed that morning.

'The bank called me up. Couldn't understand it. Then they sent this back.' But why, he wanted to ask, but why? The knotted hand pointed to the signature. What was wrong with it? 'Geoffrey', he read, admiring again the tail at the end of the 'y'. Then he looked again. 'Geofrey': he had missed out one 'f'.

'Well done but careless.' The old voice spoke heavily. The piece of paper was torn across once, then again. The pieces fluttered on the floor. So he was not going to do anything about it. Tony tried to speak, found it impossible. The voice went inexorably on.

'If you were in debt, why not come to me? I would have given you money. But I suppose you've done this before, it's a usual thing. As I said it seems a good piece of work.'

'I haven't done it before.'

'And you won't do it again? But if you didn't cheat me like this you'd do it in some other way. Through the accounts perhaps. Maybe you do that already, I don't want to know. You can keep the money, but I can't have you here. You must go.'

The face was still turned away from him, the voice was never raised a semi-tone above the even uninterested note in which you might talk about the weather. Suddenly all this was too much for him, the bloody condescension of the man saying he could keep the money, the refusal to look at him, the manner which implied that he was an inferior being. As if he hadn't earned every penny of that money and much more, as if any money could have compensated for the year he had spent listening to that interminable drivel about the war, pretending to take an interest in the attempt to cancel out mistakes by rewriting history, losing games of billiards which he could easily have won. You think you're giving me something, he wanted to say, but you aren't, I've given you one of the years of my life. He got up and almost ran out of the room, up the stairs to his bedroom. When he came back he had the Bobo letters with him. He tore open the envelope and put the letters on the desk right under the nose disdainfully turned away from him as if he were a bad smell.

'What about these, then?' he asked in the shrill tone that overcame him under any stress of emotion. It upset him to see that his own hands were shaking while those that took the letters and turned them over were perfectly steady.

Now the old man did turn and look at him. 'Where did they come from? Miriam said she had destroyed them.'

'They were in the lumber room.'

'And you kept them?'

'Don't you understand? If I'd been what you think I am I could have asked for money, I could have made you give me money.'

'Blackmail,' the quiet voice said meditatively.

He shook his head violently. 'I never asked, did I, never said anything. There are your filthy letters, you can burn them, do what you like with them.'

'They are not my letters. They were not sent to me.'

That took him aback. He did not believe it, but he was taken aback. 'My own darling G. Your name's Geoffrey. And some of them are to my darling Gee gee –'

'My son's name was Gordon. We called him Gee gee, and so did some of his friends.'

'Your son,' he repeated foolishly, and in a moment saw that he had been mistaken, that the letters had been written by one young man to another, not by a young man to a middle-aged one.

'These letters came back to us with the rest of my son's papers when he was killed. We had no idea that he was homosexual. It came as a great shock. I don't know why Miriam did not destroy them, but I shall burn them as you suggest.' He put the letters back into the envelope. 'Your assumption was wrong, these letters would have been useless for blackmailing purposes. In a way I wish you had tried. You are a scoundrel, Scott-Williams. I want you out of here at once.'

He could think of nothing to say except that he would have to pack. Now at last the General's voice was raised, raised in the kind of shout that must long ago have frightened subordinates.

'Get out, sir. Out of my sight.' The voice dropped again to its contemptuous monotone, as though a brief gale had spent itself. 'You may take a taxi to the station and charge it to my account.'

When he left the room the old man had his hands on the envelope, and was staring at the wall.

Chapter 5

On that Wednesday night he stayed at a hotel off Shaftesbury Avenue. By midday on Thursday he had found several reasons for cheerfulness. After withdrawing the money he had more than three hundred pounds in his wallet. The possession of actual cash always gave him a sense of well-being which he never had when reading a credit balance on a pass sheet. He had got away from Leathersley House showing a profit, and he was rid for ever of that boring old General. Now that he had left, it seemed to him that he could not have stood it for another week. The feeling of freedom was delightful, the knowledge that he could do exactly what he liked, walk through the West End, have lunch and take as long as he wished over it, go to the cinema, without any need to look at his watch and think that he ought to get back to play billiards or do this, that or the other. Leathersley House had seemed a cushy billet at the time, but in retrospect his duties appeared intolerably onerous.

And there was another reason for cheerfulness. The Fiona prospect.

What was the prospect exactly? You were a good-looking young man and a millionaire's daughter had shown that she was powerfully attracted by you. Putting it crudely, how did you get your hands on some of the cash? The first thing would be to find out whether she had a private income settled on her, enough to maintain them both. If she had, marriage without Papa's consent would be indicated. If she had only an allowance that might be cut off, then he would have to meet Mallory. He imagined the scene, Mallory saying that he was a fine young Englishman, offering him a job in the organization, Fiona in ecstasies, marriage in church with half London society there. But this was unhappily not probable, tycoons were notoriously tough and suspicious, his background might be investigated. Look at it another way then. Mallory saying this man's a fortune hunter, Fiona in tears, I'm going to marry him anyway, Mallory threatening to cut off her allowance – but behind the scenes taking out his cheque book and saying 'How much?' What would he settle for? Ten thousand pounds seemed a reasonable amount.

He rang up the house that evening, asked for Miss Mallory. A man's voice said, 'Who is that speaking?'

'Tony Scott-Williams.'

A pause. Then her voice, rather subdued. 'Hallo.'

'Fiona. Remember me?'

'Yes.'

'Was that your father?'

'No, the butler.'

The butler. Certainly some people knew how to live. 'I want to see you.'

'Yes.'

'Fiona, I have to see you.'

Her voice, guarded, low, said, 'I want to see you too. Are you at your uncle's?'

'In London. Can you come up? This weekend.'

'My father –'

With what he hoped was powerful urgency he said, 'I *have* to see you.'

There was a pause, so long that he thought the connection had been broken. Then her voice again. 'All right. I'll manage somehow. But I can't come till Saturday.'

Before she could ask the address of his flat he said quickly, 'Let's meet in the Ritz Bar. Can you come up for lunch?'

'Not till the evening. About six.'

'Six o'clock, the Ritz Bar, I'll be waiting.'

'Yes.'

'Darling, I long for it.'

'I do too. I have to go now.'

'Good-bye, darling.'

'Good-bye.'

She was well and truly hooked. Play your cards right, he told himself, and you've landed the fish.

He had no friend from whom he could borrow a flat, so he had to rent one. It cost him forty pounds to take a furnished flat for a week. It was high up in a modern block near Marble Arch, a marvellous position, and he regarded the money as an investment. He told the agents that he was staying over in London for only a few days and wanted to do some entertaining that couldn't be done in a hotel. Whether or not they believed him, they took the eight fivers he gave them and let him move in immediately. He got in a stock of drink – there was a cocktail cabinet, something that he'd always wanted – hung up his clothes and settled down with the feeling that he was there for ever.

When we're married, he told himself, we'll always live in places like this, places where every room is warm and you can pad about naked, and people live their own lives next door to each other without knowing the names of their neighbours, and you can get almost anything you want by lifting a telephone. He looked at London sparkling beneath him and thought, this is my world, it belongs to me and I'm going to have it. The temptation was strong to go out, find in a bar the kind of middle-aged woman who responded to his smile as if she was a fire waiting for a match, and bring her back here. But he resisted it. Anyway, the setting was wrong. Women of that sort liked to give you things, to feel that they owned you, and they would be disconcerted to find him installed in such style and at such an address. He stayed in the flat from Thursday evening until Saturday morning, having meals sent up to him.

Just after six o'clock she came into the Ritz Bar, looking slightly nervous, carrying a small suitcase, and wearing a rather unsuitable hat. He was pleased to see that she had abandoned the dark glasses. He commented on that. 'I feel I'm seeing you properly.'

She ordered gin and tonic and drank it in sips. 'Was it a job to get away?'

'Not too bad. Daddy hadn't got anyone coming down this weekend. He wanted to know where I was going. I told him I was staying with a girl-friend. I fixed it with her too.'

'Clever girl.' He patted her hand. 'For a minute on the phone I thought you didn't want to see me.'

'Tracey was there – the butler. I had to be careful.'

After a second drink her manner was perceptibly easier. 'It's wonderful to get up to London. I feel so cooped up down there.'

'I'm your good angel. I just wave my magic wand and say "Come up to London", and it's done.'

She looked round. 'It's rather quiet here.'

'Kind of traditional.' He was worried that she might have preferred to meet somewhere else, Claridge's or Hatchetts which he knew only as names. 'I often use this as a meeting place because it's so convenient.'

'Of course.' She fiddled with her handbag.

'But let's get out. Harry, my bill.' He had taken the precaution of learning the waiter's name. It was time to be masterful. He steered her up the stairs, got a taxi and kissed her ardently as soon as they were inside.

'Are we going to your flat?'

'Where else? I'm repaying hospitality.' He laughed.

She disengaged herself. 'Tony, I don't want you to think I do this with everybody.'

'Darling Fiona.'

'It's because I like you. Very much. I don't just want an affair for a weekend.'

What do you know, he thought, I believe *she's* going to propose to *me*. But the time wasn't right for anything of that sort. He took her hand and kissed it, which seemed to cover the case.

He watched when they crossed the entrance hall and went up in the lift to see if she was impressed, and there could be no doubt that she was although she tried not to show it. He was apologetic when he unlocked the door. 'It's not much like home, I'm afraid, but then I'm not here all the time.'

Inside she exclaimed with pleasure, particularly at the view. They were on the fourteenth floor and quite a lot of London was spread out beneath them.

'Yes, I do think it's something rather special myself,' he said with perfect truthfulness. 'But of course you've got your own flat in Chelsea.'

'My father has. I'm hardly ever there. Anyway, it hasn't got a view like this.'

He came up behind her, put his hands on her breasts. She turned round and her blue eyes questioned him. 'I meant what I said, Tony. I'm playing for keeps.'

Wonderful words. 'So do I, darling. I'm playing for keeps too.' In the bedroom later he asked with attempted casualness whether she had really meant it.

'You know I did.'

'Then what about meeting your father?'

Silence. Her fingers traced a pattern on his thigh. 'I don't think that would be a good idea. Not yet anyway. He doesn't want me to get married. I told you.'

'That's just damned selfish.'

'It would be no good talking to him. You don't know what he's like. I've got my own money, but he won't let me use it to take a flat in town or anything like that. Most of it just stays in the bank.'

He wanted to say that she was over twenty-one and a free agent, but refrained.

'And when I do marry he wants it to be some ghastly local. There's a boy he keeps talking about, the son of one of his friends. Marriage to him would be good for business, might even mean a merger.' She said it without irony and repeated, 'I've got my own money.'

Again he refrained from speaking, this time from asking how much. She went on, looking up at the ceiling, speaking in a sing-song voice.

'You don't understand about Daddy. I can't explain it myself, but if he told me I was to have nothing to do with you I should have to do what he said. Do you know what I dream sometimes? I dream I'm a princess and shut up in a castle where I've got everything anybody could want except freedom. People come and try to free me, to let me out because they're in love with me, but there's an invisible barrier round the castle and as soon as they pass over it their view of me changes and they see me as an old hag, toothless and dirty, so they go away. And in the dream nobody ever gets past the barrier and at the end of the dream I look in the glass and I've become what they believed me to be, filthy and dressed in rags and old.'

'That's just a dream. There aren't any barriers. You can do what you like.'

'Oh, but I can't. Someone else has to do it, someone has to help me.' She turned and clung to him, pressed her naked body to his. 'Help me, Tony.'

With everything arranging itself better than he could have hoped, he knew the importance of not saying a wrong word. It seemed best to say the serious thing he had to say lightly. 'Here's some news, Princess. Prince Charming's arrived, and guess how he got past that invisible barrier? With a special licence.'

'A special licence,' she echoed wonderingly.

'I'll get one on Monday. You come up to London and, hey presto, the deed's done, the princess is free.' He bounced off the bed, went into the bathroom. Her voice followed him. He put his head round the door. 'What's that?'

'It won't make any difference to you? I mean, to your job and all that.'

'Everyone will be delighted.'

'Shall we live here?'

'Or take a bigger flat,' he said recklessly. 'Come on, let's celebrate, go out on the town.' He felt an overwhelming euphoria at having pulled it off, a debt of gratitude towards the girl who was going to provide him with a permanent income.

They went on the town. He told her that he hardly ever used the Jag in London, driving was such hell, so they took taxis. Over dinner he learned that fifteen hundred a year was settled on her through a trust, although she couldn't touch the capital. There was quite a bit of money in her bank account, she didn't know exactly how much. He confided a few vague details of his stock-broking job, saying that it paid well but he was bored with it and thought of striking out on his own, starting a gambling club perhaps, which was a surefire way of making money. It seemed premature to mention that she would be providing the capital. He suggested that it would be fun to take a look at a club and they ended up in the Here's Sport Club in Soho. Her eyes were wide as he bought a hundred pounds' worth of chips and gave half of them to her. She asked if he could afford it.

'This is celebration night, Princess.' He had called her Princess the whole evening. 'There's plenty more. Anyway, we're going to win. We're playing my system, and it works best with a partner.'

'Was that why you lost down in Landford?'

'It could be,' he said shortly. He did not care for jokes about roulette. He explained to her the Prudential system which they would be playing. You made two bets at each spin of the wheel, a ten pound bet on passe covering the high numbers, and a five pound bet on the numbers from one to six. If a high number came up you won ten pounds and lost five, if a number from one to six turned up you were paid at odds of five to one so that you won twenty-five pounds and lost ten.

'And if it's one of the other numbers?'

'If it's seven to eighteen or zero we lose, but the odds are two to one in our favour. We'll stop when we've won a hundred.'

They very nearly did it, too. She sat on the opposite side of the table from him playing the six number transversal, and the first time she won she gave a small scream of pleasure. At one time they were seventy pounds up. Then the bank had a run in which the numbers between seven and eighteen came up half a dozen times running followed by zero. They were losing a little, Fiona was looking slightly bored, and to amuse her he committed a roulette player's cardinal sin. He changed systems, and began to play a modified version of the Capitalist's system, which involves covering every number on the board except zero and three. When zero turned up he bought another hundred pounds' worth of chips. They lost these when three came up twice in eight spins.

'Two hundred pounds,' she said, and repeated it. 'Just think, if we'd stopped when we were winning –'

'You make rules and you have to keep them,' he said sharply, although he had failed to do so. The exhilaration of gambling was so great for him that it remained for an hour or two afterwards, like the effect of drink, and he had the true gambler's dislike of complaints about losing. 'Better luck next time.'

'Next time?'

'When we're on the other side of the fence, running the club.'

'It was a lovely evening,' she said when they were back at the flat. 'But I wish we hadn't lost that money.'

Euphoria had worn off and he now wished it too, but he controlled his irritation. 'Part of the ceremony of freeing the princess. Let's have a nightcap. We're still celebrating.'

The celebration ended abruptly on Sunday morning.

He woke at half past nine. The princess was still asleep. He went into the living-room, picked up the papers from the hall – he had ordered them with the feeling that the daily delivery of newspapers gave an air of permanency – and carried them into the kitchen to look at while he made breakfast. Turning the pages idly he saw a picture and a story in the gossip column of one paper, passed it by and returned to it, looking incredulously at picture and story.

The picture showed a girl wearing a mini-skirt and a sleeveless brocaded blouse with a hooded headdress through which part of her face was visible. The story was headed: 'Millionaire's Daughter Starts Yashmak Fashion' and it began:

Fiona, up-and-coming daughter of industrial merger-maker Jacob Mallory, is touring Europe in search of something new in the fashion line to rock the younger set. Fiona's landed up in Ismir, Turkey, where she's certainly shaken the natives. It's not the mini-skirt that shocks them, they've seen those before, or even the local dress turned into something so, so sophisticated in the form of the brocaded blouse. No, its the way Fiona uses that traditionally concealing yashmak combined with the rest of the outfit that produces an effect on males. Just imagine what a glance from under that hood will do to them over here. Fiona, a working fashion-spotting for Philippa Phillips Associates, is going on looking for that elusive new something in Greece and Yugoslavia before she comes home.

He went into the living-room and sat down. He felt as dazed as somebody involved in an accident. As he read the story again his lips moved like those of a man spelling out the words. Then he got up, went into the bedroom and opened her case. She had taken clothes out of it last night, and now it was empty. Her handbag was on a chair. He opened it and spilled out the contents. Lipstick, keys – and a letter. The envelope said: 'Miss Mary Tracey, The Cottages, Frankfort Manor.' Tracey – the butler's daughter. It was like some wretched stage farce. No doubt The Cottages were the servants' quarters.

'What are you doing?' The words were whispered. She was watching him from the bed.

He handed her the paper. There was a smell of burning. It was the toast in the kitchen. The smell pervaded the flat. Tears welled into her eyes. She did not speak.

'Well?' he said questioningly, although he knew the answer. 'You're Mary Tracey. The butler's daughter.'

'He's a handyman.'

'I suppose you're a housemaid.'

'I help in the house.'

Another Doris. 'That's why you took me back. Because you knew nobody would be there.' She didn't contradict him. 'And I believed you. What a fool.'

She blew her nose. 'Sometimes she gives me clothes and I wear them when I go into town.'

'Your father's in it too? I spoke to him.'

'I told him I would speak if a friend of Fiona's rang up. I thought –' She didn't say what she thought.

'What the hell were you doing in the Golden Sovereign?'

'I know Claude.' Claude? 'Armitage. He's – he used to be a boy-friend of mine. I worked there for a bit, in the cloakroom.'

A hat check girl. How could he have failed to recognize her for what she was? She went on.

'But I do want to get away. And I do have that dream, I think of myself as a princess waiting for somebody. You've burned the toast. Shall I make some more?'

Did she think he was going to sit down to breakfast with her? The thought of all the money he had spent, the flat, the food and drink, the roulette last night, rose in his mouth like bile. 'You can leave. Any time. Now.'

'You don't want to go on with it? I suppose you wouldn't. Still, let's have breakfast.'

She got out of bed and moved towards the kitchen. He took her by the shoulders. 'I said you could leave now.'

'I don't see why you're so het up. After all, you've had some fun out of it, and you've got plenty of money.'

'Plenty of money,' he said bitterly. A moment afterwards he regretted the tone in which he had spoken, but it was too late. She began to laugh.

'Don't tell me you haven't got any money. Oh, that's good, that's really good.'

'I spent it on you.'

' "There's plenty more",' she mimicked him. 'So you were after my allowance? And I only said it because I didn't want you to think I'd be too much of a burden. It really is funny.' Her tone and accent changed so that he could not think how he had ever been deceived. 'I suppose you fiddled this place too.'

'It's rented.'

She stopped laughing. 'But you're clever. Why don't we do something together?'

'What?'

'I'm not staying at home, you know, I'm getting out. This is what I want, what we both want.' She put a finger in her mouth, bit a nail. 'Let's team up.'

'Why don't you just go?'

'After breakfast.' While she was eating her toast she continued to talk. 'I've got a thing for you. And I'm not a fool, you know. We'd make a good team.'

'I want you to leave.'

She packed her things into the little suitcase. 'Better luck next time. You might wish me that too.' He did not reply. 'Trouble is you've got no sense of humour.'

When she had gone he lay on the bed and smoked a cigarette. He had several days to run before his week's tenancy was out, but what use was the flat to him now? With less than fifty pounds of his money left he did what he had done before. He took refuge with Widgey.

PART TWO

A Dream of Loving Women

Chapter 1

Widgey had not changed in the two years since he had last seen her. The ash was long on the cigarette that stuck out of the corner of her mouth, and she sat at one side of a table in her private parlour with cards in front of her and a woman on the other side of the table. The woman was perhaps fifty, certainly younger than Widgey, and her fingers were crusted with jewels. She nervously twisted a gold bracelet on her left arm.

'A black ace, a red ten, a black queen. Not the queen of spades, that's something,' Widgey was saying as he opened the door. She said hallo to Tony without surprise, holding up her face so that he could kiss her cheek. Ash dropped on the table and she brushed it away. 'That explains part of it.'

'What does it explain?' The woman opposite panted like a Pekinese.

'Ace of clubs, ten of diamonds, queen of clubs. Means an unexpected visitor. I thought it would be for you, but it's for me. My nephew Tony. This is Mrs Harrington.'

'But it's *my* future you were reading.'

'You just can't tell, dear. Come for a visit? You can have your old room, thirteen.'

'You mean to say you don't mind?' Bulbous Pekinese eyes rolled at Tony.

'Course he doesn't, he's not superstitious any more than I am. He doesn't believe the cards and I don't really.' Widgey reshuffled expertly, stubbed out her cigarette, rolled another with paper and tobacco from an old metal case. 'Just they seem to come true, that's all.'

'Why are you starting again?'

'He disturbed the flow, and anyway when one thing's happened you always want to shuffle again, gets confused otherwise. Let's see now, two of diamonds, eight of spades, jack of hearts, not very exciting. See you later,' she called to Tony.

Room thirteen was an attic, from which across the roofs of houses you could glimpse the sea. As he looked round at the cracked wash basin, the rose-patterned paper which didn't quite cover the whole wall because Widgey had bought a discontinued line and there had not been enough of it, at the painted chest of drawers scarred by cigarette burns and the disproportionately large mahogany tallboy which she had bought with him at a sale for thirty shillings, he felt a sensation of relief. He threw himself on the bed, which was placed so that you were likely to strike your head on the coved ceiling if you got up from it hurriedly, then after a few minutes began to unpack his things. The painted chest was still uncertainly balanced because one leg was shorter than the other three and the little piece of cork under it became displaced as soon as anything was put inside. And, yes, the top drawer still contained 'The Bible For Commercial Travellers', bound in red leather with the editorial injunction on the opening page: '*Read this book* and it will bring you comfort.' He turned to the back flyleaf and saw that the old message was still there, written in a flowing commercial traveller's hand: 'If no comfort obtained try ringing Anna,' followed by what was presumably Anna's telephone number. He had come home.

He had first visited the Seven Seas Hotel when he was five years old, brought down by his father and mother to see 'the place where Belle's set up to poison people', as his father put it. That was during the war. There was barbed wire along the sea front, they had to bring ration cards, and his father complained that they did not get enough food to fill a gnat's belly. Mrs Widgeon – her name was Arabella and she was his mother's sister – was the wife of a heroic fighter pilot who had been wounded, discharged from the service, and was in the process of dying quietly. His father was of the opinion that Alec had opted for a quiet life and that there was not much wrong with him, and he did not really change this view even after Alec had proved his case by dying just after the war ended. For years they had taken their family holiday at the Seven Seas, but his father had never really liked it. It was, he contemptuously said, not a proper hotel but a boarding house, which served only breakfast and an evening meal. After his mother died and his father married again, Tony had come down alone. If room thirteen was free he always stayed in it.

He could never remember Widgey looking any different from the way she looked now, a small woman with grey untidy hair who rolled her own cigarettes and always had one in a corner of her mouth. She ran the Seven Seas with the accompaniment of a continually changing staff, and she must have been less haphazard than she seemed because people came back year after year. Or perhaps it was the haphazardness they liked. Certainly it had always delighted Tony. There was no regular time for the evening meal at the Seven Seas, or rather there was a time but it was most erratically observed. There were no rules about not taking girls, or bottles, or both up to your room. Widgey had never applied for a drinks licence but drink often appeared mysteriously on the tables. Evenings of sparse meals would alternate with occasions when the astonished guests would see a turkey or a goose brought into the dining-room, to be carved by Widgey and served with the appropriate trimmings, cranberry jelly, apple sauce, stuffing. There was no question of the door being locked at eleven. The sign in the hall 'Last In Please Lock Up' sometimes led to a reveller returning at three in the morning and finding the door locked against him, but Widgey would wave aside apologies and complaints when she staggered down in her dressing gown to open it. *Never apologize, never explain*: she might have adopted the motto had she known it. Her charm for Tony was that she was never surprised, reproachful, or disappointed by the conduct of others. In adolescence the Seven Seas became increasingly for him a home from home.

Home was a semi-detached house in Eltham, one of London's more undistinguished outer suburbs. The house was one in a long group put up during the nineteen twenties in the worst period of between-the-wars jerry building, and it fronted on to a main road where the traffic roared past both night and day. His remembrances of childhood were patchy. Going to the local school, writing his name *Anthony Jones*, and being upset because a teacher said 'Jones, that's the most *common* name there is,' wishing he had a brother or a sister, a terrible time in the school lavatories one afternoon with some older boys, good reports changing to critical ones. ('His ability is clear, but doesn't try hard . . . Can do well enough but doesn't seem interested.') His father was away a lot during the week, because he was a traveller. Tony told this to other boys, and could never understand why they were not more impressed. In his mind he saw his father travelling from one place to another, going to strange cities where wonderful things happened to him. On Friday, or sometimes Thursday, evenings when Mr Jones came home in the little car and brought a big battered brown case into the house and said that it had been a good week or a bad week and that now he must do his reports, Tony associated these reports with travel, something similar to the essays he was asked to write in school about the most exciting thing that had happened on your holidays. Not until he was eleven years old did he realize that his father's travelling was not done for pleasure but to sell things, at one time electrical equipment, at another a new kind of electric lamp, at another still a range of toys.

Mr Jones was a short stout man with a thick moustache and an ebullient way of talking. When, on returning after the week's travelling, he exclaimed 'Hallo hallo, what have we here?' and lifted Tony on to his shoulders, the boy was conscious of a pungent smell which he eventually recognized as a blend of cigarette smoke, beer and male sweat. Mr Jones was a great sportsman or at least a great watcher of sport, and in the winter they always went together on Saturday afternoons to watch a professional football match. At the match he would shout criticism freely. 'Pass, you fool,' he would cry. 'Don't fiddle faddle with the ball, man, get rid of it . . . what's happened to your eyesight, ref, go and get some glasses . . . dirty, send him off.' Occasionally they would find themselves in a nest of opposition supporters and then a verbal altercation might go on throughout the match. When the exchange of insults seemed likely to reach the point of blows Mr Jones would calm down suddenly. 'What's up then, what's the matter, it's a game, isn't it?' he would say, adding afterwards to his son, 'Just as well you were there, I almost lost my temper with that fellow, I might have done something I'd have been sorry for.' On the way home they often fell in with a bunch of home supporters and the discussion, no longer an argument, would be continued.

On Sunday mornings they would kick a ball about in the small back garden or on the nearby common. Tony would stand between a cap and a scarf placed to represent goal posts and would dive to try to save his father's rather feeble shots. 'That was great,' Mr Jones would say after these occasions, which ended with him panting hard from the reputedly weak heart which had kept him out of the armed forces. 'You're going to be a smashing little goalkeeper, you'll be playing for the school in no time.' The truth was, however, that Tony was no good at games, and didn't like them. Awareness of this was kept from his father until the day when Tony said he had been picked as goalkeeper and Mr Jones turned up to the match on Saturday morning to find that his son was not even a spectator. There was no row afterwards, but the occasion marked the end of something in their relationship. Afterwards Tony went to no more professional matches, and before long Mr Jones also stopped going.

At about the same time, when he was thirteen, Tony became aware of other things about his father. The smell that had seemed in childhood to be warm, comforting and safe, became extremely disagreeable. He learned to identify the evenings when his father came home more than usually cheerful as those on which beer could be smelt strongly on his breath, and indeed it seemed to him at times that his father's whole body reeked of beer and that the smell permeated his clothes. He associated this smell in some way with the incident in the school lavatories, which had never been repeated. And he wondered for the first time about his father's relationship with his mother. When Mr Jones came home he would embrace his wife in a bear hug and say something like 'Give us a buss, Sheila, me bonny lass. You're a sight for sore eyes and no mistake.' His mother would accept this embrace rather as if she were a statue with movable arms, which she laced in a loose and formal manner behind her husband's back. After a moment she would move away and say that she must get supper. Her husband, duty done, then dropped into an armchair, put on his slippers, and asked how every little thing was going on at school. Was this the way all mothers and fathers went on, could it be said that they loved each other. This was a question to which he never found an answer. Certainly they never had rows, there was hardly ever an argument, although Mr Jones was argumentative enough with the neighbours who came in sometimes for a drink or coffee. At any sign of family argument, however, his wife would say that she must get the lunch or the supper, or clean the bedrooms, or wash some clothes.

He saw much more of his mother than of his father, yet she was never so real a presence to him. Like her sister she was untidy and vague, but unlike Widgey she was shapelessly fat, with an indeterminate figure shrouded in sacking-like dresses of anonymous colour. Like her sister again she was interested in the unseen world, but where Widgey read the future in cards, and had once possessed a tarot pack before evolving her own system of interpreting ordinary playing cards, Mrs Jones was interested in spiritualism. She took the *Psychic News* and similar periodicals and was a member of a Spirit Circle which held regular séances. Occasionally she went to meetings in central London, and at one of these she herself had fainted after receiving a spirit message from her brother Jack who had been killed in an air raid. Sometimes Tony would come home from school and find his mother, with three or four other ladies, sitting round an ouija board or conducting spirit rapping sessions at a table. He would go into the kitchen and eat his bread and butter and jam listening to the murmur of voices, raised occasionally to small screeches of pleasure or dismay, that came from next door. When the session was over Mrs Jones would float in at the kitchen door, rather like a spirit herself, and ask whether he wanted anything more to eat. Then he did his homework, and after that in the summer went out to play with other boys on the common, in the winter stayed in and read books. Television was not yet endemic, and they had no set in their home.

When he grew up he wondered often whether she had wanted a child, and concluded that upon the whole she hadn't. She never spoke harshly to him, saw that he was clean and that his clothes were neat, but as he looked back it seemed that she had shown him no sign of love. Sometimes the ladies who came to the table rapping sessions would say what a delightful boy he was, so good looking, so quiet, so well behaved. His mother would smile vaguely and agree with them, but did she really think so? 'He's no *trouble*,' they would cry as if this were some kind of miracle, and this was true until the time of the Creighton affair, when he was fourteen years old.

Creighton was a big, rather stupid boy who had a gang of which Tony became a member. His qualification was the possession of a roulette wheel. The wheel had been bought by his mother at a sale, in a lot together with a pair of Victorian vases, which were what she really wanted, and a number of books. Among the books was one called *The Winning Rules, Or Roulette Practically Considered* by Sperienza, a gentleman who had played the game for many years at Monte Carlo. From this book Tony learned that you may bet en plein or à cheval, on a transversal or a carré or on one of the even chances. He learned also of systems that practically guaranteed you against losing, the Infallible System, the Wrangler's System, the D'Alembert System, and many others. He discovered the meaning of martingales and anti-martingales, intermittences and permanences. Why was it necessary to work, he asked his father, when you could play the Infallible System instead? His father merely said that he shouldn't believe any of that rubbish.

Was it rubbish? Tony and the gang played roulette, but few of them used any sort of system, and he could not make up his mind. After a time the rest of them got bored, and turned to other things. The gang's exploits were not remarkable. They took girls up into the nearby woods where Tony was initiated into sex, and they also pilfered goods from shops in Lewisham. The usual technique was for three of them to go in and talk to the assistant while a fourth took something off the counter or stall. The things were not of much value. Sometimes Creighton sold them, at other times they threw them away. Then four of them, including Tony, were caught in Woolworth's and brought into Juvenile Court, where they were all put on probation. The effects of the affair reverberated through the Jones household. Mr Jones came back specially from Gloucester to speak for his son in Court. Later, at home, he was almost incoherent with rage.

219

'That a son of mine should –' he began, and tried again. 'I can't understand it when you come from a good home. You all come from good homes.' Later he said, 'I should have known. Look at this last report, doesn't try. Doesn't *try*. Why don't you try, eh? You'll come to a bad end. He'll come to a bad end, Sheila, I'll tell you that.' A quick switch of attack. 'And you know whose fault it'll be. Yours.'

His wife put a hand to her wide bosom. 'Mine?'

'Too much freedom. If you hadn't given him so much freedom –'

'I must see to the potatoes.' She elevated slowly from the chair in which she had been sitting and floated out of the room.

The Creighton affair marked another turning point. In a way Tony had been terrified by the serious way in which everybody treated something so simple, something as you might say that everybody did, but what was chiefly borne in on him was the difference between practice and precept. He had often jumped off a bus with his father before the conductor had got round to collecting the fares. His father had winked and said, 'Freeman's ride, Tony, that's the best.' At Christmas time they had more than once gone to a brewery where one of the men would come out in a van and stop round a corner. Bottles of whisky would be exchanged for money, and after the van had driven away Mr Jones would chortle. 'Half price, less than half price. Makes it taste better.' How was the man able to sell them whisky at less than half price? Another wink. 'Don't ask, son. It fell off the back of the van.' When he understood what this meant he wondered: what was the difference between whisky falling off the back of the van and things disappearing from a store counter?

At fifteen he got his first job, as an insurance company clerk. He had been working for three months when he came home one evening to find supper in the oven. There was no sign of his mother. He ate supper and waited for her to come home. At eleven o'clock he went upstairs and found her lying fully dressed on the bed, with an empty bottle that had contained sleeping tablets by her side. She must have taken them immediately after putting his supper into the oven. She left no message, but there were a number of letters on the dressing-table, written to her husband by a woman who signed herself Nora. These letters, left carelessly in an old overcoat, were thought to provide the reason for her death. Tony wondered – but this was much later – whether the loss of love or of respectability had been the decisive stroke. Or had she simply wanted to move over into the spirit world about which she was so curious?

Three months after his wife's death Mr Jones married Nora, a brawny peroxide blonde with a flat Midlands voice, and soon after that Tony left the insurance company and went down to Widgey. He never returned to Eltham and never wrote to his father. He had had many jobs since then, but had held none for more than a few months before going to Leathersley House. He had sold insurance, had acted as debt collector for some book-makers, and had worked as a salesman on commission for several firms. In all of these occupations he had practised a little fiddle, something had dropped off the back of the van as it were. He had kept back some of the insurance premiums, put a percentage of the collected debts into his own pocket, and with the co-operation of somebody in the office of a firm of vacuum cleaner manufacturers had sold a number of cleaners which never passed through the company books.

Such activities meant that you could never stay in one place for long, and Tony would have accepted if he had known it the philosophical idea that life itself implies movement, a permanent flow. Every so often, when he was in the money, he would play roulette, but he had never possessed enough capital to give any system the financial backing it needed, and the result almost always showed itself on the losing side. After leaving Eltham he abandoned the undesirable Jones, and since then had called himself Scott-Williams, Lees-Partridge and Bain-Truscott. He usually placed his origin in the colonies, and said something deprecating about his name. For a short time he had cherished ideas of becoming a journalist, and had taken a course in short-hand and typing at evening classes. He had found it impossible to get a job on a paper, but these accomplishments had been useful when at times he had been compelled to do secretarial work for private employers. Most of these jobs bored him quickly. Others involved too much work, and in two cases he had been dismissed because the lady of the house made advances which were noticed by her husband. There was something hungry but yearning about Tony's looks that was especially attractive to women over forty. Such women, he slowly realized, wished to be a mother to him and at the same time wanted him to be a lover to them. There was something vaguely disagreeable about this, but the thought had crossed his mind that he might marry one of these ladies. The proposition, however, had never been a practical one because they always had husbands.

Easter was over and only half a dozen people were staying at the Seven Seas, a young couple who looked as if they were just married, a husband and wife in their seventies, he wearing a deaf aid and she tottery, a rabbit-faced clergyman whose lips moved ceaselessly perhaps in prayer, and Mrs Harrington. Supper was tomato soup, thinly sliced cold meat and salad, and ice-cream. Obviously this was one of the bad days. Widgey appeared only intermittently at meals, and was not present at this one. The food was eaten almost in silence. The young couple whispered to each other as though in church, the clergyman's lips moved, Mrs Harrington viewed food and company with a fixed smile. Only the deaf old man said, 'What's this, then, what's this?' as each course came up. 'Tomato soup . . . it's cold meat, dear, mostly ham I think,' his wife quavered and then powerfully repeated as he turned towards her the deaf aid which made a slight whistling sound.

Afterwards he signed the visitors' book firmly, 'Anthony Bain-Truscott,' with a fictitious address in London, and went to see Widgey. She sat in an armchair in the parlour reading a romance called *Love and Lady Hetty*. She put the book down, marking the place carefully.

'Just having my evening cupper. Want one?' She took the kettle off a small gas ring, got two unmatching cups from a cupboard, made tea, rolled a cigarette and said, 'Well?'

The tea was very hot, thick and in some mysterious way very sweet, although she had put in no sugar. 'How do you mean, Widgey?'

'What's up? Landing here without even a telegram. What name, by the way?'

'Bain-Truscott.'

'Tony for me.' She swilled tea round her mouth. False teeth clattered slightly. 'No need to say anything. Any real trouble, I'd like to know.'

'There's nothing.' But he felt an urgent need to talk about the way in which he had been deceived. 'It was a damned girl.' He told her about the Fiona who had turned out to be Mary and was indignant when she laughed. The laugh turned into a cough, ash dropped from her cigarette. She drank some more tea, stopped coughing.

'Glad it's no worse. You ought to settle down.' He did not answer this. 'Broke, are you?'

'I've got some money.'

'Your father wrote the other day, asked if I'd heard from you. Don't worry, I won't tell him you're here. He's had an accident, broken his leg, laid up.'

'Let him rot.'

'He's not my favourite man.'

'He killed mother.' He wondered why he spoke so fiercely when he had never been close to his mother as he had to his father.

'Sheila killed herself. She was a stupid cow. She should never have married.' She did not amplify this statement.

The conversation made him uncomfortable. He said flirtatiously, '*You* ought to marry again, Widgey.'

'Who'd have me? They'd be marrying the Seven Seas. But you should think about it, you're getting on. Sure you aren't in trouble?'

'Oh, Widgey.'

'Just I've got a feeling. Hardly ever wrong, my feelings.'

'They're wrong this time,' he said a little snappishly. As he bent to kiss her he caught her characteristic smell of tobacco blended with something both sweet and sharp like eau-de-cologne. The past rolled over him in waves, the years of bucket and spade holidays, the years when he had come down alone and walked about looking for girls. One of the rolling waves

223

was composed of pure affection. 'I won't be any trouble.'

'I don't mind a little trouble. I just wish you knew what you were doing, that's all.'

'That's ridiculous.' He made a gesture that embraced his well-cut clothes and his personality. 'What's wrong?'

'Nothing,' she said flatly. He went upstairs, and to bed.

Chapter 2

He spent the next forty-eight hours recovering his poise, as others convalesce from influenza. There could be no doubt that the Fiona-Mary affair had been a fiasco. He recalled it continually like a man exploring a sore place with his tongue, feeling each time the shock that had run through him on reading the story in the paper. The thought that he had been deceived was hard to endure.

Southbourne had grown dramatically since the war, sprouting a holiday camp and glass cliffs of flats, but it was still a small resort, a lesser Hastings rather than a miniature Brighton. He walked up and down the promenade as he had when a youth, moving very slowly like a man recovering from illness. He wandered beside the sea, played the slot machines on the pier, and on a day of blustery rain listened to the concert party in the Pier Pavilion. The season had not begun, and there was only a sprinkling of people in the canvas seats. Afterwards he went into the café under the Pavilion's dome, ordered a pot of tea and toast and sat staring through the plate glass window at the sea.

'Mr Bain-Truscott. I thought it was you.' Mrs Harrington stood beside his table. 'Isn't this the most awful weather?' She hovered, twirling a damp umbrella. At his suggestion she sat down and drank a cup of tea. They laughed together when the waitress said that a pot for two would cost more than a pot for one.

'English seaside resorts.' Tony shook his head. 'Can you wonder more and more people go abroad for holidays.'

'Are you a great traveller?'

'I know France pretty well. Mostly around Paris.' One of his secretarial jobs had taken him to France for a week. It was the only time he had been out of England.

'Ah, Paris in the spring,' Mrs Harrington sighed.

He moved off this dangerous ground. 'You're taking an early holiday.'

'Not exactly a holiday. We used to live here and Alec Widgeon was a great friend of Harrington's. I still know several people here. And of course I visit his resting place.' From a crocodile bag she drew a small lace handkerchief and delicately wiped not her eyes but her nose.

'I'm sorry.'

'How could you know. It was a motor bus. Driven by a coloured person. I miss him greatly, although of course he is over there.'

He was about to ask where, when he remembered her attention to the cards. Her brown Pekinese eyes looked into his. 'Harrington was a very vital man.'

He did not know what to say, and remained silent. 'You're Widgey's nephew, aren't you? She's a remarkable woman. Such intensity of feeling. I really think she *knows* things. Was your mother her sister?'

'Yes.' He started to explain about the colonial origins of the Bain-Truscotts. Mrs Harrington waved a jewelled hand and said it added distinction. She was wearing a diamond clasp that must be worth a lot of money if it was real, and no doubt it *was* real. And that large emerald ring – he became aware that she had said something and asked her to repeat it.

'I wondered what *you* were doing here.'

'I sometimes come down to stay with Widgey. And I've had rather a shock. I thought I was going to get married, but it was broken off.'

'You'll think I'm a prying old woman.' She gave a trill of falsetto laughter.

'You haven't been prying at all. And I think of you as just the same age as myself.'

'That's very nice even if you don't mean it. Remember, there are just as good fish in the sea.' Her hand, podgy and slightly wrinkled but ablaze with the stones she wore, touched his. As they walked back to the Seven Seas he asked her to call him Tony. He learned her name which, rather dismayingly, was Violet.

On the following day they were going out of the door at the

same time, and he accompanied her on a tour of the town's jewellery shops. She was looking for a pearl choker and examined some that cost three and four hundred pounds, but she did not neglect rings and bracelets. He was impressed by the professional way in which she looked at the things and bargained with the jewellers. In the end she placed a diamond and ruby pendant round her ample neck and asked him if he liked it. He said truthfully that it was very pretty.

'You really think so?' She said to the jeweller, 'I'll give you a hundred and fifty.'

The price was a hundred and seventy-five. The man raised his hands in despair, but she got it at her price after some haggling.

'Will you take it off, Tony.' He stood close behind her, his fingers touched the back of her neck, warm and smooth. He was aware of a faint tremor in her body as he undid the clasp. In the glass her brown eyes, warm and ardent, looked into his.

'You'll think I waste money, but you're wrong,' she said afterwards. 'I may be a fool about a lot of things but I know what I'm looking at with stones. I don't keep them for ever. I sell them after a few years, and I almost always make a profit.'

'I thought you were wonderful. I could never have got the price down like that.'

'Nothing to it. He wouldn't have liked it if I'd just said yes to the asking price.'

He decided to make his financial situation clear. 'A hundred and fifty pounds. By my standards it's a fortune.'

She patted his hand. 'Dear Tony, you're so straightforward. That's one of the things I like about you.'

That evening they had a séance, or rather a table rapping session. It was against Widgey's principles because she only approved of seeing the future in the cards, but it turned out that the deaf man and his tottery wife were interested in the world beyond, and the five of them sat at the round table in the parlour with the lights out. For some minutes nothing happened.

'What's that?' said Deaf aid. 'I heard something.'

They sat in silence. Tony repressed an inclination to giggle. Three sharp knocks were heard. Mrs Deaf aid grunted something unintelligible. Widgey said, 'Have you got a message? Is it for one of us? Two raps means you have.' Two knocks sounded. 'Is it for Mr Bennett?' So that was Deaf aid's name. One knock only. 'For Mrs Bennett?' Again one knock. 'For Mrs Harrington?' Two knocks. 'Is it a close relative?' Two knocks. 'Her husband?' Two knocks.

Tony's right hand was gripped by Mrs Harrington's left. She held it tightly, the rings pressed into his fingers. She continued to hold it as questions and answers continued, slowly because as always in table rapping the answers were confined to plain 'yes' and 'no'. When she herself began to ask questions about life over there her hot fingers slithered over his palm. It appeared that Mr Harrington was happy on the other side, although he missed Violet.

'You were always so busy down here. Are you – is there enough for you to do?' Two knocks, rather peremptory.

Falteringly Mrs Harrington continued. 'I have bought a pendant and I should like your opinion on it.'

The response to this was an absolute fusillade of knocks, irregular ones which gradually became fainter.

'Don't be angry,' Mrs Harrington said pleadingly. 'Don't go away, I have so many more questions.' She asked some, and then Mrs Bennett put a question or two, but the spirit refused to respond.

'We may as well call it a night,' Widgey said. There was the sound of chairs being pushed back. Mrs Harrington took away her hand. As often happens when lights are turned on after darkness, the blinking faces looked guilty. Mrs Harrington was flushed. 'It's strange that it becomes difficult when you reach a really interesting point.'

Widgey rolled and lit a cigarette. 'Why should they answer if they don't want to?'

Mrs Bennett agreed. 'They don't want to know about our lives. Why should we expect to know everything they think and do?'

The conversation continued in this vein. Widgey went out and made them all a cup of tea. They dispersed, the Bennetts first, then Mrs Harrington and Tony. Her room was number eleven, on the floor below his. She opened the door, turned back to him, took his hand.

'I want you to know that I'm grateful.'

'What for?'

'You were so sympathetic. I know you must think I'm foolish.' Her hand still held his, she had moved inside the room and it followed that he was now standing inside the doorway.

'I don't think anything of the sort.'

'Come in.' The injunction was not necessary for now he was quite certainly in the room. He closed the door. Around Mrs Harrington there hung always some curious scent, rather like low-lying mist clinging to the ground on a damp morning, but in the bedroom this heavy cloying smell was thick, as though he were in the lair of some powerful animal.

'Look.' She extended her arm, pointing, and for a moment he was absorbed in the spectacle of the arm itself, revealed as the sleeve of her dress moved up, a fine thick object against which the gold bracelet gleamed. The arm appeared to be pointing at the bed, but now she moved away from him and returned with a framed photograph which she pushed into his hand. It showed the head and shoulders of a tight-faced man whose brow was corrugated by a frown. What was he worried about?

'Harrington.' She spoke reverentially.

Tony returned the photograph to its place beside the bed. Beside it stood another, of a pleasant large house standing in considerable grounds. 'Is that your home?'

'Yes. It's William and Mary. Very pretty, don't you think?'

It was more than pretty, it was tangible evidence of large sums of money, which he saw suddenly adhering to her.

'Harrington was a passionate man. I am a passionate woman.'

He was overpoweringly conscious of her nearness. The scent of her somehow gave the ordinary bedroom the atmosphere of a hotel room used by dozens of men and women for sexual purposes.

'Oh, Tony, Tony.'

'Violet.' In the moment before being enclosed by those plump white arms he thought: I am lost. Then the arms clasped him firmly and bore him back on to the bed which creaked, and

229

even swayed disturbingly, under their weight. Her mouth opened like a sea anemone and sucked him in.

He went quietly up the stairs to his own room at six o'clock the following morning. Violet had told the truth in saying that she was a passionate woman.

Chapter 3

He spent much of the next two days in her company. They walked round the town together, went round the country in her solidly elegant Rover. Tony drove, and it was a pleasure to be behind the wheel of a car again, but at times he felt like a chauffeur.

'In this village there's a nice little antique shop as you go in on the left, just stop there will you,' she would say, or 'I don't think we'll have lunch at the Blue Peacock, it's no good, just take us on to the next village like a dear boy.' Not simply a chauffeur, but a chauffeur-cum-gigolo, for her manner towards him had become distinctly proprietorial, expressed in the requests she made for him to perform small services like getting her scarf and cigarettes. He did not mind her giving him money to pay for things, nor did he really resent being ordered about, but somehow it put their relationship on a footing which he did not feel they had reached. In the night she moaned for him and asked again and again if he loved her, but in the daytime she behaved as though absolutely certain of his dependence on her. What was the end of the situation, what did he want to happen? He was not sure himself.

On Saturday morning he came down just after eleven, feeling weary but looking smart in a very pale sports jacket with dark blue trousers and elegant grey suède shoes. The honeymoon couple were going home and Widgey was at the entrance to tell them good-bye. There was no sign of Violet. Widgey beckoned him with a grimy forefinger and he followed her into the parlour, which was untidier than usual. Half a dozen small receptacles were brim-full of ash and stubs, playing cards were littered over the table as if a midnight poker game had been broken up by a police raid, small bits of orange peel were scattered on the sideboard. Widgey herself was wearing an old grey skirt fastened by safety pins and a dirty blue pullover. The contrast she presented to his own elegance was somehow uncomfortable.

'Sit down.' He sat in one of the stiff rexine covered chairs at the table. She rolled around the cigarette in her mouth, perhaps a sign of embarrassment, then suddenly emitted a powerful stream of smoke from her nose, like steam coming from a horse's nostrils. 'How long are you staying?'

The question took him aback. It was something she had never said to him before. But she did not wait for an answer.

'I'm fond of Violet, known her a long time. What about you?'

'How do you mean?'

She made an irritated gesture, cigarette in hand. Ash fell to the floor. 'What are you going to do?'

He began to feel annoyed. Was he to be blamed because a woman fell in love with him? He moved his shoulders.

'Harrington had some sort of engineering firm. She still owns it. She's got plenty of money, only stays here for old times' sake.' What was she getting at? 'You going to marry her?'

'I don't know. She might not want to.'

'She'd eat you, boy, she'd eat you up alive. Don't do it.'

'It's my business.' He said it with a sharpness he did not intend.

Widgey did not answer but she turned round and he was startled to see tears in her eyes. In the next moment he felt the pricking behind his own eyes, lowered his head and moved towards her. Then she was in the old armchair that had always stood in this room, his face lay on the rough texture of the grey skirt, he was sobbing and she was stroking his hair. He had the common sensation of thinking that the whole incident had happened before, and then he remembered that this was so, that there had been a time in childhood when he had been lost for a couple of hours on the beach and had been brought back by a policeman and been scolded, and had then dirtied his pants. Rejected by his father and mother he had run into the parlour, flung himself weeping into Widgey's lap and pressed his face into the roughness of her skirt. It was as simple as that. He wiped his eyes, got up.

'You're right, it's your business,' she said huskily. 'I'm telling you, that's all. Have you got to get married?'

'I'm not pregnant.'

'You know what I mean.'

'I told you I'm not in any trouble.'

'You will be one day. I was looking at the cards.'

'Oh, the cards.'

'Don't laugh at the cards.' Her face as she said this, thin, small and malevolent, was witch-like. 'And about Violet. Remember what I said.'

'It might be nice to be eaten up.' He giggled. 'By all that money.'

She shrugged. The effect of the conversation was to make him feel that he would marry Violet if she said yes to him. Widgey, he thought, has never been short of money. But he knew that this was unjust, that she would never have done anything simply to get it.

He made the approach that afternoon, in the car, on a head-land overlooking the sea with rain pouring down outside. He had gone for a long walk – alone, because Violet did not appear until just before lunch – and had made up his mind to ignore Widgey. It was time he settled down, he needed to marry some-body with money, and Violet was everything he could reasonably expect. After all, hadn't he thought in relation to some of those Violetish ladies in the past that he could happily settle down with them if they weren't married already? And when he thought of himself as the master of that delightful house, three or four servants, no doubt the squire of the village – and of course a trip abroad every year or more often, with inevitably a flutter at the casino – why should he hesitate? And flutter was the wrong word, he would have money enough to play the Prudential or the Rational System, and with enough capital you couldn't lose. The money would bring him independence. Certainly Violet was not up to Fiona, but Fiona had not been real and Violet was unquestionably there in the flesh. You had to think about the future, and it was nonsense to talk about being eaten alive.

Afterwards he could not remember what words he had spoken in the desire to avoid the straight question, 'Will you marry me?' but whatever the words may have been they were not mis-understood. The car had a bench seat and in a moment Violet was upon him, holding him in her arms so that his very slight recoil pushed the side of his body against the door. The door handle dug into his ribs. Her mouth was on his, her warm strong scent overpowered him.

'Darling Tony, we're going to be so happy. You don't know how lonely I've been.'

'Not any more.'

'Not any more. A woman needs a man to look after her.'

He found himself being desperately honest. 'I haven't got any money.'

'What does it matter? I've got enough for two.'

He moved slightly, almost lolling back on the seat. The door handle stuck into his side just below the armpit, like a hard finger.

'We could travel abroad,' he said interrogatively.

'Yes. You'd like that, wouldn't you?'

Yes, he would like that. The hot animal breath was on him, the pop eyes looked into his own. Outside the rain changed suddenly to hail. It rattled against the windows as though somebody was firing at them with a pea shooter.

'We're cosy,' she said. They shifted positions so that both of them lay awkwardly along the bench seat. She breathed in little pants; her mouth nuzzled the side of his neck. He was incapable of making love to her. Her dress had ridden up to reveal a patch of thigh, slightly mottled. He felt terror, the sensation of being caught in a trap. A man eater, Widgey had said.

'What's the matter?'

'The door handle.' He moved again.

'Is it that woman?'

'What woman?'

'The one you told me about, that you were going to marry. You think it's just on the rebound, is that it?'

'Perhaps.'

'I don't mind. I shall understand.'

He disentangled himself and sat up behind the steering wheel. He could not go through with it. 'I think we should give ourselves time. To consider.'

'What for? We're over twenty-one.'

'You don't know anything about me.' She looked at him. He repeated feebly, 'We ought to wait.'

She sat up too, pulled down her dress. 'That's not what you were saying five minutes ago.'

The hail stopped suddenly. He looked out at the greasy sea. She said, 'Drive back. And put down the window, it's stuffy.'

That's the way it would have been, he thought on the way back.

I should have been her lackey, it would have been a terrible mistake. After their return she held out her hand for the keys, got out of the car. He got out too. They faced each other, with the car between them.

'I usually get what I want.' With these words – were they an expression of disappointment or somehow an implied threat? – she turned away from him and went into the hotel.

That night Widgey put on one of her roast turkey dinners, with an elaborate ice cream pudding afterwards. She carved the turkey herself, attacking it with frightening ferocity. Flash flash, pieces of breast fell off. Crunch – a leg had been severed and in a few moments was sliced to the bone. A spoon violated the carcass of the bird, emerging with greeny-brown stuffing. Some new guests had arrived, and the sight of the small woman making so furious an attack on the large bird stimulated them to an excited buzz of conversation. They glimpsed a series of gastronomic feasts ahead which would never be put before them. Violet did not come down to dinner, Widgey never glanced in his direction.

After dinner, the reckoning. He looked at his wallet and found that it contained only twenty pounds. He would have to get some sort of secretarial job, and get it soon.

Later in the evening he told Widgey. She was sitting in the parlour eating chocolates and reading a book called *Nancy and the Handsome Sailor*. Playing cards were spread on the table.

'I'm not going to marry her.' She nodded. 'You're right. She would have eaten me up.'

Widgey bit into a chocolate, looked at the centre, ate the rest of it. 'She's gone.'

'Gone!'

'She was staying another week, but she packed and left.'

He felt uneasiness, guilt, the need to explain. 'I only did what you said.'

'I didn't tell you to do it that way. I told you, she's a cow but I'm fond of her.' She spread out the cards again, turned them over. 'You're a Gemini.'

'What? Oh, Gemini. My birthday's on the third of June.'

'Gemini. And you're twenty-seven. Black queen after a red queen and a red king before that. It means trouble. And it means a chance.'

'I'm going to look for a job, I shan't be here much longer.'

'Stay as long as you like, it doesn't matter to me.'

Affection for her welled up in him. 'Have you got any paint? In the morning I'll paint that chest of drawers in my room.'

'I believe there's some in the store. Not sure what it's like though. Do you know something?'

'What?'

'Maybe I was wrong. Perhaps it would be good for you to be eaten up alive.'

Later, in room thirteen, he wept as he looked at the scarred chest of drawers. Was he weeping for his youth, for the lost days of football matches and kindness, for Widgey, for his present situation? He did not know. It was after three in the morning when he fell asleep.

Chapter 4

What Widgey called the store was a kind of cupboard outhouse which contained a lot of junk like old bicycles with flat tyres (he had ridden one of them when he was a child), electric hedge clippers covered with rust, dozens of empty bottles, dozens of unopened tins of tomato soup, four brass fenders, various pieces of old iron and, sure enough, some paint tins and stiff old brushes. Most of the tins were empty and the paint in the others was covered with a thick crust which had to be broken before penetrating to the liquid below. He used one of these tins to paint the chest of drawers but did not make a very good job of it because the colour, which started off as light blue, deepened steadily as he went on. The result was a parti-coloured chest, which would obviously need another coat. Widgey, however, expressed herself as delighted when she came up to see it. She looked vaguely round the room.

'Think I ought to get some new stuff in here?' She patted the tallboy. 'That's a good piece.'

'Some more wallpaper perhaps.'

'I've had people who like it, think it's original. And what the hell, they can't expect the earth for what I charge.' It was true that her charges were low. 'Know that grey haired man with the young blonde wife, came yesterday. I believe she's his niece.'

'Why?'

'She called him Uncle. Still, it's not my business.'

'I suppose not.'

'You've made a wonderful job of this.' She absent-mindedly patted the chest of drawers and paint came off on her fingers.

Sunday was the only day on which Widgey served lunch and, as always in her periods of abstraction, the food was poor. The remainder of the turkey had mysteriously vanished and the guests got pork luncheon meat and salad, followed by cold jam covering leaden pastry. Grumbles moved like distant thunder

237

round the tables. After lunch Tony went for a walk. He was approaching the pier when he heard a shout. 'Jonesy. Hey there, Jonesy.' He felt a thump between the shoulder blades and turned to see a red faced man smiling at him.

'Passed you just now and thought to myself "I know that face," and then I thought, "Of course, it's old Jonesy." ' He shook Tony's hand vigorously.

'I think you're making a mistake.'

'No, I'm not. I tell you what, I know your other name, it's Tony, right? I'm Bill Bradbury.'

And then he did remember. Bradbury had been the leader of the boys in the lavatories, the big boy who had started it all. And here he was now, a big man bursting out of his tweed suit, with horn-rimmed glasses and thinning hair. Tony hesitated for a fatal moment and then had to say 'Yes, I remember. It's been a long time.'

'And I've changed, don't I know it. Putting on weight where I shouldn't. I'd have known you anywhere. Still at Eltham, are you?'

'No. I left there long ago.'

'Same here. Shaking the old dust off the feet. Now I tell you what we'll do, you just come along with me.' And as though to enforce this policeman-like injunction Bradbury took an uncomfortable grip on Tony's arm and walked along with him. 'I've had to come in to collect a couple of things from the office, then you come back and have tea and meet the wife and family.'

'I'm not sure that —'

'Come on now, I won't take no for an answer.' They turned off down a side street. A brass plate said *South Eastern Export Company*. Bradbury unlocked the door and led the way to an office with 'Manager. Please Knock' lettered on it in black. The room had that ghostly chilliness common to offices when they are not in use.

'Sit you down.' Tony sat in the chair that was no doubt reserved for clients. Bradbury busied himself behind a big desk, then took papers from a filing cabinet and began to make notes. From time to time he would look up with an encouraging smile, and say that he wouldn't be a couple of minutes. Tony felt like a mouse being protectively watched by a cat. Suppose he started to walk out, would Bradbury pounce? Contemplating the bullet head behind the desk, pink scalp showing beneath the carefully brushed hair, he wondered also what would happen if he said, 'Do you remember a day at school . . .' and went on to recall the details of that afternoon. Bradbury had been only two or three years older than he, but at the time he had seemed like a creature from another world. No doubt he would look up and say with genuine incomprehension that he did not know what Tony was talking about. Now he took two differently coloured pens from a small battery of them on his desk and began to make notes on the papers. He returned the file to the cabinet, snapped it shut. His movements were brisk, business man style.

'That's that. One of the boys made a real cock-up on some bills of lading. Can't trust anybody nowadays, have to check everything yourself. I'll have something to say to that young gentleman tomorrow. Now then, let's get moving. I left the bus in the garage round the corner.'

'You don't live in town?'

'Not likely. I'm out in the country, good clean air, can't beat it.'

The car was a Hillman. 'What d'you drive yourself?'

'A Jaguar.'

'Do you now?' He gave a whistle between the teeth that Tony remembered. 'Things are all right, eh?'

'As a matter of fact I'm between cars at the moment.'

'Oh yes.' Bradbury gave him one quick glance and said nothing more, but Tony was suddenly conscious of the tweed-trousered leg close to his own in the car.

He said with attempted carelessness, 'By the way, I've changed my name. Lots of family complications, remarriages you know, things got difficult. It's Bain-Truscott now.'

'I see.' Again that quick glance, then he was looking at the road again. 'I'll remember. What's your line then?'

'I've just been helping a General with his memoirs. Rewriting them.'

'A writer, are you?'

'Yes.' He regretted more than ever the decision, although it had hardly been a decision, to accept Bradbury's invitation.

'Gathering material down here?'

'I'm staying with my aunt. A short holiday. What does your company do?'

The question shifted Bradbury into another gear. During the rest of the drive he talked about himself, and about his contacts with other European countries and the agencies he held. By the time they reached Beaver Close Tony had heard about Bradbury's wife Evelyn whose dad was well in with Rotary, and knew that they had decided not to have any kids for a year or two and since then had been trying without any luck. Mr Granville, Evelyn's dad, was staying the weekend with his wife and some friend of Evelyn's was coming to tea.

Beaver Close was a complex of half a dozen identical mock-Georgian houses neatly placed round their own small square of green on the outskirts of a village. It was not Tony's idea of living in the country but after getting out of the car Bradbury inflated his chest, taking in and expelling great mouthfuls of air. Each of the houses had a differently-coloured front door and Bradbury pointed this out. 'Gives that touch of originality. Come in.'

Inside there were rugs on parquet floors, a pervasive smell of newness. Bradbury tapped the parquet with his foot. 'Under-floor heating all through. Wonderful investment. Paid five thou for it three years ago, sell it for eight any day I wanted.'

A door opened and a small harassed woman appeared. 'Surprise surprise,' Bradbury cried. 'Evelyn, my dear, I ran into an old friend, brought him back to tea. This is Tony, Tony Bain-Truscott.' There was a slight pause after the Christian name.

Three people were in the neat sitting-room. Mr Granville was a larger, older image of his son-in-law, red faced and white haired. They might have been father and son. His wife had a blue rinse and a manner of painted aristocratic reserve. 'And this is –' Bradbury looked round. His wife had vanished.

'Genevieve Foster. We haven't met.'

'Charmed.' Bradbury inclined his body, then said with

tremendous formality, 'May I present my old friend, Tony Bain-Truscott.' Their how do you do's rang out at the same moment. Tony received an impression of whiteness and fragility. Evelyn wheeled in a trolley on which every article seemed to be gleaming silver, teapot, milk jug, strainer, hot water jug, sugar bowl. On a lower level there were elegant china plates, thin bread and butter, scones, jam.

'I'm afraid it's just pot luck, Mr Bain-Truscott.'

'Call him Tony,' Bradbury boomed. 'Too much of a mouthful, the other.'

He found himself sipping pale tea from a cup so frail that he feared it might break in his hands, and talking to Mr Granville. 'So you were at school with Bill. I expect he was a live-wire even in those days.'

'Yes, he was.'

'I spotted that the first time I saw him. That boy's got ideas, I said, he'll go a long way. It so happens I play golf in a foursome every week with the English director of Hispano-American Construction.' Could that be what he had said? Mr Granville sucked in his breath, winked, and went on, 'Wheels within wheels.'

Surely he must be Bradbury's father? He bit into a scone and said nothing. He saw the school lavatories with terrible clarity, the doors that were always being banged, the group of boys round him, Bradbury's big red face. Somebody spoke. He replied to Mrs Granville's blue rinse. 'I'm sorry.'

'Eldon Truscott in Shropshire. Is he –'

'My branch of the family came from Australia.'

'Colonial.' She lost interest.

'Writing, now, is there money in that?' That was her husband.

'I have an independent income.' Behind the horn-rims Bradbury was studying him curiously. Tony rose, took a plate, handed round bread and butter. Mrs Foster held out her teacup. It was refilled from the silver pot.

'I hear you're a writer. My husband writes too.'

'I'm not a professional writer. I was helping an old soldier with his war memoirs.'

'How interesting. My husband's an amateur. He is interested

in topography, which is too much for me I'm afraid.' The chair beside her was vacant, and he sat down. At least he had got away from the Granvilles. Seen more closely Mrs Foster was attractive. Her face was neat and small, the features classical, the hair cut short like a boy's. Her eyes were a strange colour, a flinty grey. The first impression of fragility was confirmed, the hand that held the teacup was small, but he had a sense of something controlled and fierce behind this delicacy.

He was wondering about her age when she said, 'You look too young to have been at school with Mr Bradbury.'

'I'm twenty-seven. He was one of the older boys.'

'But you were friends.' Something about her flinty grey gaze seemed to question it.

'Of course. We've not met for years.' He gave a start as he felt pressure applied to his upper arm. Tea spilt into his saucer, some went on to the mushroom coloured carpet. Evelyn mewed with distress.

'Startled you, old man, sorry.' It was Bradbury's hand, of course. Then Evelyn had rushed out for a cloth and he was on his knees helping her to wipe the carpet, although really only a few drops had been spilled. Evelyn kept repeating that it was perfectly all right, but her stare at the carpet said the reverse. The tea trolley was wheeled out, he was shown round the neat suburban garden, and then it was time to go.

Mrs Foster was taking him back. Bradbury accompanied them out to her car.

'It's been good to see you, but we never got a chance to talk over old times.' His leg brushed against Tony's. 'Have lunch with me one day.'

'I'm going back to town in a day or two. I'll ring you when I'm free.'

When they were out of sight of the house Mrs Foster said, 'Are you pleased to get away? I am. I'd only met Evelyn before, we're both members of the Women's Club. He was a bit of a shocker, I thought. But I forgot, you're a friend of his.'

'Not so much of a friend as all that.'

'Do you know, that's what I thought.' She flashed him a smile of what might almost have been called complicity. 'It's a pity.'

'What is?'

'That you're going back so soon. Eversley, my husband, needs help badly with his book and you do that kind of thing. Or am I wrong?'

There was the most curious kind of tension in the car. She did not look at him, she stared ahead at the ribbon of road. Why did some kind of invitation seem to lie behind those innocuous words?

'Not exactly. I told you what I did for the General'

'Eversley would expect to pay. If you wouldn't be insulted.'

He wanted to say, I am not sure, I have been much deceived in women, I am afraid of what they may do to me. Instead he said, 'I really ought to go back to London.'

'It's up to you. Where shall I drop you?' When he opened the door to get out she said, 'Don't make any mistake. I asked you because I thought you'd get on with Eversley. He's not the easiest man in the world.'

'I'm flattered.'

'There's no need to be.' She shrugged her slim shoulders. 'If you want to ring you'll find me in the book.'

He was walking away when she wound down the car window. 'Eversley likes to see references. If you've got any.'

References indeed! He tried not to show by the stiffness of his back that this really did insult him.

Chapter 5

He rang the following morning from the Seven Seas, with the daily whizzing a vacuum cleaner about under his nose. Her voice sounded cool, almost uninterested, as she asked him to come along at three o'clock. The address was Villa Majorca, Byron Avenue.

Byron Avenue was on the outskirts of Southbourne. In the bus on the way over he tried to analyse the reason for the excitement he felt. Why had he dressed with more than usual care, in a charcoal suit with a faint stripe, a plain white shirt with button down collar, a discreet blue tie? This was only a temporary job, or no job at all if Foster disliked him. He felt the tingling in his stomach which told him that Mrs Foster found him attractive, yet if Foster suspected this he might not get the job. But as the bus rattled along the sea front and then turned off, away from the hotels into a residential area of wide roads in which red brick or whitewashed houses stood detached in well kept gardens, the sense of approaching some climacteric in his life increased.

The few houses in Byron Avenue were solidly opulent in the Edwardian manner favoured by builders in seaside resorts soon after the beginning of the century, when Southbourne had been a village and these the residences of rich Londoners. He passed a plot with a 'For Sale' notice on it and then came to the Villa Majorca, which was smaller and more modern than most of its neighbours. A gravel drive led up to the front door. On the opposite side of the road were school playing fields. When he rang the bell she answered the door and took him into the drawing-room. She wore a pale dress – he was never to see her in any but pastel colours – which almost matched the grey flint of her eyes.

The room was quite small and although there were nice things in it the effect was not one of order or elegance. On the mantelpiece he saw some bits of what he recognized as Battersea enamel, a corner cupboard contained some porcelain, perhaps Dresden or Meissen, or perhaps only imitations. There was a piano with photographs on it, there were little tables studded with mother-of-pearl. An incongruous note was struck by African masks, a fur-covered shield and a pair of assegais or spears grouped in one corner. She saw his glance.

'They're my husband's, he spent some time in Africa. You were thinking his taste is different from mine? Quite right.'

'I was thinking that. At that very moment.' Where was Foster? She answered this unspoken question.

'Eversley had to go up to London, looking up references in some museum. He is so keen about this book.'

'Perhaps I should come back.'

'He wants me to interview you. Eversley is a fool about people. You said you can type. Come and show me.'

He followed her to a room at the back fitted up as a study, with a big mahogany desk, a swivel chair, a filing cabinet, books behind glass. A window looked on to the garden. There was a typewriter on the desk, paper beside it. He put the paper into the machine, typed a few lines. She nodded.

'Good. You'll think I'm being very careful, but Eversley's last secretary typed with two fingers.'

Back in the sitting-room he produced the letter from Sir Archibald Graveney and another, which he had typed on a different machine at a different time, which purported to be from Chalmsley Baker of Redmers Hall in Cumberland. Both testified to his satisfactory service as a secretary. She touched the one from Baker with her fingertips and asked if he would mind if she followed it up. He made his stock reply.

'Of course, but you won't get a reply for a week or two. Baker's yachting on the Riviera, lucky chap. He sent me a card.' He forestalled what might be her next question. 'And Sir Archibald died last year. Though I believe his widow's still at Throgmorton.'

She made no comment, but went on. 'You mentioned that you'd been helping a General with his memoirs. Eversley was particularly interested by that.'

He moved uneasily. The interview was much more businesslike than he had expected. Then he smiled. The smile was one that he had practised in the glass, and he considered it devastating. 'I practically wrote half the book. But there's something I didn't tell you. We parted on bad terms, I'm afraid.'

'I couldn't ask him for a reference?'

'He might explode if you did.'

'So there's nobody I can write to at the moment.'

This really was a little bit too much. Anybody would have thought he was applying for a job at the Bank of England. He started to get up from his chair. As he did so she folded the two letters carefully and smiled.

'I'm terribly sorry, I really am insulting you.' He did not contradict her. 'And I'm being stupid. It's just that I'm doing it for Eversley. If you'd like to take the job we should both be very pleased.'

He sat down again and she started to talk about money. She suggested an arrangement that was fair, even generous, for a job that was five days a week, mornings only, from ten o'clock each morning. 'When can you start? Will tomorrow morning be all right?'

'There's no need for an interview with your husband?'

'The problem is to keep him occupied. He's not very strong and doesn't work. He doesn't know what to do with his time.' Her tongue came out and licked her pale lips. There was again a hint of complicity, of a shared secret, in her manner as she showed him to the door.

A classic situation, he thought on the way back in the bus. Elderly valetudinarian husband, young discontented wife playing while husband's away. Yet this analysis did not satisfy him. There was something forbidding about Mrs Foster, and this was part of the attraction she held for him.

Chapter 6

He presented himself at precisely ten o'clock on the following morning, met Foster and began work.

Foster was far from the elderly valetudinarian of Tony's imagination. Mrs Foster – Jenny as he thought of her although the name was not appropriate – was about his own age, and Foster was perhaps three or four years older. He was a small man, a head shorter than Tony, of a weak Byronic handsomeness. A single white streak marked his black hair. The three of them sat in the drawing-room for half an hour talking.

'Mr Bain-Truscott really can type,' she said. 'I tested him. His fingers fairly flew over the keys. Not like the last one.'

'That's good. He was not at all satisfactory.' Foster seemed uncomfortable.

'And he has splendid references.' Her tongue crept out, touched her lips, went in again. The quick glance she gave him held no visible sign of amusement or irony.

'I leave all that to you.' Abruptly Foster said, 'Are you interested in topography?'

'To be frank I don't know the first thing about it.' The moment seemed right for his smile. 'But I can learn.'

'I rely on my wife. She doesn't often make mistakes.'

They talked about the weather and about the town and then Jenny said, 'Perhaps you should start Mr Bain-Truscott off, darling.'

Foster led him into the study, and took out several large quarto volumes from the glass-fronted case. 'What I'm trying to do is to reproduce a complete topographical survey of this area, and not only topographical but historical, so that it compares each period shown in the more important maps with every period preceding it. I want to make the comparison fully detailed about every village.'

'That sounds like quite an enterprise.'

'It's a survey of a kind that has never been attempted before,' Foster said solemnly. 'Just now I'm still in the stage of accumulating comparison notes. I'd like them typed up on separate cards and then I shall analyse them in detail.'

He proceeded to rattle off at considerable speed, so that Tony had to ask him to slow down, a variety of extracts from the volumes in front of him. They went into great detail about population details, boundary changes and physical features of each district. Then Foster showed him the form in which he wanted the notes typed up. While Tony was typing he caught the man looking at him in a way that was hard to define. It was as though he were – what? Afraid of Tony, jealous of him, assessing him as a rival? Something of all these, perhaps, with something else that he could not place.

At ten minutes to one Jenny put her head round the study door. 'Have you almost finished, Eversley?'

'For today, yes.'

'You have time for a drink before you go, Mr Bain-Truscott?'

They drank sherry in the drawing-room from small, beautiful glasses. He asked them to call him Tony because his full name was such a mouthful.

Foster was drinking his sherry in an abstracted manner, head sunk in his shoulders. When she rather sharply called him to attention he said, of course, Tony by all means. There was no reciprocal suggestion that he should use their Christian names.

'How did it go this morning?'

'Very well.' Foster gave a weak smile. 'Mr – Tony is an excellent typist.'

It was she who showed him out. 'I'm sorry not to invite you to lunch, but we have only a very light midday meal. In the afternoon Eversley often lies down for an hour. I told you he's not very strong.' As she opened the door there was the sidelong cat-like look suggesting that they shared some secret.

Wednesday morning was a repetition of Tuesday, the dictation, the typing, the glass of sherry. It seemed to Tony that Foster was reading passages from books and he suggested that if they were suitably marked he could save time by copying them without the need for dictation. Foster pulled at his upper lip dubiously.

'Perhaps. I shall have to go up to the British Museum to-morrow, and I shall leave something for copy typing. But for most of this material that wouldn't do, it wouldn't do at all. I have to select passages that fit together. I don't think I could possibly mark them all up in advance.'

He spoke with concern, almost with agitation, and Tony left it at that. If Foster liked to pay him for wasting time, why should he object? Foster continued on an apologetic note. 'I've had secretaries before who've done things their way and got into a terrible muddle. Doing them like this may take longer, but I can make sure everything is in the right order.'

'Yes, of course. How long have you been working on the book?'

'Nearly five years.'

'Since you came back from Africa, I suppose?'

A pause. 'That's right.'

'Did you live there long?'

'Quite a time.' He opened another book, started to dictate again.

Suppose Foster was thirty-five, and he certainly could not be older, had he married Jenny out there or since he returned? And did his money come from Africa? Certainly he must have money, to live here and occupy himself with a project like this. There seemed to him something odd about the marriage, but again he reflected that it was not his business. That afternoon he put a second coat of paint on the chest of drawers, and in the evening told Widgey that he had a job and would pay for his keep. She waved the suggestion aside.

'Don't want any money, I've got enough. What's the job?' She listened with a sceptical air when he told her.

'You want to look out for that Mrs Foster. Sounds to me as if she's got her hooks into you.'

'She's not like that.' He rather regretted saying anything.

'He must be pretty wet.' On this he made no comment. 'Don't get mixed up with her the way you did with Violet. Have a cuppa?'

'It would never have done,' he said as he drank the scalding liquid. 'You were quite right.' The thought of Violet's opulent flesh and of those nights in her room came back to him and he shuddered uncontrollably.

'Sometimes I think you don't like any women.'

He was indignant. 'I like them much better than men.'

'I wonder.'

'I like you. I think you're the most wonderful woman I've ever known.' He kissed the straggly hair on the top of her head.

'Thanks very much. Just don't get mixed up with this Foster female, she sounds like poison. I don't want him coming round with a shotgun.'

'He's wet, you said so yourself.'

'It's the wet ones who use guns.' There was a thunderous noise in the hall. 'Christ, it's that man O'Grady. He gets tight every night. Give me a hand.'

O'Grady was on his knees in the hall, glassy eyed, trying to right a hat-stand he had knocked over. They got him up the stairs and into his room. Widgey managed it all without removing the cigarette that drooped from her mouth. An elderly couple watched their ascent with awe, and asked if Mr O'Grady was ill.

'Drunk.' They stared after her unbelievingly. She said to Tony, 'Thanks. Don't know how I'd have managed.'

'You'd have managed. Are you going to get rid of him?'

'What for? Man's got a right to drink as long as he doesn't bother anybody.'

'The other guests won't like it.'

The cigarette moved up and down in her mouth as she spoke emphatically. 'Then they can bloody well lump it. There are too many people around who try to stop other people doing what they want.' As he was going up to bed she told him again not to get mixed up with Mrs Foster, then started to laugh, her whole body shaking. 'You see, I'm one of them.'

On Thursday he got mixed up.

It began like the other days. She opened the door to him wearing one of her pale dresses, her face colourless above it. She said simply that Eversley had left things to type. There were passages marked in books and he began work on them. Just after eleven she came in, bringing a cup of coffee. As she put it on the desk she leaned over and for a moment her slight body was close to his. There was no scent about it, no warmth. She turned away to the window and her back was towards him, slender and straight. Below the short dark hair her neck was white.

It was, or so he thought afterwards, the whiteness and vulnerability of this neck and something hopeless yet unyielding in the set of her shoulders that made him rise, move to her and put his arms round her from behind, feeling the bones of the rib cage and the small breasts. She stayed for a moment quite still like some animal unsure of its captor's intentions, then turned so that she faced him and pressed her mouth to his. The mouth was cool and dry, the body pressed against him felt hard as a board. She said nothing as they separated, but took him by the hand as if they were children and led him upstairs. In the bedroom their bodies were pressed together on one bed while another stayed unused. A dark blue medallion set like an eye in the middle of the counterpane stared at what happened.

He was amazed by the vehemence with which she made love to him, so that he was a passive rather than a dominant partner in what they did. Yet although he was surprised and in a way shocked by the passion contained in that thin white body, the sensations he experienced were more pleasurable than any he had known. To be used in this way by a woman as the vehicle of her own intense sexual desire fulfilled some emotional need in himself that he had not known to exist. Afterwards, while they lay and smoked, he took in the luxury with which the bedroom was furnished, the lacquered furniture, the smoke blue wallpaper, the silky Chinese carpet on which there was a medallion in another tint of blue.

'I know what you're thinking,' she said. 'I'll tell you the answer. Eversley's no good.'

'I understand.'

'I doubt it. I mean no good in any way, to me or to himself. He's stinking rich, that's why I married him. And he's got what he wants, he'll do anything for me. A couple of years ago I said I'd like a fast car. Next week he bought me a Jensen. When I got bored he sold it and lost a thousand pounds on the deal. A year ago he got me a motor launch. I'm bored with that too. Do you like mucking about in boats?'

'I don't know.'

'I'll show it to you one day. I'm honest, you know, I told him all this when I married him. Four years ago.'

'Soon after he came back from Africa?'

'How did you know?'

'He told me.'

'Oh yes. I was an actress in rep on and off, but it's a hell of a life, often you don't know where the next week's rent is coming from. I daresay I was no good. I can't express my feelings.' He laughed and she dug nails into his arm. 'On the stage, I mean. People say what fun it is, living in boarding houses, not having enough to eat, but I never thought so. That's why I married Eversley. I didn't know he had this heart trouble, or that he'd want to moulder away here. Topographical history.' She spoke as if it were something indecent. 'If we were married, would you want to work on topographical history?'

There was only one answer to that, and he made it. Later she stared at him with her flint grey eyes.

'It's always the wrong people who have the money. You haven't got any?'

'No.'

'Tell me about yourself.'

He gave her an edited version of his life. She listened attentively.

'I didn't think anybody could be called Bain-Truscott. What's your name?'

He said with an effort, 'Jones.'

'What's wrong with that.' She got off the bed, began to put on her clothes. 'You'd better do some typing.'

He was surprised. 'Oh. All right.'

'My woman comes in the afternoon. I don't want you here then. If you've done nothing Eversley will notice. He may be a fool but he's not stupid.'

This alternation of passion and coldness fascinated him. He left in a ferment of pleasure with which some anxiety was blended. He knew that for the first time in his life he had met a woman with whom he was emotionally involved. At one o'clock she saw him out as though he were a stranger. When he moved to kiss her good-bye she said nothing, but stepped back and away from him.

Chapter 7

On the following morning Foster opened the door to him and they went straight into the study. Jenny was nowhere to be seen. Foster had brought back new material from London, and began to dictate at once. At half past eleven he looked at his watch.

'Can you get along on your own for the rest of the morning? Some of these afforestation details are not very clear and I shall have to check on them at the local library.'

'Shall I check them for you? This afternoon I mean.'

'I prefer to do it myself.' Tony looked up and intercepted a glance that startled him, because it appeared to be one of pure dislike. It must have been a trick of the light, however, for now Foster smiled. 'You'll think I'm fussy, but this sort of thing involves checking twenty different accounts against each other, and I'd sooner make my own mistakes.'

'Are you satisfied with my work? Tell me anything I'm doing that's wrong.'

'It's fine. I'm getting along faster than I have done for a long time.' Foster gestured at the pile of cards, then pulled out his wallet. 'We'll make the payments weekly, unless you object.'

Tony said he didn't object. When he heard the front door close he came out of the study, looked in the drawing-room and the kitchen, then started up the stairs. Jenny appeared at the top of them.

'He's gone round to the library.' Why did he speak in a whisper?

She said nothing, but took his hand and led him to the bedroom. Later they came down and drank sherry from the elegant glasses. She was silent.

'What is it, Jenny? What's the matter?'

'Nothing.'

'There is something. Tell me.'

'We suit each other. Don't we?' He placed a hand on her arm.

'I don't believe you've told me everything.'

'I don't know what you mean.'

'Those references. You forged them, didn't you?' He had quite forgotten this, but now his silence was a betrayal. 'I don't mind. You're clever, they're good letters. I just wanted to know.'

He said boldly, with a sense of trusting her as he had trusted nobody since he was a child, 'Yes.'

'What was the trouble with your General. Or didn't he exist?'

At this he rebelled. It seemed to him that she wanted to probe the details of everything in his life that was most painful. 'We had an argument.'

She moved off, as it seemed, at a tangent. 'Eversley goes away on trips sometimes. On his own. For two or three weeks. He goes abroad and just wanders around. I think he's building up to one now.'

He said uncertainly, 'You mean he wouldn't want me any more?'

'Oh, he'd leave work for you. The sacred task must go on. He doesn't leave an address, just sends cards.'

What was she driving at? 'I'd be able to see you more often?'

She said coldly, 'It doesn't matter. You ought to go now.'

'I shan't see you until Monday?'

'Of course not. For God's sake don't start hanging about or come paying social calls.' The white intensity of her face could never be said to soften, but the cool lips touched his cheek. 'Until Monday.'

What was he to do with the hours until then? On the way back to the Seven Seas he bought some vividly striped wallpaper and announced to Widgey his intention of repapering his room. He started on Saturday morning but wallpapering proved more difficult than he had expected. The paper showed a tendency to crease and even to tear, and after doing half the room he could not pretend that the result was satisfactory. He was sitting on the bed contemplating what he had done when Widgey came up and stood in the doorway, hands on hips.

'I'm afraid it's a mess.' He had got paste on his trousers, and even though they were old this distressed him.

'You're not cut out for it,' she agreed. 'Something on your mind?'

'No. Why should there be?'

'I don't know. Phone call for you.'

He almost ran down the stairs, thinking of Jenny. When he heard Bradbury's voice he was irritated, and it was only because the rest of the day yawned ahead like an endless cavern that he accepted the invitation to have a drink with a couple of fellows and spend an hour or two on the town.

They met in the cocktail bar of the Grand. Bradbury's companions were a South African named Pickett and a Dutchman who was apparently connected with the European side of South Eastern Export. Pickett was lean as a greyhound, the Dutchman was thick necked and square. Both wore horn-rimmed spectacles. They drank three cocktails quickly and then went into the grill room and ate steaks. Bradbury was in great form. He winked at mention of his wife.

'Saturday's my night off. Evelyn knows that. All in the way of business, mind.'

'I like a woman who knows her place,' Pickett said.

'I am going to see swinging England.' That was the Dutchman.

'Let's hope it doesn't swing you off balance.' Bradbury roared with laughter. 'Evelyn knows a man needs a bit of relaxation. And you might not think so but you can relax in this little old town, if you know where to go.' Blood oozed from the steak.

Pickett speared two chips and began to tell a story about a man who had thought he was getting a lift from Cape Town to Durban and had ended up in Pretoria. The whole thing was connected, in some way Tony did not understand, with arms that failed to reach the Congo. Then the Dutchman, whose name was Van something, told an interminable tale about a man suspected of smuggling diamonds into Holland, who had turned out to be smuggling blue films. He was heavily fined. The joke was that he really had been smuggling diamonds too, and the films were only a cover. Bradbury shook his head over this.

'I don't know if you ought to tell such tales in front of Tony.'

He smiled. Supposing he told them about the General and the cheque, would they be shocked?

Bradbury, sitting next to him, squeezed his knee. 'Our Tony's a dark horse. You know you made quite an impression on Evelyn, she thought you might be a good influence on me.'

'What is your business?' Van something asked.

'I'm independent.'

'One of the lucky boys.' That was Pickett.

'Tony's my old school friend. He's always looked out for number one.' Bradbury ordered large brandies. When they left the Grand they were all a little drunk. They got into Bradbury's car, drove half a mile, got out, and Bradbury rang the bell of a house next to a greengrocer's shop. There was a muttered conversation and then they all went up a flight of stairs and into a room where chairs were set out in rows as though for a lecture. Was it some kind of political meeting? Half a dozen other men were in the room, most of them middle-aged. He did not realize what was going to happen until the man who had let them in, tidy and precise as a bank clerk, unrolled a screen at one end of the room and began fiddling with a projector at the other. Then he turned out the light.

Tony had never seen blue films before and now found himself unmoved by the images that flickered shakily on the screen. The men and women entwined acrobatically. He thought of Jenny and himself and the blue medallion eye watching them. Had they looked as grotesque as these figures, was the involvement he felt merely a matter of these routine embraces and postures? The actions were the same, and they were those he had performed with other women. Why did he feel that in their case it was all entirely different?

Beside him Bradbury breathed noisily. Beyond him Pickett leaned forward, lips pressed tightly together. On the other side the Dutchman sat, brawny arms folded across his chest, head sunk in his shoulders almost as though he was asleep. Bradbury's thigh pressed warmly against Tony's, and he moved his leg away. He thought of walking out, but was not sure if he could find the door. He sat through the four films, listening to the whirring of the projector and thinking about Jenny. At one point the projectionist said sharply to a man sitting in front of them, 'None of that, please, you're watching a film show,' rather as if they were in the local Odeon. Then the screen went dark, the whirring stopped, the lights were switched on again, the men filed out down the stairs.

The Dutchman said, 'What about an introduction to some of these ladies?'

The bank clerk shook his head. 'Just the film show.'

In the street Van something was critical. 'In Amsterdam we will have a house attached to such a place, a house with girls.'

'Not here, old man.' Bradbury was firm. 'I can give you an address later if you want it. Just now we're going across to Pete's Place. It's new, only been open a week.'

He disliked them all, why did he not say good-bye and go back to the Seven Seas? He could not have answered that question, but it seemed to him afterwards that if he had left at that point everything that happened later would have been different.

Had he known what Pete's Place would be? As he entered and saw the green tables under their cut-off pools of light, the counters being pushed back and forwards, the dice clattering against the sides of the board, the cards turned to show colour and picture, he blinked his eyes. Bradbury was signing them in. Tony tapped his shoulder.

'I've only got a couple of pounds with me.'

The Dutchman was taking out a wad of notes. Bradbury did not answer Tony, but handed him a pile of chips. 'Pay me back any time. Your credit's good.'

'Thanks.'

'How did you like the show? Really something, the way they got down to it.' The grinning face was close to his own. 'Old Van's randy as a goat.'

As always he played roulette. Once he was at the table he forgot Bradbury and the show and even Jenny. He had thirty pounds' worth of chips and that was not much to play with, it gave you little scope for manoeuvre, but he might make a small profit playing the Rational System. Or he could go in for a doubling-up game on the transversals. He decided on the Rational and played with some success for half an hour. The Dutchman and Pickett were playing blackjack, Bradbury was moving between two or three of the games. When Tony felt the hand on his shoulder he shrugged it off. The damned man would interfere with his game when he was trying to concentrate.

A voice whispered 'Mr Scott-Williams. Here.'

The man had a boxer's bruised face and hands like pieces of raw meat. Tony had never seen him before. He was about to say so when he saw the croupier at the blackjack table watching with a malicious smile. The man was from the Golden Sovereign. He must have been reported.

'We don't want any trouble.' The man was not whispering he simply had a hoarse voice. He decided to make whatever apologies were necessary. They went upstairs. The boxer tapped on a door, opened it, pushed Tony inside and stood with his back to the door.

The room was large and dimly lighted. A monkey-faced man in a lounge suit sat watching a closed circuit television which showed the room below. Tony could see Bradbury talking to Pickett. Were they asking where he had gone? The monkey-faced man turned off the set and looked at Tony. 'You can sit down.'

He sat in an armchair and put his hands on his knees. 'I can explain. I was with friends.'

'I'll do the talking. I'm Carlos Cotton.' A thin layer of gentility overlay the harsh Cockney voice.

Carlos Cotton? Then he remembered. This was the man Armitage had called Number One.

'I don't go looking for trouble, I was good to you. But I put a black on you, right?' In the monkey face two eyes like beads considered him.

'I told you, a friend brought me.'

'It's a new place. Why I'm down here, see, I always come down to a new place. Just to see everything's right. How many of my places you been to since I put the black on?'

'None. I told you, it's an accident, a mistake.'

'You owe me money.'

'But you said it was cancelled.'

'Now I'm saying different.'

The boxer said in his whisper 'He's got some chips.'

'Let's have them, Lefty.'

The boxer stepped forward, Tony gave the chips to him and he counted them. 'Thirty-five.'

Cotton nodded. 'You still owe me ninety.'

'But the money was only ninety –' He heard his voice becoming shrill.

'Interest.'

There was another door in the room, a door behind Cotton. Now this opened. A tall girl in a green dress came in and hesitated. Cotton saw her in the glass in front of him and beckoned with a finger. She crossed the room, stood behind the chair, and began to stroke his forehead, then his neck.

'You've got till Wednesday for the rest.'

'But I haven't got it.'

'I said don't play. You asked for trouble, you got it.'

The girl's hands rhythmically stroked Cotton's neck. 'How's the headache?'

For the first time Tony looked at the girl. She stared straight at him without recognition. It was Fiona Mallory, Mary Tracey.

In a voice of ludicrous mock-gentility Cotton said, 'It's getting better all the time, honey.'

He was still staring at the girl when Lefty half-pushed him out of the room. At the entrance to the gaming room the big man said, 'You heard what the boss said. Wednesday.'

'He had no right to take my money.'

'What's that about money?' Bradbury, red faced and smiling, stood beside them.

The big man said in his hoarse whisper 'I'll see you,' and walked away.

'I've lost the money you gave me,' Tony said. 'I can let you have it in a few days.'

'All right.' Bradbury seemed unconcerned. 'No trouble with King Kong there?'

'No.'

'Good. We've all had enough, I'm collecting up our party.'

Half an hour later the Dutchman had gone off to one of the addresses Bradbury knew, Pickett to another. Bradbury seemed disappointed that Tony refused an invitation to get himself fixed up, and drove him back to the Seven Seas.

'I don't fancy it myself as a matter of fact, but I wanted to show old Van the town.' Tony thanked him for the evening, and repeated that he would pay back the money next week.

'Don't worry about it. It means a lot to me, talking to an old friend.' He scrambled out of the car as Bradbury was saying 'I'm not a happy man, Tony.'

'Thank you for the evening,' he said again from the pavement. It seemed a ludicrously inappropriate remark. Bradbury looked at him through the window, put the car into gear and suddenly accelerated away. Tony went up to room thirteen, took off his clothes, brushed his teeth, got into bed and was immediately asleep.

On Sunday he woke with a headache and a bad taste in his mouth. He resolved not to have anything more to do with Bradbury. In the evening he attended one of Widgey's table rapping sessions. The results were disappointing.

Chapter 8

On Monday the weather changed. Rain spattered the pave-ments, a strong wind blew, people struggled along the front in plastic mackintoshes. He rode alone on the top of the bus until it turned off the promenade. Then he heard steps coming up the stairs. A body dropped into the seat beside him. He looked sideways and saw that the man was small, dark, nondescript in appearance. There was something vaguely familiar about him. What was it?

'Message for you. From Mr Cotton.' The man lighted a cigarette, blew a perfect smoke ring. 'He wants his money.'

Of course. The man had been standing at Tony's table watch-ing the play. He must have followed Bradbury's car last night, but still he seemed harmless enough. Tony felt annoyed. 'He'll get it but he'll have to wait.'

'Till Wednesday. Just to remind you. Cheerio.'

The man rose to leave the bus, pulled on his cigarette and then leaned over and pressed the burning stub on to the back of Tony's hand. He cried out. The shock was so sudden, the momentary pain so intense, that he did not rise from his seat. The man swung along the bus, clattered down the stairs, dropped off at a traffic light. Tony looked at the red mark on his hand and found it hard to believe that the incident had really taken place. Was this the shape of violence, something done casually with a 'Cheerio' at the end of it? When he got off at the end of Byron Avenue he was still shaking slightly, and looking at the red and swollen hand he felt sick. Taking deep breaths, letting wind and rain blow in his face, he walked towards the Villa Majorca. When the door opened he received his second shock of the morning. The figure confronting him was neither Foster nor Jenny but a moustached female dragon, who barred the entrance.

'I'm doing some work here. For Mr Foster.'

The dragon sniffed disapproval, but now he heard Jenny's voice. She appeared, as cool as ever.

'Sarah, this is Mr Bain-Truscott, who is doing some secretarial work.' To him she said, 'Eversley's up in London, but he's left some work for you.' Her manner was brisk, but that was natural in front of the dragon. She led the way to the study, pointed to the work arranged there, and said she had to go out. He saw nothing more of her that morning. At eleven o'clock the dragon brought in a cup of coffee and a biscuit. When he left she was still there, and Jenny had not returned.

In the afternoon the wind dropped, the rain died away, and he went for a long walk beside the sea. He had put ointment on his hand but the mark, an intrusion on the natural health of his body, was a constant reminder that his problems were real and urgent. He shivered at the thought of the knife marking his cheek, the boot in his ribs. Could Fiona, as he still thought of her, help? The problem of how she had got to know Cotton might have absorbed him at another time, but it did not seem likely that she could be of use to him and he put her out of mind. The obvious thing to do – and he had done it before, although never in quite such difficult circumstances – was to run, to take a train and bury himself in London, where it is so easy to hide. He found that he could not do this. He was frightened by the effect that Jenny had on him. He had never taken drugs, but he felt that he could understand why those who did found it impossible to give them up. The emotion that he experienced in Jenny's presence was something he had never felt before in his life.

There was one approach he could make to his immediate problem, and he made it late that evening when he and Widgey sat companionably drinking tea in the parlour, after a visit from Conway, the grey-haired man suspected of sleeping with his niece, who said that their room was too noisy and asked if he could move to the back of the house. Before Widgey's meaningful question, 'Does your *wife* find it too noisy then?' Conway faltered, and then said that the room would do and that he was sorry to have bothered her. After he had gone Widgey drank her tea noisily.

'It's none of my affair,' she said as she had done before. 'But I don't like that man. He *fawns*. I like people to have a bit of nerve. If you're going to sleep with your niece do it, but don't look as if you're apologizing for it all the time.'

Somehow it seemed to be his cue. 'Widgey, can you lend me a hundred pounds?'

She swallowed tea and sniffed. 'Yes.' Before he could express gratitude she expanded on the monosyllable. 'But I won't.'

'Why not?'

She pointed the teaspoon at him. Drops fell off it on to the carpet. 'First, I'd never see it back. And if I never saw the money I'd never see you again. You're not so much unlike old hot pants yourself, you'd feel too guilty to come and see me. And then I can't afford to lose a hundred pounds.'

'Widgey, I'd pay it back.'

She ignored this. 'But the main thing is I don't like the smell of fish. There's something fishy about it.'

He stood up and looked at himself in the fly-spotted glass over the mantelpiece. 'I owe somebody money and they want it back.'

'Tell 'em to wait.'

'They won't.'

She lighted a cigarette. 'Then do a flit. Don't tell me you've never done one before.'

'I can't. Not this time.'

She puffed smoke and looked at him. 'What have you done to your hand?'

'Grazed it. On a wall by the sea.'

'It's to do with that woman, isn't it? I told you not to get mixed up with her.'

'You've never met her.' He laughed rather shakily. 'I don't need to.'

'Did you read her character in the cards? If I don't find the money I shall get beaten up.'

'Then clear out. It isn't her character I read in the cards, it's yours.'

'Oh, go to hell,' he said, and slammed out of the room.

On the next morning, as he turned into the drive that had

become so familiar, he felt his heart thudding like a machine that operated quite independently of him. He knew that he was engaged in an affair which was essentially similar to others in the past, but the thudding machine said something different and passed on the message to his nerve ends so that every area of his body seemed unusually sensitive. When she opened the door he could have cried out with pleasure at sight of her pale face and dark hair, her eyes that in their very incommunicativeness seemed to conceal a depth of meaning that must be discovered. The questions he had meant to ask were forgotten when she led him upstairs into the bedroom where, with the beds unmade and the blue medallion eye hidden by the folded counterpane, they made love with feverish anxiety. Again he was conscious of the subordination of his passion to her own, again the feeling was pleasurable. Later he began to ask questions.

'Sarah? She usually comes in the afternoons but yesterday she couldn't, so it had to be the morning. You don't think I wanted that, do you?' She sunk her nails into his arm. 'Eversley's up in London. He needn't have gone today, at least I don't think so, but I told him I should be here to look after you.'

'And doesn't he –'

'What?'

'Suspect something?'

'I told you he was no good. He's a fool.'

'He's a fool,' he echoed happily. As they laughed together she pressed her mouth forcibly on his. The feeling of subjection overwhelmed him, he let her do what she wished.

Later he did some work and left it piled ready for Foster to see. He was aware of her presence while he typed, it seemed to him that his body reeked of her. Below the layers of clothes were spots touched by her fingers and lips, and these spots were sensitive as bruises. She did not cease to surprise him. At a quarter to one she put her head round the door and asked if he would like a glass of sherry. When they drank together she was as coolly impersonal as she had been on that first day. How could she do it? As though in answer to his question she said, 'He would expect us to have a glass of sherry. I shall leave the glasses for him to see.'

'You've done this before.' He was aware of jealousy, and astonished by it. 'Haven't you?'

'I don't like being questioned.' She spoke calmly. He could not tell whether or not she was annoyed.

'What did you mean about him going away? You said something the other day.'

'It doesn't matter.'

'But I want to know.'

'I said it doesn't matter.' Her voice was not raised, but the tone was such that he said nothing more. He knew that in any conflict of wills he was not equal to her. As she looked at him now he thought he saw in her eyes something hard and implacable, but it seemed that he must have been mistaken for in the next moment she gave one of her rare smiles. 'Turn round.'

'What for?'

'And close your eyes.' He closed them and felt paper pressed into his hand, paper with something hard inside it. 'Open them now. It's a present.'

Slowly, carefully, he unwrapped tissue paper. He kept his head down because he felt the smarting pricking sensation behind his eyes that was a prelude to tears, and he did not want her to see them. That she should have given him a present made him feel loving and grateful in a way that had nothing directly to do with sex. He remembered one year when he thought that his birthday had been forgotten and then it proved that his present, a bicycle, had been in the garden shed all day waiting for him to find it. The sensation he had felt when his father took him by the hand, led him outside and opened the door had been, like his feeling now, one of pure gratitude for being remembered.

'Open it.'

The last wrapping came off to reveal black cuff links with what looked like single diamonds set in them, and a matching tiepin.

'Do you like them?'

He made sure that there would be no tears, looked up. 'They're wonderful.' He was speaking of the act of giving not of the gift.

'I wanted to get you something, and I thought they were pretty. I have a little money of my own.'

He moved forward to take her in his arms, but she evaded

him. 'It's a present, that's all, I wanted to give you something. Now I've done it. It's after one, you'd better go.'

She was an extraordinary woman, and part of the fascination she held for him was these sudden changes from love to something like hostility. It was almost as though she wished she had not given him the present, or at least that she wanted little attention paid to it. On the way back to the Seven Seas he put the links into his cuffs. Back in his room he took them out, turned them over and looked at them. The truth, which he came to unwillingly, was that he did not like them very much. This stone that looked like a diamond set in something like an opal produced a rather vulgar effect, and when you added the tiepin it was far too flamboyant for his taste. They looked as if they might be quite old, and probably she had paid a fiver for them in some antique shop, perhaps twice that. Anyway, it was the idea of giving something that mattered.

He put them on to the painted chest of drawers and stared at them. Not for some minutes did it occur to him that the stones might be real. Once he had thought of the possibility it became important to be sure.

He was half-way to the jeweller from whom Violet had bought her diamond and ruby pendant when his conscious mind linked the possible value of the links and pin with the money he owed to Cotton. It was absurd to think that they could possibly be worth ninety pounds, but suppose they could be sold for fifty? He rejected the idea vehemently, but once contemplated it refused to be ignored, raising its head again in the form of pictures flicking through his mind like shots from old gangster films, pictures that showed him cowering at one end of a cul-de-sac while two men advanced on him with open razors, or tied up in a room at Pete's Place while lighted cigarettes were pressed into his palms, his cheeks, his testicles.

He had hardly noticed the jeweller on his previous visit. Now the man emerged as a distinct personality. He was small, with a big wart on one side of his nose which gave him an expression of cunning. He remembered Tony.

'The diamond and ruby pendant, a nice piece. Your aunt, was it?'

'A relative, yes.'

'She knew what she was looking at.' Tony suddenly noticed a larger wart, dark brown and sprouting hairs, on the man's neck just below his ear. He took the links and pin, looked at them casually, got out his glass for a closer examination, nodded. 'So what do you want, a valuation?'

'They're a kind of family heirloom. I might consider selling them.'

It was uncomfortably warm in the shop. A bird's call startled him, and then he saw that it came from a cuckoo clock on the wall. He was aware that the man had said something. 'What's that?'

'What figure did you have in mind?'

'A hundred pounds.'

With horny thumb and forefinger the jeweller pulled at his lower lip, revealing crooked and discoloured teeth. 'I could go to eighty.'

He heard this offer disbelievingly. 'They're real, then? I was never sure about it.'

'Black opals, very nice. And the diamonds, one of them has a flaw in the cutting, but still.' He looked at them again with the glass. 'I won't try to fool you, Mr –'

'Bain-Truscott.'

'You've been fair with me, I'll be fair with you. It's a nice set. If I sell it I make a profit. But how many times do I get asked for black opals, people don't like them, think they're unlucky. I could make it eighty-five.'

'No. I couldn't possibly – anything less than a hundred would be no use.' The thought of the money made him almost frantic. 'As a matter of fact it's a temporary embarrassment. If you hadn't sold them I could buy them back in a few weeks.'

'I don't do business that way. You sell them, I buy them.' He pulled again at his lip. 'All right.'

'What?'

'I take a chance, I give you a hundred.'

The jeweller's face across the counter was only a few inches distant, his breath smelled of cheese and beer. On the side of his neck three grey hairs grew like monstrous plants in the fertile dung-coloured ground of the mole. Tony swallowed violently.

'No. I've changed my mind.' He gathered up the things into their tissue, pushed them into his pocket and backed away. The jeweller rounded the counter, advanced on him with menacing crab-like slowness. Tony turned, opened the door, hurried out of the shop.

Later he felt an extreme exhilaration. He had been tested, tested as severely as possible, and he had come through. He could have taken the money and given it to Cotton. It was a kind of proof for him that his love for Jenny was something real. And hers for him was sufficiently proved by the value of her gift. Not until the evening did it occur to him that since the man had offered a hundred pounds the links and pin must be worth much more than that.

Chapter 9

Wednesday morning. He had known that Jenny would not be there, because she had said that she was going shopping, but it was still a disappointment when Foster opened the door. They went into the study and started dictation as usual. After an hour Foster said abruptly, 'I shan't be here tomorrow. I may be going away.'

It would be better not to reveal that he knew of this possibility. 'And Mrs Foster too?'

'I shall be going alone. I find it necessary sometimes to get away, there are too many pressures.'

What a fool the man was, wanting to get away from Jenny. Contemplating Foster's feebly handsome face and nervously twisting hands Tony felt both sorry for and contemptuous of him. 'Does that mean you won't want me any more.'

'I didn't say that. I may be able to leave sufficient –' His voice died away.

'If you could show me what you wanted perhaps I could do some research.'

'Perhaps, yes.' His hands coiled and uncoiled. 'I haven't made up my mind. I only know I must get away.'

'Where are you going?'

'What's that to do with you?' Foster said angrily, then recovered himself. 'I don't know. I think I shall go to South America. Peru, Chile. I should like to spend some time in the Andes.'

At midday Tony heard the front door close, and at half past twelve Jenny came in. Her usual calm was ruffled. 'Eversley, you never do a thing I ask you.'

Foster smiled nervously. 'What is it?'

She ignored him, spoke to Tony. 'Can you knock a nail in a piece of wood?'

'Yes, of course.' He looked uncertainly at Foster, who rose slowly from his chair.

Jenny still ignored him. 'Then I'd be grateful for your help.'

He followed her out into the kitchen, where she pointed to a shelf that lay on the floor and handed him a hammer and some nails. The job was simply that of nailing the shelf to wooden wall brackets, and it took no more than five minutes. She stood watching, hands on hips.

'Thanks. I've been trying to get him to do it for a couple of days.' There was something almost flirtatious and out of character in the way that she whispered, 'I told you he was useless, didn't I? Even for knocking in a nail.'

Later they went through the sherry ritual in the drawing-room. Jenny had recovered her usual coolness. Foster was moodily silent. Tony, feeling the silence awkward, admired the little Battersea enamel snuff and trinket boxes that said in ornamental copperplate, 'A gift to tell you of my love, O pray do not forget me,' with other similar sentiments. More to maintain the conversation than because he was really interested he picked up one of the photographs on the piano. Jenny joined him.

'Family group, my family that is. There I am.' She pointed to a pig-tailed girl standing meekly beside a large man with flourishing moustaches and a thin elegant woman. 'With mother and father.'

'I'd never have recognized you.'

Foster got up and poured himself another glass of sherry. She handed him another photograph, showing a mild old gentleman with an angry-looking woman beside him who wore a large floppy hat. 'Uncle William and Aunt Hilda.'

He looked at the other pictures. 'No wedding groups.'

'Eversley and I did it all as quietly as possible. No photographers, no family, no friends even.'

'Who's this?' He pointed to a portrait of an elderly erect figure with a small moustache.

'A cousin of mine. His name's Mortimer Lands.'

When he turned round a moment later to put down his sherry glass Foster was staring straight in front of him, his face white as milk. What was the matter with the man?

Chapter 10

That night he went to the theatre with Widgey and O'Grady. *'Murder in the Cathedral*,' Widgey said. 'Should be good.'

'I like a thriller.' O'Grady had close cropped grey hair and although not tall gave an impression of bulging strength.

'I believe it's poetry. A play in verse.'

'If it's got a murder in it, that's good enough for me.' O'Grady glared at Tony as though inviting him to make an issue out of this. His eyes had the slightly unfocused look of the heavy drinker.

When they got to the theatre the posters showed naked girls prancing with their legs up. 'Fine goings on in a cathedral.' O'Grady crossed himself. *Murder in the Cathedral* had been playing the previous week, and the current show was called *Guts and Garters*. There were as many almost naked girls on the stage as there had been on the posters, but the principal performers were a couple of comics who told jokes all of which ended in rude noises made by a pair of clapper boards. Widgey, wrapped in an old fur coat, watched intently. O'Grady muttered unintelligibly under his breath. Tony thought about Jenny and about the future. He felt that he ought to ask for an explanation, but what exactly did he want her to explain? 'Do you love me, did you buy those links, would you have kept a present from me which had cost a lot of money as I have kept this one from you?' It was not merely that he wanted to be reassured about her feelings for him. When he was away from her he found it difficult to believe in her existence.

At the interval they went to the bar. 'Filthy,' O'Grady said as he downed a large whisky. 'A desecration of the human body. In the old country we'd not permit it.'

'You live in Ireland?' Tony asked.

O'Grady glared at him. 'I live in Leeds. I cannot watch another moment of this filthy performance.'

Widgey gathered mouldering fur around her. 'There's a lot of tit if you like that. I'm a bit old for it myself.'

They ate fish and chips and visited three pubs on the way back, then took a short cut through an alley. O'Grady had become melancholy in the last pub and was singing 'The Minstrel Boy'. At the end of the alley a man leaned against the wall. As they walked slowly and uncertainly along their footsteps sounded curiously speedy.

There were too many footsteps. Tony's hand touched the rough brick wall beside him and found no reassurance in it. He was afraid to turn round.

'And his harp he's left *behind* him,' O'Grady wailed. Then two men were with them, standing between Tony and his companions. One of them spoke to Widgey in a low polite voice.

'You go on ahead. We just want a couple of words with our friend here.'

Widgey was not alarmed. In the darkness of the alley her face was a white blur. She began to move away, and O'Grady with her. Tony felt one of the men pushing against him, pressing him back hard against the wall. He saw, or thought he saw, the gleam of steel. He cried out. O'Grady stopped singing.

He could not have said afterwards just what happened in the next minute. O'Grady's body was launched towards them, Widgey screamed, he cried out again himself, there was a frenzied flurrying and mixing of bodies like that of fish in a pool after bait. Then one of the men was on the ground and the other was running back down the alley. O'Grady was furiously kicking the man on the ground and cursing at him. He stopped when Widgey pulled at his arm. The man slowly got to his feet and limped away.

Tony haltingly thanked O'Grady, who was immensely cheerful.

'Think nothing of it, I enjoy a scrap. I bruised my knuckle on him.' He showed a bloody fist.

'They didn't hurt you? They had knives.'

'Knives? Not they. Ah, they were just a couple of toughs. We don't have that type in the old country, I can tell you that. I could do with a drink.'

273

Tony bought them all double brandies in a pub. Widgey said nothing at the time, but after O'Grady had gone upstairs she took Tony into the parlour, rolled a cigarette, stuck it in her mouth and puffed smoke at him.

'I hate to say it but you'll have to go.'

'All right.'

'It's about the money, isn't it? The hundred pounds.'

'Yes.'

'You can have it. Tomorrow. But you'll have to go. I've got this place to run, they'll be round here.'

Something about the way she spoke, combined with her refusal to look at him, made him cry out, calling simply her name.

'What's up?'

'I'll go away. But I can come back, can't I?'

'If you want.'

'Widgey, don't –' He could not say what he felt about the severance of this tie with the past and his childhood. 'I can manage without the money, I've got enough.'

'Don't be a fool.'

'It's true.'

'You wanted it yesterday.'

'I can raise the money. If I have to. But I don't want to borrow from you.'

'Please yourself. Let's have a cuppa.' She moved to put the kettle on the gas ring. 'I still want you out, though. By the week-end. It's best for you too.'

Chapter 11

'It's finished,' Jenny said. She was alone and she had taken him straight into the drawing-room.

'Finished?'

'Eversley's made up his mind to go away. On Saturday.'

'Where to?'

'He's talking about South America, but he doesn't really tell me. I shall be lucky if I get a couple of cards.'

'And he doesn't want me to go on? I told him yesterday, I could easily do some research.'

'He doesn't like you, Tony. I think he knows.'

'But then –' He wanted to say that if Foster suspected her of carrying on an affair it would be natural for him to take her with him, but he could not phrase the words. What she said next did something to answer this unasked question.

'I told you, he's a strange man. When something like this happens, seriously I mean, he has to go away. Alone. He gives it time to burn itself out as he calls it. Then he sends me a card saying where he is, and if I want to I can join him. Otherwise he sends another card to say when he's coming back.'

He seized on the single element that was important to him. 'It's as I said, it's happened before.'

'You don't think I could live with Eversley without there being someone else?' And again in response to the question he could not ask about why she stayed with him she went on coolly, 'He has the money.'

There was something remote about her, something unreal in the whole situation that frustrated and infuriated him. The barrier between them did not fall when he stepped forward and took her unyielding body into his arms, telling her that he loved her. The words also sounded unreal to him, although he knew that they were true. The next words came more easily. 'I have to be with you, I can't leave you.'

'I want that too.'

'But the others. You felt that about the others.'

'They were nothing.' She moved out of his arms. 'Don't make a scene, I hate them. Let's have some whisky.' While she was pouring it she looked at him with the wariness of one animal watching another. 'Eversley doesn't have to come back.'

'What do you mean?'

'He doesn't have to go.'

'I don't understand.' He knew that something terrible was being proposed to him, but he did not know what it was, and he wanted her to tell him; she did not do this. Instead, sipping her whisky like a cat and looking at him over the rim of the glass, she told him things that taken by themselves did not seem significant, appeared almost to be said at random. She and Eversley had a joint account at the bank, did he know that (the question was rhetorical, for of course he didn't), but there was not a lot of money in it, not more than a few hundred pounds. But supposing, just supposing, that Eversley decided to settle in somewhere like – oh, say Venezuela or Costa Rica – and supposing he didn't come back, and that he liked South America so much that he decided to settle there for good, then naturally he'd have his securities transferred to a bank out there, wasn't that so? And Eversley was rich, his securities would last for a long time, you could say for ever.

The sun shone through the windows, yet he felt cold. The whisky tasted bitter. He had to say again that he didn't understand what she meant.

'Look.' She went out of the room, returned with a sheet of writing paper headed *Villa Majorca*. 'Don't touch,' she said. The paper was blank except for the signature at the bottom, 'Eversley Foster.' 'I asked him to sign it because I wanted to write to the telephone people about a new extension. But it could be used for typing a letter to the bank, he's signed it. I told you, he's a fool.'

'But what can we do with it, how does it help?'

'First we copy this signature until we're perfect at writing it. I mean perfect. And don't forget we'd only have to convince a bank in Venezuela.'

'I suppose that might be possible.' He spoke cautiously, he

did not want her to know of his previous experience with signatures. She gave him a smile that raised her upper lip off her teeth. 'But we couldn't keep it up, we'd be found out. One day the bank would ask to see him.'

'Of course. And they would see him. You'd be Eversley.'

'But how would –'

She talked quickly, like somebody who has rehearsed an argument many times. 'You go out there as yourself, right? You just fly abroad on a trip. Out in Caracas we get a passport that makes you Eversley.'

He began to expostulate. 'You can't get a passport just like that.'

'I know somebody out there,' she said so brusquely that he did not like to ask more questions. 'And he has contacts. It's not difficult, just a matter of money. Either we buy a passport or we use Eversley's and get the picture and the description changed. And then you're Eversley. He doesn't have any near relatives or close friends, you see the sort of life he leads. And then there's something special about Venezuela – or Costa Rica or Honduras or Dominica, it doesn't matter which. They don't have any extradition treaty with Britain. I fancy Venezuela though, from what I've read about it Caracas is a lovely city.'

'You've worked all this out. You've planned it. For a long time.' She gave him again that feline smile. 'You've talked about it to other people.'

'One.'

'He was your lover?'

'He was frightened.' Her thin shoulders shrugged under her dress.

He felt a tremor beginning in his hands and legs, and put down his glass on a table. She got up and turned away from him. Her profile seemed to him so beautiful that it took away his breath. The tremor stopped.

'I'm not frightened. Nothing frightens me.'

'I love you.' He repeated the words almost angrily, as though they were some kind of insurance against disaster.

'It's not a word I use.' The coldness and rigidity of her features frightened him. 'I told you, I want to be with you.'

'But supposing in a few months –' He could not complete the sentence.

'I didn't want to be with you. You'd be Eversley Foster, you'd be signing the cheques.'

He closed his eyes and instantly had an image of his body descending silently down an endless tunnel, twisting from side to side, bruised and torn by the speed of a descent which he was powerless to check. There was a roaring in his ears which might have been the sound of water. He thought that he was going to faint. He opened his eyes again and blinked to find himself still in the room. 'I can't bear violence.'

'There won't be any violence.' She went on, again talking with compulsive eagerness. 'I told you Eversley has a weak heart, he takes capsules to speed it up. If I slip three of them into a drink he won't wake up. I'll be responsible for all that. If it worries you. I won't need any help from you until afterwards.'

'Afterwards?'

'I said he was going away. And I told you he bought me a motor launch.'

'Yes.'

'You'll have to help me get him into it.'

'And then?'

'A sea burial. By the time he turns up he'll be unrecognizable. And anyway we shall be in Venezuela.'

'I don't know.'

'You mean you don't trust me. We want the same thing, you must see that.'

What he wanted – but how could he say this to her? – was the ideal Jenny, tender and loving, not the real woman who cloaked hard shrewdness behind an impassive beauty. As though she understood this she gave the ideal Jenny's quick gentle laugh. 'I trust you, anyway. You've got a passport?'

'Yes.'

'Why don't you fly out to Caracas on Saturday and wait for me there. I shan't be able to come for – oh, perhaps a couple of weeks. They couldn't extradite you, you'd be safe anyway.' It seemed only proper to ask about her safety. She came close to him and gripped his arm. 'I don't want to be safe, that's the difference between us. If you're going to buy a ticket you'll want some money. The single fare is a hundred and forty pounds.' He watched in amazement as she opened her handbag, took out a thick envelope and handed it to him. He put it on the table between them.

'You feel very sure of me.'

'I'm direct, you see,' she said as if she were explaining a mathematical problem to a not very bright student. 'I know what I want and what you want, and they both amount to the same thing. And I know what you're like.'

'I wonder if you do.'

'If something's made easy you'll do it as long as you feel you don't have the responsibility, isn't that right?' He could not answer. 'I'm making it easy. Have you got money to live on until I fly out to join you?' He shook his head. 'I'll draw another two hundred and fifty from the bank. You see, this trust is a one-way operation. But you don't get the rest of the money until you show me the air ticket.'

Everything she said humiliated him. 'I wouldn't steal money from you.'

'But you *have* stolen money, isn't that right?'

'Whatever I've done –' He stopped, and began again. 'Those links. I found out what they're worth, but I wouldn't sell them.'

'Oh, my sweet Tony, you priced them, did you? Don't worry, I don't mind, I wouldn't mind if you'd sold them. Being with someone like you makes it more exciting. I knew what you were like, I could tell from the first.' Her eyes sparkled as they did while making love.

'Today is Thursday. There's no time.' It was impossible, surely, that on Saturday night or Sunday morning he should be in Venezuela.

'Of course there is. You can go up to London this afternoon and buy the ticket.'

'And he's going away on Saturday?'

'That's right.'

'I can't come here tomorrow morning. To see him. I couldn't do it.'

'No, I suppose you couldn't,' she said with no hint of criticism. 'He wouldn't want to see you anyway. I'll tell him I've paid you off. He'd be pleased about that. Then come on Friday night.'

'Friday night?'

'Ten o'clock. I'll be ready by then.' He did not ask what she meant. 'Come to the back. I can't see it would matter much, but try to make sure you're not seen.'

Chapter 12

'Saturday,' the girl in the travel agency said, and tapped her pad with a pencil. 'B.O.A.C. flies Tuesdays and Thursdays, Air France on Sundays. Now, let me see.' She delved into time tables and came up with a bright smile. 'You can either fly Iberia or K.L.M., both from London Airport. Iberia leaves at eleven-fifty Saturday morning by Caravelle, arrive in Madrid fifteen o five, then you have a long stop over in Madrid, leave there o one o five Sunday morning in a Boeing, reach Caracas o seven hundred hours. K.L.M. might suit you better. Depart London o eight one o hours Saturday morning in a D.C. 8, call at Amsterdam, Zurich, Lisbon, reach Caracas twenty-two twenty-five hours Saturday evening. Depends if you mind getting up early on Saturday morning or if you'd sooner stop over half a day in Madrid.'

'I'll take the K.L.M.' As Jenny had said, there should be no danger, but the sooner he was out of the country on Saturday morning the better.

'You want to make a booking now? Single, not return? Single is a hundred and forty pounds, return can be a little cheaper. Single, right.' She got busy on the telephone, returned smiling and began to fill in a form. 'Business trip? Are you staying long?'

'Yes, it's business, and I'm not sure how long I'll be there. I may be coming back by boat.'

'Smallpox inoculation is obligatory, yellow fever is not obligatory but advised. No visa necessary.' He handed over the money, she counted it and gave him the ticket. 'Have a good trip.'

Sitting in a café afterwards, he looked at the ticket. He was going to Caracas. In less than seventy-two hours he would be in a city of which he had barely heard, and of which he knew nothing. It is so simple, then, to make your dreams come true. Yet even now he did not believe in what he was doing. It could not possibly be true that on Friday night he would go to the Villa Majorca and help Jenny to – he could not frame the words to describe it. And on the following morning was it really possible that he would walk across the tarmac at London Airport, step into the great mechanical bird, and in less than a day step out of it into a new life? He found that he was able to envisage the new life itself easily enough, the apartment in town with a villa in the hills for the hot season, scarlet bougainvillaea climbing round the terrace where they ate breakfast, orchids and jacaranda trees, continual lovemaking, the pleasure of possessing and being possessed. All this was much clearer to him than what was to happen on Friday and Saturday.

He spent most of the afternoon finding out about Caracas. 'At 3,164 feet above sea level, Caracas has one of the world's best climates. Springlike the year around, the temperature averages 64 degrees with a high of 80 degrees during April, May, September and October . . . English is spoken everywhere . . . The city has recently undergone a tremendous transformation. In the eastern part, where peons drove cattle just ten years ago, sophisticated Caracas residents now sip coffee and cocktails in chic sidewalk cafés in the best continental manner . . . the population of one and a half millions is cosmopolitan, and the faces of Italians, Spanish, Portuguese and North Americans are a familiar sight in the streets.' Not, he noted, English. As Jenny had said, the chances of recognition by anybody who knew Foster would be very small. And really, the place seemed idyllic. There was nothing about poisonous insects or snakes crawling out of bunches of bananas, only descriptions of the variety of flowering trees and the national birds, turpials, toucans and humming birds, 'resplendent in every size, colour and variety.' Photographs showed him great white skyscrapers, enormous hotels with curiously-shaped restaurants and swimming pools, eight lane highways leading out to the mountains. Altogether, Caracas seemed as dreamlike as everything else. Caracas, he read elsewhere, was one of the most expensive cities in the world, but was also 'a city where, if you have money, you can live like a king.' And he would have money, he would live like a king with the queen always by his side.

But before that happened he had to endure an eternity of

waiting. He went to the cinema and saw a Western, ate a meal, deliberately lingered in the streets so that he should take a late train back. In the Seven Seas he almost tiptoed up the stairs to avoid seeing Widgey. On the following morning he came down late, but met her coming from the dining-room to the parlour, cigarette in mouth.

'What's up, not working?' When he said that he had given up she nodded. 'Husband find out? I tell you, that woman's a fair bitch.'

'How can you possibly say that when you haven't met her.' It seemed important to defend Jenny, especially in face of attack by Widgey.

'Some women you don't have to meet. Come in, I can do with a bit of help.' The parlour table was piled with old bills, receipts, sheets on which figures had been scribbled. 'Trying to do the accounts for the year, can't make head or tail of 'em. From what I can see I made about three thousand quid last year, only I know I didn't. See if you can sort it out, there's a good boy.'

He spent the next three hours putting the bills in order and totalling them, sustained by several cups of tea and a ham sandwich. Widgey expressed her appreciation. 'Bloody marvellous you've got a real head for figures.'

'I'm going today.'

He had spoken abruptly, but she simply nodded. 'This chap, what's his name, Foster, kicked up?'

'Nothing like that. He's going away for a bit, so the job's finished for the time being.'

'He's going alone?'

'Yes.'

'And you're going too?' Without saying so Widgey implied clearly that she thought this strange. He said that it was best in every way for him to leave.

'You want to get away from those hard boys, that's a fact. But what I saw in the cards – you know? You don't want to take too much notice of that. Sometimes they work out, sometimes they don't.' It was then, perhaps out of the need to convince himself that the dream had become reality, that he showed her the air ticket. A moment later he cursed his stupidity. Widgey was rarely surprised, but this was one of the rare occasions. 'Venezuela. What the hell you going there for?'

'I've got a job there.'

Ash dropped on to the butcher's bills. 'It's to do with that woman. Isn't it?'

'You've got her on the brain. She's nothing to do with it.'

'What do you want to go to this place, what's the name of it, Caracas – for? How much did the ticket cost, two hundred quid?'

'Nothing like so much.'

'Over a hundred anyway. You've got no money, who paid for it?'

What a fool he had been to show it to her. 'I told you, I've got a job. The man who engaged me paid the fare.'

'What sort of job? You hadn't got one yesterday. That ticket means trouble, Tony, I can smell it.'

Something seemed to snap in his mind, as though a piece of elastic had been frayed until it suddenly snapped, and he was shrieking at her, using obscene words that were hardly ever in his mouth, talking about her sexual frustrations and her jealousy of him, accusing her of being like the rest of his family, wanting to rule his life, saying that he would leave now, this minute, and would never come back.

She heard him out, then started to roll another cigarette. 'Okay, you leave now if that's the way you feel.'

Upstairs in room thirteen, however, packing his suitcases among the apparatus of the past, the oversize tallboy and the wallpaper and the chest of drawers he had painted, he flung himself on the bed and wept without being able to give a better reason for his tears than that he had wanted Widgey to help in convincing him that the dream was true and that she had failed to do so. When he went down half an hour later he hesitated in front of the parlour door, then went it. She was asleep in the armchair, a copy of her latest library book, *Bettina and the Princess* on her lap. She looked small, worn, old. He put down the cases, went across and kissed her on the forehead. She opened her eyes.

'You're off, then.'

'That's right.'

'Give my love to Venezuela.' Her eyes closed again. He moved from foot to foot like a schoolboy, then walked out of the hotel and down the street with a feeling that he was walking away from the past for ever. He took a taxi to the station and left his cases in the cloakroom. Three-thirty. Six and a half hours to go.

He was on his way to the nearest cinema – time appeared in the guise of a large hole that must be plugged – when a car horn sounded behind him. Bradbury's face grinned from his car.

'Tony, old boy, what a bit of luck. Come and have a noggin.'

'At this time of day?'

'I know a place. Hop in.' Listening to Bradbury would fill time as well as anything else. A few minutes later, when they were drinking whisky in a second floor establishment called the Eldorado, he was less sure about this. Curtains were drawn over the windows and the lights were dim. In one corner two young men sat with their heads together whispering, behind the bar an ebony figure stood impassive. Bradbury's body, near to his, exuded warmth.

'The question is, old boy, filthy lucre. That money now, I don't want to press you, but when could you let me have it back?'

'You said there was no hurry.'

'That was last week. Things have changed.'

'Today's Friday. I can manage it next Monday.'

'You're sure about that.'

'No question. I said it was just a temporary loan.' On Monday he would be in one of the best hotels in Caracas, perhaps in the oval swimming pool. Now that his future was settled he could look with tolerance even upon Bradbury. He would pay the money back, Venezuelan bolivars converted into pounds and posted from Caracas. Or would that be wise? He saw with surprise that Bradbury seemed slightly disappointed.

'I had the impression you weren't too flush.'

'Next week I shall be.' It was wonderful to be able to say that.

'But you wouldn't say no to making another hundred, I take it.' Bradbury fiddled with his pony glass. A throaty giggle came from one of the young men. 'I daresay you've wondered about me.'

'Well, yes,' he said untruthfully.

'And if you did, you're right. I've got a little something going on the side. You remember old Van.'

He said that he remembered Van. Bradbury went on talking, a conversation full of half-hints, and suggestions that it would be better if he did not know too much. He did not really listen, until a word caught his attention.

'What was that?'

'A little trip abroad. On Saturday.'

He almost burst out laughing. If he could only show Bradbury the air ticket to Caracas, that would make him sit up. 'Amsterdam,' Bradbury said. 'I'll tell you the routine. Van won't meet you at the airport, but I'll give you an address to contact him. You spend a week-end there, he shows you the sights, and believe me old Van knows how to do that, Sunday evening you come back. Then we forget what you owe me and there's a hundred to come. What do you say?'

A second whisky stood in front of him. There was nothing to lose by agreement, but the drink made him feel truculent. 'What is it, diamonds or drugs?'

'Quiet.' Bradbury's hand squeezed his knee beneath the table.

'Anyway, the answer is no, thanks.'

'You don't want it?' There could be no doubt of Bradbury's surprise.

'You wouldn't be making the offer if there weren't strings attached. When I'm caught they can't touch you. That's the way you were at school. Any trouble, you slid out of it, somebody else carried the can.'

'What's up?' The mottled red face raised to his own wore an expression of injury. Tony could smell the lavatories. Should he mention them, would Bradbury know what he was talking about?

'You were a bully. At school. Don't think I've forgotten.' He stood up and Bradbury got up too. His thick cheeks were puckered with distress. He looked bewildered, like a man who has been bitten by a pet rabbit. His hand moved as though in reflex action and took its hard grip on Tony's upper arm. With one decisive blow, a man slapping a mosquito, he knocked off the hand. Bradbury's face purpled, its expression changed.

'I can be a bad enemy.'

'You just go to hell.' The cry was brave, although somehow inadequate. The face beside him, full of bad blood and reminiscent for a moment of another face he could not remember, seemed the most hateful thing in the world. He took a swing at it and missed. The whisky glass fell from the table and clattered on the floor.

'I shall want my money back. Next Monday. Or look out for trouble.'

He ignored the words, turned and, consciously bracing his shoulders, walked away. The ebony barman watched his going, the two young men raised heads for a moment and stared. Out in the street, after turning the corner he remembered whose face Bradbury had called to mind. It was that of his father, involved in argument at a football match.

He went into the nearest cinema, saw another Western, fell asleep and woke when nudged by the man in the next seat, tried to eat a sandwich in a pub but got no further than the first bite, walked about the town at random for an hour, looked at his watch. Nine-thirty.

Chapter 13

The last time, he thought as he walked up the wide sweep of Byron Avenue in a light damp mist coming off the sea, this is the last time. Even as he said this to himself it seemed impossible. The road with its cracked pavements and wide grass verge and dim street lamps now melting in mist was so utterly familiar that he seemed to have been walking up it for ever. This was where he had become a person, where love had given him some object in life. Was love the right word? 'We want the same thing,' she had said, and what did that mean but love? In his wallet the air ticket warmed him.

He passed the 'For Sale' notice, only dimly visible tonight. The Villa Majorca was completely dark. He was suddenly certain that the whole thing had been some kind of hoax. His knock at the back door would go unanswered, he would be left with the ticket and an unanswerable puzzle. A small gravel path wound away to the back of the house and he walked down this, making as little noise as possible, although what ears were there to hear? Somewhere inside the house, here at the back, a faint light showed. He rapped lightly with his knuckles on the kitchen door. Silence. He rapped again and the door opened.

The face she showed him was a white blur. As he stepped inside he saw that she was wearing gloves, a raincoat, high boots, a scarf round her head. They stood in a passage which led on the right to the kitchen, on the left to the main part of the house. The light came from a small scullery.

'All right?' She made a gesture and he saw the body, lying on the floor beside the kitchen door. It was wrapped in sacking and tied round with rope. He caught his breath in relief that he did not actually have to see the thing. Then the thought came to him that Foster might still be alive, that she had put him into the sack unconscious.

'The garage,' she said. They each picked up one end of the body, which felt horribly soft and pliable. A covered way led straight from the kitchen door into the garage and they took their burden round to the back of the car. Foster was a small man but he did not go in comfortably. He had to turn aside while she doubled up the legs and pushed them in. She closed and locked the boot, then switched on the garage light. The illumination showed her face not truly white but grey as tobacco ash, the lips drawn tensely together. They spoke in whispers.

'Are you sure?'

'What?'

'Is he really dead?'

'Don't be stupid.'

'Was it difficult? I mean to get him to take –'

'Shut up,' she said quietly but viciously. A shudder which he was unable to control passed through him. She stared, then asked if he wanted a drink. He shook his head. She whispered, 'You're not wearing gloves.'

'I forgot.'

'Do you want to leave your prints everywhere.'

She turned off the light, went back to the house and returned with a pair of woollen gloves which he put on. Then she motioned to him to open the garage doors. He did so, got in the car, and they drove away down a back road that ran into Byron Avenue. She had been driving for five minutes through the mist when he exclaimed. She turned her head.

'You've forgotten something.'

'What?'

'The weights.'

'They're in the boot.'

After that they did not speak. She drove carefully down back roads that were unknown to him. After twenty minutes she pulled the car into a natural lay-by, hidden among bushes. He looked round, bewildered.

'We can't get any nearer. The river's through the bushes.'

It was no more than thirty yards away, but the mist was thicker here, and he stumbled once or twice. The boat lay under tarpaulin. Peeled off it revealed itself as dull blue or black in colour. When she said 'Now,' he knew it meant that they would have to carry the body.

'I don't know if I can do it.'

She said without raising her voice, 'You have to.'

He could see them carrying the thing through the bushes. They slipped and the head came out of its covering, lolling free, the tongue showing. He turned and retched without vomiting. Without saying anything more she went back to the car. After a few moments he followed and helped her carry the thing. It was not as bad as he had feared, a mere inert bundle. Then he went back and got the weights, which had hooks on their ends. He cast off and began to row down the river while she sat in the stern attaching the weights to the rope round the sacking. The river bank moved past them slowly. Once he got too near to it and was brushed by the branches of a tree, which dropped moisture on to him. After that she took one of the oars. He asked how far they were from the sea.

'Less than a mile. I'll start the motor when the river broadens.'

The rowing seemed endless. Everything was dripping, it seemed to him that he was soaked in moisture. Strangely the mist cleared as they approached the sea, and when she scrambled into the bows, knelt down and pulled on the starting cord for the engine he saw in front of him black sea, felt the plash of waves on the side. When she started the motor the chugging sounded loud in his ears. Wind blew through his thin coat, a little spray went over him. The pinpoints of coastal light receded. He asked her how much farther they were going.

'Do you want them to find him?' she asked sharply. Five minutes later she cut the engine and asked if he was able to do it. The very lack of passion in her voice shamed him into action. He picked up the thing, heavy now with its weight, half-threw and half-pushed it over the side. There was a splash. She took a torch from her pocket and shone it downwards. Nothing was visible but the black sea. She turned the boat and they headed back to the mouth of the river.

With that final act accomplished his spirits were lightened. He wanted to talk, but sensed that she would not like it. The row back up the river was longer and harder than that out to sea, and he would not have known where to tie up if she had not told him. After tying up he was in a feverish hurry to be away but he helped her as, calmly and methodically, she stowed the oars and fitted the tarpaulin into place.

Walking back to the car he said, 'I'm sorry. You did everything.'

'It doesn't matter.'

'I wanted to help, it was just –' He did not finish the sentence. They reached the car. She unlocked the boot, shone the torch inside and nodded with satisfaction at its emptiness. Inside the car he produced the ticket. 'You wanted to see it.'

She took a wad of notes from her bag. 'Ten tens, twenty fives, the rest in ones.'

'Jenny.'

'Yes?'

'How am I going to get the money out there? I mean, there are currency restrictions on how much I can take out.'

'Put it in your wallet.'

'But I might be searched.'

'It's a ten thousand to one chance. If you don't want to carry it, parcel it up and post it to yourself in Venezuela. Then it's a million to one chance they won't open it.'

'There must be some way that's completely safe.'

'Not when we've got so little time. There's no risk really.' She looked at him. 'What's the matter? You've got an air ticket and two hundred and fifty pounds in your pocket. I'm the one who should worry. You could run out on me.'

'You know I shan't do that.'

'Yes.' She started the car and drove away.

'How soon will you come? In a fortnight, you said.'

'As soon as I can. I'll have to settle things here.'

'Venezuela seems to be a marvellous country. The cities, anyway. Do you know Caracas has a perfect climate? I shall stay at the Grand, it has the most wonderful swimming pool. If that's full I shall stay at the Corona. Shall I let you know where I am, I'll write poste restante to Southbourne, is that a good idea?'

'Perfect.'

He felt a need to cancel out what they had just done by speech. 'We're going to be happy.'

As they approached the town she drew in to the kerb, shut off the engine. 'I'll put you off here, you can walk to the station.'

She looked straight in front of her. He leaned forward and kissed the side of her face awkwardly, then got out of the car. She put in the clutch and moved away.

Chapter 14

He spent the following hours in a state of dazed happiness, like a small boy who has swallowed several doses of nasty medicine as prelude to a promised treat and now, with the medicine consumed, sees unalloyed pleasure ahead. He spent the night at a hotel near London Airport, arranged for a six-thirty call – the ticket said he had to report at seven-fifteen – and tried to sleep, but found it impossible. In the end he took the travel pamphlets out of his case and spent an hour looking at them.

Caracas would be wonderful for a time, but no doubt they would get tired of it. And after that? Perhaps a journey to the hinterland which revealed, so the pamphlets said, the real history of the country. He was not much interested in ruins and monuments, but probably he would learn Spanish. He saw that there were ample opportunities for gambling. He would be careful about that. Perhaps it would be a good idea for Jenny to control the money, and to make him an allowance. At the airport he would buy a Spanish phrasebook. He did not think at all of Eversley Foster, who seemed to belong already to a past so distant that it might never have existed. Nor did he think of Jenny. Strangely enough, his mind turned to recollections of the General, the book of memoirs, his own behaviour. Those wretched little fiddles he had worked, and then the business with the cheque – he felt really ashamed of them now. Yet even these thoughts were not wholly painful, for they carried with them the consolation that there would be no need for him to do anything of that kind ever again. With that in his mind he fell asleep at three o'clock in the morning.

He woke at six, and by the time his six-thirty call came had washed and shaved. He dressed with care, allowing himself to consider whether it should be the charcoal grey suit or lightweight trousers and sports jacket. He knew perfectly well that the decision had already been made in favour of informality, for in thirteen hours of travelling the suit would get rather painfully creased, but still he laid out both sets of clothes on the bed and talked to himself aloud as he weighed the possibilities, wondering what the weather would be like in Caracas when he arrived at night. Were the nights chilly? 'Even if they are I think this is going to be rather cosier, don't you?' he said to an imaginary companion before hanging up the charcoal grey again in his travelling wardrobe. As a gesture, purely as a gesture to Jenny because they were distinctly unsuitable, he put the orbicular links into the cuffs of his shirt. The money stayed in his wallet. He had decided to take Jenny's ten thousand to one chance, and not to bother with a parcel. His euphoria was such that it did not need support from food. He did no more than nibble at the toast and sip at the coffee brought to his room. Then into the car he had ordered to take him the couple of miles to the airport. The car arrived on the dot, everything was going to plan.

'European, sir, or Oceanic?' the driver asked.

'Oceanic. I'm going to Caracas. Venezuela.'

'Venezuela, eh. You want to be careful. Friend of mine, merchant seaman, unshipped a crate of bananas once, bloody snake crawled out of it, six foot long and thick as your arm.'

'I'll take my chance,' he said laughingly.

'Lot of prickly heat you get there too, they tell me.'

It was annoying that the man kept on in this way, and he told the fellow rather sharply that Caracas had one of the best climates in the world, springtime the whole year round. The faint blemish on his pleasure was removed when they pulled up outside the airport building, a friendly porter took his baggage to be weighed, and he was swept up in the delightful process of having his ticket checked and obtaining his boarding card for the plane. His bags had disappeared.

'I don't suppose I shall see them again until I get to Caracas,' he said to the girl behind the counter.

'That's right.'

'They wouldn't take them off by mistake at Amsterdam or Zurich or Lisbon?' He said it archly, not because he really feared this would happen, but to make conversation and actually to roll the names on his tongue. The girl took him seriously.

'Oh no, sir. You don't change planes, they're just stopping points. You'll find they are still on board when you get to Caracas.'

She smiled. How nice she was. He smiled back. 'I'm sure I shall.'

'Have a good trip.' What a different world this was from the one in which people threatened him because of unpaid debts and borrowed money, the world in which distasteful things had to be done. But that was all behind him, unalloyed pleasure lay ahead. He strolled about, bought newspapers and magazines and the Spanish phrase-book, felt the comfortable wad of money, looked at the people sitting in the lounge and wondered which of them would be fellow passengers. Very soon the call came and he was ready for the names which followed each other like notes in music: '... Amsterdam, Zurich, Lisbon ...' Oh yes, that's mine, he thought, those places are for me. As they moved through the final barrier two anonymous-looking men stood on either side glancing at passports and repeating the same words. 'Have a good trip, Mr da Silva ... Mr Cournos ... Mrs Walsh ... Mr Kellett ... Mr Medura ...' He waited for 'Mr Jones', but instead one of the men looked at the passport, then at him, and asked him to step aside.

'Is something wrong with my passport? How long will it take?'

'Just in here. Shan't keep you more than a couple of minutes.'

He was shown into a small office. Through the windows he could see the man pick up a telephone and hear his voice murmuring indistinguishable words. He could not sit down but paced the room, looking at the desk which had a white blotting pad and 'In' and 'Out' trays, both empty, then at a notice on the wall which listed all the articles that could not be brought into or taken out of the country, then again through the glass at the figures who were passing through the barrier. Was he being kept back deliberately so that he would miss the flight? After a space of time he could not have measured, although it was perhaps no more than the two minutes mentioned, he opened the door. The last passengers were passing through.

'Look, I've got my boarding ticket. I don't want to miss the plane.'

295

The man turned, his expression placatory. 'Very sorry, Mr Jones. They'll be here in a moment.'

'But who are they?' He did not like to be aggressive, because the man was so polite.

'Here they come.' He nodded at a point behind Tony. An abrupt turn and he confronted them, two large men wearing hats, the leading one apologetically smiling.

'Mr Jones. Sorry to have kept you.'

'What do you want?' With dismay he heard his voice rising.

'Don't suppose this will take more than a couple of minutes.' They ushered him back into the room. The first man sat in the chair behind the desk and the other stood beside the door. 'Lovely morning. Perfect day for flying.'

So there was no question of stopping him from leaving on the plane. The sense of relief he felt showed itself in a nervous laugh. He took the seat that was offered him, opposite the man.

'Mr Anthony Jones,' the man said reflectively. He was hairy, with a red, drinker's nose. 'So you're going to Caracas. Venezuela. Never been myself. Why?'

The last word, barked out, surprised him. 'What do you mean?'

'Why are you going? Business, pleasure, new job?'

'I've got a new job. But anyway, I've had enough of England,' he said recklessly.

'Have you now?' Without emphasis the big man repeated, 'Had enough of England, did you hear that?'

'I heard it,' said the man by the door. He was big too, but where his companion had taken his hat off this man kept his on. They both began to laugh.

Tony stood up. There on the desk, two feet away from him, lay the blue-covered book that was his entrance card to the new world, the new life. Leaning forward he snatched up the book from the table, and moved towards the door. Both men stared at him in amazement, their laughter cut off as suddenly as a record from which the needle has been lifted.

'Now then,' said Hatless, 'no use going on like that, you know. That won't do you any good, interfering with the course of inquiries, Mr Jones. If you want to know my authority, here it

The Man Whose Dreams Came True

is.' He produced from his wallet some kind of card and put it back again.

'Or Mr Bain-Truscott,' said Hat.

Their questions fell thick and fast as a sudden snowstorm.

'You've been working for Mr Foster, Eversley Foster, right?'

'Staying with your aunt, a Mrs Widgeon, at the Seven Seas Hotel.'

'Quarrelled with her yesterday, right?'

'Helping Mr Foster with a book he was writing, correct?'

'Packed your bags and left in a hurry.'

'Quarrelled with Mr Foster too, correct?'

'Then off to South America, funny place to go.'

'Wouldn't go there without a reason, not South America.'

'Not South America, no. Stole from him, didn't you?'

'Then when he found out, that was it. You meant it right from the start, had it in mind.'

'Or why use Bain-Truscott?'

'Why use Bain-Truscott, right. When your name's Jones.'

Silence again, and they were both looking at him. He found his voice. 'I don't understand, I don't know what you mean. I was working for Mr Foster, but the job had finished. And I – about calling myself Bain-Truscott – what's wrong about that, it's not illegal.'

'No, it isn't,' Hatless said. 'I'm a Jones myself, I can understand how you feel. Perhaps this is all a mistake.'

He felt that he must make it clear that he had not meant to insult this hairy red-nosed Jones. 'I didn't mean there was anything wrong with Jones, it's just, I've called myself Bain-Truscott for a long time.' The customs man could no longer be seen through the glass, something was being said over the speaker system, it must be the last call for the flight. 'I have to go, I shall miss my plane.'

'Don't worry about that, Mr Jones. Plenty of time.'

'But there isn't. The passengers have gone.'

'You've got ten minutes yet, we'll make sure you don't miss the flight.'

At these words from the now friendly Jones relief swept over him, and with it a vivid picture of the thing being dropped from the motor launch with the weights attached to it. There was one chance in a million, or no chance at all, that the thing had been found, these two police officers must be here because of some misunderstanding. Realization of this made him smile his own particular smile that had charmed so many women, and to speak with a serenity that could not fail to be impressive.

'That's very good of you. Tell me how I can help.'

Turn out his pockets! There were many things that he might have expected to be asked of him, but this was not one of them. Light-heartedly he complied, putting everything on the desk, loose change, a key ring with the keys of his cases on it, wallet and fountain pen, ticket – he put these things down with a confident and confiding smile, and he smiled again as he took off his watch and put it beside the other things. He picked up his topcoat, delved into the pockets and came up with some odds and ends of used bus tickets. In a final dramatic gesture he pulled out the linings of his pockets to show that nothing had been concealed.

Hat had come over to the desk and stood looking down at the things lying on it. Neither he nor Jones moved to examine them. Then Jones spoke, and his voice was no longer friendly.

'Where did you get those links?'

He made an involuntary gesture towards his sleeve. The links were invisible now, but his movement revealed them again. 'They were a present.'

'Tiepin went with them.' That was Hat. The words were a statement, not a question, and Tony did not reply. Now Hat leaned over, stretched his hand to the wallet, glanced inside and passed it to Jones who carefully took out the notes and sorted them into piles according to their denominations. Hat retreated to the door and when Jones spoke again it was in a heavy Bradbury voice, the voice of school, authority, doom.

'Where did this money come from?'

'I –' He shook his head, swallowed, started again. 'I had to have money to go abroad. It's mine.'

'I'll tell you then. Mr Foster drew them out of the bank yesterlay morning. The tenners are new, and the bank have a note of he numbers. They correspond.'

Mr Foster. He could only shake his head. 'I don't understand.'

'Don't kid me, son. These links were Foster's too, right?'

'I told you, they were a present.'

'You stole them and Foster found out, you had a row and killed him, then pinched the money, right?'

'No, no,' he said again and then, because they were so completely wrong, he was led into indiscretion. 'He's gone away, Foster, he said he was going away. Just because he's disappeared – you can't prove murder without a body.'

Jones stared at him. 'I said don't kid me, son, I don't like to be kidded. And what's the point, anyway? Show him.'

Like some malign prestidigitator Hat produced from nowhere pictures, horrible and glossy, a body in a room lying in the crumpled awkward attitude of death, the head turned away, wrecked and bloody. There were several pictures, and he could not bear to look at them.

'You wouldn't know it was Foster from those,' Jones said. 'But try this one.'

He looked at the picture and felt a roaring sound in his ears. Groping for the chair he fell rather than sat in it. He had seen the photograph before, on the piano. It showed the elderly erect figure with a small moustache who had been named by Jenny as her cousin Mortimer Lands.

PART THREE

Dreams and Realities

Chapter 1

At first the situation had so strong a flavour of absurdity that he could not take the warning, the arrest, and immurement in the prison hospital seriously. A *hospital*, of all places, did they think he was ill? Not until he was remanded did realities begin to come home to him. Had he got a solicitor? No. Had he private means, or did he wish to apply for legal aid? Legal aid.

In the cell below the Court his jailer, an elderly cougher, said: 'Clerk of the Court says would you like – cough – Washington, Maple and Hussick, they're next on the rota. Are they agreeable?'

'Agreeable?'

'Do you agree to accept their services?'

'I suppose so.' Since he knew no other solicitor there was really no choice. He asked timidly, 'Are they here?'

The man's laugh was punctuated by a cough. 'Here, no, they're not here.'

'How will they know?'

'They'll be told, don't worry.'

He was taken away to another prison hospital, Brixton this time. Everybody was very nice to him, and the food was surprisingly good. He asked the old man in the next bed, who had a cough remarkably like the jailer's, why they were in the hospital.

' 'Cause it's bloody cushy, mate, that's why, and because of my lungs. They know my lungs. I've been here before.'

'No, I meant why am I here. I'm not ill.'

' 'Cause you're up for murder, they always put 'em in hospital. The doc's got his eye on you, don't worry. You're what they call under observation.'

Tony looked round, but nobody seemed to be observing him. That evening one of the male nurses asked, 'Everything all right, no complaints?' The inquiry might have been made of a visitor in a hotel.

'Yes, thank you. But I haven't seen my solicitor.'

'Plenty of time,' the man said. 'Don't you worry.'

That night, however, he did begin to worry. He felt like somebody emerging from an anaesthetic aware that something is terribly wrong with him, but ignorant of the precise nature of his illness. Reluctantly he acknowledged that in some way he had been betrayed, and that there was only one possible betrayer, but he found it impossible to dwell on the details of what might have happened. The image of Jenny's face came before him, the neat profile, delicately pallid cheek, firm mouth and chin. What had happened to her, what was she doing, what had she said to the police? When he determined resolutely to put this image away from him he could think of nothing but the ticket to Caracas. It had been taken away with the rest of his things when he went into hospital, but where was it now? Supposing he were let out in a week, would it still be possible to use the ticket? This was the first thing he mentioned when, on the following day, he was told that his solicitor Mr Hussick had arrived. The interview took place in a small square room with flowered chintz curtains. No prison officer was present.

'Your ticket?' Mr Hussick beamed. 'I'm afraid I don't know anything about that, but I'm sure we don't need to bother about it for the moment.'

'I don't want to lose the money. I shall go there as soon as this is cleared up.'

'I'll make inquiries.' Mr Hussick wondered for a moment whether his client was showing diminished responsibility. He looked sane enough, although of course *that* was nothing to go by. Mr Hussick was a little sandy man with dancing eyebrows, and as he often said he liked to look on the bright side of things. 'How are they treating you? Best porridge in London, they tell me. Haven't sampled it myself.' Mr Hussick laughed with sheer pleasure at the thought of his sampling the porridge, and his eyebrows danced up and down.

'This is all some awful mistake,' Tony said tentatively, and was surprised by the solicitor's hearty agreement.

'I'm sure it is. That's what we've got to put right.'

'I should like – I want to get out of here.'

The eyebrows danced up and down. Mr Hussick laughed heartily, and then became momentarily grave. 'It's a serious charge, you know. The most serious charge in the book, that's what they've thrown at you.' He shook his head as though any decent sporting police force would have made the charge a lesser one, then took out what looked uncommonly like a child's exercise book, and said in the tone of a doctor asking a patient to describe his symptoms, 'If you'll just tell me exactly what happened. Take it quite easy, quite gently, there's no hurry at all. Don't leave anything out.'

Don't leave anything out. 'Has anybody else been arrested?'

'Not so far as I know.' With more assurance he said, 'Of course the police don't take me into their confidence but – nobody else at the moment, certainly.'

So Jenny was still free. *Don't leave anything out.* But it was inevitable, for his sake and for Jenny's, that he should leave things out, for how could he tell the whole story without incriminating them both? He told the solicitor of the work he had been engaged to do, of the fact that the work had ended because Foster was going abroad, and of the revelation about Foster's identity when he saw the photograph. He said nothing about the car or about the body – whose had it been? – that they had thrown into the sea. Mr Hussick made notes in a neat clerical hand. When Tony had finished he looked up, his eyebrows not dancing but apparently permanently raised.

'So you never met Foster?'

'I never met the man who was – whose photograph the police showed me.' Hopefully he said, 'There's no question that it *was* Foster?'

'None at all. Can you describe the man who was introduced to you as Foster?' Tony described him, up to the streak of white on the top of his head, and Mr Hussick noted the details, asked if Tony had any idea of the man's identity, and then tapped the exercise book with his pen.

'What it comes to is this. You were deceived by Mrs Foster from the start. Do you have any idea what might have been the object of this deception?' Tony shook his head. 'Its effect has been that you are under arrest. Are you saying that this was her purpose? It would be a serious accusation.'

'I can't believe –' What could he not believe? He started the sentence again. 'I'm not accusing her of anything.'

Mr Hussick nodded in a neutral manner. 'As you may have gathered, the body was found in the living-room. Death had been caused by head injuries. At the moment I'm rather in the dark about the police case. I shan't know what it is in detail until the Magistrate's Court hearing.'

'I see.'

'But there are two or three things we might try to clear up now. First of all have you any record, any criminal record? It wouldn't come out at the trial, but I should like to know. Nothing? That's good. Then, why Caracas?'

The words *prosecution, defence, trial,* had distracted him. 'What?'

'It seems a long way to go, but I understand you had a job waiting out there.'

'No, that isn't quite right. I'd saved the money and I'm fed up with England. I thought I could easily get a job there.'

'I see.' Hussick seemed about to say something more, but did not do so. He continued almost casually. 'The police believe that the murder weapon was a hammer, and I understand it has your prints on it. Can you tell me how they might have got there?'

It was not Mr Hussick's practice to make up his mind about any case in advance, and he regarded all his clients as innocent until they were found guilty, but he was disturbed by the look on Jones's face. He meant to wipe his prints off the hammer and then forgot, the solicitor thought, and then put the idea firmly away from him. He offered cheerful words about it being early days yet to think of counsel and said he would handle things himself in the Magistrate's Court. It would help if they could find the mysterious man with a white streak in his hair.

'You must be able to find him,' Jones said earnestly. He was a handsome young man, Hussick thought, although a little on the willowy side. He ought to make a good impression in the witness box.

'We'll do our damnedest. And let me know if you think of anything else, I'm here to help.' A wave of the hand and he was gone. The officer who had been waiting outside the door took Tony back to the ward.

Chapter 2

Life in the prison hospital seemed to be based upon a wrong conception of what he was like, for he was persistently treated as though he were an invalid or a schoolboy. One day he went to see the Medical Officer, who gave him a careful physical examination and asked how he was getting on.

'What do you think of the others, the other patients? Get on with them?'

'They're all right. But we're not patients, we're prisoners.'

'What about your general health? Ever have any serious illnesses? As a child perhaps?'

'Only the usual things, measles, mumps, chickenpox.'

'Meningitis? Any form of rheumatic fever? Nothing serious at all, you've been lucky, haven't you.' He made little ticks and crosses on a form. 'You're eating well, I'm glad to hear that.'

Back in the ward he asked the old man the reason for the examination. 'Just routine. They always like to have a look at you.' On the following day he shook hands earnestly before leaving. Tony had somehow not liked to ask what he was charged with, but after the old man had gone he spoke to the warder and learned that it was rape.

On the following day he had two visitors. When he entered the interview room a little round-shouldered man was looking out of the window into a courtyard, clinking coins in his pocket. When he turned, Tony recognized his father.

Mr Jones came forward and shook his son by the hand. His moustache was grey and he had grown fatter, but otherwise he had changed little. His characteristic smell of beer, tobacco and sweat was as strong as ever.

'How are things then? You're pretty fit from the look of you. Take any exercise?'

'An hour a day.'

'That's good. I'm keeping pretty well. Nora too, she sent her

308

regards. I've retired now, you know. Taken to watching the Codgers again, makes something to do.' The Codgers was the football team they had watched in Tony's childhood. 'Not a patch on what they were, though, shouldn't be surprised if they go down. You follow them at all?'

'No.' How could he have loved and later hated this foolish little man? 'What did you come for?'

'Just wondered if there was anything you wanted. I brought these along.' He snapped open his brief-case. The officer by the door moved forward but relaxed when Mr Jones took out a bunch of grapes.

Tony felt suddenly very angry. He flung the grapes on the floor. 'I don't want your bloody grapes.' His father looked at him in astonishment.

'Now then,' the officer said, 'that's enough of that.'

Mr Jones snapped the brief-case shut and stood with lowered head. 'That's how it is, then. You're no good, I always said it. No good and never been any good.'

Tony stood up too. 'Get out.'

His father appealed to the prison officer. 'What do you think of it, eh? You bring 'em up, you give 'em a good home, and see the way it turns out. Right from the time he was a boy I said to his mother, "You're spoiling that kid." I was away a lot, had to be you understand, business.'

'Get out, get out.' Tony advanced upon his father. The officer stepped between them, and Mr Jones went. The officer shook his head.

'You've fairly blotted your copybook, you have.'

'If he comes again, I won't see him.'

'Your own father, too. I don't know. Knock you about when you were a kid, did he? Might have been better if he had, at that.' He offered the comment in a philosophical rather than a critical manner.

The second visitor – he had grown cautious, and asked the name in advance – was Widgey. She gave him a perfunctory kiss and said, 'Looks as though the cards were right, eh? How the hell did you get into this mess?' He said truthfully that he didn't know. 'The police have been on to me asking questions. I told them we had a bit of a spat that last day. Had to when they asked me, understand?'

'I understand. It doesn't matter.'

'Don't suppose it does. Wanted to tell you though, because they're calling me as a witness. Can't really refuse.' She offered a cigarette and he took it.

'Widgey, would you do something for me?'

'What is it?'

'There's someone I want very much to see. I don't like to write because – well, I don't know what to say. Will you get in touch with her, go and see her, ask her to come.'

Widgey's thin mouth was clamped shut. She released smoke through her nostrils. 'You're a fool.'

'You've never met her, you don't know what she's like.'

'I'll tell you what she's like. This is something the police let out when they saw me, though they didn't mean to. She's the chief witness against you, that's what she's like.'

Chapter 3

'Your name is Genevieve Foster, and you are the widow of the deceased, Eversley Foster.'

'Yes.'

'What was your husband's occupation?'

'He was a director of several companies. He had spent a good deal of his life in South Africa, that was before I met him, and he had an interest in a mining company out there. Most of his directorships were connected with South Africa.'

'And he went up to London on business every weekday?'

'Yes.'

'Will you tell the Court in what circumstances you made the acquaintance of the defendant.'

'I met him one day at the house of Mr Bradbury. I knew Mrs Bradbury, and he came to tea. I brought him back to Southbourne and happened to mention that my husband wanted secretarial help on a book he was writing in his spare time. It was a book on local topography. Bain-Truscott, that was what he called himself, said he had secretarial experience. He produced references.'

'Is it a fact that the references were forgeries?'

'I understand so. I did not take them up.'

'And your husband engaged him.'

'Yes. Eversley thought he would be suitable. He left work each day for the secretary to do. Bain-Truscott came in the morning and left before lunch.'

'Was he an efficient worker?'

'I believe so. Eversley did not complain.'

'But after a few days your husband did complain to you about something, I believe. Tell us about it.'

'It was at the beginning of the second week. Eversley missed a valuable pair of cuff links and a matching tiepin.'

Tony closed his eyes, but her image remained on his retina,

pale and composed. He opened his eyes again to see the door of the Court open and a man enter silently and sit down on one of the benches. The weak handsomeness, the white streak in his hair – it was Foster! He wrote a note quickly on one of the bits of scrap paper provided for him: 'Man with white streak in hair – three rows from back – he is man I knew as Foster,' and passed it down to Mr Hussick. The solicitor's brows rose skyward. He nodded and passed over the piece of paper to his clerk, who sat next to him. The clerk got up and went out, grinning. What was there to grin about?

It is one of the peculiarities of English law that a prosecution case must be presented in full in the Magistrate's Court, where it is decided whether or not the accused person should be sent for trial, while the defence may reserve its case. The advantage to the defence is more apparent than real, because the proceedings are reported fully so that the jury empanelled to hear the trial know a great deal about the case already, and what they know is likely to favour the prosecution. The proceedings lack the tenseness of a dress rehearsal because the principal actors, the counsel, are missing. On the prosecution side a bored and sometimes in-audible young barrister appeared on behalf of the Director of Public Prosecutions, and Mr Hussick had told Tony that he proposed to handle the defence personally at this stage.

'Nothing to do really,' he had said when he saw Tony just before the hearing began. 'Hear what they've got to say, spot their weak points, bide our time, that's the way.'

'But I thought –' Tony had been about to say, '– that I should have a proper counsel,' but changed this to '– that you were engaging counsel.'

'So I shall, so I shall, and you'll have the best. But at this stage, what's the point? It's not as though we're fighting here.'

'Aren't we?'

'Certainly not. Reserve our defence, save our big guns for the time when they're needed. You'll see.' Mr Hussick spoke as though his client might be involved in many such trials, from each of which he would learn something.

So the atmosphere was undramatic, the Court was not even quite full, everything seemed to be conducted *sotto voce*, but as

one witness succeeded another and left the box unquestioned or
only cursorily challenged by Mr Hussick, Tony's spirits
dropped. There was Carlos Cotton to tell about the money Tony
owed him, and Bradbury to give an account of the loan that
remained unrepaid. There was Widgey, obviously giving evidence under protest. Then came Mr Penny, which turned out to
be the name of the little jeweller he had asked to value the links
and tiepin. A bank clerk named Podger came to say that Mr
Foster had drawn out two hundred and fifty pounds on Friday
morning, and to confirm the numbers of the ten pound notes.
Then there was Dr Dailey, who was what they called a Home
Office pathologist. He said that Foster had been killed at between eight and ten o'clock on Friday evening by several blows
struck from behind. The hammer was produced in Court and he
confirmed that it was stained with blood of Foster's group, and
had one or two hairs from Foster's head adhering to it. And Dr.
Dailey was succeeded by a stiff self-confident fingerprint man
named Moreston who said that he had found two clear prints of
Tony's fingers on the hammer, together with several other
prints too smudged for identification. Hussick questioned none
of these witnesses, but sat with a smile of apparent self-satis-
faction on his face, taking an occasional note. And now here was
Jenny, intolerably calm and beautiful. What was she saying?

'On Friday morning my husband drew out two hundred and
fifty pounds from the bank.'

'Was it unusual for him to draw so large an amount?'

'A little unusual. He had a foible for paying all the accounts
in cash each month where this was possible, rather than by
cheque. This month they were for rather large amounts.'

'Can you remember anything else he said on that morning?'

'Yes. Before leaving for London he said that he would have it
out with Bain-Truscott, that is about the links. He was convinced that Bain-Truscott had taken them.'

'Anything else?'

'Yes. He asked me to tell Bain-Truscott that he would like to
see him on Friday evening. I told him when he came that
morning, and he said all right.'

'Were you in on Friday evening?'

'No. Eversley knew that I hate scenes. I arranged to go out to dinner with my cousin at Redling, particularly so that I should not be there.'

'After that, you knew nothing more of the matter until you returned home shortly before midnight and found your husband's body?'

'That is correct.'

'And then you telephoned the police?'

'Yes.'

During this recital she had not looked at him. Once her tongue came out and quickly licked her upper lip as it had done after they made love. Remembering this, and remembering the things they had planned but which she never meant to carry out, he gripped the side of the box in which he sat so tightly that a splinter of wood went into the middle finger of his left hand. He took a piece of paper, scrawled on it in trembling capitals A L L L I E S and handed it down to Mr Hussick. The solicitor looked at it and put it aside. His clerk came back, still grinning. Would Hussick attack her, say she was lying? The solicitor rose from his chair. 'No questions,' he said. Jenny made her way out of the box. The man with the white streak in his hair rose and followed as she left the Court.

He hardly listened to the rest of the evidence. On Hussick's application he was committed for trial at the Old Bailey instead of at the local Assize near Southbourne, on the ground that there might be some local prejudice against him.

Chapter 4

After these proceedings he realized for the first time that his acquittal was not inevitable. This was made clear by Mr Hussick who came to see him and said, with no diminution of cheerfulness, that they mustn't let the other side have it all their own way.

'But you didn't challenge them. I told you, her story was all lies.'

'Tactics, tactics.' Mr Hussick shot up his eyebrows. 'Play your cards close to your chest. One thing, though. I've got to know what the cards are.'

'How do you mean?'

'You've been a little bit naughty. You never told me about Mr Penny now, did you? I'm not going to hide anything from you. They have a case, no doubt about it they have a case.'

'Everything she said was a lie.'

Mr Hussick ignored this. 'I'll tell you what I don't like. Taking those links for valuation, they'll make a lot of that. Ask how you got hold of them. Then there's the money. I mean, I don't think we can deny that it was Foster's money, can we? And of course the hammer, I don't care for the hammer. Then your appointment with Foster on Friday evening, you must have known it wouldn't be pleasant, what happened? If I could clear up those points I'd feel a lot happier.' He opened the exercise book at a blank page.

'Suppose they can't be explained.'

'Oh, but they must be,' Mr Hussick said happily. 'It would be very unwise to offer no explanation.'

'You mean I might be found guilty?'

'I mean you mustn't keep anything back. You must tell me the truth.'

'What about my ticket?'

'Ticket? Oh yes. When the time comes I don't think you'll find there will be any problem.'

'Who was the man I pointed out in Court?'

'He's Mrs Foster's cousin, the one she had dinner with on that Friday night. His name is Mortimer Lands.'

Mortimer Lands. He had been deceived, then, from the start he had been deliberately deceived. The body in the bedroom twisting like a fish above the blue eye of the medallion, the gifts, the plans for the promised land of Venezuela, all of these had been a dream. The deception was reality. This was what he had to endure and to accept.

'She planned it. She planned the whole thing.'

'What's that?' For once Mr Hussick appeared surprised.

'She gave me the cuff links, said she'd bought them for me, that they were a present.' Beginning at that point he told the whole story, Jenny's plan for disposing of Foster, the money she had given him for the fare and later for living in Caracas, the drive on Friday night out to the motor launch, the passage down the river to the sea and the thing being dropped overboard, then his own departure to London and to the airport. To tell the whole story was a relief, and he felt himself to be absolved from any consequence in doing so, because this little man was on his side.

Mr Hussick covered several pages of his notebook. When the narrative flow had stopped he rubbed his nose. He seemed for once hardly to know what to say, and when he did speak it was in a manner unusually tentative.

'If that's the complete story –'

'It is.'

'You were on your own account prepared to be accessory to a crime. It doesn't put you in a good light.' Tony made no reply to this. 'Although in fact according to you no crime was committed. What was in the sack? The thing you threw over into the water.'

'How do I know?'

'No, of course not. This line involves an outright attack on Mrs Foster, you understand that?'

'Yes.' He leaned forward. 'Somebody may have seen the car as we drove to the launch, or on the way back. Someone may have seen the launch going down the river.'

'Possibly.'

'You could make inquiries.'

'Naturally I'll do that. You must understand that while legal aid covers my costs and those of your counsel, it may be difficult to put in hand a full scale inquiry of this kind.'

'She wasn't where she says at ten o'clock that night. She was in her own house, and afterwards she was with me.'

'The police will have checked this, I'm sure. I'll have a word with them.' Mr Hussick closed the exercise book, and said with a return to his customary cheerfulness, 'Let's consider who we should brief for you. What would you say to Franklin Russell? George Pooling? Magnus Newton?'

'I don't know any of them. But if it's a matter of money –'

'Oh no no, not so far as counsel are concerned. If they aren't too busy they will be happy to take it on. It's just that legal aid won't run to a great deal of money.' He left the sentence rather hanging in air, for he had been about to add *being spent on a wild goose chase*, but refrained.

'I leave it to you.'

'The best thing you could do. I'll let you know developments. Don't worry, keep smiling.' With a pat on the shoulder he was gone.

That night Tony slept soundly. He felt that by telling the truth he had exorcised Jenny from his mind for ever.

On the following day he saw the psychiatrist, who gave him tests involving putting shapes in different relationships to each other, and then consulted some papers. He was an urbane balding man with a pleasant smile.

'Well, Anthony, you know why I'm seeing you. You've been examined by the doctor and you're in good physical condition. I have to report on you mentally.'

'Whether I'm mad, you mean?'

'That isn't a word we use. It's a question of whether you are fully responsible for your actions, and that involves all sorts of things like how easy you find it to adjust to other people and so on.' The smile said that there were no aces hidden in his sleeve. 'They tell me you've been very cooperative. There's just one little thing, what was it now? Oh yes, when your father came to see you. You got rather upset. Why was that?'

'We don't get on.'

317

'I see. What about your mother?'

'She's dead.'

'I know that, but how did you get on with her. Did you love her?'

'I suppose so.' The man was as comforting as a bedwarmer. 'She committed suicide. Took sleeping tablets. I found her.'

The psychiatrist, who had an account of the suicide on the paper in front of him, nodded. 'That upset you a lot?'

'Yes.'

'It was after her suicide that you hated your father?'

'It was his fault. He had a mistress, she found out. And then he married this woman, very soon afterwards.'

'You felt it was a betrayal of your relationship with your mother?'

'I suppose so.' Had he felt that? He didn't know. Had he ever loved his mother? Surely it had been his father who was loved. 'It was because of him that she took the pills.'

'That's what you feel.'

'It's why she took them.'

'It was a terrible experience for you,' the psychiatrist said in his warm voice. 'And soon after it you left home. Then you had several jobs, but you kept none of them for more than a short time. Tell me about those jobs . . .'

He emerged bewildered from this long session. It seemed to him that his involvement in what had happened at the Villa Majorca was being treated far too seriously. Why should it be a reason for digging into his childhood and youth, why should it be thought that they had anything to do with it? He tried to say something like this to the psychiatrist, who seemed to regard his attitude as novel and curious, and interesting chiefly because it was suggestive about Tony's state of mind. But surely it was a normal thing to think that a single incident in the present had nothing to do with the past? Lying in bed that night, fingering the coarse sheet that for some reason brought the image of Jenny before his eyes, he thought of all the things he might have said. 'I am going to be charged with murdering a man named Eversley Foster so that I could take his money. Will you tell me how that can possibly be connected with the dislike I feel for my father or with my mother's death?' Let him try to answer that one. Staring into the blackness of the ward he thought of half a dozen other questions that would have dented the psychiatrist's shell of urbanity, but of course the man was not there to answer them.

Chapter 5

During the next few days there were several developments in connection with the case, some of them important.

Franklin Russell read the papers given to him by Mr Hussick and then turned the brief down. He said that this was because he had a full plate, but Mr Hussick suspected that it was because of the nature of the defence. George Pooling was taken ill with pneumonia after playing eighteen holes in a rainstorm, and had to be ruled out. Magnus Newton, however, said yes, and if he was not the subtlest cross-examiner or the most intelligent man in the world, there was no doubt that he had a flourishing criminal practice. Hussick left the papers with him and a couple of days later had a conference at Newton's chambers.

'Extraordinary story, does this fellow know what he's doing?' Newton was a little snuffy red-faced man. He had had a good lunch and was smoking a big cigar. Mr Hussick did not care for the smell of cigar smoke.

'I've tried to show him the implications.'

'There's this to be said, that if his story's true he committed no crime at all, you realize that.' Mr Hussick smiled to show that he had realized it. 'He was prepared to commit one, but that isn't the same thing. Have you tried to check his story?'

'I've done my best. The police say that on Friday night Mrs Foster arrived at Land's house – he's some sort of farmer, a gentleman farmer I'd suppose you'd call it – at seven-thirty. That's confirmed by Lands himself and by two neighbours who came in for a drink. The housekeeper had left a cold meal and gone out for the evening to see a friend. She had to go and come back by train – Lands's place is about a mile from the local station. It was arranged that she should come back on the last train, which gets in at eleven-fifteen. Mrs Foster met her, took her back and then left. It was a drive of about fifteen miles and she got back just before midnight. It all fits.'

The Man Whose Dreams Came True

Newton blew out smoke. 'Why didn't Lands go to the station to collect his own housekeeper?'

'I'm sorry. I should have said he did go with her. His car was in the garage, so they used hers.'

'Of course, according to his story Lands is in the plot.'

'Yes.'

'Would she have had time to do the things Jones says she did and get back to, what's his name, Lands in time to meet the housekeeper?'

'Perhaps. But I don't see how we can prove it.'

'If somebody saw her car −'

'I've made inquiries, but so far there are no results.'

'It's important.'

Mr Hussick's eyebrows shot up. 'I know.'

Newton grunted, looked through the papers again, then pushed them aside. 'What his story comes to is this. She's in it with Lands, she must be Lands's mistress, he came to this house Villa Minorca −'

'Majorca.' Newton was bad about names.

'Somebody must have seen 'em together.'

Patiently Mr Hussick said, 'Certainly they were seen together, and naturally he had been to the villa. Foster knew him quite well. After all he was a relative.'

'This is the story and we have to use it.' Newton tapped the papers. 'Get somebody on to it, do some digging, what was she like before she married Foster, did she make trips to London and meet Lands there, look for a link.'

'I am doing so. But we haven't all the money in the world.'

'Yes, well, I leave it to you.' Newton got up and stood in front of an empty fireplace, cigar ash all over his waist-coat. He expanded his chest suddenly, with the effect of a frog blowing himself up. 'What's he like?'

'Jones? A good-looking young man, quiet, polite. Conceited, I daresay.'

'A good witness?'

'I should think so.' Mr Hussick hesitated, qualified this. 'Rather lacking in self-confidence. Do you want to talk to him?'

'Not unless I have to.' Newton did not care for talking to his

321

clients. In his experience such meetings were almost never useful, and they were sometimes embarrassing. 'It's all down here. If that's his story, there it is. You'll keep in touch.'

Mr Hussick took his bowler hat and got up to leave. Newton shook hands, went back to the papers again and then put them aside. They both knew that it was an open and shut case.

A couple of days later another conference was held in the chambers of Eustace Hardy, who was taking the case for the Crown. Hardy was an elegant, fastidious man, with a silver voice that matched his abundant silver hair, and an awareness of his own intellectual superiority that sometimes irritated juries. Just now it was irritating Detective Superintendent Jones, who wished that Hardy didn't have such an air of regarding the whole thing as a tedious chore. When he murmured to the Director of Public Prosecution's representative that it all seemed quite straightforward, Jones couldn't help feeling that something might go wrong.

The D.P.P.'s man, whose name was Walker, nodded. Jones felt impelled to put in a word.

'I think their line is going to be that Mrs Foster egged him on, maybe even that she took part in the murder. These things get round on the grapevine. They've been checking her movements that night – she went to dinner with a cousin, man named Lands.'

'Is there anything in that?' Hardy's fingers moved to straighten a silver cigarette box on his desk.

'As far as I can see, nothing at all.'

'What is Jones's mental condition?'

'You've got the report there, Mr Hardy.' Jones could hardly conceal his annoyance. Why didn't the bloody man look at his papers?

'Yes indeed.' Hardy glanced at it. 'Well integrated in relation to ordinary social contacts, possible inferiority complex, affected by mother's suicide, poor relationship with father, yes, well, this kind of thing doesn't mean very much. He doesn't have any doubt that the man's fit to stand trial, that's the important thing.'

'That's the important thing,' Walker echoed.

Hardy scratched a red spot on his neck. The Superintendent was not usually an uncharitable man, but he could not help thinking, you're not perfect you bastard, you have spots on your neck like anybody else. And scratch them too.

'He's got no form, although he was hard pressed for money,' Walker went on. 'But there's one thing you should know about, although we can't use it, nothing to do with this case. Just a few days before he took up residence with Old Mother Widgeon, Jones was working for a retired General, helping with his memoirs, that kind of thing. The General got rid of him after he'd forged a cheque for two hundred and fifty pounds.'

'Just got rid of him. He didn't prefer charges?'

'*And* let him keep the money,' Jones said in disgust. 'Slapped charges on him, he'd be in prison and Foster would be alive today.'

'What name was he using then, Bain-Truscott?'

'Scott-Williams.'

'Any idea why he used that name?'

Hardy was scratching the spot. Jones watched it becoming angrier. 'I think he used quite a few, mostly double-barrelled.'

'Compensating, I suppose the psychiatrist would call it. Where did you get this story from?'

'The General wrote to us. Seemed to think it would prove he wasn't a murderer.'

'Did he say why he didn't prosecute?'

'I gather he felt Jones deserved another chance, something stupid like that.'

'Interesting. He must be a persuasive young man.' Interesting, hell, the Superintendent thought, he's a villain and that's all there is to it. 'However, all the ends seem to be neatly tied up.'

'It's an open and shut case,' Walker said. Hardy smiled faintly and thanked them both.

'. . . I don't see how you could do what you did to me. You know I love you, doesn't that mean anything at all? I'm not surprised you couldn't look at me when you were giving evidence, you knew it was all lies. How could you be such a bitch, bitch, BITCH.' He read the long repetitious scrawl, then tore the sheet across. What was the good of writing? He put his hands on his knees and stared at the bed opposite. Every move she made was meant to destroy me, he thought. And I can't feel anger against her, I don't feel anything at all. When the warder came across, said he had a visitor and stuck a card under his nose he was incredulous at the name written on it.

The General was bolt upright in the uncomfortable chair that the interview room provided for visitors. Tony sat opposite him, the table between them. The prison officer stood in the corner. It was like some curious game. The General spoke.

'So your name's Jones. Don't know why you didn't say so, nothing wrong with it, had an adjutant named Jones, good chap.' Silence. 'Feeling sorry for yourself?'

'Not particularly.'

'I wrote to the police, told them about our little affair. I thought it might help you, show that you had money, had nothing to do with the other business. I suppose you got through the money in a few days. Still, I wished I hadn't written. That's why I'm here.'

Silence. He looked at the chintz curtains.

'I'm putting you on your honour now. Did you have anything to do with the death of this man?'

How was it possible to answer such a question? He did not even try. The General's head was a fine one, handsome and perfectly proportioned, but he noticed now for the first time that it was very small, almost a model of a head carved in brown and white.

'I should like to help you. I feel a certain responsibility, I don't know why. But I must know the facts.'

'You said I was a scoundrel.'

'You behaved outrageously. However, I still don't believe you capable of anything like this. Is your defence being properly conducted?'

'Legal aid.' He was bored with the whole thing. Why should he sit here and let himself be questioned by this old fool, what had his past history to do with the disastrous present? He felt a longing to be back in the ward and looked at the man beside the door. The General misinterpreted him.

'Leave us alone for five minutes.' The officer shook his head and Tony warmed to him. 'You can tell me anything, any way I can help.'

'There's nothing.' Tony stood up.

'If you refuse to accept my help –' The General stood up too, erect and neat. Again it was a shock to see that not only his head but his whole body was small, he was like a large toy soldier.

'I'd like to go back now,' he said to the officer by the door.

Strange things are found on beaches. Some boys digging for bait on the beach a couple of miles away from the place where Tony had thrown his bundle into the sea found an old pillow, a plastic hand of the kind sold in joke shops, and a partly-inflated football bladder. They were loosely joined together, and obviously other things attached to them had come away in the sea. They trod on the hand and squashed it and played beach football with the bladder. Later one of the boys took it home and kicked it about in his backyard until it hit a nail sticking out of an old toolshed and burst.

Life in the prison hospital was enjoyable in its way. The officers were overworked and Tony made himself useful in doing little jobs about the place, taking in the tea trolley and helping with the washing up. It was pleasant to find that he was respected by some of the other prisoners awaiting trial. A Cockney named Mobey who was to be charged with attempting to poison his wife with arsenic was apologetic about his own inefficiency.

'I have this bird, you see, who's fallen for me, twenty years younger than I am, you wouldn't think it possible would you?' Mobey was in his forties, and a carpenter by trade. 'When the wife got to hear of it she played up, gave me hell. Between her and Sandra, that's my bird, I didn't know whether I was coming or going. But I should never have used arsenic, that was my mistake, it happened to be handy that's all. Should have used something else.'

'Are you pleading guilty?'

'What do you take me for? My mouthpiece's going to say it was a mistake, she did it herself, cooked it with the greens.' Mobey gave Tony a wink. 'She was never much of a cook and I don't eat greens. But you, now, I can see you really gave it some thought.'

'I had nothing to do with that man being killed.'

'That's right.' Mobey winked again. 'Mum's the word. I admire you for it. Got a picture of her?'

'Who?'

'Mrs Foster, that the name? Here's Sandra.' He produced a dog-eared snap of a girl in a bikini. 'How's that for a piece of homework? And she's hot stuff. Look at this.' Tony read a letter from Sandra in which she told Mobey in detail of the pleasures they were both missing. 'Can't wait to get back to it. What's your piece like?'

He found it impossible to talk about Jenny, but Mobey was not annoyed or disconcerted, considering this rather as a further proof of Tony's superiority in sensibility as well as in the conduct of his affairs. He had an enviable certainty of his eventual release and talked continually about the splendid times he and Sandra would have when he got out.

Tony was also surprised to receive a number of letters from women who had read details of the case in the Magistrate's Court. Some called him a murderer and breaker-up of homes, but most wanted to start a correspondence and two suggested marriage after the trial. 'If your heart is still free – and I do not see how you can have any feeling for *that woman* after the way she has behaved – I want you to know that there are real loving women in the world who are keen to get something *exciting* out of life,' wrote a woman from Bedford who described herself as thirty years old and fancy free. Two or three letters asked for a signed photograph and one woman enclosed a lock of hair with the request that he should send one of his in return. He answered some of the letters and was annoyed when, apparently satisfied to have heard from him, the women didn't keep up the correspondence. At the same time there was something undoubtedly agreeable in finding himself a celebrity.

Upon the whole the days passed pleasantly enough. He seemed

to have drifted out of life and did not feel seriously disturbed even when Mr Hussick came in and reported that their attempts to disprove Mrs Foster's story had come to nothing. He looked forward to the trial with a mixture of excitement and distress. Distress because it would mean the end, one way or the other, of the hospital life that in some ways suited him very well, and also to the sessions with the psychiatrist which had continued and which he rather enjoyed. He did not allow himself to think what might happen after the trial ended if he were found guilty, and on the whole distress was submerged by excitement. It would be the first time in his life that he had ever really been given attention, and he felt the importance of doing his best in the witness box not only because (as Mr Hussick had said over and over) it was vital for his case, but because it was a real chance to show his true personality in public.

One or two experienced prisoners, men with long records, had told him that you got a lot of fan mail during the trial, especially if you made a good impression. Perhaps among those letters there would be one from a beautiful young woman, sexually demanding in just Jenny's way – he was unable quite to forget her – but a woman who really wanted all the things about which Jenny had only pretended. He called this imaginary young woman Lucinda, and the half hour in the morning that elapsed between the time he woke and the time they were called belonged to her. The trial ended with his acquittal, and she was waiting as he left the Court by a side entrance to avoid the crowd of screaming women who wanted to kiss him and to touch and tear his clothing as if he were a pop star. She moved over to the passenger seat of the sports car as he came out, he gunned the motor and they were away, driving down country roads, away, zooming at a forbidden speed down the endless lanes of the motorway, away, on and on until they reached the hotel where in the bedroom she imposed her body and her needs upon his own, using him as a man is traditionally supposed to use a woman. 'Lucinda, Lucinda,' he would whisper as he held her pillow body at this early hour of the morning when light filtered through the window into the ward and the man next to him moved and cried out in sleep. The hotel was only a stopping off place, on the following day they took the car over to Europe. When he asked where they were going she smiled and said 'Everywhere.'

Three days before the trial began he received a letter of a different kind. He had read two pages in the sprawling hand before he looked at the signature: 'Fiona.'

This is just to wish you good luck. Don't know what it's all about but it can't be nice to be in jug, and I hope you get out. It was funny seeing you with Carlos that night. Claude Armitage introduced us and I took it from there. I told you I'd never go back, didn't I? Do you know what Carlos likes most about me? I told him my father had a castle in Ayrshire but lost all his money, and he thinks I'm a nice class of girl. I thought I'd better not let on I knew you but I tried to stop Carlos doing anything. He was mad at you, said you had to be taught a lesson because you wouldn't take a warning. I'd have tipped you off if I'd known where to find you. They don't like it when people bilk and duck out, Carlos says he'd like to cut their you know what off personally. He's nice to me. He runs a whole group of clubs for the syndicate and he's put me in a flat off Curzon Street, just super. I sometimes go to the clubs but he won't let me play, says he doesn't want me getting into bad habits. He hardly lets me out of his sight, says he'd cut me up if he found me with anybody. Do you know you were one of my bad habits, or could have been. You can't say I didn't offer. Best of luck. I think about you.

Chapter 6

Dimmock dissected his grilled haddock with the care he gave to everything, first easing the large central bone away from the flesh, then meticulously attending to the smaller bones, pulling out one or two obstinate ones with his fingers, finally flaking away the succulent flesh from the skin and putting it into his mouth. He liked fish for breakfast, and had it three times a week. It was one of his few extravagances.

On this morning he ate his haddock unhurriedly, followed it with one piece of toast and two cups of tea and then said to his wife, 'If I sit here for ever I shan't get to Timbuctoo for lunch, shall I?' He had a number of such phrases, some of them nonsensical, like 'Lovely bit of haddock, brought up in a high class paddock,' or 'Every healthy growing nipper should eat each day a nice grilled kipper.' The fact that on this morning he responded to his wife's query about the haddock only by saying that it was very nice showed him to be unusually preoccupied.

'You're all packed ready. I've put in an extra shirt and socks.'

'Thank you, my dear. I'd better be getting off.'

Dimmock got up from the table, brushed his teeth, brought down his shabby suitcase, got out the old but still reliable little car, kissed his wife, and drove away from the semi-detached house in Wembley where he had lived for twenty years, ever since the war ended. He had gone in for a teachers' training scheme after being demobbed, but with a couple of small kids it just hadn't been possible to make ends meet and he had never been sorry that he gave it up to go into his present work, which wasn't exciting but provided a steady living. Now the kids, a girl and a boy, had grown up and married and Dimmock was getting on, in his fifties, with his wife the same. In a way he hadn't got much to show for his life, but then look at it another way and why should you want anything more than a decent comfortable house and a bit of garden, a couple of kids who'd never been any trouble, nice neighbours who never poked their noses into your affairs, and a good programme to watch on the telly? How many people had as much, especially in other countries? And when people had more – here Dimmock would make the point forcibly to his wife or to a neighbour if one happened to have come in for a glass of beer – did it make them happy? 'Not always, not by any manner of means. And I know what I'm talking about,' he would say.

He knew what he was talking about because, as his wife said, he was a detective. Or as Dimmock himself put it, he was an operative in a firm of inquiry agents.

Most of the work was humdrum, concerned with chasing up bad debts or trying to trace crooks who had been practising confidence tricks or long firm frauds. He had been taken off divorce work because some of the cases had shocked and disgusted him, and at the Second To None Agency he had long since been classified by Mr Clarence Newhouse, who owned it and was known to Dimmock as the Chief, as a willing workhorse, a man who was not too bright but would never fiddle his expenses or produce an imaginary report about footslogging when he had been propping up a bar all day. Such virtues are rare in the lower ranks of detection. If Dimmock was asked to find a missing woman last seen in Birmingham he would go on doggedly looking until he found her or was called off the trail. The fact that almost all disappearances are voluntary never depressed him. He would say that human nature is a funny thing, and be ready to get on with the next job. In his twenty years as an operative he had suffered violence only three times, the most serious of them being at the hands of a woman who beat him over the head with an umbrella and then threw him downstairs when he suggested that she should return to her husband.

Dimmock was assigned to the Foster case only because an operative named Berryman had been suddenly taken ill. Berryman would have known all about the case, whereas the Chief had to explain most of the details to Dimmock. However, the assignment was straightforward enough. He was to check up on the movements of Mrs Foster with the idea of disproving her story of what she had done and where she had been on the night of her husband's murder. He was also to see what he could find out about her relationship with her cousin, Mortimer Lands. As the Chief explained all this Dimmock nodded again and again.

'It's likely you'll find that the police and the defence solicitors have made inquiries already. Use your loaf when you ask questions.'

'I see.'

'It's something out of the way for us, a murder inquiry. Bit of excitement for you.'

'That's right.' Newhouse gave up in despair. He looked at the long lugubrious face with the two deep lines carved in it and thought, oh well, at least he'll go through the motions.

There is a kind of routine laid down in such cases, and Dimmock followed it. He booked in at the Commercial Hotel, drove to Byron Avenue and past the house, found the nearest shopping area and began to ask questions. He found the grocer and the butcher who delivered to the Villa Majorca, produced a photograph of Lands and asked if they had ever seen him when they called at the house. They had not. He drove round until he found the milkman, went to the Post Office and saw the postman who delivered mail at the Villa, and received similar negative replies. The postman thought he had seen a Triumph Vitesse parked in the drive, and Lands owned such a car, but the man could not be sure.

Dimmock went back to the hotel, had two drinks before dinner, bought one for the barman, and asked where he should take a young lady if he wanted a good meal and a real slap-up evening. In town? No, not in town, out in the country, some really nice place where you could have a little celebration, no expense spared. With accommodation, the barman asked slyly, and Dimmock admitted that that might be an advantage. He got the addresses of three country hotels and three restaurants. Then he went in to dinner, which was thick cornflour soup, roast lamb, and treacle pudding without very much treacle. During dinner he read the local paper and got a couple more names from that, one a restaurant and the other a country club. If Lands and Mrs Foster had gone out together, there was a good chance that they had used one of these places.

After dinner he made out his report in the bedroom. There was no writing desk or table and he wrote in a chair with a pad on his knee, in the firm copperplate hand he had been taught at school. At the end of the report he detailed the day's expenses calculated at so much a mile for the car, and including the pub lunch for which he had obtained a bill. Then he undressed, considered having a bath and decided against it because he thought that two baths a week were enough for a man of his age, put on his pyjamas which were silk, another of his little extravagances like fish for breakfast, and went to bed. He was not depressed by his failure to find out anything. He was only doing a job.

Chapter 7

Four women, Mr Hussick had said, it was splendid that they
had four women. 'Majority verdicts nowadays, you know, used
to be enough to have one, now we need three. Ten to two guilty,
nine to three innocent.'

'Do you mean women are less likely to find me guilty?'

'Depends on the case. Child cruelty, killing somebody at a
road crossing, I'd want men. Men every time in a car case. But
something like this I'd choose women. If we had eight women
and four men –' Mr Hussick raised his brows, clicked his
tongue. Eight women and four men, he seemed to imply, would
mean acquittal.

The four women did not look very promising. One sat bolt
upright and stared straight in front of her all the time. Another
had a blue rinse and spent a good deal of time contemplating her
nails. The third was pretty but fatuous, smiled often, and looked
round the Court when counsel on either side made a point as
though prepared to join in a round of applause. The fourth,
older than the rest, an iron-haired woman in her sixties, produced a notebook and made so many notes that she might have
been writing an article. At times she raised her head and looked
hard at Tony for a period of seconds. He was uncomfortably
aware of this gaze, which he found hard to meet. When he did
stare back at her, his eyes dropped first. Would she take that as
an indication of guilt?

Mr. Penny the jeweller was in the box. Where was the wart
behind his ear? Surely it had been on the left side? How extraordinary that it seemed to have vanished.

'He told me that it was a family heirloom.'

'A family heirloom.' Hardy repeated the words slowly, so that
they should sink in. 'He said that these links and pin were a
family heirloom. And then?'

'I asked if he wanted a valuation, and he said he might consider selling them. I offered eighty pounds. He said he wanted a hundred.'

'A hundred, yes, did he say anything further?'

'He said he needed the money, temporarily embarrassed were the words he used I think, and that nothing less would be any use.'

'And after that?'

'I'm not a hard man. He seemed to be a nice young fellow.' Hardy waited, eyes cast down at the papers before him, foot tapping slightly. With a quick beam at Hardy, at the judge, the jury, Penny the benevolent said, 'I said, I'll take a chance, give you a hundred.'

'Did he accept the offer?'

'No. He said he'd changed his mind, put them in his pocket and went out. Couldn't get out fast enough.'

Hardy looked at his papers again, sat down. Newton slowly shuffled to his feet, rocked on his heels. Penny turned his head and Tony saw the mole. There it was, on the left side as he had thought. He felt relieved, as though the existence of the mole proved something.

'Just one or two questions, Mr Penny, I shan't keep you long. You say you are not a hard man. Would you say you were a charitable one?'

The jeweller bristled, then gave a cunning smile. 'I give a pound for my poppy on Remembrance Day.'

There was a tiny ripple of subdued mirth. Tony looked quickly at the jury. Pretty But Fatuous put her hand over her mouth, Blue Rinse looked up in surprise and down again, Iron Hair wrote in her notebook. One or two of the men shuffled their bottoms uneasily. Newton went on rocking.

'That isn't quite what I meant. Did you think you were being charitable in offering a hundred pounds for this jewellery?'

The smile vanished. 'It was a business deal.'

'Precisely. What would you think the links and pin were worth?'

'I shouldn't like to say.'

'Perhaps I can help you. Would it surprise you to know that they had been valued at two hundred and fifty pounds?'

'What they're valued at –'

'Just answer my question, would it surprise you?'

'Black opals are unlucky, people don't like them.'

'Yes or no, Mr Penny.'

The judge, lean and birdlike, looked over the top of half moon spectacles. 'Answer counsel's question, Mr Penny.'

Mr Penny's mouth turned down in a pout. 'No.'

'You wouldn't be surprised. So when Mr Jones took the things away he might have been hoping to get a better price?'

'I offered what he asked.'

'Quite. So if he had been just concerned with money he would have accepted. Wouldn't you say that his behaviour was that of somebody who had discovered that an article he had thought worth five or ten pounds was in fact much more valuable?'

'If you say so.'

'No no, Mr Penny.' Newton scratched his wig, pulled it slightly askew. 'Do *you* say so, that is the question.'

Sulkily, still pouting, Mr Penny agreed. 'He could have been.'

'Supposing he had just been given these articles as a present and had named what he thought was an outrageous figure for them, that would explain his reactions, would it not?'

'It might have done.' Flaring up suddenly he asked, 'Then why did he say he had to have a hundred pounds?'

'I am not here to answer your questions, Mr Penny, but if he really wanted a hundred pounds why did he not take it when it was offered?' And before Hardy could intervene to protest that this was a statement rather than a question, Newton sat down.

Later that day Newton saw the accused personally, for the first and only time. He did so only because Hussick had said that the position ought to be made perfectly clear. The solicitor was also present.

'I want to make sure that you fully understand the implications of this defence,' Newton said. 'Mr Hussick has already told you that extensive inquiries have been made to check your story without result.'

'Yes.'

'We have not been able to find anybody to confirm your

story that Mrs Foster drove you to the point where the launch was kept, known as Bensley Water –'

'Bromley Water,' Hussick said.

'Bromley Water. Nor that she took you near to the station. Nor that she did anything but what she said, and spent the evening with Lands.'

'I've told you what happened.'

'Yes.' Newton lighted a cigar, then as an afterthought offered the case to Hussick and Tony. Both refused. 'You say you don't remember passing cars or people.'

'We did, of course, at least I suppose so. But not near Bromley Water. We went on side roads.'

'And you can't think of any other way in which this can be proved?'

'Only by making her tell the truth.'

'I was coming to that. When Mrs Foster goes into the box I shall cross-examine her on these lines. The questions will be severe. It is possible that she may break down under them. If not –' Newton pointed the cigar at Tony like a gun. 'The effect on your case may not be favourable. When you go into the box yourself you will certainly be subjected to a long cross-examination from the other side. It will be said that you are simply trying to blacken her reputation to save your own skin. I want you to understand that.'

He was walking across from the dock, those few momentous steps to the box, body erect and shoulders braced back. Courteous and calm he faced the inquisitor, parried the questions and slipped the sword of a decisive answer past his opponent's guard. I was stupid, I agreed to help her in a moment of madness. Slowly he turned to the judge. My lord, I was in love.

'I asked if you understood.' Newton looked at him impatiently, tapped grey ash on the floor.

He transferred his attention to the puffy little man. 'I've told you what happened.'

God help us, Newton thought, I believe you have. He felt annoyed with Hussick. What point was there in a face to face confrontation with a man who told a preposterous story like this? What was a solicitor for but to act as a barrier against such embarrassing confrontations? Yet although even by his own account Jones was nothing more than a contemptible weakling, there was something ingenuous and even innocent about him that was in its way touching. To his own surprise Newton found himself moved by the fact that Jones's fate rested in his hands.

'We shall do everything we can for you.' Inadequate words, no doubt, but he rarely said as much.

Moreston, the police fingerprint expert, took up most of the afternoon. The evidence really amounted to saying that Jones's prints had been found on the hammer and that it had certainly been used to kill Foster, but Moreston was aware of his own importance and his examination in chief took more than an hour. Newton noticed one or two jurors fidgeting, and made his own questioning brief.

'Let me say at once that the defence does not dispute that the prints on the hammer are those of the accused. What I want to ask is this. Supposing he had used the hammer for some domestic task like – oh, knocking a nail in a wall – would he not have left prints like these?'

'He might have done.'

'And then there are other blurred prints, are there not?'

'Perfectly true.'

'If the hammer had been used for this domestic task by my client and then used afterwards for the crime by somebody wearing gloves, wouldn't you expect such blurring to occur?'

Moreston considered this. 'It would be possible.'

'Whereas if the blows were simply struck by Jones, who then dropped the hammer, the prints might be expected to be much clearer?'

Moreston again took his time. 'No, I don't think so. More than one blow was struck and as the grip possibly shifted some blurring would be likely.'

'But not so much, surely, as actually took place?'

'Are you asking me that, Mr Newton?'

The judge coughed. 'It was a question, I think.'

Moreston was determined to make no concession to Newton, whom he disliked. 'I have already given my opinion, my lord, but I will repeat it. The blurring may easily have been caused by a shifting of grip on the hammer. In the purely hypothetical case that the hammer was later used by somebody else wearing gloves, that also would have caused blurring. I can go no further than that.'

The judge looked over his half-lenses. 'Does that satisfy you, Mr Newton?'

No, Newton thought, but it's all I shall get. 'Thank you, my lord. Now, the effect of these blows with the hammer was to cause a considerable amount of blood to be spilt on the sitting-room carpet and elsewhere. Is it not surprising that not a single bloodstain was found on Jones's clothing?'

'I can't give an opinion on that.'

Newton knew this perfectly well, and he put the point later to the forensic expert when he was in the box. But still, it did no harm to ask the question of this stubborn fingerprint man. Anything must be useful which helped to counteract the evidence of the prints on the hammer.

Chapter 8

There was no fish on the breakfast menu and Dimmock ate eggs and bacon while he read the morning paper with its report of the first day of the trial. In the outline of the case given him it had been suggested that he should try to trace the movements of Mrs Foster's car, but he rejected this as hopeless. What facilities did he have for making such inquiries, what could he do that had not already been done by the police? Immediately after breakfast he started on the trail of restaurants and hotels and pursued it until just after lunch, showing the photographs of Mrs Foster and Lands everywhere he went. It was after lunch when he finished. Nobody recognized either of the photographs. If the couple had spent evenings together they had not done so at any of the places on his list. It began to rain before lunch and by mid-afternoon, when he reached Beaver Close, the rain had been joined by a high wind against which he struggled in his slightly shabby coat, pushing his way up to the door with one hand clasped on his hat to prevent it from being blown away.

He's selling something, Evelyn Bradbury thought as she watched him coming up the drive, but little as she liked door to door salesmen she felt sorry for him. One of Dimmock's few advantages as an operative was that women often did feel sorry for him. He had a hangdog honesty that many women found sympathetic. When Mrs Bradbury, after looking at his card, asked what he wanted to know he flapped his arms in a hopeless way.

'I'm not sure, Mrs Bradbury. I've been asked to make inquiries, that's all.'

'On behalf of Jones, you say. But who's employing you?'

'I'm not at liberty to reveal that.' In fact Dimmock didn't know, nor was he interested.

'The police have been round, you know.' Dimmock's resigned nod said that he would always arrive second or third, never first.

'And of course my husband has had to give evidence. He was quite upset about it, you know they were at school together, but I mean you have a duty, isn't that right?'

'I would sooner talk to you,' Dimmock said truthfully. He found women much more responsive than men.

Few people said that to Evelyn Bradbury. She offered a cup of tea and took away Dimmock's damp coat and hat. When she returned with the tea trolley and little sponge cakes she asked what he wanted to know. It seemed that he was not sure.

'Well, of course you know it was here that they met. Bill says he will never forgive himself for bringing Jones back here. But they were old school friends, you see. He seemed quite a nice young man, although he spilled his tea. On the carpet, it's almost new –'

'A beautiful carpet,' Dimmock said reverently and sipped the China tea. He preferred Indian. 'Do you know Mrs Foster well?'

'There is a Women's Club in Southbourne, and we had met there. She was a new member, though she didn't seem very interested. When she became a member we were hoping that she might bring her husband along at some time, he was something in the City you know, and Bill wanted to meet him. But we never did see him.'

'You didn't meet her cousin, Mr Lands?'

'I'm afraid not,' she said reluctantly. 'Do have one of these cakes, I made them myself.'

'She never mentioned to you –' Dimmock was at a loss to know what she might be able to tell him that was useful, and continued lamely, '– anything interesting. About her husband.'

'We didn't talk about him. I am sure it was a very happy marriage.' She looked away with an expression of distaste. Dimmock humbly transferred his gaze to the carpet. 'Except that she was left alone a good deal. It may have been rather dull for her. But then I always say that if you keep busy you are never dull.'

'That's very true.'

'And she had her golf.' Dimmock looked up. It was the first he had heard about golf. 'She belonged to the Mendwich Golf Club. I have seen a bag in her car.'

'A bag.'

'Of clubs.' She spoke as if they were implements used by a primitive tribe.

The secretary of Mendwich Golf Club was red-faced and stiffish, but in the end he was softened by Dimmock's hangdog persistence. Yes, Mrs Foster had been a member of the club and came there occasionally in company with a friend of hers, or perhaps it was some sort of relative, named Lands. How often? At this point the secretary became restive and said that they did not keep a check on the presence or absence of members. Dimmock thanked him, withdrew, sat in his car and thought. There was a club within ten miles of the Villa Majorca, why hadn't she joined that instead of the Mendwich which was thirty miles away? Because her cousin belonged to the Mendwich was the obvious reply. Probably there was nothing in it, but it was the first thing he had discovered that was of any interest at all, and Mendwich was outside the area in which he had visited restaurants and hotels.

He spent the rest of the day calling on those near the golf club. At the Great South Motel the head waiter recognized the photographs as those of a couple who had come in sometimes for dinner. Had they stayed the night? About this he was emphatic. They had not. A pound note, which he contemplated with the indifference that others might show to a half-crown, changed hands. Would his story have been different if the note had been a fiver? Dimmock did not think so. At the end of a long afternoon and evening in the rain he had learned nothing of real value, yet he had the feeling that he was on the edge of some discovery. He looked at the material prepared for him by the office and read: 'Check housekeeper. Mrs Twining keeps house for Lands, lives in.' Below this was: 'Check Fosters' maid Sarah Russell.' He telephoned and found that Lands was up in London, no doubt attending the trial. It was a good opportunity to call.

It was twilight when he drove up to Land's house, a rambling building which stood a quarter of a mile off the road at the end of a squelchy drive. Heavy rain fell out of a leaden sky. He could feel it seeping through his thin coat. The house was in darkness and there was no answer to his knock. He walked round and saw a light in what must be the kitchen, heard sounds of voices raised in high-pitched argument. He knocked on a side door and knocked again. There was a click. The radio argument was extinguished. A voice from behind the door said: 'Yes?'

'My name is Dimmock.'

'Yes.'

'If you'll open the door I can give you my card.'

The door opened on a bolt and chain. A woman's body, tall and bulky, was outlined against the light. She held something in her right hand. Dimmock fumbled under his wet coat and found a card which said that he was an insurance investigator. The voice, harsh and sexually neutral, asked what he wanted.

'Could I come in for a moment and explain.'

'Is it about this business of Mr Foster?'

Subterfuge seemed useless. 'As a matter of fact it is.'

'You want Mr Lands. He's not here.'

'You're Mrs Twining, aren't you? As a matter of fact it was you I wanted to talk to.'

'I've said all I had to say. To the police.'

Rain from the guttering above was dripping steadily on to Dimmock's hat, and from the hat downwards. He could feel a cold trickle on his neck. 'It's a wet night, Mrs Twining –'

'I know your voice.' He was so disconcerted that he stopped talking. 'On the telephone. Sneaking round when Mr Lands is away.'

The drip ran under his collar. In desperation he moved forward and – a rare mistake on his part, for he was a man who respected the privacy of others – put his hand on the chain, not really with any intention of opening the door because that would not have been possible, but simply as a plea, a claim on her attention. The thing in her hand swung, and although he did not feel the blow his arm was suddenly numb. The door slammed shut, the radio voices started to argue again.

It was only the third time that he had suffered violence. Back in the car he told himself he deserved it. He should have left his call until the morning, he shouldn't have stretched out his arm. In spite of these reflections he was conscious of an unreasoning anger that lasted all the way back to the Commercial Hotel. Dinner was finished by the time he got back and he had to be content with a sandwich which was made for him with a bad grace, and a bottle of beer. When he asked for a hot water bottle in his bed the maid stared at him as though he had taken leave of his senses and said that there wasn't such a thing in the hotel. After all, she added, it was summer.

Up in his room he examined the arm, which showed a livid bruise between wrist and elbow. He wrote out his report in a hand less firm than usual, and went to bed. It was a long time before he slept. The day had been unrewarding, but that was not what kept him awake. He felt it to be monstrously unjust that a man making polite inquiries should be met with a blow on the arm.

Chapter 9

Mobey had gone. His place was taken by an inarticulate lantern-jawed man with a permanent sniff, who was charged with arson. Tony tried to find out what had happened to Mobey, but the warders were evasive. In the end he found out from Hussick.

'Mobey? The man who tried to poison his wife. He got ten years.' Mr Hussick's eyebrows danced. 'Straight-forward case. Silly fellow.'

Tony found that he was upset by this. 'He told me it was a mistake.'

'Naturally he'd say that. Not true, I'm afraid.' Mobey was dismissed. 'Mrs Foster's giving evidence today. Then Mr Newton will put your case to her.'

'What does he think of the chances?'

'We did very well yesterday, I thought. Moreston's a tough nut, doesn't give an inch unless he's forced to, but he had to agree about the blurring. It sank in with the jury, oh yes, I'm sure it sank in.' He seemed about to burst into laughter at the thought of the way it had sunk in, but refrained. 'When Mrs Foster is giving evidence, keep calm. No display of temper, judge doesn't like that and the jury don't like it either. You've been very good so far.' He might have been a dentist congratulating a patient on the way he was enduring a long session in the chair.

On the way to Court in the little van he thought about Mobey. How extraordinary it was that somebody could be in your company one day, talking cheerfully about getting rid of his wife so that he could live with his bird, and then on the next day a group of people chosen at random could decide that he was to be shut up in prison for years. Ten years – just think what it would be like to be shut up for ten years, or even seven which would allow for good conduct remission, shut up in one small room, let out only to do humiliating meaningless work, continually in the company of vulgar men, never seeing or touching a woman, your horizon bounded by the single cell, living in a world removed from bright light and colour. Would it be possible for him to endure such a world, and could it be right that anybody should be forced to suffer in that way? He saw the Morris wallpaper in his bed-room at Leathersley House, the colours brighter than they had been in actuality. When one of the two prison officers with him asked how it was going he said that he didn't know, and saw the man look at his mate as though to convey an unspoken warning: 'He's been cheerful so far, but it's getting to him now, he's beginning to realize what he's in for.' The man offered him a cigarette but he shook his head. When the two of them talked about a cricket match to be played next weekend he listened eagerly, although he was not interested in cricket.

He had been braced for Jenny's appearance, and was irritated when she did not appear in the witness box at once. Instead they had the girl from the travel agency where he had bought the ticket for Caracas. Then they had Bradbury to mention the thirty pounds he had promised to repay, and then Carlos Cotton talking about his unpaid debt to World Casino Enterprises. Newton's cross-examination was brisk.

'This debt was contracted at – ah – Landford, is that correct?'

'Yes.'

'And you subsequently agreed to forgo it?'

'I said he needn't pay.'

'But then you changed your mind, I understand.'

'I found he was playing at Southbourne after I'd put the black on him.' Cotton was wearing a tight black suit with very high lapels. His fingers played uneasily with a button.

'Put the black on. What does that mean?'

'I'd barred him from any of my gaming clubs.'

'Your clubs. That is World Casino Enterprises, those are your clubs, are they not?'

'Correct.'

'And what is your position in them, Mr Cotton?'

'Director. And general manager.'

'With some special responsibility for bad debts?'

'We don't like them. Who does?'

'Who does?' Newton echoed and continued smoothly. 'You know that gambling debts can't be enforced by law?'

'Yes.'

'So how did you propose to enforce payment?'

'I've told you. If he didn't pay up he'd be barred. I'd barred him already.' Cotton seemed to shrink into himself. He cast quick glances at Newton, the judge, the body of the Court, like a malevolent insect.

'You didn't threaten him with physical violence in any way?'

'Of course not.' Cotton turned his monkey face to the public gallery. Tony followed his gaze and saw Fiona, leaning forward in the front row.

'So there was no reason why he should be specially worried?'

The judge had been tapping gently with a pencil. Now he said, 'I don't want to interfere, Mr Newton, but isn't this line of questioning going rather far afield?'

'I hope not, my lord. My learned friend's purpose in introducing this evidence was I presume to show that my client was hard pressed for money. I am trying to bring out the point that one of these debts was to a friend and the other was not legally enforceable.'

'I think we have taken the point, Mr Newton.'

'Had threats been employed it would be a different matter. I am happy to have the assurance that there was no question of this.'

The judge bowed his head. Newton sat down and there was no re-examination. Cotton looked from one to the other of them and left the box. Shortly afterwards Fiona's head disappeared from the gallery.

In a way Tony felt indignant about this. He would have liked to ask Cotton questions himself and to say 'You threatened me, one of your thugs stubbed out his cigarette on my hand and two more tried to beat me up,' but he understood that if there had been no threats it was a good thing for him, it meant that he had no reason to worry about the money. This meant also that it didn't always pay to bring out the truth. Would it be right to say that truth was one thing and justice another? He was thinking about this when Jenny entered the box.

She walked through the Court with the care of somebody moving along a private knife edge, one foot placed before the other, her face a white blank and her head held high. She was wearing a dress in some neutral completely washed out colour, and as always she looked slight and vulnerable. The stir of anger he had been prepared to feel never flickered. He found himself as dispassionate as though he were watching a play. Hussick, looking up at his client, saw that there was no reason to worry.

For a long time the play was a repeat performance of what he had already heard, except that there were some details of her life before marriage. Most of what she had told him was true. She had been a not very successful actress, had met Foster when he returned to England from South Africa, and married him. She talked about this with a straightforwardness and simplicity that, as Tony felt, must impress the jury. Hardy led her like a dancing master through the tale she had told in the Magistrate's Court, of his engagement, her husband's discovery of the missing links, his determination to 'have things out' on Friday evening, her departure for dinner and her return to find the body in the living-room. For the first time Tony found himself wondering what had really happened. Had Lands come over, helped her, and then gone back in his own car before Tony's arrival? Or had she done the whole thing herself? He could see Foster – but then he had never met Foster, he was thinking of Lands when he used the name – turning round in the sitting-room when she asked for a drink, the hammer in her gloved hand, the first blow that staggered him, and then the hammer coming down again and again. Was there sufficient strength in those thin hands? He had felt them gripping him, and knew that there was. And remembering the look he had seen sometimes on her face when they made love, the look that made it clear she did not regard him as another human being but only as an object to be used, he had no difficulty in seeing her striking Foster, unmoved by the blood that spurted out when the eggshell head cracked.

It was these thoughts, and recollection of what Moreston had said that made him scribble a note to Hussick: 'She must have had blood on her clothes when she hit him.' Hussick read the note, nodded, folded the paper into small pieces and smiled. Tony scribbled another note: 'HAVE YOU CHECKED?' Hussick read this, nodded again, and then set his eyebrows dancing and turned down the corners of his mouth. What did that mean? At Tony's finger-beckoning the solicitor wrote a note of his own which his clerk passed up. When unfolded it read: 'We checked with laundry, etc. Nothing.'

So how had she killed him? Naked, as the Liverpool insurance agent Wallace was said to have killed his wife? That was surely not possible. He found that it was hard to concentrate on the examination.

It was after lunch when Hardy had finished and Newton rose. His tone was friendly, almost paternal.

'First of all, I wonder if you could tell me just a little more of what happened when you engaged Jones. You did engage him, isn't that so?'

'On my husband's behalf.'

'Naturally. I find that a little unusual. Why didn't your husband interview him?'

'He trusted my judgement.' She twisted her hands. 'God forgive me.'

That's a bit corny, Tony thought, a bit too actressy. He took a quick glance at his four jurywomen, but to his disgust they were behaving as usual, Blue Rinse looking at her nails, Pretty But Fatuous staring round the Court, Iron Hair waiting with pencil poised and Bolt Upright naturally bolt upright. What was Newton saying?

'He accepted your recommendation. And your impression was favourable, you engaged him on the spot.'

'He seemed pleasant. He could type. And I had met him at a friend's house.'

'You liked him?'

Thin shoulders shrugged under the colourless dress. 'I had no feelings one way or the other.'

'At least you didn't dislike him?'

Again the shrug. 'True.'

Newton looked at his notes for what seemed a long time and then spoke abruptly. 'Were you happily married?'

'Yes.'

'Your husband was twenty-five years older than you, but that made no difference?'

'None at all.'

'It was one of those marriages where age doesn't matter because husband and wife have so much in common. Is that so, Mrs Foster?'

As she repeated in a neutral voice 'We were very happy,' Tony looked again at the jury, the men as well as the women. They were all keenly attentive. There was a man who looked ominously like Clinker the builder, short and swart with hairy hands which rested on the ledge in front of him. What was he thinking, what would Tony himself think if he saw the slim woman and heard her low-voiced replies? Newton struggled on like a ship ploughing through an icefield. Tony ceased to listen. He saw instead of the courtroom the confines of a cell nine by six – was that the size? – which would be his home for years. *I shall die,* he thought, *if they shut me up in a place like that I shall die.*

Below him Newton, as he followed no particular line of questioning but probed with all the delicacy of which he was capable to find a chink in this bloodless woman's personality through which he could attack, was conscious of attempting to make bricks not only without straw but even without the basic clay. At the same time he had the feeling, which comes to all advocates at some time or another and which they know they can trust, that in some essential respects the witness was not telling the truth. The problem then is to induce the same feeling in the jury. 'You did not take up his references?'

'No.'

'We know that they were not genuine. Had you written, he would have been exposed at once.'

'Believe me, I'm sorry I didn't,' she said in a low voice.

'You engaged him after a short interview, you didn't trouble to check his references. And you still say you didn't find him attractive?'

'I had no feelings, one way or the other.'

'And then you saw him every day. Alone, since your husband was up in London.'

'Yes.'

349

'This young attractive man was alone in the house with you each day, but you still had no feelings about him?'

She raised her voice a little. 'He was there in the mornings. To do a job of work.'

Hopeless, Newton thought, hopeless. He speeded up his questions and changed his tone altogether, using the bullying peremptory manner that came naturally to him. 'I put it to you that you were bored with your elderly husband.'

'That is not true.'

'That you were bored with him, wanted to get rid of him and still enjoy his money. Isn't that the truth?'

'Certainly not.'

'And you used my client as a tool for this purpose, a tool who was like putty in your hands.'

'That is absolutely untrue,' she said without emphasis.

There it goes, Mr Hussick thought as he listened to Newton putting to her the points about the hammer, about the plan to kill Foster and about the drive to the motor launch, to be met in every case by passionless negatives and a denial that she had been to the launch for three weeks before the murder, there goes our case. You couldn't blame Newton, what could anybody do with a story that didn't have the least fragment of fact to support it.

Although Tony had felt no emotion when Genevieve Foster gave evidence, the very sight of Mortimer Lands as he walked into the box and stumbled slightly over taking the oath made him so angry that he had to grip the sides of the dock to control himself. The weak delicate features, the lock of white hair conspicuous as if it had been painted on the dark head, could this possibly be what Jenny had preferred to him? And sexual jealousy was not the only cause of his anger. The thought of those mornings when this wretched little man had dictated to him in the study and he had typed out all the meaningless details from books was really too much to be borne. The prison officers behind him exchanged meaningful glances as he leaned forward, and Mr Hussick looked up with a smile which managed to be at once reassuring and reproving.

There was really very little substance to the evidence which

Lands gave rapidly in a low voice, confirming that he was a second cousin of Mrs Foster, that he had worked for a public relations firm and had become a farmer after his father's death, had sometimes visited the Fosters at the Villa Majorca, and had given Mrs Foster dinner on the night of the murder. Hardy elicited facts and times and then sat down. When Newton rose he did so this time with a flourish. He had sensed, as a counsel can do, that Lands was easy meat.

'Was this visit of Mrs Foster's an unusual occurrence?'

Lands looked puzzled. 'I don't quite understand.'

'Was it the first time she had been to your farm for dinner?'

'Oh, I see. No, it wasn't.'

'She'd been before. Alone?'

'Yes.'

'How many times?' Lands, head down, did not reply. 'Just once? Half a dozen times? Twenty times?'

Still with his head down Lands said, 'Three or four.'

'I can't hear you.' That was the judge. Lands looked up, startled.

'I'm sorry, my lord. I said three or four times.'

'Always alone,' Newton said with relish.

'She came with Eversley once or twice I think.' Lands waved his white ladylike fingers. 'These other times, when she came alone, he was away.'

'He was away,' Newton repeated meaningfully. 'And then she dined with you. Did you ever go to dinner with her, or with them both?'

'I – I don't think so.'

'These were one way visits.' Newton looked at the jury. 'I am not implying anything wrong. It just seemed a little strange to me that she should telephone and invite herself to dinner on this Friday, but if she were a frequent visitor that explains it.'

The judge looked at Newton. 'Three or four times, the witness said, Mr Newton.'

Newton bowed his head. 'Three or four times. She had been before at all events. So you were not surprised when she telephoned and said "Can I come to dinner?" ' Suddenly he snapped. 'Did she telephone?'

351

Like a rabbit facing a wolf Lands stammered, 'Yes, on – on Friday morning.'

'And what did she say?'

'She said –' he gulped. '– there had been some unpleasantness about the man Eversley was employing, and he wanted to see the man alone that evening. Could she come over to me. Something like that.'

'This wasn't very convenient. Your housekeeper, Mrs Turner, was out for the evening.'

Lands perked up for a moment. 'Mrs Twining.'

The correction appeared to enrage Newton. He thundered: 'Mrs Twining was going out. Why not take Mrs Foster out to dinner?'

Lands stared, dumbfounded. 'I don't know.'

'Surely that would have been easier?'

'I suppose so. It never occurred to me. Mrs Twining left something, something cold.'

'And then you had dinner, *tête-à-tête*. What did you talk about?'

Lands put a hand to his head, touched his white streak as though he were touching his forelock. 'I don't remember.'

'She arrived at seven-thirty and left not long before midnight and you can't remember anything you talked about?'

'Local things,' Lands said weakly. 'And this man, Bain-Truscott. Eversley wasn't sure whether he would charge the man or not.'

'And what did Mrs Foster want him to do?'

Lands gathered a little boldness. 'I don't remember. I wasn't much interested.'

It appeared to Mr Hussick that Newton was pressing it a bit hard, and indeed this was Newton's own feeling. He went on asking questions about the times and about Mrs Twining being fetched from the station, but the effect he had made at first faded a little. Still, he had given Lands a bad quarter of an hour, although it wasn't of great importance in the long run, and he had encouraged their client. Mr Hussick raised his eyebrows and smiled at Tony, and Tony smiled shyly back.

Chapter 10

Mortimer Lands and Genevieve Foster had not really talked to each other since the trial began. They were both staying up in London, she at a hotel, he at the flat of a friend named Jerry Milton. He telephoned her that night when Milton was out.

'My housekeeper's been on the phone. Somebody's been asking questions at the farm. She sent him away.'

'Yes.'

'It wasn't the police, it was somebody else.'

'No doubt some inquiry agent for the defence.'

'One's been round already. I don't like it, Jenny.'

There was a pause. She said coldly, 'I told you not to telephone.'

'I'm worried, I have to see you.' She said nothing. 'I could come round. Now.'

'Don't be a fool.'

'I've got to see you. I can't go on if I don't.'

'I don't know what you're talking about,' she said sharply. 'It's upsetting for everybody. You don't think I liked all those questions today, do you?'

Lands had drunk a quarter of a bottle of whisky. Now he half-filled his pony glass. 'I've got to see you.'

'Very well. Tomorrow night you can take me out to dinner.'

'I could meet you somewhere quiet, nobody would –'

'I won't have anything hole and corner. Call for me here at seven o'clock.' She put down the receiver.

When Jerry Milton returned an hour later he found Mortie Lands half cut and lachrymose with it. They had been friends at Oxford and had seen a good deal of each other since then. Jerry, who was an executive in a statistical research company, disliked drunks, but he tried to be patient.

'It's ghastly the whole thing, I do see that, but after all you've given evidence now, it's over.'

353

'You don't understand,' Mortie said. His hair was mussed up, and he was sprawled all over the sofa. Jerry privately thought it was a bit much – the whisky glass had left marks on a pretty little rosewood table – but Mortie had always been a little on the hysterical side. Now he said, bleary eyed, 'It's terrible. That poor young man.'

'Jones? He's just a dirty crook. And a murderer. You're too soft-hearted, Mortie, that's your trouble. Come on, you'd better get to bed.'

With the help of his arm Mortie rose, then staggered and knocked over a Victorian glass table lamp which broke into a dozen pieces. It was really too much to be borne, and Jerry told him so pretty sharply. Mortie began to weep.

'You're all against me,' he said through sobs. 'She is too. I can't bear it, I can't go on.'

There was only one thing to do, and Jerry did it. He hauled the insensible disgusting lump into the bedroom and deposited him on top of the bed.

In the morning Mortie was apologetic, and he looked so haunted, so much like death warmed up, that Jerry didn't have the heart to say anything more.

Chapter 11

Dimmock sneezed when he got out of bed and again while he was shaving. By the time he got downstairs there could be no doubt that he had a cold. He could not have faced fish if it had been offered to him, and his breakfast was one piece of toast and marmalade and two cups of watery coffee. 'I could eat some bacon and eggs if I hadn't this pain in my pegs,' he thought, and it was true that his teeth did ache. When he set out in the car it was still raining, heavy solid stuff that came steadily down. As he drove out of town he felt distinctly ill. He did not think that there was much point in going to see the motor launch or in visiting Sarah Russell, but it did not occur to him that he might say this to the Chief. He had never yet failed to carry out the assignments given to him in every detail.

The day had begun badly with his cold, and it continued badly. He was misdirected to the place where the launch had been tied up, and when he found the place the boat was no longer there. He called at a house nearby and learned that the *Daisy Mae* had been removed by the police to the yard of a local boat builder named Clynes. It was eleven-thirty when he found the boatyard, most of the morning gone. Clynes received Dimmock in his office. He was a thin lugubrious man.

'Police have been over her,' he said. 'What you want to look at her for?'

Why did he want to look at her? Dimmock had no idea. 'It's part of an investigation I'm carrying out for somebody interested in the –' He stopped and sneezed. '– defence.'

Clynes was concerned. 'That's a nasty cold you've got. You could do with a cup of tea.'

As he drank the scalding liquid Dimmock was conscious of his wet disgusting clothes, which seemed to have lost their shape. His trousers hung round his legs like pieces of cardboard.

'Know anything about boats?' Dimmock shook his head. 'No

more did they. Bought her from me, Foster did, just because his wife wanted it. Like buying a kid a toy. Not but what she learned a bit. How to start the engine.' He laughed, and Dimmock realized that this was a joke. 'Now she wants me to sell the boat for her.'

'What sort of man was Foster?' He asked it to keep the conversation going, not because he was interested.

'Thought the sun shone out of her backside. Bloody old fool if you ask me. I've seen her sort before, out for what they can get. Gold diggers, we used to call 'em.' Clynes finished his tea. 'Interested in cricket?'

'I'm afraid not.' Hopefully, like a man excusing himself, he said, 'My son plays.'

'Local cricket club. I'm the president. Like to take some?' He pushed a book of raffle tickets across the table. Dimmock bought the whole book, twenty at a shilling each. He would charge them to expenses, but suppose he won a prize what would he do then?

Clynes did not show satisfaction, but Dimmock knew that he was pleased. 'Right then, let's go and have a look at her, shall we?'

He put on an oilskin and then squelched across the yard with the rain pouring down. Dimmock quite distinctly felt mud surge up round his left sock.

The boat was just about what he had expected. Clynes jumped in and Dimmock followed him more circumspectly, stumbling a little so that Clynes's hand had to support him. The boat builder pointed out features. 'Evinrude motor, pull starter on it easy to work. Steering wheel. Oars to use if the motor packs up. Nice little cabin, sleeps two if they're not over six foot, calor gas cooker, even a baby fridge. And that's it. She's a pleasure boat, not for serious sailors.'

'If you were taking it away from the place where it was tied up and didn't want to make a noise, you'd use the oars.'

'Of course.'

Dimmock poked about. There was nothing to see. 'I suppose the police searched it thoroughly.'

Clynes stroked his chin. 'They took a look. Not a long one. Didn't expect to find anything, you won't either.'

Dimmock went into the cabin, got down on the floor, peered under the two bunks, even put his hand under, more for the sake of appearances than anything else. Nothing. Half a dozen paperback novels stood on a small ledge above the bunk, and he read the titles idly. A small kettle was on the cooker and in an access of idiocy, disturbed by the figure of Clynes in the doorway watching, he lifted the lid. Bits of kettle fur rattled about inside.

'What you looking for, poison?' Clynes guffawed slightly. Dimmock responded with a wan smile. He was reluctant to go out again into the rain, but it had to be done. Outside again he squatted down and heard the bones crack in his knees. I shall be lucky if I don't get pneumonia, he thought. There was a little water in the bottom of the boat but to take the ache out of his knees he knelt down.

Something was attached to one of the rowlocks, if that was what you called the things in which you put the oars. You could not see it when you knelt, but he could feel something at the bottom of the rowlock. He called to Clynes, who came and bent down beside him. Dimmock gently removed the thing, a tiny piece of fabric. It was about two inches one way by an inch the other. One side was check, the other a muddy brown. It was made from some rubberized material.

'You saw me find it. I didn't put it there.'

Clynes nodded. 'We haven't cleaned her out yet. If we had done we'd have found that bit of stuff. Thrown it away most like.'

'I didn't put it there.'

'Course you bloody didn't. Think it's important?'

The discovery seemed to have changed Clynes's view of Dimmock. His stare held something approaching respect. It was unlikely that the fabric was of any importance at all, but Dimmock shrugged. He felt the heavy dampness of his topcoat. They squelched away.

'Might be a bit of mackintosh. Just what you could do with.' Clynes guffawed. 'Come in. I'll give you a tot of rum.'

They returned to the office. Dimmock drank the rum and wrote out a brief statement about the way in which he had found the bit of fabric. Clynes signed it as witness. Dimmock was a man who believed in the value of routine.

With the statement in his pocket he got into his car, removed his soaking hat and coat and drove away. It was good to have the wet things off, but there was no heater in the car and within five minutes he began to shiver.

Chapter 12

'Today's the big one then,' one of the prison officers said to him in the van that morning. 'You want to look all bright and shining, doesn't he, Bill?' The other man said that was right, get into that box and show 'em, good turn-out, bags of swank, rather as if he were going on parade in the army. One of them offered him a little pocket mirror so that he could adjust the knot of his tie. They were very friendly chaps. He had tried once or twice to tell them what his defence was, what had really happened, but they always cut him short and said that it was not their business.

He had expected to be nervous, but once he had taken the oath swearing to tell the truth (and after all he was going to do just that) and had begun to answer Newton's questions, he did not feel nervous at all. And a quick look at the jury – Bill the prison officer had told him that it was a good thing to look at them sometimes as long as you didn't overdo it – showed him that they were paying attention. Blue Rinse had abandoned her nails and was looking at him with her lips slightly parted, Pretty But Fatuous was evidently attentive, oh yes he had them on the alert as he rode the gentle swell of the questions, answering them rapidly and with firmness in a consciously clear voice. He was rather pleased with the way in which he disposed of the *name* business. Why had he called himself Bain-Truscott?

He hesitated just a moment, permitting himself just a hint of his smile. 'Snobbery, I have to admit. I did it to impress people.'

'There was no other reason?'

Firmness at this, smile vanishing. 'None at all.'

It had been raining most of the morning, but now suddenly for a quarter of an hour the sun shone through the window, casting a lean knife shadow across the Court which moved slowly in the direction of the man in the box, away from the barristers in their wigs and gowns. There were one or two moments of drama, like the one when Newton asked if he had ever met the dead man.

'Never.' Very firm, head up showing the clean line of the chin. Sunlight was strong on his face.

'But you talked to a man who called himself by that name.'

'I did.'

'He was an impostor?'

'I understand that now.'

'Do you know now who that man was?'

'It was Mortimer Lands.'

Later he admitted that he had agreed to take part in disposing of what he believed to be Foster's body.

'Are you ashamed of your conduct?'

Low voiced, but still firm. 'I am.'

'Can you explain what made you do it?'

He would have liked to look at Jenny, to search her out with his eyes, but she was not in Court. He stared boldly at the jury instead. 'I was infatuated with Mrs Foster. I thought she was in love with me.'

They went through the tale of the drive in the car, the burden dropped out of the motor launch. 'At the time you believed this to be Foster's body.'

'Yes.'

'What do you think now?'

'It must have been some kind of dummy already prepared.'

'I don't want there to be any mistake about this. You were prepared to play your part in this wretched enterprise?'

'I was.'

'You are not trying to deny that?'

'No.'

'Can you think of any word that would fit your conduct?' He said again that he was ashamed. 'When did you first learn that you had been taking part in a masquerade, that the whole thing was a sham?'

'When the detective at the airport showed me a picture of the real Eversley Foster.'

Newton repetitiously made the thing clear. 'This was a man you had never seen in your life?'

'That is so.'

'And you had no part whatever in his death?'

'Absolutely none.'

After his evidence in chief was completed the Court adjourned for lunch. Tony felt that he had done well and had impressed the jury. He ate a good meal. The prison officer with him watched him with surprise.

At just about this time Dimmock, fifty miles away, discovered the piece of fabric.

The line of defence had been fairly clear after the cross-examination of Mrs Foster, but still it seemed hardly credible, Hardy's junior Gordon Baker said to him over their chump chops and pints of bitter that such a line should be seriously advanced. Hardy smiled faintly, with the air of superiority that made him so irritating, and said that if his client insisted on the story then Newton was stuck with it.

'Yes, but I mean there are limits.' Hardy looked at him interrogatively. 'They must have given him a hint of what he was in for.'

Hardy had eaten half of his chop. He looked at the rest of it and pushed away his plate. 'And if they did?'

'Well then, surely —' Baker was at a loss how to go on.

Hardy delivered himself of one of those apothegms that made him very little loved. 'A counsel is no better than his client. Especially,' he added with the faintest gleam of a smile like sun on ice in winter, 'When the counsel is Newton.'

After Jerry Milton had gone to work Mortimer Lands felt terrible. He thought of ringing Jenny at her hotel, but he knew that she would not want to speak to him. He felt physically unable to go to Court again, although he was still worried about the man who had called at the farm. Just after midday he thought that it might do him good to go out. This proved to be a mistake. He went into a pub and felt impelled to start a discussion about the case in which he maintained that Jones might be innocent. Fortunately he did not reveal his identity, but when he left the pub he had had too much to drink and nothing to eat.

He went back to the flat and fell asleep. On waking he still felt terrible.

Genevieve Foster woke early, had her usual breakfast of orange juice and Melba toast, and then went shopping. Or rather, she went into shops and looked at clothes. She did not buy anything because she thought that it was too soon after Eversley's death for that to be wise. She had already decided that when it was all over she would not marry Mortimer. She was not worried about him, because after all he could say nothing about her which did not implicate himself, but he was a weak man and she found weakness unsympathetic. When the case was over she would tell Mortimer that what had been between them was over too and go away for a time, perhaps to one of those Greek islands that people talked about.

Looking at the round immature body of an assistant in one shop, and at the girl's equally round soft face she felt the stirrings of desire, and wondered if she were basically a Lesbian. Perhaps on the Greek island there would be a chance to find out. When she came out of the shop she took a taxi and had lunch in a salad bar. Then she took another taxi to the Old Bailey and was in Court when Hardy rose to begin his cross-examination. As Tony entered the box again she was struck by his good looks, as she had been when she first saw him. It was a pity that he was such a fool.

Chapter 13

There was not much to do at the Villa Majorca, but Sarah Russell had said that she would go in that day and in she went, cleaning and dusting as usual. Mrs Foster had told her that she might be leaving Southbourne after what had happened, but while she was there the place had to be kept clean. She put on a kettle for a cup of tea, looked at the rain shuttering down outside and thought about the Fosters. He had been a perfect gentleman, although rather old and pernickety and set in his ways, but Mrs Foster now . . . There was something that she had never quite liked about Mrs Foster, although she couldn't have said what it was, except that she never had a chat with you as in Sarah's view an employer should chat with her daily help.

As the kettle boiled the bell rang. A little man – medium-sized really, but somehow he looked small – was outside the door, and he was obviously very wet. His hat and raincoat were thoroughly sodden. 'Miss Sarah Russell,' he said, and raised the sodden hat.

The gesture touched her. Very few men had ever raised their hats to her, and he looked pathetic in his wet clothes. She had no doubt of his respectability, somehow the age of the car outside certified that, and Dimmock did not even have to produce one of his cards to get into the house. She sat him down in the kitchen, hung his wet coat in front of the electric fire and put his hat beside it. She made him take off his shoes, commented on the wetness of his trousers. Dimmock felt that she would have been quite prepared for him to take them off as well. He put them close to the fire and they steamed.

'Thank you very much.' The words came out as a crow-like croak, but the hot tea soothed his throat. 'I hope I shan't infect you. I've got a cold coming on.'

'You ought to be in bed.' She spoke angrily. She seemed a formidable old battleaxe.

'Tomorrow I shall be. Home in Wembley. And I can tell you I shan't be sorry.'

'Wembley,' she cried. Her brother and his wife lived there. Friendship was cemented, and it was not until he had had a second cup of tea and eaten a biscuit that she said, 'You're not a reporter, are you? I've had some of *them* round.' He shook his head and sneezed. 'Bless *you*,' said Sarah Russell.

He produced his card and told her that he was gathering information for the defence. She stared.

'You're too late, aren't you? The trial's half-way through. And there's been someone here already.'

'Did you tell him anything?'

'There was nothing to tell.'

Dimmock said that she knew how it was, he had been given this job to do. What use they made of any information he found – he lifted his shoulders.

'Funny the way they go on,' Sarah said, and added sharply: 'Something's burning. Your socks.'

His feet certainly were near the fire, and he withdrew them.

'My husband used to burn his socks.' In fact it came to her now that this little man reminded her of the husband who had been dead for twenty years. He too had always raised his hat to ladies. 'Do you do this all the time? Going round and talking to people, it seems a funny way to make a living.'

'I suppose it is. I don't always get so wet.' It might have been her husband John sitting in the chair opposite. And because John too had sometimes made incomprehensible jokes she was not disconcerted when he said, 'When my feet are very wet I sometimes get into a pet.' He looked at her and said, 'But not today. You've been very kind.'

'What do you want to know?'

'Well, anything – anything odd. Out of the way, you know.'

'I'll tell you something that *is* funny, something I've remembered.' At another time and in other circumstances, perhaps even if the sun had been shining, she might have sent him away with a flea in his ear. As it was she told him the something funny she had remembered and then looked with interest at the bit of material he produced, which she recognized at once as resembling Mrs Foster's raincoat. She looked for the raincoat but it wasn't where she would have expected it to be, in the hall cupboard. When they found it eventually, tucked away with some old bedding in a tiny junk room, Dimmock knew that for the first time in his life as an operative he had discovered something of importance.

Chapter 14

When Tony returned to Court after lunch he saw Jenny immediately. She sat in the row reserved for witnesses, pale and calm. He knew that in her presence it was more than ever important that he should do well.

Hardy opened quietly, almost amiably. 'Would you call yourself a truthful man?'

'On the whole, yes.'

'As truthful as most people?'

'I think so.'

'Let us see.' He consulted or pretended to consult his notes, looked up. 'You called yourself Bain-Truscott when working for Mr Foster, but that is not your real name.'

'No.'

'Have you also used the name of Scott-Williams?'

'Yes.'

'And other names too?'

'I've explained, I did it to impress people. I didn't like the name of Jones.' Just a hint of his smile there and a glance at the jury. One of them looked angry. Perhaps his name was Jones?

'Very well. Now, when you produced your references for this job, were they true or false?'

'I'd written them myself. Again, it was just to impress people.'

'The references were false?'

'They weren't genuine.'

'They weren't genuine. Very well again, since that is the phrase you prefer. Now, you will remember when you took the cuff links and pin to Mr Penny. What did you say to him?'

'I asked what they were worth.'

Hardy raised his hand into the air, then lowered it in a wearily patient manner. 'But how did you describe them? Let me remind you. Did you say they were a family heirloom?'

'Something like that.'

'True or false?' As Tony hesitated Hardy's voice rang out for a moment, clear and beautiful as a rapier blade. 'True or false, Jones?'

'It wasn't true,' he said sullenly. All this was not what he had expected, and it seemed to him unfair.

'It was not true,' Hardy repeated. 'Now, turn your mind for a moment to the time when you were interrogated at London Airport. You said you had a job in Caracas. True or false?'

He looked appealingly at the judge, who must surely understand that nobody could be expected to tell the exact truth in such circumstances, but found no help there. And Hardy was going on without waiting for his answer.

'And then you told the police that you had saved the money in your possession. True or false?'

This time the judge did speak, quietly, as Tony remained silent. His tone was kind, but the words brought no comfort.

'Just answer the question.'

'I've already explained –' he began desperately, but now the judge's voice was hard as a headmaster's.

'Answer the question.'

'I didn't tell the truth.'

'False,' Hardy said, triumphant as a man who has filled in the last clue of a crossword puzzle. 'You lied again and again. And now do you ask us to accept you as a truthful witness?'

Mr Hussick leaned back just a little, as nearly as it was possible to lean back in his hard chair. The boy was standing up for himself quite reasonably, but how long would he be able to do it when he was stuck with this hopeless story? And for the next hour Hardy, rarely raising his voice above his usual monotone, showed how hopeless that story was, going through it detail by detail, demonstrating that everything the accused man said depended on his unsupported word. He was particularly scathing about the hammer and the cuff links.

'When as you say Mrs Foster asked you to use the hammer to knock in a nail, didn't you think it odd?'

'No. She'd told me that her husband was useless about the house.'

'Did you regard knocking in nails as part of your duties as secretary?'

'Of course not.'

'So it would have been possible for you to have refused?'

There was something hateful about Hardy. The thin long-nosed patrician face, the wearily contemptuous manner, the voice enunciating its syllables with perfect clarity and style, all of them represented an attitude to life which Tony would have liked to think of as his own. He had to restrain himself from shouting his reply, but he said calmly, 'I couldn't have refused without being rude.'

'And I'm sure you are never rude.' Newton stirred uneasily at this comment, but Hardy continued swiftly. 'Supposing you had refused, one of the strongest points in the case against you would not have existed?'

With a sense of self-congratulation at his own calmness he said: 'I can only tell you what happened.'

'If you had refused Mrs Foster would have had to find some other – lethal implement – and asked you to handle that. Is that what you are asking us to believe?'

Doggedly he repeated 'I can only say what happened.'

'Just follow me for a moment. Since she was determined to incriminate you, if you had refused to handle the hammer she might have tried to get your prints on to a sharp knife – or a revolver – or a tin of weedkiller, which she would then have used as the murder instrument.' Without raising his voice Hardy managed to infuse into it a note of scorn as he said, 'Is that what you are asking the jury to believe?'

He made some kind of answer, but as he looked round the Court and found no help anywhere, in judge or jury, in his counsel or his solicitor, and as he finally found himself staring across into the pale unmoved face and the eyes that considered him indifferently, his grasp of what was being said to him vanished in a surge of hatred. He had lost the battle of wills with Hardy and his breaking point was only a question of time. The time came a quarter of an hour later when Hardy, showing the distaste of a man handling excreta with tongs, was questioning him about the sexual relations he claimed to have had with Mrs Foster.

'You have heard Mrs Foster say that hers was a happy marriage. Nobody has come here to say otherwise. But you maintain that this woman of good reputation, against whom there is no breath of suspicion, seduced you?'

'I thought she was in love with me.'

'Within a few days of your entering the house she took you to her bed, that is what you are saying?'

The sneering voice insisted, the questions came at him in endless waves, what had she said to him, when had they first done it, how many times, what precisely had she said to him about killing her husband? It seemed to him that there were now only two faces in the Court, that of his tormentor and the white beautiful face that remained like a mask while the questions were asked that destroyed his self-respect and made him seem less than a man, so that at last he shook the witness box with the thump of his fist and cried out in a high woman's voice that she had done it, she was the bitch who had got him into this, and went on to use filthy words about her, words that had hardly been in his mouth for years.

When it was over he felt spent, as he did after the sexual act. He did not hear the reproving words of the judge or take in what it was that Mr Hussick was saying to him so earnestly. Instead he looked at the jury, saw the expressions on their faces, and knew that he was lost.

Chapter 15

Mortimer Lands insisted that he must get out of London for an hour or two. He drove Jenny out to a dinner and dance place on the Great West Road. He had been drinking whisky before he picked her up and went on drinking it throughout dinner. He talked incoherently about the trial.

'That poor bastard,' he said. 'From what I read they crucified him today, really crucified him.'

'I was there.' He looked at her almost with terror.

'He loved you, the poor bastard.'

She had drunk a good deal herself and was less patient than usual. 'What are you trying to say to me?'

'We're going to get caught. I know we are.' She ate a green bean and looked at him inquiringly. 'Somebody's certain to have seen the car.'

'Nobody saw it. I told you I was careful. And I smeared mud all over the number plates.'

'Somebody will –'

'I still don't know what you're trying to say.'

'I must get out of London. I hate London.'

'Then get out. Go back tomorrow. I don't know why you stayed in town anyway.'

'I thought you wanted me to.'

'It made no difference to me.'

He leaned across the table. 'Jenny, we can't do it, he'll go to prison for life.'

The waiter came to take their plates and she did not speak until he had gone. 'He was prepared to help in killing you, that's what he thought he was doing.'

'I know. But he hasn't done anything.'

'And you did help, Mortimer. You wanted to help.' Before the intensity of her gaze he lowered his eye, mumbled something. 'Tomorrow there'll be the verdict, in a week it will all be forgotten, in three months we can be together.'

'Three months!'

'That's what we agreed.'

He looked up at her, then down again at the tablecloth.

'Are you saying you want to call it off?'

'That's what you'd like, isn't it? You've got what you wanted, now you –' She told him to lower his voice, hushing him as if he were a dog, and he finished the sentence in a ludicrous murmur. '– don't love me at all.'

'I'm trying to find out what you want. But I'll tell you this. If you come up with some different story now nobody will believe it. And if they did, then it would be as bad for you as for me. I'm ready to go.' She picked up her bag.

He stared at her drunkenly. 'I want to dance. And I want another drink.' She paused, for once uncertain. 'I want to hold you in my arms once more. The last time, I know that.'

'Oh, for God's sake, Mortimer.'

'It's my car. Shan't go home unless you dance with me.'

She thought, not for the first time, that she would have been better off with Jones. She was a reasonable, logical woman and total lack of logic was something she found it hard to deal with or understand. It was obviously not safe to leave him alone. She said that she would dance with him. He immediately called the waiter.

'A bottle of champagne. A celebration.'

They did not leave until two in the morning, and by then Jenny herself was slightly drunk.

Chapter 16

At first Mr Hussick was sceptical about the telephone call from an inquiry agency he had never heard of, and one with a ridiculous name at that, but the excitement at the other end of the line communicated itself to him during the conversation, and when he had finished talking he picked up the receiver again and rang Magnus Newton who turned out to be attending a legal dinner in London. Newton was not pleased to be called away to the telephone, but when he heard what Hussick had to say he agreed to leave after the loyal toast and before the speech. He was in fact not altogether sorry to miss the speech, which was to be given by a retired Lord of Appeal renowned for his prolixity. The four of them met at eleven o'clock that night in Newton's chambers.

Clarence Newhouse was a blustering red-faced man who wore a Guards tie. Newton listened to him for a couple of minutes and then said, 'This is the man who got the information? Then I'd like to have the story from him.'

Dimmock had been sitting in a corner, overwhelmed by the occasion. The visit to a barrister's chambers late at night, the pat on the back from the Chief and his warm words about good work, and now this request that he should take the centre of the stage – what a tale he would have to tell the wife tomorrow. He moved forward from his corner seat into the circle of light cast by Newton's desk lamp. As he did so he sneezed.

'You've got a cold,' Newton said accusingly. He produced a little inhaler from his jacket and sniffed noisily up each nostril. 'Well?'

If there was one thing that Dimmock knew he could do, it was to make a clear and succinct report, and afterwards he felt that on this evening he had really excelled himself. The great man lighted a cigar and offered the box to the rest of them (the Chief took one and lit up, but Dimmock felt that it would have been presumptuous in him to smoke at the same time as the Chief), but his keen piggy little eyes looked steadily at Dimmock even while the mouth puffed smoke from its fat tube. When he had finished Dimmock waited in awe to hear what the experts would say about it. The Chief began to expand on all the trouble that had been taken by the agency, but he was cut short by the solicitor, Mr Hussick, whose eyebrows seemed to be climbing up into his scalp.

The great man opened his mouth. What would he say?

'Take anything for those colds, do you? Is it on your chest? Or just the nose?'

'Nose. And throat.'

'This may help.' He wrote something on a piece of paper, pushed it across the desk. 'Get it made up. Use it myself.'

For a moment Dimmock thought he must be light-headed, and that he was really in a doctor's surgery. Then Newton continued. 'This woman, Russell, she'll give evidence in Court? And the boatyard man, what's his name, Clegg?'

'Clynes,' said Mr Hussick.

'I've got their signed statements.' Dimmock drew the papers from his briefcase.

'That was intelligent.' Dimmock glowed. Newton's words seemed to be a justification of his whole career.

'All our operatives are intelligent,' the Chief said with a jolly laugh. Newton swivelled to direct on him a gaze that was by no means wholly friendly.

'Who's paying you?'

'I'm afraid I can't reveal that.' The jolly laugh was slightly uneasy. 'Professional ethics.'

'Never mind, doesn't matter.'

'I believe my employer is – ah – a friend of the accused.'

'Didn't know he had any friends.' To Dimmock's bewilderment Mr Hussick and the Chief laughed heartily as though this was a good joke. 'We had a firm on to this and they turned up nothing, eh, Hussick.' Mr Hussick nodded. He seemed to find this amusing too. 'Must remember you next time. But insist that they put Mr Dimmock on to it, Hussick, insist on that.'

Newton's hand fell like an accolade on to Dimmock's shoulder as he said that they would need him also in Court. That was an exciting prospect, but Dimmock afterwards thought of the hour he had spent in those chambers, rather than the session in Court, as the crowning point of his career. He had the prescription made up, and although it had no effect upon his cold he treasured the piece of paper to the end of his life.

When they had gone Newton and Hussick got down to it. After Clynes and Sarah Russell had given evidence it would be necessary to recall Mrs Foster, and notification of this must be given to the prosecution. Then there was the matter of serving a subpoena on these two new witnesses. Hussick nodded and smiled, nodded and smiled. Newton's cigar was out before they had finished.

'About Mrs Foster,' he said at the end. 'She's still going to be a tough nut. She was in Court today. I don't want her there to-morrow.'

'I'll see to it.'

But there was no need for him to see to it.

Chapter 17

'I'll drive.' Jenny held out her hand for the keys.

'The hell you will.' Lands opened the car door and sat down heavily in the driver's seat.

'You shouldn't drive. The breathalyser. If the police stop us –'

'They won't. Are you getting in or not?'

She got in and sat sideways on the seat with the door half open. She had begun a sentence saying that she was still sober and he was not when he started the car and it shot forward so that she had to slam the door to save herself from falling out. He went out of the drive into the road, ignoring a car which swerved and hooted.

'Let me drive.'

He pushed down the accelerator. They were going at sixty. 'You know what's wrong with you? You don't like men, you hate them, want to take everything away from them. You're the boss, they dance when you tell them.' He muttered something else.

'What?'

'Not going to drive my car,' he shouted. 'Going to drive my own bloody car.' He turned on the radio and the Beatles came shrieking out of it. He hooted a Jaguar in the fast lane, then cut inside it just as the Jaguar moved into the slower lane. Lands tugged at the steering wheel to get back into the fast lane and the car responded. Their tyres screeched, the Jaguar driver yelled something as they passed him. Almost for the first time in her life she was frightened and cried out some words that he did not hear above the sound of the radio. But anger was an emotion that came to her more easily than fear, and as she heard him begin to sing some drunken accompaniment to the music she felt an access of rage against this feeble sot who was unable to carry through the small part given to him in her plan. She cried out that he should stop the car and leaned over trying to wrench the steering wheel away from him.

Mortimer held on to it, and raising his left hand chopped it down hard on hers. The cry she gave was pleasant to him. Did she think that he was not a man? Yet at the same time he wanted to tell her that he was sorry. He turned his head to say so when he heard her cry out, saw that they had strayed into the second lane, and heard the blast of the Jaguar's horn. Again he tugged at the steering, but this time the car over-responded. They went straight through the central barrier into the path of an oncoming lorry.

As they broke the barrier Jenny had time to feel one last quick surge of anger against the absurdity of what was happening. How was it possible to make plans when they were at the mercy of other people? The last thing she saw was Mortimer take his hands off the wheel and put them over his face.

The lorry struck the car head on, turning it over and over in the road. The driver was carrying a load of machine tools, and the lorry suffered nothing worse than a badly damaged radiator. The collision forced open the passenger door of the car and Jenny was thrown out into the road. It was said at the inquest that she had died instantly of a broken neck, but her body went directly in front of an oncoming car in the middle lane, and his wheels passed over it. The steering wheel went through Lands's chest, and he was trapped in the crumpled car. He was still alive when the police arrived, and it seemed to the sergeant that he was trying to say something, but in fact he never spoke. Before they had cut through the pieces of the bodywork that were holding him, he was dead.

Chapter 18

Tony stared at Mr Hussick and repeated the word. 'Dead.'

'It creates, let's be frank about it, an unusual situation.' Mr Hussick was not a man easily overborne by events, but that late session with Newton and then the news about Mrs Foster had momentarily quelled even his exuberance.

Tony stared at the short paragraph headed: *Mrs Foster Dies in Car Crash*, and read it again.

'We would of course have recalled her. And Lands. Now that won't be possible.' Mr Hussick gave a slight cough in deprecation at this statement of the obvious. 'But the vital thing is the new evidence. I had a conference with Mr Newton last night long past the witching hour –'

'What's that?' The young man looked quite dazed. Perhaps it was not surprising.

'Long past midnight. A very late night, and a very early morning. I have somebody now talking to Miss Russell.' Jones did not know the name, and he had to explain who she was. 'I don't mind telling you that Mr Newton is much more confident today than he was yesterday.' He managed a little dance with the eyebrows. Jones nodded. 'The firm involved is called the Second To None Agency. I'm bound to say that they discovered things which we had missed. I take it a friend of yours employed them?' Jones said he didn't know. Altogether, Mr Hussick was not sorry when the interview was over and he was able, as he said, to leave his client to digest the good news.

Those who were living are now dead. Those words – were they a line from a poem? – remained in Tony's mind after the lawyer had left him. Yesterday he had looked across the Court at the pale face and had felt hatred. Now that he knew he would never see her again the hatred had gone, everything had gone except a series of pictures which ran through his mind like lantern slides, showing their first meeting, the interview at the Villa Majorca, the bedroom scenes when her abandonment to pleasure had appeared complete. When people die those closely linked to them reconstitute their personalities in terms of what they wish to remember, and with her death Jenny became again instantly the woman who had loved him and whose plans were all devised for the fulfilment of their love. The dream of their life together in Caracas was omnipresent, a dream all the sweeter because now it would never know fulfilment in reality. Nothing could take the perfection of the dream away from him.

He had not really thought about the way in which the new evidence had been obtained. It was not until he was on the way to Court and one of the police officers asked how things were going and said that if there was anything he could do for Tony without stepping out of line he'd be glad to do it, that the mystery was suddenly clear to him. 'If there's anything I can do –' he remembered those as being the General's very words, and in spite of Tony's reaction he had obviously gone on to do it, he had gone to the inquiry agency. Tears welled in Tony's eyes. He murmured: 'He's a good man, a very good man.'

'What did you say?'

He shook his head, said there was nothing he wanted done, and wiped away the tears. As the police officers agreed afterwards, he was a bit of a soppy type.

Chapter 19

Sarah Russell wore her best clothes for the occasion, topped by a hat ornamented by red and white cherries. She followed Dimmock, whose evidence was confined to an account of his discoveries and the fact that he had interviewed Sarah. She was intimidated at first by the formality of it all and the fact that the lawyers were dressed so strangely, but the little man asked her such simple questions, about how long she had worked for Mrs Foster and what kind of work it was, that she soon felt at ease and even began to enjoy herself. After the preliminaries Newton got down to business.

'Now, Mrs Russell, I want you to cast your mind back to that Friday morning, the morning of the murder. Is there anything you particularly remember about that morning?'

'Something funny happened. I didn't think much of it at the time.'

'Yes?'

'There was this bit of carpet in the hall, you see. It was all rucked up because some of the tacks had come out of it, so I thought I'll tack that down. Mr Foster, he was no good at that kind of thing.'

'Yes, I see. So what did you do?'

'I looked for the hammer, it was always kept in the tool box out in the scullery. But it wasn't there. So I spoke to Mrs Foster.'

'Will you tell us what she said.'

'Told me not to bother, she had a headache. And mind you, the day before she'd been saying she must get it done.' Sarah looked round with an air of triumph and touched her hair, which she feared was untidy.

'And then what did you do?'

'I thought, what's happened to it, must be somewhere, and eventually I found it. In one of the kitchen drawers, where it had no business to be.'

'Will you tell us how you found it?'

'It was wrapped in tissue paper.'

These words created some interest. The judge made a note. Hardy listened with a frown. Newton repeated the words and asked if she could remember anything further.

'Yes, I called out to Mrs Foster and said "I've found it" and I was just taking off the paper when she came out into the kitchen and told me to leave it alone. She was quite sharp.'

'You saw the hammer?'

'Of course I did.'

'Did you touch it?'

'No, I was taking off the wrapping when she said that. Said again she had a headache and told me to leave it. So I did.'

'Exhibit fifteen, please,' Newton said. The hammer was handed to Sarah. 'Is that the hammer?'

'That's the one.'

'Had you ever known it to be put away like that before?'

'Never.'

'Can you tell the Court why you haven't mentioned this previously.'

'I didn't think anything more about it. And nobody asked me about anything funny. Not till Mr Dimmock.'

The mention of Dimmock's name launched Newton nicely on to the question of the raincoat. This was the really vital piece of evidence, for Sarah had recognized the fabric as coming from a raincoat that Mrs Foster had bought a week before her husband's death, and Dimmock had confirmed this with the shop from which it had been purchased. The inference was overwhelming that she had visited the *Daisy Mae* after buying it, although in the witness box she had sworn otherwise. And there was something else, which Newton had been allowed to bring out without objection from Hardy. There were spots on the raincoat, and an urgent forensic examination had revealed that they were blood. The blood group had been identified as AB which was Foster's blood group, although it was Mrs Foster's blood group too.

In ordinary circumstances this information would have been kept from the prosecution, but the circumstances here were remarkable. When he heard of Mrs Foster's death Newton thought it his duty to make the situation known to Hardy. There had been a conference that morning at which, slightly to Newton's surprise, Hardy had refused to acknowledge that the new evidence made much difference to the case against Jones. But this was typical of Hardy who, for all his air of languor, was not inclined to drop a case once he had his teeth into it. Now he rose and looked for a moment silently at Sarah Russell, who returned his look with some belligerence.

'Did you like Mrs Foster?'

'We never had any argument.'

'But did you like her, Mrs Russell?'

'Didn't like or dislike. She kept herself to herself, didn't talk much.'

'You know that she died tragically in a car accident last night, so that she cannot comment on your story?'

'It isn't a story. It's the truth.'

'I'm sure you are saying what you believe to be true.' Hardy smiled at the witness, but the smile came out as ironic rather than friendly. 'You say you fixed the date on which this hammer incident occurred as the morning of the murder. How can you be sure?'

'It's not a day I'm likely to forget.'

'I suppose not,' Hardy said humbly. 'And you remember all the other details too. Are you sure the hammer was wrapped in tissue paper?'

'Quite sure.'

'It wasn't just lying on it, with the tissue below?'

'I said before it was wrapped round in tissue.'

'So you did.' Hardy was apologetic. 'How did you know it was a hammer?'

'How did I know – I don't understand.'

'It's very simple.' He spoke as though to a child. 'You opened the drawer. There was some tissue paper. What made you think it was a hammer?'

'I didn't – I don't –' She made another false start and the judge told her to take her time. 'I suppose I was poking about in the drawer. I don't quite remember.'

'You don't remember that. Do you remember if you pulled aside the tissue?'

'I must have, mustn't I? To see the hammer.'

'But you don't remember doing it?' Suddenly, sharply, he said, 'You did see a hammer, you're sure of that?'

'Oh yes, I'm sure.'

'You saw the head of it? Or the handle?'

These are silly questions, she wanted to say, I know I saw the hammer and so do you, but she knew she must not say that. 'I'm not quite sure.'

'Not quite sure. But you identified the hammer, Mrs Russell.'

'It was the same hammer. I know it was.'

'Yet you can't be sure how much of it you saw. Well, we will leave it at that.' Hardy smiled at her again, then his voice hardened. 'You did forget, though, didn't you?'

She looked at him, confused. 'I don't know what you mean.'

'You'd been questioned already. And you didn't mention it.'

'Nobody asked me about anything funny. Not until I saw Mr Dimmock.'

'Mr Dimmock, ah yes, we have heard Mr Dimmock,' Hardy said in a voice implying that they wanted to hear no more of him. He went on to establish that she had seen the accused with Mrs Foster and that there was no sign of friendship between them, that the Fosters had never quarrelled in her hearing, and that Mortimer Lands had seemed on good terms with Mr Foster. But Hardy did not press this, nor did he ask more than perfunctory questions about the raincoat. His interest was not in demonstrating Mrs Foster's innocence, but in showing Jones's guilt.

Chapter 20

The passage that most struck the wise men in the Court (and there is always a number of wise men in any Court) about Hardy's final speech was that in which he ingeniously combined defence of Mrs Foster with a demonstration that even if she had lied it gave no assurance at all that Jones was telling the truth.

'Genevieve Foster, as you know, is tragically dead. She cannot be here to answer the matters raised by the last defence witnesses. But what did the points they raised really amount to? That indefatigable investigator Mr Dimmock discovered that she occasionally dined out with her cousin in a place, it was suggested, that was 'significantly far away'. But what is there significant about this when you remember that both she and Mr Lands were members of the same golf club? And then, what do you think of Sarah Russell's evidence about the hammer, that hammer which was so curiously wrapped up in tissue paper? Isn't it strange that while she recalls all this so clearly she can't remember why she thought the thing in tissue paper was a hammer at all, or whether she saw the whole of it or just the handle or the head? I am not attacking her sincerity – nobody who heard her would do that – but I suggest that what she saw was the handle of some quite different tool and that when Mrs Foster said she did not want the carpet tacked down at that moment it was simply for the reason she gave. She had a headache. When we have that good common sense explanation why should we look for something sinister?'

Hardy looked about with an air of mild triumph, and continued more seriously. 'And then we come to the raincoat. There are spots of blood on it, and you may have noticed that my learned friend was not very precise about how they may have got there. Let me be as precise as possible. If those spots on the raincoat have any meaning in the case at all Mrs Foster must have attacked her husband with the hammer while wearing the rain-coat. She must also have been wearing gloves, since her prints were not on the hammer. Now you will remember that she was a slim, I might almost say a frail woman. Can you really picture her putting on the raincoat and gloves and then using the hammer to commit this brutal murder? Isn't it far more likely that she made a mistake in saying that she hadn't visited the launch for three weeks before the murder, that she went there for some completely innocent purpose, tore the raincoat and cut her hand at the same time so that some blood spilled on to the raincoat? And that when she noticed this she stuffed it away so that her husband shouldn't notice that the new raincoat was ruined?' Hardy paused. 'And mark this. Even if you accept that she took part in her husband's savage murder, it does not follow that Jones is innocent. If her association with him was really an adulterous one, is it not overwhelmingly likely that he was a partner in her husband's murder?'

Now Hardy turned to the prisoner in the dock and appeared to be addressing him directly, using a tone of withering scorn which made him almost visibly shrink. 'If you prefer to believe the tale that Jones told, you will acquit him. But can you believe it? Didn't he impress you when he gave evidence as a rather intelligent young man, and also as one who would tell any lie to save his own skin? Listening to his account of the charade in which he says he took part, and which he says utterly deceived him, the dummy wrapped up as a body and the rest of it, ask yourselves: can any man have been as big a fool as that?'

Although Newton had the advantage of the final speech, his task was not an easy one. He had to decide just how far he could go in attacking Genevieve Foster without alienating the jury. In the end, after a long discussion with his junior, he decided to play it low and calm. As he asked the jury to accept the story told by the man in the dock, and recalled just what that story was, Newton did not once look at his client, who felt at times that he was being attacked rather than defended.

'Ladies and gentlemen, you have heard my learned friend Mr Hardy, and I will take up at once his last words: "Can any man have been as big a fool" as to act as Jones did. Just look at this question in another way. You must all of you have wondered when you heard my client give evidence why a man should concoct so clumsy and so discreditable a story in his own defence. I do not put him before you as a particularly virtuous man, or as a man whose intentions were anything but wicked. But, as my learned friend says, he quite obviously does not lack intelligence. To admit that, in the stress of passion, he entered into an agreement to murder Eversley Foster, and then to leave the country and wait for his criminal partner in a foreign land – to tell this tale that he knew would have little chance of belief because it was bound to be contradicted at every turn – can you believe that a man of reasonable intelligence would tell such a story unless it were true?

'For some time this story rested on his own word, and probably it was a word that few of you would care to accept. Happily, it is now supported by evidence. You have heard that Mrs Foster was sufficiently friendly with Lands to dine with him sometimes at a place which, in spite of what has been said to the contrary, was I repeat significantly far from her home. You have heard what Sarah Russell had to say about the hammer with which the crime was committed, and you may feel that there is no doubt at all that she did see a hammer and not the "other tool" which had been mentioned. If you accept that she did see the hammer you will make what you think right of the strange fact that, once having got Jones's fingerprints on it, Mrs Foster preserved this hammer in tissue paper. You have heard the story of the new raincoat, a small piece of which was found in the motor launch *Daisy Mae*. You will remember that Mrs Foster said at a time when the matter did not seem important, that she had not visited the launch for three weeks before the murder. You have heard that the raincoat had on it those damning spots of blood and you have heard where it was found, stuffed away in a junk room.'

Newton lowered his voice, his tone became sepulchral. 'It is painful for me to have to say these things. I do not wish to accuse the dead. But the points I have mentioned are some of those I should have questioned Mrs Foster about. Do you think, can anybody think, that she could have given satisfactory answers?'

There he left the question of Genevieve Foster, and went on to a peroration which certainly did not spare his client.

'I cannot put him before you as anything but a contemptible character, but I ask you to accept his story as true. And if you do accept it the important thing, the vital thing, that you must remember is this. He has told you frankly that he was prepared to enter into a conspiracy by which he would take part in the murder of Foster. That is, of the man he knew as Foster, for in fact he never met the real Eversley Foster. But if you accept his story *he did not take part in it*, he was deceived into thinking that he was taking part in a murder plot when in reality he was the dupe of the real murderer and of her accomplice Lands. If you find that this is really what happened, that Jones agreed to take part in a murder but really participated only in a charade, as my learned friend rightly called it, then I am telling you as a matter of law – and I am sure my lord will make reference to this later on – that he is not guilty of any crime at all, and that you must acquit him. You may think whatever you please of his character, but his character is not in question. I submit to you, members of the jury, that Anthony Jones is completely innocent of the crime of which he is accused.'

Had Newton really pitched it too low? That was the general opinion of the wise men. Looking at the jury, at Blue Rinse and Iron Hair and the others, noting slight signs of impatience while they listened to Newton in comparison with the close attention paid to Hardy's bell-like lucidity, they really hadn't much doubt about it.

Chapter 21

This assessment of the jury was quite wrong. Iron Hair had been on his side from the first. He bore a strong resemblance to a nephew of hers who had gone out to Australia and sent a splendid food parcel home to her every Christmas. Blue Rinse and Pretty But Fatuous had been inclined all along to think that Mrs Foster was too good to be true, and the man resembling Clinker, who was a director in a firm of woollen merchants, thought that Jones looked too intelligent to have behaved so stupidly and by an odd jump in reasoning therefore believed him innocent. Most of the others had thought he was guilty, but they were shaken by the raincoat evidence. They talked about it for an hour and a half, but there was never much doubt about which side the waverers would come down on.

The 'Not Guilty' verdict caused little surprise. Hardy congratulated Newton. Clerks tied up the briefs with bits of tape, white for the D.P.P.'s file, pink for all the others. Tony stepped down from the dock and Mr Hussick came over to him, eyebrows dancing. He shook hands with Mr Hussick, then with Newton and Newton's junior. Newton spoke a few words and turned away. It was all rather anticlimactic. The only people who seemed really pleased were Bill and Joe, the prison officers.

'You're away then,' said Bill. 'I knew that was the way it would be. I could feel it in my water. Had to get up to pee in the night, that's a sure sign. Never wrong, the old water.'

Tony felt like a departing guest who should thank his hosts for their hospitality, but it turned out that he had to collect various belongings from the cell below the Court.

'What'll it be then?' Bill asked. 'Off for a night on the town, a bit of a celebration?'

He shook his head. There was nobody for him to celebrate with. Bill and Joe agreed afterwards that they had never seen a man acquitted on a murder charge take it so quietly.

Standing outside the Old Bailey in summer sunlight he wondered what he should do. He owed his freedom to the General. Should he telephone to thank him, or go down to Leathersley House? A Rolls-Royce car nosed down the road and slowly drew to a halt. The judge's car, perhaps, or would he be trying the next case? A chauffeur got out and opened the rear door. Tony stared at him. The man made a gesture indicating unmistakably that he should step inside.

He got in. The woman already in the car leaned over to kiss him. It was Violet Harrington.

Chapter 22

'Aren't you going to say thank you?' She was wearing a peacock blue dress with short sleeves. Her bare brawny arms touched his.

'Thank you, yes, I didn't realize –'

'When I saw you were in real trouble I thought, I'm going to try to get him out of it even if it does cost money. When a friend's in trouble money doesn't matter.'

'This is a different car,' he said inanely.

'I'll tell you a little secret. There was a takeover bid for Harrington's companies. A handsome offer. I can afford anything I like now, Tony.' She placed a hand on his and he saw that there was a new diamond bracelet round her wrist. She indicated the neck of the chauffeur, who was separated from them by a glass partition. 'Including Meakins. I think it's a bore to drive yourself about when you can be driven.'

'Where are we going?'

'Home. To Burncourt Grange. Everything's arranged.' Her hand on his was hot and faintly moist, but the rings beneath the flesh were hard. 'You can leave it all to me now. You don't have to worry about anything.'

You don't have to worry about anything. The seat was soft, immensely luxurious. He closed his eyes.

PART FOUR

How the Dreams Came True

Chapter 1

They were married within a fortnight. There were no guests, no reception, not even a notice in *The Times*. 'We've got each other,' she said. 'We don't need anybody else.' He started to write a letter to Widgey and then tore it up. She belonged to the past, and he felt such a revulsion against the past that he could not bear to do anything that brought it back to him.

We've got each other: but the truth was, as he quickly realized, that she had him. He was not the squire of the village but a kept plaything. The servants – there were four of them, as he had imagined, although only two lived in – treated him with barely-concealed insolence. No doubt Meakins had told them about the trial, or they had seen pictures of him in the papers. Meakins himself, a spare man with slicked-down hair, had a slightly twisted lip which made his expression appear to be fixed in a sneer, and his manner had a familiarity which made it seem always that he was on the verge of asking some intimate question, like whether Mrs Harrington, now Mrs Jones, was a good lay.

About this there was in a sense no question. He was expected to be on duty at night, often in the morning and occasionally in the afternoon. It might have been like the paradise promised to believers by Mahomet, but in reality these encounters made him feel like a stallion condemned to endless servicing of a single mare. There was also something profoundly unsatisfactory to him about the form of their love-making. He closed his eyes and thought of Jenny, but the contrast between her almost angry dominance and the whimpering eagerness of Violet as her shuddering bulk lay beneath him was so disagreeable that he tried instead to make his mind completely blank.

He would have felt better if there had been any sign that she meant to carry out the promises she had made in the days before their marriage. On the second day after his release he had suggested that they go abroad. She bit into her breakfast toast and nodded. Her Pekinese eyes were bright.

'I still can't believe this is real. That prison hospital –' He left the sentence unfinished. In retrospect the hospital seemed horrific, whatever it had been like at the time.

'Poor boy.' She snapped off another piece of toast, crunched it up. 'It was lucky I decided to help, wasn't it?'

'I owe everything to you.' The words were true, although they seemed merely dutiful. 'I ought to get away. People talk.' He was aware already of the servants' attitude.

'Not if we were married.'

'You're sure you want –'

'Ever since I first saw you.'

'We could go abroad for our honeymoon. To Venice perhaps.'

'Don't you like it here?' He said truthfully that it was a wonderful house, but he meant really that it was wonderful to be waited on, to have the cook inquire in the morning about what they would like for dinner, and to order tea by ringing a bell. 'Then that's settled.'

Within a week of their marriage he knew that he had made a mistake. He should have seen to it that the tickets to Venice were bought before the ceremony, he should have made a firm arrangement about a monthly allowance. He realized too late that he had failed to realize his potential value and had sold himself for nothing. When he spoke of the honeymoon abroad she said that she hated travelling and that just to be with him was honeymoon enough for her. He had spent the last of his own money on an eternity ring, which seemed a nice symbolic touch, and he waited for her to say that they would have a joint bank account which he could use, but she said nothing of the kind. At last he raised the matter at what seemed an appropriate moment, after one of their afternoon sessions.

Her hand, with all the rings on it, including now his eternity ring, stroked his arm. 'Smooth. Not much hair on your body, is there? Harrington was a hairy man.'

It was not easy, but he said it. 'We're husband and wife. I ought to have my own bank account. Or a joint one.'

Her hand moved, touched his nipples, then moved down to

his stomach. In her brown bulging eyes he saw nothing of what he looked for, but only greed and pleasure. 'Kiss me.'

He knew that this was not what she meant, but with an effort he did as she wanted. As she lay back afterwards, panting with satisfaction, she said, 'Five pounds a week.'

He was about to protest, even to strike her. Then he saw that she would enjoy this too, and that protest would be useless.

Within a few weeks he knew that he was trapped in a net from which there was no escape. The Grange was a mile outside the village of Burncourt, and the village itself was in the Dorset countryside five miles from the nearest small town. She had told him that the Rolls was to be driven only by Meakins, but there was another car, an old one, and in this he went out two evenings a week. He spent his allowance on drink and an evening meal. It was very much like life with the General, except that he was paid less money. Violet said nothing about these evenings out, until one night he took the Rolls. Driving it gave him less pleasure than he had expected, because he had a schoolboy's feeling that there would be trouble when he returned. He came back slightly drunk to find her waiting for him.

'I told you that the Rolls was to be driven only by Meakins.' He had rehearsed a scene that began something like this, and he should have said now that as her husband he would drive any car he wished. In fact he said nothing. When she held out her hand for the keys he gave them to her. 'I have told Meakins to keep the garage locked up in future. There is another thing.' She had a glass of brandy in front of her and invited him to have some. He shook his head. She spoke slowly, savouring the words and watching him.

'You were tried and acquitted. But I remember that you admitted that you were ready to plan with that woman to kill her husband. I think I should tell you that I have made a will leaving my money to charities. Not to you. Do you understand me?' Her painted mouth curved in a smile. 'Of course it's possible that I might change my mind.'

Looking at her fat fingers twisting the stem of the glass as though she might break it, he knew what she felt for him was not love but hatred. She spoke as though she read his thoughts.

395

'You remember that afternoon in the car? I haven't forgotten. I told you, didn't I, that I usually get what I want.'

She put down the glass, got up and walked out. That night he slept in one of the spare bedrooms. In the morning he heard the maid who lived in giggling with one who came daily, no doubt telling her that husband and wife were occupying separate rooms. He went for a long walk through the woods that were part of the estate, and wondered whether any thought of Violet's death had crossed his mind. Perhaps he could withhold his services, a male Lysistrata? But he knew that his persistence was no match for hers, and that this was a fantasy. He sat on the grass in a clearing, broke up some small twigs and said aloud: 'I could leave her, I could just walk out.'

Yet he knew that this also was not possible. Something had been destroyed in him by those weeks in the prison hospital. The mainspring of his being had broken, so that he could not seriously contemplate either resisting her or leaving the undoubted comfort on which he lived to face the world again without money. He had no confidence any more in his ability to charm old Generals or to please women, and he shuddered at the thought of selling insurance again. He was imprisoned in this house as effectively as if he were in a cell. Two nights later he went back to her bedroom.

He had given his address to Hussick, and it was a week after this that the letter came. He stared unbelievingly at the cheque and then read the relevant lines of Hussick's letter. '. . . happy to say that we were able to obtain a refund on the air ticket you booked to Caracas . . . cheque for this amount is enclosed . . .' The cheque was for a hundred and forty pounds.

At lunchtime that day he said to Violet, 'I shan't be in this afternoon, I'm taking the car. Not the Rolls.' She looked at him smiling, and he felt it necessary to say something more. 'I thought I'd go to Cerne Abbas. I believe it's very pretty.'

'It is.' She crunched celery. 'You didn't ask if I wanted to come. You're looking very nice.' Her smile broadened as she saw his expression. 'Don't worry, I shan't. What is it, a girl?'

He was able to make his denial all the more convincing because it was true.

'I wouldn't mind. You can take the Rolls if you like. It might impress her.'

You're very sure of me, he thought as he said that he didn't want the Rolls, you know I'm caught. Her desire to touch him was something he had come to know and hate, and he had to restrain himself from flinching when she patted his shoulder as they got up from the table.

'If you're a good boy, Tony, you won't find I'm unreasonable.'

The bitch, he thought as he drove away down the drive, the bitch thinks she's got me but she hasn't. The feeling of elation lasted as he parked the car at the tiny Burncourt Road Station and bought his first class ticket, lasted even half the way to London. It was succeeded by a depression which deepened as the train approached Paddington Station. He had drawn a hundred pounds from the bank and it was in his pocket, but what did it give him but an illusion of freedom? He could stay away from her until the money was spent, but after that what could he do but go back? He looked at himself in the railway carriage glass and was slightly cheered to see that he was still a very good-looking young man. 'You can decide what to do when the time comes,' he said to this young man. 'What you need first of all is a good strong drink.'

From Paddington he took a taxi to the Ritz. There he settled down with a vodka-based drink called a gimlet, drank it quickly and ordered another. He could feel the horrors of Burncourt Grange peeling away from him. He had got away and he would stay away, at least for that night. Ought he to telephone Violet and tell her so?

'Tony,' a voice said. 'It *is* you.'

A girl stood beside the table, smiling down at him. She wore dark glasses as she had done long ago. Fiona.

Chapter 2

Fiona. It seemed natural that he should use her assumed name, that she should sit down at the table and let him buy her a drink. She sat there opposite him with her slim legs crossed, wearing the dark glasses, and he knew suddenly that his luck had changed and that he was being given a chance to alter all the decisions that had been made so disastrously in the spring. When he thanked her for writing she simply smiled. She had changed, she was now totally at ease, a quite different figure from the nervous girl who had come into this bar carrying her suitcase.

'Are you still with Carlos?'

'For the moment.'

'What does that mean?'

'He's an awful bastard.' She raised the glasses briefly and he saw a bruise round her left eye. Then she lowered them again. 'However. He's in Bristol opening up a new place. I'm on my own.'

'Come with me, Fiona.'

'To your flat? At Marble Arch?' She smiled and he smiled back, although impatiently.

'It's important. Don't you see I'm lucky, meeting you means I'm lucky. I want you with me when I play.' It was true, he could feel the luck in him. First the money coming from Hussick, then meeting her again, it had to mean that he was lucky.

'To *play*.' She wrinkled her nose. 'The bank always wins, you said so yourself.'

'Not if you're with me.'

'You couldn't go to one of Carlos's places. One of his boys might know you. Anyway I couldn't come with you, he'd slay me.'

'There are other places.'

'Yes.' She contemplated him for a moment. 'You're a born sucker, you know that? I want another drink.'

He ordered one and then tried to get over to her somehow the seriousness and the importance of it. 'For a gambler there's a time when things are right, you understand? I can't tell you how I know it, but this is the time. If I make a real killing I'll never play again, I shall go away, get out of England.'

'Alone?'

'It doesn't have to be alone.' She merely smiled.

They went to a club she knew in the Edgware Road called the Triple Chance. It was early, and there were only a dozen people in the club, half of them playing blackjack and the rest roulette. He bought chips for the whole of his money. She shook her head when he offered her half of them.

'I never have any luck.'

'You've got to take them. Don't you see, we repeat it all, just the way it was.'

'You're a nut.' But she took the chips and they sat down at the table. The croupier was a brass-haired boy with a broken nose. Tony began to play a modification of the Rational system. Fiona bet on the first dozen and then on the last, with occasional bets on red and black. After half an hour he had won a little, she had lost half her chips. The time was eight o'clock.

'When do we knock off work? I'm hungry.'

'We've got to stay here.'

'Like hell *we* have.' She pushed the rest of her chips towards him. He was alarmed.

'Don't leave me, Fiona. Please. Give me another half hour.'

'All right, but I'll tell you something. You're not going to get very lucky playing that way. If you finish fifty pounds up you'll be doing well.'

What she said was true. The Rational system is designed to give a regular but small profit. If he wanted to win a lot of money he would have to abandon systematic play. He began to bet à cheval, and put five pounds on the numbers 3 and 4. Number 3 came up at odds of eighteen to one. He repeated the bet and put another five pound chip between numbers 13 and 14. Number 13 came up. He enlarged the bet to include all numbers with 3 in them. In five minutes he had won five hundred pounds. His mind was quite blank. He could not have said why he pushed all the chips on to a carre of the numbers, 13, 14, 15, 16, which would pay out nine to one.

The brass-haired croupier shook his head. 'Two-fifty limit.'

Fiona spoke fiercely to the croupier, pointed to a bald man sitting next to her. 'He's been betting over that.'

'On pair and impair, madam. That's different.' His stare at her was mocking, an insult. Tony felt incapable of speech.

'If you've got a limit like that, you should put it up.'

'It's on the wall, madam. Behind you.'

Tony began to take back some of his chips. 'It doesn't matter Don't break my concentration.'

'To hell with that. It does matter. Where's the manager?'

'Do you want the manager, sir?' the croupier asked Tony.

He was about to say that he didn't, when the manager appeared. He was a willowy man with a long face. He wore a purple dinner jacket and a lilac dress shirt, and he smoked a black cigarette in a white holder. His voice had the drawl of an Oxford aesthete in the Twenties. 'Something the matter, Bob?'

Bob told him what was the matter. He said languidly to Tony 'Very happy to accommodate you.'

Did he want to bet five hundred, the whole of his money? He no longer knew. His hand moved uncertainly towards the chips and it was Fiona who gripped it. The broken nosed boy spun the wheel.

The ball rolled about and came to a stop. 'Sixteen,' the croupier said. 'Red. Even.' His glance met that of the Oxford aesthete, who removed his black cigarette from the holder and stubbed it out. The chips, black, red and white were pushed across the table.

'Leave it,' Fiona said fiercely. 'Leave it. *Now.*'

He got up from the table.

Chapter 3

Because he had known that he would win, that he must win, he was able to take it all coolly. And the same coolness marked his further actions, for he knew exactly what had to be done next. For three-quarters of an hour they drove about London in a taxi, looking for the place that he knew must exist. She sat with him in the taxi, overwhelmed. 'Five thousand pounds,' she repeated over and over again. 'You've won five thousand pounds.'

'Four thousand nine hundred. I had a hundred to start with.'

In the end they had to drive out to London Airport. It was Thursday night. He made a reservation for two on the Saturday morning K.L.M. flight to Caracas. Because it was late they gave him a reservation slip instead of the tickets, and he paid the money.

She turned down the corners of her mouth when she heard where they were going.

'Caracas. I'm not even sure where it is.'

'Venezuela. Perfect climate. You've got a passport?'

'Yes. Carlos made me get one, said I might need it sometime.'

'Get a smallpox inoculation tomorrow. It's compulsory.'

She giggled and then was serious. 'You won't be able to take all that money out.'

He had not forgotten what Jenny said, and now he was able to improve on it. 'I'm going to buy one of those dummy books that people use for cigars. I shall put the money in that and post it to myself at the Grand Hotel, Caracas. We'll be there when it arrives. It's a million to one against its being opened.'

'We shall want some –'

'I shall take two-fifty with me.' On the way back to London he said, 'You do want to come.'

'Yes. I've had Carlos. And you know that day, when you found out I wasn't Fiona Mallory. I wanted to stay. Your face then, if you could have seen it.' She began to laugh and he laughed too. It was almost the first time in his life that he had laughed at himself. 'We'll make a good partnership,' she said, and he knew she was right.

Her flat was in Hill Street. When they arrived he handed the driver a ten pound note and told him to keep the change. It was a wonderful feeling.

The flat was interior decorator's Regency, with everything possible done in stripes. She poured drinks from a cocktail cabinet done in differently striped woods. 'To Caracas. Do you know something? Hours ago I was hungry. I'll make bacon and eggs.'

'I don't want bacon and eggs.'

She giggled. 'In the bedroom the ceiling's white stars in a blue sky. You look up at it.'

'Or you do.'

In the bedroom she took off his jacket, felt inside it for the wallet, spread the money on the bed and started to kiss it. 'Doesn't it make you feel good?'

He pushed her back. 'Come on.'

'I'm keeping these glasses on.'

'It's the first time I've made love to a girl in dark glasses.'

Five minutes later they heard voices in the sitting-room. She had scrambled off the bed, but they were both still naked when the door opened. Carlos Cotton stood in the doorway. He was wearing a dark pin stripe suit and a sober tie. He stood staring at them. Then he said 'Get dressed,' and closed the door.

There were two other men with Cotton in the living-room when they entered it, and Tony had seen them both before. One was the bruiser named Lefty. The other was the small dark man who had stubbed out a cigarette in his hand. Cotton had a glass in his hand.

'I won't ask you to have a drink, I see you've helped your-selves.' He spoke to Fiona. 'It's a fine night and I decided to drive back. Just as well. Take off those glasses.'

She took them off. Her bruised eye was half-closed. The other eye was wild, frightened.

'I like to see who I'm talking to.' He turned to Tony, his manner calm, his voice quiet. 'You've given me a lot of trouble.'

Tony did not know what to say. 'And now you've had one on me, friend. You'd better go.'

Cotton was letting him go. He could hardly believe it. He moved towards the door and then turned. 'Fiona.'

'You get out. I shall be all right.' Her good eye rolled despairingly at him. He thought, once I get out I can call the police. Cotton spoke again in his mock-cultured voice.

'Lefty and Milky will see you safely away. We call him Milky because he drinks a lot of milk. That's sensible, isn't it?'

He had begun to say that it was when the two men closed on him. Lefty quickly jerked his arm up behind his back so that he cried out with pain, but he managed to turn.

'Fiona, I'm not going to leave you.' He felt the absurdity of the words as they were uttered.

'Don't be a bloody fool.' She was staring at Cotton, she did not even look at him.

Lefty gave him a push. They were outside the flat and in the lift before the hold on his arm was relaxed. 'Now we can be nice and friendly,' the big man said in his hoarse whisper.

In the flat Fiona said, 'Carlos. Please.'

'Get packed.' She stared at him. 'Nothing's going to happen to you. Just get packed and go. I thought you had class. I don't like tramps.'

'You don't like tramps.' She laughed. 'That's good. You're a tramp yourself. Do you think you fool anybody with the way you talk?'

'Get out before I change my mind.'

He followed her into the bedroom and stood watching. When she had finished she turned with her hand to her mouth. 'Carlos, what are they going to do to him?'

'Nothing. He wasn't here. Right?'

'He wasn't here,' she repeated. Her teeth were chattering. When she got outside she began to cry.

Chapter 4

At the entrance to the apartment block Tony pointed towards Shepherd Market. 'I'm going that way.'

'Why, so are we,' Lefty said. 'Just nice for a stroll, isn't it, Milky?'

'That's right.' Milky had a clear tenor voice.

There are street lights, Tony thought, it's as bright as day, they can't do anything to me here.

His arm was suddenly jerked behind his back again and now they had turned into a narrow passage between houses, big black walls reared up on either side. They're going to hurt me, he thought unbelievingly, and he put his hand into his jacket to get out the money, to tell them that he would pay them if they left him alone. He thought of that scene in the lavatories with Bradbury, of white delicate Jenny, and of the other dark alley from which he had escaped. I shall escape from this too, he thought, it's my lucky night. But the gesture he made towards his wallet had been wrongly interpreted. The karate chop across his neck was decisive. His run of luck had ended.

Milky put on a pair of gloves. He took the money from the wallet, an unexpected bonus, but left everything else. Later they gave the money to Carlos and it was split three ways. A couple of weeks afterwards Carlos met a girl named Eleonora Mainwaring, and she moved in with him. She was the daughter of a baronet and, as he said frequently, had genuine class.

It was early morning before a passer-by noticed the body. The dead man's identity was quickly established, and so was the fact that he had won a great deal of money in a gambling club. He was obviously the victim of a gang who had followed him around. The police thought it likely that the girl with him, who never came forward, was a finger for the gang but they were never able to prove this. The other contents of Jones's wallet were littered round the body. It had rained during the night and everything was sodden. A wet piece of paper which had fluttered away to the other side of the passage remained unnoticed. In due course a road sweeper picked it up, found it illegible, and pushed it down a drain. It was the air reservation for Caracas.

The Man Who Lost His Wife

Contents

PART ONE
Wife Going   411

PART TWO
Wife Lost   501

PART THREE
Wife Found   593

PART ONE

Wife Going

Chapter 1

Breakfast Conversation

A June morning, the sky blue. If anybody had asked Gilbert Welton *are you happy* and if he could have been persuaded to answer (which is unlikely, because the question would not have seemed to him meaningful) he would have said *yes*. The most serious problem confronting him seemed to be the buying of a new hat. Yet happiness is often the thinnest of veneers, and Virginia's words slightly scratched its surface. His coffee cup was raised to his lips when she spoke.

'I think I should go away.'

For a moment he did not properly hear the words, and when he heard he did not understand them. He drank some coffee, dabbed his lips with his napkin. 'What was that?'

'I said, I ought to go away.' She amended this, although with an air rather of amplifying it. 'I mean, have a holiday. To think things out.'

He pushed his plate with a half-eaten piece of toast on it firmly away from him. 'What are you talking about?'

'You heard me. I've said it twice. Just for a time.'

It occurred to him that she was ill, and had been keeping the fact from him. 'Is there something wrong? Have you been to a doctor?'

Virginia gave the question her serious consideration. 'No, I haven't. There's nothing *wrong*. Not in that way.'

Gilbert did not think of himself as an impatient man, but the conversation irritated him. 'Then I don't understand you.'

'I need to find out things. About myself. About us.'

He felt relief at the words. Virginia was a great reader of glossy magazines, and obviously her words sprang from an article in one of them. 'Do You Need a Holiday From Your Husband? ... The Strain of Being Happily Married ... Are You a Robot Wife?', he could see the headlines. He did not say this, but instead stared down at the things on the table, the blue and green cups, toast precisely cut in triangles, home-made marmalade,

413

butter in its dish. Then he looked up and out into the garden, a St John's Wood garden, small and neat, with rose-bushes and clematis trailing up the end wall. Last night Virginia had been putting fertilizer on the roses.

'Last night you were doing the roses.' It seemed a sufficient contradiction of her words.

She offered him a cigarette, but he shook his head. He never smoked before midday. She lighted one herself and blew out smoke. 'What was I doing to them?' He hesitated – had it been fertilizer, or had she been digging about with a trowel? She smiled faintly. 'You see?'

'What difference does it make what you were doing?'

'If you don't see that –'

'I don't. You're being ridiculous.'

'You think so?'

With conscious patience he went on. 'You must have a reason. What things do you want to think out?'

She blew out more smoke. 'I like marriage to be hills and valleys, a sort of switchback ride. You want to live on a plateau. But do I want that, that's what I have to find out.'

Hills, valleys, plateaux, what was she talking about? It occurred to him that if he took the conversation seriously this should be an emotional moment, one or other of them ought to be excited, throw something, burst into tears. Instead Virginia sat in her flowered dressing-gown, neat, dark, elegant, perfectly composed. They were two composed people. He took refuge in irony.

'Not immediately, I hope. We've got people coming to dinner. Max is bringing that American novelist.'

A smile curled the edges of her mouth. 'I'll be here. Everything's laid on. I thought I might go next week.'

Irritation swelled in him like a balloon, but he kept his voice down. 'Virginia, I'm a rational person –'

'Oh, so am I. I mean, you've taught me.'

'You're not making sense. You tell me you have to go away because you want to live on hills instead of plateaux. It can't be the truth.' He snatched at the packet of cigarettes which she had left on the table, took one out and lighted it.

'Would it make more sense if I said I'd been considering it for some time?'

'No.' He said what he had not intended. 'This all comes from something you've been reading.'

She did not comment on this, but stood up. The impression of delicacy given by her features was rather belied by her figure which was strong, coarse, with shapely but powerful peasant legs. 'I've got to get dressed, I'm having my hair done at ten.'

'You told me this when there was no time to talk,' he said, although there was nothing he wanted less than to talk about it.

'There'll be plenty of time for that.' She paused at the door and added reflectively, 'Though I'm not sure there's anything to say.'

He sat at the table after she had gone, touching things with his fingers, the coffee and milk jugs, the toast-rack. He reflected that some people would have gone upstairs now and as the phrase went *had it out with her*, but he was Gilbert Welton and that was not possible for him. He believed, as he often said in the office, that if you let a difficult situation alone it generally changed into an easier one. And as he listened to Virginia talking with her usual cheerfulness to their daily, Mrs Park, it was hard to believe that any 'situation' existed at all.

'I'm off, got to rush.' She blew him a kiss. 'You'll be late for the office. See you tonight. Bye.'

As he brushed his teeth and ran the comb through his hair he told himself that the whole thing was nonsensical. He still had a lot of good thick wavy hair, and the grey wings added distinction. A touch of grey was appropriate at the age of forty-five, and he had kept his figure, his face was almost unlined. People rarely realized that Virginia was twelve years his junior. Not that he minded if they did realize it. He believed that if he took some care about his appearance it was not out of vanity, but because there was nothing more wretched than a middle-aged man who had let himself go.

By the time that he had said good-bye to Mrs Park and stepped out into a fine morning he had eliminated the breakfast conversation from his conscious mind. Virginia was – he always realized the fact with surprise – a stupid woman intellectually.

At the hairdresser's she would read another magazine article and talk just as seriously about – oh, about the problems of being a second wife. Probably she would not refer again to their conversation. If she said nothing, he had no intention of mentioning it.

Chapter 2

A Bad Morning at the Office

Gilbert had a feeling for architecture. He derived pleasure every time that he looked at the proportions of their early Victorian house, the weight and shapeliness that avoided the solemn ostentation of later Victorian building. The appearance of the office, a small eighteenth-century house just off the sleazier part of Soho, gave him pleasure too, and so did the fascia which said *E.R. and Gilbert Welton* in elegant capitals. The plate glass window beneath, which carried a display of the firm's recent publications, was not so good. Not that there was anything wrong with it, or with the books discreetly displayed there, but the very idea that a publisher should set out his wares in a shop window as if he were a butcher was faintly disagreeable. Inside, he nodded to the new switchboard girl whose name he could not remember, and went upstairs.

His office was square, with a large desk almost in the middle of it. He had no sooner sat down at the desk than Miss Pinkthorn was on him. She was a large efficient woman who had been with the firm in his father's time. She surged in like a resistless tide, and bustled about the office conveying by the sense of urgency in her movements that he was late. The clock on his desk said half past ten.

'Mr Paine would like a word. As soon as you're free.' Paine was the production manager, and his words were always technical. 'And Derek Niven rang about the design for his jacket. He asked you to ring back. I don't think he likes it.'

I don't think he likes it – what a wretched way to formulate a phrase. Why not say accurately, *I think he dislikes it*? Looking down at the mercifully small mound of correspondence on his desk and then up again at the massive body confronting him, he wondered suddenly and uncharacteristically about Miss Pinkthorn's sex life. He had a vague idea that she lived with her widowed sister, but perhaps this was not true, perhaps she had spent the previous night with a man, middle-aged to elderly, to whom she had said this morning, *I think I should go away*. Was there a man, any man at all, in Miss Pinkthorn's life?

'Yes,' he said as he turned over the letters in front of him. 'Yes. Yes.'

'Shall I get Mr Niven?'

Up with her knees and down with her head, That is the way to make good cockle bread. He averted his gaze from Miss Pinkthorn's bulk.

'Let me have a copy of the jacket drawing.'

'On the desk.' A large hand unearthed it, bulging breasts were adjacent to him. The drawing was deplorable, but it was said to be the kind of thing that sold books.

'Authors never like their jackets. I sometimes wonder why we let them see anything at all.' He exhaled, a soundless sigh. 'Get me Mr Niven. And when I've done with him, ask Paine to come up.'

The day had begun. It continued like other days, with long and tedious discussions about costing figures and sales figures and a wrangle with an agent about the advance that should be paid to an author whose contract was due for renewal. He thought suddenly – and it was the kind of thought that hardly ever received admission to his mind – that publishing of this kind was not an occupation that suited him. The production of some finely printed little pamphlet containing a dozen poems by a young writer, a limited edition of a previously unknown essay by Max Beerbohm, these would have been a different matter, but the hour to hour minutiae of a business run presumably for profit was something that seemed, if he was rash enough to consider it, almost degrading. During a long discussion with Paine and Coldharbour about the costing of a travel book which seemed certain to show a loss no matter how many or how few copies were printed, his mind drifted to the breakfast conversation. It became linked with an image of Miss Pinkthorn kicking up her bulky legs.

'At three thousand copies, with this number of plates, there's nothing in it for us if we sell them all.' Paine was a small man with a disagreeable Cockney whine in his voice. 'At five thousand –'

'We shall never sell five,' Coldharbour chimed in.

'If we cut the number of plates by half –'

'We should lose sales,' Coldharbour said. 'Besides the number of plates is in the agreement.'

Silence. They looked at him. He said nothing.

'Lyme and Makepeace are expénsive,' Paine whined. 'I could try Selvers.'

That stung him. 'Could you guarantee that Selvers would do as good a job?' He knew the answer to that. 'Very well then, it's out of the question.'

In the end they agreed to print five thousand copies and hope for the sale of sheets to America. It was a faint hope. When Paine had gone Coldharbour said, 'Have you got five minutes to spare, Gilbert?'

Denis Coldharbour was a thin nervous man who had come into the firm five years earlier, as a working director providing an infusion of fresh capital. The business Gilbert inherited from his father, E.R., had been comparatively small but flourishing. It was based upon one best-selling middlebrow novelist, several useful bread-and-butter writers, some highly successful children's books and a steady selling series called 'British Sights and Scenes'. At the time that E.R. collapsed and died while making a speech to the Publishers' Association about trade terms on single order copies, he was starting to develop a series of educational books for sale in the under-developed countries. Since Gilbert took charge the best-seller had gone elsewhere, two of the bread-and-butter writers had died, the number of British Sights and Scenes about which books could be written seemed to be exhausted, and he had abandoned the educational books as too much trouble, replacing them by an idea of his own for a finely printed series of reprints of travel classics which had proved a disastrous failure. Coldharbour's money had been welcome.

That could not quite be said of Coldharbour. He was a fussy man who sprayed his office daily with some strange insecticide, ate vegetarian food and always wore a brown paper vest for warmth. His first words now were slightly startling. 'How's Virginia?'

He repeated the name as though she were a stranger. 'Very well. Why?'

'I saw her at the Moonsight Galleries yesterday. She seemed rather' – Coldharbour sought for a word and came up with – 'distrait.'

'Did you talk to her?'

'I didn't actually talk to her, no.' He moved in his chair and the brown paper crackled slightly. 'I didn't know she was interested in modern art.'

Neither did I, Gilbert refrained from saying. 'Do you mean she looked ill?'

'Not *ill*.' He spoke as if there were some area between illness and health in which he had discovered Virginia. 'Oh, certainly not ill. I didn't mean to alarm you.'

'There's no question of being alarmed,' he said with unintended sharpness. Supposing he said that Virginia had announced her intention of going away, would Coldharbour be surprised? Perhaps he had wondered for a long time why she had married a man so much older than herself. Coldharbour proceeded always by hints and suggestions. Was he saying now that there had been a man with Virginia in the gallery?

'She's a very delightful woman.' Coldharbour himself lived alone in a large basement flat in Maida Vale. Gilbert was aware that he had not heard what was being said, and asked Coldharbour to repeat it.

'Johnson, Braddock, Delaney.'

'What was that?'

'And possibly Sharkey.' Coldharbour looked coy. 'Even Heenan.'

'Who is Heenan?'

'Not hard edge. And certainly not Pop.' A surprisingly masculine chuckle rumbled up from inside him. 'A long way beyond Pop.'

'Denis, I seem to have missed something.'

'They call themselves Spatial Realists, their whole concept is one of spatial flatness. After all a canvas is originally flat, isn't that so? Any attempt to deny flatness is in a sense a fake.' Coldharbour put his fingers together. 'As you know, Gilbert, I've always maintained that we've missed the boat in the past. My belief is that the time has come . . .'

Ever since he came into the firm Coldharbour had wanted to

produce a number of monographs, first on Art Nouveau and its origins, then on abstract art, most recently on a movement called Pubism which so far as Gilbert could see would have landed them in court for reproducing obscene pictures. Obviously Pubism had been replaced by Spatial Realism. He felt inclined to say that the whole idea was nonsense, but that was not the way in which a civilized publisher talked to a colleague.

'You thought a series of monographs . . .'

'No. Oh no, not a series. I see it as one big book, *Spatial Realism and the Art of the Seventies,* something like that. Of course we should need an informed introductory essay by somebody who knows what's what, Bryan Robertson perhaps or David Sylvester.'

'Denis, what can I say? It's simply not on.' Out-of-date slang, no doubt, and he regretted it. Yet somehow the phrase was reassuring. 'It's outside our field. We're not equipped to handle it saleswise.' Not slang now but jargon, yet again it seemed expressive.

'If we never publish any art books they'll always be outside our field,' Coldharbour said reasonably. He crossed one knee over the other, showing an expanse of dead white leg. A curious scent was wafted across the room. Had Coldharbour been spraying his socks? The smell stirred some memory which he could not be bothered to place. 'I know for a fact that Studio Vista are interested, and Faber too. A Tate exhibition is a real possibility.'

'You know what our commitments are. It could be a very expensive book.'

A derisive sound came through Coldharbour's nose. 'If there is a show at the Tate we could sell ten thousand.' He pulled at the trouser, showing more leg. 'Am I to understand that you dismiss it out of hand?'

'I don't see how we can do it.'

'Then I have to say that in my view this is a practicable and profitable piece of publishing which should be most seriously considered.' He sat up and the brown paper rustled. 'Which is more than can be said for some of Bomberg's activities.'

As though on a signal the door opened and Max Bomberg's round head appeared. 'Killing two birds with one stone,' he said and entered. 'Gilbert, Denis, great news.' He spread his arms, grinning.

Max Bomberg was a Hungarian who had come into the firm two years earlier on the recommendation of Virginia's Uncle Alex, who was something to do with a merchant bank. He had had no previous direct connection with book publishing, but had been managing editor of a group of magazines and then sales director of a printing house which produced technical journals mainly for the overseas market. The magazine group had been bought up by a large corporation at what was said to be a bargain price because they were on their last legs, and there were rumours that many of the technical journals were being eaten by red ants in African warehouses, but Uncle Alex had no doubt about Bomberg's ability. The man was a business genius, he said. Had he got money? He had something better, a nose for success.

'What's your turnover?' Uncle Alex had asked, rather like a nurse asking about bowel motions, and when he heard the answer had said that Bomberg would double it within a couple of years. The business genius had been invited to dinner and under Uncle Alex's benevolent eye had talked vaguely but impressively about profitability margins and the tactics of expansion. Would he put in capital? Not exactly, but a complicated arrangement never clearly understood by Gilbert was made under which Welton's obtained a holding not in the printing house but in an allied company, and Bomberg was given what seemed to be an extremely large number of shares in Welton's. Since then – well, since then it was hard to say exactly what had happened. Certainly turnover had increased considerably, but this was because Bomberg had taken on a number of new authors, paying what were by Welton's standards enormous advances. Where was the money coming from? At such a question he would smile in a slightly pitying way.

'About this, my dear, you don't worry. It will be a bad day when Max Bomberg can't get credit for a good proposition, and this is a first-class proposition.' Max never put forward anything but first-class propositions and Gilbert, who was aware of the restraints and hesitations in his own nature, warmed to such certainties. Now Max's cherubic grin widened. He said dramatically, 'Bunce is on "People in the News" tonight. I have arranged it.'

Jake Bunce was an American novelist who had come over for the publication of his novel, *The Way They Get You Going*. He was one of Max's most dubious acquisitions. Gilbert did not see how they could recoup the advance that had been paid to lure him away from a bigger firm. When they discussed taking him on, Max had slapped a copy of *Life* on the table.

'Look there, a six-page spread, Jake Bunce on Dope, Drink and Saintliness. You see what it says, he's the hottest thing out of Brooklyn since Mailer.'

'*Brooklyn*,' Coldharbour had said, with the air of a man who has heard of the place.

They had taken Bunce on, he had arrived in England that day and was coming to dinner. Bomberg had gone to the airport to meet him, and must just have returned.

'That's very good news.' Gilbert was never able quite to convey enthusiasm.

Max pointed a finger. '*And* he has a radio interview on "World at One" in a couple of days' time. I tell you, they're falling over themselves. We've got a really hot property here.'

'Where is he now?' Coldharbour asked lugubriously. He had unhooked his leg and the scent had disappeared.

'Resting up in the hotel. Oh, I tell you he's a charmer. Can't wait to meet you.'

If Jake Bunce had really been so anxious to meet him, Gilbert reflected, he could have come to the office, but he did not say this. 'I shall see him this evening.'

'You certainly will.'

'And you'll make sure he gets to the studio.'

'You bet your life. About this evening, just one little thing.' He spoke with the casualness he always used when saying something awkward. 'Jake's brought this girl over, some kind of way out girl in films.'

'We're not paying any of her expenses, I hope.' Coldharbour spoke sharply.

'Now, Denis, would I commit us to anything like that?' Max transferred his attention back to Gilbert. 'No, the thing is this, my dear, Jake asked if he could bring Lulu along with him tonight. I said yes. He's pretty informal, you know, he's an informal kind of character, he never had any doubt it would be O.K.' In moments of embarrassment or excitement Max's speech was often infused with a slightly American flavour. 'I'm sorry as hell if it's going to put out Virginia. Should I give her a ring?'

'I'll speak to her myself. I'm sure she'll manage.' Who knew what extraordinary thing Virginia might say on the telephone?

He rang her after Max had bounced out and Coldharbour had reluctantly followed him, threatening to renew their discussion about Spatial Realism later on. Her voice had the composure and coolness he had always admired.

'It's a bore but we'll manage. Would you like me to rustle up another man?'

'No, don't bother.'

'I look forward to Mr Bunce and his Lulu. And Max is always fun.'

'It's good of you not to make a fuss.'

He thought of mentioning the breakfast conversation, even though earlier he had decided not to refer to it, but no words came out. Then Miss Pinkthorn sailed in with letters which she placed aggressively in front of him. He said good-bye and put back the receiver. As he did so he remembered the recollection roused by Coldharbour's scent-sprayed socks, if indeed it had been his socks that gave off that curious whiff. In the last few weeks Virginia had changed the scent she used, from one which was light, cool and only faintly discernible, to something distinctly heavier and sweeter. Somebody with a less keen sense of smell might not have noticed it, and his own awareness had been only semi-conscious. Why had she changed?

Chapter 3

Lunch at the Club

The club was one of those frequented in about equal proportions
by publishers, writers, lawyers, advertising and public relations
men, and rather oddly a considerable number of tennis and
cricket players and other athletes, who were attracted by the
squash and five courts and the large swimming-pool. Gilbert
lunched there on Monday, Wednesday and Friday of each week.
To do so had become part of the pattern of his life. Besides,
E.R. had lunched there three days a week. 'The best club in
London,' his father had said on first leading him into the long
dark panelled room. 'You never know who you may meet here.
Great men, little men, administrators and creators. You may sit
next at table to Stephen Spender or to the Lord Chief Justice.
Membership of the club is a liberal education.'

On that first occasion Gilbert had sat next to a barrister who
talked about the iniquities of the builders who were putting up
his new house, and he had never actually seen either Stephen
Spender or the Lord Chief Justice in the club, but he appreciated the principle of what his father said. As a young man he
had wanted above all to emulate E.R., his heavy oratorical flow
of speech, his firmness in taking decisions and refusal ever to
admit that he had been wrong. Why was he unable to acknowledge even now that he was nothing like his father? Why, he
wondered as he walked up the steps and nodded in response to
the hall porter's greeting and spent a minute looking at the
ticker-tape which did not much interest him, and another minute
in studying the details of the next club supper which interested
him even less, why did he come to the club at all?

And why was Virginia using a different scent?

At the long table he sat between an actor named Peter
Halding and Langridge-Wood, one of the partners in a large
printing firm, and a friend of E.R. Later, as they went into the
lounge, Langridge-Wood tapped his shoulder. They took their
coffee to a window seat.

'Come and play a hundred up.'

'I ought to get back.' But in the office Coldharbour might be at him again, and there was a manuscript about which he had postponed making a decision for days.

'Won't take you long to beat me. Want to have a chat.'

In the billiards room, under the lights which shone down intensely on the green baize, he felt more at home than in most other places. Playing the balls up the table as they cued for break and watching his own land almost on the back cushion, a perfect stroke, he reflected that this at least was something he had done better than his father. In the hush of the semi-darkened room, where the only sounds were the slight squeak of chalk on cue tip and the click of white on red, there was a sort of placidity. That morning on his walk to the office he had been uncustomarily disturbed by the thought that he was destined to live out his days in E.R.'s shadow, doing inefficiently what his father had done well, slowly running down the firm that his father had created. But as he put side on his ball so that it shot delicately off white and into the pocket, these things took on their proper perspective. What did it matter if the firm was running down? Was it Louis XV who had said 'It will last my time'? Welton's would certainly last his time, and Matthew had made it plain that he wanted no part in it. There would be no second descension from father to son, he thought as he admired his own skill in playing a nursery cannon and keeping the balls together. The firm had given him an easy life, an elegant house, Virginia. Thinking of Virginia he miscued. Langridge-Wood used the chalk.

'Just a word, young Gilbert. Wanted to say I was very glad to hear there are prospects.'

'Prospects?' What was the old fool talking about, the new authors on their lists?

Langridge-Wood's bald head shone under the lamps. He was a player who when in doubt hit the ball as hard as he could and hoped for the best. Now he banged white and red round the table and saw his optimism rewarded when the red dropped unexpectedly into a pocket. He followed this with two successful forcing shots and made a break of fifteen.

'Life in the old dog yet. Don't mind saying there are times when I've been worried.'

'Really?'

'About the firm. But it's a great country, America. Wide open. E.R. always said so. Accepters, not rejecters, he used to say. That's important.'

He must presumably have heard about Bunce. 'Yes, we're very pleased with what's been happening. You know he's over here?'

Langridge-Wood's hearing aid started to whistle. 'What's that? Didn't hear.'

'We're all very pleased. On this side of the water,' he added, and felt the inanity of a phrase which E.R. would have rolled out impressively.

From this point on he began to play badly. Mention of E.R. made him remember their games here, games which his father usually won when it came to a close finish. Nerve, E.R. had said to him, you're a better player than I am, my boy, but you just lack that little bit of nerve. And now Langridge-Wood, hitting the balls as though he hated them, playing uncouth strokes that sent them flying round the table to come together again miraculously for an easy shot to follow, went ahead and punctuated his play with unintelligible remarks.

'Africa too, that's opening up. Very shrewd,' he said at one point, and at another, 'You know what E.R. said? "Get your toe in you've got your foot in. Get your foot in and if you're tough enough they'll never get you out." Very true, that. True about Africa, I've always thought so.'

In the end Gilbert began to bang the balls as hard as Langridge-Wood, but with less success. He lost the game.

'They dropped for me.' Langridge-Wood racked his cue with some satisfaction. 'Soothing game. Always find it clears the head. Mind you, you were out of touch. Glad we've had a word.'

'Yes.'

'And just bear us in mind in the future. I see great things ahead.' He sounded like a seaside palmist.

'I'm delighted to hear it.'

'Glad for you, young Gilbert. I was a friend of your father's, remember. He was a great man.'

They parted on the steps. Langridge-Wood gave his hand a meaningful pressure, said, 'We'll be in touch,' and stepped into a cab. Gilbert walked back to the office. Coldharbour left him in peace. He looked again at the manuscript, the memoirs of a Second World War military leader, and decided to reject it.

Then he went home.

Chapter 4

Dinner-Party

When he turned on the set Jenny Johnson, well-known as a TV interviewer whose questions turned into speeches longer than the answers of her victims, was in full flow.

'You've written an outspoken novel about drug-taking, Mr Bunce, and another about homosexuality which shocked some people over here who thought it should be banned –'

Jake Bunce had been nodding his head as though about to fall asleep, but now he interrupted her, shoulders rocking a little in soundless mirth. 'I know, yeah, banned. Banned. I heard about that, that gave me a laugh.'

It took more than such interpolations, or the fact that Bunce's gaze was directed down at her very visible thighs, to put Jenny out of her stride. 'And now your new book, out in a few days, *The Way They Get You Going*, is likely to shock a lot more people if I'm not mistaken –'

'I shouldn't wonder.' The soundless laughter was repeated, one Bunce hand moved in the direction of Jenny's leg and drew back. 'I shouldn't wonder at all.'

Virginia came and sat beside him, watching intently.

Jenny gave one of those hopelessly ineffectual tugs at her almost non-existent skirt that had helped to make her celebrated, and leaned forward to ask one of her typical questions, projected with an air of deadliness but in content slightly anodyne. 'And what would you say is the difference between your earlier books and *The Way They Get You Going*?'

Jake Bunce fingered his lower lip and actually lifted his gaze from Jenny's thighs to her face before replying. He was not the small dark hairy man Gilbert had for some reason envisaged, but fair and gangling with one of those unfinished innocent American faces in which the features seem to be wholly amorphous, the nose from one view a blob and from another a powerful organ, the mouth a sensitive blur which changed surprisingly into a lipless pair of pincers.

'The difference is,' he began slowly, 'in those other books I had the drug scene, see, or the gay boys, but here it's the whole thing, everything's there. I'm moving to something universal and that's what I've always been after, though how can you know where home is till you're there, it's like you gotta go through these other things before you get to experience total reality.'

At the welcome, intelligible word *experience* Jenny rushed in with one of her famous interruptions. 'Experience, you said, there are scenes in your book dealing with – oh, various perversions and incest –'

Jake was a match for any interrupter. 'Incest, that's no perversion. Just a social taboo, that's all.'

Jenny gave a trill of irritated laughter. 'Very well, but you'll admit that there *are* perversions in your book, sadistic and masochistic acts and so on. Do they spring from experience?'

'Everything in my books comes from life. It's all experience.' At this point Jake actually did lean forward and place his hand on Jenny's knee. 'A novelist should experience everything, all extremes. He's all of humanity. He's a white Negro or he's nothing.'

Gilbert turned off the set. 'I hope he's not going to talk like that when he's here.'

'I thought he was rather sweet. And I never expected to see anybody actually touch Jenny Johnson, most of them think she's a sacred object. It's time to change.'

In the bedroom, when she asked him to help with the zip of her dress, he placed a hand on her back. She shivered.

'Are you a sacred object too?'

She turned to face him. 'You don't want to touch me, do you? It's a kind of duty, something expected. You always do what's expected.'

'How absurd.'

'I sometimes wonder if you're basically homosexual. Don't look so disgusted, you know we all have male and female elements. Like my moustache.' It was true that she had a faint down on her lip which had to be controlled by depilation. 'I think you may have a strong female streak, that's all.'

The remark made him unreasonably angry. 'Who's been filling your head with this nonsense? Another man?'

'Are you jealous?' She stood looking at him with her brassière partly removed, then took it off completely. Her breasts were small, with dark nipples. 'If I said yes, would you be jealous?'

'For God's sake. First of all you say I mustn't touch you and then you stand with your breasts showing and ask me if I'm jealous.'

She looked at him with that characteristic faint hint of a smile. 'I'm going to have my bath.'

She went into the bathroom. Water ran. When it stopped he heard her singing.

The arrangement of a dinner party had not been easy because Max was divorced from his wife, and was bringing Jake without (before the mention of Lulu) any feminine accompaniment. It is easy to find unattached men to put right any disbalance between the sexes but less easy to find unattached women, and Virginia had solved the problem by asking Felicity James and her friend Arabella, who was always called Arab.

They arrived while John and Sandra Sutherland were half-way through their first gin and tonic. Felicity was one of the new school of lesbian novelists, those who do not write directly about their sexual attitude in the Radclyffe Hall manner. There were lots of men in Felicity's novels, but they were always shown clearly as the weaker sex and by the end of the book were mentally or financially dependent on women, or had been ruined by them. In person Felicity, large, bony and highly coloured in dress and appearance, filled any room she entered.

'Sherry, Gilbert. Bone dry and ice cold,' she said in response to his question. When he said that the sherry would be dry but not ice cold she raised the gold lorgnette that was her single concession to old-style lesbianism and stared at him for a moment before pronouncing 'Whisky and soda.' She turned to pretty, plumpish Sandra. 'And what do you *do*?'

'I'm a housewife.'

'You find that adequate? I'm not a feminist but housework bores me. Arab likes it.' She turned away, dismissing Sandra in

431

favour of her husband, who was a lecturer in sociology at London University. Phrases drifted through their conversation: 'Balance of statistical probability . . . basically a revolt against mechanism . . . separate Pop from McLuhan . . .' Sutherland had large hornrims, and like many sociologists was a compulsive talker. Although Felicity gave him one glare through the lorgnette, she seemed upon the whole to approve of him. Arab, who was ten years her junior and had a soft crushed face, seemed content to sit watching them and saying nothing.

The Sutherlands lived almost opposite, and Sandra told Gilbert about a Swedish au pair up the road who had given a party for a dozen hippies while the advertising director who employed her was away. She described in detail and with relish the amount of drink that had been consumed, the furniture that had been smashed and the ornaments that had been stolen. The party had ended when four of the hippies, high on pot, had wandered naked into the road. Gilbert found himself thinking about Virginia. She had gone into the kitchen to superintend the cook, who had come in specially for the evening and was talented but erratic.

'You're not listening. I'm boring you.'

'Of course you're not.'

'John says I bore everybody with my tittle-tattle. Do you like tittle-tattle?'

'I call it gossip. I like it very much. How do you think Virginia is looking?'

'Marvellous. She always does. Not like me, bursting out of my clothes.'

'I've been a little worried.' Sandra, whose plump amiability concealed a rich vein of malice, looked at him eagerly, but before he could say anything rash Virginia returned. She glanced meaningfully at Felicity's empty glass and Gilbert did some re-filling. As he passed Virginia he smelled her musky scent.

Almost half an hour later things were strained. Felicity had become tired of sociology, or perhaps just tired of trying to out-talk Sutherland, and was telling Sandra, Virginia and Gilbert what was wrong with the London theatre. Sutherland, after trying to make conversation with Arab, which was almost an impossibility, had lapsed into an unusual silence. Arab, whose own silence gave her all the more time for consumption of liquor, was staring at him in a slightly glassy-eyed way. Where was Max, where was Bunce? As though in answer to the question the bell rang. There were voices in the hall. With relief Gilbert opened the door of the drawing-room to see Max's round smiling face.

'A triumph, my dear, a triumph. Did you catch it? Have you ever seen anyone deal with Jenny like that, wasn't it just terrific? Jake, this is Gilbert Welton.'

'Good to meet you. Say, Max, you call that girl tough? We got fifty in the States who'd eat her in a couple of mouthfuls and then say what's the next course.' Seen in person Bunce looked even more ingenuous, and younger, than on the TV screen. His hand seemed almost boneless.

'And this is Lulu.' Even Max's exuberance was slightly damped as he stood aside to reveal a tall dark girl with long hair, wearing a rough denim shirt and dirty-looking jeans. 'She wondered if it would be OK to come along in what she was wearing, and I said yes of course.'

The girl scowled. 'I got nothing to change into. I just wear stuff till it's finished.' Her voice sounded like a can grating over pebbles.

Max had said that it was a mistake to arrange a dinner party for anybody like Jake Bunce, and within ten minutes of sitting down at table it was evident that he had been right. Without being in any way impolite, Bunce seemed to feel that it was his duty to keep up a continual flow of conversation, and it was conversation of the utmost freedom which he addressed to the table at large. Felicity had carried the London theatre theme with her to the dinner-table, and once set on course she took a great deal of moving, but Bunce managed it.

'Osborne, Wesker, Bowen, what the hell kind of plays do they write?' he asked genially.

Felicity put down her fork, raised her lorgnette. 'They've all been produced recently on Broadway.'

'Broadway.' Bunce chuckled. 'I crap on Broadway.'

Virginia's mouth quivered slightly. 'What kind of plays do you like, Mr Bunce?'

'I reckon the theatre as such is played out, that is the theatre as a convention, you get me? Broadway, off Broadway, I mean none of it's real, it's something a lot of actors are faking up. But off off-Broadway now, we got something there that's really going. There's this cellar called Where You Are. When you go in you're blindfolded, turned round three times and told to start moving.'

'A kind of blind man's buff,' Sandra suggested. Bunce beamed 'Right. But there's this difference. You're groping around, see, and you touch other bodies or objects or whatever, and you don't know a thing. But in Where You Are there's a mediator, sometimes a man, sometimes a woman, and they act as guides.'

'What to?' Arab asked, and giggled suddenly. They were almost the first words she had spoken.

'That's it. They guide you *where they think you should go*. You might find yourself on a mattress with a girl or another fellow, or on the john, or they might take off your shoes and socks and put your feet in cold water, or stick a pin in your arm. Or you might get taken into a cinema, bandage whipped off and you're shown a horror film, Auschwitz or something. Just what they think you can take.'

Felicity glared. 'I don't call that theatre.'

'It's *living* theatre.' He pushed away his plate and made points on stubby fingers. 'It teaches lessons, like we all need to learn. One, there's the authority principle, in this world we don't any of us control what happens. Two, reality's lots of different things like pain, horror, love. Three, what life means is drama, it isn't just going to the office every day, the important things happen when everything's intense, that's what's crucial. Four.' He looked at his fingers and gave up. 'That's about it, I guess.'

'The moments when everything's intense,' Virginia repeated. 'I like that.'

'If that's theatre I can do without it,' Sandra Sutherland said. 'I go to the theatre to be amused, I don't mind saying it. And for something with a meaning I can understand.'

Lulu had been eating like a starved animal, head low over her plate, hair close to the food. She had a chicken leg in her fingers, gnawing it close to the bone. Now she put it down and said in a voice thick with chicken, 'You don't get the meaning? The meaning is, life is love.'

434

Jake beamed. 'You got it. That's the message, today and every day.'

There was silence. Then Max began to talk about the new cinema in the uncommitted or less committed Communist countries, Yugoslavia, Rumania, Bulgaria. Felicity raised her lorgnette while waiting to interrupt. Gilbert felt a nudge. It was Lulu.

'She a dyke?'

He was saved from the need to reply because Sandra on his other side spoke at the same time. He turned to her gratefully. 'What was that?'

'I only said I'm terribly old-fashioned, but I like to read novels with a story. That's why I read so many thrillers. John thinks they're an outdated form of pop culture, but I still enjoy them. Why don't you publish any?'

He started to explain that it was no use publishing just one or two crime stories, you had to go in for them in a big way. He was uneasily conscious that Lulu had returned to her bone and then rejected it, and that across the table Felicity was laying down the law about the limitations not only of Communist but of all other films. John Sutherland said something about Italian neo-realism, Virginia murmured the name of Antonioni, and Max who never cared for argument addressed himself to placating Felicity.

'Your books now, I find it quite amazing that they are not filmed. If you were Rumanian every one, every one would be filmed. As they appeared.'

'Two of my last three books have been sold for films,' Felicity said icily, but Max was not deterred.

'In Italy, Germany, Yugoslavia, it would have been all three. Your last novel –' He paused, at a loss for the title. Felicity frowned. Arab supplied it in a penetrating whisper.

'*A Particular Kind of Man.*'

'Of course. Magnificent. What a terrific part for Richard Burton or Paul Scofield.'

'That's the one which isn't being filmed,' Arab said. 'The others are being made in France.'

A toothpick twirled in Bunce's mouth. 'MGM are going into production of my last one, *The Gay Life*, next month. They've

435

got a whole cast of fags.' He moved into his soundless laughter routine.

Gilbert looked at Virginia. She rose. The other women rose with her except Lulu, who remained seated. 'Hey, what is this?' She stared at them.

One of the things that Gilbert had always admired about Virginia was her refusal to be perturbed. 'We'll have our coffee in the drawing-room and leave the men here.'

'Leave the men?' It was not Lulu's clothes but her features that were dirty, Gilbert decided. And her hair could certainly do with a wash. 'We gonna have a party on our own, is that it? I don't get my kicks that way.'

Bunce leaned forward. 'Lulu, baby, it's an English custom. You go next door for a while, see, drink some coffee, we stay here, have some port and brandy, then we meet up later. Isn't that right, Gil?'

Nobody had called him Gil for years, and the name sounded surprisingly pleasant. 'That's right.'

'So you just run along, Lulu baby.'

'Balls to them,' Lulu said. 'How do I know what that bloody great dyke might try if I get left alone with her? I'm staying here.'

Felicity raised her lorgnette and raked Lulu with one final dismissive glance. 'Arab, it is time to go.'

Across Gilbert's mind there flashed the question: what would E.R. have done? Before he could find an answer, Felicity and Arab had gone.

In the drawing-room Jake and Lulu engaged in a long wrangle about her behaviour. Virginia had disappeared. Max and Gilbert provided the audience. Neither Jake nor Lulu sat on a chair. Jake was cross-legged on a pouffe and Lulu sprawled on the floor.

'So she's a dyke, what's it matter, what you got against them?'

'I just didn't want her hands on me, is all. You see the way she looked?'

'You talk about love, you say love's the meaning. You just haven't got the meaning, you're nowhere near it. And you owe something to Gil, it's his home, how do you think he's feeling?'

Max muttered something and went out. Jake seemed really upset. His flexible nose twitched like a rabbit's. 'He brings you into his home and you insult his guests. What kind of way is that to behave? Gil's upset, isn't that so, Gil?'

Gilbert did not reply. Lulu said something inaudible. 'What's that, baby, don't keep it to yourself, say it so we can hear.'

'I said, go fuck yourself.'

'Is that a way to talk?' Jake spread out his arms appealingly. 'I ask you, Gil, is that a way to talk?' This time he did not stay for an answer. His features set into the mask of a gloomy thinker. 'I tell you the trouble with you, kid, is you've got nothing at all and you try to make it look like something. Me now, I've been through the whole works, pot, L S D and the hard stuff, boys and girls, the Eastern crap and the Russian crap, and I'm out on the other side. Way out and clear. Did you know I was three months in a monastery out in Nepal, did you know that, Gil?'

'Yes.' This was in fact one of the most-publicized periods of Jake's career.

'To know what's real you got to find out about yourself. That's what I was doing with those monks, and believe me it paid off.'

'In cash.' Lulu held up her glass for more brandy.

'But you, what did you ever do except come up from Deadsville to the Village and underground films, and believe me that's not much of a journey.' He shook his head mournfully. 'Not much of a journey at all. And now you come where it's civilized, the cradle of civilization you might say, and you don't know how to behave.'

Could Bunce's sales compensate for his conversation? And where was Max? He rose, and Bunce scrambled to his feet. Was he leaving? No, with a muttered apology he moved in the direction of the brandy. As Gilbert closed the door he heard Lulu say, 'I'll tell you something, Jake, you bore the tits off me.'

In the hall there was no sound. A sudden doubt, a feeling of disaster, sent him up the stairs two at a time. He went swiftly along the passage, flung open the bedroom door. The room was empty. He heard voices. From the bedroom window figures were faintly visible in the garden, moving towards the house.

He confronted them as they came in through the garden door. Virginia's colour was high, her manner serene. Max's hair was in

437

its usual tight curls, but then it was hair that would hardly be ruffled by a hand passing through it, and nothing would ever change his cherubic smile. He began to speak as soon as they were through the door.

'I wanted to apologize to Virginia, to tell her that I feel – I feel desolated.'

'I thought it was funny. Felicity's a first-class bitch anyway. A butch bitch.' She giggled, and that was not characteristic.

'You have a very sweet wife.' Max took Virginia's bare arm and kissed her cheek. Upon the fleshy part of her arm near the shoulder there was a small circular discoloration.

He released her. 'Jake is sweet too, the sweetest man in the world. But that girl.' He was shaking his round head when they heard the sound of breaking glass.

In the drawing-room Jake and Lulu were standing body to body, glaring at each other. Fragments of glass lay in the fireplace. They might have been figures fixed in a tableau. Then Jake raised his hand and deliberately slapped Lulu's face. She cried out something. Blood trickled from her mouth. Virginia stood beside Gilbert and he heard the indrawing of her breath.

Jake raised his hand again, lowered it. 'Max, get me out of here. I don't know what I might do to her.'

Lulu put her grubby hand to her face and looked at it wonderingly. 'The bastard's made me bleed.'

'I must apologize,' Jake said to Virginia. 'She threw her glass – your glass – at me and it broke.'

'Now then, my dears, it is time to go home.'

Such difficult circumstances always brought out the best in Max. He cajoled and bullied the pair of them out of the drawing-room, got them through the front door together yet kept them apart, pushed Lulu into the back seat of his car and Jake into the front. At the last moment Jake broke away, ran back to the house and clasped Virginia's hand.

'I apologize again. It was a *graceless* thing to do.' He kissed her on the lips and ran back to the car. His hand, with the ring on it that had cut Lulu's mouth, waved out of the car window.

Chapter 5

A Woman's Arm

'Who has not felt the beauty of a woman's arm?' George Eliot asks in *The Mill on the Floss*. 'The unspeakable suggestions of tenderness that lie in the dimpled elbow, and all the varied gently-lessening curves, down to the delicate wrist, with its tiniest, almost imperceptible nicks in the firm softness.' Virginia's arms, rich and creamy, had always held a deep sexual attraction for Gilbert. He caressed and kissed them before making love, and when the sleeve of her dress fell back as it sometimes did to reveal the whole arm from wrist to elbow, white, smooth and untouched by down, he would look at it with the intensity of feeling that other men give to breasts or buttocks. When she clasped her arms round his neck or behind his back, the vision he had of their contact with him was a vital stimulus to the act of love. It was an excitement he had never mentioned to her beyond saying that she had beautiful arms.

In the bedroom, looking at the discoloration which he surely would have noticed if it had been present when she came in to dinner, he saw clearly Max Bomberg's mouth move away from hers to kiss the upper part of her arm and then to nip the flesh between his teeth. It was something that he had never done, that he would have felt to be a desecration.

'What has happened to your arm?'

'What do you mean?'

He touched the spot. 'It wasn't there earlier this evening.'

'I must have knocked it,' she said indifferently.

He overcame his dislike of mentioning sexual matters. 'Somebody gripped your arm. Or bit it.'

'You're being ridiculous.' With her half-smile she added, 'Anyway, bites don't show that quickly.'

'How do you know?'

She shrugged. 'You don't want me to go into details. You never liked them.' And it was true that before they married she had mentioned past affairs. She had been on the editorial staff of a fashion magazine, and from what she said almost every woman in the office had had an affair with some man or other. He had always flinched from the details, saying that what she had done in the past was not his business.

'Somebody bit your arm. Max.' He could not refrain from saying it, although the words sounded absurd.

'Oh really. Do you suppose he was biting my arm in the garden?' That was just what he did suppose, but she made it sound like a bad joke. 'I went out because I'd had enough of it, that's all.'

'He followed you out there.'

'He came out to say he was sorry. Just as he told you. Anyway, I preferred the American.'

'Bunce?' he said in astonishment.

'There's a kind of sweetness about him. He's magnetic. The moments when everything's intense, I know what he means.' She pulled her dress over her head, and as she did so he saw the distinct dark hairs growing in her armpit. What was the meaning of them, why were they there when in the past she had always used depilatories to remove them? 'Why –' he began, and stopped.

'Yes?'

He put on his pyjamas. The action gave him confidence. 'Why aren't you using your cream?'

'What cream, I don't understand.'

'Under your arms.'

'Oh, that. I don't know really. Yes, I do. I read an article about men preferring women to be natural, and there's nothing more natural than letting hair grow.'

'You know I dislike it.'

'How could I know, you've never said so. Although I suppose I might have guessed.' Stretching her arms she revealed again the unsightly growth. 'Some men like it.'

'Not Englishmen.'

'If you knew what you sound like.' She turned her back as she took off her knickers and stood naked. 'I suppose you'd like it if I had no hair at all on my body. A statue, that would suit you.' She slipped a filmy nightdress over her head.

The image flashed through his mind of a statue as something

indeed desirable, the body smooth and cold, no blemishes or beauty spots, the perfect arm curving upwards into the shoulder, nothing anywhere unsightly, no drop of sweat disturbing the perfection of the form.

'The years between thirty and forty are crucial for a woman, did you know that?' This comes from a magazine too, he thought, the whole thing comes from magazines. 'It's a climacteric.' He felt certain that she had read the word for the first time recently, but it was typical of her that she pronounced it with perfect ease and naturalness. 'Perhaps something to do with the change, though it would be early for that. Anyway, it's a difficult time. You ought to realize that.'

Relief surged over him, a conviction that she was acting out the part of a sensitive woman after reading 'A Woman in Her Thirties, The Difficult Decade'. What would be the appropriate Sunday colour supplement reaction? A brusque injunction to snap out of it and remember the duty a wife owed to her husband, or readiness to talk the whole thing over? As though to confirm his thoughts she went on, 'It's all been psychologically established, you know.'

Psychologically established! He thought of her indrawn breath as she saw the blood on Lulu's mouth and felt angry. A mirror on the wall reflected his blue-pyjamaed body as he stood beside her, gripped her and turned her to him.

'All that talk about being natural, what you mean is that you want force. Violence. Isn't that so? Bunce excited you because he hit her.'

'Whether I want it, that's not important.'

'Of course it is. You've been saying how important.'

He pushed her and, taken by surprise, she fell back on the bed. Her nightdress came up to reveal the lower half of her body. He pulled at the nightdress but failed to get it off because she was lying on it. She rolled over so that the round buttocks were visible, her body more at his mercy than when she faced him. He felt the stirring of desire and tugged at his pyjama cord, pulling the wrong end so that it came into a knot. Face down, head in the eiderdown, she muttered words which he still heard quite distinctly, her voice unwaveringly calm.

'What matters is whether you want it. Violence.'

Had she read that also in a colour supplement? Desire left him, what he was doing seemed merely distasteful. He got up off the bed. Virginia turned and without haste or primness pulled down her nightdress.

'It's a matter of establishing a relationship pattern.'

'Where did you read that?'

'In a book.' There was a slightly triumphant note in her voice. Books were trump cards compared to magazine articles. 'If you don't establish the right pattern in the early years of marriage it's very bad.'

'Was it from this book that you got the idea about my being homosexual?'

'Yes. There are six basic relationships and ours –'

'Spare me the details.' They had separate beds, and he got into his own.

'I don't think you need me. You want a housekeeper. Or perhaps a hostess. But is that all I want? I'm going away to find out.'

'You mean that's all, the only reason?'

'Doesn't it seem enough?' She began to apply cream to her face and went on talking tranquilly. 'Five years and we don't have a relationship, we're just two people living together. People to whom nothing ever happens.'

'What do you want to happen?'

'I don't know. I want the moments when everything's intense, when you really feel things. You don't know me in that way, any more than I know you.'

'I think I know you pretty well.'

'You're wrong. You only know one Virginia, the one you've made, a person you've created. There might be half a dozen others. You might like one of them better.'

'And are there? Six other Virginias?'

'That's what I want to find out.'

'There's no other man?'

'No. Though at the climacteric there might be.'

'And if there were it would be someone like Bunce?'

'I don't know. Perhaps.' She got into bed and turned out the light. 'Gilbert.'

'Yes?'

'I think I should go as soon as possible really. To clear my mind. You can tell people I'm on the verge of a nervous break-down.'

'Thank you.'

'It might be true. Do you understand things better now, now I've explained?'

'I don't understand anything. I think the whole thing's idiotic.'

She did not speak again. It was a long time before he fell asleep. Thinking about the conversation he decided that what she had said was just crazy enough to be true. There had been brief periods in the past when Virginia's calm had been broken. She had once bought a sauna, had it installed, and gone into it several times a day, emerging pinkish but exhausted instead of exhilarated. She had lost interest in it when a doctor said it might be damaging her health. At another time she had spent hours every day at the Zoo, taking particular interest in the caged birds. Perhaps this was something of the same kind, something that would be forgotten in a week.

Or perhaps she was lying to him. Thinking of that intrusive hair in her armpits and the bruise that flawed the classical beauty of her arm, it seemed certain to him that she had a lover.

Chapter 6

The Anglo-Germanic Syndrome

'A veritable shambles. My dear, I'm sorry.' Max smiled.

'Never mind. How did you get on?'

'In the car not so bad, but when we got back to the hotel they started again. In the end I took them to the Out Going.'

'What's that?'

'One of those clubs. You know.' Gilbert nodded, although he didn't know. 'Jake is a very sweet person, but the girl is hell. I don't know why he has her along. She had a row with a waiter. I got to bed at four-thirty.'

'I'd never have known it.' And indeed Max looked his usual rosy self with the air of breezy freshness about him that marks many central Europeans. He tapped a finger on Gilbert's desk and said 'Eugene Ponti'.

'What?'

'*The Tigress.* The biggest European seller of the last ten years was his *Apes, Gods and Men.* A master novelist.' Was Max quoting reviews? It was never possible to be sure. 'Now he has completed *The Tigress.* And he is not happy with his English publisher, I know this for a fact. He hates the translation.' A man confiding a secret, Max said, 'Eugene is ready to move.'

'You know him?'

'I have contacts. An approach is possible, but it must be made now. Strike while the iron is hot,' he said with an air of originality.

'What do you want to do?'

'Go to Milan. Fly there, see him, make the arrangement, fly back. A few hours. I shall be away no more than that. All right?'

Was Max sexually attractive to women? The unusual colour on Virginia's cheeks when she came in from the garden, their conspiratorial air – but at this he checked himself, for had the air been conspiratorial? He could not really remember what they had looked like. Perhaps Max was the kind of man who could discover the Virginias neglected by Gilbert, Max the florid, Max the hand kisser, Max the arm biter.

'I suppose so, yes. We ought to discuss what we can offer.'

'Here are details of sales for his last book. Don't ask how I have obtained them.' A roll of the eye suggested some unmentionable piece of wickedness. He went on casually. 'Jake will be no trouble at all, I will tell him –'

'Oh no.'

'Look, my dear. This whole thing is important, I mean do we want to get hold of a European best-seller when we are on the ground floor, or not?' Max flung himself into a chair, leaned back. 'It would be possible for you to go to Milan if you wish. But not advisable. My contact is Eugene's secretary. Flavia.'

'I see.'

'That is the way things are done.' It was not the way things had been done in E.R.'s time. 'Now I can assure you Jake will be no trouble. I shall tell him that he must get in touch with you only if there is something urgently vital.'

'Perhaps Coldharbour –'

'You must be joking.' The slang sounded particularly inappropriate on his lips. 'Jake likes you, he says you are an English gentleman. Jake is a very sincere person, he wouldn't say that unless he meant it. So now let us discuss a few details and then we are all fixed.'

No sooner was Max out of the room after discussing the few details about the advance that could be offered than Miss Pinkthorn came in, her eyes gleaming with bad news.

'I've had Mr Manhood on the telephone, Mr Dexter Manhood. He hasn't received his manuscript.'

'What manuscript?'

'*A Welter of Gore.*'

'That book about a murder case? It should have gone back to him – oh, weeks ago.'

'Exactly. But it hasn't. I told him it would be looked into at once.'

'Find out who was responsible, and ask them what's happened.'

With a barely suppressed air of triumph Miss Pinkthorn said,

'I was away with influenza. Miss Steel should have sent it back.'

'Then speak to her.' Miss Steel was Max's secretary, a pretty but inefficient girl.

'I have done so. At first she remembered nothing about it, then she said she *thought* it had gone to the typing pool.' There were only two typists where in E.R.'s day there had been four, but it was still called the typing pool. 'Miss Clayton doesn't remember it, so it must have been Mrs Fairweather.'

'I didn't know we had a Mrs Fairweather.'

'She was a temporary from an agency.'

'Then speak to –'

'Of course I rang the agency. Mrs Fairweather is no longer on their books. She has moved from her last address.'

'If she didn't send it, the manuscript must be in the office.'

'We don't know that it was ever posted.' She administered this blow like a policewoman.

'It must be found.'

'I am instituting a thorough search,' Miss Pinkthorn said, still in the policewoman role. She glanced as she went out at the photograph of E.R. on the wall. Manuscripts had never disappeared in his time.

Left alone, he looked at some depressing sales figures and then at some equally depressing costing figures. Abandoning these he went over to the bookcase that housed the firm's publications and took down *Sexuality, Aggression and Nationality* by N. M. Sverdlov, a book they had published four years earlier in a brief phase of enthusiasm for the idea of starting a psychoanalytical library. His appointment with Sverdlov was for midday.

'Two and a half times a week. You don't reach that norm?'

'I'm afraid not. Not quite.' An apologetic note seemed inevitable.

'And whose responsibility is that?'

'I don't think I can say. I don't know.'

'No children,' Sverdlov said accusingly. 'Why not?'

'Virginia had an abortion. Before we were married. She can't have children. But I don't think she wants them. I've always thought we're happy as we are.'

'You think so, but does she?' Sverdlov was a small busy man with a rumpled look. 'We have to remember that she is a second wife. The first Mrs Welton was different?'

'Yes.'

'And your relationship with her, that also was different?'

'Yes.'

'You were divorced. By whose wish?'

'I think you could say it was mutual. But it was a long time ago.'

'Your first wife, do you still see her? Has she remarried?'

'I don't see her. But I'm sure I'd know if she had remarried.'

'Your son Matthew. How do you get on with him?'

'Quite well. But we don't see much of each other. He lives in Amsterdam.'

'Does your wife get on with him?'

'When she sees him, yes, very well. But I don't see what all this has to do with Virginia wanting to leave.'

'Directly, perhaps nothing. It is an essential part of the atmosphere in which both of you live. However, I am inclined to agree. Basically I have no doubt that we have here a question of national temperament.'

'I don't quite follow you.'

'I will be frank. You are an Englishman, a very typical Englishman, reserved, shy. You don't know how to express your feelings. You have the male's normal sexual aggression, but you wish all things to remain unstated. Your wife is entirely different.' He thrust out hairy wrists from a shirt distinctly dirty at the cuffs. '*Entirely.*'

'Is she?' His impression had been that Virginia's attitude was similar to his own.

'From what you have told me, undoubtedly.'

'But Virginia is English too.'

'Altogether? Absolutely and completely? You said she had an Irish grandmother.'

'Yes, but –'

'Then she is part Celtic. I divide European sexual attitudes into four main groups, Slav, Latin, Celtic, and Anglo-Germanic.'

'I know. We published your book.'

'The question is why have you come to me? Perhaps it would

447

be good for you to have children, but that is not possible. However, I am not a marriage counsellor. You wish my advice on how to put right this imbalance, how can we channel your aggression. Correct?'

'No, I don't think so.' Sverdlov looked surprised. 'We've been happily married for five years, and now she talks in this absurd way about my being homosexual.'

'You are not homosexual?'

'Of course not.'

'You have no homosexual experiences?'

'Certainly not.'

Sverdlov shook his head. 'Unusual. Significant.'

'She says she isn't in love with anybody else, she simply wants to go away. But what's happened, what's wrong?'

'*What's wrong!*' Sverdlov showed a number of discoloured teeth in a menacing way. 'My friend, we are living in a time of revolutions, that is what is wrong as you call it. The anarcho-sexual revolution is sweeping away everything that was taboo under the Anglo-Germanic code. We all have these feelings, we are all sexual revolutionaries at heart. You do not regard yourself so?'

'No, I don't.'

'Precisely. Yet there are feelings which demand release, isn't it so?'

Were there such feelings? A tight knot seemed to have formed in his stomach, he found it difficult to speak. 'I don't know of any such feelings. I am – I have been – perfectly happy.'

'Anglo-Germanism at its most obstinate.' Sverdlov moved one hand to a nostril, subsequently concealing it under his desk. 'And I am telling you it is no good. What is hidden must be acknowledged, brought into the light.' He produced his own hidden hand and tapped the desk. 'You have the sexual revolution up here.' The head was tapped. 'When it should be down here.' He appeared to indicate his stomach, but the reference was no doubt to a lower region.

'D. H. Lawrence said much the same thing.'

Sverdlov shrugged, indifferent to what D. H. Lawrence might have said. 'Quite frankly, sexual Anglo-Germanism makes me despair.'

'Perhaps it's just that Virginia is passing through a difficult time.'

'Not at all. It is *you* who are passing through a difficult time, as you call it, a period of Anglo-Germanic frustration.'

'Do you think she is telling the truth, or that she has a lover?'

'Quite possibly she has a lover. She is a Celt. She is not interested in politics?'

'Not at all.' Only in articles in glossy magazines, he felt inclined to add.

'The anarcho-sexual revolution can be expressed through politics. But if she is not interested, then her only expression is through sex. That is quite simple, inevitable. A general law.'

'You can't give me any advice?'

'I am telling you facts. General laws apply to particular cases. What is the point of *advice*, who takes it? You are suffering from the Anglo-Germanic syndrome. To use a term you may understand, it is an emotional block. Until it is removed you can have no genuine relationship. If you wish to consult me to that end, we can make an arrangement.'

'What sort of arrangement?'

'Nothing less than three sessions a week would be any use.'

'For how long?'

'A year. At least a year, perhaps more. Who can say?'

'I haven't got the time.'

'Very well.' Sverdlov rose behind his desk, a small man. His eyes flashed with anger. His finger pointed. 'But I must warn you. It is the Anglo-Germanic syndrome that led to the concentration camps.'

Chapter 7

Moonsight and Coldharbour

Little Mr Clapperton folded his hands over his round belly. 'The function of the hat, Mr Welton sir, is only partly protective. It is also ceremonial. It announces *I am that I am*, it stresses individualism and expresses a fine scorn for uniformity. It enhances and impresses.'

'Yes,' Gilbert said doubtfully. In the glass a staid middle-aged man looked at him, his head topped by a curly-brimmed dark grey bowler.

'Unquestionably. What was the object of the bear-skin shako and the tall plumed hat of the eighteenth century? To give an appearance of added height and so frighten the enemy. Not that that is necessary in your case of course, but the hat always enhances, it adds a particular flavour and style to the personality.' The bowler was whisked away and replaced by a small tweed hat which perched on the top of his head.

'No, I don't think that one.'

'This would have been your father's style.' Under the plain black bowler he looked for traces of the resolution and solidity that had marked E R's appearance, and failed to find them. His features looked longer, paler and more ineffectual than they were. 'It expressed his personality, it said "I am a man who stands foursquare, I care for nobody." If you'll forgive my making so free, Mr Welton sir, that was the way I always thought of him. He had the same hat through the years, with just the tiniest change in the brim width. The British bowler stands foursquare, as you might put it.'

'It isn't for me.'

'Perhaps not.' Mr Clapperton prowled round Gilbert, looking at his front, side and even back views, and then produced a wide-brimmed dark green trilby. 'There are other colours, but the green has what I should call a freshening effect. Nothing outrageous, but just that little touch of the unusual.'

'Certainly it isn't like what I've got.' His present hat, his invariable hat, was a black Homburg. Mr Clapperton picked it up and looked at it affectionately.

'A fine hat. It symbolizes the secure, the reliable, it says *you can trust me*. It is the hat of the man who knows his position in society and means to stay in it. A badge of position, as much as the Chinese imperial headdresses with their ornamentations showing the sun and moon or, at the other extreme, the wide-brimmed straw hat of the Mexican peon. In a sense, you can't better it.' He patted the Homburg. 'I should be sorry to see it relinquished altogether. But at the same time, if you want to have just that occasional extra edge of dash and style . . .'

Gilbert put down the dark green hat and picked up his own. 'I'll think about it. I'm sorry to have taken up your time, Mr Clapperton.'

'Always a pleasure to see you, my dear sir.' A bell tinkled as the door closed. The visit to *Clapperton, Hatter*, after a rubbery sandwich in a pub, had offered no solace. He dropped in at Sotheby's and looked at some first editions which at another time would have excited him. Now he felt no desire to possess them. He went out after five minutes and telephoned Virginia from a call box. There was no reply.

For Gilbert Welton serenity was identifiable with a settled pattern of life. Now that the pattern had been pulled apart by Virginia's behaviour, he was afflicted by a deep uneasiness which communicated itself to everything that surrounded him. He recognized the immediate cause of this uneasiness as jealousy, an emotion often most agonizing when it has no precise object on which to focus. He felt that if he had been told by Virginia that she was in love with Max he could have faced the situation. He would have asked whether she truly preferred this florid mid-European to him and if her answer had been yes, he would have tried to accept it. What had she said about the existence of six Virginias? As he looked into the window of a shop at a dummy apparently clothed only in a number of sashes he rehearsed a series of scenes with those other Virginias, lecherous or violent or untidy. Virginia advanced up Bond Street to meet him, deliberately placed his hand upon her breast and suggested that they should have sex in the taxi on the way home. Virginia, with a laddered stocking and food spots staining her dress, served an atrocious meal to half a dozen guests. Virginia, putting down her glossy magazine with a slow smile, revealed behind it Stendhal's *Le Rouge et le Noir*. That such Virginias might exist caused him more torment than the woman he visualized willingly crushed by Max's little arms.

He found another telephone box and rang again without result. In the house there would be silence except for the repeated *burr burr*. She had gone. Upstairs in the bedroom her cupboard would be tidily empty, the traditional note propped on a dressing-table clear of creams and lotions, addressed in her firm regular hand. He was aware of the absurdity of his feelings, their disproportion to the known facts. Such awareness seemed to make no difference.

When he put down the receiver and stepped out of the box a sandwich man confronted him. Long curling hair flowed to the man's shoulders, a row of beads drooped on his pullover. The board he carried said: 'The Realism of Space is the Opposition of Indivisibles.' Two others were behind him and they were parading up and down outside a picture gallery. The fascia of the gallery showed a small yellow moon and the word *sight* in childlike script. He went in.

The canvases on the walls seemed to be distinguished chiefly by a deliberate avoidance of perspective. The figures in them, brawny workers, round-faced women, idiotic-looking gaping children, were as flat as the electric cookers, refrigerators and motor cars beside which they stood, or which in some of the paintings they intersected. Heeney, Sharkey, Delaney, the signatures said, but they might as well have been the work of a single painter as far as Gilbert could see. He went into a second room and was stopped by a painting on the far wall. It was a picture of Virginia.

She was the only human figure. She stood naked, bisected by a dark brown chest of drawers which cut into her navel and eliminated one of her legs, and a large carton labelled Daz which obscured the back of her head and truncated one arm. A knife pointed at one of her breasts and a fork at the other. Her face was turned away to show a three-quarter profile, yet this incomplete body was unmistakably hers. He had seen the neck turned away from him like this a hundred times, had seen her standing with just such negligent ease, the body leaning slightly forward. The truncated arm was by her side, the marble shoulder blending into it, but the other arm was raised presumably to touch the missing back of her head. In the armpit there nestled an odious growth of hair.

'Interesting.'

Gilbert looked at the young man beside him. 'You're Mr Moon?'

'Alastair Moon.' He was not a round-faced Moon but a lantern-jawed 'one, his face encompassed with hair. He wore a corduroy suit and a string tie. 'Interesting,' he repeated, adding 'Don't you think?'

'I was looking for my wife.'

The young man glanced round with a whimsical air to indicate that they were alone. 'This is a picture of her.'

'Really?' Moon took from his pocket a pair of small spectacles, not moons but half-moons, put them on and looked again at the painting.

'She was in here the day before yesterday.' Had she come alone? 'I believe with a friend.'

'She is not here now,' Moon said gravely. 'As you see. Do please wait for her. If that's what you've arranged.'

In the studio of the Spatial Realist Virginia had stood, statuesque and beautiful. The painter walked over to her, spanned the slender wrist with his hand and raised it to reveal – a slight shudder passed through his body. He was aware that Moon had spoken.

'What?'

'Did she like the picture?'

'I don't know. I believe she may have been with my friend Coldharbour.'

'Denis Coldharbour. Of course I know him. He's most intelligent.' Gilbert agreed, although this was for him a new light on Coldharbour. 'I remember his coming along. He was most enthusiastic. Perhaps we've met at one of Denis's parties.'

'I didn't know that he gave parties.'

'Oh yes.' Within the fringe of hair Moon's mouth twitched

in a smile. 'But I don't think he came in with your wife. You'll know Jack perhaps? Jack Sharkey, who painted the picture. He's here.'

'Where?' Gilbert looked round.

'Outside.' Over the ridiculous half-moons Moon examined him as though he belonged to another species. 'The sandwich men.'

It was the one with the beads. He had narrow red-rimmed eyes, his neck was grimed with dirt, no doubt his hands also were filthy. Gilbert found it hard to know what to say.

'One of those pictures inside, one of yours –'

'Scon with your eytel.' That was what it sounded like.

'A picture of my wife. That is, she appears in it.'

Sharkey eased the board off his shoulders, rested it on the ground, said militantly, 'Grot evvy nutting.'

'I don't understand.'

'These.' He jerked a thumb at the sandwich boards and asked 'Canass four?'

'Canass four?'

'Or five?'

Gilbert spoke clearly as an elocutionist. 'I simply want to know how you came to include my wife in your picture. She is standing like this.' He raised one arm in the air and then quickly lowered it.

'Canass four. Torapic on to water room. Gotta find 'em some- where, rile bunny honey.'

'Bunny honey?'

'Sex mechanism plus. Cut and insert. Whattawant, Whistler's mum? Playboy playgirl, get it?' Sharkey dug in his clothing, found tobacco and roller, made himself the thinnest of cigarettes. 'Your wife one? Never.'

'You're telling me –?'

'A cut out, man, a cut out.'

Gilbert stared at him, turned and hurried back into the gallery. Moon had disappeared. He stood in front of the picture. Emotion ebbed away. How could he have thought this lifeless doll, an obvious cut out from a magazine, was Virginia?

On the telephone her voice was cool as water. 'Gilbert, hallo.'

'I thought – where have you been?'

454

'Making arrangements.'

'To leave?'

'For my holiday, that's right. What's the matter?'

'I thought you had gone.'

'What do you take me for, I wouldn't go without telling you. But it might be a good idea if I went tomorrow, I think I'll try to arrange that.'

The relief of hearing her voice was so great that he was almost prepared to agree. Instead he said, 'You went into an art gallery the other day. The Moonsight.'

'Oh yes, I remember. There were some boys with sandwich boards outside. I thought it might be fun, but they were boring pictures. Have you been there too?'

'Yes. I'll see you this evening then?'

'Of course.'

'There are things I want to know.' But what were they, what did he want to know when it was all so unintelligible? 'And say.'

'I thought you'd said it all last night. But I'll be here.'

The office door opened and Coldharbour came in, rustling slightly. Gilbert replaced the receiver.

'We had a little unfinished business. From yesterday. We were interrupted.'

Gilbert looked at him with disfavour. He found himself blaming Coldharbour, quite unjustly, for his ludicrous mistake at the gallery. 'I'm very busy.'

Coldharbour ignored this, sidled forward. A whiff of his characteristic smell came across the desk. 'It was about the Spatial Realists.'

'Yes. I went to see the show today.' He paused to give the next words appropriate weight. 'I thought it was rubbish.'

Coldharbour made his nose sound, but was not deterred. He sat down and crossed his legs. 'That's a point of view, but you're not an art critic. Perhaps you don't know the way in which this show has been received. The *Observer* man talked about a new concept of space.'

'Rubbish.' He repeated the word more loudly. 'And I talked to one of the artists, if that's what you call them. To Sharkey. I couldn't understand more than one word in three of what he said.'

455

'With any new movement there's a difficulty in communication.'

'There's no point in talking about it. Absolutely none.'

Coldharbour pouted, which was his extreme expression of disapproval. 'I think that's an utterly unreasonable attitude.'

'You can think what you like.'

'And if I may say so it is very different from the one you adopt towards other people.' Coldharbour always if possible avoided referring to Max by name. 'Other people are allowed to do as they wish, they have a free hand, whereas my suggestions are not given a reasonable hearing. And this is so even when other people are working perhaps quite *against* the firm's best interests.'

'What are you talking about?'

'I must warn you that I'm not prepared to put up with this kind of thing.' He walked out and slammed, quite positively slammed, the door.

Half an hour later Gilbert felt sorry about the way in which he had spoken to Coldharbour, and went down the corridor to say so. But although the small office was impregnated with insecticide so that it smelled like a conservatory Coldharbour himself was not there, and apparently had gone for the day. Walking back to his own office Gilbert reproached himself. Coldharbour was a director, and his ideas ought to receive attention. The thing to do would be to go round this evening and apologize. Denis was the kind of lonely man who was warmed by any sign of friendship.

In the corridor somebody bumped into him. A small man, almost a dwarf, with one shoulder higher than the other, said 'Sorry.'

Gilbert felt immediately the shame he always experienced when in contact with somebody physically handicapped. 'I'm very sorry.'

'Mr Welton? I'm W. Jones.'

The girl with him, one of those in the typing pool, gave a small yelp of warning or alarm.

'Very pleased to meet you. This young lady thought you were out.'

In his new spirit of charity Gilbert said 'You wanted to see me? Come in.'

He led the way into his office. W. Jones sat on the other side of the desk and beamed out of exophthalmic eyes.

'About the manuscript. You wrote some nice letters.'

'I'm afraid I don't quite –'

'I use a pseudonym. Dexter Manhood. *A Welter of Gore*.'

He looked with dismay at the beaming dwarf and pressed the button that summoned Miss Pinkthorn. When she stood in the doorway, like some implacable Eastern goddess clothed by mistake in English spinster wear, he raised his eyebrows hopefully. Still in the Eastern mode she gave a slow shake of the head. W. Jones swivelled round and directed his beam at her. She went out. Gilbert gloomily contemplated the figure opposite, who now produced some grubby sheets of paper which he flattened out. Holding them close to his nose he said, 'January 18, manuscript sent to you, acknowledged by P.C.'

'P.C.?'

'Postcard. February 27, a letter. Dear Mr Manhood, we have read your book *with great interest*, but there are just *one or two points*, which, etcetera. Signed by your good self.' The sheet was flourished in front of Gilbert and withdrawn. 'April 19, a delay of more than six weeks you observe. Dear Mr Manhood, in reply to your letter I am afraid we have still *not reached a decision . . .*'

He ceased to listen. In the Moonsight Gallery Virginia rested quietly in the arms of Coldharbour, an odalisque with the back of her head cut off, her naked body stretched like a board upon his lap. He leaned over her, smiled, murmured, 'You must be impregnated with Kilfoulair.' Gilbert gave a short bark of laughter and W. Jones looked surprised. Evidently he was expecting some reply.

'I can assure you we've been considering it very carefully.'

'But five months, Mr Welton. Five months.'

'I have my partners to consult. It doesn't rest entirely with me. Mr Bomberg is often inaccessible.' He wagged his head over the Foggish inaccessibility of Bomberg. 'He's out of the country at present.'

'Perhaps I should have used an agent. But I never touch them, man to man is the way I like it. Isn't that the best way?'

'Very often, yes.'

'It's not unreasonable now to ask for a decision. Is it?'

'A final reading,' he said desperately. 'By a most distinguished criminological expert, I mustn't tell you his name. Just give us a few more days, Mr Jones.'

Shoulder arched, eyes popping, the dwarf considered. 'Very well. But that isn't the only reason I came in, Mr Gilbert. I came to tempt you.'

Was a sexual advance to be made? But before he had time to be thankful that a desk separated them W. Jones had produced from somewhere a packet wrapped in brown paper and was undoing it, grinning.

'The Slough slaughter.'

'I beg your pardon?'

'My next book. A whole family killed for no reason, the bodies cut up and put into plastic bags you remember?' The packet was undone. Smiling, W. Jones held up photographs of disjointed legs and torsos. 'Very special photographs of the victims. Quite unique. I have my contacts.'

He lowered his gaze and saw Virginia, a bloody torso, being embraced by Sharkey.

It took him another half-hour to get rid of W. Jones. When he had done so he rang for Miss Pinkthorn and said that he was not available if Mr Jones called again. 'And it is vital that we should find his manuscript.' Her reply made it clear that she could not be responsible for the errors of others. It was after half-past five when, with the beginnings of a headache roaming round his skull, he set out for Coldharbour's flat.

He went down six dark steps to a basement area, pressed an illuminated bell. There was no sound from within, not even the sound of a bell ringing. He tapped gently on the door without result. Curtains were drawn across a window that fronted on to a basement area. Was Coldharbour out, had he made a wasted journey to Maida Vale? The irritation of the thought made his headache more distinctly perceptible. Standing at the bottom of these steps, from which the June evening light was cut away, he felt that he had been here before. On what other occasion had he stood at the bottom of steps like these, waiting with an uneasy prescience that something hateful lay behind a closed door?

Before he could trace the memory the door opened a few inches and Coldharbour's body appeared.

'Oh. It's you.'

'Denis.' He essayed a smile. 'I wanted to have a word in the office, but you'd left.'

'Yes.'

'I thought I might have offended you. I didn't mean to.'

'Not at all.' Coldharbour spoke in a formal manner. Even in the dim light it was apparent that he had on some unusually bright clothing. 'I was about to take a bath. But perhaps you'd like to come in.'

'Thank you.'

Coldharbour bent down. There was the sound of a bolt and chain sliding along a groove. A dark passage led to the sitting-room. He switched on the light. 'I always keep the curtains drawn. People can look in from the street.' In the electric light he was revealed as wearing a Japanese robe in light blue and silver, embroidered with dragons. Below it his legs showed dead white.

'I'm sorry about this afternoon. I'd had a bad day.'

'Not at all,' Coldharbour said again, uncharacteristically un-melted by the words. There were bottles on a table at the end of the room, but he did not offer a drink. Why not? And why was the door bolted and chained? Looking at the small section of bare chest visible in the vee opening of the robe Gilbert knew that there was somebody else in the flat. Could it be Virginia?

'There was something else.' He sat down. Coldharbour also sat, on the edge of a chair, ready to spring up again in a moment. 'You said something about Max working against the firm's interests.'

'I didn't mention a name.'

'No, but it was obviously Max. What exactly did you mean?'

A lavatory flushed, footsteps sounded. Coldharbour looked nervously at the door. 'I can't talk about it now.'

'You've got somebody here.'

'The people upstairs use my lavatory.' The robe came open further, revealing a surprisingly hairy chest. Modestly he drew it together. 'I have reason to believe that our partner is trying to make an arrangement with another firm. But I cannot talk about it now.'

'Denis, you can't say things like that without justifying them.'

'Tomorrow,' Coldharbour said with unusual firmness. 'Excuse me.'

The door opened. A young man came into the room. He wore a white vest and tight blue jeans with a wide black belt. His arms were splendidly muscled. His hair was thick and fair. He put his hands on slim hips, stared and said nothing.

Coldharbour gulped. 'Bill, I told you –'

'You *told* me?' The young man's voice was thick.

'I asked you – I said I shouldn't be more than five minutes.'

'I got tired of waiting.' He said to Gilbert, 'Perhaps you'd like to join the party.'

A key turned in a lock. Coldharbour put a hand to his mouth. His eyes were panic-stricken.

'I thought you'd put the bolt on,' the young man said.

'I did. But then he came.'

'You clot.'

Another figure appeared in the doorway, a hulking body with a small head, beetle-browed, grizzle-haired. Coldharbour spoke shrilly. 'Stanley, I thought I'd made it clear that you are *not* welcome here any longer. I've asked you before to give back that key.'

Stanley filled the doorway. He glanced at Bill but his gaze rested longer on Gilbert. 'Who's he?'

'I'm just going.'

Stanley's voice was surprisingly quiet in such a big man. 'You're a friend of Denny's? You'll understand then. I'm a friend too, have been for a couple of years, and now he's trying to ditch me. And for what? A pin-up out of a boysie magazine.'

'Excuse me.'

Stanley courteously made way but said emphatically, 'I ask you, is it right?'

'You can have him,' Bill said. 'I met him in a club, that's all. He's nothing in my life.'

Coldharbour started after Gilbert, who had reached the passage. 'Don't go.'

Laughter came bubbling up in him, he felt his body shaking with it. 'You wanted to get rid of me. We'll talk tomorrow.'

As he closed the door and went up the steps he heard Cold-harbour's voice raised after him in a depressing cat-like wail. He found a taxi in the street, and on the way home meditated upon the manifold tribulations of love.

Chapter 8

Wife Away

Watching the bird move along the ground, rise and slowly disappear, he looked for her face in the tiny holes that slotted its side and of course did not see her. The image of those caged Zoo birds in which she had been so deeply interested came to his mind. One day she had insisted that he should go with her and they had watched the bright creatures flying about, making love, chattering like fools, clinging to the sides of the cage.

'They're beautiful.' He had agreed. 'What do you suppose they think about?'

'I doubt if they do think. Not in the way you mean.'

'But they communicate. I read an article that said so. They can't like this, can they? For them it's like being in prison.'

'If you let them out they'd die.'

'Perhaps they'd sooner die.'

'When it comes to the point we'd all sooner live than die. Like Jews under German occupation. Most of them tried to go on living.' As soon as the words were spoken he regretted their sententiousness. 'It's a stupid comparison, people and birds.'

'I suppose so, yes.'

The conversation came back to him now that she had flown away to Yugoslavia, a bird inside another bird. Yugoslavia, he had said last night, why Yugoslavia?

'Celia Brunner says it's beautiful. And not too hot in June. But it might have been Geneva. Or Innsbruck. I just happened to be able to book a flight to Dubrovnik.'

It seemed useless to ask whether she was going alone, or would meet somebody there. 'I can't imagine what you'll do.'

'Swim. Look around.'

'You don't even know the language.'

'And think. About me. Us. You should do that too.'

'I could fly out and join you. In a couple of days you'll be bored.'

- 'Then I shall go somewhere else.'

'And if you're not?'

'I told you. I shall come back in a fortnight.'

Desperately, truthfully, he said, 'I don't see the point of it.'

'And what's the point of the way we live now? Nothing happens.'

'What do you expect to happen?'

'I don't know. But you want it that way. I have to find out if I do.'

'Supposing we'd had a child. Would it have been different?'

'How do I know? What a silly question.'

'And what is it I should think about?'

'I told you. You, me, us.'

In the morning she had everything packed and labelled, talked to Mrs Park, arranged that if he ran short of anything he would leave a note. Mrs Park accepted the whole thing as commonplace. 'Do you good,' she said. 'You've been looking peaky.'

In the morning he took her to Heathrow, kissed her cheek – at the last moment she averted her mouth – saw her walk out of the passenger lounge when the flight was called. Even when the bird rose from the ground he felt that somehow a trick had been played upon him. Surely she would walk across the tarmac and say that the whole thing was a joke? But she did not.

In the office the search for the Dexter Manhood manuscript continued unabated and unsuccessful. Mrs Fairweather had been traced and knew nothing about it. Miss Pinkthorn's eyes gleamed with pleasure. Coldharbour did not put in an appearance and there were some tiresome queries about a book he was handling. Ambiguous readers' reports on two manuscripts lay on Gilbert's desk. He sent out for sandwiches and began to read one of them himself. It was a novel purporting to be written in the first person by a deaf mute whose feelings were conveyed in an invented language which consisted of single-syllable words and exclamations. Interspersed with his narrative were extracts from a heavily ironical Report on the Sexual Customs of the Tribe supposedly composed by the psychologist who was handling the case of the deaf mute, and interpolated in the text of the Report were what amounted to quite separate novels about the problems of two couples mentioned in it. One couple were the parents of the deaf mute. He read a hundred pages, dictated on his tape recorder a letter of rejection, and turned to the other manuscript, which was concerned with the problems of a Negro dwarf who lived in a tree house and was perfectly happy until he fell in love with a white girl seven feet tall who took him home to her Gothic castle in Bigland. It was a relief when the telephone rang, although he flinched when the girl said it was Mr Bunce.

'Gil? Jake. How about Lord's?'

'What's that?'

'Up in North London. You're a cricket buff, right, isn't that where they play the top games?'

'Oh I see, Lord's. Middlesex play there, yes.'

'I wondered could we take in a match this afternoon? If you've got the time. Max said to ring you, but if you're too busy that's OK.'

There was something disarming in the apologetic hesitancy of Bunce's voice, and Gilbert agreed with a warmth that surprised himself to pick up Jake from his hotel. Before he left the office a cable came in. It was from Max in Milan and read: PROGRESS-WISE SLOWLY ABSENTEE EUGENE TRACKING THROUGH FLAVOUR WILL KEEP IN TOUCH. Flavour was presumably the secretarial Flavia, and presumably also the cable meant that Max would be away for another day or two. Well, life would be more peaceful without him.

Jake was waiting in the hotel lobby. He wore a zipping wind-cheater and levis. 'Am I dressed right? I mean, is there some special gear you wear for cricket?'

'Not the spectators, only the players.' In the taxi Gilbert explained the elements of the game and Bunce said, 'Yeah, yeah, I see, got it.' He tapped the paper under his arm. 'I've been boning up a little. I see Kent set the game alight yesterday, it says here Cowdrey hit the ball all over the ground.'

'Yes. You must be prepared for – I mean, it may be rather slow by your standards. A match can take three days.'

'Sure, sure, I know. It's like English life, a ritual. I'm interested in the symbolism. And, Gil.'

'Yes?'

'I want to say again I'm sorry about your dinner party. That Lulu should be kept locked up in a bedroom. I got rid of her.'

'You did?'

'She's moved in with Danny Knight, you know, the actor, he likes them rough. Gil, am I shocking you?'

'No.'

'I don't want you to think I got no feelings. I do have. But not about Lulu.' He gave what Gilbert thought of as an American smile, youthful and shy.

Gilbert was a member and he took Bunce into the Long Room, where the American looked with interest at the portraits round the walls. 'Old stuff,' he said. 'Respect for the past. I like it.' They sat outside the pavilion and watched Middlesex batting. There were few people in the ground, most of them small children or old men, and the play was appropriately becalmed, the batsmen pushing the ball placidly back down the pitch, occasionally dabbing it off their legs or down to third man for a single. Virginia would be settled by now in her hotel. He would telephone her tonight. With this decision he felt his eyes closing. A ripple of applause made him open them again. One of the batsmen had hit a boundary.

Jake leaned forward watching intently, his lick of fair hair hanging down. 'What does it mean to you, Gil, all this?'

'Mean?'

'It's a dance to slow music, I get that. But there's more to it, it kind of expresses British temperament, right?'

'Yes, perhaps it does if you put it that way.'

'It gets you where you live, stands to reason it must do.'

Drowsily he wondered whether this was true, and decided that there was something in it. 'Perhaps it's what I should like life to be, leisurely, with nothing unexpected happening.' It occurred to him that this was a variation on what Virginia had said last night, and Bunce's next words seemed to flow on naturally from this thought.

'I liked your wife, admired her very much. But I guess she wouldn't be too keen about cricket.'

Gilbert felt an inclination to confide in him, but resisted it. 'That's right. She thinks it's a bore.'

'Thinks it's a bore,' Bunce repeated, and laughed in what might have been a meaningful manner. He turned to the sports page in the paper, as though reading an account of the previous day's play would provide some final answer to his questions. Gilbert closed his eyes and saw the cheek he had kissed at parting, wonderfully smooth. Why had she not kissed him on the mouth, did she now find him repulsive? Such ideas were alien to him. He was startled when Bunce said emphatically, 'Sex.'

One of the batsmen had been bowled, his middle stump knocked out of the ground. 'What?'

'That's why you get a kick from it.' He tapped the paper. 'You use the ball, see, and you try to get rid of the stump. See what it says here, Herman uprooted the middle stump and that's what just happened now, right?'

'Yes, but –'

'Boy, that bowler's uprooted his middle stump all right, it's a castration symbol, see? And those pads the batter wears, he's protecting his stump with them. He wants to hit that ball, get the damn' thing away from him to the boundary, the limit. Get that ball away, he's saying, I don't want it near my stump. You read what Melanie Klein says about bat and ball games?'

'I can't say I have.'

'They symbolize a fear of sex, keep it hidden, that's the thing, destroy it if you can. And the white clothes, what do they mean but purity? It's a hell of a funny game.' The players went into the pavilion. 'That's it then, glad to have seen it.'

'They'll be coming out again. This is the tea interval.'

'I guess I've seen enough.' With cricket satisfactorily explained Bunce rose to his feet. Gilbert got up too. 'Gil, it's been great. I appreciate it, I really do. Why not stop by my hotel around seven, I'd like to have a talk. And your wife too if she's around, let's have an evening together.'

'Virginia's gone off on a short holiday.' The reticence of his own phrase was somehow decisive, and he said yes to the invitation. Bunce ambled away. Gilbert stayed watching the cricket for another half-hour, but those remarks about sexual symbolism seemed to have taken away his pleasure. He found that he could not contemplate a return to the office and went to the club where he at once fell asleep in the reading-room.

Chapter 9

A Tangible Ghost

He sat in the Out Going, aware that he had drunk too much whisky. Around him there was a tremendous noise, part of which came from The Worst, a group playing at the other end of the room. The Worst's vocalist, stripped to the waist, had the words *I Tangle* painted on his chest. Some words of his theme song came through:

. . . as we jangle
Because I . . . tangle
. . . Want to tangle . . . angle . . .
What is it . . . love . . . strangle . . .

The final line, which he fairly belted out, was perfectly clear: 'Because I got got got just got to tangle with you.' Everybody in the room appeared to be talking rather than listening, talking less to other people than to himself or herself. The Out Going was the last in a succession of similar establishments that they had visited in a group that had grown steadily larger and now numbered a dozen people. Jenny Johnson was with them, and so were Felix Perkins the photographer, who had been drinking with them at the hotel and a film producer named Lefty Leftwell. In their presence Bunce seemed a different person from the young man who had sat beside Gilbert at Lord's. In the same gangling body this other Bunce appeared, at once aggressive and self-pitying. It might have been said that he was playing to an audience, but if so he was obviously dissatisfied with his performance. Greeting Gilbert in the hotel with a kind of melancholy warmth, he had talked almost the whole evening about his own genius, and the way in which America made him suffer. At one point Jenny, rather in her televisual incarnation, had asked why he lived in the United States if he hated it that much. Bunce's mouth quivered, he looked as if he were about to cry.

'Because it turns me on, baby, the whole show turns me on,

467

because I love the goddam place, that's why.' He waved an arm, struck Felix Perkins on the chest, smiled apologetically. 'It's a great country, but it makes you suffer.'

They were all sitting round two small tables, and Jenny's thigh was pressed close against Gilbert's. 'He's a genius,' she said. 'You must be proud to publish him.'

He started to tell her that Jake was really his partner's responsibility, but she rose, slipped past him and joined a risen Bunce in the crowd of figures swaying in the centre of the room. *Why did you wear that bangle?* The Worst's vocalist asked. *Made me want to tangle.* The words became hopelessly lost.

Perkins said, 'They've got something, don't you think? A *reverberant* quality.'

'I don't know, have they?'

The photographer was thin, long-fingered, hollow-cheeked. He wore a frilled lace shirt with ruffles at the neck. 'It's a song for sad men. Like me. My wife's left me. Do you know what she said? "We're not cohering any more, and when you're not cohering what's the good." I have these rages. Do you have them?'

'I don't think so. No, I don't have rages.'

'You wouldn't think I did, would you? Once she seemed to like them. But not now. I had a card from her the other day. From Istanbul. It broke my heart.'

'Rages,' a voice said jeeringly. It came from a broad-faced ruddy man. 'Tantrums!'

'Oh Richard, please,' Perkins said.

Richard jerked a finger. 'That cow, he's on the box with Jenny, she asks him something, he has one of his tantrums and cuts loose with a load of dirty talk. And my old mum's listening, she's disgusted. "Is that the sort of thing your friends say, son?" she asks me.' He leaned across, took hold of Perkins's shirt front. 'You know what you are, don't you? A cow, a bloody liberal cow.'

'Richard, don't be fierce.'

'Don't be fierce,' Richard mimicked. 'You ought to be ashamed, using that language when old ladies are listening. You know what? They think photographers are a crowd of yobs, they think we're all like you.'

'You're tearing my shirt.' Perkins seemed rather pleased than distressed.

'You're a photographer too?' Gilbert asked.

'Too right I am.' Richard glared, released Perkins's shirt. 'You another liberal cow?'

'I don't think I'm anything at all.'

'That's right, boy, don't you be anything at all. Don't talk dirty on the box. Mind you, she asks for it.' He gestured at Jenny, who was clinging to Bunce on the floor. 'You know what my mum says about her?'

'Richard. Felix. Darlings!' A small blonde pushed her way through the crush and became visible in the dimness as an actress with a familiar face. 'Fay,' everybody cried, 'It's Fay.' The men got up and kissed her. Bunce returned sweating from his dance and kissed her too.

'Lovely,' she cried. 'But do I know you?'

'Everyone knows me, Jake Bunce.' She squealed with pleasure. 'And you're Fay. I got to prove something to myself, Fay.'

'What's that?'

'You going to bed with me tonight?'

Fay squealed again, turned to Gilbert who sat pressed within his chair and kissed him warmly. 'What do you think about that?'

'I don't know.'

She ran a hand through his hair. Behind her another woman hovered, taller, bigger. What seemed an irresistible press of bodies from behind moved Fay forward and she gently dropped into Gilbert's chair and placed an arm round his neck. The taller woman stood looking down, spoke his name.

'Gilbert, what in Christ's kind of a name is that?' Fay cried. 'That's Georgie Drake, you know Georgie.'

'I know Georgie.' He pushed Fay away, stood and faced her. He had not seen her for seven years, but she was the most tangible of ghosts. She was immediately recognizable, yet the missing years had wrecked her. The broad flat face was coarsened, the body thickened by drink, there was about her an air of bursting over-ripeness. Only the eyes of distinctive delicate blue looked at him with the openness that he remembered. It was more than seven years ago, it was ten, that he had gone down the basement steps similar to Coldharbour's and thundered on the door and pushed past the man who opened it and found her on the bed, drunk and giggling. Her mouth had wavered as it always did when she was unsure of her reception, as it was wavering now.

'Georgie,' he repeated and then said 'Mary,' and her wavering mouth smiled. His pleasure at seeing her was so great that he could have laughed or cried. He took her hands and said with perfect simplicity, as though the desert years between them did not exist, 'Mary, let's go.'

Chapter 10

The Past

'What do I think?' E.R. had asked, chalking his cue and standing beside it with his large head raised like that of a Roman senator about to pronounce sentence on an erring centurion. He bent down and played a stroke with his customary care, just missing a difficult cannon. 'It is one more absurdity added to the long list. What else is there to think? And what is the point of asking me? You are twenty-four years old. If you choose to marry a chemist's daughter from Camden Town it is your affair, not mine.'

He was intimidated, as always, by the way in which E.R. put it. Before the war his mother had been there to protect him from such weighty sarcasm, to laugh at E.R. and make him laugh too. The bit of shrapnel that killed her outright while she was making her way to a shelter after shopping had seemed unreal to him at the time, a telegram received in Africa, some words of sympathy from the Colonel. Even if it had been possible he would not have wished to go home, and in a way the fact that he did not return cushioned him from the reality of his mother's death, so that when he did come back to England he expected to find her waiting to greet him in the Chelsea house where they had lived since his childhood. Instead there was simply his father, installed there with a housekeeper to whom his manner was one of ferocious formality. Gilbert had missed university when he was called up for Army service in 1941, and four years later he felt little inclination to go. E.R. had always assumed that he would enter the business, and he did not openly question this assumption. Within a few weeks of living at home, however, he had rebelled to the point at which he said that he wanted a place of his own. E.R. had raised no objection. He got rid of the housekeeper, sold the house, and moved into a service flat in Kensington. The departure from home had been the outward mark of an estrangement that had deepened in the three years before this announcement of marriage.

471

Now he said, 'I don't see that Mary's father being a chemist has anything to do with it.'

'Ha.'

They played a few more strokes. 'I want to leave the firm.'

'Very well.'

'I'm going to start a bookshop somewhere in the country. In Gloucestershire perhaps. And set up a small private printing-press.'

With careful savagery E.R. potted the red, playing the ball so hard that it almost bounced out of the pocket. 'The New Life.' The phrase referred to the group of which Gilbert was a member.

'Yes, as a matter of fact there will be a New Life community starting near Gloucester.' What he had to say next required an effort. 'There's the matter of money.'

E.R. finished his break. 'My game.' He racked his cue and stood glaring from under great grey brows. 'I hope you don't expect me to provide it.'

'There's the money Mother left. If you approve –'

'Very well. You have my approval.'

He felt immense relief. Of course they would have got married anyway, but the money made it that much easier. 'And your blessing, I hope.'

'My blessing.' E.R. contemplated the words as he switched off the lights above the table. He hardly ever raised his voice and now his words were all the more effective for their measured weight. 'You know I wanted you to carry on the firm. Now you will not be doing so. You have involved yourself with a group of ridiculous nonentities, you propose to marry a chit of a chemist's daughter and to embark on a scheme that is as certain of failure as anything can be in this life. I am willing for you to have the money left by your mother because it is properly yours, but I should be condoning your stupidity in an unpardonable way if I gave you my blessing.' He paused and said with the sense of timing that rarely forsook him, 'Shall we go down to the bar?'

He had been right, of course, he had been dismally and painfully right in everything except in the description of Mary as a chit.

472

In the taxi, with his arm round her ampleness, he reflected that even as a girl Mary had been heavyboned and brawny. Now, with her head rolling on his shoulder, she murmured something that he failed to hear. She repeated it.

'Nothing is lost.'

'What do you mean?'

'Do you remember saying that to me? Nothing we do, think, feel together is lost, it always remains somewhere in our personalities, when people love each other it makes a link that can never be broken. Do you remember?'

'Yes,' he said untruthfully. He had said many similar things at that time. When the war ended and he came out of the Army with the rank of captain he had been sure of nothing except that the world was totally changed and that his life ought to change with it. He had seen men killed because they obeyed his orders, had glimpsed later as a staff captain something of the confusion and pettiness that marks every bureaucratic organization, and he had no intention of spending the rest of his life propping up such organizations. In the 1945 General Election a political party named Common Wealth fought using the slogan, 'What is morally wrong cannot be politically right,' and although Gilbert was not interested in politics he shared the Common Wealth feeling that a new and better society was coming into existence. Entering the firm had been understood, at least by him, as a breathing space while he discovered the nature of that society. He saw a New Life meeting advertised in a weekly paper, went to it, and joined.

The New Life group had been founded a few months before the end of the war by a dynamic bald man in his forties named George Riddiatt. The group believed in freedom. 'We must be free to share with others all that we hold most sacred in life itself,' Riddiatt would say, his dark eyes gleaming. 'What do I mean by sacred? Every one of us has his own answer to that, the sacred things are locked up here.' He would strike his barrel chest and his hearers understood that the sacred things were impalpable, it was the glimmering web of human feelings that those who lived the New Life would be sharing in a world remote from envy, jealousy and greed. Corporeal possessions were comparatively unimportant but these too would be shared in the New Life communities that were springing up all over Europe and America.

Had it all been as ridiculous as it seemed now, an old tune played to the credulous by a bald Pied Piper? It had fitted his personal needs at the time, and he had taken part with enthusiasm in the formation of the Literary, Dramatic and Psycho-Dynamic Groups and in the plans for transforming the farm which Riddiatt owned, and where he had worked during the whole of the War, into the first New Life community. He had met Mary in Psycho-Dynamics, and had been attracted at once by her rebellious innocence. The decisions that he had reached by painful effort, in making up his mind to live alone and to leave the firm, seemed to pose no problems at all for her. She regarded her parents as ignorant ogres, and agreed without any hesitation at all to come and live with him. After they had slept together at his flat she took him to see her mother and father. Gilbert was surprised to find them rather meek little people.

'I'm leaving here, we're going to live together.' Mary looked at them defiantly.

Mr Drake coughed. 'I don't know why you've thought it necessary to bring Mr Welton along –'

'His name's Gilbert.'

'Pleased to meet you, Gilbert.' They shook hands.

'Of course we should like it if you got married,' his wife said, later. They were so acquiescent that there was nothing to rebel against, as it seemed to Gilbert.

'You don't understand. They've tried to keep me down. Always. Now they can't, that's all.'

'It might be a good idea to get married.'

She disagreed. Was not marriage a negation of freedom, a completely artificial attempt to bind people together socially? Gilbert, who had in mind the effect on E.R., replied that since the ceremony was unimportant it didn't matter whether or not they conformed to it. They took the question to Riddiatt, who agreed with Gilbert. Had the question of getting his mother's money anything to do with it? Looking back years later he feared that it had. In the end they compromised by getting married in a register office with witnesses called in from the street, and announcing the fact afterwards. They bought the bookshop before marrying, and spent their honeymoon getting it straight and putting the old printing-press in the cellar in order. George Riddiatt's former farm, now the New Life centre, was only a couple of miles away, and New Lifers came in every day to chat, help, drink coffee. Within a few weeks Mary was pregnant. Broad and beaming, an image of sturdy health, she sat in the shop talking to members of the group, while Gilbert worked downstairs printing pamphlets.

When was the New Life over, when did the dream fade? Its fading had a connection, in some way that he did not understand, with the surprisingly difficult birth of Matthew, who was more than a week late. Riddiatt had said that he should be present at the birth, Mary had wanted him there, and he had sat watching horrified while she shrieked, moaned, arched her body as though bitten by a snake, and eventually excreted the messy red howling creature. And in more material terms it was of course linked to the evident failure of the bookshop to attract many people except the New Lifers, and to Gilbert's realization that George Riddiatt was not a prophet but a windbag with both eyes on the main chance.

And yet perhaps the basic reason was just the fact that Mary and he had deceived each other when they married. Slowly he understood that her broad-beamed solidity concealed a wildly romantic nature in rebellion not only against her parents but against almost every aspect of conventional society. Twenty years later Mary would have been a pot-smoking hippie with different problems. At the end of the nineteen forties she was a high flying romantic who expected him to lead her into always wilder and more imaginative areas of freedom. Were they making losses on the bookshop, was there little prospect of being paid for the New Life pamphlets? She found it impossible to feel any interest in such material matters, and used to take Matthew up to the New Life centre, leaving Gilbert to look after the shop. Sometimes she would stay there all day, these visits being succeeded by storms of remorse in which she would cling to him and assure him that he was the only man she could possibly love. This meant, as he ought to have known, that she was going to bed with Riddiatt. When he discovered this he found it impossible to blame her. She was only carrying out the principles of the group, as she pointed out to him, and any pain he felt sprang from the envious feelings that they had both forsworn. But other wives also carried out the principles, other husbands were less tolerant. Within a year the group broke up in furious dissension. Riddiatt went to the United States with a rich American girl who had recently joined, married her, and when Gilbert had last heard of him was running a School of Metaphysical Drama in California.

A few months later Gilbert sold the bookshop for less than half the price he had paid for it, and went back to work in the family firm. E.R. did not comment on what had happened beyond saying that he was glad Gilbert had come to his senses. He never came to see them in the flat that Gilbert bought with the money from the sale of the bookshop.

His arm was developing pins and needles and he withdrew it from behind her back. She turned to look at him.

'Where are we going, to your house?'

'Yes.'

'What's happened to your wife, to Vir-Virginia? Or is she there?' He had almost forgotten her occasional slight attractive stammer.

'She's away.'

'Away.' Her laugh, throaty and full of sexual promise, had not changed. 'I still love you, that's funny, isn't it, after all these years. Nothing is lost, I remember that. I remember everything.'

'Nobody remembers everything. Just what they want to remember.'

'That isn't true,' she cried with the earnestness that had always impressed him because it obviously welled up from a nature whose feelings went so much deeper than his own. 'I remember Starting Again, did you think I'd have forgotten that?'

Starting Again. It was what they had said hopefully when they moved into the flat and for two years, perhaps three, *Starting Again* had remained their motto. Then Matthew stopped being a baby and went to school, and Mary took drama classes to fill in the time and began to come back late in the evenings and Starting Again was over. How was it possible that he had endured the drink and quarrels and unfaithfulness for five years after that? There must have been a strong link, he thought now wonderingly, the link between them must have been very powerful to last so long. Now Mary sat upright on the seat, away from him.

'How's Matt?'

'Well. I had a letter a couple of weeks ago.'

'He hasn't written to me in months. No reason why he should I expect you say. But it wasn't all my fault. I did the wrong things, but it wasn't all my f-fault.'

'I never said it was.'

'I never got anywhere near to you. Except at the b-beginning perhaps. I don't know what you want from women, and I don't think you know either. That was always the t-trouble.'

'What are you doing now?'

'This and that. Telly mostly. When they want a fat middle-aged tart they think of me.' She paused. 'It would be p-polite to laugh.'

'I've seen you once or twice. And thought about you.'

'Thank you very much. To tell the truth it's absolute bloody hell. I'm through with the telly or it's through with me. I'm living with Fay.'

'Fay? Oh yes.'

'You'd never have thought I was a lizzie, would you? And butch at that. And the thing is I'm not really. Anyway I think that's finished too. Fay's bored with me, I'll be moving out before long.'

'Did you find it satisfactory?'

'Of course I bloody didn't. I told you I'm not a lizzie. Only when you're —'

'What?'

'Nothing.'

The taxi stopped. She went ahead, opening the gate while he paid the driver. As he caught up with her she looked at him.

'Why have you brought me here? Some sort of re-revenge. Is that it? It would be like you.'

The remark stung him. 'When did I ever take revenge on you?'

'Not me. Yourself.'

He opened the door and switched on the hall lights. She looked

477

around her with the inquisitiveness of a woman entering the house where a man she knows well is living with another woman. In the drawing-room she took in the striped settees, the polished tables, the pictures, the careful arrangement of everything. She turned to him with the wide trustful smile he remembered. 'She's not much like me, is she, that's for sure.'

And he remembered too – there was, after all, a great deal he had not forgotten – the chaos in which Mary lived for preference, the bits of butter left on tables and adhering to newspapers dropped on top of them, the gravy from a week-old meal gathering fur on a shelf, the bedroom's invariable disorder. He had said during one of their quarrels, 'I suppose you think you've got more important things to do than making the bed,' and she had answered, 'Yes, lying on it.' He had laughed without being appeased. For Mary order and neatness were incompatible not only with the New Life, but with everything in her nature. Outward chaos symbolized inner rebellion.

'Whisky?'

'And a drinks cupboard. Whisky, yes, with soda. I'll bet she's the kind of woman who never runs out of soda.'

'Yes. Is it a good thing to run out of soda?'

'I su-suppose not.' She sat down, crossed her legs, licked a finger and ran it over a stocking. 'A ladder, bugger it. I saw you once together. In a restaurant, you didn't see me. Pretty, but not your style I'd have thought. Though perhaps it was me who wasn't your st-style.'

'Perhaps.' He stood looking down at her, contemplating the face which retained some of the wide artlessness of youth, the body gone to seed.

'I don't see what the hell you brought me here for. Where is she, isn't she coming back?'

The words clanged in his head. He had to telephone Virginia.

'Or are we going to bed, is that it? It's been a long time. And it was never what it might have been, was it?'

'I don't know.'

'This is everything, this is what life means. Do you remember I used to say that to you. But it was never true. I had it better.'

'With a dozen others, I daresay.'

'Oh Christ, you are a bastard. All I wanted –' She gave up the sentence, drank.

In the hotel bedroom at Dubrovnik Virginia moved in a torment of pleasure beneath a body lean, brown, covered with hair, whose face was indiscernible. 'Yes. What did you want?'

'What does it matter. I shall never get it now.' With dismay he saw her take off her shoes, put her feet up on the sofa. 'Did it all mean nothing, then?'

'Did what mean nothing?'

'The things we said. Not just you and me, the Group. It can't all have been wasted, can it?' Her eyes stared at or through him, blue and innocent, asking as she had always asked for some reassurance about life or the world. 'I kept all your letters, you know that? Sentimental.'

'Yes.'

'All right then, I'm sen-sentimental. Let's go to bed.'

As she spoke the words his revulsion from her became complete, the need to speak to Virginia physically urgent. 'I'm sorry. You'll have to go.'

'She's coming back?' Again with her wide smile she said, 'I'd like to meet her. You did ask me in.'

'I've got to make a telephone call.'

'Go ahead. I'm happy here.' She held out her empty glass. 'Though I could do with another drink.'

Her presence in the house was intolerable to him. He went to the sofa, pulled her up so that she stood beside him, slapped her face. The sound was unpleasant. As he saw the look of the innocent eyes change to wonder and dismay he felt that he had done some terrible injury to an animal.

'I'm sorry.'

'Don't be sorry.' She swayed a little and he realized that she was drunk. 'You've said it too often. Where's my coat, did I have one?'

'Virginia won't be back. You can stay here. In the spare room.'

She shook her head. 'In the spare room. No, thanks.'

'Are you all right? Let me ring for a taxi.'

She shook her head again. At the door she touched her face

479

where the mark of his fingers showed, and then touched his gently. 'Good-bye, Gilbert.'

'I'm very sorry,' he repeated inanely, like a head waiter apologizing for some failure of service.

'I don't know what you want, but it's not me. It was never me. You ought to find out. It's upsetting for women when men don't know what they want. I feel sorry for Vir-Virginia.'

She walked down the steps and then up the road, a bulky middle-aged woman.

Back in the drawing-room he found himself shivering, poured more whisky and drank half of it at a gulp, then looked at his watch. The time was half-past eleven. Too late to telephone? The question was unreal, because his need was so urgent that the consideration of time did not enter into it. He dialled the operator and asked for the number.

'Yugoslavia,' a friendly man's voice said. 'That's a long way away. There'll be a delay. I'll call you back.'

He wandered round the room, putting straight the cushion on which Mary had sat, taking out her glass to the kitchen and washing it, obliterating the traces of her visit. What unbelievable stupidity it had been to bring her back here, why had he done it? And what had she meant by saying that he didn't know what he wanted? The two of them were utterly unsuited and it had taken a long time to find out, that was all.

The telephone rang.

The friendly operator said, 'Your call to Yugoslavia should be through now. Hold on a moment.' There was a series of clicks, then a tapping sound.

'Is that the Hotel Splendid?' The tapping continued, then there was an ear-splitting noise followed by a volley of what he assumed to be Serbo-Croat. 'Is that the Hotel Splendid?' More Serbo-Croat. He said loudly and slowly, 'Is there anybody who speaks English?'

A woman's voice intervened, evidently expostulating with somebody. With him? Apparently not, for the volleyer returned and spoke sharply, with rising excitement. Gilbert tried to get above them both with a shout. 'I want to speak to Madame Welton.' Silence. 'Get Madame Welton for me please.'

The two decided to ignore him and began to argue again. The operator came on, cutting them out.

'Don't seem to be doing too well, do we? Got a line crossed out there from the sound of it. Did you get any sense at all?'

'None whatever.'

'I'll try again.' He heard the same two voices, then the operator cut them out. 'I can try and get hold of Dubrovnik exchange again.'

'Thank you.'

'But that means breaking the connection. Is it urgent?'

'Yes.'

'See what I can do. Hold on.' More clicks, then a different voice. The operator, more resourceful than Gilbert had expected, spoke slowly in an unintelligible language. There was a good deal of conversation which ended with laughter on both sides.

'Look, I'm sorry, old man –'

'Please don't call me old man. We don't know each other.'

The operator became curt and formal. 'I'm sorry, subscriber, Dubrovnik say that all lines to the Hotel Splendid are engaged.'

'That's absurd. They can't be at this time of night.'

'I can only tell you what Dubrovnik reports.'

'Is that why you were laughing?'

'He made a joke about the length of time people spend on the telephone. I agreed.'

'Is he going to ring back?'

'I can ask him to do so if you wish. I couldn't guarantee that he will.'

'What do you advise?'

'If it's very urgent I should try again in half an hour. I'm going off at midnight. That's in five minutes.' A click and he was back with the dialling tone.

The idea of telephoning seemed absurd. What would he say if he spoke? 'I just rang to see if you were all right ... having a good time ... met anybody interesting ... is somebody in the room with you?' It was a stupid idea, of a piece with his behaviour during the evening. He brushed his teeth and went to bed, staring at Virginia's untouched coverlet.

He was unable to sleep. Was Bunce in bed with Jenny Johnson or with Fay, talking to her about the sexual symbolism of cricket? And what about Mary? The words were repeated in his head with tom-tom rhythm. It had been wrong to bring her back to the house, an act of deep insensitiveness. Tottering slightly, never too steady on her pins, Mary returned to the flat she shared with the actress Fay, and found it empty. From a drawer in a dressing-table she took a small packet of letters done up in pink ribbon and began to read them, her tears dropping on to the sheets. What did the letters say? They were in his writing and he strained to make out the words but was unable to do so. Mary looked up at him. 'Starting Again,' she said. She was smiling not at him but at somebody behind him, and turning he saw Virginia advancing towards her. 'Starting Again,' Virginia repeated and then bent over Mary and kissed her upturned face while he watched in horror, wanting to protest but unable to cry out. 'No,' he was able to manage at last. 'No.'

He woke shivering, his pyjamas damp with sweat, went down to the kitchen and made himself a cup of tea, returned to bed. A phrase of Scott Fitzgerald's, changed and no doubt debased, was repeated in his mind. 'When you wake and remember the past you never go back to sleep.'

It was after three o'clock when he slept. In his dreams the telephone seemed to be ringing.

Chapter 11

Telephone, Newspaper, Cable

The agonies and terrors of the night vanish in the light of morning. Gilbert Welton woke, bathed, shaved, dressed, made himself toast and coffee, spoke to Mrs Park, walked to the office in bright sunshine. Over the toast and coffee he skimmed through a letter from Amsterdam in Matthew's round hand. 'How are you both? Very sorry I haven't written recently but we've been very busy, however better busy than slack . . .' Matthew was a stolid, pleasant, rather boring young man, not bright enough for university, who had gone into an Anglo-Dutch engineering combine as a trainee and had then come out of it to start a firm for the sale of some gadget used in the operation of concrete mixers. His partner was the inventor of the gadget and, surprisingly to Gilbert, they seemed to be doing very well.

Surprisingly also, Matthew got on very well with Virginia, who had adapted herself easily to the idea of having a grown-up stepson. Something about this humdrum letter helped to set the preceding night into perspective. He had drunk too much and behaved foolishly, but nothing had been done that could not be undone, and his need to telephone now seemed incomprehensible. You were married, your wife had gone away for a while because she was feeling the sort of strain that all married couples suffered from time to time. To make a telephone call in the middle of the night was just about the worst possible course of action. He decided that he would stop behaving stupidly. He would not telephone Virginia, but would wait for her to get in touch with him. It was Friday. No doubt he would hear from her before the week-end was over.

He spent the next seventy-two hours in the semi-anaesthetized condition of a man waiting for an operation. The office on Friday was somnolent. There was no word from Max. He left at three o'clock, went to the Zoo and watched the sea-lions being fed. They positioned themselves on rocks and caught in their mouths the fishes thrown to them. Later he found himself standing in

front of the aviary and contemplating the birds in a fixed meaningless way. On Saturday he went to the club and played squash,
on Sunday the Sutherlands invited him to lunch. He told them
that Virginia had gone away for a short holiday, and that pressure
of work prevented him from going with her. Sandra said nothing
further about her departure, but started to talk about the attractiveness of Bunce. What food had they given him, what else
had been said? Half an hour after leaving them he could not
remember.

He went home and began to turn out old clothes from his
bedroom drawers and then to throw away papers. Then he tried
to open the small desk in which Virginia kept her correspondence. It was locked. He tried several keys without success and
eventually forced the lock with a chisel, searching in it with an
eagerness he could not explain. He found nothing but bills,
cheque book stubs and half a dozen old letters of his own.

The telephone did not ring. That night he drank a good deal
of whisky, and on Monday morning woke with a headache. There
was no letter from Virginia. Well, she had left on Thursday so
she would hardly have had time to write, but he decided to ring
her at midday. As he entered his office on Monday morning
the telephone was ringing.

'Mel Branksom.' The voice on the telephone was American,
deep and warm. 'Branksom Associates. I don't know whether
Max told you we'd had a chat.'

'As a matter of fact he didn't. He's in Italy at the moment.'

'That's too bad.' The voice was slightly ruffled, velvet rubbed
the wrong way. 'I guess he left in a hurry. I was putting, you
know, a little idea to Max that he thought would interest you,
and I wondered if you'd do me the honour of having lunch one
day. Just to discuss it.'

'Can you give me some idea –' He paused as Coldharbour's
face, with a bruise showing on one cheek, appeared at the door.
He beckoned to the face before completing the sentence. '– what
it's all about?'

'Well now, I'd sooner not do that on the telephone. I'd sooner
put it face to face.'

What had Max been up to? Remembering that conversation
with Langridge-Wood he became suddenly anxious to know.

His diary pad was blank for the day. He suggested that Branksom should have lunch with him at the club. The voice became richer and warmer.

'I'd enjoy that, I really would. I look forward to meeting you.'

He put down the telephone and said to Coldharbour, 'Branksom Associates. Something to do with Max.'

Coldharbour shifted in his chair. 'Precisely. You remember I mentioned it.'

'I can't say I do.'

'I heard in a roundabout way that our friend had been discussing matters with them. Behind our backs. It is *not* the sort of thing that inspires confidence. I mean, are Branksom the sort of firm we want to get mixed up with?'

Gilbert nodded in a placatory manner. Branksom Associates were an American firm who had recently set up in England as publishers of sensational non-fiction books dealing with sex, crime and prison camp atrocities. They were said to have made a good deal of money. 'You don't know what they've got in mind?'

'Certainly not. If I had known I should have told you.'

'We may as well find out. There's no harm in talking.'

Coldharbour's sniff said that there might be harm in anything connected with Branksom. He moved one leg restlessly. 'About the other night. I don't want you to have the wrong idea.'

'Please, Denis.' The embarrassment he always felt at any suggestion of admission to the private lives of other people operated immediately. 'It had nothing to do with me.'

'That's perfectly true. I just wanted you to understand. Life is not always easy.' He suddenly scratched his neck. 'Stanley *was* a good friend of mine, but we had rather fallen out.' He seemed to find the phrase reassuring enough for repetition.

'I'm sorry to hear it.'

'However, our difference of opinion was only temporary. Bill proved to be very much what Stanley suggested, I'm afraid. Not a very agreeable fellow.'

'Denis, I must insist. I don't want to know anything more about it.'

He was surprised by the look Coldharbour gave him. 'You never want to know, do you?'

'What?'

'About other people.'

'I don't know what you mean.'

'That's all right,' Coldharbour said obscurely. He stood up. 'I take it your mind is quite made up. About the Spatial Realists.'

'The Spatial Realists?' For a moment he failed to make the connection. 'I'm sorry I put it so strongly, but – well, yes. It's outside our field.'

'Very well.' A hand strayed to his bruised cheek. 'Since you're completely opposed there's no point in discussing it further. No doubt you'll keep me apprised of any developments in connection with Branksom.' With a bob of the head he was gone.

The intercom buzzed. Miss Pinkthorn said with relish, 'I have Mr Manhood on the line.'

'I'm out.'

'I have told him. He says that he wants a decision in the next week, otherwise he must ask for the return of the manuscript.'

'Say you'll speak to me about it. And Miss Pinkthorn –'

'Yes.'

'That manuscript must be found, do you understand?'

Between the understanding and the discovery falls the shadow. It was possible to admit frankly to W. Jones that his manuscript had been lost, but such an admission was repugnant, and what if he said that he had no carbon copy? And hadn't a set of lurid pictures been sent along with it? His early morning euphoria had disappeared and it was with a sensation of deepening gloom that he settled down to a session with Coldharbour and Treval- lion, the sales manager, about the weekly figures. These were not often encouraging, and the only bright spot in this particular week was a rush of orders for Bunce's novel. Coldharbour, no doubt nursing his Spatial Realist grievance, hardly spoke. Trevallion, a cherubic pipe-smoking figure, was on the other hand only too eloquently full of praise for the persistence of the sales staff. 'That's a difficult book,' he said of a novel which had received long reviews but sold a derisorily small number of copies. 'You gave us a tough one there, but the boys are really getting down to brass tacks.'

'I don't see much sign of it.'

'It's no good expecting miracles with a book like that. I tried it myself. Hard going.' Removing his pipe, Trevallion showed his teeth as though the toughness were a literal matter of digestion.

This weekly conference was usually enlivened by the presence of Max, who could conjure up miraculous possibilities out of the most unlikely books. In his absence it was a dull affair. Half-way through it the receptionist came in with a cable. Gilbert tore it open and read: MISSED TIGRESS HERE BY HOURS STILL STALKING PROBABLY GENEVA HUNT WORTH WHILE MAX. The cable had been sent from Salzburg. He read it to them. Coldharbour sniffed and rustled. Trevallion said, 'He's a live wire, Mr Bomberg, a real live wire.'

'Live wires cause short circuits,' Coldharbour commented with gloomy wit. Upon this note the conference ended.

Looking again at the cable he realized he had expected it to be from Virginia. He put through a call to Yugoslavia and was told that there would be an hour's delay. Should they keep the call in? He said that he would try again. Was there a connection between Max's tigress hunt and Virginia's holiday. 'Ridiculous,' he said aloud. 'Simply ridiculous.' The words did not banish the thought, which stayed with him like an ulcer pain until he went out to lunch.

'This is a real pleasure, Mr Welton.' Mel Branksom was tall and fresh-faced, his eyes solemn behind rimless spectacles. 'You know what I admire most about England? You're a people who know how to live.'

Gilbert smiled and handed his guest the menu. Branksom nodded as though it confirmed his view, and expanded on the statement.

'A place like this, it's got that blend of informality and what I can only call, you know, stateliness, that we don't seem able to manage in the States. It's friendly, it's relaxed, but it still says keep your distance, let's not be too familiar.'

He remembered Coldharbour's wounding words. 'Some people would say we keep our distance too much.'

'That isn't true. English tradition, that's something very valuable. Don't ever lose it.' The words were spoken seriously, as though tradition might be stolen like a diamond ring. 'I always say there are just two cities where I feel completely at home. One's New York and the other's London.'

Through the prawn cocktail and the steak Branksom expanded on his love for Britain and his respect for tradition. In what Gilbert had come to recognize as one American style he left a good deal of food on his plate while saying that it had been wonderful, refused pudding and cheese and asked, 'How's my good friend Max?'

'I think I told you. In Italy. Or Geneva.'

'A dynamic figure. A man who gets things done. I have a great respect for him. If I may say so you made an inspired choice when you took him in as a partner.'

'Not exactly a partner, a director. We're a family firm. My father founded Welton's.'

'Indeed I know that. Yours is a name we hold in the highest respect. A true independent British publishing house. That's what interests me.'

'What is, Mr Branksom?'

'Mel is what my friends call me. Or is that being too informal? I don't want to say anything that's, you know, out of line. I wish Max was here, he's got all that at his fingertips.' It occurred to Gilbert that anybody who thought Max had English manners at his fingertips must have an odd view of them, but he did not comment. 'What do you think about Africa?'

'The colour problem?'

'I mean as a market. The underdeveloped countries. But I needn't ask, it's a field you've explored already.' Gilbert still said nothing. He had no idea what Branksom was talking about. 'That series of educational textbooks you produced for Africa was really something.'

'Oh yes, I see what you mean.'

'You were one of the first in the field. A pity it was dropped, but still your name is known, you've got contacts. Now look, Gilbert, I'm a straightforward man, I like all the cards to be on the table, you know, face up. Then we know where we are, agreed?' It seemed safe to say that he agreed. 'Branksom, what do you think about when you hear the name? Don't tell me, I know. *Love Slaves of the Camps, How I Fooled the FBI, A Geisha Girl's Story*. That's not all we publish, mind. But it's not good enough.' This time it seemed safe not to say agreed. 'And I know it's not good enough. That's a bad image, I said to the Board, and we're going to change it.' Behind the rimless spectacles his eyes gleamed with determination. 'We're going into the educational field, and we're going into it in a big way. That's where you come in.'

'I see.'

'You've got a foothold in Africa. We haven't. I admit it. I'm playing the cards face up.'

'Yes.'

'Now the lines I'm thinking on are these. You've got the foothold, we've got the know-how. You produce a line of text-books covering the whole educational field. We back them. Welton name, Branksom money. And we really push them, which, you know, I don't think you were able to do. How does it sound?'

'Very interesting.'

'I like that.' Branksom slapped his knee and almost upset his coffee cup. 'There's your traditional British reserve. We've carried out market research, and believe me it's a wide-open market. There's room for everybody.'

'I should like to think about it.'

'Just what Max said your reaction would be. Of course we'd reckon to buy into Welton's.'

'You mean you'd want a majority shareholding?'

'Not necessarily.' He said vaguely, 'Leave it to the lawyers, all that. But this is the point. Whatever arrangement was made wouldn't affect the books you publish. Welton's stands for something that's entirely and absolutely British and I hope I've shown my respect for that.' Langridge-Wood passed their table, looked meaningfully at Branksom, smiled. No doubt knowledge of his interest was responsible for those cryptic phrases the other day. The American went on expressing his admiration of tradition for another twenty minutes. When they parted his handshake had the firmness of a partner sealing a verbal agreement to a gold claim.

Gilbert walked meditatively back to the office. This was the fate of British publishing houses no doubt, to be taken over by rimless-spectacled Americans who talked about tradition but would turn the Welton list into a blend of pornography and vulgar adventure. Or was Branksom genuinely interested in the export market and the profits to be made from it? In any case, what should he do? Obviously Max was in favour of considering the idea, and what Coldharbour thought was neither here nor there. Should he sell out, take the cash in hand and waive the rest? The rest, after all, was E.R.'s creation and had never been truly his own concern.

'Got you.' Where had the words come from? He was thirty yards from the office and the pavements seemed empty. The wild thought occurred to him that messages were being sent to his brain by remote control. Then W. Jones stepped out of a doorway, grinning. 'This morning they said you were out.'

'Quite right, I was.'

'So I came back after lunch. I waited.' He had difficulty in keeping pace with Gilbert and did so by means of hurried little steps alternating with an occasional leap. 'But you were in this morning. Come on, Mr Gilbert, admit it.'

'No.'

'Never mind.' He tapped with his left hand the briefcase that swung in his right. 'This will interest you.'

They were in front of the office. Reluctantly he faced W. Jones.

'Look, Mr Jones, I'm extremely sorry we've kept your manuscript so long. You'll have a decision on it quite positively in the next week. You have a carbon copy, of course?'

'Never mind. Let me show you this. It will make your hair stand on end.'

'I'm sorry. We can't consider any other manuscript until we've decided on this one.' He went through the door. W. Jones was at his heels, like some two-legged terrier. 'You'll have to take that as final.'

'I'm disappointed, Mr Gilbert. I thought at least you'd look at these.' Faithful Fido rejected, W. Jones turned away, then brightened. 'I shall come every day for news of my book. Every day. Five months, you know.'

Gilbert made his way furiously into the room where Miss Pinkthorn ruled the roost.

'I've just been pestered again by that man Jones. Has his manuscript been found?' She shook her head. 'This is intolerable. It must be in the office.'

'Since I was not here I can't express an opinion.'

'There's no need to look so pleased about it.' Miss Pinkthorn looked startled by these harsh words, worthy of E.R. himself, and responded by a faint simper. 'Type out a memo to everybody saying they're to make a thorough search through the whole of their files, in every desk and cupboard and so on. They're to drop everything except the most urgent work and then report personally to me. I'll sign it at once.'

In the office he again put through the call to Yugoslavia. Max's secretary brought in the evening paper and put it on his desk. He drew the paper towards him and leafed through the pages while listening to the small explosions and fragments of switchboard conversation that seemed inseparable from an overseas call. In less than a minute the operator said, 'Your number is ringing.'

Burr burr burr. The burring stopped.

'Is that the Hotel Splendid? Do you speak English?'

A pause. A voice said carefully, 'I speak English.'

'I want to speak to Mrs Welton. She is staying in your hotel.' Another pause. Heavy breathing. 'Do you understand?'

'I am writing down. Now I go away.'

He nodded and turned another page of the paper. There was something that might have caught his attention, but it had not done so and he could not be bothered to turn back and look for it. He began to read a paragraph about the American political situation. The writer seemed to think it was pretty gloomy.

'Hallo. Reception, Hotel Splendid.' This was a different voice, a woman's. Had he not been speaking to reception earlier?

'I wish to speak to my wife, Mrs Welton.'

'Veltin, Mrs Veltin?'

'Welton. W-e-l-t-o-n.'

'A moment.' He read the paragraph about America again. The voice said, 'No.'

'What's that?'

'No. Mrs Veltin. Not staying.'

'But that's impossible. She came last Thursday.' I remember the baggage, he wanted to say, it was clearly labelled. 'There must be some mistake.'

'I do not think so. A moment.'

She was replaced by a man's voice, hard and vigorous, which blasted away at him in French. He caught a phrase or two, which seemed to be to the effect that Virginia was not staying there, but most of it was unintelligible. He broke in, in English. 'I'm sorry, I haven't understood. Can you tell me in English?'

Pips sounded. The operator asked, 'Are you still connected?'

'Yes, yes, of course. In English,' he pleaded.

'Not so good.' A deprecating laugh. 'My English not so good. Name is Kornaro. Manager.'

'Mr Kornaro, listen. Is my wife staying at your hotel?'

'Yes.'

'Then can you fetch her to the telephone?'

'No. Not possible.'

'You mean she's out, on the beach or something.'

'I do not think so. Not on beach, I think.'

'Never mind then, if she's in the town. Ask her to ring me when she comes in. I'll give you the number.'

'Not in the town, I do not think.'

'Mr Kornaro, what are you telling me?'

'I beg your pardon.'

With what he felt to be conscious restraint he asked, 'Is my wife staying at your hotel or not?'

'She is staying.' Gilbert sighed with relief. 'But is not present now, I do not think.'

What the hell did the man mean? 'Do you mean she's left?'

Carefully explanatory, the voice said, 'She is here, but was not.'

'Don't you mean she was here but is not?' he said, with the feeling of playing an idiotic verbal game.

'I beg your pardon?'

There was a sputter of Serbo-Croat, succeeded by pips and severe crackling on the line. Then the dialling tone. He looked at the instrument in despair and returned it to the cradle. What was the piece in the paper that had not quite caught his attention, like a latch that just fails to engage? He turned back a page and then another without finding anything, then saw a heading and read the paragraph beneath it:

ACTRESS'S FLAT-MATE DIES FROM OVERDOSE

Fay Percival, well-known stage and TV actress, returned to her flat in Gayhill Gardens, Chelsea, early this morning to discover Georgie Drake, a friend sharing the flat with her, in an unconscious condition. She was suffering from barbiturate poisoning and died three hours later without recovering consciousness. Miss Drake had also appeared on TV and will be remembered as the landlady Mrs Potter in the long-running series 'Down Our Street.'

He closed his eyes. He saw not blackness but colours zigzagging across from left to right, blue, red, yellow. A voice said 'Mr Welton.'

He looked at the formidable bosom of Miss Pinkthorn. 'Are you feeling ill?'

'I'm all right. What do you want?'

'These are the memos you asked for. And here is a cable.'

From Virginia? He tore it open and read: STALKING OVER HOPE TO RIDE THAT TIGRESS TOMORROW MAX. He looked at the place of despatch. It had been sent from Zagreb in Yugoslavia. He made his decision.

'I want you to book me a flight to Dubrovnik. Tonight if there is one, if not as early as possible tomorrow.'

Raised eyebrows showed Miss Pinkthorn's disapproval. 'How long will you be away?'

'I'm not sure. Not more than two or three days. I'll arrange the return flight myself.'

'Mr Bomberg is also away. Will he be back tomorrow?'

'I'm not sure.'

'That leaves Mr Coldharbour.' She spoke with the air of one saying that left nothing at all. 'Shall I tell him?'

'I'll do it myself.' He signed the memos.

Chapter 12

The Departure

'Hello,' Fay Percival said. She was wearing skin-tight red pants and a man's jersey which flapped over her wrists. 'You're –'

'Gilbert Welton. I was married to Mary. Georgie.'

She stood staring at him, then said, 'Come in.'

He followed her into an untidy living-room where, without much surprise, he saw Bunce sitting cross-legged on the floor reading a book. He raised a hand without speaking and returned to the book. Looking at the cover Gilbert saw that it was a translation of the Koran.

Fay splashed whisky into a glass, handed it to him. 'We've been drinking. I wanted to smoke a little pot, but Jake said no. So what's on your mind, love? Why come to the wake?'

'I saw her on Thursday night.' Fay stared at him. 'We were talking at my house until, I don't know, after eleven. I think perhaps she rang me during the night.'

'Maybe she did. What about it?'

'I just wondered –' He could not have said what he wondered. 'Was she trying to get in touch with me?'

'Not that I know of.'

'Did she leave anything, any message?'

Fay plucked at the folds of the pullover. Her face was angry. 'No note, nothing. She'd been drinking ever since – for days.' Had she been about to say, since Thursday night? 'Yesterday the doctor says she drank herself silly, then took the pills. The phone was off the hook. Poor fat cow.' She poured more whisky into her own glass. 'It was about seven this morning when I found her. This stuff does nothing for me, you know that?'

Bunce closed the Koran. The lock of hair hung down. He looked serious and youthful. 'Interesting book. We ought to find an Arab priest.'

'Georgie had this idea she wanted to become a Muslim,' Fay said. 'It was a lot of crap.'

'You can't say that, Fay, how do you know? It might have

494

changed her life.' Bunce was at his quietest and most reasonable.

'Darling, she'd been with me a long time. She's been a scientologist, a priestess of a lot called Heaven on Earth and a member of something called the Order of St Bridget where they all used to beat each other with wet towels.'

'Nevertheless,' Bunce said mildly.

'Darling, you know *nothing* about it. She was a poor fat cow, that's all. And she's dead.' Fay burst into tears and ran from the room.

'Guilt,' Bunce said. 'We were at a party. Supposing we'd been here and all that.'

'And supposing I'd answered the telephone that night.'

'It was Thursday, you said? If she'd wanted, she could have rung you on Friday. Or at the week-end. If she'd wanted to.'

'I suppose so.' But he did not suppose so at all. Remembering that question, *did it all mean nothing?*, he could not doubt that she was asking for his help. From the New Life you could take steps in a dozen different directions, but all of them led downwards as you looked for instant ecstasy through loving your own sex or moving into a non-corporeal world or being beaten with wet towels. And the end of it was that you were laid out flat, hands folded, the whole thing was over and it had meant nothing. He was led to say, 'She wasn't a believer, you know. She expected heaven here, not somewhere else. It would be absurd to look for that Arab priest.'

'If you say so, Gil.' Bunce stretched out his hand towards the Koran.

'She's not here?'

'Gil, get a hold on yourself. They took her away to the hospital and then the morgue.'

'I see.'

'And I wouldn't go around talking about seeing her that night and her calling you. It can't have anything to do with anything, but once the cops get to asking questions.' Bunce, a youthful father-confessor, shook a sage head. Fay appeared in the doorway. 'She has to hold the shitty end of the stick, the inquest and all that. You don't.'

The picture of Mary blended with that of Virginia. Wavewashed, the face bloated, body rolled up on foreign shingle. Had

495

Mary looked peaceful, or had the pills blown up and distorted her features? Had she gone willingly or was there a moment when she wanted desperately to be saved? He longed to be away from the untidy room that somehow reeked of Mary, from the red-eyed actress in her floppy pullover and solemn pragmatical Bunce. Feeble rational good manners took over.

'If you're sure there's nothing I can do –'

Fay's laughter was raucous. 'Do, what did you ever do? You should hear the things Georgie told me. We had some good laughs. What kind of man is he, I'd say? And she'd answer, I only wish I knew. Poor bloody Georgie.'

'I came in because I have to go away. To join my wife. She's on holiday in Yugoslavia.'

'Virginia is certainly a lovely woman,' Bunce said.

With conscious pomposity he addressed a vacant space between them. 'I don't think there's any point in delaying my flight.'

'No point!' A great deal of laughter came out of Fay's small body. 'Darling, whatever you do there's no point.'

'Shut it, Fay.' New-style father figure Bunce did not speak unkindly. His unmade features had coalesced into a portrait of the Serious Young American, the one who understands that other people in the world have troubles and wants to help out. 'You can't do any good here, Gil. Forget you ever saw her that night, it didn't mean anything. And say hallo to your wife for me.' The Serious Young American shook hands, English-style. Fay gave him a bark of despairing laughter.

Forget you ever saw her that night: excellent advice, but how could he follow it? Hate, love, anger, ecstasy, are regarded as irrational states of feeling, but there is nothing more rational about remorse. On the way back to the office, to which he returned because of a compulsive need to clear his desk, he recalled in detail Mary's visit to the house. It was he who had taken her there quite deliberately, had exposed her to the sight of the apparently settled life he had made with another woman. That now seemed terrible. Perhaps the hour in his house had, on top of everything else, finally broken the small grip she still kept on life. Perhaps if he had gone to bed with her (but that would have been useless), if he had let her stay in the house, she would not have taken the pills. What had she said at the end? *You've said sorry too often,* and then *Good-bye, Gilbert.* Those last two words seemed now intensely meaningful, yet they had meant nothing at the time.

When he got out of the taxi it was raining. It was nearly six o'clock and his footsteps rang in the hall with the dead sound particular to empty offices. He went upstairs, switched on the light in his office, which already had the musty smell of evening. On his desk was the ticket for his flight at eight o'clock on the following morning and a memo from Miss Pinkthorn, with the points neatly tabulated:

(i)   Here is ticket.

(ii) You have no hotel booking. Will you please inform me of whereabouts, so that you can be reached if urgent.

(iii) Hope you have a good trip.

At the bottom was her clerically neat signature and a P.S. *Here is my home number in case you want it.* It occurred to him again that he knew nothing about Miss Pinkthorn. He could not believe that she existed as a person outside the office, living with the widowed sister. Or was she alone in a bedsitter, cooking supper each evening and then sitting in the room's single easy chair to watch life on the television screen? How much had E.R. known about Miss Pinkthorn, would he have known her telephone number?

In a calligraphy as neat as her own he wrote a reply saying that he would be at the Hotel Splendid, Dubrovnik, but that he expected to be back within forty-eight hours. He added details about two or three letters to be written, and then paused. It seemed that he should leave a message addressed to the unknown Miss Pinkthorn, but he found nothing to say.

He telephoned Coldharbour, but got no reply. No doubt he was gallivanting with Stanley. This meant another note, which he left on Coldharbour's desk. Then there was nothing to do but go home and pack.

Entering the empty house, choosing clothes with care and packing them neatly into the travelling wardrobe, he was aware

497

of loneliness. It came on him as a physical sensation, an aching in the stomach, as influenza may be preceded by a tickling in the throat and slight pains in the limbs which are warnings of the fever to come. The ache was associated with Mary, but it was much more deeply linked with the idea that he had lost Virginia and would never see her again. As he thought about her words and actions they seemed explicable only upon the basis that she had gone to meet a lover, but this disturbed him less than his inability to summon up the physical details of her appearance. Quite simply, he could not remember what she looked like.

He rummaged in a cupboard and found some photographs, one taken on holiday when she had her head thrown back laughing, another in a group at a publisher's cocktail party, but they were no help in explaining the discoloured arm that had so much disturbed him, the cold cheek he had kissed at parting. Among the pile of photographs he came upon one of Mary in the bookshop days, hands on hips, broadly smiling. Then there was another picture of her looking down with no particular pleasure at Matthew, a small bundle in her arms.

He had not written to Matthew. Drawing a sheet of paper out of the pigeon-hole in his desk he sat down to do so, and was conscious of overwhelming distaste and weariness. 'Dear Matthew,' he wrote, and stopped. What did you say? 'Your mother, whom you never much cared about, is dead, and your stepmother has disappeared'? Was it true that Matthew had never cared much about Mary and that she really hadn't wanted him? In Gilbert's recollection the stolid young man had been originally a stolid baby and then a stolid child, eating greedily everything put before him, crying rarely under the stresses of the New Life and Starting Again, accepting separation from his mother without many questions, asking about her only occasionally and showing affection for Virginia. Yet could all that really be true, and was it true that the only too vulnerable Mary had not cared about her son? He crumpled up the sheet of paper, threw it away, telephoned the club and found that they had a room free for the night. Before leaving the house he ran his hands over the sofa, then looked at the fingertips. It seemed to him that they tingled with some vibration from Mary's body.

He wrote ten lines to Matthew on the club paper, telling him about Mary, ordered an early morning call, played a game of snooker and then went to bed. He slept uneasily. At seven-fifteen in the morning he was at London Airport and at eight o'clock precisely the plane rose into the air.

PART TWO

Wife Lost

Chapter 1

Dubrovnik

The plane was no more than half full. Gilbert sat on the aisle. Beyond the empty seat next to him a thin faced beaky nosed man smiled encouragingly. He did not answer the smile but looked away over the aisle where a turbaned Sikh stared straight in front of him. A feeling that something terrible was waiting at the end of this journey oppressed him, like potential sickness. He considered the idea of going to the lavatory and rejected it.

'I am engaged on a quest as endless as that for the Holy Grail,' he said. 'If Virginia is in Dubrovnik she may not be pleased to see me and my journey will have been useless. It will be equally useless if she is deceiving me. I shall either learn nothing or I shall find out something I do not want to know.' As he spoke these words aloud one of the stewardesses passed by and flashed a smile at him, yet it did not seem that she heard him. Was something wrong with his vocal cords? He coughed experimentally, and was alarmed to hear no sound. Listening for the airplane engines he was met by blank silence. His hearing must have been affected by the height at which they were flying, even though the cabin was pressurized.

The Sikh across the aisle slowly turned his head and smiled, offering a gaping red mouth, then spoke. The words were not audible. He leaned across interrogatively and the Sikh bent over too so that their faces were almost touching. Two words came from the smiling lips: 'Only connect.'

Staring astonished at the face that grinned into his own he was aware of the body of the stewardess, navy blue thighs pressed against his leaning head, hand holding out a piece of paper. The Sikh jerked his own head back, returned to his eyes front position, and now it was the stewardess who bent over him and whose mouth opened to show pink gum, white teeth. She was saying, what was it she was saying? He strove to understand the ribbons of words in her mouth but then she closed it with a snap and her fingers significantly touched his palm as she pressed into it the piece of paper she held. It was a cable and as he read the words SCREWING YOUR WIFE HERE WHAT A TIGRESS his throat protested, choking him as he tried to speak, to protest to the stewardess who said nothing but put her hand on his shoulder. Is it from Dubrovnik? was what he wanted to say, but the pressure of her hand distracted him. Why was he unable to speak?

'All right, old boy?' It was the beaky nosed man. He removed his hand from Gilbert's shoulder.

'Thank you.' He sat up. He had fallen over sideways and had a crick in his neck.

'Feeling a bit Harry groggers? You sounded desperate. Funny noises.' He put his head to one side and made gurgling sounds.

'I apologize.'

'Not to worry. Name's Painter, Jerry Painter. Not that I paint jerries, mind you.'

'Gilbert Welton.'

'Business or pleasure bound?'

'A little of both, I suppose.'

'Business for me.' He whipped out a card and handed it over. Gilbert read: *G. R. Painter, Topline Car Hire*. 'Started up a few months ago out there and something's rotten in the state of Denmark. Touch of the old Slav temperament I expect. Painter the troubleshooter, here I come. Sure you're all right?'

'Thank you.'

'Just have a zizz myself.' He nodded, closed his eyes. Within five minutes his mouth was slightly open, he looked like a dead man. On the other side of the gangway the Sikh stared expressionlessly ahead of him.

Heat shimmered on the tarmac as he walked across it with Painter. Gilbert's ears were tuned, as always at airports and railway stations, to catch a message for him on the Tannoy, a message that never came.

'Where are you staying, old boy?'

'The Splendid.'

'I'm at the Imperial. What about painting the old place a bit red tonight?' He laughed heartily. 'Joke. But I hear they've got a casino.'

'I'm afraid I can't manage that. I'm meeting my wife.'

'Oh well. Here's my bus and there's yours. See you around.'

He got into the bus labelled *Hotel Splendid*. As they moved out of the forecourt and jolted along the road to the city his journey seemed totally absurd. Two clear, different but equally embarrassing pictures came into his mind. In the first he went up to Virginia's room, entered and found her tussling on the bed with a man. In the second she lay on the beach wearing dark glasses which she slowly removed. The most disturbing thing about these encounters was that when she stared at him from the bed or took off the dark glasses she showed no sign of recognition.

As they rounded a bend he had a glimpse of the walled city, looking like a bit of a film set. The Splendid Hotel, however, proved to be a few hundred yards short of the old city, a modern slab overlooking the sea. His bus companions murmured their approval as they drove into the entrance. The place had the reassuring anonymity of an international hotel. There was nothing too offensively Yugoslav about it.

In the foyer he was plunged at once into a tourist holiday world. Men and women wearing briefs and bikinis, sometimes covered by gay dressing-gowns, came up the steps from the beach, stalking over to the lift. All German or English, bronzed and with an air of suppressed energy, they seemed of a different species from the pallid bus passengers, who looked at them enviously. A travel courier, a bronzed girl with long dark hair and some organizational badge pinned on her, marshalled them over to the reception desk behind which two girls allotted rooms, handing out keys as though they were performing a conjuring trick. When his time came a small dark girl said, 'Your passport, please.'

'I don't have a reservation. My name is Welton. My wife is staying here.'

'Please, your passport.'

'If you can just tell me the number of her room.'

'Your passport.'

Furiously he slapped his passport on the counter. A disapproving murmur rose from those behind him at this display of petulance. The girl took it and pushed a pad towards him. 'You will please to complete this.'

'No no.' He shoved back the pad. 'Look, let me speak to Mr Kornaro. We've talked already on the telephone.'

'Telephone.' She pointed across the hall. He snatched back the passport, relinquished his place in the queue and followed the direction of her finger to find that she had directed him to a telephone kiosk. With an awareness of his own inanity he entered the box and ruffled the pages of the directory it contained, then came out and stood on the steps, looking down at the small iron tables where groups of men and women sat in the sun. He did not see Virginia. He returned to the desk when the last of the party had gone. The girl said, 'Your passport, please.'

'All I want is the number of Mrs Welton's room.'

'You do not have a reservation, then I must have your passport.'

Playing the next move in this repeated gambit, but omitting mention of the telephone, he said 'I want to speak to Mr Kornaro.'

'Mr Kornaro.' She appeared to be assessing his qualifications for an interview, then lifted the flap of the reception counter and emerged from behind it. 'Come.'

He followed her down a corridor. She knocked on a door filled with frosted glass and went in. Then she came out and opened the door. As Gilbert passed her she gave him a hostile look.

Mr Kornaro shook hands warmly. His smile showed three gold teeth. 'I understand you have a complaint about our hotel. I am sorry.'

'No, no, I have no complaint.'

'I am glad.' His smile broadened. 'This is the finest hotel in Yugoslavia.'

'Mr Kornaro, I don't think the receptionist understood –'

'A very fine lady, very efficient. Is that word correct?'

'Quite correct. We talked on the telephone. I rang you up from London.'

Mr Kornaro, one admonitory finger lifted, walked round to a cupboard behind his desk. A key from the bunch at his waist opened it and he produced a bottle of colourless liquid and two glasses which he carefully filled to the brim. He handed over one of these glasses with an inclination of the head that was almost a bow. Gilbert recognized the faint oiliness of slivovitz.

'Cheers. Down the hatch.' He drank half the glassful in one

swallow. Gilbert sipped and felt the liquid run over his tongue and burn his gullet. 'You like our beautiful city of Dubrovnik,' the manager stated rather than asked. 'It is the most beautiful city in Yugoslavia.'

'Mr Kornaro.' He spoke desperately and with unusual speed. 'I'm pleased to be here, but I want to talk to my wife. Mrs Welton, Virginia Welton. She's staying in this hotel. I talked to you about it yesterday. That's all I want, I have no complaints of any kind. I'm sure the Hotel Splendid is – splendid,' he finished feebly.

'Ah *ha*.' Mr Kornaro threw back his head and laughed. 'You make a joke. Very good.'

'What's that?'

'The Hotel Splendid is – splendid. Very good, I shall not forget.' He drank the rest of his slivovitz, poured a refill. 'And we spoke before, I remember it well.' He patted the telephone on his desk affectionately, it might have been an old friend. 'Mrs Welton, your wife, she was a very beautiful woman.'

'If you'll just give me her room number.' He stopped. Mr Kornaro was shaking his head. 'What's wrong?'

'I have told you on the telephone. She was not here.'

'What do you mean?'

'She has no complaints. But she is left.'

'That's impossible.' He knew that it was not at all impossible.

'She stays here three days. Then she goes. But not with complaints. I think she is not knowing that you come here, wasn't it so? So perhaps she is sad.'

'She didn't know, that's right. My plans were changed. What forwarding address did she leave?'

'I am sorry, English is not good.' Was there something inimical about the manager's stare?

'Where did she go to?'

'Ah yes. I think she is going to Mostar. A beautiful city, very Turkish. Perhaps then on to Sarajevo.'

The change in Gilbert Welton could have been timed from this moment. As he continued to ask Kornaro questions, about the best way of reaching Mostar and the hotels Virginia might have stayed at there, about the precise details of her departure (but he learned nothing more except that on Saturday she had said that she was tired of staying in one place, she was going to wander around), he was conscious that he had acquired the kind of knowledge that brings with it freedom. He knew now that Virginia had left him. She had gone to meet somebody in Mostar, in Sarajevo, what did it matter? She was lost to him, and he was able to accept the fact of loss. He remembered lines from a poem read long ago:

> For he is no Orpheus,
> She no Eurydice.
> She has truly packed and gone
> To live with someone
> Else, in pleasures of the sun,
> Far from his kingdoms of despair
> Here, there, or anywhere.

But the emotion he felt in a strange city, a new country, was not despair but relief.

'Today you look at our beautiful city of Dubrovnik,' Kornaro said masterfully. 'Tomorrow you take the bus at eleven hundred hours, arrive Mostar fifteen thirty hours, find your wife, very good.' Gilbert agreed, although he was not sure that he would go to Mostar. *He is no Orpheus, she no Eurydice.* He lacked the will for pursuit of her into those underground regions of the heart. He went up to the small neat room provided for him, which had a balcony overlooking the sea, unpacked his travelling wardrobe, lay down on the bed and fell asleep. He woke an hour later refreshed, changed into sleeveless shirt and thin trousers and went to look at Mr Kornaro's beautiful city of Dubrovnik.

It was in fact a beautiful place. He walked through the Ploce gate into the carless city and was aware at once of the friendly buzzing sound which comes from a group of human beings together, when it is not overlaid by the noise of vehicles. The prevailing colour was grey, everything was or looked old. He stood outside a café staring down the long central Placa filled with human beings and empty of traffic, then walked slowly down the street looking into the shop windows that seemed to be selling almost exactly the same hats, scarves and blouses, silverware, wooden trays and salad bowls. The sun was hot on his head and seemed to be burning his eyes. He entered a building on his right to get away from the glare and found himself in a cloister. In the middle of it was a small garden with a fountain playing. The coupled columns were surmounted with stone heads and curious animal figures.

When he married Virginia they had taken a car across the Channel and spent their honeymoon touring Brittany. Somewhere, in a small town the name of which he could not remember, they had walked hand in hand down a street like the Placa and entered a small cloister garden like this one, with a central fountain. Thinking themselves alone they had embraced and kissed passionately, to see a moment later that they were being watched by a withered old woman who carried a basket of flowers. As he thought of this there was a movement at the end of the cloister. Two monks in brown habits appeared and walked slowly past him. '*Dobro veche*,' they said, and bared their heads. It occurred to him that he was able to think about this memory without emotion. A small but vital operation had been performed, the surgeon's scissors had said *snip* and removed suffering.

On the hotel terrace the pallid passengers had gathered round the travel girl, who flashed leaflets at them. Phrases came over to the table where he sat with eyes half closed looking out across the sea. 'Half day on Lokrum . . . caves of Kotor . . . lobster for lunch . . .' There were murmurs of delighted laughter.

'Will you come with us, Lucy?' one of the men asked.

'Of course. I am here to show you the ropes.'

'I'd love to see them. If my wife weren't here, that is. How about it, Helen, is it all right for Lucy to show me the ropes?' Loud laughter. This was what they had paid for, the holiday spirit. He closed his eyes completely. His body seemed light, even empty. Perhaps this was the way women felt after having a baby.

There was the sound of chairs scraping back. Feet moved past him. A voice said 'Hallo.'

He opened his eyes. The courier was standing beside his chair. The badge on her shirt said *Paradise Travel*. 'Hope I didn't wake you up.' He shook his head. 'You were on the bus. Are you with Paradise? No, well, I thought you might be. Some people don't like to crowd round. You're independent?'

The phrase amused him. 'Yes.'

'You looked a bit out of things. But perhaps you don't like being organized.'

Something decisive about the way she spoke appealed to him. 'Why don't you sit down? Have a drink.'

She considered the idea, and ordered Cinzano and soda. 'It's the Yugo substitute really, but drinkable.'

She was dark with lots of long hair, and what he could see of her body was completely brown. It was almost too much of an effort to speak to her, but he managed it. 'Lucy, that's a very English name, you don't look English.'

'Basically I'm Israeli. No, that's wrong, basically I'm Australian but I was born in Israel, lived there till I was sixteen.'

'Not now?' He heard his distant voice asking, although he did not care about the answer.

'I got away. I'll never go back.' Something about the tone startled him. He looked at her. In the gaze of her blue eyes staring at him from under thick brows there seemed to be a sexual invitation. He asked whether she lived in England.

'Sometimes. I'm going to change and swim. Coming?'

She cut the water with firm attacking strokes, so that he had a job to keep up with her. Later they lay side by side on the concrete stage belonging to the hotel that pushed out into the water.

'You don't look as if you're here on holiday.'

Should he say *I came to look for my wife but have given up the search*? 'I'm a publisher.'

'Yes?'

'I came out to look for a colleague.' The effort of constructing a reasonable story defeated him.

'I don't care, you know. There's no need to tell me lies.'

'I'm not.' He raised himself on one arm to deny it. Her navel winked at him. 'You might say I'm at a loose end. It's hard to explain.'

'Then don't.' Her eyes were remarkably fine, a piercing blue. 'You're going to burn. I'll oil you. Turn over.'

As her hands moved on his back and shoulders, then along his legs, he felt the stirring of desire. With the decisiveness that marked her most trivial actions she put back the top on the bottle.

'My father looked like you. That withdrawn look. It says don't come too near. Is that what you're like?'

'I suppose it is, in a way. Do you think it's a bad way to be?'

'I think perhaps I do. He's dead, my father. Five years ago.'

'I'm sorry.'

'Why be sorry, why should you care? Though he was a good man in lots of ways. A super person, they said at my English school.'

'You went to school in England?'

'For a bit. When I said I wouldn't stay in the kibbutz. All the girls said *super* and *I fancy him.*' She looked at him fiercely. 'I expect they do still.'

'It can't be that long ago.'

'Five years. I'm twenty-two.' A voice said 'Lucy.' She got up. 'Do you think I'm father-fixated?'

'I shouldn't think it likely.'

'Because I fancy you, you know that don't you?'

'Lucy.' A large bouncing girl stood beside them. She wore an incongruous pinafore dress with a badge that said *Irma, Goethe Travel.* Her blonde hair burst out from a yachting cap. 'Lucy, it is about the trip to Lokrum. Some people who want tickets, they say you promised. Hallo,' she said to Gilbert who scrambled up.

'My name's Gilbert Welton.'

'English manners, I love them. We shake hands, isn't that right?' They shook hands.

He felt that he should say something to Lucy, but she waved an arm, said that she would see him around and was gone. He watched the two girls going along the concrete and up the steps, then sank back on to his cushions and closed his eyes. Lucy, fierce-eyed and dramatic, and surely a little ridiculous, appeared behind the lids.

He saw her again that evening after dinner. She stopped beside his table. She wore a dark blue sleeveless linen dress which accentuated the darkness of her skin. The fat man who had talked about being shown the ropes was by her side. 'There is a little party going to the casino this evening. If you'd like to come along you will be welcome.'

'Thanks. I'll think about it.'

The fat man said, 'Don't worry about losing, Lucy's coming as our mascot. Can't lose with her.'

'I don't give any guarantee. You might lose the shirt off your back.' Her tone was almost coquettish. 'We meet at eight-thirty in the entrance hall.'

What am I doing here, he asked himself, what am I thinking of? He felt nothing more in relation to Lucy than the mild sexual interest natural for a man in his forties who has received instead of making advances, or so he told himself, but at eight-thirty he was in the entrance hall.

He was not attracted by the idea of winning a quantity of dinars which, as notices made clear to him and as Lucy emphasized, could not be taken out of the country, but in any case he lost small sums steadily. When he was a couple of pounds down he stopped playing and watched the others. The fat man, whose name was Briars, reacted to every drop of the ball with shrieks of laughter in which his wife joined him. It was as though they were applause machines at a TV comedy show.

'There's ten dinars down the drain,' Briars roared. 'Ten smackers right down the plughole.'

'No dear, I'm *winning*,' his wife said. 'Three times now I've won on red, what do you think this time?'

'You've been winning on red, I've been losing on black,' Mr Briars cried in an ecstasy of mirth.

Nails dug into the palm of his hand. Lucy said, 'Not having fun?'

'I shouldn't call it exactly gay.' He indicated a particularly grim-looking croupier who was pushing chips towards one of their party. 'He might smile.'

'It is against their principles, you see. They think gambling is wrong, but they want dollars and pounds and German marks, so they allow it. But it all has to be respectable and dull, don't expect them to smile.' Her forefinger explored his palm, curled round his own index finger, moved gently up and down, was withdrawn. She moved away.

'How's it going, old man?' He turned to confront Painter. 'Made your fortune yet? You don't have to tell me, nobody ever made a fortune here. Where's the better half?'

'My wife is not here.'

'On your Franchot Tone? I tell you what, young Milo in my office here told me of a little place in the Old Town where you can see a bit of life. What do you say?' About Painter's confiding beaky look there was something manic.

'I've had me chips.' Briars had two chips left, one red and one white. He stuck them over his eyes and whined, 'Can anyone spare a dinar for a poor blind man?' Heads were turned, a group of muscle-bound Germans spoke to each other and laughed. They're saying it's the English, Gilbert thought, not the mad but the poverty-stricken English who don't know how to lose a few dinars.

Briars dropped the chips out of his eyes, caught them neatly. 'Let's get away before they take me shirt. Lucy, I thought you were going to be our mascot, I thought you never lost.'

Lucy's smile was slightly foxy, it made her look wary and showed her small even teeth. 'I never lose because I don't bet.'

General laughter. 'Got you there, Tom,' said Mrs Briars.

'There's a café by the water where you can get slivovitz. Or a cup of tea,' Lucy announced. A chorus of joyful yelps greeted these last words.

'How about it?' Painter asked. 'Might have some fun, bring on the dancing girls kind of thing.'

'No, thanks. I'm really with the hotel party.'

'I expect you're right.' He sank from manic to depressive in a moment. 'Bound to be a washout here, girls dancing in a blanket. Dead and alive hole.' As Gilbert moved away he called, 'Give my regards to the trouble and strife.'

Tea at the café was approved, it was agreed that Lucy knew her way around. Gilbert found himself next to Briars.

'Very very nice little kid. No flies on her, either. Man in one of those shops in the what d'ye call it, main street, tried to overcharge the wife, she was on to it, you should have heard her. Of course she's clever. Father's a diplomat.'

'Really?'

'She told Mrs Craxton. Somewhere out in the Far East. Hong Kong is it? You can see she's got class.'

Had she got class? Watching her talking easily to the party of a dozen men and women, keeping them amused, responding with apparent pleasure to the idiotic jokes of the men and listening patiently to the women as they talked about their homes in Woking or Bromley, he wondered if that was the right word and decided that it was not. She had a feral quality, there was something uncontrolled about her, she gave the impression of playing a part. In the café he was content to sit and let the waves of conversation roll over him. His body felt anaesthetized so that a pin stuck in it would have remained unperceived, and as they left the café in a noisy group and went on making their ugly English noise as they walked through the quiet town, he seemed to be removed from any conscious sensation. On the way back Lucy did not acknowledge his individual presence in any way. In the entrance hall they parted, with assurances that it had been a good day.

'So tomorrow is this place called Kotor, is that right?' asked anxious Mrs Strong, or perhaps it was Long, because confusingly there was one of each in the party.

'No. Tomorrow is Lokrum, an afternoon trip.'

'But what shall we do in the morning?' Mrs Strong/Long asked. 'I mean, there's not much to *do*, is there? Will you be here?'

He left half a dozen of them talking in the hall, with Lucy in the middle of them. In his room he put away his clothes tidily as usual, got into bed and fell asleep at once. The sleep must have been light, for it was only twenty minutes later that he was wakened by a gentle tapping.

He opened the door which he had locked. She moved quickly inside and stood with her back against the wall, looking at him. The room was still in darkness and he could not see the expression on her face as she said 'You certainly took your time.'

'I'm sorry, I didn't realize.' He abandoned that sentence. 'I fell asleep.'

She began to laugh.

Chapter 2

The Second Day of Love

Is there a technique of seduction? Books have been written about it, but it often seems that they are evasions rather than discussions of reality. Many couples have the *Kama Sutra* on their shelves, but how many practise the activities described in it? Few significant variations of the sex act are possible, the refinements are elaborations of a central theme. This at least would have been his view if he had been compelled to formulate it. Certainly he performed no physical act with Lucy that he had not undertaken at some time with Mary or Virginia. Yet the sensations he felt were unlike anything he could remember.

It was four-thirty when she said, 'I must go.'

In the dawn light he looked at the dark hair hiding her face, pushed it aside. 'Love,' he said, and repeated the word questioningly. 'Love?'

'I've got to go.'

'We must talk.'

'What about?'

'We haven't talked.' This was not literally true, but their conversation like that of most people making love had been partly specific, about what they were doing, and partly inane.

She ran her hand over his body, then touched his face, fingers wandering about nose and eye sockets. 'I don't know what it is about you, some bloody thing. I think it must be that you're like my father, don't you?'

'We ought to talk about things. I've got a wife, I told you that. I don't know anything about you.'

'I've got all the right things in the right places. What else do you want to know?'

'Everything. I want to know everything about you.'

'I think –'

'What?'

'Nothing.' She rolled over on top of him, found his mouth, bit his lip. 'Christ, I do fancy you. I'd better get out of here.' She dressed nervously, almost angrily, while he lay in bed and watched. 'I look a wreck.'

He got out of bed and moved towards her. She averted her face.

'I never kiss good-bye. Bad luck.'

'When am I going to see you?'

'I'll be busy most of the morning. You saw what it's like. Half-past eleven or as near as I can make it. On the terrace.'

After she had gone he opened the french windows and stood on the balcony, looking at the city in the pearly light of early morning. It was already warm, but when he got back into bed he was shivering. The shivers were pleasurable, they ran through his body as though created by fingers. His lips felt twice as thick as usual, the soft tissue inside them was swollen when he ran his tongue over it. His body felt as though it had been bruised by hers. Was he deceiving himself in thinking that his feelings had little to do with sex, when they were so firmly grounded on it? He embraced this contradiction, although he had no idea of how it would be possible to phrase what he wanted to say. 'What begins as sex ends as love' – something like that? The feeling of well-being he had, as though his body had been simultaneously drained and satisfied, was no doubt sexual in origin . . .

It was nine-thirty when he woke again.

Conflation of red and green umbrellas, blue sea, brown or white bodies, grey of city walls. A mess of colours. Conflation also of shapes, forked people, circular tables, wedge shaped concrete nose pushing into the sea. A mess of shapes. Colours and shapes merging into one. Down the steps strode Mr Kornaro, incongruous in black jacket and striped trousers, the Yugoslav manager's wear.

'Telephone. For you.'

How long ago it was that he had sat in Mr Kornaro's office. He looked at the receiver standing on the table with disquiet. What did its blackness contain?

'Mr Welton. I thought you should know that –'

'Who is that?' The voice was completely strange.

Silence, then outraged tones. 'This is Miss Pinkthorn. Mr Welton, is that you?'

No one of that name or character known here, disappeared I'm afraid, Mr Welton has disintegrated, the phrases went through his mind but were not on his tongue. 'Hallo, Miss Pinkthorn. I didn't recognize your voice.'

'Are you enjoying yourself? Did you find Mrs Welton quite well?'

Both questions were unanswerable in Pinkthorn terms. A simple affirmative seemed proper and he gave it.

'I thought you should know that we've had another cable from Mr Bomberg. He is at the Hotel Europa, in Sarajevo. He wants to get in touch with you. I haven't given him your address, because I didn't know if you'd still be there.'

'Yes.'

'What shall I do then? Shall I give him your number, or will you telephone him?'

'Yes.' The affirmative repeated.

'Mr Welton? Mr Welton, what would you like me to do?'

He ran his tongue round swollen tissue. 'You can leave it to me.'

'You'll get in touch yourself?' He did not reply. 'Are you there?'

'Certainly, yes.' *And how is every little thing in your life, Miss Pinkthorn?* 'And how is everything, Miss Pinkthorn?'

'Mr Welton, can you hear me properly?'

'I have to go now. Wanted here. Urgently. Keep in touch.' He put back the receiver. How easy it is to cut yourself off from the boring and disagreeable, how easy after all to make a new start. He laughed at the thought. Mr Kornaro laughed with him. The slivovitz bottle was produced. There was a little joke about the Hotel Splendid being splendid, an inquiry about his wife. He said that he would stay another day, perhaps two.

She was sitting on the terrace drinking Cinzano and soda, with an open folder in front of her. She put away the folder.

'I'd forgotten what you looked like. Your eyes. I've never seen eyes so blue.' She did not acknowledge the remark. 'There are lots of things I wanted to say. For me this kind of thing is not – not casual.'

'I don't know what you mean. Nothing is casual.' She took a sip of her drink. 'You want to know about me.' He had meant to talk about himself, but he listened. 'My father was a Jew, did you know that? I told you I was brought up on a kibbutz.'

'Yes, you said that. It must have been interesting.'

'Awful. I ran away when I was fourteen. They found me and brought me back. When I was sixteen I ran away again. For good.'

'To school in England?'

She took out a packet of cigarettes, lighted one, talked between puffs. 'The kibbutz, do you know what it does to you? You aren't a person any more, you do what everybody else does, you're part of the group. The collective ego, they call it. You want to break something, you don't do it because it's anti-social. You want to make love, you don't do that, because that might be anti-social too, it would disturb the group. Love, it just doesn't exist, it isn't there. Do you know what I wanted more than anything else when I was eight? For my mother to tuck me up in bed at night. In my kibbutz it wasn't allowed, mothers weren't allowed to be possessive.'

He remembered Mary's indifference to Matthew. 'Sometimes mothers don't want to have much to do with their children.'

'All right. But in the kibbutz it wasn't *allowed*. It broke my mother's heart, she died when I was eleven. He was a bastard.'

'Who?'

'My father.'

'Somebody told me he was a diplomat.'

'Yes. He gave it up, joined the kibbutz.'

'What sort of diplomat?'

'Consul. In Hong Kong.'

'And you said he was a super person.' He found *super* a difficult word to say.

'I said he was a good man. He just had this thing about permissiveness, the kibbutz way of life and all that. I'll never be part of any group, I'm a separate person.'

'You're unique.' Idiotic, idiotic.

'But are you separate too?' She did not wait for him to reply. 'Are you coming to Lokrum after lunch? Over there.'

She pointed to an island covered by pines that spread over it like a green helmet. He wanted to ask if it would be possible for them to be alone there, but did not do so when she added that of course it would be with the hotel party. He said that he would go. Simply to be near her, to watch her, would be a pleasure.

'Super.' She opened the folder, made a note.

'Lucy.' He wanted to say that their talk had been inadequate. Instead he asked, 'What's your other name?'

'Spandrell. That's what I call myself here. I took it out of a book. By Aldous Huxley.'

'Lucy too?'

'Yes, she's in the book too.'

'But why? What's your real name?'

'Too hard to pronounce. You can call it Anna.'

'After Karenina?'

She laughed. 'As a matter of fact, yes. I've got to go. See you.'

On the short boat journey he sat next to the brawny Irma, no-where near Lucy whom he now thought of as Anna, and as soon as they stepped ashore she was surrounded by the hotel party, talking, making crude jokes. Accompanied by hairy-legged Englishmen wearing shorts that came down to their knees, and trailed by their wives, she set off up a path through the pine woods without so much as a glance at him. He stood sulkily waiting for her to turn and suggest that he should join them, but she did not look back. Instead Irma pounced on him.

'Mr Welton, you will come along with me.'

'I was with the other party.'

'I am going to better places. And I have not so many.'

Unwillingly he joined her cortège, which was German instead of English. All the men carried cameras, the formidable thighs of the women strained their tight shorts, their brawny shoulders reddened like meat in the sun. She strode along, arms swinging like a sergeant-major's, talking all the time in German. He left them and went down a path on his own.

For the next three hours he wandered through pine woods, scrambled down from one of them into a small bay in which he swam, and then lay on his back in the sun thinking about Anna. Had she been telling him the truth about the kibbutz, was her father ever consul in Hong Kong, what was she really like? One part of his mind fastened on these questions while another was aware of their irrelevance to his feelings. Most of us under the stress of passion are capable of believing two different things at the same time. So Gilbert was now able to build an image of Anna which ignored oddities of speech and behaviour.

On the beach at Lokrum he constructed a relationship between them which involved Starting Again. The idea was not only possible but easy. By selling out to the American he would have enough money to live on for at least ten years. They would settle in a small English country town, he would open an antique shop, selling only things that he enjoyed seeing and touching. In time he would become in his own small way celebrated, people would say, 'You can be sure that anything you buy from Gilbert Welton will be marked by his own impeccable taste.' Anna would go on fancying him. A satisfied vanity took possession of him as he dwelt on the fact that at the time he married Mary, Anna could not have been born. To have slept with her was a kind of triumph, although their sexual contact was only the beginning of the unsuspected tenderness that he felt opening out in him.

When he returned to the landing stage she was the first person he saw. 'Where the hell have you been all this time, where have you *been*?'

'Sunbathing. Swimming. On my own.'

'You knew I couldn't come with you. Don't tell me you thought we could go off on our own. I'm conducting tours to Paradise, remember?'

He smiled and said that he knew it. On the way back in the boat he sat next to Craxton, a puffy man whose forehead and legs were turning beetroot colour. 'You missed a most interesting tour, very instructive. This island, Lokrum, belonged to the Archduke Maximilian, the one who was killed in Mexico. I saw a film about him once. Did you get to the park?'

'No, I didn't.'

'Very keen on plants, he was, Maximilian. I've got quite a collection myself, but there were some I'd never even heard of. She knew, though, knew all the names.' He pointed to Anna who was talking to Briars and his wife in the stern. 'Of course she ought to.'

'She'd learned them, you mean?'

'Her father was a botanist, spent a lot of time up the Amazon. Took her with him when she was so high, taught her all the names.'

What can be more conventional than an account of the second day of love? Passion has been succeeded by reflection. Will the pleasures you enjoyed be repeated, did they ever happen at all or were they partly imaginary? Gilbert lay in his bed staring at the dark ceiling, the door this time unlocked, and by midnight was convinced that she would not come to him. Ten minutes later she was in his bed.

The physical transports of the second day of love, how are they to be described, and what is the point of describing them since inevitably they repeat the first? The uses of mouths, hands, penis, vagina, were all as they had been before. There was a difference for him, however, in that he felt the tenderness that had pervaded him upon the beach at Lokrum. He spoke the word love to her, said positively *I love you* for the first time to the black hair spread out beside him and the turned-away face. She did not reply.

'I love you, Karenina. Anna Karenina.'

'It's sex you're talking about. What about your wife?'

'She's gone.'

'What do you mean, gone?'

'I don't know where she is. But it doesn't matter. I thought it did, but it doesn't.'

'I know the name for you. The man who lost his wife.'

'No, that's not the name.'

'What is, then?'

'The man who found himself. I want to live with you.'

'How would we live? Tell me.'

He told her about Gilbert Welton, the man who had made a first foolish marriage and thought that he wanted to be a bookseller, and then married again and lived in St John's Wood and ran a publishing firm in which he was not interested, the man whose tedious skin would be sloughed off when they started again in the English countryside. He talked about the antique shop and the selectiveness with which they would choose the things that they cared to stock.

'I don't know anything about antiques.'

'I should teach you.' That would be part of the pleasure in their relationship. He said easily the kind of thing he had never said before to any woman. 'You are so beautiful that you would be certain to love beautiful things.'

'Wouldn't it all be like what you did before? With your first wife, I mean?' It seemed sufficient answer to say that she was not Mary. She yawned. 'It might be rather a drag. But you're sweet, you know that?'

'I don't like sweet. It means old. I like "I fancy you."'

'Age has nothing to do with it,' she said vehemently. 'I hate young men, they're boring.' She touched his face. 'I don't much fancy the country, not in England. Couldn't we live in Italy, I'm mad about Italy?'

'Perhaps,' he said doubtfully. 'As long as you're with me. We'd have enough to live on anyway.' He turned her head with his hands so that she faced him. The shutters were open, her wide eyes looked into his own. 'Do you want to be with me, Anna Karenina?'

'Yes. I can't really speak Italian, only a few words. Could I have a poodle?'

'What?'

'A poodle. I do think they're super dogs, I'm mad about them. So artificial, and still they're real.'

'You can have what you like, as long as you go on fancying me.'

Their conversation went on like this, conventional, repetitive. She sighed when he asked if her father had been a botanist, and said he had been fifty different things. 'We'll go away from here then, go together? You'll give up Paradise?'

'They won't like it.'

'I thought you didn't care about that kind of thing.'

'Hell, no, why should I? Let's go straight to Italy.'

'I ought to go back to England first. But I want you to come with me.' He felt that once out of his sight she would disappear.

She left him again at half past four, but before doing so she woke him up. 'Something I wanted to say. We're separate people. I don't like the way you try to make us the same.'

'Separate people,' he said drowsily.

'You're not responsible for me, I'm not responsible for you. I do what I want.' Her voice was shaking with emotion. He agreed. She kissed him, dressed, briefly touched his face again with her lips, left.

This time he did not fall asleep.

Chapter 3

The Last Day of Love

In the morning he felt the need of action, action that would make the happenings of the night irrevocable. Boats must be burned, bonds cut. He ought to speak to Coldharbour, speak to Max, tell them that he wanted to accept the American offer and was going to resign from the firm. A shrinking from action went with this desire for it. He felt that if he let the past come into contact with the present it would destroy the world in which he was going to live with Anna. It was with reluctance that after breakfast he made a call to Max in Sarajevo, with relief that he learned that all the lines were engaged. Afterwards he looked for Anna, and found her in the foyer with Briars, the Strong/Longs and half a dozen others. The English contingent was in a rebellious and inharmonious mood. Fat Briars, no longer jolly, was their spokesman.

'It's a bit much, don't you agree? One of the best hotels in the place, or supposed to be. You would think they might make an effort.' He appealed directly to Gilbert.

'What sort of effort?'

'Eggs and bacon. Bacon and tomato. Something more than the old bread and marmalada.'

'You must understand that they don't eat things of that kind for breakfast,' Anna said patiently. 'You can have boiled eggs, or cheese. They won't offer anything else.'

'Cheese for breakfast, I ask you,' said Mr Strong/Long.

'I'm not blaming this little girl.' Briars patted Anna's shoulder. 'She's doing a grand job, as they say. But you take the trip this morning to – what's it called?'

'Cilipi. They wear local costumes.'

'On our booking it says tours included.'

He listened to her explaining that some trips were included, others had to be paid for. She barely looked at him, and in the end he called her aside, and asked how she could bear to go on with this. She gave him what seemed almost a hostile glance.

'Why not?'

'You know what we talked about.'

'Yes.'

'Why don't you say you don't care what they do?'

'Are you asking me to go away now? This morning?'

'Not this morning.'

'All right. This morning I shall take the party to Cilipi. Are you coming?' He shook his head. 'All right then. You don't have to come.' She went back to Briars and the Strong/Longs.

He turned away, to be confronted by a smiling Kornaro. His call to Sarajevo had come through. It was strange to hear Max's voice.

'Tremendous news.' He spoke as if they were continuing a discussion begun half an hour ago. 'Eugene is excited, he wants very much to join us.'

'Eugene?'

'Eugene Ponti, *The Tigress*, you remember. The thing is you're here, it's an ideal chance for you to meet him and clinch the deal. Can you get here today?'

Are you asking me to go away now? This morning? 'I don't know if I can manage today. I'll let you know later on.' Why should Anna not come with him? 'Perhaps today. Or early tomorrow.'

'Teriffic. For you to meet Eugene, that will be the clincher. We'll see him tomorrow, OK by you?'

'Yes.' Perhaps the last problem of the old world could be disposed of. 'How's Virginia?'

Silence. Then Max's voice, less bouncing than usual, said 'I thought she was with you.'

'She's not here. She said something about going on to Sarajevo.'

'Is that so? Where's she staying? I sure would like to see Virginia.' The voice had taken on Max's mock American intonation.

'I thought she might be with you.'

Silence again before Max spoke, his voice perfectly clear. 'I can hardly hear a word on this damned line. It's just hopeless. Look, my dear, did you say you were coming tonight?'

'I'm not sure. Tonight or tomorrow.'

'All right then, I'll fix –' The click of disengagement. Had Max been cut off before saying good-bye, or had he replaced the receiver?

He sat on the terrace of the Gradska Kavana, at the Ploce end of the town, a small cup of bitter coffee in front of him, thinking about the past night and understanding for the first time the phrase, *You're getting under my skin.* Anna was not perhaps under his skin, but it seemed that his skin was impregnated with her. When he sniffed his hand what he smelt was her body. He had always disliked what he thought of as the fleshy scent associated with lovemaking, but this smell was not disagreeable. It was a long way removed from anything he had felt after making love to Virginia. These impressions occupied his mind, although they could not have been classified as thinking. He tried to visualize Starting Again with Anna, but could think of nothing but his desire for her and his tenderness about her.

He drained the coffee cup and thought, I must go back to England, I must see Max in Sarajevo, I must find out what Anna is really like. Of these, only the last seemed important. He closed his eyes.

'Snatching a spot of shut-eye?' Painter stood by the table. He wore very tight dark blue trousers and a shirt striped in blue and green with a cut-out panel in the centre which said ILUVIT. He sat down. 'How's everything? Feeling a bit Harry groggers myself, you should have been with me last night. Les girls. Something about old King Sol that gets them. But I forgot, you were otherwise engaged. How's the wife?'

'Not here.'

'You didn't meet her?'

'She's gone on to Sarajevo.'

'Sarajevo. Going there myself. What about joining forces, two's company. Shake up the office there, they don't know their arse from their elbow. Do you know what the chap servicing our Topline cars here used to be? Guide to the jolly old Rector's Palace there.' He pointed to the Renaissance portico of the building beside them. 'Calls himself an engineer, looked down at his feet when I asked if he'd checked the brake linings. Read this?' He laid a paperback book on the table, *The Monkey's*

Puzzle. Gilbert shook his head. 'This chappie has a monkey, trains it to fix a gadget on a lift so that cyanide gets pumped into the cage, kills the chap inside. Works with a kind of bellows effect, little nozzle in the lift connected to some tubing. Monkey sets it going, pulls out the tubing afterwards. Dead clever.'

Two large glasses filled with red liquid appeared on the table. Painter's large nose pointed questioningly. '*Koliko?*'

'*Dvadeset jedan,*' said the waiter.

'Twenty-one, that is. Daylight robbery, but it's a good drink. Try it.' He put down some notes and waved away the change. The drink was strong and sweet. 'And the accounting system was all to pot as well. Yes, I can tell you I've put a bomb under their backsides here. Going to do the same at Sarajevo, then Split, then Zagreb. Then home. How about it?'

'How about what?'

'Bit of a burn up to Sarajevo. You said your wife was there.'

For some reason he found himself almost unable to speak. 'The thing is –' he said and stopped.

Painter looked at him. 'All right, old man? You look as if the sun's knocked you a bit skew whiff.'

'I'm all right. The thing is, I'm not sure, I may have someone with me.'

'Plenty of room in the old jalopy.' He looked at Gilbert again, gave a cackle of manic laughter. 'Don't tell me it's a native damsel? Slipped her a length, have you? You want to watch it, old man, they're very sniffy about these things here, her Montenegrin boyfriend'll do you.'

'Nothing like that.' The need to confide in somebody was intense, and he gave way to it, aware of his foolishness. 'My wife and I have parted, she's gone off with someone else. I've met a girl here.'

Painter whistled, long and low. 'You're a quick worker, old man. Never have thought it. Why Sarajevo, though? Having it out with your wife there, if I may coin a joke?'

'I'm not sure. I have to go there. On business.'

'Say no more. Mine not to peek or pry and all that.' He winked. 'This deserves another. Hey, what's your name, *gospodin.*' The waiter came over. 'What the hell's two?'

'*Dua.*'

'Dua more of the same then. Give you and your girl a lift, no trouble at all.'

'The thing is, I'm not sure about the time. It might –' He was already regretting what he had said.

'I tell you what, old man. I'm at the Imperial, I told you, old-fashioned sort of place, just outside the Pile Gate. You come along there. This afternoon I'm reading the riot act again to the clot here who calls himself a manager, then I'll have a zizz. Be ready around four. If you're not there by six I'm off.' He drank what remained in his glass, refused another. 'This stuff's stronger than it looks, you want to watch it. I'll have the other half tonight.'

'I'm not sure I shall be able to come.'

'OK, old man, leave it flexible.' Painter picked up his crime story, tapped the message on his shirt. 'Don't do anything I wouldn't.' He moved off down the Placa. The panel on the back of his shirt asked: 'DO YOU?'

Climbing up the steps of the Ulica od Sigurat towards the ramparts, houses overhanging menacingly from both sides, he approached a figure in green stepping daintily down. The identity and even the sex of this figure remained uncertain, and it was uncertain also whether Gilbert or somebody behind him was being acknowledged with a wave of the arm. At half a dozen steps' distance the figure was identifiably masculine – a long white face, a faint smile – and recognizable also as somebody he had met, but who was it? The eyes were hidden behind an owl's dark glasses, a camera hung loosely over one shoulder.

'Hallo.' They stood beneath a stonework balcony. 'What a delightful surprise.' The voice was thin and slightly fluting.

'Hallo.'

'Isn't this place simply *spectacular*? But exhausting. Are you going round the ramparts?'

'No, just filling in time.' He turned and they went down the steps together. *Filling in time*, a curious phrase, which covered all the recent years of his life. And what was he doing filling in time here? Perhaps he should have gone to Cilipi with Anna or taken her away this morning, perhaps he had failed some vital test set for him. As they moved downwards his unidentified companion, picking his way as delicately as if he were moving on stepping stones through mud, talked on.

'I mean, what can you do with a place like this? It's all too much, don't you think so? It just *is* a picture postcard. Though I must say I was tempted.' They emerged into the Placa. The green clothing was revealed as a two piece in tussore silk, the jacket hanging loosely, the trousers voluminous. 'It's just not my scene. This little beauty believes that life is real and earnest, she's truly at home in Whitechapel or Saint-Denis.' He patted the camera. The gesture brought recognition. This was Felix Perkins, the photographer.

'We met at that night club.'

'The Out Going, yes.' Perkins turned and looked back up the steps. A child stood looking at them, fingers in mouth. 'I think I must succumb.' The camera clicked and clicked. Perkins said apologetically, 'Ridiculous, but I just couldn't resist.' They walked up towards the Ploce Gate. Heads were turned to look at the green silk. 'You simply vanished that night, very wise. I was in rather a state, I know, Richard became *so* offensive. At the end I got into one of my rages. Would you like a drink?'

'No, thanks. I ought to get back to my hotel.' He felt a consuming meaningless anxiety. 'You're not here on an assignment, I take it?'

'Oh no, *quite* the contrary. By appointment you might say. Journey's end, you know.' He giggled. They crossed the bridge to the Ploce Gate and walked up the Put Frana Supila into the hotel courtyard. Perkins stayed with him buzzing away with speech, a harmless but irritating fly. He was talking about a book of East London pictures he had coming out in the autumn, a book for which somebody whose name Gilbert didn't catch had written a scrumptious text, when the buses drove in. The Briars got off and the Strong/Longs, but where was Anna? Again anxiety paralyzed him. Everybody got off the bus. Then he saw her blue dress, and realized that of course she would see the rest of the passengers away first. Now she looked around, saw him, waved, smiled, began to walk towards him. He felt his heart distinctly flutter.

What happened after that was a passage of corny film comedy. Her smile widened as she approached, she said 'Hallo,' and moved into Perkins's green tussore silk arms. He took off his glasses and spoke reprovingly.

'Naughty, naughty little Dolly.'

'What super gear.' She stepped back and looked at him. 'Fantastic.'

'Do you like it? *Really?*' He turned to Gilbert. 'Dolly's my wife. Dorothy Perkins. Well, that's her name, though she's been calling herself Lucy lately. Did she tell you her name was Lucy?'

Gilbert stared at her and she looked back at him, frowning. 'You two know each other, do you? That's a bit awkward. I've been having rather a thing with him.'

'And after you'd written to me too.' He spoke to Gilbert. 'You know you can't believe a word she says, don't you? She's just a naughty Dolly Perkins, you can't *rely* on her. I do hope you haven't been relying on her? Oh dear, I'm afraid you have. You remember my saying I was madly unhappy because she'd gone away? In the Out Going, you must remember. Well, being on her lonesome didn't work out, did it, Doll? So she sent a veritable *cri de coeur* to her loving husand. And out I flew.' He waved green arms. 'But the point is, she's so unreliable. I didn't know for sure she'd be here. She might have taken off.'

'You didn't say you were coming.'

'You know if I had you'd have flown away.' He went on flapping his arms.

Gilbert said ineptly, 'Why didn't you say you were married?'

She did not look at him. Perkins said, 'I do assure you she is. Off and on anyway. Now I think the thing to do is to leave this picture postcard scene as soon as possible and get back to reality. If all the bugs are out of your head, that is.'

'They are for now.'

'Then let's take the first plane back, Dolly darling.'

'What about my job?'

'You know very well you don't care about your job, you're only playing.' He said to Gilbert, 'She's very good at playing.'

'Don't you even want to go in the sea, now you're here?'

'Dolly darling, why should I? I know it's wet.'

'You didn't tell me you were married,' Gilbert repeated. 'And you said your name was really Anna.'

Perkins replaced his dark glasses. 'Are we going to have a

scene? I think I'd better leave you. I shall be in the way. I'll see what unspeakable concoction they're offering for lunch.'

'Sitting down is allowed,' she said when they were alone. They sat at one of the iron tables.

'Are you going back with him?' It seemed that he could ask nothing but foolish questions.

'He isn't queer, you know, or not very. And he's mad on me in his way. I'd never have gone back if he'd not flown out to get me, he's quite right.' She gave her foxy smile.

'How can you? After what we said.'

'What did we say?' She stuck out a leg, examined its burnished brown.

'You said you loved me.'

'It's what you say. I mean, how can you say anything else?'

'You lied to me, all the time.'

'Oh, come on.'

'Even your name. And all that about your father being an Australian diplomat and a botanist and so on, all lies.'

She swung her leg, looking down at it with her smile. 'Not all.'

'You mean about being brought up on a kibbutz?'

'It doesn't matter, does it?' She lighted a cigarette, puffed, met his gaze. 'This morning I would have gone away with you if you'd wanted, do you know that?'

'Suppose I said it now.'

'You always say *suppose*. Felix is here, no suppose for him. I'll tell you something. You're lucky, we both are. It would never have done, we'd have split in a week.'

'It isn't true,' he said hopelessly.

'You must know it is.'

'You mean you'd sooner be with him?'

She looked at the hotel. 'He's a person, I'm a person, he understands me.'

'And I don't?'

'You don't understand anything,' she said brutally.

He reproached her like an adolescent, the words bitter on his tongue. 'I don't understand people like you. You lie, you lie all the time. About everything.' Conscious of his own absurdity, of the game being lost, he cried, 'You said you fancied me.'

'I did. I do.'

531

'Well then?'

'Well then what?'

'Didn't it mean anything to you?' He felt the old dislike of naming sexual parts and routines.

'Yes, it was fine. Put your hand on the table.' He did so and she covered it with her own. 'I get the feeling. You know. I get it with you all the time and I love it. But there's something about you I can't take.' Still with her hand covering his she said, 'You want it but you can't give it back. You're detached, but you don't want me to be. It's like sucking blood or something. I don't know what it is, but it makes me shudder.'

He snatched away his hand at the same moment that hers was withdrawn. She rose. 'That's it then. Ciao.' She went into the hotel. As she entered the foyer a shade in green silk rose to meet her.

'How about that? Isn't she a beaut?' Gilbert looked at an ordinary grey car and nodded. 'I'm a patriot, old man, but on the production line for the old combustion engine we have to give Jerry best over an awful lot of things.' He stowed the cases, unlocked the door. 'Hop in and let's get going. Listen to that, doesn't she purr? Like a three-month-old kitten.'

'Very nice.'

'I'll say. Very nice, she's beautiful, if she were a woman she'd be lying down for me. What happened to your little filly?'

'Her husband arrived. He's taking her back to England.'

Painter roared with laughter. 'The lady's husband arrived. And you and your wife have packed it in already. Forgive me, old man, but I find that funny. I've got a peculiar sense of humour.'

As the car moved out of Dubrovnik's dull suburbs Painter muttered to himself. The muttering emerged in a phrase or two. 'Lazy buggers . . . no, not lazy . . . all of them . . . glad to be . . .' They reached the Adriatic Highway and he raised his voice. 'Good-bye, Dubrovnik. Sarajevo, here I come. Be another shambles I expect. Had much to do with them?'

'Croats, you mean, the people here? Not much.'

'You're lucky. Croats, are they, I'd cut their croats. I call them all bloody Slavs. They're not lazy like wogs, just inefficient.

Work hard but don't know what they're doing. They can build a dam but they can't run an office. I'll bet I have to light a few more bombs under them in Sarajevo. They don't watch the clock, just don't know it's there. Like the country?'

'What I've seen of it, yes, very much.'

'Give me the Sussex Downs and the Lakes any time.' The car in front of them was slowing down. Painter sounded his horn. 'Come on now, don't play silly buggers.' He shot past, through the gap between the car and an oncoming lorry, braked sharply and cut in, then took a bend with a cry of tyres.

Good-bye Dubrovnik. How was it possible to be so greatly deceived, to hold the body of love at one moment and find yourself empty-handed the next? One of the tyres made a flicking noise, repeated over and over again, the sound formed itself into the pattern of two lines from Housman:

> Possess, as I possessed a season,
> The country I resign

The lines were inaccurate. Anna was a country he had never possessed, and he had not resigned from it but been expelled. Extraordinary to think that he had slept with her last night and that they had talked about Starting Again. He became aware that Painter had asked a question.

'What's that?' He realized that the question was about how long he had been married. 'Five years.'

'I've been hitched fifteen.' Taking one hand from the wheel he fumbled with a wallet in front of him, extracted a photograph. 'Moira. And the kids. In the garden.'

The snapshot showed a harassed-looking woman holding a watering-can, and two small boys, one in a paddling-pool. A suburban lawn stretched around them, the neighbour's fence could be seen to one side. 'David and Jonathan. Little devils, fight like tigers, but I wouldn't be without them. Got any children?'

'One son. But he's grown up. It's my second marriage,' he added to forestall further questions.

'I'd die for my family, you know that.' Painter half-turned to him, inviting contradiction. 'But a man wants his freedom. Different for a woman, but a man has to have it. I'm a free man, my own master, that's what I like about this job. Shall I tell you something? Most people don't know what to do with freedom, they stick their arses in the air and ask you to give 'em a kick. But not Jerry Painter. Last job I had working for somebody else, I was a car salesman. Do you know the boss asked me to wash a car one day. I said to him take that and stick it up your jumper.' He blew a loud raspberry. 'Did he look surprised! I was pleased when he fired me. Never been able to stick working for other people. In Topline I'm not just a rep, I'm a partner. And there are pickings on the side if you want them.' He glanced at Gilbert. 'Not saying I do, mind you, never step out of line. You wouldn't say they were free in this country, would you?'

'I don't know. There are different kinds of freedom.'

'Too deep for me, that is. Either you're free or you're not. Tell you something, I've been in France, Belgium, Holland, Spain, Italy, Germany, Ireland. Seven countries, and in every one of 'em I've dipped my wick. And I haven't paid for it either. Here's our turnoff.'

The sign said *Opuzen, Metkovic*. They ran across an open plain, with a river on one side. Painter looked at his watch. 'The sixty-four-thousand dollar question is whether we stop the night at Mostar and look for local talent, or push on to Sarajevo.'

'I'd like to get there tonight if possible.' He wondered why he said this. What did it matter when he reached Sarajevo, or whether he got there at all?

'All right with your Uncle Jerry. They say the road's a bit rough later on, but she'll get through all right, won't you, my beauty?' He patted the steering-wheel affectionately. 'Been reading a very clever story about a car – *First Gear Murder*.'

'That isn't the one I saw you reading.'

'No, I get through three a day.' He went off into one of his gusts of laughter. 'Long as there's a body and some clues I'm happy. But this one really has something, it's about a chap who crashes into a brick wall when his brakes pack up. Thing is, you see, this other bugger, that's the local doctor, hates him because he cheated the doctor over a share deal when they were young out in Australia. So he ups the bonnet, drains his brake fluid, brakes won't work. Trick of it is, the doctor's first on the scene, carries a bottle of brake fluid in his black bag, tops it up again.'

'How does he get found out?'

'Detective, very bright geezer named Verity Glendenning, pinches the doctor's bag, examines it, finds traces of brake fluid. Can't think why you don't publish detective stories, you'd make a mint. Read another good one this week, *Open Wide Please*, about a dentist who gets patients to make a will in his favour, then knocks 'em off with a drug in the injection which doesn't take effect for the next half-hour. You're not listening.'

'I'm sorry.'

Painter was silent. Then he said, 'Funny thing, love, have you ever thought that? Doesn't matter how many times I dip my wick, it's only the wife and kids who mean anything to me. Don't you agree?'

'I'm not sure. I don't think I've had that much experience.'

'Believe me it's true. The one you poke isn't always the one you love, not by any means.'

'I'm not sure I know what love is. It seems to me just a word.'

'That's very true too, old man.' Painter sighed. 'Mostar coming up.'

Chapter 4

The Hitch-Hikers

Just outside Mostar the plain ended. They began to climb along narrow roads, through gashed and fissured mountains, with the Neretva running fast in a ravine below them, and beyond it the railway line stretching along like a toy. Painter kept up a flow of comment on the scenery and the road, comparing both unfavourably with the Lakes. The heat of the day died, and he produced from the boot a black and white striped blazer which he put on. A toy train, four crawling coaches behind a puffer, passed along on the other side of the ravine and vanished in a tunnel. Gilbert drifted into a daydream in which he was travelling in the train with Anna. It stopped often, and at one of the tiny stations they bought grapes, bread and rough sausage. They ate these in the carriage, sharing them with a Yugoslav couple. No conversation was possible, but the Yugoslavs made it clear that they thought Gilbert and Anna were man and wife. Something about this made him uneasy, but he did not know what it was. Perhaps the train was going to crash, perhaps the man's friendly look would change to a snarl . . .

Painter whistled. 'Did you see what I saw?'

'What was that?'

'Two birds, two luscious birds thumbing a lift as I live and breathe.' He pulled up, opened the door and jumped out. 'I think we're in, old man, I think we're in. Here they come.'

The sky had become perceptibly darker, light was failing. Two long-haired figures with packs on their backs hastened towards them. Something about the appearance of one made him say 'I think —'

Painter realized it at the same moment. 'Christ, it's a man.'

The two reached them. They were both young, the girl a round-faced blonde, the boy darkly handsome with hair that came down almost to his shoulders. 'Are we glad to see you,' he said. 'Another hour and we'd have settled for camping out.'

'And there's some snake they warned us of around here. What

536

do they call it, the poskok? Snuggles up to you for warmth.' The girl shivered. Like the boy, she was American.

In the fading light they confronted each other. Painter's big nose jutted out belligerently. The girl eased off her pack.

'You want to get your hair cut,' Painter said to the boy. 'You could get into trouble that way.' The boy did not reply. 'The boot's pretty full, I don't know if we can get all that gear into it.'

The boy seemed about to say something. The girl said 'David,' and he stayed silent. She went on. 'We'll get the stuff in somehow, it can go on our knees in the back if we have to put it there. If you can take us somewhere we can stay the night, we'll be grateful.'

The boot easily took the two rucksacks. The boy and girl got into the back of the car. 'Bloody hippies,' Painter whispered out of the corner of his mouth to Gilbert, and drove off with jolting energy. 'What's the idea then, what's it supposed to prove?' he shouted.

'I'm sorry?' That was the girl. Gilbert turned round. They were sitting very consciously apart on the back seats. The boy's dark narrow head was still, his eyes were watchful.

'Like my Aunt Agatha said when she produced quintuplets, in somebody else I'd call this excessive but when I've never been with a man it's just ridiculous.' There was no laughter from the back. 'I mean, jeans, long hair, you look the same, you dress the same, it takes the kick out of everything. Hell, maybe you are the same, maybe hippies just don't have anything down there.'

'We're not hippies.'

'You just want to look like a girl, eh? When I was at school we used to call that cissy.'

'Look, mister –' That was the girl again.

'Jerry, my love. Not to be confused with the homely utensil that used to be found under the bed. And this is Gilbert.'

'You don't have to give us a lift if you don't want.'

'Who said I don't want to? I stopped, didn't I?'

'We're not hippies, we're students.'

'Your boy friend said so. American university, eh? Which one?'

'Berkeley.'

537

'I might have known it.' Painter groaned. 'You heard of Berkeley, Gilbert?'

'I've heard of it, yes.'

'Where they write up four-letter words in the classrooms and call the police pigs. Anyway it's June, why aren't you at home?'

'We just dropped out for a year. David thought it was more culturally important to see things for ourselves.'

There was a sharp crack, the windscreen became blind. Painter jammed on his brakes, switched off the engine. 'Bloody *hell*,' he said, and opened his door. 'There's a torch in the glove compartment, let's have it.'

The torch revealed a windscreen still intact but split into a thousand opaque pieces. Painter went to the boot, rummaged, shouted: 'Don't just sit there, get out and do something. And watch it. We're only a few feet from the side.'

They got out. It was almost dark, a steep drop on the right was faintly visible. Warmth had gone out of the air. 'What happened?' Gilbert asked.

Painter threw the two rucksacks out on to the road and emerged with the car jack. He got inside the car and swung it twice. The splintered windscreen crackled out, with only a few jagged fragments left. 'Some flint on the bastard sodding road came up and hit the windscreen, what do you think happened? If you've got anything warm you'd better put it on. We're going to have a lot of mountain air blowing through and it's a long way to Sarajevo.' He chuckled, and began to sing 'It's a long way to Sarajevo' to the tune of 'Tipperary'.

The boy opened the rucksacks and asked, 'Babs, are the pullovers in yours or mine?'

'Babs,' Painter said. 'That's good, you look like a baby.' His hand moved out to touch the girl. She shrank back from him.

'Stop it,' Gilbert said. 'Just stop that.' He was surprised by the passion in his voice. David, bent over a rucksack, paused. Painter looked surprised.

'What did you think I was doing, old man? Believe me, all Jerry Painter wants to do is get to jolly old Sarajevo and get his head down.'

'Just leave her alone.' He had heard the remark in a hundred bad films, how did he happen to be saying it?

'Right you are. If the deadly snake comes slithering out of the rocks I won't –' He stopped and shouted, 'Look out. Behind you.'

The girl screamed, the boy pushed her aside and stood staring. Laughter welled up in Painter, rocking his body.

'If you could have seen, if you could just have seen your face. 'Ware snakes. Oh dear me.'

The boy and girl put on thick pullovers, and Painter found a pullover which went under the sports blazer. Gilbert wore his raincoat. Babs and David moved round the car. Painter opened the front passenger's seat and bowed gallantly. David got into this seat himself and Gilbert sat in the back with the girl. They drove on.

Round some bends they hugged the mountain, and bits of rock and scree lay in the road, occasionally the drop to the river could be seen on the other side. There was little traffic. Once a lorry passed them with much loud preliminary hooting. They were rising most of the time, and it became colder. At one point they bumped over a shaky-looking log bridge. A hundred yards beyond it the road narrowed so that it was impossible for cars to pass. Headlights showed in the distance, became brighter. Painter hooted and was met by a hoot in reply. He put on speed. The lights approached nearer, and were dazzling.

The boy spoke. 'What are you trying to do, get us killed?'

'Let 'em go back then.' Painter kept his thumb on the horn. The hooting from the other car stopped, the lights became less bright. 'That's it, my beauty, back you go.'

The other car backed for a quarter of a mile before the road widened and it was able to pull into the cliff side. As they passed a window was opened, shouts of abuse rang on the night air. Painter played 'Colonel Bogey' on his horn and roared back, 'And the same to you.'

'You could have gone back,' the boy said. 'The road was wide enough to pass after we'd crossed the bridge.'

'An Englishman never retreats. The Yanks may, they're a mongrel lot anyway, but an Englishman always goes forward.' With cheerful belligerence he asked, 'Do you mean to tell me they let you drop out and then go back again?'

'At Berkeley, yes. I'm majoring in European sociology and

they agreed it would be useful for me to have a year in Europe. Mind you, I've got good grades.'

'Never went to the varsity myself. People couldn't afford it. You don't know how lucky you are.'

'The States is different. If you want to go, you go, just a matter of where.'

In the back seat the girl's leg pressed against Gilbert's with unerotic warmth, or perhaps he was no longer capable of being erotically roused. He tried to summon up thoughts of Anna. Supposing she was beside him now in this car, her leg pressed against his, would he feel different? The girl put her arm through his. She shivered, and whispered something.

'What's that?'

'Your friend? What's the matter with him, why is he so angry?' He thought of saying that Painter was not his friend, but before he could do so she continued. 'He shouldn't ride Dave that way, Dave's got a temper.'

'So has Painter.'

'Dave can be nasty, he doesn't like anyone trying to ride him. What do you do?'

Hardly believing it, he said, 'I'm a publisher.'

'I'm majoring in English, the twentieth-century novel.'

'We publish Bunce, Jake Bunce.'

'Well, what do you know?' She leaned forward, the whole upper part of her body touched him. 'Dave, this guy is a publisher, he publishes Jake Bunce.'

Dave said something, but with the air rushing through the gap of the windscreen it was not possible to hear the words. Only snatches of conversation from the front were audible, but they seemed reasonably friendly. 'I'm going to sleep,' Babs said. She curled up to him like a kitten.

In the front Painter was laughing. A good sign or a bad one? As he bent forward to hear, Babs accommodated herself to him.

'I'll tell you what I'd do,' Painter was saying. 'The first hundred I caught, they'd go up against a wall, then –' He made a clicking noise with his tongue. 'The next hundred I'd say do you want the same, or are you going back to work with your professors like good little boys? And I can tell you the answer.' Dave murmured something. 'Are you trying to tell me they're such democrats themselves? I'd say to them, I'd say to you, you've got a job to do, so get in there and do it.' Another murmur. 'I'm a free man, I'm one of the lucky ones. That's what free enterprise means, my son, those who deserve it get to the top.' His laugh boomed out, his head was turned. 'Jablanica, getting on now. Bloody great dam they've built somewhere around. Half-way there, I'd say. Everything okey-dokey there in the back, snuggling up to you is she?' He said something to Dave and laughed again.

The girl's hand was pushed inside his raincoat. She whispered complainingly, 'Dave, I'm cold.'

'It's not Dave.'

She pressed herself closer to him. Quite impersonally he considered what her reaction would be if he put a hand on her thigh. The idea surprised him. He did nothing.

While his mind wandered vaguely around such thoughts he must have dozed. He was aware of voices in the front, of the cutting wind, the noise of the car engine, the body beside him giving and receiving warmth. Then all this stopped. There was silence. Perhaps he was asleep? The silence was broken by Painter's voice cursing loudly, monotonously, repetitiously. Doors slammed. He reluctantly roused himself, pushed the sleeping Babs aside, opened the door and got out.

The night was full of stars. The silence had some quality – of depth, should it be called? – that was quite different from what one thinks of as silence in a city. At once, and ridiculously, he thought of Anna. Would she have understood the quality of this silence, would she have looked up at the stars, said *Good-bye Felix* and walked away with him? He rubbed a hand across his face as if it were a damp flannel, and was surprised to find the hand warm. Painter was shining a torch at the engine. Dave stood by his side.

'Why did I ever trust that stupid lazy bugger who called himself an engineer? Trust a Slav, I'd sooner trust the blind school.' He put his head inside the engine, grunted, leaned over, emerged and shone the torch on his blazer sleeve. Something dark showed on it. 'That's oil, how am I going to get oil off?' he said in an indignant whine. 'I ask you, how am I going to get oil off?'

Dave was leaning over too. 'Have you checked the distributor head?'

'You just get out of there. I don't want any American layabout fiddling with my car.' He put a hand on the boy's shoulder and pushed him away. For a moment it seemed that Dave would react, but he did nothing. 'If you want to make yourself useful get inside and try the starter.'

Dave got into the driver's seat and switched on and off half a dozen times. The engine did not respond. Painter glared at Gilbert, who yawned uncontrollably.

'Is there anything I can do?'

'You've done enough already.'

'I have?'

Dave was still trying the starter. 'Stop that, you bloody clot, you'll run the battery flat,' Painter shouted. To Gilbert he said accusingly, 'Who was it wanted to get to Sarajevo tonight? I could have been in Mostar drinking the old slivovitz if it weren't for you. And I wouldn't be lumbered with these deadbeat love-birds either.' He gave the mudguard a kick. 'Bloody sodding rotten car.'

'Do you mean we're stuck here for the night?'

Painter smacked his forehead. 'God give me patience, what do you think I mean? What shall I do, ring up the nearest garage and ask 'em to send a breakdown van? This isn't civilization, it's Yugoslavia.'

'It couldn't be that you've run out of petrol?'

Painter stared at him, his great nose shining in the moonlight. Then he gripped Gilbert's arm, led him round to the dashboard and pointed. 'Three-quarters full. And don't say it might be empty. I filled up at Mostar, remember?'

'I thought you knew about cars?'

'Are you trying to be funny? I don't crawl about underneath 'em, I let the peasants do that.'

Dave joined them. 'I've checked the distributor head and the points. Nothing wrong there that I can see.' A car's headlights shone round a bend in the road and then showed dazzlingly bright as it neared them. Dave moved out waving his arms, jumped back as the car hooted and accelerated.

'Nobody's going to stop, they're all afraid of getting their throats cut,' Painter said. 'We're stuck till morning.' Grotesque in his blazer he stood glaring from one to the other of them. The absurdity of his appearance moved Gilbert to facetiousness.

'You're sure it isn't escaping brake fluid? Like *First Gear Murder?*'

Painter gave the car another kick. 'That stupid young devil in Dubrovnik, I'll have him for this. What the hell are you doing?'

Dave was taking the rucksacks out of the boot. He said cheerfully, 'Getting out the tent and stuff. I'll wake up Babs and we'll go and search for a bit of flat ground.' He shone the torch. 'Looks as if there might be something away there on the left.'

'Some people have all the luck. A nice bit of nooky in the sack, that's your name for it, isn't it? What's she like in the sack? Quite a handful, I should imagine.'

'I don't like the way you talk,' Dave said. 'I don't like you, I tell you that.'

'But you share and share alike nowadays, don't you? Seen her on the job with a dozen other boys, I expect.'

Dave turned abruptly away from them and went round the other side of the car. 'What are you trying to do, get him to hit you?' Gilbert asked.

Painter grinned. 'I'd like that. Used to be middle-weight champion in the Terriers.'

There was a shout. Dave came running round the car, got into the driver's seat, switched on. The engine started. He jumped out, thumbs up, grinning. 'Vacuum built up in the petrol-tank. Just thought of it, had it in another car once. Take off the petrol cap, she goes whoosh, and it's clear.'

'That's wonderful,' Gilbert said, although upon the whole he would have preferred to be left here in the limbo of a Yugoslav mountain rather than face the problems waiting in Sarajevo.

One of the car doors slammed, there was a noise. 'What the hell?' Dave said and left Gilbert, who followed him. Painter was holding the girl, Dave was pulling at him, Painter pushed her away. She staggered and slipped to the ground. Painter brushed away the vague swing that Dave made at him.

'Juicy, very juicy,' he said with satisfaction, and then spoke to Gilbert. 'Had to get her out.'

'What do you mean?'

'End of the road. Thought I'd kiss her good-bye.'

'You can't turn them out.'

'Who says? I like your face, I give you a lift. I don't like it any more, I say that's enough. My car, my privilege. Smarty pants here had got their gear out already, saved me the trouble.'

'You can't do it.'

He could not see Painter's face clearly, but he knew the grin that would be stretching it. 'You want to call a halt too, old man? Perfectly free to do that if you like, that's what freedom means. Expect you'd find it very snug, three of you in one sleeping-bag.'

The torch in Dave's hand shone on Painter's grinning teeth, flicked to Gilbert and then to the girl. His voice was still quiet. 'Get back into the car, Babs. Back seat.'

'Oh no you don't.' Painter moved forward.

'Look at my hand.' The words were still not loud. The boy's left hand held the torch, which shone on to his right. The right hand showed no stigmata, it was smooth and white in the torch-light, but the fingers were curled round a small revolver.

Painter laughed and moved towards the girl. 'All right then,' Dave said, and at the strangled note in his voice Painter's hand jerked back as though he had been burned.

'He would, you know. The little bastard means it,' Painter said to Gilbert. Then he spoke to the girl. 'You'd better do what Superman says, get back into the car and catch up with your beauty sleep.'

'Dave,' she said quaveringly. Gilbert became aware that Painter was close to him and had said something. It took a few moments for the words to penetrate, and then he realized that they had been something about rushing him together. Dave told Gilbert to get in the back seat.

Painter said conversationally, 'Are you going to let this little thug tell you what to do? If we rush him he won't have a chance.'

Gilbert did not answer him. He opened the car door. Dave's even voice said, 'I don't think we'll take you with us, I think I'll give it you now. After all, why wouldn't I? You know the kind we are, Babs is on grass and I'm on acid, we think it's shit funny when one of the pigs gets it, why wouldn't I give it to you?'

He held the torch on Painter, who was sweating. 'You heard him.'

With a confidence he did not feel, Gilbert said, 'He's kidding, don't worry.' As he got into the car he had the feeling of shutting out something disagreeable. What happened next he saw through the barrier of glass.

Painter cried out something and dived forward, in what Gilbert vaguely recalled as a rugger tackle. Dave must have been expecting something of the kind. He sidestepped and hit Painter with the butt of the revolver. Painter fell down.

Gilbert stared through the car window. The moon was obscured and the impression of things outside the glass was confused. The body on the ground appeared to shift slightly, but he could not be sure. Beside him Babs made a sound between a whimper and a giggle.

'He shouldn'ta talked to Dave that way, should he?'

The back door was flung open. 'Help me get him in,' Dave said.

'But he can't drive.'

'I'll drive.'

'He may be badly hurt.'

'Look, I've had all I can take. I could leave you both on the road, the way he was going to leave us. Is that what you want?'

They lifted Painter and put him in the front passenger seat. A trickle of blood ran from his scalp to his forehead. Gilbert wiped it away. Dave started the engine and ground the gears as he drove off.

He drove along the mountain roads with the headlights full on, never dipping them, and ignoring the hooting of the few cars they met. Glancing back occasionally over his shoulder he talked to Gilbert as though to himself.

'I don't want you to get the wrong idea. That's only the second time I've ever hit anybody, to hurt them I mean. The other was a boy I had a fight with at school. But a bastard like that, what can you do but look after yourself? It's you or him.' He said reflectively, 'Babs's father is Judge Deeley, one of the best-known men in Northern California, isn't that so, Babs?'

'Daddy's famous,' Babs claimed. 'He's stuffy, you know, but kind of sweet.'

'He let you come on this trip.' Dave spoke earnestly, turning again to emphasize the words. 'And he let you come with me. He wouldn't've done that if he'd thought I was just a drop-out, don't you see?'

'You don't have to convince me,' Gilbert said.

'It's true though, isn't it Babs? Her father trusts me.'

'Daddy just loves Dave. He said to me, "I wouldn't let you go to Europe with just anybody but Dave's a fine boy. A little wild maybe, but I like a boy to have some spunk." And I tell you something else Daddy said. He said to me, "I reckon that boy loves you. If you love him too, then that makes it all right by me." And he gave me funds for the trip. Not too much, mind you.'

'He doesn't sound stuffy to me.'

'Some ways he is. I had to promise him I'd never drink wine, he said it would heat my blood and it was hot enough anyway.' She giggled.

'Her dad's a great guy.' Dave's voice in front was solemn. 'And what he said, you know that's true. We love each other. We're going to get married.' The word *marriage* jarred him like a dentist's drill touching a nerve. Dave negotiated a bend and went on. 'He said to me, "I trust you, you'll look after my daughter." This gun now, I'll tell you something funny, Judge Deeley gave me this gun. It's his. Just in case we ran into trouble. I guess he didn't mean this sort of trouble. He a friend of yours?'

'No. He just gave me a lift.'

'I don't reckon he's got any friends. Hell, he didn't have to give us a lift, he didn't have to stop. And then pawing Babs about that way. Saying those things.'

'I hope he's all right.'

As though at a signal Painter groaned and sat up. He put his hand to his head, looked at Dave and then round into the back seat.

'Dave,' the girl said. 'He's with us.'

'He hit me on the head, you're a witness to that.' Gilbert said nothing. 'And now he's driving my car. Without a licence, I'll bet.'

'International driving licence,' the boy said.

'You're driving without my permission. You can just stop the car and get out.'

'You'd never have got it started. And you're not fit to drive.'

They crossed a bridge and came into a large village. 'What's this place, I didn't see?'

Gilbert peered out. 'Konjic.'

Painter's hands were clasped tightly together. 'I'll tell you what I'm going to do with you if you stay in the car. When we stop I'm giving you both in charge.'

'What for?'

'Stealing my car, kidnapping me, grievous bodily harm or whatever they call it here. And let me tell you, sonny, they don't like your sort. Nobody likes your sort.' Dave did not reply. 'You're in trouble up to your neck. Stop the car and get out.' He put his hand on the steering-wheel. 'Stop the car.'

Dave cut the engine, but left the headlights on. Ahead lay rock, scrub, the winding road. The moon was showing again and illuminated Painter's beaky profile turned towards Dave, the stripes of his blazer, the boy's flowing hair.

'Now, out,' Painter said. The boy rested his arms on the steering-wheel. 'I said o, u, t, out.'

Dave turned to face him. He had a look of surprise. 'So easy, that's what I can't get over, it's so easy. Just a little tap on the head and he falls down. You have a gun, you can do anything. Why don't I shoot them, Babs, what do you say? Take their money and then ditch the car. Why don't we do that?'

The girl made her giggling noise.

'Don't be such a clot,' Painter said. 'They'd have you in a few hours.'

'Why would they?' He turned to the back. His voice was still quiet and reasonable. 'I don't see it. Nobody was there when he picked us up, nobody sees us leave the car. We run it over one of these big drops, go on a bit and pitch our tent for the night, clean the gun and ditch that somewhere too, take the bus in the morning. I don't see anything wrong with it, it's easy.'

'I never know when you're kidding,' she said.

'I'm not kidding. At least I don't think so.'

Painter shouted something incoherent to Gilbert, leaned over and tried to pinion Dave's arms. Again he must have been expecting the move, for in a moment he had the door open and was standing outside with the revolver held loosely in his hand. The interior light came on, revealing Painter with his arms stretched forward. 'Don't you move, don't you try to get in that other seat or I swear I'll let you have it.'

Not since he was a young man, a quarter of a century ago, had Gilbert experienced any situation which placed him in physical danger. Now there seemed to be within him a block of some kind, a solid mass of material which precluded fear. He opened his own car door.

'You too,' Dave said. 'You stay where you are.'

'Why should I? You're not going to shoot me.' He felt an absolute confidence that this was true. Outside he breathed in the mountain air, invigorating and clear. A car passed on the way to Mostar, flashing its lights. They showed Dave's face, dark and desperate. 'I mean, you don't have any reason to.'

'It's so damned easy. They shouldn't make it so easy.'

Painter started to say something. Gilbert cut him off sharply. 'Be quiet, you've said enough.' If Anna saw me now she'd be surprised, he thought. 'It isn't easy, it's impossible. You'd never get away with it and you know you couldn't do it. You'd better get in and start driving. And give me that.' He put out a hand towards the revolver.

'No.'

'All right, keep it. But start driving.'

'Why can't I do it?' His voice now was petulant, appealing. 'He thinks we're drop-outs, why not?'

Supposing the gun were fired, the bullet would bounce back off the block within him. He felt impermeable to harm. 'Think about Judge Deeley. That's not why he gave you the gun.'

'He wouldn't ever know.'

'You're not like me, you've got something to live for.' In the night air his thought process seemed wonderfully clear. 'It doesn't matter to me. Or to him, all he's after is a quick lay in every country in Europe. We don't have a future, but you do and so does she.'

Painter said something. From outside the car he looked like a striped fish in a tank. He wound down the window. 'He left some native bit back in Dubrovnik, that's why he talks such a load of cobblers.'

About the glance that the boy directed at him there was something betrayed, something wounded. Out of some inner feeling that he had not known he possessed, Gilbert cried, 'Things are different for you, different for Americans.'

A long stare, then his words were approved by a nod. 'I guess you're right, they are.' He held out the revolver. In Gilbert's hand it felt small, cold, disagreeable.

'I'll be damned.' Painter began to laugh, a jarring nasal sound. He began to shift over to the driver's seat. Gilbert made an imperative gesture.

'Let him drive.'

'Christ, man, it is my bloody car.' But he made no further protest when Dave got into the driving-seat. The engine buzzed. They moved away.

An hour and a half later they reached Ilidza, a few kilometres from Sarajevo. Hardly a word had been spoken during the whole of that time by Dave or Painter. In the back seat Babs put her hand over Gilbert's. 'You were so right, you know that, so right. I don't know what came over Dave, except he's got a temper, I told you.'

'Yes.'

'But I don't believe he'd ever have used that. I've never seen him that way before. It was kind of frightening. You know.' She shivered, and her shoulder touched his.

'I had a girl. In Dubrovnik.' He wanted to say *she was not much older than you*, but what would she care?

'Yes.'

'Nothing. I don't know what I wanted to say. She went off with someone else.'

'That's what made you talk the way you did. About not caring. Isn't that so?'

'Perhaps. I just don't know.'

'I like you.' Her mouth shaped itself towards him, he went to meet it, but found the kiss planted on his cheek. Her right hand, a warm hostage, remained in his left one. His right hand still held the revolver.

At Ilidza Dave parked the car in a small square beside a hotel. He got out, stretched himself, said 'Come on, Babs,' and unloaded their bags.

'It's all right if I drive my own car now?' Painter held out his hand for the keys. Dave dropped them into his palm.

Gilbert gave back the revolver. 'Thanks,' he said without smiling. He weighed it in his hand, put it into his hip pocket and said 'Thanks,' again.

The hotel said *Serbija* over the front. 'Are we going to be able to get in here?' the girl said. 'I'm pooped.'

'We'll soon find out.' He bounded up the steps, opened the swing doors, disappeared. They stood about awkwardly without speaking. He came back. 'OK.'

'Well folks, it was nice knowing you,' Babs said. She kissed Gilbert's cheek again. 'Some of you.'

They passed through the swing doors.

Painter drove for a mile without saying anything. When he did speak his voice had the geniality of their early encounters. 'Very dicey there for a bit. The old tick-tick was working overtime. You handled him perfectly.' His tone changed. 'Bloody young psycho. He should be shut up.' The lights of Sarajevo could be seen now, blue and white stars ahead of them. Painter went on talking.

'Americans are two sorts like anybody else. Good and bad, and he's one of the rotten apples in the barrel. And that girl. Just a little tart. They'll find they can't muck about with Jerry Painter. Now that he's got the taste for it that boy's not going to stop. I got away with a crack on the head, the next chap may not be so lucky.'

'What are you going to do?'

'Just what I told them I'd do, old man. Go to the police, tell them what happened, the crack on the head, the way he stuck us up, everything. They can't say I didn't warn 'em.'

'No.'

Painter jerked the wheel in his surprise so that they skidded. 'What do you mean, no?'

'You'd need me as a witness. I wouldn't support you.'

'Wouldn't *support* me? What kind of weirdo are you, you like being threatened with a gun?'

They were coming into the outskirts of the city. Blue sodium lights were strung along endlessly in the middle of the road. On either side white cliffs of flats loomed up and were passed.

'You were going to turn them out of the car. That's why it happened.'

'And that means it was all right for them to hold me up?'

Behind the round neutral face of Babs he saw that of Anna. What were the last words she had said to him? He groped for them unsuccessfully, yet he knew that they had left an open wound. 'I shouldn't give evidence against them. Not in any circumstances.'

He was thrown forward joltingly, so that his face almost came into contact with the jagged bits of glass round the empty space of the windscreen. The car stopped. Painter turned to him a face violently red with anger. 'Then not in any circumstances will I have you in my car. You can get out and walk, and I hope you bloody well walk for ever.'

Gilbert opened the door, got out, bent to take things from the boot. A blow on the shoulder sent him spinning.

'Let my car alone.' He opened the boot, took out Gilbert's case and threw it on the ground. A shirt and pyjamas fell out on to the road. Painter laughed. His words sprayed saliva into Gilbert's face. 'If there's anyone I hate it's weirdos who're soft on crime. I don't wonder your wife left you, and your piece in Dubrovnik too. If you ever had one, which I doubt.' He put two fingers up in a Churchillian gesture, got back into the car and drove away. Gilbert knelt on the pavement, repacked his bag, looked at his watch. The time was half-past nine. He felt as if he had been in Painter's company for a week.

He walked a few hundred yards, and after waiting twenty minutes caught a bus which took him through wide anonymous streets into the centre of the town. At the Hotel Europa they understood and even spoke English. They told him that Mr Bomberg was out and had left no message, although he had given instructions that a room should be reserved for Mr Welton if he arrived. Gilbert became aware that he was hungry, and ate some kind of meal in the restaurant. Then, depressed and overwhelmingly tired, he went to bed.

Chapter 5

Max

What voice was at the other end of the bedside telephone? He envisioned it as Anna, saying that she was waiting in the lobby. But of course it was Max.

'Hallo, my dear. The top of the morning to you. They told me you were here, but I was late last night. I had fish to fry. You know?' His laugh was warm and easy. 'Shall we breakfast together? In fifteen minutes.'

Rosy-faced, euphoric, wearing a very thin suit of some shimmering material, Max was more himself than usual. 'You have not been here before? A wonderful place in its way. The Turkish quarter is terrific. The covered market, do you know what the top of it looks like? Pressure cookers, big pressure cookers. And the mosques, you just have to see them. What's the matter, you don't look up to the mark.'

'I'm all right.' The sight of Max had dissipated the block of indifference within him as though hot water had been poured on to ice. Twinges of feeling that he had thought dead moved into action with the painfulness of unused muscles.

'You're angry because I've spent a lot of time on this? But wait till you read *The Tigress*, it just has everything. Adventure and sex and tenderness, and all – all *infused* with such a perfect historical sense.' He touched his finger to his lips. 'We meet Eugene for drinks before lunch today, OK?'

'Yes.' He did not mention Virginia, but remembered another reason why he should be angry with Max. 'I had a call from a man named Melvyn Branksom. I don't appreciate your conducting negotiations behind my back.'

'The silly devil.' Max seemed genuinely annoyed. 'I wasn't conducting negotiations, just having a chat. But I told him he must on no account talk to you before I had a chance to see you.'

At another time he might have left it at that, but irritation made him go on. 'I should think half London knows about it.

552

Somebody in the club spoke to me.' Something in Max's open face, something un-put-down-able in his bouncing optimism, pushed him further forward. 'It's not what I expect. If you're going on like this we've come to the parting of the ways. You'd better realize it.'

'My dear, what's up?' The open-eyed astonishment seemed ingenuous and genuine. 'If I've offended you I'm very sorry. I apologize. I shoot off my big mouth, I know I do, but what I said to Mel was in confidence and he should have respected it.' He paused, but Gilbert did not express forgiveness. Max flung out his arms. 'I apologize, it won't happen again, what more can I say? You know me, I'm impetuous, I rely on your judgement.'

He said, 'All right,' feeling the response to have a school-boy's sulkiness. He was right, but in some way Max had put him in the wrong.

'You're not yourself. Do you want me to put off seeing Eugene, shall I see him alone and make your excuses?'

'No.'

'He has a villa near the top of Trebevic. Marvellous view. You can go up in the funicular, but we will use my little hired car. So sad that Eugene cannot see the view, he is blind, you know that?' Max spoke with his usual liveliness, but Gilbert sensed that he was being watched, assessed. 'You told me you would send a telegram.'

'I didn't have time.'

'And you mentioned something about Virginia. I thought you said she was with you.'

Enunciating carefully he said, 'I don't know that she is even in the country any longer. I don't know where she is.'

Max made no reply. Looking at him, catching what seemed to be a quick-suppressed smile, Gilbert knew that he was concealing something, and that the something was connected with Virginia. A moment later Max took out a handkerchief and blew his nose. Gilbert recognized the handkerchief. It had on it a strongly-marked pattern in light blue and dark blue, and Virginia had given him half a dozen of these handkerchiefs on his birthday last year, telling him that they could be bought at only one shop in London. With the production of the handkerchief there came also the powerful odour of her new scent. The smell lingered, but was much less strong, when the handkerchief was replaced.

The sight of the handkerchief, the smell of the scent. It was these things, combined perhaps with what had happened on the drive to Sarajevo, that made him think of killing Max.

They spent the morning wandering round the Bascarsija, the old Turkish quarter, and in the Brusa Bezistan, the covered market whose semi-circular domes Max had likened to the tops of pressure cookers. The immense quality of carved wooden ashtrays, salad servers and small wind instruments in the market reminded Gilbert strongly of Heal's, and the tumbledown shacks outside in the doors of which tailors sat cross-legged stitching at unidentifiable garments, or metal and leather workers added a burnish to some undistinguished bit of metal seemed to him merely sordid. Max, however, was in transports of pleasure. He haggled lengthily over the price of some broad copper pans, left them with a regretful shake of the head and bought a wedge of sticky pastry which he ate with the greatest relish. He forced a small piece on Gilbert. The nuts and syrup were cloying in his mouth. He gulped the rest of it and felt sick.

Max drove the car, a Morris, with characteristic dash, and kept up a flow of chatter as they crossed the shallow lively Miljacka and went out through the suburbs.

'Bistrik,' he said. 'Austro-Hungarian. The mixture of Muslim and Frank Joseph is interesting, don't you think? Some of this, you know, it's what I was brought up in.'

'Here, you mean?'

'No, but the old building was the same everywhere, heavy, dignified, but not graceful. Like old Franz Joseph himself. Though I've been here. My father was a construction worker and he spent six months in Sarajevo before the war. Of course I was a child then, and it was winter. In winter it's cold here. This is the gipsy quarter, they call it Dajanli.' They passed through steep winding streets where the little wooden houses clung to each other for support and muddy streams ran along between the narrow alleys. The houses were filled with small lean children and hungry-looking cats. 'Muslims,' Max said. 'They never kill cats, you know, they say that Mahomet cut off a part of his robe rather than disturb a cat who was sleeping on it. Not much like England.' He glanced at Gilbert.

'No.'

'In a way I love all this, in another way it's what I wanted to get away from more than anything in the world. Being poor in central Europe, that's no fun. You wouldn't know about that.'

'I suppose not.'

'In England everybody is a gentleman or they pretend to be. When you know you're not one it gives you an advantage. But this is where I belong. I've got away from it, but it says something to me.'

'You're not a Muslim?'

'My mother was. Half-Turkish. By religion, you mean? I'm nothing.' They moved out of Dajanli, up a corkscrew hill. He moved into lower gear, gunned the engine. 'I'll never understand you, Gilbert. People like you.'

They went up and up. The scenery changed to scrub, with occasional pine trees. They then moved out of this, the landscape opened, Sarajevo was spread out below them, the domes of two dozen mosques gleaming in the sunlight. 'That's something, isn't it? But barbaric, you'd call it barbaric.' He turned a bend at a right angle, came almost to a dead stop. A lorry was in front of them, the driver on the road changing the wheel. A car shot down the hill going too fast. The Morris pulled over to the left, towards a hundred-foot drop, came with shuddering uncertainty to a halt. 'Damn' thing pulls over if you have to make a quick stop. Needs new brake linings.'

As Max spoke the word 'brake' Gilbert remembered *First Gear Murder* and what Painter had said about brake fluid. You let out the brake fluid and the brakes just didn't work. 'Suppose you had no brake fluid,' he said almost before he knew he had spoken the words.

'Then I should just have the hand brake which is distinctly dicey.' Max grinned at him. 'Like everything about this car. You know I don't mind that, I like taking chances. But it might be good-bye two members of old-established English publishing firm, one a foreign upstart. Are you wishing you'd taken the funicular? Not much farther now, but most of it in first.'

The road went round and round as they climbed. Five minutes later they stopped at a pair of elaborate wrought-iron gates which said 'Villa Garibaldi'. A bent old woman wearing drab clothes came out of a small stone building, said, *'Dobre danya'* and opened them. They drove into an enclosed courtyard to the front of a sprawling villa, whose generally Italianate style was blended with Moorish arches. Max jumped out and spread his arms.

'We have arrived. It's OK, don't you think?'

'Somebody's here before us.' An Alfa-Romeo stood by an open garage at one end of the courtyard.

'Flavia's. She uses it to go down into town.'

The effect was rather what Gilbert thought of as Hollywood architecture, and this was for some reason enhanced when a maid wearing a white cap and frilled apron led them through a dark large hall with a green and white terrazzo flooring into a large drawing-room full of books and Italian china, opened french windows and stood aside to let them pass.

'I thought this was a Communist country, hard-living and high-thinking.'

'Not for Eugene. He is a sympathizer, an honoured guest.'

From the wide stone-flagged terrace the ground dropped steeply away, so that you had the impression of the terrace being built on air. Below it Sarajevo shone, the Miljacka running through it like a vein in a hand. Three people sat out there, a white-haired man talking into a tape-recorder, a dark girl who sat at a table reading a set of proofs and a blonde in a bikini wearing dark glasses stretched flat on a sun bed. The man switched off the tape-recorder as they approached, and stood up. The white hair was disorderly around his powerful head. Max said formally, 'May I present my managing director Gilbert Welton, Signor Eugene Ponti.' They shook hands. 'And this is Janet Ponti.' The dark girl looked up from the proof. 'And Flavia Orsini.' The girl in the dark glasses took them off, looked at him and put them on again.

'A perfect view, isn't it, Mr Welton? Unhappy for me that I cannot see it, and yet I know this view because Janet has described it to me. It is printed in here.' He touched his forehead with a hand flecked by liver spots.

'It's marvellous. Your English is very good.'

'I learned it in the best possible way, among Englishmen. In the war. I was your prisoner.' The proud head reared up, the white hair looking like a cock's crest.

They sat down. The smiling maid came out with a tray of drinks and then left them. Ponti said interrogatively, 'Janet?'

'Why the hell doesn't she do it, I'm working.'

Ponti said something in Italian to the blonde girl, who answered him with a couple of laconic phrases. 'You do it, Janet.'

'She's too busy, I suppose.'

'She will have letters to type later on.'

'She can't speak English, she doesn't know enough French to correct proofs, she has only one talent.' She slapped down the drinks in front of them. A little spilled on to the table.

Ponti raised his glass to them. He drank only Perrier water. 'I am happy to learn that you will publish my book.'

'We are honoured,' Gilbert said. Something about Ponti's manner made this kind of tone obligatory. 'Do you want to discuss the terms in detail? I understand we deal with you direct.'

'I have done with agents. The terms content me perfectly.' They had contented Gilbert too, when Max outlined them. For an author with so high a reputation Ponti had asked for surprisingly little money. 'But I must mention the translation.'

'Eugene was dissatisfied with his English translation,' Max said easily.

'I was disgusted. Have you heard of Abraham J. Cohen?'

'I have explained that that was an American translation. Ours, now –' Max sucked in his breath to show the stylistic purity and academic correctness of the translation they would sponsor. Ponti looked directly at Gilbert. The look was not comfortable to meet, because his eyes had apparently an assessing gaze. The whites were clear, the irises a vivid blue.

'You understand that money no longer is of importance. My life is simple, my wants are few.'

'Just a house outside Amalfi, a flat in Rome and this villa for the summer,' Janet Ponti interjected. Ponti gave no sign that he had heard.

'I am an old man now, I have lost my sight, of what importance is money? My life is over, it is time to contemplate what is eternal.'

Janet drew back her chair, the noise harsh on the stone. Her pale skin was blotchy. She gave Max a single glance, then her feet made a rattling sound as she went back into the villa. Ponti looked inquiring. Flavia said something, and Max for a moment appeared to be about to protest but stayed silent.

'You must forgive my daughter.' It was almost as if he were a priest forgiving sins. 'Your partner here tells me that the translator will be Angus Wilson. That is satisfactory.'

Max gave Gilbert an enormous wink. He was too stunned to do more than repeat feebly, 'Angus Wilson.'

'I was speaking to Angus just after the last PEN Congress,' Max said smoothly. 'I think I told you that he has the greatest possible admiration for your work.'

'I was gratified. I have read his novels with interest.'

Recovering a little from the shock, Gilbert decided that he must be firm. 'I must make it clear that at present it is impossible to say who will do the translation.' Rather lamely he went on, 'We shall certainly get the best possible translator, and he will be most carefully chosen.'

'Exactly. You've really hit the nail on the head,' Max agreed heartily.

'You spoke of Angus Wilson.' Ponti's voice was accusing. 'Who are you speaking of now?'

The blonde got up and stretched like a cat, then walked delicately across the terrace. She halted by the easy chair in which the old man sat, kissed the top of his head and put one hand on his knee. She ran this hand up his thigh until it reached his crotch, where it deliberately lingered. Bending over, she murmured something into his ear, then went inside the villa.

'We are speaking of the very best,' Max said earnestly. 'You want the best translator, nobody else is good enough, we understand that. If it is not Angus Wilson, it will be somebody of equal distinction. Perhaps Iris Murdoch.'

When Ponti stood up it seemed natural for them to stand up too. 'I shall have to consider. I regret that my household arrangements make it impossible for me to ask you to stay to lunch.'

'Eugene –'

'Mr Bomberg, I shall have to consider. I have said this, I repeat it.'

'May I call on you later – this evening – to discuss the whole thing. And make other suggestions. I assure you that we shall give you a translator of your choice, a real interpreter. Like Scott-Moncrieff with Proust.'

'I shall be happy to see you.'

'Would eight o'clock be all right?'

'My appetite is that of a sparrow, but if you wish you may come to dinner. The food will be the simplest.' With a noticeable lack of warmth he added, 'Mr Welton, if you are free, I shall be happy to see you.'

'Too bad you've got that date this evening,' Max said. With a feeling that he was being rather weak, Gilbert agreed that he had a date.

Ponti moved uncertainly towards the french windows. Max put out a hand to help him, then withdrew it. Janet appeared as though she had been waiting, and took his arm. He shook off her hand. Max and Gilbert followed them through the sitting-room and out to the hall. At the bottom of a curving staircase Ponti shook hands with them ceremoniously. Flavia appeared and said something. Slowly he moved up the stairs. The audience was over.

As soon as he was at the top of the stairs Janet turned on them. 'Do you know what will happen now? He will make my life miserable for a week. Why did you do it?'

'Do what?' Gilbert asked stupidly.

'Let him think that Angus Wilson is translating his book; what does it matter? Who is going to tell him anything different? Me? And I'll tell you something else, he hates the English anyway.' She turned and went through a swing door which evidently led to the kitchen.

By the time they had driven out through the iron gates Max had recovered his bounce. 'An unusual household.'

'Ghastly. How long has he been blind?'

'Oh, quite a while. His wife was English, you know that? She left him twenty years ago when Janet was a little girl. That was her misfortune.'

'How do you mean?'

'For someone like Eugene it is unthinkable that a woman should leave him. He sent Janet away to school in England, to get her out of his sight. Then he brought her back here to work for him. Fortunately as you saw she is ugly, not like her mother. She has not left him. Eugene has, you know, a certain reputation with women. His wife insulted him, and he takes it out of Janet. With Flavia, and no doubt others.'

'How do you know all this?'

'I have my methods, Watson, as old Sherlock used to say. And then he is very mean, you gathered that?'

'We are going back a different way.'

'Ah ha.' They went through a small pine forest and came out almost at the top of Mount Trebevic. Max paused for a moment to admire the view, which he seemed to regard proprietorially. 'Isn't that just something?' he asked. Then he drove on to a small restaurant near the top of the cable railway. 'Have you ever eaten roast boar? Then you will do so today.'

The roast boar was flavoursome but tough, rather like venison, and it was Max's attitude in relation to it, his central European air of instructing the ignorant, that was the immediate cause of their quarrel. Or perhaps it was the powerful locally made red wine that they drank with it. Sitting under the restaurant awnings, looking at yet another unquestionably magnificent view and remembering the scent on the handkerchief, he felt hatred for Max.

'When you go up there this evening I want it made perfectly clear that all this talk about Angus Wilson or Iris Murdoch translating the book is nonsense. Neither of them is a translator as far as I know.'

Max nodded, smiling. He took out a cigar case, offered a cigar to Gilbert and when it was refused lighted one himself. With the large tube rolling between his red lips he looked, Gilbert thought, like an East End Jew who had made it.

'After all, they may not even know Italian,' Max offered. He rocked with laughter. 'A joke. You should have seen your face. But actually, my dear, you have made what might be called rather a balls-up of the whole thing.'

'*I* have?'

'Precisely. Now look. That girl is perfectly right. All we want from Eugene is a piece of paper with his signature on it. It is one of our standard agreement forms. Oh yes, I have brought one with me. It gives terms, publication price, advance and so on. Everything we have discussed. He signs it, I come home, and we have a best-seller.'

'But our agreement says nothing about a translator.'

'Precisely,' Max said again. 'As Janet said, how would he know?'

Gilbert felt rising in him a full-blooded anger worthy of E.R. Did it spring from sexual jealousy, the Anglo-Germanic syndrome, a knowledge that Max would always succeed with women while in the end he would always fail? Was it hatred of all that Max represented, his unEnglish gift of easy friendship and his unEnglish vice of easy adjustment to dishonesty? He managed to keep his voice quiet.

'We could never do anything like that, surely you must realize it?' Max shrugged. 'To cheat a poor old blind man, with the help of his daughter because she hates him — that's plain disgusting fraud.' Max did not stop smiling and Gilbert fleetingly wondered, *Does he hate me as I hate him*?

'Eugene isn't poor, he's rich. He's not a poor old man, he's a tyrant who sleeps with his secretary and makes life a misery for his daughter. But what you don't understand, what you most don't understand, my dear, is that this is a game he is playing. Eugene is not a fool, he knows quite well he will not get Angus Wilson to translate his book, he simply wants to make sure we understand his importance. It is a game, he enjoys it.'

'It's fraud. It may be the kind of thing you have done before, perhaps it is commonplace for somebody with your background. You may as well understand that I should never consent to it. If you come back with an agreement I shall want a specific letter signed by Ponti to say that the choice of a translator is left to us.'

Max stubbed out his cigar and rose from the table. He paid the bill. They did not speak on the drive back. The Europa car park was full, and Max put the car in a back yard where bricks and bits of concrete lay scattered about, looking as though they were part of a simultaneous process of building and demolition. In the hotel lobby Max spoke.

'I shall go up there this evening, and I shall come back with an agreement.'

Gilbert could not stop his voice from rising. The clerk at the desk, the one who knew English, looked amused.

'You know what I said about that. I mean it.'

'But I am not so foolish as to think you have insulted me because of that. There is something wrong with you, and you connect it with me.'

He turned away. Gilbert gripped his arm. 'I connect you with Virginia.' He shouted the next words. 'What have you done with Virginia?'

'Take care. People will look at us, you would not like that.' And in fact the clerk was now watching with fascination this uncharacteristic, unEnglish show of temper. 'Virginia would love you, if you would permit it. That is my opinion. I can't be responsible for your delusions. But I want to say this. I intend to remain in the firm. You won't find it easy to get rid of me.'

Would he not find it easy? You unscrewed two nuts near the front tyres, was that what Painter had said? He bent down, looked and saw nothing. It occurred to him that he ought to open the bonnet, which had a spring catch arrangement. Peering in, he saw that there did seem to be some nuts beside the wheels, but he had no idea whether they were the ones Painter had meant. In any case, how did you undo them? Nothing had been said about that, but presumably there must be a spanner among the tools. He rummaged hurriedly in the boot, found an all-purpose spanner and fitted it to the nuts. They turned easily. One turn, two turns, three turns. Should he make it half a dozen? He had no idea. Were there similar nuts at the back? He had no idea about that either.

He stood in the empty yard, surrounded by builders' rubble, trying to decide whether he should look for nuts at the back of the car and undo them, or tighten up again those he had loosened. There was a sound. Somebody was behind him, somebody had disturbed the rubble. He closed the boot, straightened and walked away. A black cat came out of the rubble and stared at him, then ran off. He saw nobody as he came out of the yard and returned to the hotel.

In the hotel room he wondered whether he should go back and try to screw up the nuts again. He decided against it. What would he say if Max found him bent over the car? What idiotic feeling had possessed him, that he should try to tamper with a car about which he knew nothing in a way derived from a ridiculous crime story? It seemed to him impossible that Gilbert Welton could have done any such thing.

While he washed his hands he remembered Max's last words, something about Virginia loving him if he would permit it, and he suddenly realized that if she had returned home and was trying to reach him she would be unable to do so. He put in a call to his house and lay on the bed for half an hour, to be told that they had not been able to get through. Had the number actually been rung, or was it not possible to make the London connection? There was no point in staying any longer in Sarajevo, or indeed in Yugoslavia. Nor was there any point in seeing Max again. He had made his position about the translation clear, and another meeting would no doubt end in another quarrel.

He went down to the lobby, and discovered that it was impossible to fly direct from Sarajevo back to England. The best connection was via Zagreb, with a four hour wait, and he made a booking on this for the morning. With all this done he went out, partly to avoid seeing Max. As he walked past the yard the car still stood there, with two others now beside it. A man and a woman got out of one of them.

At half past nine he was in a night-club called the Bosna, in a narrow street off the long Marsala Tito. He had found it by wandering about the streets, after eating in a fish restaurant a good but rather expensive lobster. It was not much like what he thought of as a night-club, and certainly resembled very little the Out Going. Young men and women danced what he recognized as a local version of the twist, in a manner both more whole-hearted and more decorous than anything he had seen in England. The musicians played an adulterated version of Western pop songs, with occasional solos of quite a different kind, languorous and passionate. There was a sprinkling of tourists, mostly German but with one or two American couples. They did not speak to Gilbert, and he sat alone at a small table. Once he asked

563

a girl to dance, but she smiled and turned away her head and a moment later her escort appeared. He was a fierce-looking young man who wore earrings, and under the strength of his glare Gilbert went back to his table.

He sat there drinking something called prepecenica, which he had picked at random from the list offered by a bald, gloomy waiter wearing dark trousers and an embroidered waistcoat, topped by a fez. The first glass seemed to burn away the lining of his throat. He drank a second to see if it could really be as atrocious as he had thought, and discovered that it was comparatively agreeable when accompanied by Turkish coffee.

'What ho, we meet again.' The voice was unmistakable, but his eyes needed to confirm the evidence of his ears. Jerry Painter stood beside his table, wearing a shirt of which the whole front was in the pattern of the Union Jack. He was smiling broadly. A small girl hung on to his arm as though she might lose it.

'International collaboration.' He turned and revealed that the back of his shirt showed the Stars and Stripes. 'Bright but not gaudy. And I've been doing a spot of the old fraternizing. This is Maria. Maria, meet Gilbert. She's an assistant in our Topline office here.'

'I am sorry, my English is not good.' The girl smiled.

'We use the old sign language.' Painter patted her bottom and sat down. 'Mind if we park here? I owe you an apology, old man. Those weirdos drove me round the bend, I don't mind admitting it. I apologize, I grovel, I bow my head before you.' His head touched the table top. 'Two Englishmen in a strange land. Mustn't quarrel. Shake on it. What's your poison?'

In the club, in St John's Wood, anywhere in England he would have got up and walked away. Even here he did not touch the hand held out to him but placed in it his empty glass, at the same time saying accusingly, either to Painter or to the girl, 'You left me to walk into Sarajevo, he dumped my case in the road.'

'How could I ever have done such a bloody rotten thing?' He said to the girl, 'It was these weirdos, I told you the boy held us up with a gun. You know I don't think she believed me if she understood what I was talking about at all, but it's true, isn't it?'

'You told me you were going to report them.'

The girl had been sniffing his glass. She said gravely, 'Prepe-cenica, not good.'

'If Maria says it's not good it must be terrible. Her stomach's made of cast iron. I know, I've felt it.'

'Did you report them?'

'What do you take me for? Anglo-American solidarity for ever, that's what I say. Let's drink to that.'

Gilbert asked Maria to dance. He found with surprise that standing up demanded a good deal of his attention. They staggered about on the floor.

'Jerry is a funny man. He makes me laugh. He is an old friend, yes?'

'No, we met out here. Not a friend at all really.'

'You think he is hard? I think he is very hard. He has booted here a lot of people.'

'Booted? Oh yes, I see.'

'The order of the boot, he said. I think it is an idiom?'

'Yes.'

'Here in Sarajevo it was very bad, Topline, sometimes we send out the cars and they are very bad. Jerry gives the order of the boot.' A couple bumped into them. He lurched and almost fell. Her arm was raised to hold him, and he saw the dark hair in the armpit.

'I should like very much to go to England, do you think he will take me? He says yes, perhaps.' He was about to express scepticism when he stumbled again. 'Perhaps we go back.'

'Isn't she the most wonderful little thing you've ever held in your arms?' Painter asked as they returned.

Gilbert sat down heavily. His head was clear although his movements seemed not perfectly co-ordinated. He felt a militant dislike of Painter, a desire to insult him. 'She says you're talking about taking her to England. I was going to tell her, want to tell her, don't believe a word he says.' Painter looked injured.

'Maria knows I'm a man of my word.'

The prepecenica went down easily this time, although he was glad to have finished it. Then disconcertingly, mysteriously, his glass was full and he felt bound to raise it again. He heard the girl say something about leaving, and although he hated Painter and wanted to insult him, he wanted also to keep them there, not to go back to his hotel. He remembered his plane booking.

'Flying back tomorrow. To Zagreb. Got to wait at Zagreb. Glad to get out of the country.'

Painter leaned across. The Union Jack glared at him. 'I agree, old man, but I shouldn't say it too loud. Not here. You don't know who might be listening.'

'Bloody rotten country, it's brought me no luck.' The lines of the Union Jack wavered, he blinked to keep them straight. 'Good books lately, read any?'

'I think we'd better get you home. Which hotel is it?'

He could see the flecks of broken blood vessels in Painter's nose. 'Any more first gear murders?'

'I don't know what you're talking about.'

'Know what you said about me, a weirdo who was soft on crime. Never do anything, you said. Well, I've done it.'

'Of course you have. Up you come now.' His hands were on the table. Painter's hand was placed over one of them, tried to disengage what turned out to be his grip on the table. With his other hand, made into a fist, he smacked down on it. Painter yelped and let go.

'Your brake fluid nonsense, I've done it all. Doesn't mean a thing, any of it. Just books. Bad books lately.'

'*Jerry*,' the girl said. 'Jerry, I must not have trouble.'

Painter wrenched away Gilbert's left arm from the table, pulling him up. Almost instinctively he struck out with the right. He was astonished to feel the flesh of Painter's face, delighted to see blood appear in the nostrils of his detested nose. A couple of drops went on to the Union Jack. A look of rage replaced the amiability of Painter's expression, he said some inaudible words and one of his fists – or was it both? – came forward. Gilbert felt a blow in his stomach and then a grinding pain in his mouth as though all his teeth were being shaken in his head. Then he knew nothing more.

Chapter 6

The Interrogation

His head ached, he was lying flat on his back, two commission-aires were looking at him upside down. He closed his eyes to take away this illusion and when he opened them again the faces were the right way up. They had been standing behind the bed on which he lay and now they had moved round to the head of it, that was all. They wore rather pretty blue uniforms, and at their waists were holsters from which the handles of revolvers pro-truded. The revolvers settled the question of identity. They were not commissionaires but policemen.

He was prepared to take the presence of police officers quite equably until he saw a blue passport in the hands of the younger one, a fresh-faced boy who looked as if he should have been in a school choir. He sat up and pointed at the passport. A searing pain split his head through the middle. He became aware at the same time that he was fully dressed except for his shoes. With a great effort he moved his head and saw that the drawers of his dressing-table had been opened, and that his bags were open too. The other policeman, a grizzled man with an unfriendly ex-pression, held up his keys. They must have been taken from him while he slept. He pointed at the keys.

'How dare you take my keys and open my bags?' The words came out in a croak.

The grizzled man held out a hand for the passport, which was given to him. Slowly and disdainfully as a strip dancer he re-moved dark gloves, looked at it, and said, 'Jil-bear-vel-ton.'

'That's right. But what are you doing with my passport?'

'*Zasto posjecujete Jugoslaviju? Sto je svrha Vase posjete Sara-jevu?*'

Unintelligible. 'Give me my passport,' he retorted. Grizzle stared at him contemptuously, flicked open the passport again and then put it in his pocket, taking care not to crease his jacket.

'*Navedeno je da ste Vi izdavac. Da li je Vasa posjeta u vezi publikacije?*'

'I don't understand you. Speak English.' The pain in his head became too great to bear and he sank back, groaning. Grizzle snapped something at his youthful partner, who came across and held out one hand with a boyish smile. Gilbert unwisely took it, to find himself briskly hauled to his feet. For a moment he thought he would faint, and for another that he would be sick. Then he recovered, and actually standing up made him feel better.

'I can't understand a word you say, and you can't understand me. Why don't you get some linguists in your police?' he asked.

Grizzle stared at him and then spoke rapidly to Round Face, who went out of the room. Gilbert looked at his drawers and case. Everything appeared intact, and indeed what was there that might have been taken? Then he saw his wallet, which lay open on a small table beside Grizzle. He moved towards it. Grizzle divined his intention, picked up the wallet and calmly slipped it into his other jacket pocket.

It was not until the desk clerk appeared from down below, looking apologetic and nervous, that it occurred to him to wonder why the police were searching his room. As soon as he thought about it he knew the answer. There had been a row last night which had involved the police, either in the Bosna or at the hotel.

'Did I cause trouble last night?' he asked the desk clerk. The man stared at him. 'When I came back, perhaps there was a fight. If so, will you say I apologize.'

'Your friends brought you here. You were –' He mimed unconsciousness and then discovered the word '– sleeping.'

The trouble had been in the Bosna then, and perhaps that was worse. He started to ask about this, but was interrupted by a spate of questions, or perhaps accusations, from Grizzle, which seemed to startle the clerk. Gilbert waited until this fusillade of phrases had subsided and then asked, 'What did he say?'

He could not hear the reply, because Grizzle started again. '*On ce poci sa nama*,' he said, and added as an afterthought, '*Sad*.'

'He wishes you to go with them.' The clerk had become pale.

'To the police station, I suppose. What for?'

'Naturally, to answer some questions.'

He looked at his watch. It was on his wrist, but the glass had splintered and the hand was not moving. He had no idea of the time, and as always this disturbed him. He spoke with a sharpness that was the product of uncertainty.

'Tell him that I am ready to answer questions here, but I do not wish to go with him. And tell him that whatever happened last night, it does not justify his searching my room and taking my wallet and passport. Do you understand?'

The desk clerk shrugged and shook his head, although Gilbert felt certain that he understood. 'I want my wallet,' he said loudly and angrily. The clerk said something. Grizzle put a hand on his revolver holster, then seemed to change his mind and held out the wallet with a shrug.

'That's better,' Gilbert said. He looked at the wallet. His money was intact.

Grizzle said, *'Gospodin Velton molim podjite sa nama da odgovorite na neka pitanja.'*

'He says you must accompany them to the police station.'

'This is absurd.' The throbbing in his head had lessened, but now it became suddenly worse again. He sat down on the bed. Grizzle made a sign and Round Face heaved him up, started to pull him towards the door.

Gilbert pointed a shaking hand at the desk clerk. 'You are a witness that they are taking me away under protest. I shall complain to the British consul. And I want to know what this is all about.'

'Sta on kaze?' This was evidently a question. The clerk made a long speech to Grizzle and then said to Gilbert, 'I do not understand.'

'You mean you don't understand what I'm saying? Nonsense.'

The man wiped his forehead and said pleadingly, 'If you will go with them, please. I am sure it will not be for long.'

He gave up. 'Perhaps at least they'll have somebody there who can speak English.'

The desk clerk smiled in relief and nodded emphatically.

He sat in the back of a little black car, with Grizzle in the front seat and Round Face by his side. The driver might have been Round Face's brother. They crossed one of the bridges over the river into an area that looked like Bistrik, although he could not be sure. After ten minutes' driving the car turned into the courtyard of a large grey building. The driver got out and opened the front passenger door for Grizzle, then the back door for Gilbert. He looked up to see the sun almost directly overhead. It must be about midday. He walked between Grizzle and Round Face through swing doors, and followed Grizzle into an office where half a dozen men sat at desks. They did not look like policemen, or like anything except clerks. Grizzle spoke to one of them, who made a note.

'*Ovamo*,' Grizzle said, and beckoned. They went in convoy, Grizzle in front and Round Face behind, along a passage with doors at either side. There were no names on these doors. Grizzle stopped suddenly in front of one door, and Round Face moved from behind Gilbert to open it. With a trace of a smile showing beneath his clipped moustache Grizzle made a gesture indicating that Gilbert should precede him. What was waiting for him inside the room, a man at a desk waiting to question him? He hesitated momentarily, and a hand on his back gently pushed him inside. The door closed.

There was no desk, and nobody else in the room. It contained a bed, a chair, a small table, a curtained recess. A window set high up in the wall had bars on it. There was no handle on the door. He was in a cell.

Or at least he was shut up. Looking at the furniture, which was of light oak and rather similar to the utility furniture made in Britain during and immediately after the war, and discovering behind the curtain a lavatory, wash-basin and towel, he had the impression that he was in a rather low-grade hotel. Or perhaps in a waiting-room from which, after a few minutes, he would be called to some disagreeable appointment of an orthodontic kind. This impression was enhanced by the fact that the toilet recess had in it a shelf containing half a dozen books, most of them Marxist classics in Serbo-Croat, but including a Penguin edition of Evelyn Waugh's *Decline and Fall*.

Its presence was a kind of reassurance, implying as it surely did an English visitor, somebody who had spent an hour or two here and, his spirit enlivened by Llanabba Castle, Captain Grimes and Margot Beste-Chetwynde, had thoughtfully left his

copy of the book to entertain other possible English readers. He
opened it and read the name 'Frosic' written on the inside cover
in a neat cribbed hand. Looking at the chapter headings he saw
one that said, 'Stone Walls do not a Prison Make', and turned to
it:

The next four weeks of solitary confinement were among the hap-
piest of Paul's life. The physical comforts were certainly meagre, but
at the Ritz Paul had learned to appreciate the inadequacy of purely
physical comfort. It was so exhilarating, he found, never to have to
make any decision on any subject, to be wholly relieved from the
smallest consideration of time, meals or clothes, to have no anxiety
ever about what kind of impression he was making; in fact, to be free.

He put back the book on the shelf, feeling intense anxiety. What
nonsense it all was. There were no stone walls, this was not the
Lubianka, but the light oak and the lavatory did not conceal its
identity as a prison. He was shut up and could not get out, how
could anybody possibly identify that as freedom?

He stood on a chair in an attempt to see out of the window,
from which a gleam of sunlight shone, but was unable to reach
the bars. He felt a need to urinate in the wash-basin instead of the
lavatory, did so, and was at once ashamed and alarmed. Was this
what happened to you in prison, was his need like that of the
housebreaker to defecate on valuable carpets, slash pictures,
scrawl obscenities on walls? He sat on the bed, which creaked
beneath him, and tried to concentrate on images from the reality
of his past life, Virginia, Coldharbour, even old Langridge-
Wood. They were only names, which summoned up no pictures
of any kind. He got up, went to the door, banged on it and then
kicked it. Nothing happened for a minute or two and then a slot
which he had not previously noticed was pushed aside. A voice
said, '*Sto zelite?*'

He went to the grille revealed in the door and looked through
it. An eye, bloodshot and rolling, stared at him. 'How long am I
to be kept here? I demand to see somebody in charge.'

'*Mirujte,*' the voice said.

He felt the frustration of somebody unable to make himself
understood. The alien character of this fragment of Europe had
been hidden from him by his situation as a tourist, smiled at and
agreed with by hotel managers and waiters. Now it seemed to

him that he might as well try to make himself understood by a central African tribe.

He continued to look through the grille until the bloodshot eye disappeared and the gap was decisively shut. The little wooden panel closed over it perfectly from both sides, so that the join was almost indiscernible. He lay down on the bed, but found that various twitchings were taking place in the calf of his right leg and arm that he was unable to control. He walked about the cell, noting that he covered it each way in three strides, so that the area must be approximately nine feet by nine. He seemed to have read that this was the size of an English prison cell, although of course in England there was no curtained-off lavatory. It occurred to him that the curtaining off, presumably to conceal the prisoner on the lavatory seat from the warder's eye, was a surprising piece of prudishness or carelessness. Suppose you tried to commit suicide by putting your head in the lavatory bowl? The thought was slightly cheering, for it seemed to imply that these were cells for only temporary habitation.

The sunlight had gone from the window when the grille moved again. He stopped pacing and looked at it. The door opened. Two men stood there, one in uniform who was no doubt the warder, and a younger fair-haired man wearing a grey suit. This man beckoned him with one finger. Gilbert stepped out of the cell and they began to walk down the passage, in the opposite direction from the way they had come.

'Where am I being taken?' he asked. 'I demand to see some-body in charge.'

The fair-haired man said, 'You will see the President himself.'

Did that mean he was being taken to see Tito? His bewilder-ment made it seem possible.

Upstairs, along a corridor, over an internal bridge that joined his building to another, at last to a door with a name written on it that he had no time to read. The fair-haired man tapped on the door and they went in.

He was seeing at last a man behind a desk, a man looking at papers. He put them aside, and made a motion for Gilbert to sit down. The fair-haired man also sat down at a smaller desk near the door. Gilbert did not sit down. He asked, 'Do you speak English?'

'Pretty well, yes. Do you smoke – English cigarettes?' The accent was only slight.

'I won't smoke. I want to know why I was taken forcibly from my hotel, brought here and kept in detention for several hours.'

'Forcibly, Mr Welton?' He took a cigarette and drew on it. 'Was force used? I gave no such instruction.'

'Against my will, then. And without an explanation.'

'Let me introduce myself. Ivan Radonic. I am the President of Police.' Radonic had a large smooth face. He wore heavy horn-rims. His expression was mild, even friendly. 'I really should advise you to sit down. You may be here some time.'

The maintenance of an indignant attitude is always difficult for an Englishman. Gilbert sat down.

'Your name is Gilbert Welton, you are the director of an English publishing company. Why are you in this country?'

A strong sense of his own rights had returned to Gilbert with the relief of being able to make himself understood. 'I have no intention of answering questions until you have told me why I am here.' Tapping in the corner distracted him. Radonic followed his glance.

'He is making a note of your interrogation, that is all. An old English custom. Perhaps we have a more up-to-date machine than those in your country.'

'I've told you, I shan't answer questions –'

'You do not understand the situation. Or perhaps even my own position. I am the President of Police. That means I am in charge of this district. I am like – oh, say, one of your Superintendents, although my powers are a little wider. You will have to talk to me.'

'I don't see why I should. You've had me brought here against my will, why should I say anything. I refuse to say anything at all.' He folded his arms.

'You are angry as well as ignorant. I am trying to make excuses for you, but please do not make it too difficult.' He went on, speaking more rapidly. 'You are not in England now. Do you know the old saying that a foreigner who drives a car in this country has one foot in prison and the other in the grave? A foreigner in trouble with the police is in a worse position. If he behaves himself he will never see us, except occasionally in the street on traffic duty, but if he comes here to commit a crime we dislike that very much. *I* dislike it, Mr Welton. I do not like our own criminals, but I like much less those who come from another country to commit their crime here because they think we are foolish. I take pleasure in showing them – yes, I take pleasure, Mr Welton – that this is not at all the case.'

He said with genuine bewilderment, 'I don't know what you mean. I'm not sure what I said last night, or who got mixed up in the little fight I had –'

'Do you really think that for just a fight we should search your room, look at your passport?' Radonic took off his glasses, pinched his nose where they had been, and spoke gently. 'Mr Max Bomberg is your partner, is he not? You went with him yesterday to see Eugene Ponti, the distinguished novelist who makes his summer home in our country. I have to say to you that we are delighted for Signor Ponti to visit us. We are concerned for his welfare. I, personally, am concerned.' He put on his glasses again. 'And I have also to give you the sad news that your partner Mr Bomberg is dead. His car went off the road coming down Mount Trebevic last night and it fell a hundred feet or more. He and his companion were killed immediately.'

'His companion?'

'Her name was Flavia Orsini. She acted as secretary to Signor Ponti.'

'But why was she in the car?'

'She was your partner's mistress. She had stayed in his hotel room the past three nights, returning in the morning. The hotel staff knew this, but of course she did not care. And we knew it too, but we also did not care. We are used to the immorality of foreigners and we tolerate it.' Radonic's mouth turned down at the corners. 'It is natural for you to be surprised, Mr Welton, but why are you so disturbed?'

Two thoughts emerged from the confusion in his mind. He had committed a double murder, he had killed a woman utterly unconnected with him. And the murder itself had been pointless. It had been committed in error, for if Max had taken Flavia back to his room for the last three nights, Virginia could not have been staying with him. Perhaps she had never even come to Sarajevo. He closed his eyes.

'Mr Welton.' The fair-haired young man was holding out the national receipt for all ills, a glass of slivovitz. He drank it in two gulps and felt better.

'You see we do not practise the third degree.' Radonic slapped the table with his hand. 'Now I will tell you what is the matter, Mr Welton, why you are here. You were expecting this, were you not, it is not a surprise to you at all. You are only surprised to be caught.'

He stared dumbfounded at the large smooth face across the table. Radonic said, in a lowered voice, 'There was a brake failure. That was something you arranged. You know what I am talking about, don't try to pretend.'

'I don't understand.' He felt a desire to confide in the man on the other side of the table. Was not confession followed by submission the way to grace? Radonic had about him the kind of benevolence, the air of tolerance towards more fallible human beings, that is said to have been possessed by the Spanish Inquisitors who were truly sorry that those who came before them should be so foolish and so unrepentant. About the knowledge he possessed there seemed something miraculous. Why should Gilbert have been linked at once with the brake trouble on the car? But when put to the point Gilbert, like other modern men, did not believe in miracles, and it was for this reason that he repeated, 'I don't understand.'

'Then this will take even longer than I thought.' He picked up a telephone and spoke in a low voice. A dumpy middle-aged woman came in carrying a tray which she put on the desk. It contained a teapot, two cups, a milk jug, and four thin biscuits on a plate. Radonic smiled. 'A dish of tea with biscuits, English style. I shall be mother.'

The tea was thin and weak, the biscuits tasted like straw. Radonic watched him steadily as though the way in which he drank tea would in itself provide the answers to questions. 'The tea is refreshing, is that the right word?'

'Yes.'

'Very well.' The tray was pushed aside. 'So you don't understand. Well, fortunately we have the rest of the day, we have many days. You might say that we have all the time in the world, although the time will pass more slowly for you than for me. Do you admire my English? I was in your country during my naval service. Edinburgh, Liverpool, fine places.'

'Very good. Your English.'

'You had a quarrel with your partner yesterday.'

'I did? Certainly not.'

'At the Vjdikovac Restaurant, on Trebevic. Ah, I see you remember. Why did you quarrel?'

'I'd entirely forgotten. It was nothing.'

'That is not what I was told by Lieutenant Andric. What did you quarrel about?'

'It was an argument, not a quarrel. About what translator we should get for Ponti's work.'

'A literary matter. Not about your wife?' He stared at Radonic. 'Your wife's name is Virginia?'

'Yes.'

The President of Police laughed. 'Do not look at me like that, I have no supernatural powers.' He read from a paper in front of him. 'Statement of Janos Vujic, desk clerk. "I saw the two Englishmen in the hotel lobby at about fifteen-thirty hours. The taller one was shouting at the other. It was something to do about his wife – with his wife, I am sorry. At one point he shouted out, 'What have you done with Virginia?' I think that was the name, it was a difficult English name." That is part of his statement. Correct?'

'Yes. I'd forgotten.'

'Two things you had forgotten. But I should not have thought you were forgetful, I should have said you were a careful man.'

'It meant nothing.'

'I should not have thought you were a man who said things that meant nothing.' Radonic got up from his chair and began to walk about the room. He was a big man with a slight limp, which made his walk seem eager and predatory. 'This fight you say you had last night, tell me about it.'

'It was in a night-club.'

'The Bosna, yes.'

'You know about it already.'

'Just tell me.' He stood looking down at Gilbert. 'Believe me, it will be best to tell me. Tell me everything. Your position is not comfortable.'

'I'd had too much to drink. Well, not so very much, but it affected me. I was with a man named Painter and we had a row, I don't remember every word.'

'Did you say you would be glad to be out of this country?' He laughed at the look on Gilbert's face. 'Do not worry, my friend, we are used to the rudeness of foreigners. There is freedom of speech for everybody in the Yugoslav Republics.'

The words were spoken with infuriating smugness. In England, far away, he would not have been moved to reply. Now he said, 'Including Milovan Djilas?'

'*Ovo nemoje da zapisujete.*' The tapping stopped. 'Do not make things worse than they are. You have nothing to do with Djilas. His pronouncements are political.'

'So freedom of speech doesn't apply in his case.'

'You have a gift for making enemies, Mr Welton. I do not advise you to make one of me. Be thankful that I have not had your remark noted.' He nodded to the fair-haired man. The tapping continued with the next question.

'I repeat, we are tolerant. You are not here because you insulted my country in a public place, although you would be unwise to do so again. Tell me what else happened in the Bosna.'

'You know it all.' And indeed it did seem to him that Radonic had traced with impossible speed and accuracy his words and movements. 'I had a fight with Painter. I hit him and he hit me. After that I don't remember.'

'You were both asked to leave. Then your friend brought you here. If he is your friend. The night porter got you to your room.' The President spoke absently, as though his mind was on something else. 'What else did you say to Painter?'

It was then that he remembered (although had he ever really forgotten?) that he had said something to Painter about *First Gear Murder* and brake fluid. If he told the inquisitor, what would happen? The urge to confess was so strong that he did not trust himself to speak. He shook his head and stared at the floor. He felt a hand placed beneath his chin, and strangely this gave him comfort. His head was lifted. Radonic was squatting beside him. Behind the thick horn-rims brown eyes looked into his own. A hand patted his head. It was a moment of comradeship so poignant that he could have cried.

'No third degree. A pity in a way that we are civilized, not like the gangster Americans.' He stood up again, loped round to his chair. The moment had passed. 'I shall be frank with you, why should I be anything else? We are efficient, but in spite of appearances we do not work miracles. I do not care for this whole affair. We have here Autoservis and Putnik, why did your friend have to hire a car from these people called Topline? I am speaking of your friend Bomberg. It was because of this that we talked to Mr Painter. He calls himself a *trouble-shooter*.' With heavy irony he added, 'I should rather call him a *trouble-maker*.'

'I see.' Like all conjuring tricks this one was disappointing when revealed.

'We talked to him. And he talked about you. He had already made a complaint about –' He looked through the papers '– two American tourists. That they held him up with a gun. In his car. An extraordinary story.'

'I was with him in the car.'

'So he said.'

'It's not true. He behaved badly to them. He is a very unpleasant man.' When had he told so many lies in so short a time?

'I thought he was your friend. He took you back to the hotel.' Gilbert shrugged. Radonic tapped the papers. 'Here is an interesting thing. Andric talked to him early this morning. He told us then something you had said about interfering with the brakes, some nonsense about a detective story.' He paused on a interrogative note. '*After* this we checked the brakes, and found that the controlling nuts had been loosened. How do you explain what he said, if he was not telling the truth?'

'It is not for me to explain it.' Almost happily he said, 'He still had the hand brake.'

'No doubt he tried to apply it. There were skid marks on the road. The point is that Painter told us this story *before* we checked the brakes. Do you suggest that he interfered with them himself?'

'I don't suggest anything.' From some point outside himself he listened to the answer and was pleased by it. Was it a totally new Gilbert Welton who spoke, one who had relinquished the past?

Or was it a game he was playing, based on his reluctance to face reality?

'I see.' Radonic sighed, perhaps a little theatrically. 'You are not being helpful.'

'I'm sorry.'

'Perhaps you do not understand the difficulty of my position. You thought I should say "your position," no doubt, but I am an open person, not a deceiver. There are several aspects here, the affair is not simple. One, we – and I am speaking not of our Sarajevo commune alone but of important people in Belgrade – are anxious that nothing should disturb Signor Ponti, our distinguished visitor. Any kind of scandal would be regretted. Two, an Englishman has died violently, and his woman companion also. It would be unfortunate if this appeared to reflect on the state of our roads, if any local negligence were implied. Three, I have the statement of your friend – I know you say he is not your friend, but you were travelling and drinking with him – your friend Mr Painter. If I pursue what he has said, there will be some undesirable scandal, if I do not, perhaps scandal will be caused also. This Flavia Orsini, she was well connected. A whore, but well connected,' he said without heat.

'There is also the question of justice. That seems to have escaped your attention.'

'Naïve.' The President sounded irritable. 'Justice is not an abstraction, Mr Welton. Juries in your country reach their verdicts on the basis of bourgeois prejudice, judges pass sentence to protect their own kind of society. The sort of justice you are speaking of does not exist. The question is, where is the balance of advantage?' He spoke to the young man, and then said to Gilbert, 'I have told him there is no need to record this, it is merely conversation.'

There was a switchboard beside Radonic, and now a green light showed on it. He picked up one of three telephones in front of him and talked for a couple of minutes, giving an occasional speculative glance at Gilbert. With the receiver replaced he said, 'Very well. Thank you.'

The fair young man stood up. Gilbert stood too. 'We've finished?'

579

'We have finished.'

'And I can go?'

'I did not say that. We shall resume our conversation later.'

'Then I want to see the British consul.'

'Later. Perhaps it will not be necessary.'

'What do you mean?'

'This is a chat, that is the English word. No more. But in this chat you have not told the truth. Be quiet, listen to me. We shall talk again. If I am satisfied with your story, very well. If not, you will appear before the examining magistrate. When that is decided, is the time to see your representative.'

'You were talking about the balance of advantage. You mean you've made up your mind what it is?'

'I did not say that. You have not been helpful.'

'I want to see the English representative, somebody official.'

'Later.' Suddenly Radonic seemed cold, unfriendly. He pushed a button on his desk and a buzzer sounded.

Back in the cell he realized how confidently he had expected to be set free, and how little that expectation was justified by anything Radonic had said. There might be two, three, a dozen interrogations, and if the balance of advantage appeared to justify it they would end by his being placed on trial. No doubt the British authorities would intervene, but in practice what could they do? He faced for the first time the prospect that this cell might for the next several months be his home. The prospect did not alarm him. Perhaps Paul Pennyfeather had been right after all.

The room became darker, an electric light behind a wire casing was switched on from outside, he was inspected through the grille and a plate of food brought in. It was some sort of stewed meat with vegetables. He ate it all with relish, and drank the mug of thin coffee that came with it. As he chewed the stringy but by no means tasteless beef he wondered why he did not feel distress and guilt. He had been responsible for killing a man because of the mistaken idea that the man was his wife's lover, and also for the death of an absolutely innocent woman. Yet he felt no responsibility for this, remained quite unworried by it. Had the local air created a man anaesthetized to Western ideas of liberal justice because of what he had been through, his ludicrous but still agonizing affair with Anna and the incident with the American hitch-hikers?

What would he have done if the boy had carried out his threat and killed Painter? Contemplating it quite coolly he knew that he would have done nothing, and that his inaction would not have been caused by fear but by what Radonic called the balance of advantage. Perhaps the boy and girl were now in prison because of the complaint that Painter had sworn he did not make. If that was the case, would he prefer that they had killed Painter? He decided that he would. Everything that had happened to him in this country was a contradiction of the ideas he had lived by for at least a decade. Shut up in this small box he did not worry about where Virginia was, or about the crime he had committed, or how long he would stay here. He took down *Decline and Fall* from the shelf again, lay on the bed and began to read it, but found himself too sleepy.

The thought of going to bed filled him with pure unsensual pleasure, and he was indignant to find that he had no pyjamas. Had they been left at the hotel by accident, or was this an indication that he was not expected to stay the night? He banged on the door with one shoe and managed to make the warder understand what was needed. The man returned with a large coarse nightshirt which Gilbert put on. The rough texture of it was comforting. He had his toothbrush and now slowly brushed his teeth and got between the blankets of the hard bed. He felt affection for Radonic, who had been fatherly and kind, and was sorry that he had been a disappointment by his unhelpfulness. Tomorrow, or at their next interview, whenever it was, he would tell Radonic everything and leave him to work out which way the balance of advantage rested. He took off his watch, as he always did at night, and put it on the floor. It was for some reason a comfort that the watch did not work, with its implication that time had been permanently stopped. A feeling of luxuriant emotional ease spread through his body.

He stayed in the cell for another thirty-six hours before being called again to see Radonic. During this not precisely happy but certainly contented time he ate and slept well, re-read *Decline*

and Fall and asked his guardian for a Serbo-Croat dictionary
with which he tried to puzzle out a few words in the other books.
He also prepared in full detail the statement he would make, so
that he could hardly conceal his pleasure when he was taken
again along the corridors. Radonic awaited him, plump and
smiling. The fair-haired young man was in his place.

Gilbert began immediately to make his statement. He said
that he had reason to' believe that Bomberg was carrying on an
affair with his wife, and described briefly his inexpert tampering
with the braking system. The statement was quite short. It
ended with an expression of regret for what he had done, and
praise for Radonic. 'I should like to thank President of Police
Radonic for the courtesy with which he has conducted my
interrogation, to apologize for the trouble I have given him by
not making this statement before, and to emphasize that everything I have said has been entirely voluntary.'

He finished almost on a note of triumph, but something was
lacking. What was it? The stenographer's fingers were still, the
tapping sound was missing. He said appealingly to Radonic,
'You said before that I was not helpful. You can't say that this
time.'

Radonic raised his eyebrows. 'Can I not?'

'I have told you everything, everything I know.'

'You have told me a story, but is it the truth?'

'Of course it is.'

'The motives of people like yourself are often obscure to me
but a desire to confess to crimes that have not been committed is
not unknown. This is done to gain attention, to impress. There is
also the desire to be loved. Such confessions, for such reasons,
are rare in our country but not in bourgeois society. They
express a wish also to suffer, they are a compensation for social
guilt.'

'What I said – you didn't even have it taken down.'

'It was not necessary.'

Outraged, he cried, 'How dare you say that?'

'What you have to say is no longer relevant. A good word, is it
the right one?' He smiled. 'We had learned the cause of the
unhappy accident in which your partner and Miss Orsini lost
their lives. The steering of the car was faulty, very faulty indeed.

It was by this defectiveness that the accident was caused. This our experts have established.'

'But the brakes. You told me yourself about them.'

'A statement based upon a mistaken assumption, correct that, I should say a preliminary examination.' The tapping faltered, was resumed. Radonic looked at Gilbert, but sounded as if he were addressing a meeting. 'In fact it is true to say that the level of the brake fluid was low, but this did not cause the accident. There was very little lining left on the brakes, it was dangerous to drive this car in any circumstances, even along a straight flat road. The basic reason for this tragedy was the use of a car hired from a foreign agency whose vehicles did not conform to the standard of efficiency demanded in this country. The English representative of this agency, the Topline, is at present under interrogation.'

He felt dazed, deprived. 'You mean he may be charged with negligence, something like that?'

'It is dependent upon the result of his further interrogation. There is also a question of currency offences with which he may be charged.' Radonic almost twinkled across the desk. 'For you. Mr Welton, it remains for us to thank you for your cooperation with us, to express very great regret for the trouble caused you, This trouble was caused by the misleading statements of the man Painter.'

'You don't want me any more, I can go?'

'At any time. And thank you.' The twinkle became a smile. His passport appeared. He took it angrily.

'The balance of advantage you talked about, this is an example of it?'

Again the clicking stopped. The President regarded him tolerantly, almost with pity. 'You assume too many things, you feel too much and think too little. Everything one says is not to be taken seriously. Some things are for effect, isn't that the phrase?' He came round his desk, laughing. 'Come now, you will make me think you are sorry to be out of here. We are friends, isn't it so? Put your passport in your pocket.' They shook hands. 'There have been some messages, isn't it so, Paul? Here they are. From your office somebody rang, Miss Pinkthorn – is that the name? And Mr Bunce – is that also correct? – wished to speak with you. I think your firm had told him that you were here in Sarajevo.'

'How did they know –' He did not complete the sentence.

'They did not of course know that you were our guest. The hotel said simply that you were not available.'

'Nobody knows I've been here?'

'Helping the police with their investigations, isn't that your English phrase? We still have much to learn from the English. Shall we try to reach your office for you, now? It is Monday morning.' He shook his head. It seemed to him that he would never again have anything to say to Miss Pinkthorn. 'Your partner's death has of course been reported in the English Press. Paul.'

The fair-haired young man had already poured glasses of slivovitz. 'Your health, Mr Welton. I hope we shall meet again on a happier occasion.' As they put down the glasses he said, 'One thing more. The burial of your friend is this afternoon. You will no doubt wish to attend. Signor Ponti would like to see you afterwards. I believe you have reached agreement to publish a book of his. Isn't it so?'

'It's not finally fixed. He was arranging it.'

'I should like you to see Signor Ponti.' For a moment his look was stern again. 'He is a good friend of my country. I very much hope that nothing happens to disturb Signor Ponti.'

Chapter 7

The Funeral

Paul accompanied him to the cemetery. The driver misunderstood the instructions, so that they went first to the Jewish cemetery Alijakovac, and when they reached the new cemetery in Jukiceva they were late. Paul got out and walked along not exactly with him but just behind, like an old-style Oriental wife. They went through a maze of gravestones, some with crosses, others with pictures of the dead under glass, flanked by artificial flowers. He thought this too might be the wrong place until he saw a little group at the far end of one of the long avenues.

From a few feet away he saw that a service was being conducted at the graveside. Perhaps this was the wrong funeral? But on the other side of the hole in the ground into which the coffin was at this moment being lowered he saw Janet Ponti, looking pale in a black dress and hat. She glanced up at him and then lowered her head. He joined the group and bent his own head. A voice beside him whispered, 'There you are.' It was Coldharbour.

He whispered back. 'What are you doing here?'

'Somebody had to represent the firm. We spent a *fortune* trying to get in touch with you, most inconsiderate.' As his voice rose the priest's rose also, soaring over it in some beautiful incomprehensible incantation. Appropriately to this image of soaring, his arms waved like a bird's wings.

'But why?'

'Why *what*?'

'This service. Max had no religion.'

'We were in touch with Louise. She thought he was a Catholic.' Louise was Max's divorced wife, but whatever Coldharbour had been going to say about her was checked by a harsh 'Quiet,' spoken by somebody on the other side of him. Leaning forward a little he saw that the word had been spoken by Bunce.

Earth was thrown on the coffin, the priest crossed himself, the service was over. A group of what appeared to be official mourners – for surely they could have had no connection with Max? – accompanied the priest as he moved slowly away.

'Gil, it's good to see you.' Bunce shook his hand. 'It's moving, don't you find that? There's something about putting a body in the ground that gets you, it has meaning.'

'Mr Bunce wanted to accompany me when he heard that I was flying out. That is, after we were unable to contact you.' Reproachfully he said, 'I was sick on the plane.'

'It isn't that I wanted to intrude,' Bunce said earnestly. 'Just to pay my little tribute to a good guy, is all. Most people, you know, they're just nobodies from nowhere, but Max was really somebody.'

'Excuse me.' Paul had gone over to Janet Ponti and was saying something to her. He introduced her and said, 'This is Paul.'

Paul shook hands with them both and clicked his heels slightly. Gilbert said, 'I think Signor Ponti is expecting us. Max was negotiating about our publishing his book, *The Tigress*.'

Coldharbour sniffed. He was looking at Paul in a speculative way, and it occurred to Gilbert that a Christian name introduction was no doubt odd. 'Mr Coldharbour is one of my co-directors, would your father mind if –'

Before she could reply, Paul spoke. 'Signor Ponti is very tired, I think he wishes only to see you.' He turned to Coldharbour. 'Perhaps another day.'

Coldharbour's shrug conveyed that to be deprived of seeing Ponti was in accordance with the treatment generally meted out to him. Bunce asked, 'You his secretary or something?'

'I have not that honour.' They were approaching the cemetery gate.

'Then just you button your mouth.' Paul looked mystified. Bunce said to Janet, 'Miss Ponti, I'd be honoured to meet your father, speaking personally. He's a traditional writer, you might say out of date, but I respect him.'

Outside the cemetery two cars were drawn up, both with drivers, the black car they had come in and a large red Fiat behind it. The drivers got out and moved like automata to open the passenger doors.

'I'm sorry,' Janet said to Bunce. She got into the Fiat and Gilbert followed her.

Coldharbour said, almost in a wail, 'But where shall we see you afterwards?'

'I will arrange,' Paul said. He pointed to the black car. The Fiat was away.

They passed again through Dajanli and began to climb. Janet looked out of the window. He said, 'Why does your father want to see me?'

'He made an agreement that night with Mr Bomberg. He wants to make sure it holds good.'

'If it was made under false pretences it doesn't.'

Now she turned. The black dress made her more unattractive, accentuating the coarseness of her skin and the blotches on it. 'You are a fool, you still don't know what it's about, do you? I should have thought that policeman –'

'Radonic, you mean?'

'I should have thought he would have told you. They said you'd been talking to him.'

'Told me what? I don't understand.'

'This is where they went off the road, just here.' It was on a sharp bend. To the left there was a steep drop, green slopes succeeded by pine trees. He thought of the car turning over and over, and looked for skid marks on the road or a scar on the green lushness, but saw nothing. Then they were round the bend.

'That bitch. Flavia Orsini. Her father is the Minister for Export Trade.'

'I thought she was Italian.'

'In Italy, of course. Now do you see?'

'I'm afraid not.'

'There is some big trade deal going on between this country and Italy. Supposing there were an investigation and questions were asked about what Signorina Orsini was doing as a permanent guest of the famous novelist Eugene Ponti, why she spent half her nights in Sarajevo and who she spent them with – you don't suppose your friend was the only one, do you? And do you see now? There must be no trouble, everything must be hushed up, it does not matter what lies are told.' From her tight throat there was wrenched a single dry sob.

'Radonic knew all this?'

'He has been up at the house talking to my father. My father

587

is old, he does not care what happens as long as he gets what he wants. At the moment he wants this agreement. He is like a child. It will make him happy and then he will cause no trouble. Radonic wants that. I suppose you will be happy too.'

What about the steering, he wanted to ask, had it been faulty or was that just a convenient invention? But she would not know what he was talking about. Only Radonic knew, and whatever Radonic said was not to be believed. He would never know the truth.

'I don't see why you're so concerned. You can hardly have been fond of Flavia.'

She was looking away from him again as they went through the wrought iron gates. 'No, I was not fond of her,' she said as they stepped out into the sunshine. He remembered that single long look she had given Max, and understood. As he followed her out to the terrace he wondered again what quality it was that made a man like Max a sexual magnet, no matter what he said or how badly he behaved. And why was Gilbert Welton anti-magnetic? Thoughts of the Anglo-Germanic syndrome passed across his mind like thunder clouds. Then he was again in Ponti's presence, and the white cock's crest was turned to him.

'Come and sit. Beside me.' There was a chair close to his. 'Sit and enjoy the view.'

'Wonderful.' Much the same thing had been said when he came up here with Max. With conscious banality he spoke about a terrible tragedy.

'The old get used to tragedy, they understand that it is the meaning of life. When I lost these, that was tragic.' He touched his eyes. 'Tragedy is the nature of life, death is a commonplace. It has no power to disturb me. I confront human tragedy with the power of art.'

To this rotund wisdom Gilbert did not reply. Ponti's rich voice changed from complacency to complaint. 'What does disturb me is to be woken in the middle of the night, to be asked questions by police officials, impertinent questions about my life.' The liver-spotted hands quivered, he broke into a rush of Italian. Janet, who had been sitting a few feet away from them looking at a magazine, got up, came over and spoke to him. Her pale face contorted with anger. She said to Gilbert, 'I have said to him do not worry, you will find another secretary, there are plenty like her to fawn around famous men.' She went into the house.

Ponti listened to her retreating footsteps. 'Tragedy and ingratitude, an old man is used to both. But the official stupidity and the, what is the word, is it prying? – that must not be tolerated. Their inquiries! I could say things, I could say many things that would cause trouble.' His lips puffed in and out. The maid brought tea things. Janet reappeared, poured the tea and offered biscuits, placed an envelope between them on the table and went away again. 'She thinks she can be a tyrant now that I am alone, all human beings wish to be tyrants, but I shall not submit. I do not like tyrants.' Yourself excepted, Gilbert thought. The old man took a biscuit, crumbled it, put pieces in his mouth. Without faltering he placed a hand on the agreement. 'This is the paper I signed. Will you read it to me?'

Gilbert opened the envelope, began to read. It was their standard form of agreement for translation. Ponti stopped him after a few lines. 'Tell me about the name. Does it name Mr Angus Wilson?'

He turned the page. Inserted in typewriting were the words: 'The translation shall be undertaken by Angus Wilson, if that is possible and he is agreeable, or if not by another translator of the publisher's choice, who will make a true rendering of the original into the English language.' It meant nothing at all. But what had Max said and promised?

'It names Angus Wilson.'

'Very well. I have signed it. Are you prepared to sign also?'

He remembered Radonic's last words: 'I very much hope that nothing happens to disturb Signor Ponti.' He was not sure whether he loved or hated Radonic, but he knew that he did not want to sit again on the other side of the table from the President of Police who did not use third-degree methods, with Paul tapping in his corner. His confession, what seemed now his stupid and astonishing confession, had not been typed, but perhaps it had been recorded on tape. What the old man thought he was getting was ridiculous, but the result of saying no to him might be unpleasant.

'I am prepared to sign it.' Ponti looked for a moment almost disappointed. 'But I must tell you that the name of Angus Wilson inserted in the agreement means nothing. I don't know what my partner said, but this is the full clause.' He read it.

There was silence. Ponti's hand slowly stretched for another biscuit, put it on his plate, broke it. Crumbs fell to the ground. Then he threw back his head and laughed. His chair tilted perilously backwards and righted itself. Gilbert looked at him in bewilderment.

'A test,' he said. 'I was testing you. Give me the agreement.' Gilbert handed it to him. 'Now the envelope.' He put the agreement into the envelope, handed it across the table. 'It is yours. You have the right to publish Eugene Ponti in Britain.'

'I don't understand.'

'Your partner, Max Bomberg. I liked him very much.'

'I know.'

'But I did not trust him. I knew he was playing a trick on an old man. I do not like you, Mr Welton. But I trust you.'

'I think I am entitled to ask for an explanation,' Coldharbour said. It was raining. They sat in the large lounge of the hotel and watched the rain fall on the terrace. 'The office has been turned really *upside down*. It was quite inexcusable not to let us know where we could find you. When I received the news from the Yugoslav Embassy –'

'The Yugoslav Embassy?'

'They got in touch with me through the caretaker at Max's flat. I naturally supposed that you would handle the matter since you were in Sarajevo. You had said that you would be getting in touch with Max.' Coldharbour rustled a little. Obviously he had made no concession to the local climate. 'Anna has been very worried. And upset.'

'Anna?'

'Miss Pinkthorn. She has been a tower of strength. I can't imagine what you've been doing in the last forty-eight hours, why you didn't get in touch.'

'Let's have a drink.' A waiter bore down on them, smiling. They were back in the world where the tourist was deferred to. Gilbert found that the thought of slivovitz revolted him, and ordered beer. Coldharbour drank mineral water, which he sipped cautiously, eyeing Gilbert as though he were a wayward animal. 'Where's Bunce?'

'He went off. To look at the Turkish market, he *said*. I must say I was glad to be rid of him. Do you know, on the plane he became very familiar with a stewardess? I am afraid Americans are lecherous by nature.'

'Not all of them, surely.'

'Perhaps not. Who was that man?'

'What man?'

With a slight smirk Coldharbour pronounced the name. 'Paul.'

Foolishly unprepared for this question, he improvised. 'He's something to do with an official department, the Home Office I think.'

'Bunce said he was a policeman, that he had all the signs of being the law.' He sniffed. 'I thought myself that he was rather nice.'

'Yes. Quite nice.'

'Gilbert, what have you been doing, why did you just turn up at the funeral? I think I have a right to know.'

For this question he was prepared. 'We have an agreement with Ponti for publishing *The Tigress*. Max and I arranged it. Really it was Max's doing,' he said truthfully. He drew out the agreement, but Coldharbour was not to be deflected.

'And then?'

'How do you mean?'

'After Max had his accident, where were you? Why couldn't the hotel find you?'

'I went off on my own for a short time, I only learned about it when I got back.'

'But how did Paul –' Coldharbour began, obviously dissatisfied. He was checked by the appearance of Bunce, exhausted but enthusiastic.

'What a town, what a wonderful little town. It's where history began. I've been standing in the assassin's footprints.'

Gilbert was startled. 'What's that?'

'The assassin or the hero. Princip, the guy who knocked off the old Archduke and got things moving. They've got footprints let in the pavement. You know they named a bridge after him and put up a museum. He had small feet, mine fitted exactly.

Something symbolic there.' Somehow Bunce had obtained a glass full of what looked like whisky. 'Max would have appreciated it, he was like me, he had a foot in both worlds, the old and the new. A great man, Max. It's a hell of a thing to die, but that's the way to go if you're going.' He raised the glass. 'Max.'

They drank. Bunce relaxed in his chair. 'What are you doing here, Gil? I'd have thought you'd be with Virginia.'

'With Virginia?'

'I quite forgot.' Coldharbour wriggled uncomfortably. 'She rang the office, wanted to get hold of you. I told her you'd be here. With Max.'

'You've spoken to her, you know where she is?'

'If you hadn't done so much chasing about and going off on your own, you'd have talked to her yourself.'

'Where is she, Denis?'

'There's no need to look like that,' Coldharbour said pettishly. 'She rang from Amsterdam. She's staying with your son.'

PART THREE

Wife Found

Chapter 1

Matthew

Out of the bird's belly at Schiphol: the return to reality. The feeling was strengthened when he saw his son in the reception hall. A strong handshake, a hand lifting his baggage out to the car.

'Good to see you.' Was this square man in a double-breasted suit really his son, anybody's son? Matthew lighted a pipe as they got into the car, tamped it down, got it going. From adolescence he had been a pipe-smoking man. 'Got your telegram,' he said as he started the car and they drove on the exit road from the airport.

'I couldn't reach you on the telephone.' He hesitated to ask why Virginia had not come to meet him.

'Sorry to hear about your partner. Rotten business. You flew out to clear things up, I suppose.' At a traffic light Matthew gave him a glance. 'You knew Virginia was here?'

'Yes. You mean she isn't with you now?'

'Flew back yesterday. You haven't spoken to her then?'

'No, we haven't been in touch. I've been trying to find her.' It seemed to be the understatement of his life. 'How is she?'

'Fine, fine. I gather she's been in Yugoslavia too.'

'Yes. How's Miriam?'

'Couldn't be better.' Matthew removed the pipe. 'You're going to be a grandfather.' He put back the pipe.

For a moment he did not take in the meaning of the circumlocution. Then he said, 'That's wonderful news. Congratulations to you both.'

'We're very pleased. Virginia was pleased too.'

Miriam was waiting in their apartment on the Herrengracht. When he saw her, small, dark, not pretty but elegant, and conspicuously foreign, he wondered as he had done before how Matthew had come to marry this rather exotic plant. It occurred to him that he had never speculated on the attraction Matthew held for her. He had always automatically assumed that British stolidity had its charm for the butterfly foreigner. Was this an indirect product of the Anglo-Germanic syndrome, or was Matthew really an entirely different person from the tractable child and adolescent who had grown into the solemnly boring young man now telling him in detail about the firm's turnover increase in the past six months? He wondered about this while he drank a single glass of sherry and ate a delicate lunch.

Miriam waved away his congratulations. 'It's going to be a bore really, because I'll have to give up my job.' She was secretary to the director of an industrial trust and, he felt sure, very competent. 'But Matthew thought we ought to have a child while we were young.' Was Matthew young? It seemed hard to believe. 'I shall have to leave in another couple of months but then I shall go back when Reuben is at nursery school. They have wonderful nurseries here.'

'Reuben?'

'It was my grandfather's name.'

'Suppose it's a girl.'

'It won't be. Matthew says it will be a son, and he is always right.' The look she gave her husband was so melting that something within Gilbert twanged like a piano wire. 'If you will forgive me, I have to go back to work now. But I shall see you later, you'll stay with us of course.'

'Thank you, but I must get back to London. I really have to talk to Virginia.' He had already made a telephone call and heard that discouraging double ring going on and on.

'She is so delightful, so gay. I like her very much. By the way –'

'Yes?'

'Reuben's other name will be Gilbert.' There was a smile, a quick brush on the cheek. Then she had gone, and he was alone with his son.

'More coffee? Glass of port? Or try some of this Dutch liqueur, Van der Hum they call it, don't know if it is Dutch really.' Tiny liqueur glasses sat in a cupboard along with sherry glasses, wine glasses, brandy snifters, everything was in its place. 'Glad of this chance to have a chat.'

It struck Gilbert that their roles were reversed, and that Matthew was speaking to him like a father, or perhaps like a housemaster at school. The feeling was heightened when they took their drinks to the small room that Matthew (but of course) called his den, and he said, 'Everything all right?'

'How do you mean?'

'Virginia said she'd been off on a bit of a holiday. On her own. That seemed rather funny to me. And then you being out there too. If anything's going on I'd like to know.'

'Of course nothing's going on, as you put it.'

'Because we're very fond of you both, Miriam and I. We'd be very sorry if anything was wrong.' He took out his pipe, looked at it, laid it to one side with a gesture appropriate to a TV serial. Then he picked up the pipe again and began to fill it slowly, still in the best televisual manner. 'She didn't stay long, Virginia. Just the one night. Then she rang the office to find you and somebody told her about your partner's death. After that she went back.'

'Was she upset?'

'What about?' Matthew gave his father the young executive's inquiring glance.

'Max's death.'

'I didn't notice. Should she have been?' He did not wait for a reply to that. 'She was jolly pleased about Reuben, I can tell you that.'

The walls of the den were covered with photographs in the manner of a housemaster's study. Or were housemasters' studies now covered with pictures of the Rolling Stones and Julie Felix? And for that matter school photographs like these, groups rock-climbing in the Lakes, Matthew in the school play, a photograph of his prep school soccer team, were not generally preserved by schoolboys but by their parents. It was with a shock that he saw a family group below a picture of Matthew in the tennis team, Mary, Matthew and himself. It must have been taken after Starting Again, on a desperate and unsuccessful family holiday in Devon. Mary was sprawled on the sand in an ungainly fashion, he was bent over digging with a tiny spade, the child examined them with an astonished expression. He had not thought of Mary for days. Now he said, 'You got my letter. About your mother.'

'Yes. That, was what I wanted to have a word about.'

He turned from the photograph. Matthew's square face, set

in the solid and reliable lines that would deepen with the years, the hair already thinning a little, looked up at him from the chair. He felt and controlled a spasm of irritation. 'About Mary? I told you she died in a friend's flat where she'd been living. Sleeping tablets. You probably saw the details in reports of the inquest.'

'I only read the Dutch papers now. If you're living in a country you ought to read their press.' He felt another spasm, more intense. 'I had your letter, yes. But I'd already heard.'

'What do you mean? I know I didn't write at once, but how could you have heard –'

'From Mother. She wrote to me that night, before she took the pills. She wrote to me. She told me she'd seen you.'

He sat down and looked at Matthew. He wanted desperately to see the letter. It seemed to him that it contained the answer to the whole of his behaviour, the things he had done and the things that had been done to him.

'She must have written it, posted it straightaway and then gone on drinking and swallowed the pills.' His tone was matter of fact. 'It was pretty maudlin. And very scrawly, she must have been extremely drunk.' He sipped his Van der Hum.

'Where is it?'

'I only saw her a few times after leaving school, but she wasn't an unhappy person, was she? I think she was a happy person, though I don't remember her that way.'

'You mean I made her unhappy?'

'Oh no. I only know – I never minded going back to school, that's all. She was rather feckless perhaps. I suppose that's why you didn't get on.'

Gilbert looked at him. He was amazed that Matthew had ever thought about his father and mother at all. 'Can I see the letter?'

'No. I destroyed it.'

'Destroyed it!'

'What was the point of doing anything else? Drunken ramblings, that's all.'

The final answer had been denied to him. He was angry, yet behind the anger lay fear of what he would have found. 'She must have said something important, something about why she was going to do it.' Matthew shook his head. 'She was my wife, you should have sent it to me. Or kept it for me.'

'She was your wife, she was my mother, but that was all a long time ago. When she wrote that letter she was just a drunk. A good deal of it didn't make sense.'

'She said something about me. I want to know what it was.'

'I told you, nothing important.'

'What was it?'

'She said she'd met you somewhere, she'd been to see you, you'd turned her out. There was a lot about not wanting to make a mess of your home.'

'What else?'

'Nothing I remember. I shouldn't have mentioned it.' His word-searching manner became more deliberate than usual. 'But there's one thing. You must have asked her back to the house. You saw the state she was in. Why did you turn her out?'

The serious ponderous face carried only inquiry, not condemnation, but he could not endure his son's company or stay in the apartment any longer. 'I must go. I'll get a taxi to the airport.'

'Why don't you ring Virginia again?'

'No, I must go.'

'I'll drive you there. If I've said something to upset you I'm sorry.'

'It's what you are that upsets me,' he said in a rare moment of openness. 'And what I am. I'll get a taxi.'

'No no, please let me take you.'

In the end it was less trouble to let Matthew take him. On the way out to Schiphol Matthew said what a pity it was that his father could not stay and have a look at the pleasures of Amsterdam, the canals, the shopping in the Kalverstraat, the night life. He wanted to wait, but Gilbert refused to let him. They shook hands at parting. There was a flight to London in three-quarters of an hour, and he got on to it with a standby ticket.

599

Chapter 2

Virginia

In London lances of rain struck at the pavements. His sense of moving from one life to another was enhanced. On the way to St John's Wood in the taxi he wondered whether he would be permitted to return.

Light showed in the hall, filtered through the drawn drawing-room curtains. He walked up the path in the rain, opened the front door, and stopped when he heard voices. The last voice he had heard here was Mary's: *It's upsetting for women when men don't know what they want. I feel sorry for Vir-Virginia.* Grotesque thoughts passed through his mind. Would he find Mary and Virginia talking in the drawing-room, would Max be there? He put down his suitcase and turned the handle of the door.

Virginia was in there with the Sutherlands. She got up, came over and embraced him. He noticed at once that her scent was fresh and mild, 'Darling, did you have a good flight?'

'You were expecting me?'

'Matthew rang and said you were on your way. Are you mad with hunger? John and Sandra are staying to dinner, isn't that nice? Now you're here I won't have to pour drinks.'

'I hear you and Virginia have been following each other round Yugoslavia,' John Sutherland said. 'Very similar thing happened to me in Greece, damned funny.' He told a long story about a time when he and Sandra in a motorized caravan had arrived a day late to meet friends in a village near Athens, and had spent the next fortnight narrowly missing them. 'Of course communications are bad in these countries.'

'I always say that's part of their charm.' Sandra could be relied on for the safe confirmatory remark. 'You must be pleased to be home.' He said that he was, and when John said that it was terrible about Max's death he agreed. They went on asking questions.

'I saw him out there, the afternoon before it happened. We went to see an Italian novelist, Eugene Ponti.'

'Oh yes, about the book you were so keen on,' Virginia said. 'You told me about it.'

Had he told her? He could not remember it. He asked if she had seen Max.

'No, I didn't even know he was there. Anyway, I never got to Sarajevo.'

'At the Dubrovnik hotel they seemed to think you were going there.'

'I thought about it, but never went. We're ready to eat.' She linked her arm in his and whispered, 'I'll get rid of them as soon as I can.'

This was not very soon. They talked about the relationship between soft drugs and violence, the connection of pop groups with American protest songs, the limitations of comprehensive education, where the Sutherlands might go for their summer holiday, about a new theory that autistic children could be helped by leaving them entirely alone for long periods at a time. It was an average evening for their class, age and income group, one that he found exhausting, although he would have taken it in its stride in the past.

'They're nice but boring,' Virginia said when they had gone. 'I wouldn't have asked them if I'd known you'd be back. I didn't actually know you were going away.'

'I flew out to Dubrovnik because I wanted to see you.'

'It was dull there, so I left. If I'd known you were coming –'

'I telephoned. Or tried to. Where did you go?'

'Oh, all over. A couple of the islands, Korcula and Brac, then to Split. Up to Lake Bled, that was heavenly.'

'But not to Sarajevo.'

'Not to Sarajevo.'

The showdown, the final explanation he had been looking for, where was it? It seemed that there was nothing to explain.

'Did you do what you wanted, make up your mind?'

'Yes. I don't know what I was thinking about. A woman's place is with her husband. I mean, she should live his life, not the other way round.' It crossed his mind that this low-grade magazine wisdom could have been obtained without going abroad, but he did not say so. 'Gilbert.'

'Yes?'

'Something has happened to you. Did you have an *adventure*?' Her eyes sparkled with pleasure.

'I didn't go looking for adventure. I was looking for you.'

'Don't be stuffy, I was joking. Let's make love.'

As they lay in the bedroom afterwards, she said, 'How was that?'

'Fine.' How was it compared with Anna, how had it really been? 'Marvellous.' He kissed her shoulder.

'I was sorry about Mary, I heard when I got back.' Why had she chosen that precise moment to mention Mary? 'She was a lush at the end, wasn't she? I shall never be like that.'

'You won't go away again?'

'Only with you.' She stroked his hair. 'Are you pleased you'll be a grandfather?'

'I don't think I mind either way.'

'Miriam wrote and told me, that's why I went to see them. I wish I could have had a child.'

'Matthew was quite enough.'

'Hold me.' He held her, nipples pressed against him, legs wound over his. 'Something happened while you were away, I feel sure it did.'

'Did anything happen to you?'

'No. I had a boring time.'

'Nothing happened to me either. I'm the same person that I was when you left.' He broke from their interlocking grasp, took her by the throat. 'You have to believe that.'

She pulled at his hands. 'You don't have to strangle me. Whatever happened –'

'I've told you, nothing happened. Nothing at all.'

'We're the kind of people to whom nothing ever happens. That's what you wanted me to say, isn't it?'

'It isn't just what I wanted. It's true.'

'Yes, it's true.'

Just before she turned out the light he saw the inside of her raised arm. It was perfectly smooth and white.

Chapter 3

Da Capo

On the following morning he looked at the exterior of the house and felt his usual small but distinct sense of pleasure at its elegant lack of ostentation. This was a kind of test, which he passed successfully. He savoured the mild orderliness of England in walking to the office through Regent's Park. The day was warm without a hint of heat, an old man wearing a very long tattered sweater fed the ducks.

At the office everybody seemed genuinely pleased to see him. Even the lugubrious Paine smiled and said, 'You're back, Mr Welton.' It was as though he had been away for months, not a few days. Miss Pinkthorn (Anna) charged in head down and planked on to his desk a thick wad of manuscript. It was *A Welter of Gore*.

'*Mr Bomberg* was responsible.' She spoke as though he were in the next room and not under earth in Sarajevo. 'He gave it to J. Wilson Arkwright to read without saying a word. Not a word to anybody.' Pause. 'He seems to think it's good.'

J. Wilson Arkwright, a barrister who had found writing about crime more profitable than the law, was a name to conjure with. His enthusiasm for *A Welter of Gore* seemed total, his view of its prospects was optimistic. Gilbert dictated on the spot a letter to Dexter Manhood accepting the book.

'Very sad about Mr Bomberg,' Miss Pinkthorn said after they had disposed of the rubbish that had accumulated in his absence. 'Mr Coldharbour said he saw you at the funeral, though I don't suppose it was anything, being in an atheist country. He should have been brought back.' Gilbert suggested that Max wouldn't have minded. Miss Pinkthorn glared at him. 'Did you enjoy yourself?' It was impossible to say anything but yes. 'And I hope you found Mrs Welton well.' He said that he had.

'We shall miss Mr Bomberg. He had some funny ways but you couldn't help liking him.' She brushed away a tear.

He lunched at the club and received more condolences. After

603

lunch he went to a sale of jewellery at Christie's and bought a diamond necklace. In the evening he took Virginia to the theatre. The play was a sexy comedy, at which they both laughed. When they returned he gave her the necklace. It was the most expensive present he had ever bought her, and she said she loved it. On the following day she made arrangements to invite to dinner an ex-Minister whose book about his resignation from the Government was being published by the firm. Getting together politico-literary guests to meet him was a problem that she seemed to face with relish.

The telephone call from Mel Branksom came a week later. 'Hi there. I should have called before, but I've been in the States. I wanted to say I was just horrified, and I mean horrified, to hear about Max. It was one of those goddam stupid things that just shouldn't happen. A man like that, he had flair. You might call it genius. It must be a blow.'

'We're carrying on.'

'I've had conferences with our parent company. When are you free for lunch?'

Coldharbour also came to lunch, in a restaurant called the New American, which as Mel said lacked English dignity. There, in his own words, he laid it on the line. Branksom Associates would either buy out the existing directors completely, or they would take a fifty-one per cent shareholding. In this case they would want financial but not editorial control. The terms proposed were generous. He showed Gilbert a report from their financial advisers which said that the firm was under-capitalized. The Spatial Realists were mentioned. Mel was enthusiastic, he was an enthusiastic man.

'Why not? I hear these Spatial Realists are the latest thing. And how about a book on the erotic art of the East, Indian temple paintings, old Chinese work, some of the Louis Fifteen stuff? You think it's too near to our old image, maybe you're right. But we ought to do half a dozen art books, make it a series. You'll edit them, won't you, Denis?' Coldharbour wriggled with pleasure. 'This is a great deal, one of my lifelong ambitions fulfilled. I'm only sorry Max is not here to see it. He was a genius.'

Coldharbour nodded in a solemn concurrence.

Virginia arranged a dinner-party for Mel and his wife, who wore pince-nez and chainsmoked. She found some people to go with them.

Perhaps Max really had been a genius. The film rights of *The Way They Get You Going* were sold. It was said that Richard Burton, Elizabeth Taylor and Dustin Hoffman were to star. An offer for the paperback rights was received which staggered Gilbert. He queried the offer and it was immediately increased. Welton's got nothing from the film but a great deal of money from the paperback.

The calligraphy had a bold flourish, the postmark said N.W.6. He read the letter at the breakfast table and put it into his pocket. Virginia looked at him with eyebrows slightly raised.

'Pass the marmalade.'

She did so. 'Bad news?'

'No news at all.'

'You looked rather – I don't know – the way you looked when you first came back.'

'It's a man who pestered me before. Now he's writing to me at home.'

A half-truth he reflected, as he read the letter:

Hallo there!

Saw a bit in the paper about some merger or other you were in with the Yanks, pity we can't keep anything British these days but that's the way it goes. Anyway, couldn't resist writing a line to tell you that I'm back in the Old Country safe and sound, after a spot of what they call interrogation because of a little bother over some Swiss francs. Least said soonest mended! The old tick-tock was going pit-a-pat, I can tell you. A couple of sessions with that cold-blooded police chief and anybody would be feeling a bit Harry groggers. Gather you got some of the same, afraid I said a couple of things I shouldn't in the heat of the moment, but all's well that ends well, as the bard put it.

In the end they decided to let me off with a caution, after trying to put the blame for that accident on Topline. Trust the foreigners for that. However, the upshot was we've closed down our operations in a certain country, and yours truly can't say he's sorry. Must say, though, looking back I enjoyed our trip together and that little night-club session – what a dump! Nice little piece, Maria, keen on me too. I'd have dipped my wick if unforeseen circumstances hadn't intervened, as they say. Back with the wife and kids now, a good thing too.

Well, here's hoping we'll meet again one of these days. I move around a good deal, as the girl in the newspaper shop said when the man asked if she kept stationery, but if you give a tinkle to the office number they'll always get a message through. All the very best.

Jerry

When he had read the letter again he tore it up and flushed the pieces down the lavatory.

'Gil.' Bunce had been swanning around unreachably in Europe when the paperback deal was made, but his voice on the telephone was warm and fresh. 'Gil, how are you?'

'We've been trying to get hold of you. Where have you been?'

'Crete, Minorca, up in Castile, pretty much every place I guess. Oh, and I forgot, Algeria, the boys there are really something. Now I'm going back to Mother.'

'To Mother?'

'My only Mother, the tart New York and the virgin Kansas, the mother country.' He sounded a little high. 'Gil, I'm at the Ritz. Come up and say good-bye.'

It turned out that the highness was natural Bunce, a euphoria engendered by anticipation of his return. 'Saks and Macy's I can't wait to get my arms around you, Yorkville you dreary old German slut I love you,' he said. 'Honestly Gil, Europe's finished, sucked dry.'

'That's not what you were saying a few weeks ago.'

'That could be. But whatever number you use to dial the future it'll be America who answers. How about that for the title of my next book?'

'Rather long.'

The bedroom in the suite opened and a girl came out of it. 'This is Hedda. She's coming to the States with me. Hedda, say hallo to my publisher. Hedda, Gil.'

'Hallo, we've met.' It was Anna. She had had her hair cut very short, almost a skinhead crop.

Gilbert said, 'The hair and the name were different, but we've met.'

'She's married to some half-arsed photographer named

Perkins. He calls her Dorothy, but her name's Hedda all right. She was born half-way through a performance of *Hedda Gabler*, that's how she got it.'

'She used to call herself Anna. After Anna Karenina.'

'Oh, for God's sake,' she said.

'She's a temperamental girl,' Bunce said seriously. 'What we all need is some brandy.' He sent down for a bottle and they drank quite a lot of it. Anna and Gilbert hardly said a word to each other, but that did not matter because Bunce talked all the time. Gilbert said an affectionate good-bye to him. He had become fond of Bunce. At the last moment Anna, or Hedda came up and kissed him on the mouth. Her lips were hot, the effect slightly repellent.

'You've made up your mind then,' Virginia said. 'About the offer.' She was in a nightdress at her dressing-table, preparing for bed.

'Yes. They can have their fifty-one per cent. Coldharbour agrees. There'll be a couple of Americans breathing over our shoulders, but I don't think that matters.'

'You won't sell out altogether?'

'No. What for, what should we do?'

'I think that's right,' she said with her air of stating a profound truth, 'A man needs an occupation.'

'Virginia.'

'Yes?'

'Whatever it was made you go away – it's all over now?'

'Of course. I told you, I needed a change. To think about things.' She patted her cheeks. 'You must have thought too. You know, you're different.'

'In what way?'

'More considerate, I suppose. Something like that.'

'Virginia.'

'Yes?'

'If I said I'm still not sure what happened, what would you say?'

'I don't want to talk about it any more, do you mind?' She turned on her chair. 'I love my necklace.'

'Good.'

'Gilbert, can I have something? Something I want.'

'I expect so, what?'

'A dog. I'd take it for walks in the park.'

'A poodle?'

'No, I hate little dogs. A retriever or labrador, something like that.'

'All right.'

The next day he bought a new hat. It was a Russian-style fur hat. Mr Clapperton thought that he looked very dashing in it.

When he got home a golden retriever puppy jumped up and licked eagerly at his hand.

'Max,' Virginia called. She came out into the hall, smiling. 'I'm calling him Max. In memory,' she said.